From the Pages of The Legend of Sleepy Hollow and Other Writings

From the moment you lose sight of the land you have left all is vacancy until you step on the opposite shore, and are launched at once into the bustle and novelties of another world.

(from "The Voyage," page 52)

"There is in every true woman's heart a spark of heavenly fire, which lies dormant in the broad daylight of prosperity; but which kindles up, and beams and blazes in the dark hour of adversity. No man knows what the wife of his bosom is—no man knows what a ministering angel she is—until he has gone with her through the fiery trials of this world."

(from "The Wife," page 68)

A tart temper never mellows with age, and a sharp tongue is the only edged tool that grows keener with constant use.

(from "Rip Van Winkle," page 77)

"Surely," thought Rip, "I have not slept here all night."

(from "Rip Van Winkle," page 81)

There are certain half-dreaming moods of mind, in which we naturally steal away from noise and glare, and seek some quiet haunt, where we may indulge our reveries and build our air castles undisturbed.

(from "The Mutability of Literature," page 107)

There is no duenna so rigidly prudent, and inexorably decorous, as a superannuated coquette.

(from "The Spectre Bridegroom," page 121)

The spectre is known, at all the country firesides, by the name of the Headless Horseman of Sleepy Hollow.

(from "The Legend of Sleepy Hollow," page 164)

In this by-place of nature, there abode, in a remote period of American history, that is to say, some thirty years since, a worthy wight of the name of Ichabod Crane; who sojourned, or, as he expressed it, "tarried," in Sleepy Hollow, for the purpose of instructing the children of the vicinity.

(from "The Legend of Sleepy Hollow," pages 164–165)

On mounting a rising ground, which brought the figure of his fellow-traveller in relief against the sky, gigantic in height, and muffled in a cloak, Ichabod was horror-struck, on perceiving that he was headless!—but his horror was still more increased, on observing that the head, which should have rested on his shoulders, was carried before him on the pommel of the saddle.

(from "The Legend of Sleepy Hollow," pages 187–188)

"It may be one of the royal family for aught I know, for they are all stout gentlemen!"

(from "The Stout Gentleman," page 210)

"A man is never a man till he can defy wind and weather, range woods and wilds, sleep under a tree, and live on bass-wood leaves!"

(from "Dolph Heyliger," page 251)

I am always at a loss to know how much to believe of my own stories.

(from "To the Reader," page 289)

"To rescue from oblivion the memory of former incidents, and to render a just tribute of renown to the many great and wonderful transactions of our Dutch progenitors, Diedrich Knickerbocker, native of the city of New York, produces this historical essay."

(from *A History of New York*, page 383)

It has already been hinted in this most authentic history, that in the domestic establishment of William the Testy "the gray mare was the better horse"; in other words, that his wife "ruled the roast," and in governing the governor, governed the province, which might thus be said to be under petticoat government.

(from *A History of New York*, page 438)

THE LEGEND OF SLEEPY HOLLOW

and Other Writings

Washington Irving

*Selected, with an Introduction
and Notes, by Peter Norberg*

George Stade
Consulting Editorial Director

BARNES & NOBLE CLASSICS
NEW YORK

$\mathcal{B}$

BARNES & NOBLE CLASSICS

NEW YORK

Published by Barnes & Noble Books
122 Fifth Avenue   New York, NY 10011

www.barnesandnoble.com/classics

See "A Note on the Text" for original publication information
on the works included in this volume.

Published in 2006 by Barnes & Noble Classics with new Introduction,
Notes, Note on the Text, Biography, Chronology, Inspired By,
Comments & Questions, and For Further Reading.

The Legend of Sleepy Hollow and Other Writings
ISBN-13: 978-1-59308-225-3
ISBN-10: 1-59308-225-8
LC Control Number 2005932486

Produced and published in conjunction with:
Fine Creative Media, Inc.
322 Eighth Avenue
New York, NY 10001

Michael J. Fine, President and Publisher

Printed in the United States of America
QM
3 5 7 9 10 8 6 4

Washington Irving

Washington Irving, arguably the first American author to earn international literary acclaim, was born on April 3, 1783, in New York City. The Americans had won independence from Britain (the Treaty of Paris would be signed in September), and William Irving, a well-to-do merchant who had emigrated from Scotland, named his eleventh and youngest child after General George Washington. When Irving was seventeen, he began apprenticing in New York legal firms, including that of a former attorney general of New York, Josiah Hoffman. Irving soon realized, however, that his true interests lay in writing.

By the age of nineteen he was writing witty stories and sketches for local journals. His series *Letters of Jonathan Oldstyle, Gent.* was published in 1802 in the *Morning Chronicle*, a weekly edited by his brother Peter. In 1807, after a two-year tour of Europe, he began a similarly tongue-in-cheek series of sketches, *Salmagundi; or, The Whim-Whams and Opinions of Launcelot Langstaff & Others*, which he coauthored with his brother William and their friend James Kirke Paulding. Two years later Irving's mock history of Dutch colonization, *A History of New York*, was published; full of fascinating historical details and ribald comic portraits, it gained instant notoriety. This period was also one of personal hardship and depression for Irving. His fiancée, Matilda Hoffman, died of tuberculosis in 1809; a few years later, the War of 1812 devastated the family import business. Irving sailed to London in 1815 to begin a second tour of Europe but found himself instead in Liverpool, helping his brother attempt to salvage the remains of their company.

When P. & E. Irving went bankrupt in 1818, Irving determined to earn a living through his writing. He met Scottish novelist Sir Walter Scott, who took the young author under his wing, introducing him to such literati as Mary Shelley and Lord Byron. Irving scored an immediate triumph with *The Sketch-Book of Geoffrey Crayon*, published in 1819. The work—which contains his best-known tales,

"The Legend of Sleepy Hollow" and "Rip Van Winkle"—was an international success.

In 1826 Irving was appointed a diplomatic attaché to the American embassy in Madrid. Ever curious to understand his environment, he began researching Spanish history and customs. *The Conquest of Granada* was published in 1829, and *The Alhambra* followed in 1832.

Irving finally returned to America in 1832, after a seventeen-year absence. He made an adventurous trip through the American West, which he chronicled in *A Tour of the Prairies* (1835), and then built his home, Sunnyside, along the picturesque banks of the Hudson River north of New York City. Irving traveled again to Europe in 1842 to serve as the American minister to Spain, a position he held until 1846. Otherwise he remained at Sunnyside, where he continued to write. He published many more stories and sketches as well as a five-volume biography of his namesake, George Washington. Washington Irving died at home on November 28, 1859.

Table of Contents

The World of Washington Irving and
The Legend of Sleepy Hollow

1783   Washington Irving is born in New York City on April 3, the youngest of eleven children. His father, a Scottish immigrant and well-to-do merchant, names him after General George Washington. The American Revolution ends with the Treaty of Paris, signed on September 3, in which Great Britain formally recognizes the independence of the United States.

1787   Irving attends several schools in the New York area and develops a love of plays and histories.

1788   English poet and satirist George Gordon, Lord Byron, is born.

1789   The French Revolution begins. *Songs of Innocence*, by English poet and artist William Blake, is published. George Washington is inaugurated as first president of the United States.

1790   Conservative English statesman Edmund Burke publishes *Reflections on the Revolution in France*, in which he opposes the French Revolution.

1791   American political writer Thomas Paine publishes part 1 of his treatise in defense of the French Revolution, *Rights of Man*; part 2 will be published in 1792.

1798   *Lyrical Ballads*, by English poets Samuel Taylor Coleridge and William Wordsworth, is published.

1799   Irving begins studying law in the offices of Henry Masterton and, two years later, Brockholst Livingston.

1802   Irving continues his law studies clerking for Judge Josiah Hoffman, a former attorney general of New York. In his spare time, Irving begins writing for newspapers and literary journals. His *Letters of Jonathan Oldstyle, Gent.*, witty send-ups of Manhattan culture written in the voice of a disapproving elder, are published in the *Morning Chronicle*, which is edited by his brother Peter.

1804   Irving embarks on a two-year tour of Europe.

1806   He returns to the United States in 1806 and is admitted to the bar.

1807   Irving, his brother William, and his friend James Kirke Paulding collaborate to publish a series of satirical writings entitled *Salmagundi; or, The Whim-Whams and Opinions of Launcelot Langstaff, Esq. & Others.*

1809   Irving's *A History of New York* is published under the pen name Diedrich Knickerbocker. The book, a wry and comedic mock-political history of New Amsterdam (the Dutch settlement that became New York) is a great success. Irving's fiancée, Matilda (the daughter of Judge Hoffman), dies, and Irving enters into a deep depression; he will never marry. American author Edgar Allan Poe is born.

1811   English novelist Jane Austen's *Sense and Sensibility* is published.

1812   The War of 1812, between Great Britain and the United States, begins. Irving serves as military aide to New York Governor Daniel Tompkins. He travels to Washington, D.C., to seek relief from the trade embargoes that are crippling his family's import business. *Grimm's Fairy Tales*, a collection of German folk tales by Jakob and Wilhelm Grimm, is published.

1814   American poet Francis Scott Key writes "The Star-spangled Banner."

1815   Irving travels to England intending to begin another tour of Europe. With the family business still foundering, however, he remains in Liverpool to help his brother Peter, who is director of the company's British office. The Napoleonic Wars end with the defeat of Napoleon I at the Battle of Waterloo.

1817   Irving tours England and Scotland, and meets Scottish author Sir Walter Scott. Construction begins on the Erie Canal, an artificial waterway connecting New York City with the Great Lakes.

1818   When his family's business collapses, Irving determines to make a living through his writing. *Frankenstein*, by English author Mary Wollstonecraft Shelley, is published.

1819   Serialization begins of *The Sketch-Book of Geoffrey Crayon, Gent.*, a collection of sketches and stories that includes Irving's tales "The Legend of Sleepy Hollow" and "Rip Van Winkle." The work is immensely popular in America, Britain, and Europe. Irving's newfound celebrity makes

him a popular guest in London's most exclusive literary sa-
lons, where he counts such writers as Scott and Byron
among his friends. Scott's novel *Ivanhoe* and Byron's satirical poem *Don Juan* are published.

1820   *The Sketch-Book of Geoffrey Crayon, Gent.* is published in
book form.

1822   Another collection of Irving's sketches and stories, *Bracebridge Hall*, is published.

1823   The Monroe Doctrine is established to curtail European
advancement into the Western Hemisphere.

1824   Irving publishes *Tales of a Traveller*, inspired by his visits to
Europe.

1825   While in England, he becomes romantically involved with
novelist Mary Shelley.

1826   Irving becomes a diplomatic attaché to the American embassy in Madrid. *The Last of the Mohicans*, by American
novelist James Fenimore Cooper, is published.

1828   While in Spain, Irving publishes *A History of the Life and
Voyages of Christopher Columbus* in several volumes. Amer-
ican lexicographer Noah Webster publishes *An American
Dictionary of the English Language*.

1829   The historical novel *A Chronicle of the Conquest of Granada*,
written by Irving under the pseudonym Fray Antonio
Agapida, is published.

1831   American abolitionist William Lloyd Garrison begins publication of his anti-slavery newsletter *The Liberator*.

1832   Irving returns to America after a seventeen-year absence
and is welcomed as a celebrity. He publishes *The Alhambra*,
a series of sketches about Spain.

1833   Slavery is abolished in the British Empire.

1835   Irving's *A Tour of the Prairies*, based on a recent trip
through the American West, is published. He buys land in
Tarrytown, New York, along the Hudson River, and builds a
house he names Sunnyside. Samuel Langhorne Clemens
(pseudonym Mark Twain) is born.

1836   *Astoria*, Irving's history of American financier John Jacob
Astor's Pacific Fur Company, is published. Davy Crockett is
killed at the Alamo during the Texas Revolution.

1837   Irving's novel about the American frontier, *The Adventures
of Captain Bonneville, U.S.A.*, is published.

1839   American poet Henry Wadsworth Longfellow publishes *Hyperion*.

1840   After spending months doing research for a book on the conquest of Mexico, Irving abandons the project when he finds that noted historian William Prescott is writing a similar work. Irving becomes a regular contributor to the monthly *Knickerbocker Magazine*, a literary publication.

1841   American essayist and transcendentalist Ralph Waldo Emerson publishes *Essays*.

1842   Irving is appointed American minister to Spain, a position he holds until 1846. English author Charles Dickens's *American Notes* (a criticism of America) appears.

1844   Emerson publishes a second series of *Essays*.

1845   Edgar Allan Poe's *The Raven, and Other Poems* appears.

1848   Irving becomes president of the Astor Library (now the New York Public Library).

1849   Irving's *Life of Oliver Goldsmith* is published.

1850   Herman Melville's *Moby-Dick* and Nathaniel Hawthorne's *The Scarlet Letter* are published.

1852   *Uncle Tom's Cabin*, by American novelist and abolitionist Harriet Beecher Stowe, is published in book form.

1854   *Walden; or, Life in the Woods*, by Henry David Thoreau, is published.

1855   *Wolfert's Roost*, a compilation of Irving's contributions to the *Knickerbocker*, is published. Irving begins publishing his five-volume biography of George Washington, *The Life of George Washington*.

1859   Shortly after finishing the final volume of *The Life of George Washington*, Washington Irving dies at Sunnyside on November 28.

The First American Man of Letters

In April 1789, George Washington arrived in New York City for his inauguration as the first president of the newly formed republic of the United States. He met with a hero's welcome. In the weeks that followed, well-wishers and admirers regularly approached him in the streets, among them a Scottish-born woman who cornered him in a shop on Broadway. Drawing before her a six-year-old child, she exclaimed, "Please, Your Excellency, here's a bairn that's called after ye." It was Washington Irving. In retrospect, the scene seemed prophetic. Later in life, after having established a reputation as the first American man of letters, Irving recalled in an interview how Washington "laid his hand upon my head, and gave me his blessing" (Williams, *The Life of Washington Irving*, vol. 1, p. 10; see "For Further Reading"). Three generations after the Revolutionary War, George Washington was revered as the father of our country. Irving likewise was recognized as a founding father of America's national literature.

Such a title might strike today's reader as an exaggeration. Irving's best-known characters, Rip Van Winkle and Ichabod Crane, do not seem substantial enough to serve as foundational figures in an American literary tradition. However, the stories Irving set in Sleepy Hollow, a secluded village in the Hudson River Valley, provided American culture with a local habitation and a name. Along with James Fenimore Cooper and William Cullen Bryant, Irving was one of America's pioneer writers. He helped sketch the contours of a cultural landscape that was unique to the United States, not a pale imitation of the literature of England and Europe. Sleepy Hollow is an early example of American authors self-consciously setting out to create an imaginative space for artistic creativity. Nathaniel Hawthorne described this sort of space in his introduction to *The Scarlet Letter* as "a neutral territory, somewhere between the real-world and fairy-land, where the Actual and the Imaginary may meet, and each imbue itself with the nature of the other" (Hawthorne, *The Centenary Edition of the Works of Nathaniel*

Hawthorne, vol. 1, p. 36). By providing such a "neutral territory" for his readers, Irving contributed to the new nation's efforts to generate a collective cultural memory from native sources.

In the wake of the American Revolution, as the Constitution was being ratified, the general public sentiment was that a distinctively American literature was essential for the success of America's democratic experiment. For what did the states share in common other than their opposition to colonial rule? As Alexander Hamilton, James Madison, and John Jay were publishing *The Federalist* to promulgate common political principles and beliefs for the nation's citizens, American authors were also being called on to promote a common set of cultural values. "America must be as independent in *literature* as she is in *politics*," Noah Webster declared, "as famous for arts as she is for arms" (Spencer, *The Quest for Nationality*, p. 27). However, the barriers to such cultural independence were formidable. Because there was no international copyright law, American booksellers could reprint English editions without paying royalties. As a result, the literary marketplace was flooded with foreign works. Why publish—or purchase, for that matter—the work of an American writer when one could have the writings of the best-known authors of Britain and Europe for little more than the cost of paper and ink? Magazines and newspapers also capitalized on this situation by reprinting poetry, essays, and criticism culled from the latest British periodicals. An odd phenomenon began to occur: In order for American authors to win approval from the American public, they first had to establish a critical reputation in the British press.

The extent of the public's reliance on British critical opinion is captured succinctly in Philip Freneau's satirical advice "To a New England Poet."

> Dear bard, I pray you, take the hint,
> In England what you write and print,
> Republished here in shop, or stall,
> Will perfectly enchant us all:
> It will assume a different face,
> And post your name at every place.

Cultural subservience to England was further compounded by the British disdain for all things American in the decade following the War of 1812. In the January 1820 issue of the *Edinburgh Review*, Sydney Smith famously posed the rhetorical question: "In the four quarters of the globe, who reads an American book? Or goes to an American play? Or looks at an American picture or statue?" Washington Irving responded directly to such criticisms in *The Sketch-Book of Geoffrey Crayon, Gent*. Published in England in the same year as Smith's notorious taunt, *The Sketch-Book* established Irving's reputation, according to John Gibson Lockhart in the February 1820 issue of *Blackwood's Edinburgh Magazine*, as an author whose writings "should be classed with the best English writings of our day." It was hailed as evidence that America possessed the raw materials necessary to produce a culture of its own. In his review, Lockhart wrote, "[*The Sketch-Book*] proves to us distinctly that there is *mind* working in America, and that there are materials, too, for it to work upon, of a very singular and romantic kind."

While helping American literature gain legitimacy in England and Europe, Irving's *Sketch-Book* also introduced British and European romanticism into American culture. In post-Revolutionary America, literature was considered part of public discourse rather than the unique expression of an individual artist. Poetry and fiction had a well-defined civic purpose: to educate readers in the virtues of citizenship. This was especially important in the newly formed republic, where common law practices were being implemented across regions with widely divergent social customs, from puritan New England to the plantation-based South. Writers were expected to produce stories and poems that were morally instructive, domestic and national allegories that illustrated how and why individuals should subordinate their personal interests and inclinations to the public good. Purely imaginative literature, and especially the novel, was suspect, because it elicited from readers emotional and psychological responses that were unregulated by principles of community. However, the public conception of literature began to change as British and European romanticism made its way across the Atlantic. The works of Thomas Carlyle, Samuel Taylor Coleridge, William Wordsworth, and other prominent romantic writers were printed and reprinted by American booksellers and magazine editors. Gradually, fiction came to represent a space of imaginative freedom, a setting suitable for the self-reliant individualism championed by Ralph Waldo Emerson and Henry David Thoreau. What appeared as a dangerous and seductive wilderness to the citizen of the early republic came to be perceived as a symbolic space of unlimited possibility.

Washington Irving's writings were an integral part of this transformation. He was among the first American writers to separate literary fiction from public discourse. Although his early writings contain elements of social and political satire, he refused to put his writing in the service of a single party or cause. Evidence of this can be found in his 1848 "Preface to the Revised Edition of *The Sketch-Book*," in which Irving relates his struggle to find a publisher. He appealed to Sir Walter Scott for help; Scott, after reading some parts of the manuscript, offered Irving the editorship of a weekly periodical but warned him that it would have "somewhat of a political bearing." Irving's reply makes clear that he preferred to write when and what he pleased.

> [I am] peculiarly unfitted for the situation offered to me, not merely by my political opinions, but by the very constitution and habits of my mind. . . . I am unfitted for any periodically recurring task, or any stipulated labor of body or mind. I have no command of my talents, such as they are, and have to watch the varyings of my mind as I would those of a weather cock. Practice and training may bring me more into rule; but at present I am as useless for regular service as one of my own country Indians, or a Don Cossack.
>
> I must, therefore, keep on pretty much as I have begun; writing when I can, not when I would. I shall occasionally shift my residence and write whatever is suggested by objects before me, or whatever rises in my imagination; and hope to write better and more copiously by and by (Irving, *The Complete Works of Washington Irving*, vol. 8, p. 5).

What is remarkable about this retrospective account of his correspondence with Scott is the extent to which Irving identified as his own character traits he attributed to Geoffrey Crayon, the narrative persona he constructed for *The Sketch-Book*. In "The Author's Account of Himself," Irving describes how he spent the "holiday afternoons" of his youth "in rambles about the surrounding country [making himself] familiar with all its places famous in history or fable [and] neglect[ing] the regular exercises of the school" (pp. 49–50). These idle, romantic habits informed his peculiar narrative perspective, that of an outside observer of "the shifting scenes of life."

In describing this point of view, Irving presents writing as an activity that affords an aesthetic pleasure akin to travel or to shopping for prints.

> I have wandered through different countries, and witnessed many of the shifting scenes of life. I cannot say that I have studied them with the eye of a philosopher; but rather with the sauntering gaze with which humble lovers of the picturesque stroll from the window of one print-shop to another; caught sometimes by the delineations of beauty, sometimes by the distortions of caricature, and sometimes by the loveliness of landscape (p. 51).

More than a simple pun on the title of his book, this description exemplifies a significant shift in the public conception of reading. The subjects of his sketches are not meant to illustrate ethical norms for citizenship. They are meant to provide some distraction and relief from the pressures and anxieties of modern, professional life. Literature had become a leisure activity rather than a moral exercise in character formation.

If Geoffrey Crayon is a self-portrait, then Irving clearly thought of himself as a romantic writer recording his unique impressions with little regard for instructing readers in the political or moral truths of the moment. In so doing, he assumed a narrative persona that Nathaniel Hawthorne later imitated when he wrote in his introduction to *The Scarlet Letter*, "I am a citizen of somewhere else" (Hawthorne, vol. 1, p. 44). Irving's Geoffrey Crayon inaugurated a literary tradition of interiority and introspection that led subsequent writers such as Henry David Thoreau to declare that the true American frontier was to be found within each individual's experience. "The frontiers are not east or west, north or south," Thoreau wrote in *A Week on the Concord and Merrimack Rivers*, "[they are] wherever a man *fronts* a fact, though that fact be his neighbor. . . . Let him build himself a log-house with the bark on where he is, *fronting* IT" (Thoreau, *The Writings of Henry David Thoreau*, vol. 1, pp. 323–324). Irving's insistence that literature was a species of imaginative entertainment rather than a means of moral or political instruction helped usher in a new conception of artistry that contributed to the formation of an American literary culture conducive to democratic individualism.

Irving grew up in a post-Revolutionary America torn between its democratic aspirations for the future and its memories of the colonial era. During his boyhood, British sympathizers lived next door to veterans of the Continental army. Memories of the hardships endured while quartering British troops during the occupation of New York were mixed with frustration over financial losses incurred from the severing of ties with Great Britain. The War of 1812, often referred to as the Second War of American Independence, rekindled and put to rest some of these memories, but the early republic continued to be haunted by its British colonial past. The story "Rip Van Winkle" wonderfully illustrates Irving's strategy for putting these ghosts to rest. Set in Sleepy Hollow, "a little village of great antiquity . . . founded by some of the Dutch colonists, in the early times of the province," this story conjures up the ghosts of New York's Dutch colonial past in a way designed to erase the memory of America's subservience to British rule. Rip wanders from the village and out into the Kaatskill Mountains at a time when "the country was yet a province of Great Britain" (p. 74). When he returns after a twenty-year nap in the wilderness, the Revolutionary War is over and the signs of British colonial rule have been replaced by symbols of American independence. The village inn, which used to be "designated by a rubicund portrait of His Majesty George the Third" (p. 77), has been renamed the Union Hotel, and the sign bearing the portrait of King George has been repainted to look like George Washington. "The red coat was changed for one of blue and buff, a sword was held in the hand instead of a sceptre, the head was decorated with a cocked hat, and underneath was painted in large characters, GENERAL WASHINGTON" (p. 84).

Irving's story exemplifies the shift in public discourse that coincided with this transformation of the signs of colonial rule into the symbols of American nationalism. When he returns to the village Rip walks into the midst of a political debate led by "a lean, bilious-looking fellow . . . haranguing vehemently about rights of citizens—elections—members of congress—liberty—Bunker's

Hill—heroes of seventy-six—and other words, which were a perfect Babylonish jargon to the bewildered Van Winkle" (p. 84). When asked " 'Whether he was a Federal or Democrat,' " Rip is equally bewildered (p. 84). Irving's story, at this point, becomes a satire on the American public's preoccupation with political matters. The explanation for Rip's mysterious twenty-year absence turns out to be a legend derived from New York's Dutch colonial past. It is given by "old Peter Vanderdonk," whom we are told was "a descendant of the historian of that name, who wrote one of the earliest accounts of the province" (p. 87). He assures the villagers of "a fact, handed down from his ancestor," namely, that the Dutch explorer "Hendrick Hudson, the first discoverer of the river and country," returned to Sleepy Hollow every twenty years to "keep a guardian eye upon the river, and the great city called by his name" (p. 87).

Oddly, Hudson's protective intervention takes the form of playing nine-pins and drinking from "a stout keg" of Hollands gin. Rip, being "naturally a thirsty soul" joins in the carousing, and after repeated draughts from the flagon, "his senses were overpowered" (p. 81) and he passed out for the duration of the Revolutionary War and its political aftermath. Rip's long nap leads him to forget—or better, to never know   the traumatic separation from the land of their fathers that marks the memories of his fellow citizens. Moreover, in the story's conclusion, Irving cast Rip in the role of a storyteller so that his fellow citizens could share the bliss of forgetting. Loafing on the bench outside the Union Hotel, Rip tells his story to every stranger who arrives in the village and, in so doing, becomes a kind of living history that provides the younger generation with an alternative to the political turmoil of the post-Revolutionary period. He prefers "making friends among the rising generation, with whom he soon grew into great favor," and soon becomes "reverenced as one of the patriarchs of the village, and a chronicle of the old times 'before the war' " (p. 88). Those old times constitute a pre-history for the new republic free of the emotional scars of its having severed ties with England. By having Rip take up the task of the historian, Irving turns his story into an allegory of how to construct a "legendary" past, one that presents the origins of the nation as idyllic and therefore free of the political conflict that is inherently part of democracy (Horwitz, " 'Rip Van Winkle' and Legendary National Memory," p. 37).

Irving grew up in a time without a history. The youngest of eight surviving children, he was born on April 3, 1783, the same year British troops formally withdrew from New York. His father, William Irving, was a merchant of moderate means, whose business fluctuated with the political climate of the newly formed nation. His mother, Sarah Sanders Irving, was a devoted wife and mother, whom Irving remembered dearly throughout his life. He was the pampered favorite of his sisters, Ann, Catherine, and Sarah, and throughout his adolescence and early adulthood, his four brothers, William, Peter, Ebenezer, and John Treat, also watched over him. He was not spoiled, but latitude was allowed him conducive to his development as an artist. With four brothers already set to work in the family business, there was no need for him to be pressured into a practical education for a career. Irving showed quick intelligence in his schooling but little discipline. Instead of applying himself to Dillworth's *Arithmetic* or translations of Virgil, he was more apt to bury himself in books culled from his father's library. He found popular travel narratives especially appealing. He absorbed *The World Displayed*, a collection of travel narratives, along with fictional works such as *The Arabian Nights* and *Robinson Crusoe*. His religious upbringing also left him lukewarm. His father, a deacon in the Presbyterian Church, imposed rigorous theological training on his children. Irving later recalled that "religion was forced upon me before I could understand or appreciate it. I was forced to swallow it whether I would or not . . . until I was disgusted with all its forms and observances" (Williams, vol. 1, p. 7). He never attended Columbia College (now Columbia University), as did his brothers Peter and John, and eventually decided to study law less from ambition than to escape "the risks and harassing cares of commerce" (Irving, *The Complete Works of Washington Irving*, vol. 25, p. 1,008).

His knowledge of the law rendered him competent to attend to some aspects of the family's importing business, while still allowing him time to indulge his idle inclination for literature. By the time he was nineteen, he was employed in the offices of Judge Josiah Hoffman, former attorney general of New York. Irving found relief from the monotony of legal work in penning a series of letters under the pseudonym "Jonathan Oldstyle, Gent." He probably had the encouragement of his brother Peter who, as editor of the New York weekly *Morning Chronicle*, agreed to publish them. A light satire on the fashionable circles of New York's emerging middle class, these letters earned the young Irving some notoriety for his wit. The narrative persona he constructed—that of an elderly gentleman nostalgic for the social mores of the pre-Revolutionary period—anticipates his later narrators, Diedrich Knickerbocker and Geoffrey Crayon. The satire of the "Letters" is light, written for humor rather than for purposes of social reform, and this contributed to their success. The new nation was not yet ready for the goading criticisms of an Emerson or a Thoreau, and Irving's portrayal of New York manners allowed readers to laugh at themselves without feeling the sting of self-criticism. In this regard, the "Letters" initiate a pattern Irving would develop in his subsequent literary endeavors. His desire to appeal to the tastes of his audience caused him to avoid overtly controversial issues almost by instinct.

In his legal career, Irving experienced a similar mild success. He became a close friend of the Hoffman family, and especially enjoyed the company of the daughters, Ann and Matilda. He traveled with their father up the Hudson River to Albany, and then on to Montreal, through landscape he later described in "Rip Van Winkle" and "Dolph Heyliger." Soon after his return, he became ill and worried that he might be developing tuberculosis. His brothers arranged for him to travel to Europe in the hope that the climate would improve his health. Irving took full advantage of this opportunity and traveled extensively through France and Italy. While in Rome, he made the acquaintance of the landscape painter Washington Allston and briefly considered becoming a painter himself. Language, however, would remain Irving's chosen medium, even while he continued to experiment in his journals with scenic descriptions meant to parallel the picturesque style of his compatriot, Allston.

He returned to New York in March 1806 with a more worldly perspective on his native city of New York. That perspective narrowed to a satirical point in his contributions to *Salmagundi*, the series of twenty pamphlets he coauthored with his brother William and their friend James Kirke Paulding. *Salmagundi* was essentially a fictional newspaper complete with an editorial column and a variety of regular features, including theatrical criticism by "William Wizard, Esq.," satirical verse by "Pindar Cockloft," and political correspondence from "Mustapha Rub-a-Dub Keli Khan." Joseph Addison's *Spectactor* and Oliver Goldsmith's *Citizen of the World* surely served as models for the substance and form of this pamphlet, but there were a number of publications closer to home that also inspired these young wits—first among them, the Philadelphia *Port Folio*, edited by Joseph Dennie.

The idea for *Salmagundi* emerged out of a social club called by various names, including "the lads of Kilkenny" and "the nine worthies." Irving's brothers, William, Peter, and Ebenezer, were all members, along with Paulding, Henry Brevoort, and other young bachelors of New York's merchant class. Their gossip and banter about literary, theatrical, social, and political issues provided the raw material for the early numbers of the pamphlet, which quickly gained notoriety from New York to Philadelphia. The success of *Salmagundi* may have inspired Irving's next project. Along with his brother Peter, he began to write a parody of a well-known guidebook of New York, Samuel Mitchill's *The Picture of New York; or, The Traveller's Guide, through the Commercial Metropolis of the United States* (1809). What began as a simple spoof grew into Irving's first significant work, his Rabelaisian epic *A History of New York*.

The composition of *A History* coincided with his courtship of Matilda Hoffman, and his literary enthusiasm grew under the influence of their love. In his notebooks, Irving recalled their courtship.

> I would read to her from some favorite poet . . . and dwell upon his merits when I came to some tender passage [that] seemed to catch my excited feelings. I would close the book and launch forth into his praises and when I had wrought myself up into some strain of enthusiasm I would turn to her pale dark eyes beaming upon me . . . I would drink in new inspiration from them—until she suddenly seemed to recollect herself—& throw them down upon the earth with a sweet pensiveness and a full drawn sigh (quoted in Williams, vol. 2, p. 195).

When Josiah Hoffman learned of the young couple's budding relationship, he offered Irving a partnership in his law firm to ensure that the dilettante author settled into a regular career. Tragically, though, Matilda suffered from tuberculosis, the consumptive disease Irving's brothers had sent him to Europe to escape. As their courtship progressed her health deteriorated, and on April 26, 1809, she died, at the age of seventeen. Irving was overwhelmed.

> I cannot tell you what a horrid state of mind I was in for a long time—I seemed to care for nothing—the world was a blank to me—I abandoned all thoughts of the Law—I went into the country, but could not bear solitude yet could not enjoy society—There was a dismal horror continually in my mind that made me fear to be alone—I had often to get up in the night & seek the bedroom of my brother, as if having a human being by me would relieve me of the frightful gloom of my thoughts (Williams, vol. 2, pp. 257–258).

He found solace in working on *A History*, spending long days in the libraries of New York and Philadelphia. The source material he gleaned from European travel narratives and early colonial histories would give his manuscript a verisimilitude that added to its popularity.

This air of realism was heightened by a promotional stunt Irving pulled off with the help of Henry Brevoort and James Kirke Paulding. In the weeks prior to publication, he published a report in the New York *Evening Post* that an elderly gentleman by the name of Knickerbocker had wandered off from his lodgings without paying his rent, leaving behind only a collection of papers in manuscript. In a subsequent issue, a letter to the editor reported that a gentleman matching Knickerbocker's description had been seen in the Hudson River Valley, walking north toward Albany. A week and a half later, under the pseudonym "Seth Handaside, Landlord of the Independent Columbian Hotel," Irving announced that the manuscript Knickerbocker left behind was to be published in order to "pay off his bill for boarding and lodging" (p. 374). This hoax was remarkably successful, so much so that for a time Irving's narrator gained greater notoriety than the author himself. The historical accuracy of his narrative of New York's history as the Dutch colony of New Amsterdam made his mock-heroic epic more than a Swiftean satire. It provided the newly formed nation with a basis for history that was free of associations with British colonial rule. In so doing, *A History* anticipates on a grand scale the historical displacement that is a central theme of Irving's better-known story, "Rip Van Winkle."

America's need to declare its cultural independence from Britain intensified in the decade following the War of 1812. In August 1814, after the British burned Washington, D.C., Irving enlisted. He served as aide-de-camp to New York's Governor Daniel Tompkins, but the war was in its final stages and he never saw action. However, he did gain experience in politics and diplomacy that served him well later in life (he was appointed secretary to the American legation in London in 1829, and minister to Spain in 1842). Unfortunately, his political talents could not help save the family importing business. P. & E. Irving foundered after the war, largely due to Peter Irving's mismanagement of purchasing in Liverpool. The demand for imported goods had evaporated as public sentiment became decidedly anti-British and manufacturing increased in the mid-Atlantic region. Irving sailed to Liverpool in June 1815 intending to travel through England and Europe for a second time, but he found himself caught up in the financial collapse of the firm. He remembered this period as one of the darkest of his life.

> This new calamity seemed more intolerable even than [Matilda's death]. That was solemn and sanctifying, it seemed while it prostrated my spirits, to purify & elevate my soul. But this was vile and sordid and humiliated me to the dust. . . . I lost all appetite, I scarcely slept— I went to my bed every night as to a grave (Williams, vol. 2, p. 259).

To drive off his despondency, Irving again turned to writing. He had the good fortune to meet up with Washington Allston who, along with his fellow American artist Charles Leslie, had been commissioned to illustrate a British edition of *A History*. Irving became their regular companion, and they encouraged him to pursue the literary "sketches" he had begun to write. To gain some relief from the anxieties of impending bankruptcy, he traveled to Scotland and met Sir Walter Scott, whom he had long admired. Scott invited Irving to spend a few days with him at Abbotsford, and this visit had a decisive influence on Irving's conception of *The Sketch-Book*. Scott's deep interest in folklore as the foundational element of a national culture confirmed Irving's intuition that a legend of Sleepy Hollow might merit as much attention as Rob Roy.

When Irving returned to Liverpool to appear before the Commissioners of Bankruptcy with his brother Peter, he already had decided to pursue a career in literature. His brother William, a congressman back in Washington, D.C., made arrangements for him to serve as first clerk in the Navy Department at a comfortable salary, but Irving declined the post, for he was determined "to raise myself once more by my talents, and owe nothing to compassion" (Williams, vol. 2, p. 260). In a letter of explanation to his brother Ebenezer, he declared, "My talents are merely literary," and pleaded "to be left for a little while entirely to the bent of my own inclination, and not agitated by new plans for subsistence, or by entreaties to come home" (Irving, vol. 23, p. 541). The brothers honored his request, and by June 1819 the first installment of *The Sketch-Book* was in print in America. Irving had more difficulty finding a publisher in England and eventually made arrangements to print the first volume at his own expense. The early reviews were positive, praising Irving for his style and recognizing him as that hitherto unheard of thing, a genuine American man of letters. Now confident that the book would pay for itself, London publisher John Murray agreed to take over publication of the remaining volumes, and Irving's reputation was assured.

The Sketch-Book marks the apex of Irving's career. Having declared his independence from his family, he was confident enough to declare independence for American literature as well, which he did overtly in "English Writers on America" (p. 91). More importantly, his narrator, Geoffrey Crayon, was a prototypical figure of the American individual. In the opening sketch, "The Voyage," Crayon's passage across the Atlantic leaves him doubly detached from family and place. Crossing the Atlantic is like opening "a blank page in existence" that "severs" the chain of memories that otherwise would "[grapple] us to home" (p. 52). His arrival in Liverpool is no joyous return of a prodigal son to the land of his forefathers. It only deepens his isolation. While preparing to disembark from the ship, he witnesses a dying sailor being carried ashore and feels himself "a stranger in the land" (p. 57). The melancholy Irving evokes from Crayon's situation as an aimless tourist suggests a feeling of placelessness often associated with American individualism. Crayon's alienation is the other side of Emerson's self-reliant assertion that "Whoso would be a man must be a nonconformist" (Emerson, *The Collected Works of Ralph Waldo Emerson*, vol. 2, p. 29). The poignant detachment of Crayon's point of view anticipates such first-person narrators as Nathaniel Hawthorne's Miles Coverdale, Herman Melville's Ishmael, or F. Scott Fitzgerald's Nick Carraway. Yet it was Irving's displacement from home that caused him to imagine Sleepy Hollow as an ideal "retreat, whither I might steal from the world and its distractions, and dream quietly away the remnant of a troubled life" (p. 163).

Two-thirds of *The Sketch-Book* is made up of observational essays that fall into the genre of travel literature. Only five of its "sketches" are recognizably what we would call short stories (if we include "The Wife" and "The Mutability of Literature" along with "Rip Van Winkle," "The Spectre Bridegroom," and "The Legend of Sleepy Hollow"). Yet it is these few stories that make Irving an innovative artist whom some have called the inventor of the short story in America. As Fred Lewis Pattee observed, Irving "was the first prominent writer to strip the prose tale of its moral and didactic elements and to make of it a literary form solely for entertainment" (*The Development of the American Short Story*, p. 21). The short stories in *The Sketch-Book* are regularly interspersed among sketches of daily life and social customs in Great Britain and provide imaginative relief from what might otherwise become a mundane travel narrative. Irving actively pursued the commercialization of literature in his next two works as well, enlarging the fictional component of both *Bracebridge Hall* (1822) and *Tales of a Traveller* (1824). In *Bracebridge Hall*, he capitalized on the success of his descriptions of rural England, while at the same time pursuing his interest in prose fiction. The premise for *Bracebridge Hall* is simple. Geoffrey Crayon returns to the fictional manor he had described in some sections of *The Sketch-Book* to spend a few weeks there while preparations are being made for the marriage of Julia, "the daughter of a favorite college friend" of Simon Bracebridge. Like *The Sketch-Book*, a majority of *Bracebridge Hall* is made up of descriptions of the Hall and its environs and character sketches of the family, their guests, and the inhabitants of the local village. As the book proceeds, Irving regularly creates opportunities for characters to relate stories, the longest of which, "Dolph Heyliger," Crayon presents as "a manuscript tale from the pen of my fellow-countryman, the late Mr. Diedrich Knickerbocker, the historian of New York" (p. 214).

Irving is doing more than simply filling out the pages of his book with an occasional story set in America. He is using the conventional genres that were popular with readers of magazines and gift books—the observational essay or character sketch written in a confessional mode—as a platform for staging stories mildly Gothic in tone and content. He would take this method a step further in *Tales of a Traveller*, the first of his collections in which fiction predominates over travel narrative. Divided into four books, *Tales* lacks the unity that a common setting gives to *Bracebridge Hall*, but Irving compensates for this by creating tale-telling contests, or by using frame-narratives to nest a story within a story, as with the interrelated series that includes "Adventure of the Mysterious Picture," "Adventure of the Mysterious Stranger," and "The Story of the Young Italian." Although Irving originally intended to use his travels through Germany and Italy as the organizational premise for *Tales*, he abandoned this realist narrative framework and told his stories as he would. He felt that the final manuscript was uneven but also believed it contained some of his best writing. Critics in England and America unfortunately did not agree. They found it imitative and even vulgar for its moments of sexual innuendo and for the darker psychological strain of tales such as "Adventure of the German Student." As a critic in the October 1824 issue of the *Westminster Review* made painfully clear, Irving's vogue in literary London had passed.

> Geoffrey's fame was occasioned by the fact of his being a *prodigy*; a prodigy for show—such as La Belle Sauvage, or the learned pig: up to the time of Geoffrey, there were no Belles Lettres in America, no native *litterateurs*, and he shot up at once with true American growth, a triumphant proof of what had so long been doubted and denied, namely, that the sentimental plant may flourish even on that republican soil.

But now, this critic continued, Irving catered to the tastes of a shallow, bourgeois audience, providing them with "a little pathos, a little sentiment to excite tears as a pleasurable emotion," yet little of "solid matter." Still, *Tales* sold well and Irving's reputation with the public was not spoiled by the poor critical reception it received.

His interest in writing fiction was dampened, though, and he turned to popular history and biography instead, like that which he had written in *A History of New York* but without the satirical overtone. He traveled to Madrid in 1826 and, at the suggestion of Alexander Everett, the American minister to Spain, began translating Martín Fernández de Navarette's history of Columbus. He eventually abandoned the idea of a direct translation, choosing to write a biography of his own from sources he culled from the private library of Obadiah Rich, an American consul in Madrid to whom Everett introduced him. His *A History of the Life and Voyages of Christopher Columbus* was published in 1828, and the other works associated with Irving's Spanish period soon followed: *A Chronicle of the Conquest of Granada* (1829), *Voyages and Discoveries of the Companions of Columbus* (1831), and *The Alhambra* (1832).

With *The Alhambra*, Irving returned to fiction, and in that same year, he returned to America after a seventeen-year absence. He continued to write prolifically, producing dozens of stories for the *Knickerbocker*, a magazine named after one of his most famous narrators, and three novel-length books—*A Tour of the Prairies* (1835), *Astoria* (1836), and *The Adventures of Captain Bonneville, U.S.A.* (1837). None of these, however, captured the depth of emotion Irving was able to distill into *The Sketch-Book*. In 1842 he returned to Europe, having agreed to serve as minister to Spain under the Tyler administration. When he returned to America for good in 1846, he retired to Sunnyside, the "neglected cottage" situated on the banks of the Hudson, which he had renovated as his own Sleepy Hollow retreat. The major work of his later years was a five-volume biography of his namesake, *The Life of George Washington*. In 1859 he finished the final volume with the help of his nephew Pierre Irving, who had taken over the management of his literary estate. He died that same year, having completed this last great memorial to the nation whose birth coincided with his own.

Peter Norberg received his Ph.D. from Rice University in 1998. Since 1997 he has been Assistant Professor of English at Saint Joseph's University in Philadelphia. A specialist on the writers associated with the transcendentalist movement, he has written and lectured extensively on Ralph Waldo Emerson, Henry David Thoreau, Margaret Fuller, and the critical reaction to transcendentalism in the writings of Nathaniel Hawthorne and Edgar Allan Poe. He also has published articles on Herman Melville and the poetry of Richard Henry Stoddard. His future projects include a history of Emerson's career as a public lecturer.

A Note on the Text

This edition contains stories from three of Irving's collections, *The Sketch-Book* (1820), *Bracebridge Hall* (1822), and *Tales of a Traveller* (1824), as well as selections from his early writings: *Letters of Jonathan Oldstyle, Gent.* (1802), *Salmagundi* (1807–1808), and *A History of New York* (1809). The text of this edition is based on the Author's Revised Edition that was issued by Putnam in New York in 1848. With the exception of *A History of New York*, the selections are arranged chronologically in the order in which Irving published them. In the Author's Revised Edition, Irving made substantial changes to the style and content of *A History*. Accordingly, the selections from that volume are placed at the end of this edition. Readers interested in the 1809 edition of *A History* and any other textual matters should consult *The Complete Works of Washington Irving*, completed under the general editorship of Henry A. Pochmann, Herbert L. Kleinfield, and Richard Dilworth Rust (see "For Further Reading").

THE LEGEND OF
SLEEPY HOLLOW

and Other Writings

Contents

SELECTIONS FROM

LETTERS OF
JONATHAN OLDSTYLE, GENT.[1]

Letter I

Mr. Editor,—If the observations of an odd old fellow are not wholly superfluous, I would thank you to shove them into a spare corner of your paper.

It is a matter of amusement to an uninterested spectator like myself, to observe the influence fashion has on the dress and deportment of its votaries,* and how very quick they fly from one extreme to the other.

A few years since the rage was,—very high crowned hats with very narrow brims, tight neckcloth, tight coat, tight jacket, tight small-clothes, and shoes loaded with enormous silver buckles; the hair craped, plaited, queued, and powdered;—in short, an air of the greatest spruceness and tightness diffused over the whole person.

The ladies, with their tresses neatly turned up over an immense cushion; waist a yard long, braced up with stays into the smallest compass, and encircled by an enormous hoop; so that the fashionable belle resembled a walking bottle.

Thus dressed, the lady was seen, with the most bewitching languor, reclining on the arm of an extremely attentive beau, who, with a long cane, decorated with an enormous tassel, was carefully employed in removing every stone, stick, or straw that might impede the progress of his tottering companion, whose high-heeled shoes just brought the points of her toes to the ground.

What an alteration has a few years produced! We now behold our gentlemen, with the most studious carelessness and almost slovenliness of dress; large hat, large coat, large neckcloth, large pantaloons, large boots, and hair scratched into every careless direction, lounging along the streets in the most apparent listlessness and vacuity of thought; staring with an unmeaning countenance at every passenger, or leaning upon the arm of some kind fair one for support, with the other hand crammed into his breeches' pocket. Such is the picture of a

---

*Followers.

modern beau,—in his dress stuffing himself up to the dimensions of a Hercules,* in his manners affecting the helplessness of an invalid.

The belle who has to undergo the fatigue of dragging along this sluggish animal has chosen a character the very reverse,—emulating in her dress and actions all the airy lightness of a sylph, she trips along with the greatest vivacity. Her laughing eye, her countenance enlivened with affability and good-humor, inspire with kindred animation every beholder, except the torpid being by her side, who is either affecting the fashionable sangfroid,† or is wrapt up in profound contemplation of himself.

Heavens! how changed are the manners since I was young! Then, how delightful to contemplate a ball-room,—such bowing, such scraping, such complimenting; nothing but copperplate speeches‡ to be heard on both sides; no walking but in minuet measure;§ nothing more common than to see half a dozen gentlemen knock their heads together in striving who should first recover a lady's fan or snuff-box that had fallen.

But now, our youths no longer aim at the character of pretty gentlemen; their greatest Ambition is to be called lazy dogs, careless fellows, &c., &c. Dressed up in the mammoth style, our buck saunters into the ball-room in a surtout, hat under arm, cane in hand; strolls round with the most vacant air; stops abruptly before such lady as he may choose to honor with his attention; entertains her with the common slang of the day, collected from the conversation of hostlers, footmen, portors, &c., until his string of smart sayings is run out, and then lounges off to entertain some other fair one with the same unintelligible jargon. Surely, Mr. Editor, puppyism** must have arrived to a climax; it must turn; to carry it to a greater extent seems to me impossible.

JONATHAN OLDSTYLE
NOVEMBER 15, 1802

---

*Mythical hero of ancient Greece who possessed remarkable strength and the courage to accomplish any task.
†Cool indifference; literally, "cold blood" (French).
‡Ornate speeches, such as those printed from engraved copper printing plates.
§As in the slow, stately pace of the minuet.
**That is, the conceited arrogance of young men.

Letter II

Sir,—Encouraged by the ready insertion you gave my former communication, I have taken the liberty to intrude on you a few more remarks.

Nothing is more intolerable to an old person than innovation on old habits. The customs that prevailed in our youth become dear to us as we advance in years; and we can no more bear to see them abolished than we can to behold the trees cut down under which we have sported in the happy days of infancy.

Even I myself, who have floated down the stream of life with the tide,—who have humored it in all its turnings, who have conformed in a great measure to all its fashions,—cannot but feel sensible of this prejudice. I often sigh when I draw a comparison between the present and the past; and though I cannot but be sensible that, in general, times are altered for the better, yet there is something, even in the imperfections of the manners which prevailed in my youthful days, that is inexpressibly endearing.

There is nothing that seems more strange and preposterous to me than the manner in which modern marriages are conducted.[2] The parties keep the matter as secret as if there was something disgraceful in the connection. The lady positively denies that anything of the kind is to happen; will laugh at her intended husband, and even lay bets against the event, the very day before it is to take place. They sneak into matrimony as quietly as possible, and seem to pride themselves on the cunning and ingenuity they have displayed in their manœuvres.

How different is this from the manners of former times! I recollect when my aunt Barbara was addressed by 'Squire Stylish; nothing was heard of during the whole courtship but consultations and negotiations between her friends and relatives; the matter was considered and reconsidered, and at length the time set for a final answer. Never, Mr. Editor, shall I forget the awful solemnity of the scene. The whole family of the Oldstyles assembled in awful conclave: my aunt Barbara dressed out as fine as hands could make

11

her,—high cushion, enormous cap, long waist, prodigious hoop, ruffles that reached to the end of her fingers, and a gown of flame-colored brocade, figured with poppies, roses, and sunflowers. Never did she look so sublimely handsome. The 'Squire entered the room with a countenance suited to the solemnity of the occasion. He was arrayed in a full suit of scarlet velvet, his coat decorated with a profusion of large silk buttons, and the skirts stiffened with a yard or two of buckram; a long pig-tailed wig, well powdered, adorned his head; and stockings of deep blue silk, rolled over the knees, graced his extremities; the flaps of his vest reached to his knee-buckles, and the ends of his cravat, tied with the most precise neatness, twisted through every button-hole. Thus accoutred, he gravely walked into the room, with his ivory-headed ebony cane in one hand, and gently swaying his three-cornered beaver with the other. The gallant and fashionable appearance of the 'Squire, the gracefulness and dignity of his deportment, occasioned a general smile of complacency through the room; my aunt Barbara modestly veiled her countenance with her fan, but I observed her contemplating her admirer with great satisfaction through the sticks.

The business was opened with the most formal solemnity, but was not long in agitation. The Oldstyles were moderate; their articles of capitulation few; the 'Squire was gallant, and acceded to them all. In short, the blushing Barbara was delivered up to his embraces with due ceremony. Then, Mr. Editor, then were the happy times: such oceans of arrack,*—such mountains of plumcake,—such feasting and congratulating,—such fiddling and dancing,—ah me! who can think of those days, and not sigh when he sees the degeneracy of the present: no eating of cake nor throwing of stockings,— not a single skin filled with wine on the joyful occasion,—nor a single pocket edified by it but the parson's.

It is with the greatest pain I see those customs dying away, which served to awaken the hospitality and friendship of my ancient comrades,—that strewed with flowers the path to the altar, and shed a ray of sunshine on the commencement of the matrimonial union.

The deportment of my aunt Barbara and her husband was as decorous after marriage as before; her conduct was always regulated

---

*A sweet alcoholic drink.

by his,—her sentiments ever accorded with his opinions; she was always eager to tie on his neckcloth of a morning,—to tuck a napkin under his chin at meal-times,—to wrap him up warm of a winter's day, and to spruce him up as smart as possible of a Sunday. The 'Squire was the most attentive and polite husband in the world; would hand his wife in and out of church with the greatest ceremony,—drink her health at dinner with particular emphasis, and ask her advice on every subject,—though I must confess he invariably adopted his own;—nothing was heard from both sides but dears, sweet loves, doves, &c. The 'Squire could never stir out of a winter's day, without his wife calling after him from the window to button up his waistcoat carefully. Thus, all things went on smoothly; and my relations Stylish had the name—and, as far as I know, deserved it,—of being the most happy and loving couple in the world.

A modern married pair will, no doubt, laugh at all this; they are accustomed to treat one another with the utmost carelessness and neglect. No longer does the wife tuck the napkin under her husband's chin, nor the husband attend to heaping her plate with dainties;—no longer do I see those little amusing fooleries in company where the lady would pat her husband's cheek, and he chuck her under the chin; when dears, and sweets were as plenty as cookies on a New-year's day. The wife now considers herself as totally independent,—will advance her own opinions, without hesitation, though directly opposite to his,—will carry on accounts of her own, and will even have secrets of her own, with which she refuses to entrust him.

Who can read these facts, and not lament with me the degeneracy of the present times;—what husband is there but will look back with regret to the happy days of female subjection.

JONATHAN OLDSTYLE
NOVEMBER 20, 1802

SELECTIONS FROM

SALMAGUNDI[1]

As everybody knows, or ought to know, what a SALMAGUND* is, we shall spare ourselves the trouble of an explanation; besides, we despise trouble as we do everything low and mean, and hold the man who would incur it unnecessarily as an object worthy our highest pity and contempt. Neither will we puzzle our heads to give an account of ourselves, for two reasons; first, because it is nobody's business; secondly, because if it were, we do not hold ourselves bound to attend to anybody's business but our own; and even *that* we take the liberty of neglecting when it suits our inclination. To these we might add a third, that very few men can give a tolerable account of themselves, let them try over so hard; but this reason, we candidly avow, would not hold good with ourselves.

There are, however, two or three pieces of information which we bestow gratis on the public, chiefly because it suits our own pleasure and convenience that they should be known, and partly because we do not wish that there should be any ill will between us at the commencement of our acquaintance.

Our intention is simply to instruct the young, reform the old, correct the town, and castigate the age; this is an arduous task, and therefore we undertake it with confidence. We intend for this purpose to present a striking picture of the town; and as everybody is anxious to see his own phiz† on canvas, however stupid or ugly it may be, we have no doubt but the whole town will flock to our exhibition. Our picture will necessarily include a vast variety of figures; and should any gentleman or lady be displeased with the inveterate truth of their likenesses, they may ease their spleen by laughing at those of their neighbors—this being what *we* understand by *poetical justice*.

---

*Or salmagundi: dish made up of an assortment of meats, eggs, and vegetables; a miscellany.
†Face; shortened from "physiognomy."

Like all true and able editors, we consider ourselves infallible; and therefore, with the customary diffidence of our brethren of the quill, we shall take the liberty of interfering in all matters either of a public or a private nature. We are critics, amateurs, dilettanti, and cognoscenti; and as we know "by the pricking of our thumbs," that every opinion which we may advance in either of those characters will be correct, we are determined though it may be questioned, contradicted, or even controverted, yet it shall never be revoked.

We beg the public particularly to understand that we solicit no patronage. We are determined, on the contrary, that the patronage shall be entirely on our side. We have nothing to do with the pecuniary concerns of the paper; its success will yield us neither pride nor profit—nor will its failure occasion to us either loss or mortification. We advise the public, therefore, to purchase our numbers merely for their own sakes; if they do not, let them settle the affair with their consciences and posterity.

To conclude, we invite all editors of newspapers and literary journals to praise us heartily in advance, as we assure them that we intend to deserve their praises. To our next-door neighbor, "Town,"* we hold out a hand of amity, declaring to him that, after ours, his paper will stand the best chance for immortality. We proffer an exchange of civilities: he shall furnish us with notices of epic poems and tobacco; and we in return will enrich him with original speculations on all manner of subjects, together with "the rummaging of my grandfather's mahogany chest of drawers," "the life and amours of mine Uncle John," "anecdotes of the Cockloft family,"† and learned quotations from that unheard of writer of folios, *Linkum Fidelius*.‡

---

*The title of a newspaper published in New York, the columns of which, among other miscellaneous topics, occasionally contained strictures on the performances at the theatres.—*Paris Ed.* [Irving's note].
†Fictional family whose exploits are depicted in subsequent numbers of *Salmagundi*.
‡This sentence concludes with a list of the regular features and columns of *Salmagundi*.

FROM MY ELBOW-CHAIR

As I delight in everything novel and eccentric, and would at any time give an old coat for a new idea, I am particularly attentive to the manners and conversation of strangers, and scarcely ever a traveller enters this city whose appearance promises anything original, but by some means or another I form an acquaintance with him. I must confess I often suffer manifold afflictions from the intimacies thus contracted: my curiosity is frequently punished by the stupid details of a blockhead, or the shallow verbosity of a coxcomb.* Now, I would prefer at any time to travel with an ox-team through a Carolina sand-flat, rather than plod through a heavy, unmeaning conversation with the former; and as to the latter, I would sooner hold sweet converse with the wheel of a knife-grinder than endure his monotonous chattering. In fact, the strangers who flock to this most pleasant of all earthly cities are generally mere birds of passage, whose plumage is often gay enough, I own, but their notes,† "heaven save the mark" are as unmusical as those of that classic night-bird which the ancients humorously selected as the emblem of wisdom.‡ Those from the South, it is true, entertain me with their horses, equipages, and puns; and it is excessively pleasant to hear a couple of these *four-in-hand*§ gentlemen detail their exploits over a bottle. Those from the East have often induced me to doubt the existence of the wise men of yore, who are said to have flourished in that quarter; and as for those from parts beyond seas—O! my masters, ye shall hear more from me anon.

---

*Flamboyant, ostentatious man.
†That is, their colloquial expressions.
‡That is, an owl.
§Coach drawn by four horses.

Heaven help this unhappy town! hath it not goslings enow of its own hatching and rearing, that it must be overwhelmed by such an inundation of ganders from other climes? I would not have any of my courteous and gentle readers suppose that I am running *a muck*, full tilt, cut and slash, upon all foreigners indiscriminately. I have no national antipathies, though related to the Cockloft family. As to honest John Bull,* I shake him heartily by the hand, assuring him that I love his jolly countenance, and, moreover, am lineally descended from him; in proof of which I allege my invincible predilection for roast beef and pudding. I therefore look upon all his children as my kinsmen; and I beg, when I tickle a cockney, I may not be understood as trimming an Englishman;—they being very distinct animals, as I shall clearly demonstrate in a future number. If any one wishes to know my opinion of the Irish and Scotch, he may find it in the characters of those two nations, drawn by the first advocate of the age. But the French, I must confess, are my favorites; and I have taken more pains to argue my cousin Pindar† out of his antipathy to them than I ever did about any other thing. When, therefore, I choose to hunt a Monsieur for my own particular amusement, I beg it may not be asserted that I intend him as a representative of his countrymen at large. Far from this; I love the nation, as being a nation of right merry fellows, possessing the true secret of being happy; which is nothing more than thinking of nothing, talking about anything, and laughing at everything. I mean only to tune up those little thingimys,‡ who represent nobody but themselves; who have no national trait about them but their language, and who hop about our town in swarms, like little toads after a shower.

Among the few strangers whose acquaintance has entertained me, I particularly rank the magnanimous Mustapha Rub-a-dub Keli Khan, a most illustrious captain of a ketch,§ who figured, some time since, in our fashionable circles, at the head of a ragged

---

*Stereotypical Englishman.
†Greek lyric poet (c.518–c.438 B.C.).
‡Variant of "thingamajigs" or "what-do-you-call-them."
§Coastal sailing vessel.

regiment of Tripolitan prisoners.* His conversation was to me a perpetual feast; I chuckled with inward pleasure at his whimsical mistakes and unaffected observations on men and manners, and I rolled each odd conceit "like a sweet morsel under my tongue."

Whether Mustapha was captivated by my iron-bound physiognomy, or flattered by the attentions which I paid him, I won't determine; but I so far gained his confidence, that, at his departure, he presented me with a bundle of papers, containing, among other articles, several copies of letters, which he had written to his friends at Tripoli. The following is a translation of one of them. The original is in Arabic-Greek; but by the assistance of Will Wizard, who understands all languages, not excepting that manufactured by Psalmanazar,[3] I have been enabled to accomplish a tolerable translation. We should have found little difficulty in rendering it into English, had it not been for Mustapha's confounded pot-hooks and trammels.

LETTER FROM MUSTAPHA RUB-A-DUB KELI KHAN,

CAPTAIN OF A KETCH, TO ASEM HACCHEM,
PRINCIPAL SLAVE-DRIVER TO HIS HIGHNESS
THE BASHAW OF TRIPOLI

Thou wilt learn from this letter, most illustrious disciple of Mahomet,[†] that I have for some time resided in New York; the most polished, vast, and magnificent city of the United States of America. But what to me are its delights! I wander a captive through its splendid streets, I turn a heavy eye on every rising day

---

*Several Tripolitan prisoners, taken by an American squadron, in an action off Tripoli, were brought to New York, where they lived at large, objects of the curiosity and hospitality of the inhabitants, until an opportunity presented to restore them to their own country.—*Paris Ed.* [Irving's note].[2]

†Or Muhammad (570?–632), prophet and founder of Islam, whose revelations are recorded in the Qur'an. In 1850 Irving published *Lives of Mahomet and His Successors*, a biography he worked on sporadically for years.

that beholds me banished from my country. The Christian husbands here lament most bitterly any short absence from home, though they leave but one wife behind to lament their departure; what then, must be the feelings of thy unhappy kinsman, while thus lingering at an immeasurable distance from three-and-twenty of the most lovely and obedient wives in all Tripoli! O Allah! shall thy servant never again return to his native land, nor behold his beloved wives, who beam on his memory beautiful as the rosy morn of the east, and graceful as Mahomet's camel!

Yet beautiful, O most puissant slave-driver, as are my wives, they are far exceeded by the women of this country. Even those who run about the streets with bare arms and necks (*et cetera*), whose habiliments are too scanty to protect them from the inclemency of the seasons, or the scrutinizing glances of the curious, and who it would seem belong to nobody, are lovely as the houris* that people the elysium of true believers. If, then, such as run wild in the highways, and whom no one cares to appropriate, are thus beauteous, what must be the charms of those who are shut up in the seraglios,[†] and never permitted to go abroad! surely the region of beauty, the Valley of the Graces,[‡] can contain nothing so inimitably fair!

But, notwithstanding the charms of these infidel women, they are apt to have one fault, which is extremely troublesome and inconvenient. Wouldst thou believe it, Asem, I have been positively assured by a famous dervise,[§] or doctor, as he is here called, that at least one-fifth part of them—have souls! Incredible as it may seem to thee, I am the more inclined to believe them in possession of this monstrous superfluity, from my own little experience, and from the information which I have derived from others. In walking the streets I have actually seen an exceedingly good-looking woman, with soul enough to box her husband's ears to his heart's content, and my very whiskers trembled with indignation at the abject state of these

---

*Beautiful young women who inhabit the Muslim paradise.
[†]Harems.
[‡]A landscape in *The Citizen of the World; or, Letters from a Chinese Philosopher, Residing in London, to His Friends in the East* (1762), by English poet Oliver Goldsmith (letter 76, "The Preference of Grace to Beauty: An Allegory").
[§]Or dervishes; mendicant ascetics and religious teachers of Islam.

wretched infidels. I am told, moreover, that some of the women have soul enough to usurp the breeches of the men, but these I suppose are married and kept close; for I have not, in my rambles, met with any so extravagantly accoutred: others, I am informed, have soul enough to swear!—yea! by the beard of the great Omar, who prayed three times to each of the one hundred and twenty-four thousand prophets of our most holy faith, and who never swore but once in his life—they actually swear!

Get thee to the mosque, good Asem! return thanks to our most holy prophet, that he has been thus mindful of the comfort of all true Mussulmans, and has given them wives with no more souls than cats and dogs, and other necessary animals of the household.

Thou wilt doubtless be anxious to learn our reception in this country, and how we were treated by a people whom we have been accustomed to consider as unenlightened barbarians.

On landing we were waited upon to our lodgings, I suppose according to the directions of the municipality, by a vast and respectable escort of boys and negroes, who shouted and threw up their hats, doubtless to do honor to the magnanimous Mustapha, captain of a ketch; they were somewhat ragged and dirty in their equipments, but this we attributed to their republican simplicity. One of them, in the zeal of admiration, threw an old shoe, which gave thy friend rather an ungentle salutation on one side of the head, whereat I was not a little offended, until the interpreter informed us that this was the customary manner in which great men were honored in this country; and that the more distinguished they were, the more they were subjected to the attacks and peltings of the mob. Upon this I bowed my head three times, with my hands to my turban, and made a speech in Arabic-Greek, which gave great satisfaction, and occasioned a shower of old shoes, hats, and so forth, that was exceedingly refreshing to us all.

Thou wilt not as yet expect that I should give thee an account of the laws and politics of this country. I will reserve them for some future letter, when I shall be more experienced in their complicated and seemingly contradictory nature.

This empire is governed by a grand and most puissant bashaw, whom they dignify with the title of president. He is chosen by persons, who are chosen by an assembly, elected by the people—hence the mob is called the sovereign people—and the country, free; the body politic doubtless resembling a vessel, which is best governed by its tail. The present bashaw[4] is a very plain old gentleman—something they say of a humorist, as he amuses himself with impaling butter-flies and pickling tadpoles; he is rather declining in popularity, having given great offense by wearing red breeches and tying his horse to a post.* The people of the United States have assured me that they themselves are the most enlightened nation under the sun; but thou knowest that the barbarians of the desert, who assemble at the summer solstice, to shoot their arrows at that glorious luminary, in order to extinguish his burning rays, make precisely the same boast—which of them have the superior claim, I shall not attempt to decide.

I have observed, with some degree of surprise, that the men of this country do not seem in haste to accommodate themselves even with the single wife which alone the laws permit them to marry; this backwardness is probably owing to the misfortune of their ab-solutely having no female mutes among them. Thou knowest how valuable are these silent companions—what a price is given for them in the East, and what entertaining wives they make. What delightful entertainment arises from beholding the silent eloquence of their sighs and gestures; but a wife possessed both of a tongue and a soul—monstrous! monstrous! is it astonishing that these unhappy infidels should shrink from a union with a woman so preposterously endowed!

Thou hast doubtless read in the works of Abul Faraj,[†] the Arabian historian, the tradition which mentions that the muses were once upon the point of falling together by the ears about the admission of a tenth among their number, until she assured them, by signs, that

---

*This is another allusion to the primitive habits of Mr. Jefferson [see endnote 4], who, even while the first magistrate of the Republic, and on occasions when a little of the "pomp and circumstance" of office would not have been incompatible with that situation, was accustomed to dress in the plainest garb, and when on horseback to be without an attendant; so that it not unfrequently happened that he might be seen, when the business of the state required his personal presence, riding up alone to the government house at Washington, and having tied his steed to the nearest post, proceed to transact the important business of the nation.—*Paris Ed.* [Irving's note].
[†]Possibly Abu al-Faraj Ali of Esfahan (897–967), Arabic scholar known for his *Kitab al-Aghani*, or Book of Songs.

she was dumb; whereupon they received her with great rejoicing. I should, perhaps, inform thee that there are but nine Christian muses, who were formerly pagans, but have since been converted, and that in this country we never hear of a tenth, unless some crazy poet wishes to pay a hyperbolical compliment to his mistress; on which occasion it goes hard, but she figures as a tenth muse, or fourth grace, even though she should be more illiterate than a Hottentot,* and more ungraceful than a dancing bear! Since my arrival in this country, I have met with not less than a hundred of these supernumerary muses and graces—and may Allah preserve me from ever meeting with any more!

When I have studied this people more profoundly, I will write thee again: in the meantime watch over my household, and do not beat my beloved wives unless you catch them with their noses out at the window. Though far distant and a slave, let me live in thy heart as thou livest in mine; think not, O friend of my soul, that the splendors of this luxurious capital, its gorgeous palaces, its stupendous mosques, and the beautiful females who run wild in herds about its streets, can obliterate thee from my remembrance. Thy name shall still be mentioned in the five-and-twenty prayers which I offer up daily; and may our great prophet, after bestowing on thee all the blessings of this life, at length, in good old age, lead thee gently by the hand, to enjoy the dignity of bashaw of three tails[†] in the blissful bowers of Eden.

MUSTAPHA

---

*Name given by Dutch colonizers to some of the native peoples of South Africa.
†The rank of some Turkish officials was indicated by the number of horsetails tied to their standards.

LETTER FROM MUSTAPHA RUB-A-DUB KELI KHAN,
TO ASEM HACCHEM, PRINCIPAL SLAVE-DRIVER
TO HIS HIGHNESS THE BASHAW OF TRIPOLI

I promised in a former letter, good Asem, that I would furnish thee with a few hints respecting the nature of the government by which I am held in durance. Though my inquiries for that purpose have been industrious, yet I am not perfectly satisfied with their results; for thou mayst easily imagine that the vision of a captive is overshadowed by the mists of illusion and prejudice, and the horizon of his speculations must be limited indeed. I find that the people of this country are strangely at a loss to determine the nature and proper character of their government. Even their dervises are extremely in the dark as to this particular, and are continually indulging in the most preposterous disquisitions on the subject; some have insisted that it savors of an aristocracy; others maintain that it is a pure democracy; and a third set of theorists declare absolutely that it is nothing more or less than a mobocracy. The latter, I must confess, though still wide in error, have come nearest to the truth. You of course must understand the meaning of these different words, as they are derived from the ancient Greek language, and bespeak loudly the verbal poverty of these poor infidels, who cannot utter a learned phrase without laying the dead languages under contribution. A man, my dear Asem, who talks good sense in his native tongue, is held in tolerable estimation in this country; but a fool, who clothes his feeble ideas in a foreign or antique garb, is bowed down to as a literary prodigy. While I conversed with these people in plain English, I was but little attended to; but the moment I prosed away in Greek, every one looked up to me with veneration as an oracle.

Although the dervises differ widely in the particulars above mentioned, yet they all agree in terming their government one of the most pacific in the known world. I cannot help pitying their ignorance, and smiling, at times, to see into what ridiculous errors those nations will wander, who are unenlightened by the precepts of Mahomet, our divine prophet, and uninstructed by the five hundred and forty-nine books of wisdom of the immortal Ibrahim Hassan al Fusti. To call this nation pacific! Most preposterous! it reminds me of the title assumed by the sheik of that murderous tribe of wild Arabs, that desolate the valleys of Belsaden, who styles himself "Star of Courtesy—Beam of the Mercy-Seat."

The simple truth of the matter is, that these people are totally ignorant of their own true character; for, according to the best of my observation, they are the most warlike, and I must say, the most savage nation that I have as yet discovered among all the barbarians. They are not only at war, in their own way, with almost every nation on earth, but they are at the same time engaged in the most complicated knot of civil wars that ever infested any poor unhappy country on which Allah has denounced his malediction!

To let thee at once into a secret, which is unknown to these people themselves, their government is a pure unadulterated *logocracy*, or government of words. The whole nation does everything *viva voce*, or by word of mouth; and in this manner is one of the most military nations in existence. Every man who has what is here called the gift of the gab, that is, a plentiful stock of verbosity, becomes a soldier outright; and is forever in a militant state. The country is entirely defended *vi et linguâ*; that is to say, by force of tongues. The account which I lately wrote to our friend, the snorer, respecting the immense army of six hundred men, makes nothing against this observation; that formidable body being kept up, as I have already observed, only to amuse their fair countrywomen by their splendid appearance and nodding plumes; and are, by way of distinction, denominated the "defenders of the fair."

In a logocracy thou well knowest there is little or no occasion for fire-arms, or any such destructive weapons. Every offensive or defensive measure is enforced by wordy battle, and paper war; he who has the longest tongue or readiest quill is sure to gain the victory—will carry horror, abuse, and ink-shed into the very trenches of the enemy; and, without mercy or remorse, put men, women, and children to the point of the—pen!

There is still preserved in this country some remains of that Gothic spirit of knight-errantry which so much annoyed the faithful in the middle ages of the Hegira.* As, notwithstanding their martial disposition, they are a people much given to commerce and agriculture, and must, necessarily, at certain seasons be engaged in these employments, they have accommodated themselves by appointing knights, or constant warriors, incessant brawlers, similar to those who, in former ages, swore eternal enmity to the followers of our divine prophet. These knights, denominated editors or *slang-whangers*, are appointed in every town, village, or district, to carry on both foreign and internal warfare, and may be said to keep up a constant firing "in words." O my friend, could you but witness the enormities sometimes committed by these tremendous slang-whangers, your very turban would rise with horror and astonishment. I have seen them extend their ravages even into the kitchens of their opponents, and annihilate the very cook with a blast; and I do assure thee, I beheld one of these warriors attack a most venerable bashaw, and at one stroke of his pen lay him open from the waistband of his breeches to his chin!

There has been a civil war carrying on with great violence for some time past, in consequence of a conspiracy, among the higher classes, to dethrone his highness, the present bashaw,† and place another in his stead. I was mistaken when I formerly asserted to thee that this dissatisfaction arose from his wearing red breeches. It is true, the nation have long held that color in great detestation, in consequence of a dispute they had some twenty years since with the barbarians of the British Islands.‡ The color, however, is again rising into favor, as the ladies have transferred it to their heads from the bashaw's—body. The true reason, I am told, is, that the bashaw absolutely refuses to believe in the deluge,§ and in the story of

---

*Muhammad's journey from his native city of Mecca to Medina in the year 622.
†See endnote 4 to *Salmagundi*.
‡Reference to the American Revolutionary War.
§Flood described in the Bible, Genesis 7.

Balaam's ass;* maintaining that this animal was never yet permitted to talk except in a genuine logocracy; where, it is true, his
voice may often be heard, and is listened to with reverence, as "the
voice of the sovereign people." Nay, so far did he carry his obstinacy,
that he absolutely invited a professed antediluvian from the Gallic
empire,† who illuminated the whole country with his principles—
and his nose. This was enough to set the nation in a blaze—
every slang-whanger resorted to his tongue or his pen; and for
seven years have they carried on a most inhuman war, in which
volumes of words have been expended, oceans of ink have been
shed, nor has any mercy been shown to age, sex, or condition. Every
day have these slang-whangers made furious attacks on each other
and upon their respective adherents; discharging their heavy artillery, consisting of large sheets, loaded with scoundrel! villain! liar!
rascal! numskull! nincompoop! dunderhead! wiseacre! blockhead!
jackass! and I do swear by my beard, though I know thou wilt
scarcely credit me, that in some of these skirmishes the grand
bashaw himself has been wofully pelted! yea, most ignominiously
pelted! and yet have these talking desperadoes escaped without the
bastinado!‡

Every now and then a slang-whanger, who has a longer head, or
rather a longer tongue than the rest, will elevate his piece and discharge a shot quite across the ocean, leveled at the head of the emperor of France, the king of England, or, wouldst thou believe it, O
Asem, even at his sublime highness the bashaw of Tripoli! These
long pieces are loaded with single ball, or language, as tyrant!
usurper! robber! tiger! monster! and thou mayst well suppose they
occasion great distress and dismay in the camps of the enemy, and
are marvelously annoying to the crowned heads at which they are
directed. The slang-whanger, though perhaps the mere champion of
a village, having fired off his shot, struts about with great self-
congratulation, chuckling at the prodigious bustle he must have
occasioned, and seems to ask of every stranger, "Well, sir, what do

---

*See the Bible, Numbers 22:21–35.
†That is, a scholar from France who challenged the historical accuracy of the Bible.
‡Punishment in which the soles of one's feet are beaten with a stick.

they think of me in Europe?"* This is sufficient to show you the manner in which these bloody, or rather windy fellows fight; it is the only mode allowable in a logocracy or government of words. I would also observe that their civil wars have a thousand ramifications.

While the fury of the battle rages in the metropolis, every little town and village has a distinct broil, growing like excrescences out of the grand national altercation, or rather agitating within it, like those complicated pieces of mechanism where there is a "wheel within a wheel."

But in nothing is the verbose nature of this government more evident than in its grand national divan, or Congress, where the laws are framed; this is a blustering, windy assembly, where everything is carried by noise, tumult, and debate; for thou must know, that the members of this assembly do not meet together to find wisdom in the multitude of counselors, but to wrangle, call each other hard names, and hear themselves talk. When the Congress opens, the bashaw first sends them a long message, *i. e.*, a huge mass of words— *vox et prœterea nihil*, all meaning nothing; because it only tells them what they perfectly know already. Then the whole assembly are thrown into a ferment, and have a long talk about the quantity of words that are to be returned in answer to this message; and here arise many disputes about the correction and alteration of "if so be's" and "how so ever's." A month, perhaps, is spent in thus determining the precise number of words the answer shall contain; and then another, most probably, in concluding whether it shall be

---

*The sage Mustapha, when he wrote the above paragraph, had probably in his eye the following anecdote, related either by Linkum Fidelius, or Josephus Millerius, vulgarly called Joe Miller, of facetious memory.

The captain of a slave-vessel, on his first landing on the coast of Guinea, observed under a palm-tree a negro chief, sitting most majestically on a stump; while two women, with wooden spoons, were administering his favorite pottage of boiled rice; which, as his imperial majesty was a little greedy, would part of it escape the place of destination and run down his chin. The watchful attendants were particularly careful to intercept these scape-grace particles, and return them to their proper port of entry. As the captain approached, in order to admire this curious exhibition of royalty, the great chief clapped his hands to his sides, and saluted his visitor with the following pompous question—"Well, sir! what do they say of me in England?" [Irving's note].

carried to the bashaw on foot, on horseback, or in coaches. Having settled this weighty matter, they next fall to work upon the message itself, and hold as much chattering over it as so many magpies over an addled egg. This done, they divide the message into small portions, and deliver them into the hands of little juntos of talkers, called committees; these juntos have each a world of talking about their respective paragraphs, and return the results to the grand divan, which forthwith falls to and retalks the matter over more earnestly than ever. Now, after all, it is an even chance that the subject of this prodigious arguing, quarreling, and talking is an affair of no importance, and ends entirely in smoke. May it not then be said, the whole nation have been talking to no purpose? The people, in fact, seem to be somewhat conscious of this propensity to talk, by which they are characterized, and have a favorite proverb on the subject, viz., "all talk and no cider;" this is particularly applied when their Congress, or assembly of all the sage chatterers of the nation, have chattered through a whole session, in a time of great peril and momentous event, and have done nothing but exhibit the length of their tongues and the emptiness of their heads. This has been the case more than once, my friend; and to let thee into a secret, I have been told in confidence, that there have been absolutely several old women smuggled into Congress from different parts of the empire; who, having once got on the breeches, as thou mayst well imagine, have taken the lead in debate, and overwhelmed the whole assembly with their garrulity; for my part, as times go, I do not see why old women should not be as eligible to public councils as old men who possess their dispositions; they certainly are eminently possessed of the qualifications requisite to govern in a logocracy.

Nothing, as I have repeatedly insisted, can be done in this country without talking; but they take so long to talk over a measure, that by the time they have determined upon adopting it, the period has elapsed which was proper for carrying it into effect. Unhappy nation! thus torn to pieces by intestine* talks! never, I fear, will it be restored to tranquillity and silence. Words are but breath; breath is but air; and air put into motion is nothing but wind. This vast

---

*Pun on "intestate" (having no legal will).

empire, therefore, may be compared to nothing more or less than a mighty windmill, and the orators, and the chatterers, and the slang-whangers, are the breezes that put it in motion; unluckily, however, they are apt to blow different ways, and their blasts counteracting each other—the mill is perplexed, the wheels stand still, the grist is unground, and the miller and his family starved.

Everything partakes of the windy nature of the government. In case of any domestic grievance, or an insult from a foreign foe, the people are all in a buzz; town-meetings are immediately held where the *quidnuncs** of the city repair, each like an *Atlas,*† with the cares of the whole nation upon his shoulders, each resolutely bent upon saving his country, and each swelling and strutting like a turkey-cock; puffed up with words, and wind, and nonsense. After bustling, and buzzing, and bawling for some time, and after each man has shown himself to be indubitably the greatest personage in the meeting, they pass a string of resolutions, *i. e.* words, which were previously prepared for the purpose; these resolutions are whimsically denominated the sense of the meeting, and are sent off for the instruction of the reigning bashaw, who receives them graciously, puts them into his red breeches pocket, forgets to read them—and so the matter ends.

As to his highness, the present bashaw, who is at the very top of the logocracy, never was a dignitary better qualified for his station. He is a man of superlative ventosity, and comparable to nothing but a huge bladder of wind. He talks of vanquishing all opposition by the force of reason and philosophy: throws his gauntlet at all the nations of the earth, and defies them to meet him—on the field of argument! Is the national dignity insulted, a case in which his highness of Tripoli would immediately call forth his forces, the bashaw of America—utters a speech. Does a foreign invader molest the commerce in the very mouth of the harbors, an insult which would induce his highness of Tripoli to order out his fleets, his highness of America—utters a speech. Are the free citizens of America dragged from on board the vessels of their country, and forcibly detained in

*Newsmongers, gossips.
†In Greek mythology, the Titan who was condemned to hold the sky on his shoulders.

the war ships of another—his highness utters a speech. Is a peaceable citizen killed by the marauders of a foreign power, on the very shores of his country—his highness utters a speech. Does an alarming insurrection break out in a distant part of the empire—his highness utters a speech!—nay, more, for here he shows his "energies"—he most intrepidly despatches a courier on horseback, and orders him to ride one hundred and twenty miles a day, with a most formidable army of proclamations, *i. e.* a collection of words, packed up in his saddle-bags. He is instructed to show no favor nor affection; but to charge the thickest ranks of the enemy, and to speechify and batter by words the conspiracy and the conspirators out of existence. Heavens, my friend, what a deal of blustering is here! It reminds me of a dunghill cock in a farmyard, who, having accidentally in his scratchings found a worm, immediately begins a most vociferous cackling—calls around him his hen-hearted companions, who run chattering from all quarters to gobble up the poor little worm that happened to turn under his eye. O, Asem! Asem! on what a prodigious great scale is everything in this country!

Thus, then, I conclude my observations. The infidel nations have each a separate characteristic trait, by which they may be distinguished from each other; the Spaniards, for instance, may be said to sleep upon every affair of importance; the Italians to fiddle upon everything; the French to dance upon everything; the Germans to smoke upon everything; the British islanders to eat upon everything; and the windy subjects of the American logocracy to talk upon everything.

Forever thine,

MUSTAPHA

No. XI.—*Tuesday, June 2, 1807*

LETTER FROM MUSTAPHA RUB-A-DUB KELI KHAN,

CAPTAIN OF A KETCH, TO ASEM HACCHEM,
PRINCIPAL SLAVE-DRIVER TO HIS HIGHNESS
THE BASHAW OF TRIPOLI

The deep shadows of midnight gather around me; the footsteps of the passengers have ceased in the streets, and nothing disturbs the holy silence of the hour save the sound of the distant drums, mingled with the shouts, the bawlings, and the discordant revelry of his majesty, the Sovereign Mob. Let the hour be sacred to friendship, and consecrated to thee, O thou brother of my inmost soul!

O Asem! I almost shrink at the recollection of the scenes of confusion, of licentious disorganization which I have witnessed during the last three days. I have beheld this whole city, nay, this whole State, given up to the tongue and the pen; to the puffers, the bawlers, the babblers, and the slang-whangers. I have beheld the community convulsed with a civil war, or civil talk; individuals verbally massacred, families annihilated by whole sheets full, and slangwhangers coolly bathing their pens in ink and rioting in the slaughter of their thousands. I have seen, in short, that awful despot, the People, in the moment of unlimited power, wielding newspapers in one hand, and with the other scattering mud and filth about, like some desperate lunatic relieved from the restraints of his strait waistcoat. I have seen beggars on horseback, ragamuffins riding in coaches, and swine seated in places of honor; I have seen liberty; I have seen equality; I have seen fraternity. I have seen that great political puppet-show—an Election.

A few days ago the friend, whom I have mentioned in some of my former letters, called upon me to accompany him to witness this grand ceremony; and we forthwith sallied out to the polls, as he called them. Though for several weeks before this splendid exhibition nothing else had been talked of, yet I do assure thee I was entirely ignorant of its nature; and when, on coming up to a church, my companion informed me we were at the polls, I supposed that an election was some great religious ceremony, like the fast of Ramazan,* or the great festival of Haraphat,† so celebrated in the East.

My friend, however, undeceived me at once, and entered into a long dissertation on the nature and object of an election, the substance of which was nearly to this effect:—

"You know," said he, "that this country is engaged in a violent internal warfare, and suffers a variety of evils from civil dissensions. An election is the grand trial of strength, the decisive battle when the belligerents draw out their forces in martial array; when every leader, burning with warlike ardor, and encouraged by the shouts and acclamations of tatterdemalions, buffoons, dependents, parasites, toad-eaters, scrubs, vagrants, mumpers, ragamuffins, bravoes, and beggars in his rear; and puffed up by his bellows-blowing slang-whangers, waves gallantly the banners of faction, and presses forward *to office and immortality!*

"For a month or two previous to the critical period which is to decide this important affair, the whole community is in a ferment. Every man, of whatever rank or degree—such is the wonderful patriotism of the people—disinterestedly neglects his business to devote himself to his country; and not an insignificant fellow but feels himself inspired, on this occasion, with as much warmth in favor of the cause he has espoused, as if all the comfort of his life, or even his life itself, was dependent on the issue. Grand councils of war are, in the first place, called by the different powers, which are dubbed general meetings, where all the head workmen of the party collect, and arrange the order of battle—appoint their different commanders, and their subordinate instruments, and furnish the funds indispensable for supplying the expenses of the war. Inferior

---

*Or Ramadan, ninth month of the Islamic year, in which Muslims fast from dawn to dusk to commemorate the revelation of the Qur'an to Muhammad.
†Celebration that occurs on the pilgrim route to Mecca.

councils are next called in the different classes or wards, consisting of young cadets, who are candidates for offices; idlers who come there for mere curiosity; and orators who appear for the purpose of detailing all the crimes, the faults, or the weaknesses of their opponents, and *speaking the sense of the meeting*, as it is called; for as the meeting generally consists of men whose quota of sense, taken individually, would make but a poor figure, these orators are appointed to collect it all in a lump; when, I assure you, it makes a very formidable appearance, and furnishes sufficient matter to spin an oration of two or three hours.

"The orators who declaim at these meetings are, with a few exceptions, men of the most profound and perplexed eloquence; who are the oracles of barbers' shops, market-places, and porter-houses; and whom you may see every day at the corners of the streets, taking honest men prisoners by the button, and talking their ribs quite bare without mercy and without end. These orators, in addressing an audience, generally mount a chair, a table, or an empty beer barrel, which last is supposed to afford considerable inspiration, and thunder away their combustible sentiments at the heads of the audience, who are generally so busily employed in smoking, drinking, and hearing themselves talk, that they seldom hear a word of the matter. This, however, is of little moment: for as they come there to agree, at all events, to a certain set of resolutions, or articles of war, it is not at all necessary to hear the speech; more especially as few would understand it if they did. Do not suppose, however, that the minor persons of the meeting are entirely idle. Besides smoking and drinking, which are generally practiced, there are few who do not come with as great a desire to talk as the orator himself; each has his little circle of listeners, in the midst of whom he sets his hat on one side of his head, and deals out matter-of-fact information, and draws self-evident conclusions with the pertinacity of a pedant, and to the great edification of his gaping auditors. Nay, the very urchins from the nursery, who are scarcely emancipated from the dominion of birch, on these occasions strut pigmy great men, bellow for the instruction of gray-bearded ignorance, and, like the frog in the fable,* endeavor to puff

---

*Aesop's fable "The Frog and the Ox."

themselves up to the size of the great object of their emulation—the principal orator."

"But is it not preposterous to a degree," cried I, "for those puny whipsters to attempt to lecture age and experience? They should be sent to school to learn better."

"Not at all," replied my friend; "for as an election is nothing more than a war of words, the man that can wag his tongue with the greatest elasticity, whether he speaks to the purpose or not, is entitled to lecture at ward meetings and polls, and instruct all who are inclined to listen to him; you may have remarked a ward meeting of politic dogs, where, although the great dog is, ostensibly, the leader, and makes the most noise, yet every little scoundrel of a cur has something to say; and in proportion to his insignificance, fidgets, and worries, and puffs about mightily, in order to obtain the notice and approbation of his betters. Thus it is with these little, beardless, bread-and-butter politicians, who on this occasion escape from the jurisdiction of their mammas to attend to the affairs of the nation. You will see them engaged in dreadful wordy contest with old cartmen, cobblers, and tailors, and plume themselves not a little if they should chance to gain a victory. Aspiring spirits! how interesting are the first dawnings of political greatness! An election, my friend, is a nursery or hot-bed of genius in a logocracy; and I look with enthusiasm on a troop of these Liliputian* partisans, as so many chatterers, and orators and puffers, and slangwhangers in embryo, who will one day take an important part in the quarrels and wordy wars of their country.

"As the time for fighting the decisive battle approaches, appearances become more and more alarming; committees are appointed, who hold little encampments from whence they send out small detachments of tattlers, to reconnoitre, harass, and skirmish with the enemy, and, if possible, ascertain their numbers; everybody seems big with the mighty event that is impending; the orators, they gradually swell up beyond their usual size; the little orators, they grow greater and greater; the secretaries of the ward committees

---

*Small-minded and self-important; from English author Jonathan Swift's satire *Gulliver's Travels* (1726), in which Lemuel Gulliver is captured by the Lilliputians, a race of people who are only six inches tall.

strut about, looking like wooden oracles; the puffers put on the airs of mighty consequence; the slangwhangers deal out direful innuendoes, and threats of doughty import, and all is buzz, murmur, suspense, and sublimity!

"At length the day arrives. The storm that has been so long gathering and threatening in distant thunders, bursts forth in terrible explosion; all business is at an end; the whole city is in a tumult; the people are running helter-skelter, they know not whither, and they know not why; the hackney coaches rattle through the streets with thundering vehemence, loaded with recruiting sergeants who have been prowling in cellars and caves, to unearth some miserable minion of poverty and ignorance, who will barter his vote for a glass of beer, or a ride in a coach with such *fine gentlemen!* the buzzards of the party scamper from poll to poll, on foot or on horseback; and they worry from committee to committee, and buzz, and fume, and talk big, and—*do nothing*; like the vagabond drone, who wastes his time in the laborious idleness of *see-saw-song* and busy nothingness."

I know not how long my friend would have continued his detail, had he not been interrupted by a squabble which took place between two *old continentals,** as they were called. It seems they had entered into an argument on the respective merits of their cause, and not being able to make each other clearly understood, resorted to what is called knock-down arguments, which form the superlative degree of *argumentum ad hominem*;† but are, in my opinion, extremely inconsistent with the true spirit of a genuine logocracy. After they had beaten each other soundly, and set the whole mob together by the ears, they came to a full explanation; when it was discovered that they were both of the same way of thinking; whereupon they shook each other heartily by the hand, and laughed with great glee at their humorous misunderstanding.

I could not help being struck with the exceeding great number of ragged, dirty-looking persons that swaggered about the place, and

---

*Veteran soldiers who fought for the Continental army during the American Revolution.

†Argument to the man (Latin); attacking the person giving an argument rather than attacking the argument itself.

seemed to think themselves the bashaws of the land. I inquired of my friend if these people were employed to drive away the hogs, dogs, and other intruders that might thrust themselves in and interrupt the ceremony?

"By no means," replied he; "these are the representatives of the sovereign people, who come here to make governors, senators, and members of assembly, and are the source of all power and authority in this nation."

"Preposterous!" said I; "how is it possible that such men can be capable of distinguishing between an honest man and a knave; or, even if they were, will it not always happen that they are led by the nose by some intriguing demagogue, and made the mere tools of ambitious political jugglers? Surely it would be better to trust to Providence, or even to chance, for governors, than resort to the discriminating powers of an ignorant mob. I plainly perceive the consequence. A man, who possesses superior talents, and that honest pride which ever accompanies this possession, will always be sacrificed by some creeping insect who will prostitute himself to familiarity with the lowest of mankind; and, like the idolatrous Egyptian, worship the wallowing tenants of filth and mire."

"All this is true enough," replied my friend, "but after all, you cannot say but that this is a free country, and that the people can get drunk cheaper here, particularly at elections, than in the despotic countries of the East." I could not, with any degree of propriety or truth, deny this last assertion; for just at that moment a patriotic brewer arrived with a load of beer, which, for a moment, occasioned a cessation of argument. The great crowd of buzzards, puffers, and "old continentals" of all parties, who throng to the polls, to persuade, to cheat, or to force the freeholders into the right way, and to maintain the freedom of suffrage, seemed for a moment to forget their antipathies, and joined heartily in a copious libation of this patriotic and argumentative beverage.

These beer-barrels, indeed, seem to be most able logicians, well stored with that kind of sound argument best suited to the comprehension, and most relished by the mob, or sovereign people, who are never so tractable as when operated upon by this convincing liquor, which, in fact, seems to be imbued with the very spirit of a logocracy. No sooner does it begin its operation, than the tongue waxes exceeding valorous, and becomes impatient for some mighty conflict. The puffer puts himself at the head of his body-guard of buzzards, and his legion of ragamuffins, and woe then to every unhappy adversary who is uninspired by the deity of the beer-barrel—he is sure to be talked, and argued, into complete insignificance.

While I was making these observations, I was surprised to observe a bashaw, high in office, shaking a fellow by the hand, that looked rather more ragged than a scarecrow, and inquiring with apparent solicitude concerning the health of his family; after which he slipped a little folded paper into his hand and turned away. I could not help applauding his humility in shaking the fellow's hand, and his benevolence in relieving his distresses, for I imagined the paper contained something for the poor man's necessities; and truly he seemed verging toward the last stage of starvation. My friend, however, soon undeceived me by saying that this was an elector, and that the bashaw had merely given him the list of candidates for whom he was to vote.

"Ho! ho!" said I, "then he is a particular friend of the bashaw?"

"By no means," replied my friend, "the bashaw will pass him without notice, the day after the election, except, perhaps, just to drive over him with his coach."

My friend then proceeded to inform me that for some time before, and during the continuance of an election, there was a most delectable courtship, or intrigue carried on between the great bashaws and the mother Mob. That mother Mob generally preferred the attentions of the rabble, or of fellows of her own stamp; but would sometimes condescend to be treated to a feasting, or anything of that kind, at the bashaw's expense! Nay, sometimes when she was in good humor, she would condescend to toy with him in her rough way: but woe to the bashaw who attempted to be familiar with her, for she was the most petulant, cross, crabbed, scolding, thieving, scratching, toping, wrongheaded, rebellious, and abominable termagant that ever was let loose in the world to the confusion of honest gentlemen bashaws.

Just then a fellow came round and distributed among the crowd a number of handbills, written by the ghost of Washington,* the

---

*Irving was named after George Washington (1732–1799), first president of the United States and commander-in-chief of the Continental army during the American Revolution.

fame of whose illustrious actions, and still more illustrious virtues, have reached even the remotest regions of the East, and who is venerated by this people as the Father of his country. On reading this paltry paper, I could not restrain my indignation. "Insulted hero," cried I, "is it thus thy name is profaned, thy memory disgraced, thy spirit drawn down from heaven to administer to the brutal violence of party rage? It is thus the necromancers of the East, by their infernal incantations, sometimes call up the shades of the just, to give their sanction to frauds, to lies, and to every species of enormity?" My friend smiled at my warmth, and observed, that raising ghosts, and not only raising them but making them speak, was one of the miracles of election. "And believe me," continued he, "there is good reason for the ashes of departed heroes being disturbed on these occasions, for such is the sandy foundation of our government, that there never happens an election of an alderman, or a collector, or even a constable, but we are in imminent danger of losing our liberties, and becoming a province of France, or tributary to the British islands." "By the hump of Mahomet's camel," said I, "but this is only another striking example of the prodigious great scale on which everything is transacted in this country!"

By this time I had become tired of the scene; my head ached with the uproar of voices, mingling in all the discordant tones of triumphant exclamation, nonsensical argument, intemperate reproach, and drunken absurdity. The confusion was such as no language can adequately describe, and it seemed as if all the restraints of decency, and all the bands of law, had been broken and given place to the wide ravages of licentious brutality. These, thought I, are the orgies of liberty! these are manifestations of the spirit of independence! these are the symbols of man's sovereignty! Head of Mahomet! with what a fatal and inexorable despotism do empty names and ideal phantoms exercise their dominion over the human mind! The experience of ages has demonstrated, that in all nations, barbarous or enlightened, the mass of the people, the mob, must be slaves, or they will be tyrants; but their tyranny will not be long: some ambitious leader, having at first condescended to be their slave, will at length become their master; and in proportion to the vileness of his former servitude, will be the severity of his subsequent tyranny. Yet, with innumerable examples staring them in the face, the people still bawl out liberty; by which they mean nothing but freedom from every species of legal restraint, and a warrant for all kinds of licentiousness: and the bashaws and leaders, in courting the mob, convince them of their power; and by administering to their passions, for the purposes of ambition, at length learn, by fatal experience, that he who worships the beast that carries him on his back, will sooner or later be thrown into the dust, and trampled under foot by the animal who has learnt the secret of its power, by this very adoration.

Ever thine,

MUSTAPHA

FROM MY ELBOW-CHAIR (A SELECTION)

In compliance with[6] an ancient and venerable custom, sanctioned by time and our ancestors, and more especially by my own inclinations, I will take this opportunity to salute my readers with as many good wishes as I can possibly spare for, in truth, I have been so prodigal of late, that I have but few remaining. I should have offered my congratulations sooner; but, to be candid, having made the last New-Year's campaign, according to custom, under Cousin Christopher, in which I have seen some pretty hard service, my head has been somewhat out of order of late, and my intellects rather cloudy for clear writing. Besides, I may allege as another reason, that I have deferred my greetings until this day, which is exactly one year since we introduced ourselves to the public; and surely periodical writers have the same right of dating from the commencement of their works, that monarchs have from the time of their coronation, or our most puissant republic from the declaration of its independence.

These good wishes are warmed into more than usual benevolence by the thought that I am now, perhaps, addressing my old friends for the last time. That we should thus cut off our work in the very vigor of its existence, may excite some little matter of wonder in this enlightened community. Now, though we could give a variety of good reasons for so doing, yet it would be an ill-natured act to deprive the public of such an admirable opportunity to indulge in their favorite amusement of conjecture; so we generously leave them to flounder in the smooth ocean of glorious uncertainty. Besides, we have ever considered it as beneath persons of our dignity to account for our movements or caprices; thank heaven, we are not like the unhappy rulers of this enlightened land, accountable to the mob for our actions, or dependent on their smiles for support!—this much, however, we will say, it is not for want of subjects that we stop our career. We are not in the situation of poor Alexander the Great,* who wept, as well indeed he might, because there were no more worlds to conquer; for, to do justice to this queer, odd, rantipole city, and to this whimsical country, there is matter enough in them to keep our risible muscles and our pens going till doomsday.

Most people, in taking a farewell which may, perhaps, be forever, are anxious to part on good terms; and it is usual, on such melancholy occasions, for even enemies to shake hands, forget their previous quarrels, and bury all former animosities in parting regrets. Now, because most people do this, I am determined to act in quite a different way; for, as I have lived, so I should wish to die, in my own way, without imitating any person, whatever may be his rank, talents, or reputation. Besides, if I know our trio, we have no enmities to obliterate, no hatchet to bury; and as to all injuries—those we have long since forgiven. At this moment there is not an individual in the world, not even the Pope himself, to whom we have any personal hostility. But if, shutting their eyes to the many striking proofs of good-nature displayed through the whole course of this work, there should be any persons so singularly ridiculous as to take offense at our strictures, we heartily forgive their stupidity; earnestly entreating them to desist from all manifestations of ill-humor, lest they should, peradventure, be classed under some one of the denominations of recreants we have felt it our duty to hold up to public ridicule. Even at this moment, we feel a glow of parting philanthropy stealing upon us; a sentiment of cordial good-will toward the numerous host of readers that have jogged on at our heels during the last year; and in justice to ourselves must seriously protest, that if at any time we have treated them a little ungently, it was purely in that spirit of hearty affection, with which a schoolmaster drubs an unlucky urchin, or a humane muleteer his recreant animal, at the very moment when his heart is brimful of loving-kindness. If this is not considered an ample justification, so much the worse; for in that case I fear we shall remain forever unjustified—a most desperate extremity, and worthy of every man's commiseration!

---

*Alexander III (356–323 B.C.), king of Macedon; he conquered much of Asia.

One circumstance, in particular, has tickled us mightily as we jogged along; and that is, the astonishing secrecy with which we have been able to carry on our lucubrations! fully aware of the profound sagacity of the public of Gotham, and their wonderful faculty of distinguishing a writer by his style, it is with great self-congratulation we find that suspicion has never pointed to us as the authors of SALMAGUNDI. Our gray-beard speculations have been most bountifully attributed to sundry smart young gentlemen, who, for aught we know, have no beards at all; and we have often been highly amused when they were charged with the sin of writing what their harmless minds never conceived, to see them affect all the blushing modesty and beautiful embarrassment of detected virgin authors. The profound and penetrating public, having so long been led away from truth and nature by a constant perusal of those delectable histories, and romances, from beyond seas, in which human nature is, for the most part, wickedly mangled and debauched, have never once imagined this work was a genuine and most authentic history; that the Cocklofts were a real family, dwelling in the city, paying scot and lot, entitled to the right of suffrage, and holding several respectable offices in the corporation. As little do they suspect that there is a knot of merry old bachelors seated snugly in the old-fashioned parlor of an old-fashioned Dutch house, with a weather-cock on the top that came from Holland; who amuse themselves of an evening by laughing at their neighbors, in an honest way, and who manage to jog on through the streets of our ancient and venerable city, without elbowing or being elbowed by a living soul.

When we first adopted the idea of discontinuing this work, we determined, in order to give the critics a fair opportunity for dissection, to declare ourselves, one and all, absolutely defunct; for it is one of the rare and invaluable privileges of a periodical writer, that by an act of innocent suicide he may lawfully consign himself to the grave, and cheat the world of posthumous renown. But we abandoned this scheme for many substantial reasons. In the first place, we care but little for the opinion of critics, whom we consider a kind of freebooters in the republic of letters; who, like deer, goats, and divers other graminivorous animals, gain subsistence by gorging upon the buds and leaves of the young shrubs of the forest, thereby robbing them of their verdure, and retarding their progress to maturity.

It also occurred to us, that though an author might lawfully, in all countries, kill himself outright, yet this privilege did not extend to the raising himself from the dead, if he was ever so anxious; and all that is left him in such a case, is to take the benefit of the metempsychosis act, and revive under a new name and form.

Far be it, therefore, from us to condemn ourselves to useless embarrassments, should we ever be disposed to resume the guardianship of this learned city of Gotham, and finish this invaluable work, which is yet but half completed. We hereby openly and seriously declare, that we are not dead, but intend, if it please Providence, to live for many years to come, to enjoy life with the genuine relish of honest souls, careless of riches, honors, and everything but a good name, among good fellows, and with the full expectation of shuffling off the remnant of existence after the excellent fashion of that merry Grecian, who died laughing.*

---

*The Greek painter Zeuxis (fifth century B.C.) is said to have died from laughter caused by his viewing of the picture he had completed during a competition with Parrhasius to see who could paint a more realistic picture.

THE SKETCH-BOOK[1]

The Author's Account of Himself[2]

> "I am of this mind with Homer, that as the snaile that crept out
> of her shel was turned eftsoons into a toad, and thereby was
> forced to make a stoole to sit on; so the traveller that stragleth
> from his owne country is in a short time transformed into so
> monstrous a shape, that he is faine to alter his mansion with his
> manners, and to live where he can, not where he would."
>
> LYLY'S EUPHUES.*

I was always fond of visiting new scenes, and observing strange
characters and manners. Even when a mere child I began my
travels, and made many tours of discovery into foreign parts and
unknown regions of my native city, to the frequent alarm of my
parents, and the emolument† of the town-crier. As I grew into
boyhood, I extended the range of my observations. My holiday
afternoons were spent in rambles about the surrounding country.
I made myself familiar with all its places famous in history or fable.
I knew every spot where a murder or robbery had been committed,
or a ghost seen. I visited the neighboring villages, and added greatly
to my stock of knowledge, by noting their habits and customs, and
conversing with their sages and great men. I even journeyed one
long summer's day to the summit of the most distant hill, whence
I stretched my eye over many a mile of terra incognita,‡ and was
astonished to find how vast a globe I inhabited.

This rambling propensity strengthened with my years. Books of
voyages and travels became my passion, and in devouring their contents, I neglected the regular exercises of the school. How wistfully
would I wander about the pier-heads in fine weather, and watch the

---

*Quotation from *Euphues and His England* (1580), one book of a two-part work
(with *The Anatomy of Wit*, 1578) by English writer John Lyly; the term "euphuism"
(referring to an elaborate and artificial writing style) is derived from Lyly's style.
†Profit from employment.
‡Parts unknown.

parting ships, bound to distant climes—with what longing eyes would I gaze after their lessening sails, and waft myself in imagination to the ends of the earth!

Further reading and thinking, though they brought this vague inclination into more reasonable bounds, only served to make it more decided. I visited various parts of my own country; and had I been merely a lover of fine scenery, I should have felt little desire to seek elsewhere its gratification, for on no country have the charms of nature been more prodigally lavished. Her mighty lakes, like oceans of liquid silver; her mountains, with their bright aerial tints; her valleys, teeming with wild fertility; her tremendous cataracts, thundering in their solitudes; her boundless plains, waving with spontaneous verdure; her broad deep rivers, rolling in solemn silence to the ocean; her trackless forests, where vegetation puts forth all its magnificence; her skies, kindling with the magic of summer clouds and glorious sunshine;—no, never need an American look beyond his own country for the sublime and beautiful of natural scenery.

But Europe held forth the charms of storied and poetical association. There were to be seen the masterpieces of art, the refinements of highly-cultivated society, the quaint peculiarities of ancient and local custom. My native country was full of youthful promise: Europe was rich in the accumulated treasures of age. Her very ruins told the history of times gone by, and every mouldering stone was a chronicle. I longed to wander over the scenes of renowned achievement—to tread, as it were, in the footsteps of antiquity—to loiter about the ruined castle—to meditate on the falling tower—to escape, in short, from the commonplace realities of the present, and lose myself among the shadowy grandeurs of the past.

I had, beside all this, an earnest desire to see the great men of the earth. We have, it is true, our great men in America: not a city but has an ample share of them. I have mingled among them in my time, and been almost withered by the shade into which they cast me; for there is nothing so baleful to a small man as the shade of a great one, particularly the great man of a city. But I was anxious to see the great men of Europe; for I had read in the works of various philosophers, that all animals degenerated in America, and man among the number.[3] A great man of Europe, thought I, must therefore be as superior to a great man of America, as a peak of the Alps to a highland of the Hudson, and in this idea I was confirmed, by observing the comparative importance and swelling magnitude of many English travellers among us, who, I was assured, were very little people in their own country. I will visit this land of wonders, thought I, and see the gigantic race from which I am degenerated.

It has been either my good or evil lot to have my roving passion gratified. I have wandered through different countries, and witnessed many of the shifting scenes of life. I cannot say that I have studied them with the eye of a philosopher; but rather with the sauntering gaze with which humble lovers of the picturesque[4] stroll from the window of one print-shop to another; caught sometimes by the delineations of beauty, sometimes by the distortions of caricature, and sometimes by the loveliness of landscape. As it is the fashion for modern tourists to travel pencil in hand, and bring home their port-folios filled with sketches, I am disposed to get up a few for the entertainment of my friends. When, however, I look over the hints and memorandums I have taken down for the purpose, my heart almost fails me at finding how my idle humor has led me aside from the great objects studied by every regular traveller who would make a book. I fear I shall give equal disappointment with an unlucky landscape painter, who had travelled on the continent, but, following the bent of his vagrant inclination, had sketched in nooks, and corners, and by-places. His sketch-book was accordingly crowded with cottages, and landscapes, and obscure ruins; but he had neglected to paint St. Peter's, or the Coliseum; the cascade of Terni, or the bay of Naples;* and had not a single glacier or volcano in his whole collection.

---

*List of sites in Italy commonly visited by those making a "grand tour" of Europe.

The Voyage[5]

Ships, ships, I will descrie you
Amidst the main,
I will come and try you,
What you are protecting,
And projecting,
What's your end and aim.
One goes abroad for merchandise and trading,
Another stays to keep his country from invading,
A third is coming home with rich and wealthy lading.
Halloo! my fancie, whither wilt thou go?

OLD POEM.*

To an American visiting Europe, the long voyage he has to make is an excellent preparative. The temporary absence of worldly scenes and employments produces a state of mind peculiarly fitted to receive new and vivid impressions. The vast space of waters that separates the hemispheres is like a blank page in existence. There is no gradual transition, by which, as in Europe, the features and population of one country blend almost imperceptibly with those of another. From the moment you lose sight of the land you have left all is vacancy until you step on the opposite shore, and are launched at once into the bustle and novelties of another world.

In travelling by land there is a continuity of scene and a connected succession of persons and incidents, that carry on the story of life, and lessen the effect of absence and separation. We drag, it is true, "a lengthening chain,"† at each remove of our pilgrimage; but the chain is unbroken: we can trace it back link by link; and we feel that the last still grapples us to home. But a wide sea voyage severs

---

*From the anonymous poem "Halloo My Fancie," found in *English Minstrelsy* (vol. 2, 1810), edited by Sir Walter Scott.
†Quotation from "The Traveler; or, A Prospect of Society" (1764), by English poet Oliver Goldsmith (line 10).

us at once. It makes us conscious of being cast loose from the secure anchorage of settled life, and sent adrift upon a doubtful world. It interposes a gulf, not merely imaginary, but real, between us and our homes—a gulf subject to tempest, and fear, and uncertainty, rendering distance palpable, and return precarious.

Such, at least, was the case with myself. As I saw the last blue line of my native land fade away like a cloud in the horizon, it seemed as if I had closed one volume of the world and its concerns, and had time for meditation, before I opened another. That land, too, now vanishing from my view, which contained all most dear to me in life; what vicissitudes might occur in it—what changes might take place in me, before I should visit it again! Who can tell, when he sets forth to wander, whither he may be driven by the uncertain currents of existence; or when he may return; or whether it may ever be his lot to revisit the scenes of his childhood?

I said that at sea all is vacancy; I should correct the expression. To one given to day-dreaming, and fond of losing himself in reveries, a sea voyage is full of subjects for meditation; but then they are the wonders of the deep, and of the air, and rather tend to abstract the mind from worldly themes. I delighted to loll over the quarter-railing, or climb to the main-top, of a calm day, and muse for hours together on the tranquil bosom of a summer's sea; to gaze upon the piles of golden clouds just peering above the horizon, fancy them some fairy realms, and people them with a creation of my own;—to watch the gentle undulating billows, rolling their silver volumes, as if to die away on those happy shores.

There was a delicious sensation of mingled security and awe with which I looked down from my giddy height, on the monsters of the deep at their uncouth gambols. Shoals of porpoises tumbling about the bow of the ship; the grampus* slowly heaving his huge form above the surface; or the ravenous shark, darting, like a spectre, through the blue waters. My imagination would conjure up all that I had heard or read of the watery world beneath me; of the finny herds that roam its fathomless valleys; of the shapeless monsters that lurk among the very foundations of the earth; and of those wild phantasms that swell the tales of fishermen and sailors.

---

*Whale.

Sometimes a distant sail, gliding along the edge of the ocean, would be another theme of idle speculation. How interesting this fragment of a world, hastening to rejoin the great mass of existence! What a glorious monument of human invention; which has in a manner triumphed over wind and wave; has brought the ends of the world into communion; has established an interchange of blessings, pouring into the sterile regions of the north all the luxuries of the south; has diffused the light of knowledge and the charities of culti-vated life; and has thus bound together those scattered portions of the human race, between which nature seemed to have thrown an insurmountable barrier.

We one day descried some shapeless object drifting at a distance. At sea, every thing that breaks the monotony of the surrounding expanse attracts attention. It proved to be the mast of a ship that must have been completely wrecked; for there were the remains of handkerchiefs, by which some of the crew had fastened themselves to this spar, to prevent their being washed off by the waves. There was no trace by which the name of the ship could be ascertained. The wreck had evidently drifted about for many months; clusters of shell-fish had fastened about it, and long sea-weeds flaunted at its sides. But where, thought I, is the crew? Their struggle has long been over—they have gone down amidst the roar of the tempest—their bones lie whitening among the caverns of the deep. Silence, oblivion, like the waves, have closed over them, and no one can tell the story of their end. What sighs have been wafted after that ship! What prayers offered up at the deserted fireside of home! How often has the mistress, the wife, the mother, pored over the daily news, to catch some casual intelligence of this rover of the deep! How has expecta-tion darkened into anxiety—anxiety into dread—and dread into despair! Alas! not one memento may ever return for love to cherish. All that may ever be known, is, that she sailed from her port, "and was never heard of more!"

The sight of this wreck, as usual, gave rise to many dismal anec-dotes. This was particularly the case in the evening, when the weather, which had hitherto been fair, began to look wild and threatening, and gave indications of one of those sudden storms which will sometimes break in upon the serenity of a summer voyage. As we sat round the dull light of a lamp in the cabin, that made the gloom more ghastly, every one had his tale of shipwreck and disaster. I was particularly struck with a short one related by the captain.

"As I was once sailing," said he, "in a fine stout ship across the banks of Newfoundland, one of those heavy fogs which prevail in those parts rendered it impossible for us to see far ahead even in the daytime; but at night the weather was so thick that we could not distinguish any object at twice the length of the ship. I kept lights at the mast-head, and a constant watch forward to look out for fishing smacks, which are accustomed to lie at anchor on the banks. The wind was blowing a smacking breeze, and we were going at a great rate through the water. Suddenly the watch gave the alarm of a sail ahead!'—it was scarcely uttered before we were upon her. She was a small schooner, at anchor, with her broadside towards us. The crew were all asleep, and had neglected to hoist a light. We struck her just amidships. The force, the size, the weight of our vessel bore her down below the waves; we passed over her and were hurried on our course. As the crashing wreck was sinking beneath us, I had a glimpse of two or three half naked wretches rushing from her cabin; they just started from their beds to be swallowed shrieking by the waves. I heard their drowning cry mingling with the wind. The blast that bore it to our ears swept us out of all farther hearing. I shall never forget that cry! It was some time before we could put the ship about, she was under such headway. We returned, as nearly as we could guess, to the place where the smack had anchored. We cruised about for several hours in the dense fog. We fired signal guns, and listened if we might hear the halloo of any survivors: but all was silent—we never saw or heard anything of them more."

I confess these stories, for a time, put an end to all my fine fancies. The storm increased with the night. The sea was lashed into tremendous confusion. There was a fearful, sullen sound of rushing waves, and broken surges. Deep called unto deep.* At times the black volume of clouds overhead seemed rent asunder by flashes of lightning which quivered along the foaming billows, and made the succeeding darkness doubly terrible. The thunders bellowed over the wild waste of waters, and were echoed and prolonged by the

*See the Bible, Psalms 42:7.

mountain waves. As I saw the ship staggering and plunging among these roaring caverns, it seemed miraculous that she regained her balance, or preserved her buoyancy. Her yards would dip into the water: her bow was almost buried beneath the waves. Sometimes an impending surge appeared ready to overwhelm her, and nothing but a dexterous movement of the helm preserved her from the shock.

When I retired to my cabin, the awful scene still followed me. The whistling of the wind through the rigging sounded like funereal wailings. The creaking of the masts, the straining and groaning of bulk-heads, as the ship labored in the weltering sea, were frightful. As I heard the waves rushing along the sides of the ship, and roaring in my very ear, it seemed as if Death were raging round this floating prison, seeking for his prey: the mere starting of a nail, the yawning of a seam, might give him entrance.

A fine day, however, with a tranquil sea and favoring breeze, soon put all these dismal reflections to flight. It is impossible to resist the gladdening influence of fine weather and fair wind at sea. When the ship is decked out in all her canvas, every sail swelled, and careering gayly over the curling waves, how lofty, how gallant she appears—how she seems to lord it over the deep!

I might fill a volume with the reveries of a sea voyage, for with me it is almost a continual reverie—but it is time to get to shore.

It was a fine sunny morning when the thrilling cry of "land!" was given from the mast-head. None but those who have experienced it can form an idea of the delicious throng of sensations which rush into an American's bosom, when he first comes in sight of Europe. There is a volume of associations with the very name. It is the land of promise, teeming with every thing of which his childhood has heard, or on which his studious years have pondered.

From that time until the moment of arrival, it was all feverish excitement. The ships of war, that prowled like guardian giants along the coast; the headlands of Ireland, stretching out into the channel; the Welsh mountains, towering into the clouds; all were objects of intense interest. As we sailed up the Mersey, I reconnoitred the shores with a telescope. My eye dwelt with delight on neat cottages, with their trim shrubberies and green, grass plots. I saw the mouldering ruin of an abbey overrun with ivy, and the taper spire of a village church rising from the brow of a neighboring hill—all were characteristic of England.

The tide and wind were so favorable that the ship was enabled to come at once to the pier. It was thronged with people; some, idle lookers-on, others, eager expectants of friends or relatives. I could distinguish the merchant to whom the ship was consigned. I knew him by his calculating brow and restless air. His hands were thrust into his pockets; he was whistling thoughtfully, and walking to and fro, a small space having been accorded him by the crowd, in deference to his temporary importance. There were repeated cheerings and salutations interchanged between the shore and the ship, as friends happened to recognize each other. I particularly noticed one young woman of humble dress, but interesting demeanor. She was leaning forward from among the crowd; her eye hurried over the ship as it neared the shore, to catch some wished-for countenance. She seemed disappointed and agitated; when I heard a faint voice call her name. It was from a poor sailor who had been ill all the voyage, and had excited the sympathy of every one on board. When the weather was fine, his messmates had spread a mattress for him on deck in the shade, but of late his illness had so increased, that he had taken to his hammock, and only breathed a wish that he might see his wife before he died. He had been helped on deck as we came up the river, and was now leaning against the shrouds, with a countenance so wasted, so pale, so ghastly, that it was no wonder even the eye of affection did not recognize him. But at the sound of his voice, her eye darted on his features; it read, at once, a whole volume of sorrow; she clasped her hands, uttered a faint shriek, and stood wringing them in silent agony.

All now was hurry and bustle. The meetings of acquaintances—the greetings of friends—the consultations of men of business. I alone was solitary and idle. I had no friend to meet, no cheering to receive. I stepped upon the land of my forefathers—but felt that I was a stranger in the land.

Roscoe[6]

—In the service of mankind to be
A guardian god below; still to employ
The mind's brave ardor in heroic aims,
Such as may raise us o'er the grovelling herd,
And make us shine forever—that is life.

THOMSON*

One of the first places to which a stranger is taken in Liverpool is the Athenæum.[†] It is established on a liberal and judicious plan; it contains a good library, and spacious reading-room, and is the great literary resort of the place. Go there at what hour you may, you are sure to find it filled with grave-looking personages, deeply absorbed in the study of newspapers.

As I was once visiting this haunt of the learned, my attention was attracted to a person just entering the room. He was advanced in life, tall, and of a form that might once have been commanding, but it was a little bowed by time—perhaps by care. He had a noble Roman style of countenance; a head that would have pleased a painter; and though some slight furrows on his brow showed that wasting thought had been busy there, yet his eye still beamed with the fire of a poetic soul. There was something in his whole appearance that indicated a being of a different order from the bustling race around him.

I inquired his name, and was informed that it was Roscoe. I drew back with an involuntary feeling of veneration. This, then, was an author of celebrity; this was one of those men, whose voices have gone forth to the ends of the earth; with whose minds I have communed even in the solitudes of America. Accustomed, as we are in our country, to know European writers only by their works, we

---

*Quotation from the 1730 tragedy *Sophonisba* (act 2, scene 1), by Scottish poet and dramatist James Thomson.
[†]Building that keeps books, periodicals, and such.

cannot conceive of them, as of other men, engrossed by trivial or sordid pursuits, and jostling with the crowd of common minds in the dusty paths of life. They pass before our imaginations like superior beings, radiant with the emanations of their genius, and surrounded by a halo of literary glory.

To find, therefore, the elegant historian of the Medici,* mingling among the busy sons of traffic, at first shocked my poetical ideas; but it is from the very circumstances and situation in which he has been placed, that Mr. Roscoe derives his highest claims to admiration. It is interesting to notice how some minds seem almost to create themselves, springing up under every disadvantage, and working their solitary but irresistible way through a thousand obstacles. Nature seems to delight in disappointing the assiduities† of art, with which it would rear legitimate dulness to maturity; and to glory in the vigor and luxuriance of her chance productions. She scatters the seeds of genius to the winds, and though some may perish among the stony places of the world, and some be choked by the thorns and brambles of early adversity, yet others will now and then strike root even in the clefts of the rock, struggle bravely up into sunshine, and spread over their sterile birthplace all the beauties of vegetation.

Such has been the case with Mr. Roscoe. Born in a place apparently ungenial to the growth of literary talent; in the very market-place of trade; without fortune, family connections, or patronage; self-prompted, self-sustained, and almost self-taught, he has conquered every obstacle, achieved his way to eminence, and, having become one of the ornaments of the nation, has turned the whole force of his talents and influence to advance and embellish his native town.

Indeed, it is this last trait in his character which has given him the greatest interest in my eyes, and induced me particularly to point him out to my countrymen. Eminent as are his literary merits, he is but one among the many distinguished authors of this intellectual nation. They, however, in general, live but for their own fame, or their own pleasures. Their private history presents no lesson to the world, or, perhaps, a humiliating one of human frailty and inconsistency.

---

*See endnote 6 to *The Sketch-Book*.
†Diligent attention to detail.

At best; they are prone to steal away from the bustle and common-place of busy existence; to indulge in the selfishness of lettered ease; and to revel in scenes of mental, but exclusive enjoyment.

Mr. Roscoe, on the contrary, has claimed none of the accorded privileges of talent. He has shut himself up in no garden of thought, nor elysium of fancy; but has gone forth into the highways and thor-oughfares of life; he has planted bowers by the way-side, for the re-freshment of the pilgrim and the sojourner, and has opened pure fountains, where the laboring man may turn aside from the dust and heat of the day, and drink of the living streams of knowledge. There is a "daily beauty in his life,"* on which mankind may meditate and grow better. It exhibits no lofty and almost useless, because inim-itable, example of excellence; but presents a picture of active, yet simple and imitable virtues, which are within every man's reach, but which, unfortunately, are not exercised by many, or this world would be a paradise.

But his private life is peculiarly worthy the attention of the citizens of our young and busy country, where literature and the elegant arts must grow up side by side with the coarser plants of daily necessity; and must depend for their culture, not on the exclu-sive devotion of time and wealth, nor the quickening rays of titled patronage, but on hours and seasons snatched from the pursuit of worldly interests, by intelligent and public-spirited individuals.

He has shown how much may be done for a place in hours of leisure by one master spirit, and how completely it can give its own impress to surrounding objects. Like his own Lorenzo De' Medici,[†] on whom he seems to have fixed his eye as on a pure model of an-tiquity, he has interwoven the history of his life with the history of his native town, and has made the foundations of its fame the mon-uments of his virtues. Wherever you go in Liverpool, you perceive traces of his footsteps in all that is elegant and liberal. He found the tide of wealth flowing merely in the channels of traffick; he has diverted from it invigorating rills to refresh the garden of literature. By his own example and constant exertions he has effected

---

*From Shakespeare's *Othello, the Moor of Venice* (act 5, scene 1).
†Italian merchant prince (1449–1492) who ruled in the city of Florence at the height of the Renaissance.

that union of commerce and the intellectual pursuits, so eloquently recommended in one of his latest writings:* and has practically proved how beautifully they may be brought to harmonize, and to benefit each other. The noble institutions for literary and scientific purposes, which reflect such credit on Liverpool, and are giving such an impulse to the public mind, have mostly been originated, and have all been effectively promoted, by Mr. Roscoe; and when we consider the rapidly increasing opulence and magnitude of that town, which promises to vie in commercial importance with the metropolis, it will be perceived that in awakening an ambition of mental improvement among its inhabitants, he has effected a great benefit to the cause of British literature.

In America, we know Mr. Roscoe only as the author—in Liverpool he is spoken of as the banker; and I was told of his having been unfortunate in business. I could not pity him, as I heard some rich men do. I considered him far above the reach of pity. Those who live only for the world, and in the world, may be cast down by the frowns of adversity; but a man like Roscoe is not to be overcome by the reverses of fortune. They do but drive him in upon the resources of his own mind; to the superior society of his own thoughts; which the best of men are apt sometimes to neglect, and to roam abroad in search of less worthy associates. He is independent of the world around him. He lives with antiquity and posterity; with antiquity, in the sweet communion of studious retirement; and with posterity, in the generous aspirings after future renown. The solitude of such a mind is its state of highest enjoyment. It is then visited by those elevated meditations which are the proper *aliment* of noble souls, and are, like manna, sent from heaven, in the wilderness of this world.†

While my feelings were yet alive on the subject, it was my fortune to light on further traces of Mr. Roscoe. I was riding out with a gentleman, to view the environs of Liverpool, when he turned off, through a gate, into some ornamented grounds. After riding a short distance, we came to a spacious mansion of freestone, built in the

---

*Address on the opening of the Liverpool Institution [Irving's note].
†See the Bible, Exodus 16.

Grecian style. It was not in the purest taste, yet it had an air of elegance, and the situation was delightful. A fine lawn sloped away from it, studded with clumps of trees, so disposed as to break a soft fertile country into a variety of landscapes. The Mersey was seen winding a broad quiet sheet of water through an expanse of green meadow-land; while the Welsh mountains, blended with clouds, and melting into distance, bordered the horizon.

This was Roscoe's favorite residence during the days of his prosperity. It had been the seat of elegant hospitality and literary retirement. The house was now silent and deserted. I saw the windows of the study, which looked out upon the soft scenery I have mentioned. The windows were closed—the library was gone. Two or three ill-favored beings were loitering about the place, whom my fancy pictured into retainers of the law. It as like visiting some classic fountain, that had once welled its pure waters in a sacred shade, but finding it dry and dusty, with the lizard and the toad brooding over the shattered marbles.

I inquired after the fate of Mr. Roscoe's library, which had consisted of scarce and foreign books, from many of which he had drawn the materials for his Italian histories. It had passed under the hammer of the auctioneer, and was dispersed about the country. The good people of the vicinity thronged like wreckers to get some part of the noble vessel that had been driven on shore. Did such a scene admit of ludicrous associations, we might imagine something whimsical in this strange irruption in the regions of learning. Pigmies rummaging the armory of a giant, and contending for the possession of weapons which they could not wield. We might picture to ourselves some knot of speculators, debating with calculating brow over the quaint binding and illuminated margin of an obsolete author; of the air of intense, but baffled sagacity, with which some successful purchaser attempted to dive into the black-letter bargain he had secured.

It is a beautiful incident in the story of Mr. Roscoe's misfortunes, and one which cannot fail to interest the studious mind, that the parting with his books seems to have touched upon his tenderest feelings, and to have been the only circumstance that could provoke the notice of his muse. The scholar only knows how dear these silent, yet eloquent, companions of pure thoughts and innocent hours become in the seasons of adversity. When all that is worldly turns to dross around us, these only retain their steady value. When friends grow cold, and the converse of intimates languishes into vapid civility and commonplace, these only continue the unaltered countenance of happier days, and cheer us with that true friendship which never deceived hope, nor deserted sorrow.

I do not wish to censure; but, surely, if the people of Liverpool had been properly sensible of what was due to Mr. Roscoe and themselves, his library would never have been sold. Good worldly reasons may, doubtless, be given for the circumstance, which it would be difficult to combat with others that might seem merely fanciful; but it certainly appears to me such an opportunity as seldom occurs, of cheering a noble mind struggling under misfortunes, by one of the most delicate, but most expressive tokens of public sympathy. It is difficult, however, to estimate a man of genius properly who is daily before our eyes. He becomes mingled and confounded with other men. His great qualities lose their novelty, we become too familiar with the common materials which form the basis even of the loftiest character. Some of Mr. Roscoe's townsmen may regard him merely as a man of business; others as a politician; all find him engaged like themselves in ordinary occupations, and surpassed, perhaps, by themselves on some points of worldly wisdom. Even that amiable and unostentatious simplicity of character, which gives the nameless grace to real excellence, may cause him to be undervalued by some coarse minds, who do not know that true worth is always void of glare and pretension. But the man of letters, who speaks of Liverpool, speaks of it as the residence of Roscoe.— The intelligent traveller who visits it inquires where Roscoe is to be seen.—He is the literary landmark of the place, indicating its existence to the distant scholar.—He is, like Pompey's column at Alexandria,* towering alone in classic dignity.

The following sonnet, addressed by Mr. Roscoe to his books on parting with them, is alluded to in the preceding article. If anything can add effect to the pure feeling and elevated thought here displayed, it is the conviction, that the whole is no effusion of fancy, but a faithful transcript from the writer's heart.

---

*Column erected in honor of the Roman emperor Diocletian to commemorate the conquest of Alexandria in A.D. 296.

To My Books*

As one who, destined from his friends to part,
 Regrets his loss, but hopes again erewhile
 To share their converse and enjoy their smile,
And tempers as he may affliction's dart;

Thus, loved associates, chiefs of elder art,
 Teachers of wisdom, who could once beguile
 My tedious hours, and lighten every toil,
I now resign you; nor with fainting heart;

For pass a few short years, or days, or hours,
 And happier seasons may their dawn unfold,
 And all your sacred fellowship restore:
When, freed from earth, unlimited its powers,
 Mind shall with mind direct communion hold,
 And kindred spirits meet to part no more.

---

*This poem was first published in *Gentleman's Magazine*, vol. 86 (1816).

The Wife[7]

The treasures of the deep are not so precious
As are the conceal'd comforts of a man
Locked up in woman's love. I scent the air
Of blessings, when I come but near the house.
What a delicious breath marriage sends forth . . .
The violet bed's not sweeter.

MIDDLETON*

I have often had occasion to remark the fortitude with which women sustain the most overwhelming reverses of fortune. Those disasters which break down the spirit of a man, and prostrate him in the dust, seem to call forth all the energies of the softer sex, and give such intrepidity and elevation to their character, that at times it approaches to sublimity. Nothing can be more touching than to behold a soft and tender female, who had been all weakness and dependence, and alive to every trivial roughness, while treading the prosperous paths of life, suddenly rising in mental force to be the comforter and support of her husband under misfortune, and abiding, with unshrinking firmness, the bitterest blasts of adversity.

As the vine, which has long twined its graceful foliage about the oak, and been lifted by it into sunshine, will, when the hardy plant is rifted by the thunderbolt, cling round it with its caressing tendrils, and bind up its shattered boughs; so is it beautifully ordered by Providence, that woman, who is the mere dependent and ornament of man in his happier hours, should be his stay and solace when smitten with sudden calamity; winding herself into the rugged recesses of his nature, tenderly supporting the drooping head, and binding up the broken heart.

I was once congratulating a friend, who had around him a blooming family, knit together in the strongest affection. "I can wish

*From the 1625 tragedy *Women Beware Women*, by English dramatist Thomas Middleton (act 3, scene 2, lines 3–8).

you no better lot," said he, with enthusiasm, "than to have a wife and children. If you are prosperous, there they are to share your prosperity; if otherwise, there they are to comfort you." And, indeed, I have observed that a married man falling into misfortune is more apt to retrieve his situation in the world than a single one; partly because he is more stimulated to exertion by the necessities of the helpless and beloved beings who depend upon him for subsistence; but chiefly because his spirits are soothed and relieved by domestic endearments, and his self-respect kept alive by finding, that though all abroad is darkness and humiliation, yet there is still a little world of love at home, of which he is the monarch. Whereas a single man is apt to run to waste and self-neglect; to fancy himself lonely and abandoned, and his heart to fall to ruin like some deserted mansion, for want of an inhabitant.

These observations call to mind a little domestic story, of which I was once a witness. My intimate friend, Leslie,* had married a beautiful and accomplished girl, who had been brought up in the midst of fashionable life. She had, it is true, no fortune, but that of my friend was ample; and he delighted in the anticipation of indulging her in every elegant pursuit, and administering to those delicate tastes and fancies that spread a kind of witchery about the sex.—"Her life," said he, "shall be like a fairy tale."

The very difference in their characters produced an harmonious combination: he was of a romantic and somewhat serious cast; she was all life and gladness. I have often noticed the mute rapture with which he would gaze upon her in company, of which her sprightly powers made her the delight; and how, in the midst of applause, her eye would still turn to him, as if there alone she sought favor and acceptance. When leaning on his arm, her slender form contrasted finely with his tall manly person. The fond confiding air with which she looked up to him seemed to call forth a flush of triumphant pride and cherishing tenderness, as if he doted on his lovely burden for its very helplessness. Never did a couple set forward on the flowery path of early and well-suited marriage with a fairer prospect of felicity.

---

*Charles Robert Leslie (1794–1859), biographer and painter, who illustrated scenes from Irving's *A History of New York*. This sketch, however, is based on events in the life of Washington Allston (see endnote 4 to *The Sketch-Book*).

It was the misfortune of my friend, however, to have embarked his property in large speculations; and he had not been married many months, when, by a succession of sudden disasters, it was swept from him, and he found himself reduced almost to penury. For a time he kept his situation to himself, and went about with a haggard countenance, and a breaking heart. His life was but a protracted agony; and what rendered it more insupportable was the necessity of keeping up a smile in the presence of his wife; for he could not bring himself to overwhelm her with the news. She saw, however, with the quick eyes of affection, that all was not well with him. She marked his altered looks and stifled sighs, and was not to be deceived by his sickly and vapid attempts at cheerfulness. She tasked all her sprightly powers and tender blandishments to win him back to happiness; but she only drove the arrow deeper into his soul. The more he saw cause to love her, the more torturing was the thought that he was soon to make her wretched. A little while, thought he, and the smile will vanish from that cheek— the song will die away from those lips—the lustre of those eyes will be quenched with sorrow; and the happy heart, which now beats lightly in that bosom, will be weighed down like mine, by the cares and miseries of the world.

At length he came to me one day, and related his whole situation in a tone of the deepest despair. When I heard him through I inquired, "Does your wife know all this?"—At the question he burst into an agony of tears. "For God's sake!" cried he, "if you have any pity on me, don't mention my wife; it is the thought of her that drives me almost to madness!"

"And why not?" said I. "She must know it sooner or later; you cannot keep it long from her, and the intelligence may break upon her in a more startling manner, than if imparted by yourself; for the accents of those we love soften the hardest tidings. Besides, you are depriving yourself of the comforts of her sympathy; and not merely that, but also endangering the only bond that can keep hearts together—an unreserved community of thought and feeling. She will soon perceive that something is secretly preying upon your mind; and true love will not brook reserve; it feels undervalued and outraged, when even the sorrows of those it loves are concealed from it."

"Oh, but, my friend! to think what a blow I am to give to all her future prospects—how I am to strike her very soul to the earth, by telling her that her husband is a beggar! that she is to forego all the elegancies of life—all the pleasures of society—to shrink with me into indigence and obscurity! To tell her that I have dragged her down from the sphere in which she might have continued to move in constant brightness—the light of every eye—the admiration of every heart!—How can she bear poverty? She has been brought up in all the refinements of opulence. How can she bear neglect? she has been the idol of society. Oh! it will break her heart—it will break her heart!—"

I saw his grief was eloquent, and I let it have its flow; for sorrow relieves itself by words. When his paroxysm had subsided, and he had relapsed into moody silence, I resumed the subject gently, and urged him to break his situation at once to his wife. He shook his head mournfully, but positively.

"But how are you to keep it from her? It is necessary she should know it, that you may take the steps proper to the alteration of your circumstances. You must change your style of living——nay," observing a pang to pass across his countenance, "don't let that afflict you. I am sure you have never placed your happiness in outward show—you have yet friends, warm friends, who will not think the worse of you for being less splendidly lodged: and surely it does not require a palace to be happy with Mary——"

"I could be happy with her," cried he, convulsively, "in a hovel!—I could go down with her into poverty and the dust!—I could—I could—God bless her!—God bless her!" cried he, bursting into a transport of grief and tenderness.

"And believe me, my friend," said I, stepping up, and grasping him warmly by the hand, "believe me she can be the same with you. Ay, more: it will be a source of pride and triumph to her—it will call forth all the latent energies and fervent sympathies of her nature; for she will rejoice to prove that she loves you for yourself. There is in every true woman's heart a spark of heavenly fire, which lies dormant in the broad daylight of prosperity; but which kindles up, and beams and blazes in the dark hour of adversity. No man knows what the wife of his bosom is—no man knows what a ministering angel she is—until he has gone with her through the fiery trials of this world."

There was something in the earnestness of my manner, and the figurative style of my language, that caught the excited imagination of Leslie. I knew the auditor I had to deal with; and following up the impression I had made, I finished by persuading him to go home and unburden his sad heart to his wife.

I must confess, notwithstanding all I had said, I felt some little solicitude for the result. Who can calculate on the fortitude of one whose life has been a round of pleasures? Her gay spirits might revolt at the dark downward path of low humility suddenly pointed out before her, and might cling to the sunny regions in which they had hitherto revelled. Besides, ruin in fashionable life is accompanied by so many galling mortifications, to which in other ranks it is a stranger.—In short, I could not meet Leslie the next morning without trepidation. He had made the disclosure.

"And how did she bear it?"

"Like an angel! It seemed rather to be a relief to her mind, for she threw her arms round my neck, and asked if this was all that had lately made me unhappy.—But, poor girl," added he, "she cannot realize the change we must undergo. She has no idea of poverty but in the abstract; she has only read of it in poetry, where it is allied to love. She feels as yet no privation; she suffers no loss of accustomed conveniences nor elegancies. When we come practically to experience its sordid cares, its paltry wants, its petty humiliations—then will be the real trial."

"But," said I, "now that you have got over the severest task, that of breaking it to her, the sooner you let the world into the secret the better. The disclosure may be mortifying; but then it is a single misery, and soon over: whereas you otherwise suffer it, in anticipation, every hour in the day. It is not poverty so much as pretence, that harasses a ruined man—the struggle between a proud mind and an empty purse—the keeping up a hollow show that must soon come to an end. Have the courage to appear poor and you disarm poverty of its sharpest sting." On this point I found Leslie perfectly prepared. He had no false pride himself, and as to his wife, she was only anxious to conform to their altered fortunes.

Some days afterwards he called upon me in the evening. He had disposed of his dwelling house, and taken a small cottage in the country, a few miles from town. He had been busied all day in sending out furniture. The new establishment required few articles, and those of the simplest kind. All the splendid furniture of his late residence had been sold, excepting his wife's harp. That, he said, was too closely associated with the idea of herself; it belonged to the little story of their loves; for some of the sweetest moments of their courtship were those when he had leaned over that instrument, and listened to the melting tones of her voice. I could not but smile at this instance of romantic gallantry in a doting husband.

He was now going out to the cottage, where his wife had been all day superintending its arrangement. My feelings had become strongly interested in the progress of this family story, and, as it was a fine evening, I offered to accompany him.

He was wearied with the fatigues of the day, and, as we walked out, fell into a fit of gloomy musing.

"Poor Mary!" at length broke, with a heavy sigh, from his lips.

"And what of her?" asked I: "has any thing happened to her?"

"What," said he, darting an impatient glance, "is it nothing to be reduced to this paltry situation—to be caged in a miserable cottage—to be obliged to toil almost in the menial concerns of her wretched habitation?"

"Has she then repined at the change?"

"Repined! she has been nothing but sweetness and good humor. Indeed, she seems in better spirits than I have ever known her; she has been to me all love, and tenderness, and comfort!"

"Admirable girl!" exclaimed I. "You call yourself poor, my friend; you never were so rich—you never knew the boundless treasures of excellence you possessed in that woman."

"Oh! but, my friend, if this first meeting at the cottage were over, I think I could then be comfortable. But this is her first day of real experience; she has been introduced into a humble dwelling—she has been employed all day in arranging its miserable equipments— she has, for the first time, known the fatigues of domestic employment—she has, for the first time, looked round her on a home destitute of every thing elegant,—almost of every thing convenient; and may now be sitting down, exhausted and spiritless, brooding over a prospect of future poverty."

There was a degree of probability in this picture that I could not gainsay, so we walked on in silence.

After turning from the main road up a narrow lane, so thickly shaded with forest trees as to give it a complete air of seclusion, we came in sight of the cottage. It was humble enough in its appearance for the most pastoral poet; and yet it had a pleasing rural look. A wild vine had overrun one end with a profusion of foliage; a few trees threw their branches gracefully over it; and I observed several pots of flowers tastefully disposed about the door, and on the grass-plot in front. A small wicket gate opened upon a footpath that wound through some shrubbery to the door. Just as we approached, we heard the sound of music—Leslie grasped my arm; we paused and listened. It was Mary's voice singing, in a style of the most touching simplicity, a little air of which her husband was peculiarly fond.

I felt Leslie's hand tremble on my arm. He stepped forward to hear more distinctly. His step made a noise on the gravel walk. A bright beautiful face glanced out at the window and vanished—a light footstep was heard—and Mary came tripping forth to meet us: she was in a pretty rural dress of white; a few wild flowers were twisted in her fine hair; a fresh bloom was on her cheek; her whole countenance beamed with smiles—I had never seen her look so lovely.

"My dear George," cried she, "I am so glad you are come! I have been watching and watching for you; and running down the lane, and looking out for you. I've set out a table under a beautiful tree behind the cottage; and I've been gathering some of the most delicious strawberries, for I know you are fond of them—and we have such excellent cream—and everything is so sweet and still here— Oh!" said she, putting her arm within his, and looking up brightly in his face, "Oh, we shall be so happy!"

Poor Leslie was overcome. He caught her to his bosom—he folded his arms round her—he kissed her again and again—he could not speak, but the tears gushed into his eyes; and he has often assured me, that though the world has since gone prosperously with him, and his life has, indeed, been a happy one, yet never has he experienced a moment of more exquisite felicity.

Rip Van Winkle[8]

A POSTHUMOUS WRITING OF DIEDRICH KNICKERBOCKER.*

By Woden, God of Saxons,
From whence comes Wensday, that is Wodensday,
Truth is a thing that ever I will keep
Unto thylke day in which I creep into
My sepulchre—

CARTWRIGHT[†]

[The following Tale was found among the papers of the late Diedrich Knickerbocker, an old gentleman of New York, who was very curious in the Dutch history of the province, and the manners of the descendants from its primitive settlers. His historical researches, however, did not lie so much among books as among men; for the former are lamentably scanty on his favorite topics; whereas he found the old burghers, and still more their wives, rich in that legendary lore, so invaluable to true history. Whenever, therefore, he happened upon a genuine Dutch family, snugly shut up in its low-roofed farmhouse, under a spreading sycamore, he looked upon it as a little clasped volume of black-letter,[‡] and studied it with the zeal of a book-worm.

The result of all these researches was a history of the province during the reign of the Dutch governors, which he published some years since. There have been various opinions as to the literary

---

*Fictional narrator of Irving's *A History of New York*.
†Quotation from *The Ordinary* (1635), by English dramatist William Cartwright; Irving may have taken it from Sir Walter Scott's 1816 novel *The Antiquary* (chapter 16).
‡Heavy, ornamental printing typeface.

character of his work, and, to tell the truth, it is not a whit better than it should be. Its chief merit is its scrupulous accuracy, which indeed was a little questioned on its first appearance, but has since been completely established; and it is now admitted into all historical collections, as a book of unquestionable authority.

The old gentleman died shortly after the publication of his work, and now that he is dead and gone, it cannot do much harm to his memory to say that his time might have been much better employed in weightier labors. He, however, was apt to ride his hobby* his own way; and though it did now and then kick up the dust a little in the eyes of his neighbors, and grieve the spirit of some friends, for whom he felt the truest deference and affection; yet his errors and follies are remembered "more in sorrow than in anger," and it begins to be suspected, that he never intended to injure or offend. But however his memory may be appreciated by critics, it is still held dear by many folks, whose good opinion is well worth having; particularly by certain biscuit-bakers, who have gone so far as to imprint his likeness on their new-year cakes; and have thus given him a chance for immortality, almost equal to being stamped on a Waterloo Medal, or a Queen Anne's Farthing.]†

W hoever has made a voyage up the Hudson must remember the Kaatskill mountains. They are a dismembered branch of the great Appalachian family, and are seen away to the west of the river, swelling up to a noble height, and lording it over the surrounding country. Every change of season, every change of weather, indeed, every hour of the day, produces some change in the magical hues and shapes of these mountains, and they are regarded by all the good wives, far and near, as perfect

---

*That is, his hobbyhorse.
†Waterloo Medals, issued to soldiers who had participated in various battles of the Napoleonic Wars, commemorated Napoleon's final defeat at the Battle of Waterloo (June 18, 1815) by the Allies under English and Prussian generals Wellington and Blücher. Queen Anne farthings were issued only in 1714, during the last year of Queen Anne's reign in Great Britain and Ireland, and were thought to be rare.

barometers. When the weather is fair and settled, they are clothed in blue and purple, and print their bold outlines on the clear evening sky; but, sometimes, when the rest of the landscape is cloudless, they will gather a hood of gray vapors about their summits, which, in the last rays of the setting sun, will glow and light up like a crown of glory.

At the foot of these fairy mountains, the voyager may have descried the light smoke curling up from a village, whose shingle-roofs gleam among the trees, just where the blue tints of the upland melt away into the fresh green of the nearer landscape. It is a little village of great antiquity, having been founded by some of the Dutch colonists, in the early times of the province, just about the beginning of the government of the good Peter Stuyvesant,* (may he rest in peace!) and there were some of the houses of the original settlers standing within a few years, built of small yellow bricks brought from Holland, having latticed windows and gable fronts, surmounted with weather-cocks.

In that same village, and in one of these very houses (which, to tell the precise truth, was sadly time-worn and weather-beaten), there lived many years since, while the country was yet a province of Great Britain, a simple good-natured fellow of the name of Rip Van Winkle. He was a descendant of the Van Winkles who figured so gallantly in the chivalrous days of Peter Stuyvesant, and accompanied him to the siege of Fort Christina.† He inherited, however, but little of the martial character of his ancestors. I have observed that he was a simple good-natured man; he was, moreover, a kind neighbor, and an obedient hen-pecked husband. Indeed, to the latter circumstance might be owing that meekness of spirit which gained him such universal popularity; for those men are most apt to be obsequious and conciliating abroad, who are under the discipline of shrews at home. Their tempers, doubtless, are rendered pliant and malleable in the fiery furnace of domestic tribulation; and a curtain

---

*The last Dutch director-general of New Netherland (1646–1664); unpopular for his harsh leadership, he was forced to surrender the colony to Great Britain in 1664, when it was subsequently renamed New York.
†Swedish settlement on the Delaware River; it was captured by the Dutch under Stuyvesant in 1655.

lecture* is worth all the sermons in the world for teaching the virtues of patience and long-suffering. A termagant† wife may, therefore, in some respects, be considered a tolerable blessing; and if so, Rip Van Winkle was thrice blessed.

Certain it is, that he was a great favorite among all the good wives of the village, who, as usual, with the amiable sex, took his part in all family squabbles; and never failed, whenever they talked those matters over in their evening gossipings, to lay all the blame on Dame Van Winkle. The children of the village, too, would shout with joy whenever he approached. He assisted at their sports, made their playthings, taught them to fly kites and shoot marbles, and told them long stories of ghosts, witches, and Indians. Whenever he went dodging about the village, he was surrounded by a troop of them, hanging on his skirts, clambering on his back, and playing a thousand tricks on him with impunity; and not a dog would bark at him throughout the neighborhood.

The great error in Rip's composition was an insuperable aversion to all kinds of profitable labor. It could not be from the want of assiduity or perseverance; for he would sit on a wet rock, with a rod as long and heavy as a Tartar's lance, and fish all day without a murmur, even though he should not be encouraged by a single nibble. He would carry a fowling-piece on his shoulder for hours together, trudging through woods and swamps, and up hill and down dale, to shoot a few squirrels or wild pigeons. He would never refuse to assist a neighbor even in the roughest toil, and was a foremost man at all country frolics for husking Indian corn, or building stone-fences; the women of the village, too, used to employ him to run their errands, and to do such little odd jobs as their less obliging husbands would not do for them. In a word Rip was ready to attend to anybody's business but his own; but as to doing family duty, and keeping his farm in order, he found it impossible.

In fact, he declared it was of no use to work on his farm; it was the most pestilent little piece of ground in the whole country; every thing about it went wrong, and would go wrong, in spite of him. His fences were continually falling to pieces; his cow would either go

---

*That is, one given behind the curtains, out of sight of neighbors.
†Argumentative and nagging.

astray, or get among the cabbages; weeds were sure to grow quicker in his fields than anywhere else; the rain always made a point of setting in just as he had some out-door work to do; so that though his patrimonial estate had dwindled away under his management, acre by acre, until there was little more left than a mere patch of Indian corn and potatoes, yet it was the worst conditioned farm in the neighborhood.

His children, too, were as ragged and wild as if they belonged to nobody. His son Rip, an urchin begotten in his own likeness, promised to inherit the habits, with the old clothes of his father. He was generally seen trooping like a colt at his mother's heels, equipped in a pair of his father's cast-off galligaskins,* which he had much ado to old up with one hand, as a fine lady does her train in bad weather.

Rip Van Winkle, however, was one of those happy mortals, of foolish, well-oiled dispositions, who take the world easy, eat white bread or brown, whichever can be got with least thought or trouble, and would rather starve on a penny than work for a pound. If left to himself, he would have whistled life away in perfect contentment; but his wife kept continually dinning in his ears about his idleness, his carelessness, and the ruin he was bringing on his family. Morning, noon, and night, her tongue was incessantly going, and everything he said or did was sure to produce a torrent of household eloquence. Rip had but one way of replying to all lectures of the kind, and that, by frequent use, had grown into a habit. He shrugged his shoulders, shook his head, cast up his eyes, but said nothing. This, however, always provoked a fresh volley from his wife; so that he was fain to draw off his forces, and take to the outside of the house—the only side which, in truth, belongs to a hen-pecked husband.

Rip's sole domestic adherent was his dog Wolf, who was as much hen-pecked as his master; for Dame Van Winkle regarded them as companions in idleness, and even looked upon Wolf with an evil eye, as the cause of his master's going so often astray. True it is, in all points of spirit befitting an honorable dog, he was as courageous an animal as ever scoured the woods—but what courage can withstand the ever-during and all-besetting terrors of a woman's tongue?

---

*Loose-fitting breeches.

The moment Wolf entered the house his crest fell, his tail drooped to the ground, or curled between his legs, he sneaked about with a gallows air, casting many a sidelong glance at Dame Van Winkle, and at the least flourish of a broomstick or ladle, he would fly to the door with yelping precipitation.

Times grew worse and worse with Rip Van Winkle as years of matrimony rolled on; a tart temper never mellows with age, and a sharp tongue is the only edged tool that grows keener with constant use. For a long while he used to console himself, when driven from home, by frequenting a kind of perpetual club of the sages, philosophers, and other idle personages of the village; which held its sessions on a bench before a small inn, designated by a rubicund portrait of His Majesty George the Third.* Here they used to sit in the shade through a long lazy summer's day, talking listlessly over village gossip, or telling endless sleepy stories about nothing. But it would have been worth any statesman's money to have heard the profound discussions that sometimes took place, when by chance an old newspaper fell into their hands from some passing traveller. How solemnly they would listen to the contents, as drawled out by Derrick Van Bummel, the schoolmaster, a dapper learned little man, who was not to be daunted by the most gigantic word in the dictionary; and how sagely they would deliberate upon public events some months after they had taken place.

The opinions of this junto were completely controlled by Nicholas Vedder, a patriarch of the village, and landlord of the inn, at the door of which he took his seat from morning till night, just moving sufficiently to avoid the sun and keep in the shade of a large tree; so that the neighbors could tell the hour by his movements as accurately as by a sun-dial. It is true he was rarely heard to speak, but smoked his pipe incessantly. His adherents, however (for every great man has his adherents), perfectly understood him, and knew how to gather his opinions. When any thing that was read or related displeased him, he was observed to smoke his pipe vehemently, and to send forth short, frequent and angry puffs; but when pleased, he would inhale the smoke slowly and tranquilly, and emit it in light

---

*British king (1760–1820) against whom the colonists rebelled in the American Revolution.

and placid clouds; and sometimes, taking the pipe from his mouth, and letting the fragrant vapor curl about his nose, would gravely nod his head in token of perfect approbation.

From even this stronghold the unlucky Rip was at length routed by his termagant wife, who would suddenly break in upon the tranquillity of the assemblage and call the members all to naught; nor was that august personage, Nicholas Vedder himself, sacred from the daring tongue of this terrible virago,* who charged him outright with encouraging her husband in habits of idleness.

Poor Rip was at last reduced almost to despair; and his only alternative, to escape from the labor of the farm and clamor of his wife, was to take gun in hand and stroll away into the woods. Here he would sometimes seat himself at the foot of a tree, and share the contents of his wallet† with Wolf, with whom he sympathized as a fellow-sufferer in persecution. "Poor Wolf," he would say, "thy mistress leads thee a dog's life of it; but never mind, my lad, whilst I live thou shalt never want a friend to stand by thee!" Wolf would wag his tail, look wistfully in his master's face, and if dogs can feel pity I verily believe he reciprocated the sentiment with all his heart.

In a long ramble of the kind on a fine autumnal day, Rip had unconsciously scrambled to one of the highest parts of the Kaatskill mountains. He was after his favorite sport of squirrel shooting, and the still solitudes had echoed and re-echoed with the reports of his gun. Panting and fatigued, he threw himself, late in the afternoon, on a green knoll, covered with mountain herbage, that crowned the brow of a precipice. From an opening between the trees he could overlook all the lower country for many a mile of rich woodland. He saw at a distance the lordly Hudson, far, far below him, moving on its silent but majestic course, with the reflection of a purple cloud, or the sail of a lagging bark,‡ here and there sleeping on its glassy bosom, and at last losing itself in the blue highlands.

On the other side he looked down into a deep mountain glen, wild, lonely, and shagged, the bottom filled with fragments from the impending cliffs, and scarcely lighted by the reflected rays of the

---

*Quarrelsome, shrewish woman.
†Knapsack.
‡Small sailing ship.

setting sun. For some time Rip lay musing on this scene; evening was gradually advancing; the mountains began to throw their long blue shadows over the valleys; he saw that it would be dark long before he could reach the village, and he heaved a heavy sigh when he thought of encountering the terrors of Dame Van Winkle.

As he was about to descend, he heard a voice from a distance, hallooing, "Rip Van Winkle! Rip Van Winkle!" He looked round, but could see nothing but a crow winging its solitary flight across the mountain. He thought his fancy must have deceived him, and turned again to descend, when he heard the same cry ring through the still evening air; "Rip Van Winkle! Rip Van Winkle!"—at the same time Wolf bristled up his back, and giving a low growl, skulked to his master's side, looking fearfully down into the glen. Rip now felt a vague apprehension stealing over him; he looked anxiously in the same direction, and perceived a strange figure slowly toiling up the rocks, and bending under the weight of something he carried on his back. He was surprised to see any human being in this lonely and unfrequented place, but supposing it to be some one of the neighborhood in need of his assistance, he hastened down to yield it.

On nearer approach he was still more surprised at the singularity of the stranger's appearance. He was a short square-built old fellow, with thick bushy hair, and a grizzled beard. His dress was of the antique Dutch fashion—a cloth jerkin strapped round the waist—several pair of breeches, the outer one of ample volume, decorated with rows of buttons down the sides, and bunches at the knees. He bore on his shoulder a stout keg, that seemed full of liquor, and made signs for Rip to approach and assist him with the load. Though rather shy and distrustful of this new acquaintance, Rip complied with his usual alacrity; and mutually relieving one another, they clambered up a narrow gully, apparently the dry bed of a mountain torrent. As they ascended, Rip every now and then heard long rolling peals, like distant thunder, that seemed to issue out of a deep ravine, or rather cleft, between lofty rocks, toward which their rugged path conducted. He paused for an instant, but supposing it to be the muttering of one of those transient thunder-showers which often take place in mountain heights, he proceeded. Passing through the ravine, they came to a hollow, like a small amphitheatre, surrounded by perpendicular precipices, over the brinks of which impending trees shot their branches, so that you only caught glimpses of the azure sky and the bright evening cloud. During the whole time Rip and his companion had labored on in silence; for though the former marvelled greatly what could be the object of carrying a keg of liquor up this wild mountain, yet there was something strange and incomprehensible about the unknown, that inspired awe and checked familiarity.

On entering the amphitheatre, new objects of wonder presented themselves. On a level spot in the centre was a company of odd-looking personages playing at nine-pins. They were dressed in a quaint outlandish fashion; some wore short doublets, others jerkins, with long knives in their belts, and most of them had enormous breeches, of similar style with that of the guide's. Their visages, too, were peculiar: one had a large beard, broad face, and small piggish eyes: the face of another seemed to consist entirely of nose, and was surmounted by a white sugar-loaf hat set off with a little red cock's tail. They all had beards, of various shapes and colors. There was one who seemed to be the commander. He was a stout old gentleman, with a weather-beaten countenance; he wore a laced doublet, broad belt and hanger, high-crowned hat and feather, red stockings, and high-heeled shoes, with roses in them. The whole group reminded Rip of the figures in an old Flemish painting, in the parlor of Dominie* Van Shaick, the village parson, and which had been brought over from Holland at the time of the settlement.†

What seemed particularly odd to Rip was, that though these folks were evidently amusing themselves, yet they maintained the gravest faces, the most mysterious silence, and were, withal, the most melancholy party of pleasure he had ever witnessed. Nothing interrupted the stillness of the scene but the noise of the balls, which, whenever they were rolled, echoed along the mountains like rumbling peals of thunder.

As Rip and his companion approached them, they suddenly desisted from their play, and stared at him with such fixed statue-like gaze, and such strange, uncouth, lack-lustre countenances, that his

---

*Clergyman.
†The Dutch established the settlement of New Amsterdam in 1625; its history is the subject of Irving's *A History of New York*.

heart turned within him, and his knees smote together. His companion now emptied the contents of the keg into large flagons, and made signs to him to wait upon the company. He obeyed with fear and trembling; they quaffed the liquor in profound silence, and then returned to their game.

By degrees Rip's awe and apprehension subsided. He even ventured, when no eye was fixed upon him, to taste the beverage, which he found had much of the flavor of excellent Hollands.* He was naturally a thirsty soul, and was soon tempted to repeat the draught. One taste provoked another; and he reiterated his visits to the flagon so often that at length his senses were overpowered, his eyes swam in his head, his head gradually declined, and he fell into a deep sleep.

On waking, he found himself on the green knoll whence he had first seen the old man of the glen. He rubbed his eyes—it was a bright sunny morning. The birds were hopping and twittering among the bushes, and the eagle was wheeling aloft, and breasting the pure mountain breeze. "Surely," thought Rip, "I have not slept here all night." He recalled the occurrences before he fell asleep. The strange man with a keg of liquor—the mountain ravine—the wild retreat among the rocks—the woe-begone party at nine-pins—the flagon—"Oh! that flagon! that wicked flagon!" thought Rip—"what excuse shall I make to Dame Van Winkle!"

He looked round for his gun, but in place of the clean well-oiled fowling-piece, he found an old firelock lying by him, the barrel incrusted with rust, the lock falling off, and the stock worm-eaten. He now suspected that the grave roysters† of the mountain had put a trick upon him, and, having dosed him with liquor, had robbed him of his gun. Wolf, too, had disappeared, but he might have strayed away after a squirrel or partridge. He whistled after him and shouted his name, but all in vain; the echoes repeated his whistle and shout, but no dog was to be seen.

He determined to revisit the scene of the last evening's gambol, and if he met with any of the party, to demand his dog and gun. As he rose to walk, he found himself stiff in the joints, and wanting in his usual activity. "These mountain beds do not agree with me,"

---

*Sweet-tasting gin produced by the Dutch.
†Revelers.

thought Rip, "and if this frolic should lay me up with a fit of the rheumatism, I shall have a blessed time with Dame Van Winkle." With some difficulty he got down into the glen: he found the gully up which he and his companion had ascended the preceding evening; but to his astonishment a mountain stream was now foaming down it, leaping from rock to rock, and filling the glen with babbling murmurs. He, however, made shift to scramble up its sides, working his toilsome way through thickets of birch, sassafras, and witch-hazel, and sometimes tripped up or entangled by the wild grapevines that twisted their coils or tendrils from tree to tree, and spread a kind of network in his path.

At length he reached to where the ravine had opened through the cliffs to the amphitheatre; but no traces of such opening remained. The rocks presented a high impenetrable wall over which the torrent came tumbling in a sheet of feathery foam, and fell into a broad deep basin, black from the shadows of the surrounding forest. Here, then, poor Rip was brought to a stand. He again called and whistled after his dog; he was only answered by the cawing of a flock of idle crows, sporting high in air about a dry tree that overhung a sunny precipice; and who, secure in their elevation, seemed to look down and scoff at the poor man's perplexities. What was to be done? the morning was passing away, and Rip felt famished for want of his breakfast. He grieved to give up his dog and gun; he dreaded to meet his wife; but it would not do to starve among the mountains. He shook his head, shouldered the rusty firelock, and, with a heart full of trouble and anxiety, turned his steps homeward.

As he approached the village he met a number of people, but none whom he knew, which somewhat surprised him, for he had thought himself acquainted with every one in the country round. Their dress, too, was of a different fashion from that to which he was accustomed. They all stared at him with equal marks of surprise, and whenever they cast their eyes upon him, invariably stroked their chins. The constant recurrence of this gesture induced Rip, involuntarily, to do the same, when, to his astonishment, he found his beard had grown a foot long!

He had now entered the skirts of the village. A troop of strange children ran at his heels, hooting after him, and pointing at his gray beard. The dogs, too, not one of which he recognized for an old acquaintance, barked at him as he passed. The very village was altered; it was larger and more populous. There were rows of houses which he had never seen before, and those which had been his familiar haunts had disappeared. Strange names were over the doors—strange faces at the windows—every thing was strange. His mind now misgave him; he began to doubt whether both he and the world around him were not bewitched. Surely this was his native village, which he had left but the day before. There stood the Kaatskill mountains—there ran the silver Hudson at a distance—there was every hill and dale precisely as it had always been—Rip was sorely perplexed—"That flagon last night," thought he, "has addled my poor head sadly!"

It was with some difficulty that he found the way to his own house, which he approached with silent awe, expecting every moment to hear the shrill voice of Dame Van Winkle. He found the house gone to decay—the roof fallen in, the windows shattered, and the doors off the hinges. A half-starved dog that looked like Wolf was skulking about it. Rip called him by name, but the cur snarled, showed his teeth, and passed on. This was an unkind cut indeed—"My very dog," sighed poor Rip, "has forgotten me!"

He entered the house, which, to tell the truth, Dame Van Winkle had always kept in neat order. It was empty, forlorn, and apparently abandoned. This desolateness overcame all his connubial* fears—he called loudly for his wife and children—the lonely chambers rang for a moment with his voice, and then all again was silence.

He now hurried forth, and hastened to his old resort, the village inn—but it too was gone. A large rickety wooden building stood in its place, with great gaping windows, some of them broken and mended with old hats and petticoats, and over the door was painted, "the Union Hotel, by Jonathan Doolittle." Instead of the great tree that used to shelter the quiet little Dutch inn of yore, there now was reared a tall naked pole, with something on the top that looked like a red night-cap, and from it was fluttering a flag, on which was a singular assemblage of stars and stripes—all this was strange and

---

*Concerning marriage.

incomprehensible. He recognized on the sign, however, the ruby face of King George, under which he had smoked so many a peaceful pipe; but even this was singularly metamorphosed. The red coat was changed for one of blue and buff, a sword was held in the hand instead of a sceptre, the head was decorated with a cocked hat, and underneath was painted in large characters, GENERAL WASHINGTON.*

There was, as usual, a crowd of folk about the door, but none that Rip recollected. The very character of the people seemed changed. There was a busy, bustling, disputatious tone about it, instead of the accustomed phlegm and drowsy tranquillity. He looked in vain for the sage Nicholas Vedder, with his broad face, double chin, and fair long pipe, uttering clouds of tobacco-smoke instead of idle speeches; or Van Bummel, the schoolmaster, doling forth the contents of an ancient newspaper. In place of these, a lean, bilious-looking fellow, with his pockets full of handbills, was haranguing vehemently about rights of citizens—elections—members of congress—liberty—Bunker's Hill†—heroes of seventy-six—and other words, which were a perfect Babylonish jargon‡ to the bewildered Van Winkle.

The appearance of Rip, with his long grizzled beard, his rusty fowling-piece, his uncouth dress, and an army of women and children at his heels, soon attracted the attention of the tavern politicians. They crowded round him, eyeing him from head to foot with great curiosity. The orator bustled up to him, and, drawing him partly aside, inquired "on which side he voted?" Rip stared in vacant stupidity. Another short but busy little fellow pulled him by the arm, and, rising on tiptoe, inquired in his ear, "Whether he was Federal or Democrat?"§ Rip was equally at a loss to comprehend the question; when a knowing, self-important old gentleman, in a sharp cocked hat, made his way through the crowd, putting them to the right and left with his elbows as he passed, and planting himself before

---

*See footnote on p. 40.
†The Battle of Bunker Hill (June 17, 1775) was one of the earliest of the American Revolution.
‡Like the confusion of tongues said to have followed the fall of the Tower of Babel; see the Bible, Genesis 11.
§The two major political parties of the early Republic.

Van Winkle, with one arm akimbo, the other resting on his cane, his keen eyes and sharp hat penetrating, as it were, into his very soul, demanded in an austere tone, "what brought him to the election with a gun on his shoulder, and a mob at his heels, and whether he meant to breed a riot in the village?"—"Alas! gentlemen," cried Rip, somewhat dismayed, "I am a poor quiet man, a native of the place, and a loyal subject of the king, God bless him!"

Here a general shout burst from the by-standers—"A tory!* a tory! a spy! a refugee! hustle him! away with him!" It was with great difficulty that the self-important man in the cocked hat restored order; and, having assumed a tenfold austerity of brow, demanded again of the unknown culprit, what he came there for, and whom he was seeking? The poor man humbly assured him that he meant no harm, but merely came there in search of some of his neighbors, who used to keep about the tavern.

"Well—who are they?—name them."

Rip bethought himself a moment, and inquired, "Where's Nicholas Vedder?"

There was a silence for a little while, when an old man replied, in a thin piping voice, "Nicholas Vedder! why, he is dead and gone these eighteen years! There was a wooden tombstone in the church-yard that used to tell all about him, but that's rotten and gone too."

"Where's Brom Dutcher?"

"Oh, he went off to the army in the beginning of the war; some say he was killed at the storming of Stony Point—others say he was drowned in a squall at the foot of Antony's Nose.† I don't know—he never came back again."

"Where's Van Bummel; the schoolmaster?"

"He went off to the wars too, was a great militia general, and is now in congress."

Rip's heart died away at hearing of these sad changes in his home and friends, and finding himself thus alone in the world. Every answer puzzled him too, by treating of such enormous lapses of time, and of matters which he could not understand: war—congress—Stony

---

*Derogatory term for an American who advocated allegiance to Great Britain during the American Revolution.

†Or Anthony's Nose; headland on the Hudson River near Peekskill.

Point;—he had no courage to ask after any more friends, but cried out in despair, "Does nobody here know Rip Van Winkle?"

"Oh, Rip Van Winkle!" exclaimed two or three, "Oh, to be sure! that's Rip Van Winkle yonder, leaning against the tree."

Rip looked, and beheld a precise counterpart of himself, as he went up the mountain: apparently as lazy, and certainly as ragged. The poor fellow was now completely confounded. He doubted his own identity, and whether he was himself or another man. In the midst of his bewilderment, the man in the cocked hat demanded who he was, and what was his name?

"God knows," exclaimed he, at his wit's end; "I'm not myself— I'm somebody else—that's me yonder—no—that's somebody else got into my shoes—I was myself last night, but I fell asleep on the mountain, and they've changed my gun, and every thing's changed, and I'm changed, and I can't tell what's my name, or who I am!"

The by-standers began now to look at each other, nod, wink significantly, and tap their fingers against their foreheads. There was a whisper, also, about securing the gun, and keeping the old fellow from doing mischief, at the very suggestion of which the self-important man in the cocked hat retired with some precipitation. At this critical moment a fresh comely woman pressed through the throng to get a peep at the gray-bearded man. She had a chubby child in her arms, which, frightened at his looks, began to cry. "Hush, Rip," cried she, "hush, you little fool; the old man won't hurt you." The name of the child, the air of the mother, the tone of her voice, all awakened a train of recollections in his mind. "What is your name, my good woman?" asked he.

"Judith Gardenier."

"And your father's name?"

"Ah, poor man, Rip Van Winkle was his name, but it's twenty years since he went away from home with his gun, and never has been heard of since—his dog came home without him; but whether he shot himself, or was carried away by the Indians, nobody can tell. I was then but a little girl."

Rip had but one question more to ask; but he put it with a faltering voice:

"Where's your mother?"

"Oh, she too had died but a short time since; she broke a blood-vessel in a fit of passion at a New-England peddler."

There was a drop of comfort, at least, in this intelligence. The honest man could contain himself no longer. He caught his daughter and her child in his arms. "I am your father!" cried he—"Young Rip Van Winkle once—old Rip Van Winkle now!—Does nobody know poor Rip Van Winkle?"

All stood amazed, until an old woman, tottering out from among the crowd, put her hand to her brow, and peering under it in his face for a moment, exclaimed, "Sure enough! it is Rip Van Winkle—it is himself! Welcome home again, old neighbor—Why, where have you been these twenty long years?"

Rip's story was soon told, for the whole twenty years had been to him but as one night. The neighbors stared when they heard it; some were seen to wink at each other, and put their tongues in their cheeks: and the self-important man in the cocked hat, who, when the alarm was over, had returned to the field, screwed down the corners of his mouth, and shook his head—upon which there was a general shaking of the head throughout the assemblage.

It was determined, however, to take the opinion of old Peter Vanderdonk, who was seen slowly advancing up the road. He was a descendant of the historian of that name,* who wrote one of the earliest accounts of the province. Peter was the most ancient inhabitant of the village, and well versed in all the wonderful events and traditions of the neighborhood. He recollected Rip at once, and corroborated his story in the most satisfactory manner. He assured the company that it was a fact, handed down from his ancestor the historian, that the Kaatskill mountains had always been haunted by strange beings. That it was affirmed that the great Hendrick Hudson,[9] the first discoverer of the river and country, kept a kind of vigil there every twenty years, with his crew of the Half-moon; being permitted in this way to revisit the scenes of his enterprise, and keep a guardian eye upon the river, and the great city called by his name. That his father had once seen them in their old Dutch dresses

---

*Adriaen Van Der Donck (1620–1655?), Dutch lawyer and a colonist to America, whose *Description of the New Netherlands* was used as a promotional tract to encourage emigration to the colony.

playing at nine-pins in a hollow of the mountain; and that he himself had heard, one summer afternoon, the sound of their balls, like distant peals of thunder.

To make a long story short, the company broke up, and returned to the more important concerns of the election. Rip's daughter took him home to live with her; she had a snug, well-furnished house, and a stout cheery farmer for a husband, whom Rip recollected for one of the urchins that used to climb upon his back. As to Rip's son and heir, who was the ditto* of himself, seen leaning against the tree, he was employed to work on the farm; but evinced an hereditary disposition to attend to any thing else but his business.

Rip now resumed his old walks and habits; he soon found many of his former cronies, though all rather the worse for the wear and tear of time; and preferred making friends among the rising generation, with whom he soon grew into great favor.

Having nothing to do at home, and being arrived at that happy age when a man can be idle with impunity, he took his place once more on the bench at the inn door, and was reverenced as one of the patriarchs of the village, and a chronicle of the old times "before the war." It was some time before he could get into the regular track of gossip, or could be made to comprehend the strange events that had taken place during his torpor. How that there had been a revolutionary war—that the country had thrown off the yoke of old England—and that, instead of being a subject of his Majesty George the Third, he was now a free citizen of the United States. Rip, in fact, was no politician; the changes of states and empires made but little impression on him; but there was one species of despotism under which he had long groaned, and that was—petticoat government. Happily that was at an end; he had got his neck out of the yoke of matrimony, and could go in and out whenever he pleased, without dreading the tyranny of Dame Van Winkle. Whenever her name was mentioned, however, he shook his head, shrugged his shoulders, and cast up his eyes; which might pass either for an expression of resignation to his fate, or joy at his deliverance.

He used to tell his story to every stranger that arrived at Mr. Doolittle's hotel. He was observed, at first, to vary on some points every time he told it, which was, doubtless, owing to his having

---

*Duplicate.

so recently awaked. It at last settled down precisely to the tale I have related, and not a man, woman, or child in the neighborhood, but knew it by heart. Some always pretended to doubt the reality of it, and insisted that Rip had been out of his head, and that this was one point on which he always remained flighty. The old Dutch inhabitants, however, almost universally gave it full credit. Even to this day they never hear a thunderstorm of a summer afternoon about the Kaatskill, but they say Hendrick Hudson and his crew are at their game of nine-pins; and it is a common wish of all hen-pecked husbands in the neighborhood, when life hangs heavy on their hands, that they might have a quieting draught out of Rip Van Winkle's flagon.

Note

The foregoing Tale, one would suspect, had been suggested to Mr. Knickerbocker by a little German superstition about the Emperor Frederick *der Rothbart*, and the Kypphaüser mountain:[10] the subjoined note, however, which he had appended to the tale, shows that it is an absolute fact, narrated with his usual fidelity: "The story of Rip Van Winkle may seem incredible to many, but nevertheless I give it my full belief, for I know the vicinity of our old Dutch settlements to have been very subject to marvellous events and appearances. Indeed, I have heard many stranger stories than this, in the villages along the Hudson; all of which were too well authenticated to admit of a doubt. I have even talked with Rip Van Winkle myself, who, when last I saw him, was a very venerable old man, and so perfectly rational and consistent on every other point, that I think no conscientious person could refuse to take this into the bargain; nay, I have seen a certificate on the subject taken before a country justice and signed with a cross, in the justice's own handwriting. The story, therefore, is beyond the possibility of doubt.

D. K."

Postscript

The following are travelling notes from a memorandum-book of Mr. Knickerbocker: The Kaatsberg, or Catskill mountains, have always been a region full of fable. The Indians considered them the abode of spirits, who influenced the weather, spreading sunshine or clouds over the landscape, and sending good or bad hunting seasons. They were ruled by an old squaw spirit, said to be their mother. She dwelt on the highest peak of the Catskills, and had charge of the doors of day and night to open and shut them at the proper hour. She hung up the new moons in the skies, and cut up the old ones into stars. In times of drought, if properly propitiated, she would spin light summer clouds out of cobwebs and morning dew, and send them off from the crest of the mountain, flake after flake, like flakes of carded cotton, to float in the air; until, dissolved by the heat of the sun, they would fall in gentle showers, causing the grass to spring, the fruits to ripen, and the corn to grow an inch an hour. If displeased, however, she would brew up clouds black as ink, sitting in the midst of them like a bottle-bellied spider in the midst of its web; and when these clouds broke, woe betide the valleys!

In old times, say the Indian traditions, there was a kind of Manitou or Spirit, who kept about the wildest recesses of the Catskill Mountains, and took a mischievous pleasure in wreaking all kinds of evils and vexations upon the red men. Sometimes he would assume the form of a bear, a panther, or a deer, lead the bewildered hunter a weary chase through tangled forests and among ragged rocks; and then spring off with a loud ho! ho! leaving him aghast on the brink of a beetling precipice or raging torrent.

The favorite abode of this Manitou is still shown. It is a great rock or cliff on the loneliest part of the mountains, and, from the flowering vines which clamber about it, and the wild flowers which abound in its neighborhood, is known by the name of the Garden Rock. Near the foot of it is a small lake, the haunt of the solitary bittern, with water-snakes basking in the sun on the leaves of the pond-lilies which lie on the surface. This place was held in great awe by the Indians, insomuch that the boldest hunter would not pursue his game within its precincts. Once upon a time, however, a hunter who had lost his way, penetrated to the garden rock, where he beheld a number of gourds placed in the crotches of trees. One of these he seized and made off with it, but in the hurry of his retreat he let it fall among the rocks, when a great stream gushed forth, which washed him away and swept him down precipices, where he was dashed to pieces, and the stream made its way to the Hudson, and continues to flow to the present day; being the identical stream known by the name of the Kaaters-kill.

English Writers On America[11]

"Methinks I see in my mind a noble and puissant nation, rousing herself like a strong man after sleep, and shaking her invincible locks: methinks I see her as an eagle, mewing her mighty youth, and kindling her undazzled eyes at the full midday beam."

MILTON ON THE LIBERTY OF THE PRESS*

It is with feelings of deep regret that I observe the literary animosity daily growing up between England and America. Great curiosity has been awakened of late with respect to the United States, and the London press has teemed with volumes of travels through the Republic; but they seem intended to diffuse error rather than knowledge; and so successful have they been, that, notwithstanding the constant intercourse between the nations, there is no people concerning whom the great mass of the British public have less pure information, or entertain more numerous prejudices.

English travellers are the best and the worst in the world. Where no motives of pride or interest intervene, none can equal them for profound and philosophical views of society, or faithful and graphical descriptions of external objects; but when either the interest or reputation of their own country comes in collision with that of another, they go to the opposite extreme, and forget their usual probity and candor, in the indulgence of splenetic remark, and an illiberal spirit of ridicule.

Hence, their travels are more honest and accurate, the more remote the country described. I would place implicit confidence in an Englishman's descriptions of the regions beyond the cataracts of the Nile; of unknown islands in the Yellow Sea; of the interior of India; or of any other tract which other travellers might be apt to

---

*Quotation from *Areopagitica* (1644), a prose work by English poet John Milton arguing for freedom of the press.

picture out with the illusions of their fancies; but I would cautiously receive his account of his immediate neighbors, and of those nations with which he is in habits of most frequent intercourse. However I might be disposed to trust his probity, I dare not trust his prejudices.

It has also been the peculiar lot of our country to be visited by the worst kind of English travellers. While men of philosophical spirit and cultivated minds have been sent from England to ransack the poles, to penetrate the deserts, and to study the manners and customs of barbarous nations, with which she can have no permanent intercourse of profit or pleasure; it has been left to the broken-down tradesman, the scheming adventurer, the wandering mechanic, the Manchester and Birmingham agent, to be her oracles respecting America. From such sources she is content to receive her information respecting a country in a singular state of moral and physical development; a country in which one of the greatest political experiments* in the history of the world is now performing; and which presents the most profound and momentous studies to the statesman and the philosopher.

That such men should give prejudicial accounts of America is not a matter of surprise. The themes it offers for contemplation are too vast and elevated for their capacities. The national character is yet in a state of fermentation; it may have its frothiness and sediment, but its ingredients are sound and wholesome; it has already given proofs of powerful and generous qualities; and the whole promises to settle down into something substantially excellent. But the causes which are operating to strengthen and ennoble it, and its daily indications of admirable properties, are all lost upon these purblind observers; who are only affected by the little asperities incident to its present situation. They are capable of judging only of the surface of things; of those matters which come in contact with their private interests and personal gratifications. They miss some of the snug conveniences and petty comforts which belong to an old, highly-finished, and over-populous state of society; where the ranks of useful labor are crowded, and many earn a painful and servile subsistence by studying the very caprices of appetite and self-indulgence. These minor comforts, however, are all-important in the estimation of

---

*That is, democracy.

narrow minds; which either do not perceive, or will not acknowledge, that they are more than counterbalanced among us by great
and generally diffused blessings.

They may, perhaps, have been disappointed in some unreasonable expectation of sudden gain. They may have pictured America to
themselves an *El Dorado*,* where gold and silver abounded, and the
natives were lacking in sagacity; and where they were to become
strangely and suddenly rich, in some unforeseen, but easy manner.
The same weakness of mind that indulges absurd expectations produces petulance in disappointment. Such persons become embit-
tered against the country on finding that there, as everywhere else, a
man must sow before he can reap; must win wealth by industry and
talent; and must contend with the common difficulties of nature,
and the shrewdness of an intelligent and enterprising people.

Perhaps, through mistaken, or ill-directed hospitality, or from
the prompt disposition to cheer and countenance the stranger,
prevalent among my countrymen, they may have been treated with
unwonted respect in America; and having been accustomed all their
lives to consider themselves below the surface of good society, and
brought up in a servile feeling of inferiority, they become arrogant
on the common boon of civility: they attribute to the lowliness of
others their own elevation; and underrate a society where there are
no artificial distinctions,† and where, by any chance, such individuals
as themselves can rise to consequence.

One would suppose, however, that information coming from
such sources, on a subject where the truth is so desirable, would be
received with caution by the censors of the press; that the motives of
these men, their veracity, their opportunities of inquiry and
observation, and their capacities for judging correctly, would be rig-
orously scrutinized before their evidence was admitted, in such
sweeping extent, against a kindred nation. The very reverse, however, is the case, and it furnishes a striking instance of human inconsistency. Nothing can surpass the vigilance with which English
critics will examine the credibility of the traveller who publishes an

---

*Legendary territory sought by European explorers of the Americas, said to be rich
in gold and precious stones.
†That is, hereditary class distinctions.

account of some distant, and comparatively unimportant country. How warily will they compare the measurements of a pyramid, or the descriptions of a ruin; and how sternly will they censure any inaccuracy in these contributions of merely curious knowledge: while they will receive, with eagerness and unhesitating faith, the gross misrepresentations of coarse and obscure writers, concerning a country with which their own is placed in the most important and delicate relations. Nay, they will even make these apocryphal* volumes text-books, on which to enlarge with a zeal and an ability worthy of a more generous cause.

I shall not, however, dwell on this irksome and hackneyed topic; nor should I have adverted to it, but for the undue interest apparently taken in it by my countrymen, and certain injurious effects which I apprehend it might produce upon the national feeling. We attach too much consequence to these attacks. They cannot do us any essential injury. The tissue of misrepresentations attempted to be woven round us are like cobwebs woven round the limbs of an infant giant. Our country continually outgrows them. One falsehood after another falls off of itself. We have but to live on, and every day we live a whole volume of refutation.

All the writers of England united, if we could for a moment suppose their great minds stooping to so unworthy a combination, could not conceal our rapidly-growing importance, and matchless prosperity. They could not conceal that these are owing, not merely to physical and local, but also to moral causes—to the political liberty, the general diffusion of knowledge, the prevalence of sound moral and religious principles, which give force and sustained energy to the character of a people; and which, in fact, have been the acknowledged and wonderful supporters of their own national power and glory.

But why are we so exquisitely alive to the aspersions of England? Why do we suffer ourselves to be so affected by the contumely she has endeavored to cast upon us? It is not in the opinion of England alone that honor lives, and reputation has its being. The world at large is the arbiter of a nation's fame; with its thousand eyes it

---

*Not genuine; spurious.

witnesses a nation's deeds, and from their collective testimony is national glory or national disgrace established.

For ourselves, therefore, it is comparatively of but little importance whether England does us justice or not; it is, perhaps, of far more importance to herself. She is instilling anger and resentment into the bosom of a youthful nation, to grow with its growth and strengthen with its strength. If in America, as some of her writers are laboring to convince her, she is hereafter to find an invidious rival, and a gigantic foe, she may thank those very writers for having provoked rivalship and irritated hostility. Every one knows the all-pervading influence of literature at the present day, and how much the opinions and passions of mankind are under its control. The mere contests of the sword are temporary; their wounds are but in the flesh, and it is the pride of the generous to forgive and forget them; but the slanders of the pen pierce to the heart; they rankle longest in the noblest spirits; they dwell ever present in the mind, and render it morbidly sensitive to the most trifling collision. It is but seldom that any one overt act produces hostilities between two nations; there exists, most commonly, a previous jealousy and ill-will; a predisposition to take offence. Trace these to their cause, and how often will they be found to originate in the mischievous effusions of mercenary writers; who, secure in their closets, and for ignominious bread, concoct and circulate the venom that is to inflame the generous and the brave.

I am not laying too much stress upon this point; for it applies most emphatically to our particular case. Over no nation does the press hold a more absolute control than over the people of America,[*] for the universal education of the poorest classes makes every individual a reader. There is nothing published in England on the subject of our country that does not circulate through every part of it. There is not a calumny[†] dropped from English pen, nor an unworthy sarcasm uttered by an English statesman, that does not go to blight good-will, and add to the mass of latent resentment. Possessing, then, as England does, the fountain-head whence the literature

---

[*]Compare this with Irving's characterization of America as a "logocracy" in *Salmagundi*, pp. 27 and 36.
[†]Slander.

of the language flows, how completely is it in her power, and how truly is it her duty, to make it the medium of amiable and magnanimous feeling—a stream where the two nations might meet together, and drink in peace and kindness. Should she, however, persist in turning it to waters of bitterness, the time may come when she may repent her folly. The present friendship of America may be of but little moment to her; but the future destinies of that country do not admit of a doubt; over those of England there lower some shadows of uncertainty. Should, then, a day of gloom arrive; should these reverses overtake her, from which the proudest empires have not been exempt; she may look back with regret at her infatuation, in repulsing from her side a nation she might have grappled to her bosom, and thus destroying her only chance for real friendship beyond the boundaries of her own dominions.

There is a general impression in England, that the people of the United States are inimical to the parent country. It is one of the errors which have been diligently propagated by designing writers. There is, doubtless, considerable political hostility, and a general soreness at the illiberality of the English press; but, generally speaking, the prepossessions of the people are strongly in favor of England. Indeed, at one time, they amounted, in many parts of the Union, to an absurd degree of bigotry. The bare name of Englishman was a passport to the confidence and hospitality of every family, and too often gave a transient currency to the worthless and the ungrateful. Throughout the country there was something of enthusiasm connected with the idea of England. We looked to it with a hallowed feeling of tenderness and veneration, as the land of our forefathers—the august repository of the monuments and antiquities of our race—the birthplace and mausoleum of the sages and heroes of our paternal history. After our own country, there was none in whose glory we more delighted—none whose good opinion we were more anxious to possess—none towards which our hearts yearned with such throbbings of warm consanguinity.* Even during the late war, whenever there was the least opportunity for kind feelings to spring forth, it was the delight of the generous spirits of our

---

*Common blood.

country to show that, in the midst of hostilities, they still kept alive the sparks of future friendship.

Is all this to be at an end? Is this golden band of kindred sympathies, so rare between nations, to be broken for ever?—Perhaps it is for the best—it may dispel an illusion which might have kept us in mental vassalage; which might have interfered occasionally with our true interests, and prevented the growth of proper national pride. But it is hard to give up the kindred tie! and there are feelings dearer than interest—closer to the heart than pride—that will still make us cast back a look of regret, as we wander farther and farther from the paternal roof, and lament the waywardness of the parent that would repel the affections of the child.

Short-sighted and injudicious, however, as the conduct of England may be in this system of aspersion, recrimination on our part would be equally ill-judged. I speak not of a prompt and spirited vindication of our country, nor the keenest castigation of her slanderers—but I allude to a disposition to retaliate in kind; to retort sarcasm, and inspire prejudice; which seems to be spreading widely among our writers. Let us guard particularly against such a temper, for it would double the evil instead of redressing the wrong. Nothing is so easy and inviting as the retort of abuse and sarcasm; but it is a paltry and an unprofitable contest. It is the alternative of a morbid mind, fretted into petulance, rather than warmed into indignation. If England is willing to permit the mean jealousies of trade, or the rancorous animosities of politics, to deprave the integrity of her press, and poison the fountain of public opinion, let us beware of her example. She may deem it her interest to diffuse error, and engender antipathy, for the purpose of checking emigration; we have no purpose of the kind to serve. Neither have we any spirit of national jealousy to gratify, for as yet, in all our rivalships with England, we are the rising and the gaining party. There can be no end to answer, therefore, but the gratification of resentment—a mere spirit of retaliation; and even that is impotent. Our retorts are never republished in England; they fall short, therefore, of their aim; but they foster a querulous and peevish temper among our writers; they sour the sweet flow of our early literature, and sow thorns and brambles among its blossoms. What is still worse, they circulate through our own country, and, as far as they have effect, excite virulent national prejudices. This last is the evil most especially to be deprecated. Governed, as we are, entirely by public opinion, the utmost care should be taken to preserve the purity of the public mind. Knowledge is power, and truth is knowledge; whoever, therefore, knowingly propagates a prejudice, wilfully saps the foundation of his country's strength.

The members of a republic, above all other men, should be candid and dispassionate. They are, individually, portions of the sovereign mind and sovereign will, and should be enabled to come to all questions of national concern with calm and unbiased judgments. From the peculiar nature of our relations with England, we must have more frequent questions of a difficult and delicate character with her than with any other nation; questions that affect the most acute and excitable feelings; and as, in the adjusting of these, our national measures must ultimately be determined by popular sentiment, we cannot be too anxiously attentive to purify it from all latent passion or prepossession.

Opening, too, as we do, an asylum for strangers from every portion of the earth, we should receive all with impartiality. It should be our pride to exhibit an example of one nation, at least, destitute of national antipathies, and exercising not merely the overt acts of hospitality, but those more rare and noble courtesies which spring from liberality of opinion.

What have we to do with national prejudices? They are the inveterate diseases of old countries, contracted in rude and ignorant ages, when nations knew but little of each other, and looked beyond their own boundaries with distrust and hostility. We, on the contrary, have sprung into national existence in an enlightened and philosophic age, when the different parts of the habitable world, and the various branches of the human family, have been indefatigably studied and made known to each other; and we forego the advantages of our birth, if we do not shake off the national prejudices, as we would the local superstitions of the old world.

But above all let us not be influenced by any angry feelings, so far as to shut our eyes to the perception of what is really excellent and amiable in the English character. We are a young people, necessarily an imitative one, and must take our examples and models, in a great degree, from the existing nations of Europe. There is no country more worthy of our study than England. The spirit of her constitution is most analogous to ours. The manners of her people—their intellectual activity—their freedom of opinion—their habits of thinking on those subjects which concern the dearest interests and most sacred charities of private life, are all congenial to the American character; and, in fact, are all intrinsically excellent; for it is in the moral feeling of the people that the deep foundations of British prosperity are laid; and however the superstructure may be time-worn, or overrun by abuses, there must be something solid in the basis, admirable in the materials, and stable in the structure of an edifice, that so long has towered unshaken amidst the tempests of the world.

Let it be the pride of our writers, therefore, discarding all feelings of irritation, and disdaining to retaliate the illiberality of British authors, to speak of the English nation without prejudice, and with determined candor. While they rebuke the indiscriminating bigotry with which some of our countrymen admire and imitate every thing English, merely because it is English, let them frankly point out what is really worthy of approbation. We may thus place England before us as a perpetual volume of reference, wherein are recorded sound deductions from ages of experience; and while we avoid the errors and absurdities which may have crept into the page, we may draw thence golden maxims of practical wisdom, wherewith to strengthen and to embellish our national character.

The Art of Book-Making[12]

"If that severe doom of Synesius be true—'It is a greater offence to steal dead men's labor, than their clothes,' what shall become of most writers?"

BURTON'S ANATOMY OF MELANCHOLY*

I have often wondered at the extreme fecundity of the press, and how it comes to pass that so many heads, on which nature seemed to have inflicted the curse of barrenness, should teem with voluminous productions. As a man travels on, however, in the journey of life, his objects of wonder daily diminish, and he is continually finding out some very simple cause for some great matter of marvel. Thus have I chanced, in my peregrinations† about this great metropolis, to blunder upon a scene which unfolded to me some of the mysteries of the book-making craft, and at once put an end to my astonishment.

I was one summer's day loitering through the great saloons of the British Museum, with that listlessness with which one is apt to saunter about a museum in warm weather; sometimes lolling over the glass cases of minerals, sometimes studying the hieroglyphics on an Egyptian mummy, and sometimes trying, with nearly equal success, to comprehend the allegorical paintings on the lofty ceilings. Whilst I was gazing about in this idle way, my attention was attracted to a distant door, at the end of a suite of apartments. It was closed, but every now and then it would open, and some strange-favored being, generally clothed in black, would steal forth, and glide through the rooms, without noticing any of the surrounding objects. There was an air of mystery about this that piqued my languid curiosity, and I determined to attempt the passage of that strait, and

---

*Quotation from *The Anatomy of Melancholy* (1621), by English clergyman Robert Burton (from the author's preface, "Democritus Junior to the Reader")
†Walks.

to explore the unknown regions beyond. The door yielded to my hand, with that facility with which the portals of enchanted castles yield to the adventurous knight-errant. I found myself in a spacious chamber, surrounded with great cases of venerable books. Above the cases, and just under the cornice, were arranged a great number of black-looking portraits of ancient authors. About the room were placed long tables, with stands for reading and writing, at which sat many pale, studious personages, poring intently over dusty volumes, rummaging among mouldy manuscripts, and taking copious notes of their contents. A hushed stillness reigned through this mysterious apartment, excepting that you might hear the racing of pens over sheets of paper, or occasionally, the deep sigh of one of these sages, as he shifted his position to turn over the page of an old folio; doubtless arising from that hollowness and flatulency incident to learned research.

Now and then one of these personages would write something on a small slip of paper, and ring a bell, whereupon a familiar would appear, take the paper in profound silence, glide out of the room, and return shortly loaded with ponderous tomes, upon which the other would fall tooth and nail with famished voracity. I had no longer a doubt that I had happened upon a body of magi, deeply engaged in the study of occult sciences. The scene reminded me of an old Arabian tale, of a philosopher shut up in an enchanted library, in the bosom of a mountain, which opened only once a year; where he made the spirits of the place bring him books of all kinds of dark knowledge, so that at the end of the year, when the magic portal once more swung open on its hinges, he issued forth so versed in forbidden lore, as to be able to soar above the heads of the multitude, and to control the powers of nature.

My curiosity being now fully aroused, I whispered to one of the familiars, as he was about to leave the room, and begged an interpretation of the strange scene before me. A few words were sufficient for the purpose. I found that these mysterious personages, whom I had mistaken for magi, were principally authors, and in the very act of manufacturing books. I was, in fact, in the reading-room of the great British Library—an immense collection of volumes of all ages and languages, many of which are now forgotten, and most of which are seldom read: one of these sequestered pools of obsolete literature, to which modern authors repair, and draw buckets full of classic lore, or "pure English, undefiled,"* where-with to swell their own scanty rills of thought.

Being now in possession of the secret, I sat down in a corner, and watched the process of this book manufactory. I noticed one lean, bilious-looking wight, who sought none but the most worm-eaten volumes, printed in black-letter. He was evidently constructing some work of profound erudition, that would be purchased by every man who wished to be thought learned, placed upon a conspicuous shelf of his library, or laid open upon his table; but never read. I observed him, now and then, draw a large fragment of biscuit out of his pocket, and gnaw; whether it was his dinner, or whether he was endeavoring to keep off that exhaustion of the stomach produced by much pondering over dry works, I leave to harder students than myself to determine.

There was one dapper little gentleman in bright-colored clothes, with a chirping, gossiping expression of countenance, who had all the appearance of an author on good terms with his bookseller. After considering him attentively, I recognized in him a diligent getter-up of miscellaneous works, which bustled off well with the trade. I was curious to see how he manufactured his wares. He made more stir and show of business than any of the others; dipping into various books, fluttering over the leaves of manuscripts, taking a morsel out of one, a morsel out of another, "line upon line, precept upon precept, here a little and there a little."† The contents of his book seemed to be as heterogeneous as those of the witches' caldron in *Macbeth*. It was here a finger and there a thumb, toe of frog and blind-worm's sting, with his own gossip poured in like "baboon's blood," to make the medley "slab and good."‡

After all, thought I, may not this pilfering disposition be implanted in authors for wise purposes; may it not be the way in which Providence has taken care that the seeds of knowledge and wisdom shall be preserved from age to age, in spite of the inevitable decay of

---

*Quotation from *The Faerie Queene* (1589–1596), by English poet Edmund Spenser (book 2, canto 2, stanza 32).
†See the Bible, Isaiah 28:10 (King James Version).
‡Allusion to Shakespeare's *Macbeth* (act 4, scene 1).

the works in which they were first produced? We see that nature has wisely, though whimsically, provided for the conveyance of seeds from clime to clime, in the maws of certain birds; so that animals, which, in themselves, are little better than carrion, and apparently the lawless plunderers of the orchard and the cornfield, are, in fact, nature's carriers to disperse and perpetuate her blessings. In like manner, the beauties and fine thoughts of ancient and obsolete authors are caught up by these flights of predatory writers, and cast forth again to flourish and bear fruit in a remote and distant tract of time. Many of their works, also, undergo a kind of metempsychosis, and spring up under new forms. What was formerly a ponderous history revives in the shape of a romance—an old legend changes into a modern play—and a sober philosophical treatise furnishes the body for a whole series of bouncing and sparkling essays. Thus it is in the clearing of our American woodlands; where we burn down a forest of stately pines, a progeny of dwarf oaks start up in their place: and we never see the prostrate trunk of a tree mouldering into soil, but it gives birth to a whole tribe of fungi.

Let us not, then, lament over the decay and oblivion into which ancient writers descend; they do but submit to the great law of nature, which declares that all sublunary shapes of matter shall be limited in their duration, but which decrees, also, that their elements shall never perish. Generation after generation, both in animal and vegetable life, passes away, but the vital principle is transmitted to posterity, and the species continue to flourish. Thus, also, do authors beget authors, and having produced a numerous progeny, in a good old age they sleep with their fathers, that is to say, with the authors who preceded them—and from whom they had stolen.

Whilst I was indulging in these rambling fancies, I had leaned my head against a pile of reverend folios. Whether it was owing to the soporific emanations from these works; or to the profound quiet of the room; or to the lassitude arising from much wandering; or to an unlucky habit of napping at improper times and places, with which I am grievously afflicted, so it was, that I fell into a doze. Still, however, my imagination continued busy, and indeed the same scene remained before my mind's eye, only a little changed in some of the details. I dreamt that the chamber was still decorated with the portraits of ancient authors, but that the number was increased.

The long tables had disappeared, and, in place of the sage magi, I beheld a ragged, threadbare throng, such as may be seen plying about the great repository of cast-off clothes, Monmouth-street.* Whenever they seized upon a book, by one of those incongruities common to dreams, methought it turned into a garment of foreign or antique fashion, with which they proceeded to equip themselves. I noticed, however, that no one pretended to clothe himself from any particular suit, but took a sleeve from one, a cape from another, a skirt from a third, thus decking himself out piecemeal, while some of his original rags would peep out from among his borrowed finery.

There was a portly, rosy, well-fed parson, whom I observed ogling several mouldy polemical writers through an eye-glass. He soon contrived to slip on the voluminous mantle of one of the old fathers, and, having purloined the gray beard of another, endeavored to look exceedingly wise; but the smirking commonplace of his countenance set at naught all the trappings of wisdom. One sickly-looking gentleman was busied embroidering a very flimsy garment with gold thread drawn out of several old court-dresses of the reign of Queen Elizabeth. Another had trimmed himself magnificently from an illuminated manuscript, had stuck a nosegay in his bosom, culled from "The Paradise of Daintie Devices,"† and having put Sir Philip Sidney's‡ hat on one side of his head, strutted off with an exquisite air of vulgar elegance. A third, who was but of puny dimensions, had bolstered himself out bravely with the spoils from several obscure tracts of philosophy, so that he had a very imposing front; but he was lamentably tattered in rear, and I perceived that he had patched his small-clothes with scraps of parchment from a Latin author.

There were some well-dressed gentlemen, it is true, who only helped themselves to a gem or so, which sparkled among their own ornaments, without eclipsing them. Some, too, seemed to contemplate the costumes of the old writers, merely to imbibe their principles of taste, and to catch their air and spirit; but I grieve to say, that

---

*Street in London known for its old-clothes shops.
†Popular verse miscellany published in 1576.
‡Also spelled Sydney; English Elizabethan poet and courtier (1554–1586), whose works include the sonnet cycle *Astrophel and Stella* and the unfinished prose romance *Arcadia*.

too many were apt to array themselves from top to toe in the patchwork manner I have mentioned. I shall not omit to speak of one genius, in drab breeches and gaiters, and an Arcadian* hat, who had a violent propensity to the pastoral, but whose rural wanderings had been confined to the classic haunts of Primrose Hill, and the solitudes of the Regent's Park. He had decked himself in wreaths and ribbons from all the old pastoral poets, and, hanging his head on one side, went about with a fantastical lack-a-daisical air, "babbling about green fields."† But the personage that most struck my attention was a pragmatical old gentleman, in clerical robes, with a remarkably large and square, but bald head. He entered the room wheezing and puffing, elbowed his way through the throng, with a look of sturdy self-confidence, and having laid hands upon a thick Greek quarto, clapped it upon his head, and swept majestically away in a formidable frizzled wig.

In the height of this literary masquerade, a cry suddenly resounded from every side, of "Thieves! thieves!" I looked, and lo! the portraits about the wall became animated! The old authors thrust out, first a head, then a shoulder, from the canvas, looked down curiously, for an instant, upon the motley throng, and then descended with fury in their eyes, to claim their rifled property. The scene of scampering and hubbub that ensued baffles all description. The unhappy culprits endeavored in vain to escape with their plunder. On one side might be seen half a dozen old monks, stripping a modern professor; on another, there was sad devastation carried into the ranks of modern dramatic writers. Beaumont and Fletcher,‡ side by side, raged round the field like Castor and Pollux,§ and sturdy Ben Jonson** enacted more wonders than when a volunteer with the army in Flanders. As to the dapper little compiler of

---

*That is, rustic or pastoral.

†See Shakespeare's *The Life of Henry the Fifth* (act 2, scene 1).

‡English dramatists Francis Beaumont (1584?–1616) and John Fletcher (1579–1625) collaborated on a number of plays, including *The Maides Tragedy*, *Phylaster*, and *A King and No King*.

§In Roman mythology, Castor and Pollux were the twin sons of Jupiter and Leyda (in Greek myth, Zeus and Leda).

**English playwright and poet (1572–1637), perhaps the best known of Shakespeare's contemporaries.

farragos, mentioned some time since, he had arrayed himself in as many patches and colors as Harlequin,* and there was as fierce a contention of claimants about him, as about the dead body of Patroclus.† I was grieved to see many men, to whom I had been accustomed to look up with awe and reverence, fain to steal off with scarce a rag to cover their nakedness. Just then my eye was caught by the pragmatical old gentleman in the Greek grizzled wig, who was scrambling away in sore affright with half a score of authors in full cry after him! They were close upon his haunches: in a twinkling off went his wig; at every turn some strip of raiment was peeled away; until in a few moments, from his domineering pomp, he shrunk into a little, pursy, "chopped bald shot,"‡ and made his exit with only a few tags and rags fluttering at his back.

There was something so ludicrous in the catastrophe of this learned Theban,§ that I burst into an immoderate fit of laughter, which broke the whole illusion. The tumult and the scuffle were at an end. The chamber resumed its usual appearance. The old authors shrunk back into their picture-frames, and hung in shadowy solemnity along the walls. In short, I found myself wide awake in my corner, with the whole assemblage of book-worms gazing at me with astonishment. Nothing of the dream had been real but my burst of laughter, a sound never before heard in that grave sanctuary, and so abhorrent to the ears of wisdom, as to electrify the fraternity.

The librarian now stepped up to me, and demanded whether I had a card of admission. At first I did not comprehend him, but I soon found that the library was a kind of literary "preserve," subject to game-laws, and that no one must presume to hunt there without special license and permission. In a word, I stood convicted of being an arrant poacher, and was glad to make a precipitate retreat, lest I should have a whole pack of authors let loose upon me.

---

*Figure of mischief and frivolity in the pantomime tradition, often dressed in parti-colored clothes.

†Greek warrior in Homer's *Iliad* who was killed by Hector at Troy, sparking Achilles' outrage and grief (see books 16–18).

‡See Shakespeare's *The First Part of Henry the Fourth* (act 3, scene 2).

§See Shakespeare's *King Lear* (act 3, scene 4).

The Mutability of Literature[13]

A COLLOQUY IN WESTMINSTER ABBEY

I know that all beneath the moon decays,
And what by mortals in this world is brought,
In time's great period shall return to nought.
I know that all the muse's heavenly lays,
With toil of sprite which are so dearly bought,
As idle sounds, of few or none are sought,
That there is nothing lighter than mere praise.

DRUMMOND OF HAWTHORNDEN*

There are certain half-dreaming moods of mind, in which we naturally steal away from noise and glare, and seek some quiet haunt, where we may indulge our reveries and build our air castles undisturbed. In such a mood I was loitering about the old gray cloisters of Westminster Abbey, enjoying that luxury of wandering thought which one is apt to dignify with the name of reflection; when suddenly an interruption of madcap boys from Westminster School, playing at foot-ball, broke in upon the monastic stillness of the place, making the vaulted passages and mouldering tombs echo with their merriment. I sought to take refuge from their noise by penetrating still deeper into the solitudes of the pile, and applied to one of the vergers for admission to the library. He conducted me through a portal rich with the crumbling sculpture of former ages, which opened upon a gloomy passage leading to the chapter-house and the chamber in which doomsday book† is

---

*Scottish poet William Drummond (1585–1649); Irving inaccurately quotes from a sonnet in his *Poems* (1616).
†The Domesday Book contains the results of a survey ordered by William the Conqueror (King William I of England) in 1086 to verify tax revenues.

deposited. Just within the passage is a small door on the left. To this the verger applied a key; it was double locked, and opened with some difficulty, as if seldom used. We now ascended a dark narrow staircase, and, passing through a second door, entered the library.

I found myself in a lofty antique hall, the roof supported by massive joists of old English oak. It was soberly lighted by a row of Gothic windows at a considerable height from the floor, and which apparently opened upon the roofs of the cloisters. An ancient picture of some reverend dignitary of the church in his robes hung over the fireplace. Around the hall and in a small gallery were the books, arranged in carved oaken cases. They consisted principally of old polemical writers, and were much more worn by time than use. In the centre of the library was a solitary table with two or three books on it, an inkstand without ink, and a few pens parched by long disuse. The place seemed fitted for quiet study and profound meditation. It was buried deep among the massive walls of the abbey, and shut up from the tumult of the world. I could only hear now and then the shouts of the schoolboys faintly swelling from the cloisters, and the sound of a bell tolling for prayers, echoing soberly along the roofs of the abbey. By degrees the shouts of merriment grew fainter and fainter, and at length died away; the bell ceased to toll, and a profound silence reigned through the dusky hall.

I had taken down a little thick quarto, curiously bound in parchment, with brass clasps, and seated myself at the table in a venerable elbow-chair. Instead of reading, however, I was beguiled by the solemn monastic air, and lifeless quiet of the place, into a train of musing. As I looked around upon the old volumes in their mouldering covers, thus ranged on the shelves, and apparently never disturbed in their repose, I could not but consider the library a kind of literary catacomb, where authors, like mummies, are piously entombed, and left to blacken and moulder in dusty oblivion.

How much, thought I, has each of these volumes, now thrust aside with such indifference, cost some aching head! how many weary days! how many sleepless nights! How have their authors buried themselves in the solitude of cells and cloisters; shut themselves up from the face of man, and the still more blessed face of nature; and devoted themselves to painful research and intense reflection! And all for what? to occupy an inch of dusty shelf—to have the title of their works read now and then in a future age, by some drowsy churchman or casual straggler like myself; and in another age to be lost, even to remembrance. Such is the amount of this boasted immortality. A mere temporary rumor, a local sound; like the tone of that bell which has just tolled among these towers, filling the ear for a moment—lingering transiently in echo—and then passing away like a thing that was not.

While I sat half murmuring, half meditating these unprofitable speculations with my head resting on my hand, I was thrumming with the other hand upon the quarto, until I accidentally loosened the clasps; when, to my utter astonishment, the little book gave two or three yawns, like one awaking from a deep sleep; then a husky hem; and at length began to talk. At first its voice was very hoarse and broken, being much troubled by a cobweb which some studious spider had woven across it; and having probably contracted a cold from long exposure to the chills and damps of the abbey. In a short time, however, it became more distinct, and I soon found it an exceedingly fluent conversable little tome. Its language, to be sure, was rather quaint and obsolete, and its pronunciation, what, in the present day, would be deemed barbarous; but I shall endeavor, as far as I am able, to render it in modern parlance.

It began with railings about the neglect of the world—about merit being suffered to languish in obscurity, and other such commonplace topics of literary repining, and complained bitterly that it had not been opened for more than two centuries. That the dean only looked now and then into the library, sometimes took down a volume or two, trifled with them for a few moments, and then returned them to their shelves. "What a plague do they mean," said the little quarto, which I began to perceive was somewhat choleric, "what a plague do they mean by keeping several thousand volumes of us shut up here, and watched by a set of old vergers, like so many beauties in a harem, merely to be looked at now and then by the dean? Books were written to give pleasure and to be enjoyed; and I would have a rule passed that the dean should pay each of us a visit at least once a year; or if he is not equal to the task, let them once in a while turn loose the whole school of Westminster among us, that at any rate we may now and then have an airing."

"Softly, my worthy friend," replied I, "you are not aware how much better you are off than most books of your generation. By being stored away in this ancient library, you are like the treasured remains of those saints and monarchs, which lie enshrined in the adjoining chapels; while the remains of your contemporary mortals, left to the ordinary course of nature, have long since returned to dust."

"Sir," said the little tome, ruffling his leaves and looking big, "I was written for all the world, not for the bookworms of an abbey. I was intended to circulate from hand to hand, like other great contemporary works; but here have I been clasped up for more than two centuries, and might have silently fallen a prey to these worms that are playing the very vengeance with my intestines, if you had not by chance given me an opportunity of uttering a few last words before I go to pieces."

"My good friend," rejoined I, "had you been left to the circulation of which you speak, you would long ere this have been no more. To judge from your physiognomy, you are now well stricken in years: very few of your contemporaries can be at present in existence; and those few owe their longevity to being immured like yourself in old libraries; which, suffer me to add, instead of likening to harems, you might more properly and gratefully have compared to those infirmaries attached to religious establishments, for the benefit of the old and decrepit, and where, by quiet fostering and no employment, they often endure to an amazingly good-for-nothing old age. You talk of your contemporaries as if in circulation—where do we meet with their works? what do we hear of Robert Groteste, of Lincoln?* No one could have toiled harder than he for immortality. He is said to have written nearly two hundred volumes. He built, as it were, a pyramid of books to perpetuate his name: but, alas! the pyramid has long since fallen, and only a few fragments are scattered in various libraries, where they are scarcely disturbed even by the antiquarian. What do we hear of Giraldus Cambrensis,† the historian, antiquary,

---

*That is, Robert Grosseteste (c.1175–1253), bishop of Lincoln; he wrote numerous works on science, geometry, and optics as well as commentaries on Aristotle.
†Or Gerald de Barri (c.1147–1223), Welsh clergyman and historian, perhaps best known for his history of the Norman conquest of Ireland.

philosopher, theologian, and poet? He declined two bishoprics, that he might shut himself up and write for posterity; but posterity never inquires after his labors. What of Henry of Huntingdon,* who, besides a learned history of England, wrote a treatise on the contempt of the world, which the world has revenged by forgetting him? What is quoted of Joseph of Exeter,[†] styled the miracle of his age in classical composition? Of his three great heroic poems one is lost forever, excepting a mere fragment; the others are known only to a few of the curious in literature; and as to his love verses and epigrams, they have entirely disappeared. What is in current use of John Wallis, the Franciscan, who acquired the name of the tree of life? Of William of Malmsbury;—of Simeon of Durham;—of Benedict of Peterborough;—of John Hanvill of St. Albans;—of——"[‡]

"Prithee, friend," cried the quarto, in a testy tone, "how old do you think me? You are talking of authors that lived long before my time, and wrote either in Latin or French, so that they in a manner expatriated themselves, and deserved to be forgotten;[§] but I, sir, was ushered into the world from the press of the renowned Wynkyn de Worde.** I was written in my own native tongue, at a time when the language had become fixed; and indeed I was considered a model of pure and elegant English."

---

*Archdeacon and historian of early medieval England (c.1084–1155); Irving refers to his treatise *Epistola de Contemptu Mundi*.

[†]Latin poet (died c.1210), author of *De Bello Trojano*, and an epic, now lost, on the deeds of Richard I.

[‡]John Wallis is possibly a reference to the Oxford mathematician whose *A Treatise of Algebra Both Historical and Practical* (London, 1685) includes a history of mathematics in medieval England; English historian William of Malmesbury (c.1090–c.1143) was known for his history of English kings entitled *Gesta regum Anglorum*; Simeon (c.1060–1130) was a Benedictine monk and precentor of Durham Cathedral; Benedict (died 1193) was abbot of Peterborough; John Hanville of St. Albans (born c.1180) was a Dominican monk and archdeacon of Oxford.

[§]In Latin and French hath many soueraine wittes had great delyte to endite, and have many noble thinges fulfilde, but certes there ben some that speaken their poisye in French, of which speche the Frenchmen have as good a fantasye as we have in hearing of Frenchmen's Englishe.—Chaucer's *Testament of Love* [Irving's note]. The *Testament of Love* was actually written by English author Thomas Usk (died 1388) while he was incarcerated in Newgate Prison.

**British printer (died c.1535) who succeeded William Caxton in 1491 to become the second printer in England.

(I should observe that these remarks were couched in such intolerably antiquated terms, that I have had infinite difficulty in rendering them into modern phraseology.)

"I cry your mercy," said I, "for mistaking your age; but it matters little: almost all the writers of your time have likewise passed into forgetfulness; and De Worde's publications are mere literary rarities among book-collectors. The purity and stability of language, too, on which you found your claims to perpetuity, have been the fallacious dependence of authors of every age, ever back to the times of the worthy Robert of Gloucester,* who wrote his history in rhymes of mongrel Saxon.† Even now many talk of Spenser's 'well of pure English undefiled,'‡ as if the language ever sprang from a well or fountain-head, and was not rather a mere confluence of various tongues, perpetually subject to changes and intermixtures. It is this which has made English literature so extremely mutable, and the reputation built upon it so fleeting. Unless thought can be committed to something more permanent and unchangeable than such a medium, even thought must share the fate of every thing else, and fall into decay. This should serve as a check upon the vanity and exultation of the most popular writer. He finds the language in which he has embarked his fame gradually altering, and subject to the dilapidations of time and the caprice of fashion. He looks back and beholds the early authors of his country, once the favorites of their day, supplanted by modern writers. A few short ages have covered them with obscurity, and their merits can only be relished by the quaint taste of the bookworm. And such, he anticipates, will be the fate of his own work, which, however it may be admired in its day, and held up as a model of purity, will in the course of years grow antiquated and obsolete; until it shall become almost as unintelligible

---

*Robert of Gloucester (flourished 1260–1300), author of a chronicle of England.

†Holinshed, in his Chronicle, observes, "afterwards, also, by deligent travell of Geffry Chaucer and of John Gowre, in the time of Richard the Second, and after them of John Scogan and John Lydgate, monke of Berrie, our said toong was brought to an excellent passe, norwithstanding that it never came unto the type of perfection until the time of Queen Elizabeth, wherein John Jewell, Bishop of Sarum, John Fox, and sundrie learned and excellent writers, have fully accomplished the ornature of the same, to their great praise and immortal commendation" [Irving's note].[14]

‡See footnote on p. 102.

in its native land as an Egyptian obelisk, or one of those Runic inscriptions said to exist in the deserts of Tartary. I declare," added I, with some emotion, "when I contemplate a modern library, filled with new works, in all the bravery of rich gilding and binding, I feel disposed to sit down and weep; like the good Xerxes,* when he surveyed his army, pranked out in all the splendor of military array, and reflected that in one hundred years not one of them would be in existence!"

"Ah," said the little quarto, with a heavy sigh, "I see how it is; these modern scribblers have superseded all the good old authors. I suppose nothing is read now-a-days but Sir Philip Sydney's Arcadia, Sackville's stately plays, and Mirror for Magistrates, or the fine-spun euphuisms of the 'unparalleled John Lyly.' "†

"There you are again mistaken," said I; "the writers whom you suppose in vogue, because they happened to be so when you were last in circulation, have long since had their day. Sir Philip Sydney's Arcadia, the immortality of which was so fondly predicted by his admirers,‡ and which, in truth, is full of noble thoughts, delicate images, and graceful turns of language, is now scarcely ever mentioned. Sackville has strutted into obscurity; and even Lyly, though his writings were once the delight of a court, and apparently perpetuated by a proverb, is now scarcely known even by name. A whole crowd of authors who wrote and wrangled at the time, have likewise gone down, with all their writings and their controversies. Wave after wave of succeeding literature has rolled over them, until they are buried so deep, that it is only now and then that some

---

*Xerxes I (c.519–465 B.C.), king of ancient Persia; the anecdote that follows is taken from the Greek historian Herodotus' *Histories* (7.44–46).

†For Sir Philip Sydney, see footnote on p. 104. English poet Thomas Sackville (1536–1608) contributed to the collection *The Mirror for Magistrates* (1563) and is credited with its arrangement. John Lyly (see footnote on p. 49) is described as "unparalleled" in a collection of his plays published by Edward Blount in 1632.

‡Live ever sweete booke; the simple image of his gentle witt, and the golden-pillar of his noble courage; and ever notify unto the world that thy writer was the secretary of eloquence, the breath of the muses, the honey-bee of the daintyest flowers of witt and arte, the pith of morale and intellectual virtues, the arme of Bellona in the field, the tonge of Suada in the chamber, the sprite of Practise in esse, and the paragon of excellency in print.—*Harvey, Pierce's Supererogation* [Irving's note]. Gabriel Harvey (c.1550–1631) was an English poet and scholar.

industrious diver after fragments of antiquity brings up a specimen for the gratification of the curious.

"For my part," I continued, "I consider this mutability of lan-guage a wise precaution of Providence for the benefit of the world at large, and of authors in particular. To reason from analogy, we daily behold the varied and beautiful tribes of vegetables springing up, flourishing, adorning the fields for a short time, and then fading into dust, to make way for their successors. Were not this the case, the fecundity of nature would be a grievance instead of a blessing. The earth would groan with rank and excessive vegetation, and its surface become a tangled wilderness. In like manner the works of genius and learning decline, and make way for subsequent produc-tions. Language gradually varies, and with it fade away the writings of authors who have flourished their allotted time; otherwise the creative powers of genius would overstock the world, and the mind would be completely bewildered in the endless mazes of literature. Formerly there were some restraints on this excessive multiplication. Works had to be transcribed by hand, which was a slow and labori-ous operation; they were written either on parchment, which was expensive, so that one work was often erased to make way for another; or on papyrus, which was fragile and extremely perishable. Authorship was a limited and unprofitable craft, pursued chiefly by monks in the leisure and solitude of their cloisters. The accumula-tion of manuscripts was slow and costly, and confined almost entirely to monasteries. To these circumstances it may, in some measure, be owing that we have not been inundated by the intellect of antiquity; that the fountains of thought have not been broken up, and modern genius drowned in the deluge. But the inventions of paper and the press have put an end to all these restraints. They have made every one a writer, and enabled every mind to pour itself into print, and diffuse itself over the whole intellectual world. The consequences are alarming. The stream of literature has swollen into a torrent—augmented into a river—expanded into a sea. A few centuries since, five or six hundred manuscripts constituted a great library; but what would you say to libraries such as actually exist, containing three or four hundred million volumes; legions of authors at the same time busy; and the press going on with fearfully increasing activity, to double and quadruple the number? Unless some unforeseen mortality should break out among the progeny of the muse, now that she has become so prolific, I tremble for posterity. I fear the mere fluctuation of language will not be sufficient. Criticism may do much. It increases with the increase of literature, and resembles one of those salutary checks on population spoken of by economists. All possible encouragement, therefore, should be given to the growth of critics, good or bad. But I fear all will be in vain; let criticism do what it may, writers will write, printers will print, and the world will inevitably be overstocked with good books. It will soon be the employment of a lifetime merely to learn their names. Many a man of passable information, at the present day, reads scarcely anything but reviews; and before long a man of erudition will be little better than a mere walking catalogue."

"My very good sir," said the little quarto, yawning most drearily in my face, "excuse my interrupting you, but I perceive you are rather given to prose. I would ask the fate of an author who was making some noise just as I left the world. His reputation, however, was considered quite temporary. The learned shook their heads at him, for he was a poor half-educated varlet, that knew little of Latin, and nothing of Greek,* and had been obliged to run the country for deer-stealing. I think his name was Shakspeare. I presume he soon sunk into oblivion."

"On the contrary," said I, "it is owing to that very man that the literature of his period has experienced a duration beyond the ordinary term of English literature. There rise authors now and then, who seem proof against the mutability of language, because they have rooted themselves in the unchanging principles of human nature. They are like gigantic trees that we sometimes see on the banks of a stream; which, by their vast and deep roots, penetrating through the mere surface, and laying hold on the very foundations of the earth, preserve the soil around them from being swept away by the ever-flowing current, and hold up many a neighboring plant, and, perhaps, worthless weed, to perpetuity. Such is the case with Shakspeare, whom we behold defying the encroachments of time,

---

*Ben Jonson's famous jibe against his rival Shakespeare—"Thou hadst small Latin, and less Greek"—is from his poem "To the Memory of My Beloved, the Author, Mr. William Shakespeare, and What He Hath Left Us."

retaining in modern use the language and literature of his day, and giving duration to many an indifferent author, merely from having flourished in his vicinity. But even he, I grieve to say, is gradually assuming the tint of age, and his whole form is overrun by a profusion of commentators, who, like clambering vines and creepers, almost bury the noble plant that upholds them."

Here the little quarto began to heave his sides and chuckle, until at length he broke out in a plethoric* fit of laughter that had well nigh choked him, by reason of his excessive corpulency. "Mighty well!" cried he, as soon as he could recover breath, "mighty well! and so you would persuade me that the literature of an age is to be perpetuated by a vagabond deer-stealer! by a man without learning; by a poet, forsooth—a poet!" And here he wheezed forth another fit of laughter.

I confess that I felt somewhat nettled at this rudeness, which, however, I pardoned on account of his having flourished in a less polished age. I determined, nevertheless, not to give up my point.

"Yes," resumed I, positively, "a poet; for of all writers he has the best chance for immortality. Others may write from the head, but he writes from the heart, and the heart will always understand him. He is the faithful portrayer of nature, whose features are always the same, and always interesting. Prose writers are voluminous and unwieldy; their pages are crowded with common places, and their thoughts expanded into tediousness. But with the true poet every thing is terse, touching, or brilliant. He gives the choicest thoughts in the choicest language. He illustrates them by every thing that he sees most striking in nature and art. He enriches them by pictures of human life, such as it is passing before him. His writings, therefore, contain the spirit, the aroma, if I may use the phrase, of the age in which he lives. They are caskets which inclose within a small compass the wealth of the language—its family jewels, which are thus transmitted in a portable form to posterity. The setting may occasionally be antiquated, and require now and then to be renewed, as in the case of Chaucer; but the brilliancy and intrinsic value of the gems continue unaltered. Cast a look back over the long reach of

---

*Excessive, or profuse.

literary history. What vast valleys of dulness, filled with monkish legends and academical controversies! what bogs of theological speculations! what dreary wastes of metaphysics! Here and there only do we behold the heaven-illuminated bards, elevated like beacons on their widely-separate heights, to transmit the pure light of poetical intelligence from age to age."*

I was just about to launch forth into eulogiums upon the poets of the day, when the sudden opening of the door caused me to turn my head. It was the verger, who came to inform me that it was time to close the library. I sought to have a parting word with the quarto, but the worthy little tome was silent; the clasps were closed: and it looked perfectly unconscious of all that had passed. I have been to the library two or three times since, and have endeavored to draw it into further conversation, but in vain; and whether all this rambling colloquy actually took place, or whether it was another of those odd day-dreams to which I am subject, I have never to this moment been able to discover.

---

*Thorow earth and waters deepe,
The pen by skill doth passe:
And featly nyps the worldes abuse,
And shoes us in a glasse,
The vertu and the vice
Of every wight alyve;
The honey comb that bee doth make
Is not so sweet in hyve,
As are the golden leves
That drop from poet's head!
Which doth surmount our common talke
As farre as dross doth lead.

Churchyard [Irving's note]. English writer Thomas Churchyard (c.1520–1604).

The Inn Kitchen[15]

Shall I not take mine ease in mine inn?

FALSTAFF*

D uring a journey that I once made through the Netherlands,
I arrived one evening at the *Pomme d'Or*,[†] the principal inn of
a small Flemish village. It was after the hour of the *table
d'hôte*,[‡] so that I was obliged to make a solitary supper from the relics
of its ampler board. The weather was chilly; I was seated alone in one
end of a great gloomy dining-room, and, my repast being over, I had
the prospect before me of a long dull evening, without any visible
means of enlivening it. I summoned mine host, and requested something to read; he brought me the whole literary stock of his household,
a Dutch family Bible, an almanac in the same language, and a number
of old Paris newspapers. As I sat dozing over one of the latter, reading
old and stale criticisms, my ear was now and then struck with bursts of
laughter which seemed to proceed from the kitchen. Every one that has
travelled on the continent must know how favorite a resort the kitchen
of a country inn is to the middle and inferior order of travellers; particularly in that equivocal kind of weather, when a fire becomes agreeable toward evening. I threw aside the newspaper, and explored my way
to the kitchen, to take a peep at the group that appeared to be so merry.
It was composed partly of travellers who had arrived some hours before in a diligence, and partly of the usual attendants and hangers-on
of inns. They were seated round a great burnished stove, that might
have been mistaken for an altar, at which they were worshipping. It was
covered with various kitchen vessels of resplendent brightness; among
which steamed and hissed a huge copper tea-kettle. A large lamp threw
a strong mass of light upon the group, bringing out many odd features

---

*Quotation from Shakespeare's *The First Part of Henry the Fourth* (act 3, scene 3).
†The Golden Apple (French).
‡Meal served to guests at a fixed time and price.

in strong relief. Its yellow rays partially illumined the spacious kitchen, dying duskily away into remote corners; except where they settled in mellow radiance on the broad side of a flitch of bacon, or were reflected back from well-scoured utensils, that gleamed from the midst of obscurity. A strapping Flemish lass, with long golden pendants in her ears, and a necklace with a golden heart suspended to it, was the presiding priestess of the temple.

Many of the company were furnished with pipes, and most of them with some kind of evening potation. I found their mirth was occasioned by anecdotes, which a little swarthy Frenchman, with a dry weazen face and large whiskers, was giving of his love adventures; at the end of each of which there was one of those bursts of honest unceremonious laughter, in which a man indulges in that temple of true liberty, an inn.

As I had no better mode of getting through a tedious blustering evening, I took my seat near the stove, and listened to a variety of traveller's tales, some very extravagant, and most very dull. All of them, however, have faded from my treacherous memory except one, which I will endeavor to relate. I fear, however, it derived its chief zest from the manner in which it was told, and the peculiar air and appearance of the narrator. He was a corpulent old Swiss, who had the look of a veteran traveller. He was dressed in a tarnished green travelling-jacket, with a broad belt round his waist, and a pair of overalls, with buttons from the hips to the ankles. He was of a full, rubicund countenance, with a double chin, aquiline nose, and a pleasant, twinkling eye. His hair was light, and curled from under an old green velvet travelling-cap stuck on one side of his head. He was interrupted more than once by the arrival of guests, or the remarks of his auditors; and paused now and then to replenish his pipe; at which times he had generally a roguish leer, and a sly joke for the buxom kitchen-maid.

I wish my readers could imagine the old fellow lolling in a huge arm-chair, one arm akimbo, the other holding a curiously twisted tobacco pipe, formed of genuine *écume de mer*,* decorated with silver chain and silken tassel—his head cocked on one side, and the whimsical cut of the eye occasionally, as he related the following story.

---

*Meerschaum (literally, "seafoam" in French); a claylike mineral used to make tobacco pipes.

The Spectre Bridegroom[16]

A TRAVELLER'S TALE*

He that supper for is dight,
He lyes full cold, I trow, this night!
Yestreen to chamber I him led,
This night Gray-Steel has made his bed.
SIR EGER, SIR GRAHAME,
AND SIR GRAY-STEEL[†]

On the summit of one of the heights of the Odenwald, a wild and romantic tract of Upper Germany, that lies not far from the confluence of the Main and the Rhine, there stood, many, many years since, the Castle of the Baron Von Landshort. It is now quite fallen to decay, and almost buried among beech trees and dark firs; above which, however, its old watchtower may still be seen, struggling, like the former possessor I have mentioned, to carry a high head, and look down upon the neighboring country.

The baron was a dry branch of the great family of Katzenellenbogen,[‡] and inherited the relics of the property, and all the pride of his ancestors. Though the warlike disposition of his predecessors had much impaired the family possessions, yet the baron still endeavored to keep up some show of former state. The times were peaceable, and the German nobles, in general, had abandoned

---

*The erudite reader, well versed in good-for-nothing lore, will perceive that the above Tale must have been suggested to the old Swiss by a little French anecdote, a circumstance said to have taken place at Paris [Irving's note].

[†]From *The History of Sir Eger, Sir Grahame, and Sir Gray-Steel* (1687), an early metrical romance; Irving's source is unidentified.

[‡]*i. e.*, CAT'S-ELBOW. The name of a family of those parts very powerful in former times. The appellation, we are told, was given in compliment to a peerless dame of the family, celebrated for her fine arm [Irving's note].

their inconvenient old castles, perched like eagles' nests among the mountains, and had built more convenient residences in the valleys: still the baron remained proudly drawn up in his little fortress, cherishing, with hereditary inveteracy, all the old family feuds; so that he was on ill terms with some of his nearest neighbors, on account of disputes that had happened between their great-great-grandfathers.

The baron had but one child, a daughter; but nature, when she grants but one child, always compensates by making it a prodigy; and so it was with the daughter of the baron. All the nurses, gossips, and country cousins, assured her father that she had not her equal for beauty in all Germany; and who should know better than they? She had, moreover, been brought up with great care under the superintendence of two maiden aunts, who had spent some years of their early life at one of the little German courts, and were skilled in all the branches of knowledge necessary to the education of a fine lady. Under their instructions she became a miracle of accomplishments. By the time she was eighteen, she could embroider to admiration, and had worked whole histories of the saints in tapestry, with such strength of expression in their countenances, that they looked like so many souls in purgatory. She could read without great difficulty, and had spelled her way through several church legends, and almost all the chivalric wonders of the Heldenbuch.* She had even made considerable proficiency in writing; could sign her own name without missing a letter, and so legibly, that her aunts could read it without spectacles. She excelled in making little elegant good-for-nothing lady-like nicknacks of all kinds; was versed in the most abstruse dancing of the day; played a number of airs on the harp and guitar; and knew all the tender ballads of the Minnelieders† by heart.

Her aunts, too, having been great flirts and coquettes in their younger days, were admirably calculated to be vigilant guardians and strict censors of the conduct of their niece; for there is no duenna‡ so rigidly prudent, and inexorably decorous, as a superannuated coquette. She was rarely suffered out of their sight; never

---

Das Heldenbuch, or Book of Heroes, a collection of thirteenth-century German metrical romances.

†Or Minnesingers; medieval German troubadours.

‡Chaperone, or governess.

went beyond the domains of the castle, unless well attended, or rather well watched; had continual lectures read to her about strict decorum and implicit obedience; and, as to the men—pah!—she was taught to hold them at such a distance, and in such absolute distrust, that, unless properly authorized, she would not have cast a glance upon the handsomest cavalier in the world—no, not if he were even dying at her feet.

The good effects of this system were wonderfully apparent. The young lady was a pattern of docility and correctness. While others were wasting their sweetness in the glare of the world, and liable to be plucked and thrown aside by every hand, she was coyly blooming into fresh and lovely womanhood under the protection of those im-maculate spinsters, like a rose-bud blushing forth among guardian thorns. Her aunts looked upon her with pride and exultation, and vaunted that though all the other young ladies in the world might go astray, yet, thank Heaven, nothing of the kind could happen to the heiress of Katzenellenbogen.

But, however scantily the Baron Von Landshort might be pro-vided with children, his household was by no means a small one; for Providence had enriched him with abundance of poor relations. They, one and all, possessed the affectionate disposition common to humble relatives; were wonderfully attached to the baron, and took every possible occasion to come in swarms and enliven the castle. All family festivals were commemorated by these good people at the baron's expense; and when they were filled with good cheer, they would declare that there was nothing on earth so delightful as these family meetings, these jubilees of the heart.

The baron, though a small man, had a large soul, and it swelled with satisfaction at the consciousness of being the greatest man in the little world about him. He loved to tell long stories about the dark old warriors whose portraits looked grimly down from the walls around, and he found no listeners equal to those that fed at his expense. He was much given to the marvellous, and a firm believer in all those su-pernatural tales with which every mountain and valley in Germany abounds. The faith of his guests exceeded even his own: they listened to every tale of wonder with open eyes and mouth, and never failed to be astonished, even though repeated for the hundredth time. Thus lived the Baron Von Landshort, the oracle of his table, the absolute monarch of his little tèrritory, and happy, above all things, in the persuasion that he was the wisest man of the age.

At the time of which my story treats, there was a great family gathering at the castle, on an affair of the utmost importance: it was to receive the destined bridegroom of the baron's daughter. A negotiation had been carried on between the father and an old nobleman of Bavaria, to unite the dignity of their houses by the marriage of their children. The preliminaries had been conducted with proper *punctilio.** The young people were betrothed without seeing each other; and the time was appointed for the marriage ceremony. The young Count Von Altenburg had been recalled from the army for the purpose, and was actually on his way to the baron's to receive his bride. Missives had even been received from him, from Wurtzburg, where he was accidentally detained, mentioning the day and hour when he might be expected to arrive.

The castle was in a tumult of preparation to give him a suitable welcome. The fair bride had been decked out with uncommon care. The two aunts had superintended her toilet, and quarrelled the whole morning about every article of her dress. The young lady had taken advantage of their contest to follow the bent of her own taste; and fortunately it was a good one. She looked as lovely as youthful bridegroom could desire; and the flutter of expectation heightened the lustre of her charms.

The suffusions that mantled her face and neck, the gentle heaving of the bosom, the eye now and then lost in reverie, all betrayed the soft tumult that was going on in her little heart. The aunts were continually hovering around her; for maiden aunts are apt to take great interest in affairs of this nature. They were giving her a world of staid counsel how to deport herself, what to say, and in what manner to receive the expected lover.

The baron was no less busied in preparations. He had, in truth, nothing exactly to do; but he was naturally a fuming bustling little man, and could not remain passive when all the world was in a hurry. He worried from top to bottom of the castle with an air of infinite anxiety; he continually called the servants from their work to

*Attention to ceremony or formality.

exhort them to be diligent; and buzzed about every hall and chamber, as idly restless and importunate as a blue-bottle fly on a warm summer's day.

In the mean time the fatted calf had been killed; the forests had rung with the clamor of the huntsmen; the kitchen was crowded with good cheer; the cellars had yielded up whole oceans of *Rhein-wein** and *Ferne-wein*;[†] and even the great Heidelburg tun[‡] had been laid under contribution. Every thing was ready to receive the distinguished guest with *Saus und Braus*[§] in the true spirit of German hospitality—but the guest delayed to make his appearance. Hour rolled after hour. The sun, that had poured his downward rays upon the rich forest of the Odenwald, now just gleamed along the summits of the mountains. The baron mounted the highest tower, and strained his eyes in hope of catching a distant sight of the count and his attendants. Once he thought he beheld them; the sound of horns came floating from the valley, prolonged by the mountain echoes. A number of horsemen were seen far below, slowly advancing along the road; but when they had nearly reached the foot of the mountain, they suddenly struck off in a different direction. The last ray of sunshine departed—the bats began to flit by in the twilight—the road grew dimmer and dimmer to the view; and nothing appeared stirring in it but now and then a peasant lagging homeward from his labor.

While the old castle of Landshort was in this state of perplexity, a very interesting scene was transacting in a different part of the Odenwald.

The young Count Yon Altenburg was tranquilly pursuing his route in that sober jog-trot way, in which a man travels toward matrimony when his friends have taken all the trouble and uncertainty of courtship off his hands, and a bride is waiting for him, as certainly as a dinner at the end of his journey. He had encountered at Wurtzburg, a youthful companion in arms, with whom he had seen

---

*Wine from the Rhine region of Germany.
†That is, old, tainted wine.
‡One of the largest wine vats in the world, the Heidelburg Tun, found in the castle at Heidelberg, Germany, held approximately 58,000 gallons.
§Revel and riot.

some service on the frontiers; Herman Von Starkenfaust, one of the stoutest hands, and worthiest hearts, of German chivalry, who was now returning from the army. His father's castle was not far distant from the old fortress of Landshort, although an hereditary feud rendered the families hostile, and strangers to each other.

In the warm-hearted moment of recognition, the young friends related all their past adventures and fortunes, and the count gave the whole history of his intended nuptials with a young lady whom he had never seen, but of whose charms he had received the most enrapturing descriptions.

As the route of the friends lay in the same direction, they agreed to perform the rest of their journey together; and, that they might do it the more leisurely, set off from Wurtzburg at an early hour, the count having given directions for his retinue to follow and overtake him.

They beguiled their wayfaring with recollections of their military scenes and adventures; but the count was apt to be a little tedious, now and then, about the reputed charms of his bride, and the felicity that awaited him.

In this way they had entered among the mountains of the Odenwald, and were traversing one of its most lonely and thickly-wooded passes. It is well known that the forests of Germany have always been as much infested by robbers as its castles by spectres; and, at this time, the former were particularly numerous, from the hordes of disbanded soldiers wandering about the country. It will not appear extraordinary, therefore, that the cavaliers were attacked by a gang of these stragglers, in the midst of the forest. They defended themselves with bravery, but were nearly overpowered, when the count's retinue arrived to their assistance. At sight of them the robbers fled, but not until the count had received a mortal wound. He was slowly and carefully conveyed back to the city of Wurtzburg, and a friar summoned from a neighboring convent, who was famous for his skill in administering to both soul and body; but half of his skill was superfluous; the moments of the unfortunate count were numbered.

With his dying breath he entreated his friend to repair instantly to the castle of Landshort, and explain the fatal cause of his not keeping his appointment with his bride. Though not the most ardent of lovers, he was one of the most punctilious of men, and appeared earnestly solicitous that his mission should be speedily and courteously executed. "Unless this is done," said he, "I shall not sleep quietly in my grave!" He repeated these last words with peculiar solemnity. A request, at a moment so impressive, admitted no hesitation. Starkenfaust endeavored to soothe him to calmness; promised faithfully to execute his wish, and gave him his hand in solemn pledge. The dying man pressed it in acknowledgment, but soon lapsed into delirium—raved about his bride—his engagements—his plighted word; ordered his horse, that he might ride to the castle of Landshort; and expired in the fancied act of vaulting into the saddle.

Starkenfaust bestowed a sigh and a soldier's tear on the untimely fate of his comrade; and then pondered on the awkward mission he had undertaken. His heart was heavy, and his head perplexed; for he was to present himself an unbidden guest among hostile people, and to damp their festivity with tidings fatal to their hopes. Still there were certain whisperings of curiosity in his bosom to see this far-famed beauty of Katzenellenbogen, so cautiously shut up from the world; for he was a passionate admirer of the sex, and there was a dash of eccentricity and enterprise in his character that made him fond of all singular adventure.

Previous to his departure he made all due arrangements with the holy fraternity of the convent for the funeral solemnities of his friend, who was to be buried in the cathedral of Wurtzburg, near some of his illustrious relatives; and the mourning retinue of the count took charge of his remains.

It is now high time that we should return to the ancient family of Katzenellenbogen, who were impatient for their guest, and still more for their dinner; and to the worthy little baron, whom we left airing himself on the watch-tower.

Night closed in, but still no guest arrived. The baron descended from the tower in despair. The banquet, which had been delayed from hour to hour, could no longer be postponed. The meats were already overdone; the cook in an agony; and the whole household had the look of a garrison that had been reduced by famine. The baron was obliged reluctantly to give orders for the feast without the presence of the guest. All were seated at table, and just on the point of commencing, when the sound of a horn from without the gate gave notice of the approach of a stranger. Another long blast filled the old courts of the castle with its echoes, and was answered by the warder from the walls. The baron hastened to receive his future son-in-law.

The drawbridge had been let down, and the stranger was before the gate. He was a tall, gallant cavalier, mounted on a black steed. His countenance was pale, but he had a beaming, romantic eye, and an air of stately melancholy. The baron was a little mortified that he should have come in this simple, solitary style. His dignity for a moment was ruffled, and he felt disposed to consider it a want of proper respect for the important occasion, and the important family with which he was to be connected. He pacified himself, however, with the conclusion, that it must have been youthful impatience which had induced him thus to spur on sooner than his attendants.

"I am sorry," said the stranger, "to break in upon you thus unseasonably—"

Here the baron interrupted him with a world of compliments and greetings; for, to tell the truth, he prided himself upon his courtesy and eloquence. The stranger attempted, once or twice, to stem the torrent of words, but in vain, so he bowed his head and suffered it to flow on. By the time the baron had come to a pause, they had reached the inner court of the castle; and the stranger was again about to speak, when he was once more interrupted by the appearance of the female part of the family, leading forth the shrinking and blushing bride. He gazed on her for a moment as one entranced; it seemed as if his whole soul beamed forth in the gaze, and rested upon that lovely form. One of the maiden aunts whispered something in her ear; she made an effort to speak; her moist blue eye was timidly raised; gave a shy glance of inquiry on the stranger; and was cast again to the ground. The words died away; but there was a sweet smile playing about her lips, and a soft dimpling of the cheek that showed her glance had not been unsatisfactory. It was impossible for a girl of the fond age of eighteen, highly predisposed for love and matrimony, not to be pleased with so gallant a cavalier.

The late hour at which the guest had arrived left no time for parley. The baron was peremptory, and deferred all particular conversation until the morning, and led the way to the untasted banquet.

It was served up in the great hall of the castle. Around the walls hung the hard-favored portraits of the heroes of the house of

Katzenellenbogen, and the trophies which they had gained in the field and in the chase. Hacked corslets, splintered jousting spears, and tattered banners, were mingled with the spoils of sylvan warfare; the jaws of the wolf, and the tusks of the boar, grinned horribly among cross-bows and battle-axes, and a huge pair of antlers branched immediately over the head of the youthful bridegroom.

The cavalier took but little notice of the company or the entertainment. He scarcely tasted the banquet, but seemed absorbed in admiration of his bride. He conversed in a low tone that could not be overheard—for the language of love is never loud; but where is the female ear so dull that it cannot catch the softest whisper of the lover? There was a mingled tenderness and gravity in his manner, that appeared to have a powerful effect upon the young lady. Her color came and went as she listened with deep attention. Now and then she made some blushing reply, and when his eye was turned away, she would steal a sidelong glance at his romantic countenance, and heave a gentle sigh of tender happiness. It was evident that the young couple were completely enamored. The aunts, who were deeply versed in the mysteries of the heart, declared that they had fallen in love with each other at first sight.

The feast went on merrily, or at least noisily, for the guests were all blessed with those keen appetites that attend upon light purses and mountain air. The baron told his best and longest stories, and never had he told them so well, or with such great effect. If there was any thing marvellous, his auditors were lost in astonishment; and if any thing facetious, they were sure to laugh exactly in the right place. The baron, it is true, like most great men, was too dignified to utter any joke but a dull one; it was always enforced, however, by a bumper of excellent Hockheimer;* and even a dull joke, at one's own table, served up with jolly old wine, is irresistible. Many good things were said by poorer and keener wits, that would not bear repeating, except on similar occasions; many sly speeches whispered in ladies' ears, that almost convulsed them with suppressed laughter; and a song or two roared out by a poor, but merry and broad-faced cousin of the baron, that absolutely made the maiden aunts hold up their fans.

---

*Famous German wine.

Amidst all this revelry, the stranger guest maintained a most singular and unseasonable gravity. His countenance assumed a deeper cast of dejection as the evening advanced; and, strange as it may appear, even the baron's jokes seemed only to render him the more melancholy. At times he was lost in thought, and at times there was a perturbed and restless wandering of the eye that bespoke a mind but ill at ease. His conversations with the bride became more and more earnest and mysterious. Lowering clouds began to steal over the fair serenity of her brow, and tremors to run through her tender frame.

All this could not escape the notice of the company. Their gayety was chilled by the unaccountable gloom of the bridegroom; their spirits were infected; whispers and glances were interchanged, accompanied by shrugs and dubious shakes of the head. The song and the laugh grew less and less frequent; there were dreary pauses in the conversation, which were at length succeeded by wild tales and supernatural legends. One dismal story produced another still more dismal, and the baron nearly frightened some of the ladies into hysterics with the history of the goblin horseman that carried away the fair Leonora;* a dreadful story, which has since been put into excellent verse, and is read and believed by all the world.

The bridegroom listened to this tale with profound attention. He kept his eyes steadily fixed on the baron, and, as the story drew to a close, began gradually to rise from his seat, growing taller and taller, until, in the baron's entranced eye, he seemed almost to tower into a giant. The moment the tale was finished, he heaved a deep sigh, and took a solemn farewell of the company. They were all amazement. The baron was perfectly thunder-struck.

"What! going to leave the castle at midnight? why, every thing was prepared for his reception; a chamber was ready for him if he wished to retire."

The stranger shook his head mournfully and mysteriously; "I must lay my head in a different chamber tonight!"

There was something in this reply, and the tone in which it was uttered, that made the baron's heart misgive him; but he rallied his forces, and repeated his hospitable entreaties.

---

*"Lenore," a ballad by German poet Gottfried August Bürger (1747–1794), is one of Irving's sources for "The Spectre Bridegroom."

The stranger shook his head silently, but positively, at every offer; and, waving his farewell to the company, stalked slowly out of the hall. The maiden aunts were absolutely petrified—the bride hung her head, and a tear stole to her eye.

The baron followed the stranger to the great court of the castle, where the black charger stood pawing the earth, and snorting with impatience.—When they had reached the portal, whose deep archway was dimly lighted by a cresset, the stranger paused, and addressed the baron in a hollow tone of voice, which the vaulted roof rendered still more sepulchral.

"Now that we are alone," said he, "I will impart to you the reason of my going. I have a solemn, an indispensable engagement—"

"Why," said the baron, "cannot you send some one in your place?"

"It admits of no substitute—I must attend it in person—I must away to Wurtzburg cathedral—"

"Ay," said the baron, plucking up spirit, "but not until to-morrow—to-morrow you shall take your bride there."

"No! no!" replied the stranger, with tenfold solemnity, "my engagement is with no bride—the worms! the worms expect me! I am a dead man—I have been slain by robbers—my body lies at Wurtzburg—at midnight I am to be buried—the grave is waiting for me—I must keep my appointment!"

He sprang on his black charger, dashed over the drawbridge, and the clattering of his horse's hoofs was lost in the whistling of the night blast.

The baron returned to the hall in the utmost consternation, and related what had passed. Two ladies fainted outright, others sickened at the idea of having banqueted with a spectre. It was the opinion of some, that this might be the wild huntsman, famous in German legend. Some talked of mountain sprites, of wood-demons, and of other supernatural beings, with which the good people of Germany have been so grievously harassed since time immemorial. One of the poor relations ventured to suggest that it might be some sportive evasion of the young cavalier, and that the very gloominess of the caprice seemed to accord with so melancholy a personage. This, however, drew on him the indignation of the whole company, and especially of the baron, who looked upon him as little better than an infidel; so that he was fain to abjure his heresy as speedily as possible, and come into the faith of the true believers.

But whatever may have been the doubts entertained, they were completely put to an end by the arrival, next day, of regular missives, confirming the intelligence of the young count's murder, and his interment in Wurtzburg cathedral.

The dismay at the castle may well be imagined. The baron shut himself up in his chamber. The guests, who had come to rejoice with him, could not think of abandoning him in his distress. They wandered about the courts, or collected in groups in the hall, shaking their heads and shrugging their shoulders, at the troubles of so good a man; and sat longer than ever at table, and ate and drank more stoutly than ever, by way of keeping up their spirits. But the situation of the widowed bride was the most pitiable. To have lost a husband before she had even embraced him—and such a husband! if the very spectre could be so gracious and noble, what must have been the living man. She filled the house with lamentations.

On the night of the second day of her widowhood, she had retired to her chamber, accompanied by one of her aunts, who insisted on sleeping with her. The aunt, who was one of the best tellers of ghost stories in all Germany, had just been recounting one of her longest, and had fallen asleep in the very midst of it. The chamber was remote, and overlooked a small garden. The niece lay pensively gazing at the beams of the rising moon, as they trembled on the leaves of an aspen-tree before the lattice. The castle-clock had just tolled midnight, when a soft strain of music stole up from the garden. She rose hastily from her bed, and stepped lightly to the window. A tall figure stood among the shadows of the trees. As it raised its head, a beam of moonlight fell upon the countenance. Heaven and earth! she beheld the Spectre Bridegroom! A loud shriek at that moment burst upon her ear, and her aunt, who had been awakened by the music, and had followed her silently to the window, fell into her arms. When she looked again, the spectre had disappeared.

Of the two females, the aunt now required the most soothing, for she was perfectly beside herself with terror. As to the young lady, there was something, even in the spectre of her lover, that seemed endearing. There was still the semblance of manly beauty; and though the shadow of a man is but little calculated to satisfy the affections of a love-sick girl, yet, where the substance is not to be had, even that is consoling. The aunt declared she would never sleep in that chamber again; the niece, for once, was refractory, and declared as strongly that she would sleep in no other in the castle: the consequence was, that she had to sleep in it alone: but she drew a promise from her aunt not to relate the story of the spectre, lest she should be denied the only melancholy pleasure left her on earth— that of inhabiting the chamber over which the guardian shade of her lover kept its nightly vigils.

How long the good old lady would have observed this promise is uncertain, for she dearly loved to talk of the marvellous, and there is a triumph in being the first to tell a frightful story; it is, however, still quoted in the neighborhood, as a memorable instance of female secrecy, that she kept it to herself for a whole week; when she was suddenly absolved from all further restraint, by intelligence brought to the breakfast table one morning that the young lady was not to be found. Her room was empty—the bed had not been slept in—the window was open, and the bird had flown!

The astonishment and concern with which the intelligence was received, can only be imagined by those who have witnessed the agitation which the mishaps of a great man cause among his friends. Even the poor relations paused for a moment from the indefatigable labors of the trencher; when the aunt, who had at first been struck speechless, wrung her hands, and shrieked out, "The goblin! the goblin! she's carried away by the goblin."

In a few words she related the fearful scene of the garden, and concluded that the spectre must have carried off his bride. Two of the domestics corroborated the opinion, for they had heard the clattering of a horse's hoofs down the mountain about midnight, and had no doubt that it was the spectre on his black charger, bearing her away to the tomb. All present were struck with the direful probability; for events of the kind are extremely common in Germany, as many well authenticated histories bear witness.

What a lamentable situation was that of the poor baron! What a heart-rending dilemma for a fond father, and a member of the great family of Katzenellenbogen! His only daughter had either been rapt away to the grave, or he was to have some wood-demon for a son-in-law, and, perchance, a troop of goblin grandchildren. As usual, he was completely bewildered, and all the castle in an uproar. The men were ordered to take horse, and scour every road and path and glen of the Odenwald. The baron himself had just drawn on his jack-boots, girded on his sword, and was about to mount his steed to sally forth on the doubtful quest, when he was brought to a pause by a new apparition. A lady was seen approaching the castle, mounted on a palfrey, attended by a cavalier on horseback. She galloped up to the gate, sprang from her horse, and falling at the baron's feet, embraced his knees. It was his lost daughter, and her companion—the Spectre Bridegroom! The baron was astounded. He looked at his daughter, then at the spectre, and almost doubted the evidence of his senses. The latter, too, was wonderfully improved in his appearance since his visit to the world of spirits. His dress was splendid, and set off a noble figure of manly symmetry. He was no longer pale and melancholy. His fine countenance was flushed with the glow of youth, and joy rioted in his large dark eye.

The mystery was soon cleared up. The cavalier (for, in truth, as you must have known all the while, he was no goblin) announced himself as Sir Herman Von Starkenfaust. He related his adventure with the young count. He told how he had hastened to the castle to deliver the unwelcome tidings, but that the eloquence of the baron had interrupted him in every attempt to tell his tale. How the sight of the bride had completely captivated him, and that to pass a few hours near her, he had tacitly suffered the mistake to continue. How he had been sorely perplexed in what way to make a decent retreat, until the baron's goblin stories had suggested his eccentric exit. How, fearing the feudal hostility of the family, he had repeated his visits by stealth—had haunted the garden beneath the young lady's window—had wooed—had won—had borne away in triumph—and, in a word, had wedded the fair.

Under any other circumstances the baron would have been inflexible, for he was tenacious of paternal authority, and devoutly obstinate in all family feuds; but he loved his daughter; he had lamented her as lost; he rejoiced to find her still alive; and, though her husband was of a hostile house, yet, thank Heaven, he was not a goblin. There was something, it must be acknowledged, that did not exactly accord with his notions of strict veracity, in the joke the knight had passed upon him of his being a dead man; but several old friends present, who had served in the wars, assured him that every stratagem was excusable in love, and that the cavalier was entitled to especial privilege, having lately served as a trooper.

Matters, therefore, were happily arranged. The baron pardoned the young couple on the spot. The revels at the castle were resumed. The poor relations overwhelmed this new member of the family with loving kindness; he was so gallant, so generous—and so rich. The aunts, it is true, were somewhat scandalized that their system of strict seclusion, and passive obedience should be so badly exemplified, but attributed it all to their negligence in not having the windows grated. One of them was particularly mortified at having her marvellous story marred, and that the only spectre she had ever seen should turn out a counterfeit; but the niece seemed perfectly happy at having found him substantial flesh and blood—and so the story ends.

Traits of Indian Character[17]

> "I appeal to any white man if ever he entered Logan's cabin hungry, and he gave him not to eat; if ever he came cold and naked, and he clothed him not."

SPEECH OF AN INDIAN CHIEF*

There is something in the character and habits of the North American savage, taken in connection with the scenery over which he is accustomed to range, its vast lakes, boundless forests, majestic rivers, and trackless plains, that is, to my mind, wonderfully striking and sublime. He is formed for the wilderness, as the Arab is for the desert. His nature is stern, simple, and enduring; fitted to grapple with difficulties, and to support privations. There seems but little soil in his heart for the support of the kindly virtues; and yet, if we would but take the trouble to penetrate through that proud stoicism and habitual taciturnity, which lock up his character from casual observation, we should find him linked to his fellow-man of civilized life by more of those sympathies and affections than are usually ascribed to him.

It has been the lot of the unfortunate aborigines of America, in the early periods of colonization, to be doubly wronged by the white men. They have been dispossessed of their hereditary possessions by mercenary and frequently wanton warfare: and their characters have been traduced by bigoted and interested writers. The colonist often treated them like beasts of the forest; and the author has endeavored to justify him in his outrages. The former found it easier to exterminate than to civilize; the latter to vilify than to discriminate. The appellations of savage and pagan were deemed suffcient to sanction

---

*Version of a speech given in 1774 by Native American Mingo chief Logan after his family was massacred by white settlers; various versions of Logan's speech—often published under the title "Logan's Lament"—were written by white Americans during the eighteenth and nineteenth centuries to exemplify the noble sentiments of the "savage."

the hostilities of both; and thus the poor wanderers of the forest were persecuted and defamed, not because they were guilty, but because they were ignorant.

The rights of the savage have seldom been properly appreciated or respected by the white man. In peace he has too often been the dupe of artful traffic; in war he has been regarded as a ferocious animal, whose life or death was a question of mere precaution and convenience. Man is cruelly wasteful of life when his own safety is endangered, and he is sheltered by impunity; and little mercy is to be expected from him, when he feels the sting of the reptile and is conscious of the power to destroy.

The same prejudices, which were indulged thus early, exist in common circulation at the present day. Certain learned societies have, it is true, with laudable diligence, endeavored to investigate and record the real characters and manners of the Indian tribes; the American government, too, has wisely and humanely exerted itself to inculcate a friendly and forbearing spirit towards them, and to protect them from fraud and injustice.* The current opinion of the Indian character, however, is too apt to be formed from the miserable hordes which infest the frontiers, and hang on the skirts of the settlements. These are too commonly composed of degenerate beings, corrupted and enfeebled by the vices of society, without being benefited by its civilization. That proud independence, which formed the main pillar of savage virtue, has been shaken down, and the whole moral fabric lies in ruins. Their spirits are humiliated and debased by a sense of inferiority, and their native courage cowed and daunted by the superior knowledge and power of their enlightened neighbors. Society has advanced upon them like one of those withering airs that will sometimes breed desolation over a whole region of fertility. It has enervated their strength, multiplied their diseases, and super-induced upon their original barbarity the low vices

---

*The American government has been indefatigable in its exertions to ameliorate the situation of the Indians, and to introduce among them the arts of civilization, and civil and religious knowledge. To protect them from the frauds of the white traders, no purchase of land from them by individuals is permitted; nor is any person allowed to receive lands from them as a present, without the express sanction of government. These precautions are strictly enforced [Irving's note].

of artificial life. It has given them a thousand superfluous wants, whilst it has diminished their means of mere existence. It has driven before it the animals of the chase, who fly from the sound of the axe and the smoke of the settlement, and seek refuge in the depths of remoter forests and yet untrodden wilds. Thus do we too often find the Indians on our frontiers to be the mere wrecks and remnants of once powerful tribes, who have lingered in the vicinity of the settlements, and sunk into precarious and vagabond existence. Poverty, repining and hopeless poverty, a canker of the mind unknown in savage life, corrodes their spirits, and blights every free and noble quality of their natures. They become drunken, indolent, feeble, thievish, and pusillanimous. They loiter like vagrants about the settlements, among spacious dwellings replete with elaborate comforts, which only render them sensible of the comparative wretchedness of their own condition. Luxury spreads its ample board before their eyes; but they are excluded from the banquet. Plenty revels over the fields; but they are starving in the midst of its abundance: the whole wilderness has blossomed into a garden; but they feel as reptiles that infest it.

How different was their state while yet the undisputed lords of the soil! Their wants were few, and the means of gratification within their reach. They saw every one around them sharing the same lot, enduring the same hardships, feeding on the same aliments, arrayed in the same rude garments. No roof then rose, but was open to the homeless stranger; no smoke curled among the trees, but he was welcome to sit down by its fire, and join the hunter in his repast. "For," says an old historian of New England,* "their life is so void of care, and they are so loving also, that they make use of those things they enjoy as common goods, and are therein so compassionate, that rather than one should starve through want, they would starve all; thus they pass their time merrily, not regarding our pomp, but are better content with their own, which some men esteem so meanly of." Such were the Indians, whilst in the pride and energy of their primitive natures: they resembled those wild plants, which thrive

---

*Thomas Morton (c.1579–1647), who established the colony at Merry Mount (now Quincy, Massachusetts); Irving quotes from his *New English Canaan* (book 1).

best in the shades of the forest, but shrink from the hand of cultivation, and perish beneath the influence of the sun.

In discussing the savage character, writers have been too prone to indulge in vulgar prejudice and passionate exaggeration, instead of the candid temper of true philosophy. They have not sufficiently considered the peculiar circumstances in which the Indians have been placed, and the peculiar principles under which they have been educated. No being acts more rigidly from rule than the Indian. His whole conduct is regulated according to some general maxims early implanted in his mind. The moral laws that govern him are, to be sure, but few; but then he conforms to them all;—the white man abounds in laws of religion, morals, and manners, but how many does he violate?

A frequent ground of accusation against the Indians is their disregard of treaties, and the treachery and wantonness with which, in time of apparent peace, they will suddenly fly to hostilities. The intercourse of the white men with the Indians, however, is too apt to be cold, distrustful, oppressive, and insulting. They seldom treat them with that confidence and frankness which are indispensable to real friendship; nor is sufficient caution observed not to offend against those feelings of pride or superstition, which often prompts the Indian to hostility quicker than mere considerations of interest. The solitary savage feels silently, but acutely. His sensibilities are not diffused over so wide a surface as those of the white man; but they run in steadier and deeper channels. His pride, his affections, his superstitions, are all directed towards fewer objects; but the wounds inflicted on them are proportionably severe, and furnish motives of hostility which we cannot sufficiently appreciate. Where a community is also limited in number, and forms one great patriarchal family, as in an Indian tribe, the injury of an individual is the injury of the whole; and the sentiment of vengeance is almost instantaneously diffused. One council fire is sufficient for the discussion and arrangement of a plan of hostilities. Here all the fighting men and sages assemble. Eloquence and superstition combine to inflame the minds of the warriors. The orator awakens their martial ardor, and they are wrought up to a kind of religious desperation, by the visions of the prophet and the dreamer.

An instance of one of those sudden exasperations, arising from a motive peculiar to the Indian character, is extant in an old record of the early settlement of Massachusetts.* The planters of Plymouth had defaced the monuments of the dead at Passonagessit, and had plundered the grave of the Sachem's mother of some skins with which it had been decorated. The Indians are remarkable for the reverence which they entertain for the sepulchres of their kindred. Tribes that have passed generations exiled from the abodes of their ancestors, when by chance they have been travelling in the vicinity, have been known to turn aside from the highway, and, guided by wonderfully accurate tradition, have crossed the country for miles to some tumulus, buried perhaps in woods, where the bones of their tribe were anciently deposited; and there have passed hours in silent meditation. Influenced by this sublime and holy feeling, the Sachem, whose mother's tomb had been violated, gathered his men together, and addressed them in the following beautifully simple and pathetic harangue; a curious specimen of Indian eloquence, and an affecting instance of filial piety in a savage.

"When last the glorious light of all the sky was underneath this globe, and birds grew silent, I began to settle, as my custom is, to take repose. Before mine eyes were fast closed, methought I saw a vision, at which my spirit was much troubled; and trembling at that doleful sight, a spirit cried aloud, 'Behold, my son, whom I have cherished, see the breasts that gave thee suck, the hands that lapped thee warm, and fed thee oft. Canst thou forget to take revenge of those wild people who have defaced my monument in a despiteful manner, disdaining our antiquities and honorable customs? See, now, the Sachem's grave lies like the common people, defaced by an ignoble race. Thy mother doth complain, and implores thy aid against this thievish people, who have newly intruded on our land. If this be suffered, I shall not rest quiet in my everlasting habitation.' This said, the spirit vanished, and I, all in a sweat, not able scarce to speak, began to get some strength, and recollect my spirits that were fled, and determined to demand your counsel and assistance."

I have adduced this anecdote at some length, as it tends to show how these sudden acts of hostility, which have been attributed to caprice and perfidy, may often arise from deep and generous

*Morton's *New English Canaan* (book 1, "Of a Vision and a Battle").

motives, which our inattention to Indian character and customs prevents our properly appreciating.

Another ground of violent outcry against the Indians is their barbarity to the vanquished. This had its origin partly in policy and partly in superstition. The tribes, though sometimes called nations, were never so formidable in their numbers, but that the loss of several warriors was sensibly felt; this was particularly the case when they had frequently been engaged in warfare; and many an instance occurs in Indian history, where a tribe, that had long been formidable to its neighbors, has been broken up and driven away, by the capture and massacre of its principal fighting men. There was a strong temptation, therefore, to the victor to be merciless; not so much to gratify any cruel revenge, as to provide for future security. The Indians had also the superstitious belief, frequent among barbarous nations, and prevalent also among the ancients, that the manes* of their friends who had fallen in battle were soothed by the blood of the captives. The prisoners, however, who are not thus sacrificed, are adopted into their families in the place of the slain, and are treated with the confidence and affection of relatives and friends; nay, so hospitable and tender is their entertainment, that when the alternative is offered them, they will often prefer to remain with their adopted brethren, rather than return to the home and the friends of their youth.

The cruelty of the Indians towards their prisoners has been heightened since the colonization of the whites. What was formerly a compliance with policy and superstition, has been exasperated into a gratification of vengeance. They cannot but be sensible that the white men are the usurpers of their ancient dominion, the cause of their degradation, and the gradual destroyers of their race. They go forth to battle, smarting with injuries and indignities which they have individually suffered, and they are driven to madness and despair by the wide-spreading desolation, and the overwhelming ruin of European warfare. The whites have too frequently set them an example of violence, by burning their villages, and laying waste their slender means of subsistence: and yet they wonder that savages do not show moderation and magnanimity towards those who have left them nothing but mere existence and wretchedness.

------

*Souls.

We stigmatize the Indians, also, as cowardly and treacherous, because they use stratagem in warfare, in preference to open force; but in this they are fully justified by their rude code of honor. They are early taught that stratagem is praiseworthy; the bravest warrior thinks it no disgrace to lurk in silence, and take every advantage of his foe: he triumphs in the superior craft and sagacity by which he has been enabled to surprise and destroy an enemy. Indeed, man is naturally more prone to subtilty than open valor, owing to his physical weakness in comparison with other animals. They are endowed with natural weapons of defence: with horns, with tusks, with hoofs, and talons; but man has to depend on his superior sagacity. In all his encounters with these, his proper enemies, he resorts to stratagem; and when he perversely turns his hostility against his fellow-man, he at first continues the same subtle mode of warfare.

The natural principle of war is to do the most harm to our enemy with the least harm to ourselves; and this of course is to be effected by stratagem. That chivalrous courage which induces us to despise the suggestions of prudence, and to rush in the face of certain danger, is the offspring of society, and produced by education. It is honorable, because it is in fact the triumph of lofty sentiment over an instinctive repugnance to pain, and over those yearnings after personal ease and security, which society has condemned as ignoble. It is kept alive by pride and the fear of shame; and thus the dread of real evil is overcome by the superior dread of an evil which exists but in the imagination. It has been cherished and stimulated also by various means. It has been the theme of spirit-stirring song and chivalrous story. The poet and minstrel have delighted to shed round it the splendors of fiction; and even the historian has forgotten the sober gravity of narration, and broken forth into enthusiasm and rhapsody in its praise. Triumphs and gorgeous pageants have been its reward: monuments, on which art has exhausted its skill, and opulence its treasures, have been erected to perpetuate a nation's gratitude and admiration. Thus artificially excited courage has risen to an extraordinary and factitious degree of heroism: and arrayed in all the glorious "pomp and circumstance of war,"* this turbulent

---

*See Shakespeare's *Othello, the Moor of Venice* (act 3, scene 3).

quality has even been able to eclipse many of those quiet, but invaluable virtues, which silently ennoble the human character, and swell the tide of human happiness.

But if courage intrinsically consists in the defiance of danger and pain, the life of the Indian is a continual exhibition of it. He lives in a state of perpetual hostility and risk. Peril and adventure are congenial to his nature; or rather seem necessary to arouse his faculties and to give an interest to his existence. Surrounded by hostile tribes, whose mode of warfare is by ambush and surprisal, he is always prepared for fight, and lives with his weapons in his hands. As the ship careers in fearful singleness through the solitudes of ocean;—as the bird mingles among clouds and storms, and wings its way, a mere speck, across the pathless fields of air;—so the Indian holds his course, silent, solitary, but undaunted, through the boundless bosom of the wilderness. His expeditions may vie in distance and danger with the pilgrimage of the devotee, or the crusade of the knight-errant. He traverses vast forests, exposed to the hazards of lonely sickness, of lurking enemies, and pining famine. Stormy lakes, those great inland seas, are no obstacles to his wanderings: in his light canoe of bark he sports, like a feather, on their waves, and darts, with the swiftness of an arrow, down the roaring rapids of the rivers. His very subsistence is snatched from the midst of toil and peril. He gains his food by the hardships and dangers of the chase: he wraps himself in the spoils of the bear, the panther, and the buffalo, and sleeps among the thunders of the cataract.

No hero of ancient or modern days can surpass the Indian in his lofty contempt of death, and the fortitude with which he sustains its cruellest infliction. Indeed we here behold him rising superior to the white man, in consequence of his peculiar education. The latter rushes to glorious death at the cannon's mouth; the former calmly contemplates its approach, and triumphantly endures it, amidst the varied torments of surrounding foes and the protracted agonies of fire. He even takes a pride in taunting his persecutors, and provoking their ingenuity of torture; and as the devouring flames prey on his very vitals, and the flesh shrinks from the sinews, he raises his last song of triumph, breathing the defiance of an unconquered heart, and invoking the spirits of his fathers to witness that he dies without a groan.

Notwithstanding the obloquy* with which the early historians have overshadowed the characters of the unfortunate natives, some bright gleams occasionally break through, which throw a degree of melancholy lustre on their memories. Facts are occasionally to be met with in the rude annals of the eastern provinces, which, though recorded with the coloring of prejudice and bigotry, yet speak for themselves; and will be dwelt on with applause and sympathy, when prejudice shall have passed away.

In one of the homely narratives of the Indian wars in New England,† there is a touching account of the desolation carried into the tribe of the Pequod Indians. Humanity shrinks from the cold-blooded detail of indiscriminate butchery. In one place we read of the surprisal of an Indian fort in the night, when the wigwams were wrapped in flames, and the miserable inhabitants shot down and slain in attempting to escape, "all being despatched and ended in the course of an hour." After a series of similar transactions, "our soldiers," as the historian piously observes, "being resolved by God's assistance to make a final destruction of them," the unhappy savages being hunted from their homes and fortresses, and pursued with fire and sword, a scanty, but gallant band, the sad remnant of the Pequod warriors, with their wives and children, took refuge in a swamp.

Burning with indignation, and rendered sullen by despair, with hearts bursting with grief at the destruction of their tribe, and spirits galled and sore at the fancied ignominy of their defeat, they refused to ask their lives at the hands of an insulting foe, and preferred death to submission.

As the night drew on they were surrounded in their dismal retreat, so as to render escape impracticable. Thus situated, their enemy "plied them with shot all the time, by which means many were killed and buried in the mire." In the darkness and fog that preceded the dawn of day some few broke through the besiegers and escaped into the woods: "the rest were left to the conquerors, of which many were killed in the swamp, like sullen dogs who would

---

*Abusive language.
†Reference to *A Narrative of the Troubles with the Indians in New England* (1677), by William Hubbard.

rather, in their self-willedness and madness, sit still and be shot through, or cut to pieces," than implore for mercy. When the day broke upon this handful of forlorn but dauntless spirits, the soldiers, we are told, entering the swamp, "saw several heaps of them sitting close together, upon whom they discharged their pieces, laden with ten or twelve pistol bullets at a time, putting the muzzles of the pieces under the boughs, within a few yards of them; so as, besides those that were found dead, many more were killed and sunk into the mire, and never were minded more by friend or foe."

Can any one read this plain unvarnished tale, without admiring the stern resolution, the unbending pride, the loftiness of spirit, that seemed to nerve the hearts of these self-taught heroes, and to raise them above the instinctive feelings of human nature? When the Gauls laid waste the city of Rome, they found the senators clothed in their robes, and seated with stern tranquillity in their curule chairs;* in this manner they suffered death without resistance or even supplication. Such conduct was, in them, applauded as noble and magnanimous; in the hapless Indian it was reviled as obstinate and sullen! How truly are we the dupes of show and circumstance! How different is virtue, clothed in purple and enthroned in state, from virtue, naked and destitute, and perishing obscurely in a wilderness!

But I forbear to dwell on these gloomy pictures. The eastern tribes have long since disappeared; the forests that sheltered them have been laid low, and scarce any traces remain of them in the thickly-settled states of New England, excepting here and there the Indian name of a village or a stream. And such must, sooner or later, be the fate of those other tribes which skirt the frontiers, and have occasionally been inveigled from their forests to mingle in the wars of white men. In a little while, and they will go the way that their brethren have gone before. The few hordes which still linger about the shores of Huron and Superior, and the tributary streams of the Mississippi, will share the fate of those tribes that once spread over Massachusetts and Connecticut, and lorded it along the proud banks of the Hudson; of that gigantic race said to have existed on the

---

*Backless chairs with curved legs, reserved for Roman civil magistrates.

borders of the Susquehanna; and of those various nations that flourished about the Potomac and the Rappahannock, and that peopled the forests of the vast valley of Shenandoah. They will vanish like a vapor from the face of the earth; their very history will be lost in forgetfulness; and "the places that now know them will know them no more for ever." Or if, perchance, some dubious memorial of them should survive, it may be in the romantic dreams of the poet, to people in imagination his glades and groves, like the fauns and satyrs and sylvan deities of antiquity. But should he venture upon the dark story of their wrongs and wretchedness; should he tell how they were invaded, corrupted, despoiled, driven from their native abodes and the sepulchres of their fathers, hunted like wild beasts about the earth, and sent down with violence and butchery to the grave, posterity will either turn with horror and incredulity from the tale, or blush with indignation at the inhumanity of their forefathers.—"We are driven back," said an old warrior,* "until we can retreat no farther—our hatchets are broken, our bows are snapped, our fires are nearly extinguished:—a little longer, and the white man will cease to persecute us—for we shall cease to exist!"

---

*These words are attributed to Tenskwatawa, the Shawnee shaman and brother of Chief Tecumseh.

Philip of Pokanoket[18]

AN INDIAN MEMOIR

As monumental bronze unchanged his look:
A soul that pity touch'd but never shook:
Train'd from his tree-rock'd cradle to his bier,
The fierce extremes of good and ill to brook
Impassive—fearing but the shame of fear—
A stoic of the woods—a man without a tear.

CAMPBELL*

It is to be regretted that those early writers, who treated of the discovery and settlement of America, have not given us more particular and candid accounts of the remarkable characters that flourished in savage life. The scanty anecdotes which have reached us are full of peculiarity and interest; they furnish us with nearer glimpses of human nature, and show what man is in a comparatively primitive state, and what he owes to civilization. There is something of the charm of discovery in lighting upon these wild and unexplored tracts of human nature; in witnessing, as it were, the native growth of moral sentiment, and perceiving those generous and romantic qualities which have been artificially cultivated by society, vegetating in spontaneous hardihood and rude magnificence.

In civilized life, where the happiness, and indeed almost the existence, of man depends so much upon the opinion of his fellow-men, he is constantly acting a studied part. The bold and peculiar traits of native character are refined away, or softened down by the levelling influence of what is termed good-breeding; and he practises so many petty deceptions, and affects so many generous sentiments, for

---

*From *Gertrude of Wyoming* (1809), by British poet Thomas Campbell (part 1, stanza 23, lines 4–9).

the purposes of popularity, that it is difficult to distinguish his real from his artificial character. The Indian, on the contrary, free from the restraints and refinements of polished life, and, in a great degree, a solitary and independent being, obeys the impulses of his inclination or the dictates of his judgment; and thus the attributes of his nature, being freely indulged, grow singly great and striking. Society is like a lawn, where every roughness is smoothed, every bramble eradicated, and where the eye is delighted by the smiling verdure of a velvet surface; he, however, who would study nature in its wildness and variety, must plunge into the forest, must explore the glen, must stem the torrent, and dare the precipice.

These reflections arose on casually looking through a volume of early colonial history, wherein are recorded, with great bitterness, the outrages of the Indians, and their wars with the settlers of New England. It is painful to perceive even from these partial narratives, how the footsteps of civilization may be traced in the blood of the aborigines; how easily the colonists were moved to hostility by the lust of conquest; how merciless and exterminating was their warfare. The imagination shrinks at the idea, how many intellectual beings were hunted from the earth, how many brave and noble hearts, of nature's sterling coinage, were broken down and trampled in the dust!

Such was the fate of PHILIP OF POKANOKET, an Indian warrior, whose name was once a terror throughout Massachusetts and Connecticut. He was the most distinguished of a number of contemporary Sachems who reigned over the Pequods, the Narragansets, the Wampanoags, and the other eastern tribes, at the time of the first settlement of New England; a band of native untaught heroes, who made the most generous struggle of which human nature is capable; fighting to the last gasp in the cause of their country, without a hope of victory or a thought of renown. Worthy of an age of poetry, and fit subjects for local story and romantic fiction, they have left scarcely any authentic traces on the page of history, but stalk, like gigantic shadows, in the dim twilight of tradition.*

---

*While correcting the proof sheets of this article, the author is informed that a celebrated English poet has nearly finished an heroic poem on the story of Philip of Pokanoket [Irving's note]. The poet Irving refers to is Robert Southey (1774–1843), English poet laureate, who in 1837 published "Oliver Newman, A New England Tale," which is set in the events surrounding King Philip's War.

When the pilgrims, as the Plymouth settlers are called by their descendants, first took refuge on the shores of the New World, from the religious persecutions of the Old, their situation was to the last degree gloomy and disheartening. Few in number, and that number rapidly perishing away through sickness and hardships; surrounded by a howling wilderness and savage tribes; exposed to the rigors of an almost arctic winter, and the vicissitudes of an ever-shifting climate; their minds were filled with doleful forebodings, and nothing preserved them from sinking into despondency but the strong excitement of religious enthusiasm. In this forlorn situation they were visited by Massasoit, chief Sagamore of the Wampanoags, a powerful chief, who reigned over a great extent of country. Instead of taking advantage of the scanty number of the strangers, and expelling them from his territories, into which they had intruded, he seemed at once to conceive for them a generous friendship, and extended towards them the rites of primitive hospitality. He came early in the spring to their settlement of New Plymouth, attended by a mere handful of followers, entered into a solemn league of peace and amity; sold them a portion of the soil, and promised to secure for them the good-will of his savage allies. Whatever may be said of Indian perfidy, it is certain that the integrity and good faith of Massasoit have never been impeached. He continued a firm and magnanimous friend of the white men; suffering them to extend their possessions, and to strengthen themselves in the land; and betraying no jealousy of their increasing power and prosperity. Shortly before his death he came once more to New Plymouth, with his son Alexander, for the purpose of renewing the covenant of peace, and of securing it to his posterity.

At this conference he endeavored to protect the religion of his forefathers from the encroaching zeal of the missionaries; and stipulated that no further attempt should be made to draw off his people from their ancient faith; but, finding the English obstinately opposed to any such condition, he mildly relinquished the demand. Almost the last act of his life was to bring his two sons, Alexander and Philip (as they had been named by the English), to the residence of a principal settler, recommending mutual kindness and confidence; and entreating that the same love and amity which had existed between the white men and himself might be continued afterwards with his children. The good old Sachem died in peace, and was happily gathered to his fathers before sorrow came upon his tribe; his children remained behind to experience the ingratitude of white men.

His eldest son, Alexander, succeeded him. He was of a quick and impetuous temper, and proudly tenacious of his hereditary rights and dignity. The intrusive policy and dictatorial conduct of the strangers excited his indignation; and he beheld with uneasiness their exterminating wars with the neighboring tribes. He was doomed soon to incur their hostility, being accused of plotting with the Narragansets to rise against the English and drive them from the land. It is impossible to say whether this accusation was warranted by facts or was grounded on mere suspicion. It is evident, however, by the violent and overbearing measures of the settlers, that they had by this time begun to feel conscious of the rapid increase of their power, and to grow harsh and inconsiderate in their treatment of the natives. They despatched an armed force to seize upon Alexander, and to bring him before their courts. He was traced to his woodland haunts, and surprised at a hunting house, where he was reposing with a band of his followers, unarmed, after the toils of the chase. The suddenness of his arrest, and the outrage offered to his sovereign dignity, so preyed upon the irascible feelings of this proud savage, as to throw him into a raging fever. He was permitted to return home, on condition of sending his son as a pledge for his reappearance; but the blow he had received was fatal, and before he had reached his home he fell a victim to the agonies of a wounded spirit.

The successor of Alexander was Metacomet, or King Philip, as he was called by the settlers, on account of his lofty spirit and ambitious temper. These, together with his well-known energy and enterprise, had rendered him an object of great jealousy and apprehension, and he was accused of having always cherished a secret and implacable hostility towards the whites. Such may very probably, and very naturally, have been the case. He considered them as originally but mere intruders into the country, who had presumed upon indulgence, and were extending an influence baneful to savage life. He saw the whole race of his countrymen melting before them from the face of the earth; their territories slipping from their hands, and their tribes becoming feeble, scattered and dependent. It may be said that the soil was originally purchased by the settlers; but who does not know the nature of Indian purchases, in the early periods of colonization? The Europeans always made thrifty bargains through their superior adroitness in traffic; and they gained vast accessions of territory by easily provoked hostilities. An uncultivated savage is never a nice inquirer into the refinements of law, by which an injury may be gradually and legally inflicted. Leading facts are all by which he judges; and it was enough for Philip to know that before the intrusion of the Europeans his countrymen were lords of the soil, and that now they were becoming vagabonds in the land of their fathers.

But whatever may have been his feelings of general hostility, and his particular indignation at the treatment of his brother, he suppressed them for the present, renewed the contract with the settlers, and resided peaceably for many years at Pokanoket, or, as it was called by the English, Mount Hope,* the ancient seat of dominion of his tribe. Suspicions, however, which were at first but vague and indefinite, began to acquire form and substance; and he was at length charged with attempting to instigate the various Eastern tribes to rise at once, and, by a simultaneous effort, to throw off the yoke of their oppressors. It is difficult at this distant period to assign the proper credit due to these early accusations against the Indians. There was a proneness to suspicion, and an aptness to acts of violence, on the part of the whites, that gave weight and importance to every idle tale. Informers abounded where talebearing met with countenance and reward; and the sword was readily unsheathed when its success was certain, and it carved out empire.

The only positive evidence on record against Philip is the accusation of one Sausaman, a renegado Indian, whose natural cunning had been quickened by a partial education which he had received among the settlers. He changed his faith and his allegiance two or three times, with a facility that evinced the looseness of his principles. He had acted for some time as Philip's confidential secretary and counsellor, and had enjoyed his bounty and protection. Finding, however, that the clouds of adversity were gathering round

*Now Bristol, Rhode Island [Irving's note].

his patron, he abandoned his service and went over to the whites; and, in order to gain their favor, charged his former benefactor with plotting against their safety. A rigorous investigation took place. Philip and several of his subjects submitted to be examined, but nothing was proved against them. The settlers, however, had now gone too far to retract; they had previously determined that Philip was a dangerous neighbor; they had publicly evinced their distrust; and had done enough to insure his hostility; according, therefore, to the usual mode of reasoning in these cases, his destruction had become necessary to their security. Sausaman, the treacherous informer, was shortly afterwards found dead, in a pond, having fallen a victim to the vengeance of his tribe. Three Indians, one of whom was a friend and counsellor of Philip, were apprehended and tried, and, on the testimony of one very questionable witness, were condemned and executed as murderers.

This treatment of his subjects, and ignominious punishment of his friend, outraged the pride and exasperated the passions of Philip. The bolt which had fallen thus at his very feet awakened him to the gathering storm, and he determined to trust himself no longer in the power of the white men. The fate of his insulted and broken-hearted brother still rankled in his mind; and he had a further warning in the tragical story of Miantonimo, a great Sachem of the Narragansets, who, after manfully facing his accusers before a tribunal of the colonists, exculpating himself from a charge of conspiracy, and receiving assurances of amity, had been perfidiously despatched at their instigation. Philip, therefore, gathered his fighting men about him; persuaded all strangers that he could, to join his cause; sent the women and children to the Narragansets for safety; and wherever he appeared, was continually surrounded by armed warriors.

When the two parties were thus in a state of distrust and irritation, the least spark was sufficient to set them in a flame. The Indians, having weapons in their hands, grew mischievous, and committed various petty depredations. In one of their maraudings a warrior was fired on and killed by a settler. This was the signal for open hostilities; the Indians pressed to revenge the death of their comrade, and the alarm of war resounded through the Plymouth colony.

In the early chronicles of these dark and melancholy times we meet with many indications of the diseased state of the public mind.

The gloom of religious abstraction, and the wildness of their situation, among trackless forests and savage tribes, had disposed the colonists to superstitious fancies, and had filled their imaginations with the frightful chimeras of witchcraft and spectrology. They were much given also to a belief in omens. The troubles with Philip and his Indians were preceded, we are told, by a variety of those awful warnings which forerun great and public calamities. The perfect form of an Indian bow appeared in the air at New Plymouth, which was looked upon by the inhabitants as a "prodigious apparition." At Hadley, Northampton, and other towns in their neighborhood, "was heard the report of a great piece of ordnance, with a shaking of the earth and a considerable echo."* Others were alarmed on a still, sunshiny morning, by the discharge of guns and muskets; bullets seemed to whistle past them, and the noise of drums resounded in the air, seeming to pass away to the westward; others fancied that they heard the galloping of horses over their heads; and certain monstrous births, which took place about the time, filled the superstitious in some towns with doleful forebodings. Many of these portentous sights and sounds may be ascribed to natural phenomena: to the northern lights which occur vividly in those latitudes; the meteors which explode in the air; the casual rushing of a blast through the top branches of the forest; the crash of fallen trees or disrupted rocks; and to those other uncouth sounds and echoes which will sometimes strike the ear so strangely amidst the profound stillness of woodland solitudes. These may have startled some melancholy imaginations, may have been exaggerated by the love of the marvellous, and listened to with that avidity with which we devour whatever is fearful and mysterious. The universal currency of these superstitious fancies, and the grave record made of them by one of the learned men of the day, are strongly characteristic of the times.

The nature of the contest that ensued was such as too often distinguishes the warfare between civilized men and savages. On the part of the whites it was conducted with superior skill and success;

---

*The Rev. Increase Mather's History [Irving's note]. This and subsequent passages are taken from *A Brief History of the War with the Indians* (1676), by American Puritan clergyman Increase Mather.

but with a wastefulness of the blood, and a disregard of the natural rights of their antagonists: on the part of the Indians it was waged with the desperation of men fearless of death, and who had nothing to expect from peace, but humiliation, dependence, and decay.

The events of the war are transmitted to us by a worthy clergyman of the time; who dwells with horror and indignation on every hostile act of the Indians, however justifiable, whilst he mentions with applause the most sanguinary atrocities of the whites. Philip is reviled as a murderer and a traitor; without considering that he was a true born prince, gallantly fighting at the head of his subjects to avenge the wrongs of his family; to retrieve the tottering power of his line; and to deliver his native land from the oppression of usurping strangers.

The project of a wide and simultaneous revolt, if such had really been formed, was worthy of a capacious mind, and, had it not been prematurely discovered, might have been overwhelming in its consequences. The war that actually broke out was but a war of detail, a mere succession of casual exploits and unconnected enterprises. Still it sets forth the military genius and daring prowess of Philip; and wherever, in the prejudiced and passionate narrations that have been given of it, we can arrive at simple facts, we find him displaying a vigorous mind, a fertility of expedients, a contempt of suffering and hardship, and an unconquerable resolution, that command our sympathy and applause.

Driven from his paternal domains at Mount Hope, he threw himself into the depths of those vast and trackless forests that skirted the settlements, and were almost impervious to anything but a wild beast, or an Indian. Here he gathered together his forces, like the storm accumulating its stores of mischief in the bosom of the thunder cloud, and would suddenly emerge at a time and place least expected, carrying havoc and dismay into the villages. There were now and then indications of these impending ravages, that filled the minds of the colonists with awe and apprehension. The report of a distant gun would perhaps be heard from the solitary woodland, where there was known to be no white man; the cattle which had been wandering in the woods would sometimes return home wounded; or an Indian or two would be seen lurking about the skirts of the forests, and suddenly disappearing; as the lightning will sometimes be seen playing silently about the edge of the cloud that is brewing up the tempest.

Though sometimes pursued and even surrounded by the settlers, yet Philip as often escaped almost miraculously from their toils, and, plunging into the wilderness, would be lost to all search or inquiry, until he again emerged at some far distant quarter, laying the country desolate. Among his strongholds, were the great swamps or morasses, which extend in some parts of New England; composed of loose bogs of deep black mud; perplexed with thickets, brambles, rank weeds, the shattered and mouldering trunks of fallen trees, overshadowed by lugubrious hemlocks. The uncertain footing and the tangled mazes of these shaggy wilds, rendered them almost impracticable to the white man, though the Indian could thrid their labyrinths with the agility of a deer. Into one of these, the great swamp of Pocasset Neck, was Philip once driven with a band of his followers. The English did not dare to pursue him, fearing to venture into these dark and frightful recesses, where they might perish in fens and miry pits, or be shot down by lurking foes. They therefore invested the entrance to the Neck, and began to build a fort, with the thought of starving out the foe; but Philip and his warriors wafted themselves on a raft over an arm of the sea, in the dead of the night, leaving the women and children behind; and escaped away to the westward, kindling the flames of war among the tribes of Massachusetts and the Nipmuck country, and threatening the colony of Connecticut.

In this way Philip became a theme of universal apprehension. The mystery in which he was enveloped exaggerated his real terrors. He was an evil that walked in darkness; whose coming none could foresee, and against which none knew when to be on the alert. The whole country abounded with rumors and alarms. Philip seemed almost possessed of ubiquity;* for, in whatever part of the widely-extended frontier an irruption from the forest took place, Philip was said to be its leader. Many superstitious notions also were circulated concerning him. He was said to deal in necromancy, and to be attended by an old Indian witch or prophetess, whom he consulted, and who assisted him by her charms and incantations. This indeed

---

*Omnipresence.

was frequently the case with Indian chiefs; either through their own credulity, or to act upon that of their followers: and the influence of the prophet and the dreamer over Indian superstition has been fully evidenced in recent instances of savage warfare.

At the time that Philip effected his escape from Pocasset, his fortunes were in a desperate condition. His forces had been thinned by repeated fights, and he had lost almost the whole of his resources. In this time of adversity he found a faithful friend in Canonchet, chief Sachem of all the Narragansets. He was the son and heir of Miantonimo, the great Sachem, who, as already mentioned, after an honorable acquittal of the charge of conspiracy, had been privately put to death at the perfidious instigations of the settlers. "He was the heir," says the old chronicler, "of all his father's pride and insolence, as well as of his malice towards the English;"—he certainly was the heir of his insults and injuries, and the legitimate avenger of his murder. Though he had forborne to take an active part in this hopeless war, yet he received Philip and his broken forces with open arms; and gave them the most generous countenance and support. This at once drew upon him the hostility of the English; and it was determined to strike a signal blow that should involve both the Sachems in one common ruin. A great force was, therefore, gathered together from Massachusetts, Plymouth, and Connecticut, and was sent into the Narraganset country in the depth of winter, when the swamps, being frozen and leafless, could be traversed with comparative facility, and would no longer afford dark and impenetrable fastnesses to the Indians.

Apprehensive of attack, Canonchet had conveyed the greater part of his stores, together with the old, the infirm, the women and children of his tribe, to a strong fortress; where he and Philip had likewise drawn up the flower of their forces. This fortress, deemed by the Indians impregnable, was situated upon a rising mound or kind of island, of five or six acres, in the midst of a swamp; it was constructed with a degree of judgment and skill vastly superior to what is usually displayed in Indian fortification, and indicative of the martial genius of these two chieftains.

Guided by a renegado Indian, the English penetrated, through December snows, to this stronghold, and came upon the garrison by surprise. The fight was fierce and tumultuous. The assailants were repulsed in their first attack, and several of their bravest officers were shot down in the act of storming the fortress sword in hand. The assault was renewed with greater success. A lodgment was effected. The Indians were driven from one post to another. They disputed their ground inch by inch, fighting with the fury of despair. Most of their veterans were cut to pieces; and after a long and bloody battle, Philip and Canonchet, with a handful of surviving warriors, retreated from the fort, and took refuge in the thickets of the surrounding forest.

The victors set fire to the wigwams and the fort; the whole was soon in a blaze; many of the old men, the women and the children perished in the flames. This last outrage overcame even the stoicism of the savage. The neighboring woods resounded with the yells of rage and despair, uttered by the fugitive warriors, as they beheld the destruction of their dwellings, and heard the agonizing cries of their wives and offspring. "The burning of the wigwams," says a contemporary writer, "the shrieks and cries of the women and children, and the yelling of the warriors, exhibited a most horrible and affecting scene, so that it greatly moved some of the soldiers." The same writer cautiously adds, "they were in *much doubt* then, and afterwards seriously inquired, whether burning their enemies alive could be consistent with humanity, and the benevolent principles of the Gospel."*

The fate of the brave and generous Canonchet is worthy of particular mention: the last scene of his life is one of the noblest instances on record of Indian magnanimity.

Broken down in his power and resources by this signal defeat, yet faithful to his ally, and to the hapless cause which he had espoused, he rejected all overtures of peace, offered on condition of betraying Philip and his followers, and declared that "he would fight it out to the last man, rather than become a servant to the English." His home being destroyed; his country harassed and laid waste by the incursions of the conquerors; he was obliged to wander away to the banks of the Connecticut; where he formed a rallying point to the whole body of western Indians, and laid waste several of the English settlements.

---

*MS. of the Rev. W. Ruggles [Irving's note]. Possibly the Rev. Thomas Ruggles, Jr., who wrote a history of Guilford, Connecticut, in 1763.

Early in the spring he departed on a hazardous expedition, with only thirty chosen men, to penetrate to Seaconck, in the vicinity of Mount Hope, and to procure seed corn to plant for the sustenance of his troops. This little band of adventurers had passed safely through the Pequod country, and were in the centre of the Narraganset, resting at some wigwams near Pawtucket River, when an alarm was given of an approaching enemy.—Having but seven men by him at the time, Canonchet despatched two of them to the top of a neighboring hill, to bring intelligence of the foe.

Panic-struck by the appearance of a troop of English and Indians rapidly advancing, they fled in breathless terror past their chieftain, without stopping to inform him of the danger. Canonchet sent another scout, who did the same. He then sent two more, one of whom, hurrying back in confusion and affright, told him that the whole British army was at hand. Canonchet saw there was no choice but immediate flight. He attempted to escape round the hill, but was perceived and hotly pursued by the hostile Indians and a few of the fleetest of the English. Finding the swiftest pursuer close upon his heels, he threw off, first his blanket, then his silver-laced coat and belt of peag,* by which his enemies knew him to be Canonchet, and redoubled the eagerness of pursuit.

At length, in dashing through the river, his foot slipped upon a stone, and he fell so deep as to wet his gun. This accident so struck him with despair, that, as he afterwards confessed, "his heart and his bowels turned within him, and he became like a rotten stick, void of strength."

To such a degree was he unnerved, that, being seized by a Pequod Indian within a short distance of the river, he made no resistance, though a man of great vigor of body and boldness of heart. But on being made prisoner the whole pride of his spirit arose within him; and from that moment, we find, in the anecdotes given by his enemies, nothing but repeated flashes of elevated and prince-like heroism. Being questioned by one of the English who first came up with him, and who had not attained his twenty-second year, the proud-hearted warrior, looking with lofty contempt upon his youthful countenance, replied, "You are a child—you cannot understand

---

*Shell beads used by some Native Americans as money.

matters of war—let your brother or your chief come—him will I answer."

Though repeated offers were made to him of his life, on condition of submitting with his nation to the English, yet he rejected them with disdain, and refused to send any proposals of the kind to the great body of his subjects; saying, that he knew none of them would comply. Being reproached with his breach of faith towards the whites; his boast that he would not deliver up a Wampanoag nor the paring of a Wampanoag's nail; and his threat that he would burn the English alive in their houses; he disdained to justify himself, haughtily answering that others were as forward for the war as himself, and "he desired to hear no more thereof."

So noble and unshaken a spirit, so true a fidelity to his cause and his friend, might have touched the feelings of the generous and the brave; but Canonchet was an Indian; a being towards whom war had no courtesy, humanity no law, religion no compassion—he was condemned to die. The last words of him that are recorded, are worthy the greatness of his soul. When sentence of death was passed upon him, he observed "that he liked it well, for he should die before his heart was soft, or he had spoken any thing unworthy of himself." His enemies gave him the death of a soldier, for he was shot at Stoningham, by three young Sachems of his own rank.

The defeat at the Narraganset fortress, and the death of Canonchet, were fatal blows to the fortunes of King Philip. He made an ineffectual attempt to raise a head of war, by stirring up the Mohawks to take arms; but though possessed of the native talents of a statesman, his arts were counteracted by the superior arts of his enlightened enemies, and the terror of their warlike skill began to subdue the resolution of the neighboring tribes. The unfortunate chieftain saw himself daily stripped of power, and his ranks rapidly thinning around him. Some were suborned by the whites; others fell victims to hunger and fatigue, and to the frequent attacks by which they were harassed. His stores were all captured; his chosen friends were swept away from before his eyes; his uncle was shot down by his side; his sister was carried into captivity; and in one of his narrow escapes he was compelled to leave his beloved wife and only son to the mercy of the enemy. "His ruin," says the historian, "being thus gradually carried on, his misery was not prevented, but augmented thereby; being himself made acquainted with the sense and experimental feeling of the captivity of his children, loss of friends, slaughter of his subjects, bereavement of all family relations, and being stripped of all outward comforts, before his own life should be taken away."

To fill up the measure of his misfortunes, his own followers began to plot against his life, that by sacrificing him they might purchase dishonorable safety. Through treachery a number of his faithful adherents, the subjects of Wetamoe, an Indian princess of Pocasset, a near kinswoman and confederate of Philip, were betrayed into the hands of the enemy. Wetamoe was among them at the time, and attempted to make her escape by crossing a neighboring river: either exhausted by swimming, or starved by cold and hunger, she was found dead and naked near the water side. But persecution ceased not at the grave. Even death, the refuge of the wretched, where the wicked commonly cease from troubling, was no protection to this outcast female, whose great crime was affectionate fidelity to her kinsman and her friend. Her corpse was the object of unmanly and dastardly vengeance; the head was severed from the body and set upon a pole, and was thus exposed at Taunton, to the view of her captive subjects. They immediately recognized the features of their unfortunate queen, and were so affected at this barbarous spectacle, that we are told they broke forth into the "most horrible and diabolical lamentations."

However Philip had borne up against the complicated miseries and misfortunes that surrounded him, the treachery of his followers seemed to wring his heart and reduce him to despondency. It is said that "he never rejoiced afterwards, nor had success in any of his designs." The spring of hope was broken—the ardor of enterprise was extinguished—he looked around, and all was danger and darkness; there was no eye to pity, nor any arm that could bring deliverance. With a scanty band of followers, who still remained true to his desperate fortunes, the unhappy Philip wandered back to the vicinity of Mount Hope, the ancient dwelling of his fathers. Here he lurked about, like a spectre, among the scenes of former power and prosperity, now bereft of home, of family and friend. There needs no better picture of his destitute and piteous situation, than that furnished by the homely pen of the chronicler, who is unwarily enlisting the feelings of the reader in favor of the hapless warrior whom he reviles. "Philip," he says, "like a savage wild beast, having been hunted by the English forces through the woods, above a hundred miles backward and forward, at last was driven to his own den upon Mount Hope, where he retired, with a few of his best friends, into a swamp, which proved but a prison to keep him fast till the messengers of death came by divine permission to execute vengeance upon him."

Even in this last refuge of desperation and despair, a sullen grandeur gathers round his memory. We picture him to ourselves seated among his care-worn followers, brooding in silence over his blasted fortunes, and acquiring a savage sublimity from the wildness and dreariness of his lurking-place. Defeated, but not dismayed— crushed to the earth, but not humiliated—he seemed to grow more haughty beneath disaster, and to experience a fierce satisfaction in draining the last dregs of bitterness. Little minds are tamed and sub- dued by misfortune; but great minds rise above it. The very idea of submission awakened the fury of Philip, and he smote to death one of his followers, who proposed an expedient of peace. The brother of the victim made his escape, and in revenge betrayed the retreat of his chieftain. A body of white men and Indians were immediately despatched to the swamp where Philip lay crouched, glaring with fury and despair. Before he was aware of their approach, they had begun to surround him. In a little while he saw five of his trustiest followers laid dead at his feet; all resistance was vain; he rushed forth from his covert, and made a headlong attempt to escape, but was shot through the heart by a renegado Indian of his own nation.

Such is the scanty story of the brave, but unfortunate King Philip; persecuted while living, slandered and dishonored when dead. If, however, we consider even the prejudiced anecdotes furnished us by his enemies, we may perceive in them traces of amiable and lofty character sufficient to awaken sympathy for his fate, and respect for his memory. We find that, amidst all the harassing cares and fero- cious passions of constant warfare, he was alive to the softer feelings of connubial love and paternal tenderness, and to the generous sentiment of friendship. The captivity of his "beloved wife and only son" are mentioned with exultation as causing him poignant misery: the death of any near friend is triumphantly recorded as a new blow on his sensibilities; but the treachery and desertion of many of his followers, in whose affections he had confided, is said to have desolated his heart, and to have bereaved him of all further comfort. He was a patriot attached to his native soil—a prince true to his subjects, and indignant of their wrongs—a soldier, daring in battle, firm in adversity, patient of fatigue, of hunger, of every variety of bodily suffering, and ready to perish in the cause he had espoused. Proud of heart, and with an untamable love of natural liberty, he preferred to enjoy it among the beasts of the forests or in the dismal and famished recesses of swamps and morasses, rather than bow his haughty spirit to submission, and live dependent and despised in the ease and luxury of the settlements. With heroic qualities and bold achievements that would have graced a civilized warrior, and have rendered him the theme of the poet and the historian; he lived a wanderer and a fugitive in his native land, and went down, like a lonely bark foundering amid darkness and tempest—without a pitying eye to weep his fall, or a friendly hand to record his struggle.

The Legend of Sleepy Hollow[19]

FOUND AMONG THE PAPERS OF THE LATE
DIEDRICH KNICKERBOCKER*

> A pleasing land of drowsy head it was,
>   Of dreams that wave before the half-shut eye;
> And of gay castles in the clouds that pass,
>   For ever flushing round a summer sky.

CASTLE OF INDOLENCE[†]

In the bosom of one of those spacious coves which indent the eastern shore of the Hudson, at that broad expansion of the river denominated by the ancient Dutch navigators the Tappan Zee, and where they always prudently shortened sail, and implored the protection of St. Nicholas[‡] when they crossed, there lies a small market-town or rural port, which by some is called Greensburgh, but which is more generally and properly known by the name of Tarry Town. This name was given, we are told, in former days, by the good housewives of the adjacent country, from the inveterate propensity of their husbands to linger about the village tavern on market days. Be that as it may, I do not vouch for the fact, but merely advert to it, for the sake of being precise and authentic. Not far from this village, perhaps about two miles, there is a little valley, or rather lap of land, among high hills, which is one of the quietest places in the whole world. A small brook glides through it, with just murmur enough to lull one to repose; and the occasional whistle of a quail, or tapping of a woodpecker, is almost the only sound that ever breaks in upon the uniform tranquillity.

---

*See the discussion that begins on page xxiii of the Introduction.
[†]From *The Castle of Indolence* (1748), by Scottish poet and dramatist James Thomson (canto 1, stanza 6, lines 1–4).
[‡]Patron saint of travelers and sailors and of all those in distress.

I recollect that, when a stripling, my first exploit in squirrel-shooting was in a grove of tall walnut-trees that shades one side of the valley. I had wandered into it at noon time, when all nature is peculiarly quiet, and was startled by the roar of my own gun, as it broke the Sabbath stillness around, and was prolonged and reverberated by the angry echoes. If ever I should wish for a retreat, whither I might steal from the world and its distractions, and dream quietly away the remnant of a troubled life, I know of none more promising than this little valley.

From the listless repose of the place, and the peculiar character of its inhabitants, who are descendants from the original Dutch settlers, this sequestered glen has long been known by the name of SLEEPY HOLLOW, and its rustic lads are called the Sleepy Hollow Boys throughout all the neighboring country. A drowsy, dreamy influence seems to hang over the land, and to pervade the very atmosphere. Some say that the place was bewitched by a high German doctor, during the early days of the settlement; others, that an old Indian chief, the prophet or wizard of his tribe, held his powwows there before the country was discovered by Master Hendrick Hudson.* Certain it is, the place still continues under the sway of some witching power, that holds a spell over the minds of the good people, causing them to walk in a continual reverie. They are given to all kinds of marvellous beliefs; are subject to trances and visions; and frequently see strange sights, and hear music and voices in the air. The whole neighborhood abounds with local tales, haunted spots, and twilight superstitions; stars shoot and meteors glare oftener across the valley than in any other part of the country, and the nightmare, with her whole nine fold,† seems to make it the favorite scene of her gambols.

The dominant spirit, however, that haunts this enchanted region, and seems to be commander-in-chief of all the powers of the air, is the apparition of a figure on horseback without a head. It is said by some to be the ghost of a Hessian trooper,‡ whose head had been carried away by a cannon-ball, in some nameless battle during the

---

*See endnote 9 to *The Sketch-Book*.
†Allusion to Shakespeare's *King Lear* (act 3, scene 4).
‡German mercenary soldier who fought on the side of the British in the American Revolution.

revolutionary war; and who is ever and anon seen by the country folk, hurrying along in the gloom of night, as if on the wings of the wind. His haunts are not confined to the valley, but extend at times to the adjacent roads, and especially to the vicinity of a church at no great distance. Indeed, certain of the most authentic historians of those parts, who have been careful in collecting and collating the floating facts concerning this spectre, allege that the body of the trooper having been buried in the church-yard, the ghost rides forth to the scene of battle in nightly quest of his head; and that the rushing speed with which he sometimes passes along the Hollow, like a midnight blast, is owing to his being belated, and in a hurry to get back to the church-yard before daybreak.

Such is the general purport of this legendary superstition, which has furnished materials for many a wild story in that region of shadows; and the spectre is known, at all the country firesides, by the name of the Headless Horseman of Sleepy Hollow.

It is remarkable that the visionary propensity I have mentioned is not confined to the native inhabitants of the valley, but is unconsciously imbibed by every one who resides there for a time. However wide awake they may have been before they entered that sleepy region, they are sure, in a little time, to inhale the witching influence of the air, and begin to grow imaginative—to dream dreams, and see apparitions.

I mention this peaceful spot with all possible laud; for it is in such little retired Dutch valleys, found here and there embosomed in the great State of New-York, that population, manners, and customs, remain fixed; while the great torrent of migration and improvement, which is making such incessant changes in other parts of this restless country, sweeps by them unobserved. They are like those little nooks of still water which border a rapid stream; where we may see the straw and bubble riding quietly at anchor, or slowly revolving in their mimic harbor, undisturbed by the rush of the passing current. Though many years have elapsed since I trod the drowsy shades of Sleepy Hollow, yet I question whether I should not still find the same trees and the same families vegetating in its sheltered bosom.

In this by-place of nature, there abode, in a remote period of American history, that is to say, some thirty years since, a worthy wight of the name of Ichabod Crane; who sojourned, or, as he expressed it, "tarried," in Sleepy Hollow, for the purpose of instructing the children of the vicinity. He was a native of Connecticut; a State which supplies the Union with pioneers for the mind as well as for the forest, and sends forth yearly its legions of frontier woodsmen and country schoolmasters. The cognomen of Crane was not inapplicable to his person. He was tall, but exceedingly lank, with narrow shoulders, long arms and legs, hands that dangled a mile out of his sleeves, feet that might have served for shovels, and his whole frame most loosely hung together. His head was small, and flat at top, with huge ears, large green glassy eyes, and a long snipe nose,* so that it looked like a weather-cock, perched upon his spindle neck, to tell which way the wind blew. To see him striding along the profile of a hill on a windy day, with his clothes bagging and fluttering about him, one might have mistaken him for the genius† of famine descending upon the earth, or some scarecrow eloped from a cornfield.

His school-house was a low building of one large room, rudely constructed of logs; the windows partly glazed, and partly patched with leaves of old copy-books. It was most ingeniously secured at vacant hours, by a withe‡ twisted in the handle of the door, and stakes set against the window shutters; so that, though a thief might get in with perfect ease, he would find some embarrassment in getting out; an idea most probably borrowed by the architect, Yost Van Houten, from the mystery of an eel-pot. The school-house stood in a rather lonely but pleasant situation, just at the foot of a woody hill, with a brook running close by, and a formidable birch tree growing at one end of it. From hence the low murmur of his pupils' voices, conning§ over their lessons, might be heard in a drowsy summer's day, like the hum of a beehive; interrupted now and then by the authoritative voice of the master, in the tone of menace or command; or, peradventure, by the appalling sound of the birch, as he urged some tardy loiterer along the flowery path of knowledge. Truth to say, he was a

---

*Long, thin, and hooked, like the bills of certain shorebirds known as snipe.
†Embodiment.
‡Slender, flexible twig.
§Studying.

conscientious man, and ever bore in mind the golden maxim, "Spare the rod and spoil the child."*—Ichabod Crane's scholars certainly were not spoiled.

I would not have it imagined, however, that he was one of those cruel potentates of the school, who joy in the smart of their subjects; on the contrary, he administered justice with discrimination rather than severity; taking the burthen off the backs of the weak, and laying it on those of the strong. Your mere puny stripling, that winced at the least flourish of the rod, was passed by with indulgence; but the claims of justice were satisfied by inflicting a double portion on some little, tough, wrong-headed, broad-skirted Dutch urchin, who sulked and swelled and grew dogged and sullen beneath the birch. All this he called "doing his duty by their parents;" and he never inflicted a chastisement without following it by the assurance, so consolatory to the smarting urchin, that "he would remember it, and thank him for it the longest day he had to live."

When school hours were over, he was even the companion and playmate of the larger boys; and on holiday afternoons would convoy some of the smaller ones home, who happened to have pretty sisters, or good housewives for mothers, noted for the comforts of the cupboard. Indeed it behooved him to keep on good terms with his pupils. The revenue arising from his school was small, and would have been scarcely sufficient to furnish him with daily bread, for he was a huge feeder, and though lank, had the dilating powers of an anaconda; but to help out his maintenance, he was, according to country custom in those parts, boarded and lodged at the houses of the farmers, whose children he instructed. With these he lived successively a week at a time; thus going the rounds of the neighborhood, with all his worldly effects tied up in a cotton handkerchief.

That all this might not be too onerous on the purses of his rustic patrons, who are apt to consider the costs of schooling a grievous burden, and schoolmasters as mere drones, he had various ways of rendering himself both useful and agreeable. He assisted the farmers occasionally in the lighter labors of their farms; helped to make hay; mended the fences; took the horses to water; drove the cows from

---

*See the Bible, Proverbs 13:24: "He that spareth his rod hateth his son: but he that loveth him chasteneth him betimes" (King James Version).

pasture; and cut wood for the winter fire. He laid aside, too, all the dominant dignity and absolute sway with which he lorded it in his little empire, the school, and became wonderfully gentle and ingratiating. He found favor in the eyes of the mothers, by petting the children, particularly the youngest; and like the lion bold, which whilom so magnanimously the lamb did hold,* he would sit with a child on one knee, and rock a cradle with his foot for whole hours together.

In addition to his other vocations, he was the singing-master of the neighborhood, and picked up many bright shillings by instructing the young folks in psalmody. It was a matter of no little vanity to him, on Sundays, to take his station in front of the church gallery, with a band of chosen singers; where, in his own mind, he completely carried away the palm from the parson. Certain it is, his voice resounded far above all the rest of the congregation; and there are peculiar quavers still to be heard in that church, and which may even be heard half a mile off, quite to the opposite side of the mill-pond, on a still Sunday morning, which are said to be legitimately descended from the nose of Ichabod Crane. Thus, by divers little make-shifts in that ingenious way which is commonly denominated "by hook and by crook," the worthy pedagogue got on tolerably enough, and was thought, by all who understood nothing of the labor of headwork, to have a wonderfully easy life of it.

The schoolmaster is generally a man of some importance in the female circle of a rural neighborhood; being considered a kind of idle gentlemanlike personage, of vastly superior taste and accomplishments to the rough country swains, and, indeed, inferior in learning only to the parson. His appearance, therefore, is apt to occasion some little stir at the tea-table of a farmhouse, and the addition of a supernumerary dish of cakes or sweetmeats, or, peradventure, the parade of a silver tea-pot. Our man of letters, therefore, was peculiarly happy in the smiles of all the country damsels. How he would figure among them in the church-yard, between services on Sundays! gathering grapes for them from the wild vines that overrun the surrounding trees; reciting for their amusement all the

---

*This phrase comes from the illustration of the letter L in the *New England Primer* (c.1683), a spelling book.

epitaphs on the tombstones or sauntering, with a whole bevy of them, along the banks of the adjacent mill-pond; while the more bashful country bumpkins hung sheepishly back, envying his superior elegance and address.

From his half itinerant life, also, he was a kind of travelling gazette, carrying the whole budget of local gossip from house to house; so that his appearance was always greeted with satisfaction. He was, moreover, esteemed by the women as a man of great erudition, for he had read several books quite through, and was a perfect master of Cotton Mather's history of New England Witchcraft,* in which, by the way, he most firmly and potently believed.

He was, in fact, an odd mixture of small shrewdness and simple credulity. His appetite for the marvellous, and his powers of digesting it, were equally extraordinary; and both had been increased by his residence in this spellbound region. No tale was too gross or monstrous for his capacious swallow. It was often his delight, after his school was dismissed in the afternoon, to stretch himself on the rich bed of clover, bordering the little brook that whimpered by his school-house, and there con over old Mather's direful tales, until the gathering dusk of the evening made the printed page a mere mist before his eyes. Then, as he wended his way, by swamp and stream and awful woodland, to the farmhouse where he happened to be quartered, every sound of nature, at that witching hour, fluttered his excited imagination: the moan of the whip-poor-will† from the hillside; the boding cry of the tree-toad, that harbinger of storm; the dreary hooting of the screech-owl, or the sudden rustling in the thicket of birds frightened from their roost. The fire-flies, too, which sparkled most vividly in the darkest places, now and then startled him, as one of uncommon brightness would stream across his path; and if, by chance, a huge blockhead of a beetle came winging his blundering flight against him, the poor varlet was ready to give up

---

*Puritan clergyman Cotton Mather (1663–1728), the son of Increase Mather (see footnote on p. 152), participated in the Salem witch trials and wrote a number of works concerning witchcraft, including *Memorable Providences, Relating to Witchcrafts and Possessions* (1689) and *The Wonders of the Invisible World* (1693).

†The whip-poor-will is a bird which is only heard at night. It receives its name from its note, which is thought to resemble those words [Irving's note].

the ghost, with the idea that he was struck with a witch's token. His only resource on such occasions, either to drown thought, or drive away evil spirits, was to sing psalm tunes;—and the good people of Sleepy Hollow, as they sat by their doors of an evening, were often filled with awe, at hearing his nasal melody, "in linked sweetness long drawn out,"* floating from the distant hill, or along the dusky road.

Another of his sources of fearful pleasure was, to pass long winter evenings with the old Dutch wives, as they sat spinning by the fire, with a row of apples roasting and spluttering along the hearth, and listen to their marvellous tales of ghosts and goblins, and haunted fields, and haunted brooks, and haunted bridges, and haunted houses, and particularly of the headless horseman, or galloping Hessian of the Hollow, as they sometimes called him. He would delight them equally by his anecdotes of witchcraft, and of the direful omens and portentous sights and sounds in the air, which prevailed, in the earlier times of Connecticut; and would frighten them wofully with speculations upon comets and shooting stars; and with the alarming fact that the world did absolutely turn round, and that they were half the time topsy-turvy!

But if there was a pleasure in all this, while snugly cuddling in the chimney corner of a chamber that was all of a ruddy glow from the crackling wood fire, and where, of course, no spectre dared to show his face, it was dearly purchased by the terrors of his subsequent walk homewards. What fearful shapes and shadows beset his path amidst the dim and ghastly glare of a snowy night!—With what wistful look did he eye every trembling ray of light streaming across the waste fields from some distant window!—How often was he appalled by some shrub covered with snow, which, like a sheeted spectre, beset his very path!—How often did he shrink with curdling awe at the sound of his own steps on the frosty crust beneath his feet; and dread to look over his shoulder, lest he should behold some uncouth being tramping close behind him!—and how often was he thrown into complete dismay by some rushing blast, howling among the trees, in the idea that it was the Galloping Hessian on one of his nightly scourings!

---

*From "L' Allegro" (1631), by English poet John Milton (line 140).

All these, however, were mere terrors of the night, phantoms of the mind that walk in darkness; and though he had seen many spectres in his time, and been more than once beset by Satan in divers shapes, in his lonely perambulations, yet daylight put an end to all these evils; and he would have passed a pleasant life of it, in despite of the devil and all his works, if his path had not been crossed by a being that causes more perplexity to mortal man than ghosts, goblins, and the whole race of witches put together, and that was— a woman.

Among the musical disciples who assembled, one evening in each week, to receive his instructions in psalmody, was Katrina Van Tassel, the daughter and only child of a substantial Dutch farmer. She was a blooming lass of fresh eighteen; plump as a partridge; ripe and melting and rosy cheeked as one of her father's peaches, and universally famed, not merely for her beauty, but her vast expectations. She was withal a little of a coquette, as might be perceived even in her dress, which was a mixture of ancient and modern fashions, as most suited to set off her charms. She wore the ornaments of pure yellow gold, which her great-great-grandmother had brought over from Saardam; the tempting stomacher of the olden time; and withal a provokingly short petticoat, to display the prettiest foot and ankle in the country round.

Ichabod Crane had a soft and foolish heart towards the sex; and it is not to be wondered at, that so tempting a morsel soon found favor in his eyes; more especially after he had visited her in her paternal mansion. Old Baltus Van Tassel was a perfect picture of a thriving, contented, liberal-hearted farmer. He seldom, it is true, sent either his eyes or his thoughts beyond the boundaries of his own farm; but within those every thing was snug, happy, and well-conditioned. He was satisfied with his wealth, but not proud of it; and piqued himself upon the hearty abundance, rather than the style in which he lived. His stronghold was situated on the banks of the Hudson, in one of those green, sheltered, fertile nooks, in which the Dutch farmers are so fond of nestling. A great elm-tree spread its broad branches over it; at the foot of which bubbled up a spring of the softest and sweetest water, in a little well, formed of a barrel; and then stole sparkling away through the grass, to a neighboring brook, that bubbled along among alders and dwarf willows. Hard by the farmhouse was a vast barn, that might have served for a church; every window and crevice of which seemed bursting forth with the treasures of the farm; the flail was busily resounding within it from morning to night; swallows and martins skimmed twittering about the eaves; and rows of pigeons, some with one eye turned up, as if watching the weather, some with their heads under their wings, or buried in their bosoms, and others swelling, and cooing, and bowing about their dames, were enjoying the sunshine on the roof. Sleek unwieldy porkers were grunting in the repose and abundance of their pens; whence sallied forth, now and then, troops of sucking pigs, as if to snuff the air. A stately squadron of snowy geese were riding in an adjoining pond, convoying whole fleets of ducks; regiments of turkeys were gobbling through the farmyard, and guinea fowls fretting about it, like ill-tempered housewives, with their peevish discontented cry. Before the barn door strutted the gallant cock, that pattern of a husband, a warrior, and a fine gentleman, clapping his burnished wings, and crowing in the pride and gladness of his heart—sometimes tearing up the earth with his feet, and then generously calling his ever-hungry family of wives and children to enjoy the rich morsel which he had discovered.

The pedagogue's mouth watered, as he looked upon this sumptuous promise of luxurious winter fare. In his devouring mind's eye, he pictured to himself every roasting-pig running about with a pudding in his belly, and an apple in his mouth; the pigeons were snugly put to bed in a comfortable pie, and tucked in with a coverlet of crust; the geese were swimming in their own gravy; and the ducks pairing cosily in dishes, like snug married couples, with a decent competency of onion sauce. In the porkers he saw carved out the future sleek side of bacon, and juicy relishing ham; not a turkey but he beheld daintily trussed up, with its gizzard under its wing, and, peradventure, a necklace of savory sausages; and even bright chanticleer himself lay sprawling on his back, in a side-dish, with uplifted claws, as if craving that quarter which his chivalrous spirit disdained to ask while living.

As the enraptured Ichabod fancied all this, and as he rolled his great green eyes over the fat meadow-lands, the rich fields of wheat, of rye, of buckwheat, and Indian corn, and the orchards burthened with ruddy fruit, which surrounded the warm tenement of Van Tassel, his heart yearned after the damsel who was to inherit these domains, and his imagination expanded with the idea, how they might be readily turned into cash, and the money invested in immense tracts of wild land, and shingle palaces in the wilderness. Nay, his busy fancy already realized his hopes, and presented to him the blooming Katrina, with a whole family of children, mounted on the top of a wagon loaded with household trumpery, with pots and kettles dangling beneath; and he beheld himself bestriding a pacing mare, with a colt at her heels, setting out for Kentucky, Tennessee, or the Lord knows where.

When he entered the house the conquest of his heart was complete. It was one of those spacious farmhouses, with high-ridged, but lowly-sloping roofs, built in the style handed down from the first Dutch settlers; the low projecting eaves forming a piazza along the front, capable of being closed up in bad weather. Under this were hung flails, harness, various utensils of husbandry, and nets for fishing in the neighboring river. Benches were built along the sides for summer use; and a great spinning-wheel at one end, and a churn at the other, showed the various uses to which this important porch might be devoted. From this piazza the wondering Ichabod entered the hall, which formed the centre of the mansion and the place of usual residence. Here, rows of resplendent pewter, ranged on a long dresser, dazzled his eyes. In one corner stood a huge bag of wool ready to be spun; in another a quantity of linsey-woolsey just from the loom; ears of Indian corn, and strings of dried apples and peaches, hung in gay festoons along the walls, mingled with the gaud of red peppers; and a door left ajar gave him a peep into the best parlor, where the claw-footed chairs, and dark mahogany tables, shone like mirrors; and irons, with their accompanying shovel and tongs, glistened from their covert of asparagus tops; mock-oranges and conch-shells decorated the mantelpiece; strings of various colored birds' eggs were suspended above it: a great ostrich egg was hung from the centre of the room, and a corner cupboard, knowingly left open, displayed immense treasures of old silver and well-mended china.

From the moment Ichabod laid his eyes upon these regions of delight, the peace of his mind was at an end, and his only study was how to gain the affections of the peerless daughter of Van Tassel.

In this enterprise, however, he had more real difficulties than generally fell to the lot of a knight-errant of yore, who seldom had any thing but giants, enchanters, fiery dragons, and such like easily-conquered adversaries, to contend with; and had to make his way merely through gates of iron and brass, and walls of adamant, to the castle keep, where the lady of his heart was confined; all which he achieved as easily as a man would carve his way to the centre of a Christmas pie; and then the lady gave him her hand as a matter of course. Ichabod, on the contrary, had to win his way to the heart of a country coquette, beset with a labyrinth of whims and caprices, which were for ever presenting new difficulties and impediments; and he had to encounter a host of fearful adversaries of real flesh and blood, the numerous rustic admirers, who beset every portal to her heart; keeping a watchful and angry eye upon each other, but ready to fly out in the common cause against any new competitor.

Among these the most formidable was a burly, roaring, roystering blade, of the name of Abraham, or, according to the Dutch abbreviation, Brom Van Brunt, the hero of the country round, which rang with his feats of strength and hardihood. He was broad-shouldered and double-jointed, with short curly black hair, and a bluff, but not unpleasant countenance, having a mingled air of fun and arrogance. From his Herculean frame and great powers of limb, he had received the nickname of BROM BONES, by which he was universally known. He was famed for great knowledge and skill in horsemanship, being as dexterous on horseback as a Tartar. He was foremost at all races and cock-fights; and, with the ascendency which bodily strength acquires in rustic life, was the umpire in all disputes, setting his hat on one side, and giving his decisions with an air and tone admitting of no gainsay or appeal. He was always ready for either a fight or a frolic; but had more mischief than ill-will in his composition; and, with all his overbearing roughness, there was a strong dash of waggish good humor at bottom. He had three or four boon companions, who regarded him as their model, and at the head of whom he scoured the country, attending every scene of feud or merriment for miles round. In cold weather he was distinguished by a fur cap, surmounted with a flaunting fox's tail; and when the folks at a country gathering descried this well-known crest at a distance, whisking about among a squad of hard riders, they always stood by for a squall. Sometimes his crew would be heard dashing along past the farmhouses at midnight, with whoop and halloo, like a troop of Don Cossacks; and the old dames, startled out of their sleep, would listen for a moment till the hurry-scurry had clattered by, and then exclaim, "Ay, there goes Brom Bones and his gang!" The neighbors looked upon him with a mixture of awe, admiration, and good will; and when any madcap prank, or rustic brawl, occurred in the vicinity, always shook their heads, and warranted Brom Bones was at the bottom of it.

This rantipole* hero had for some time singled out the blooming Katrina for the object of his uncouth gallantries, and though his amorous toyings were something like the gentle caresses and endearments of a bear, yet it was whispered that she did not altogether discourage his hopes. Certain it is, his advances were signals for rival candidates to retire, who felt no inclination to cross a lion in his amours; insomuch, that when his horse was seen tied to Van Tassel's paling, on a Sunday night, a sure sign that his master was courting, or, as it is termed, "sparking," within, all other suitors passed by in despair, and carried the war into other quarters.

Such was the formidable rival with whom Ichabod Crane had to contend, and, considering all things, a stouter man than he would have shrunk from the competition, and a wiser man would have despaired. He had, however, a happy mixture of pliability and perseverance in his nature; he was in form and spirit like a supple-jack†—yielding, but tough; though he bent, he never broke; and though he bowed beneath the slightest pressure, yet, the moment it was away—jerk! he was as erect, and carried his head as high as ever.

To have taken the field openly against his rival would have been madness; for he was not a man to be thwarted in his amours, any more than that stormy lover, Achilles.‡ Ichabod, therefore, made his advances in a quiet and gently-insinuating manner. Under cover of his character of singing-master, he made frequent visits at the farmhouse; not that he had any thing to apprehend from the

---

*Boisterous, merrymaking.
†Strong, flexible climbing shrub used to make walking sticks.
‡Greek hero of the *Iliad* who fought with Agamemnon over who would claim the captured girl Briseis.

meddlesome interference of parents, which is so often a stumbling-block in the path of lovers. Balt Van Tassel was an easy indulgent soul; he loved his daughter better even than his pipe, and, like a reasonable man and an excellent father, let her have her way in every thing. His notable little wife, too, had enough to do to attend to her housekeeping and manage her poultry; for, as she sagely observed, ducks and geese are foolish things, and must be looked after, but girls can take care of themselves. Thus while the busy dame bustled about the house, or plied her spinning-wheel at one end of the piazza, honest Balt would sit smoking his evening pipe at the other, watching the achievements of a little wooden warrior, who, armed with a sword in each hand, was most valiantly fighting the wind on the pinnacle of the barn. In the mean time, Ichabod would carry on his suit with the daughter by the side of the spring under the great elm, or sauntering along in the twilight, that hour so favorable to the lover's eloquence.

I profess not to know how women's hearts are wooed and won. To me they have always been matters of riddle and admiration. Some seem to have but one vulnerable point, or door of access; while others have a thousand avenues, and may be captured in a thousand different ways. It is a great triumph of skill to gain the former, but a still greater proof of generalship to maintain posses-sion of the latter, for the man must battle for his fortress at every door and window. He who wins a thousand common hearts is there-fore entitled to some renown; but he who keeps undisputed sway over the heart of a coquette, is indeed a hero. Certain it is, this was not the case with the redoubtable Brom Bones; and from the mo-ment Ichabod Crane made his advances, the interests of the former evidently declined; his horse was no longer seen tied at the palings on Sunday nights, and a deadly feud gradually arose between him and the preceptor of Sleepy Hollow.

Brom, who had a degree of rough chivalry in his nature, would fain have carried matters to open warfare, and have settled their pretensions to the lady, according to the mode of those most concise and simple reasoners, the knights-errant of yore—by single combat; but Ichabod was too conscious of the superior might of his adver-sary to enter the lists against him: he had overheard a boast of Bones, that he would "double the schoolmaster up, and lay him on a shelf of his own school-house;" and he was too wary to give him an opportunity. There was something extremely provoking in this obstinately pacific system; it left Brom no alternative but to draw upon the funds of rustic waggery in his disposition, and to play off boorish practical jokes upon his rival. Ichabod became the object of whimsical persecution to Bones, and his gang of rough riders. They harried his hitherto peaceful domains; smoked out his singing school, by stopping up the chimney; broke into the school-house at night, in spite of its formidable fastenings of withe and window stakes, and turned every thing topsy-turvy: so that the poor school-master began to think all the witches in the country held their meet-ings there. But what was still more annoying, Brom took all opportunities of turning him into ridicule in presence of his mis-tress, and had a scoundrel dog whom he taught to whine in the most ludicrous manner, and introduced as a rival of Ichabod's to instruct her in psalmody.

In this way matters went on for some time, without producing any material effect on the relative situation of the contending powers. On a fine autumnal afternoon, Ichabod, in pensive mood, sat enthroned on the lofty stool whence he usually watched all the concerns of his little literary realm. In his hand he swayed a *ferule*,* that sceptre of despotic power; the birch of justice reposed on three nails, behind the throne, a constant terror to evil doers; while on the desk before him might be seen sundry contraband articles and pro-hibited weapons, detected upon the persons of idle urchins; such as half-munched apples, popguns, whirligigs, fly-cages, and whole legions of rampant little paper game-cocks. Apparently there had been some appalling act of justice recently inflicted, for his scholars were all busily intent upon their books, or slyly whispering behind them with one eye kept upon the master; and a kind of buzzing still-ness reigned throughout the school-room. It was suddenly inter-rupted by the appearance of a negro, in tow-cloth jacket and trowsers, a round-crowned fragment of a hat, like the cap of Mercury,[†] and mounted on the back of a ragged, wild, half-broken colt, which

---

*Ruler used for punishing children.
[†]Messenger of the gods in Roman mythology, traditionally represented as wearing a hat with wings.

he managed with a rope by way of halter. He came clattering up to the school door with an invitation to Ichabod to attend a merry-making or "quilting frolic," to be held that evening at Mynheer Van Tassel's; and having delivered his message with that air of importance, and effort at fine language, which a negro is apt to display on petty embassies of the kind, he dashed over the brook and was seen scampering away up the hollow, full of the importance and hurry of. his mission.

All was now bustle and hubbub in the late quiet school-room. The scholars were hurried through their lessons, without stopping at trifles; those who were nimble skipped over half with impunity, and those who were tardy, had a smart application now and then in the rear, to quicken their speed, or help them over a tall word. Books were flung aside without being put away on the shelves, inkstands were overturned, benches thrown down, and the whole school was turned loose an hour before the usual time, bursting forth like a legion of young imps, yelping and racketing about the green, in joy at their early emancipation.

The gallant Ichabod now spent at least an extra half hour at his toilet, brushing and furbishing up his best, and indeed only suit of rusty black, and arranging his looks by a bit of broken looking-glass, that hung up in the school-house. That he might make his appearance before his mistress in the true style of a cavalier, he borrowed a horse from the farmer with whom he was domiciliated, a choleric old Dutchman, of the name of Hans Van Ripper, and, thus gallantly mounted, issued forth, like a knight-errant in quest of adventures. But it is meet I should, in the true spirit of romantic story, give some account of the looks and equipments of my hero and his steed. The animal he bestrode was a broken-down plough-horse, that had outlived almost every thing but his viciousness. He was gaunt and shagged, with a ewe neck and a head like a hammer; his rusty mane and tail were tangled and knotted with burrs; one eye had lost its pupil, and was glaring and spectral; but the other had the gleam of a genuine devil in it. Still he must have had fire and mettle in his day, if we may judge from the name he bore of Gunpowder. He had, in fact, been a favorite steed of his master's, the choleric Van Ripper, who was a furious rider, and had infused, very probably, some of his own spirit into the animal; for, old and broken-down as he looked, there was more of the lurking devil in him than in any young filly in the country.

Ichabod was a suitable figure for such a steed. He rode with short stirrups, which brought his knees nearly up to the pommel of the saddle; his sharp elbows stuck out like grasshoppers'; he carried his whip perpendicularly in his hand, like a sceptre, and, as his horse jogged on, the motion of his arms was not unlike the flapping of a pair of wings. A small wool hat rested on the top of his nose, for so his scanty strip of forehead might be called; and the skirts of his black coat fluttered out almost to the horse's tail. Such was the appearance of Ichabod and his steed, as they shambled out of the gate of Hans Van Ripper, and it was altogether such an apparition as is seldom to be met with in broad daylight.

It was, as I have said, a fine autumnal day, the sky was clear and serene, and nature wore that rich and golden livery which we always associate with the idea of abundance. The forests had put on their sober brown and yellow, while some trees of the tenderer kind had been nipped by the frosts into brilliant dyes of orange, purple, and scarlet. Streaming files of wild ducks began to make their appearance high in the air; the bark of the squirrel might be heard from the groves of beech and hickory nuts, and the pensive whistle of the quail at intervals from the neighboring stubble-field.

The small birds were taking their farewell banquets. In the fulness of their revelry, they fluttered, chirping and frolicking, from bush to bush, and tree to tree, capricious from the very profusion and variety around them. There was the honest cock-robin, the favorite game of stripling sportsmen, with its loud querulous note; and the twittering blackbirds flying in sable clouds; and the golden-winged woodpecker, with his crimson crest, his broad black gorget, and splendid plumage; and the cedar bird, with its red-tipt wings and yellow-tipt tail, and its little monteiro cap of feathers; and the blue-jay, that noisy coxcomb, in his gay light-blue coat and white under-clothes; screaming and chattering, nodding and bobbing and bowing, and pretending to be on good terms with every songster of the grove.

As Ichabod jogged slowly on his way, his eye, ever open to every symptom of culinary abundance, ranged with delight over the treasures of jolly autumn. On all sides he beheld vast store of apples;

some hanging in oppressive opulence on the trees; some gathered into baskets and barrels for the market; others heaped up in rich piles for the cider-press. Farther on he beheld great fields of Indian corn, with its golden ears peeping from their leafy coverts, and holding out the promise of cakes and hasty pudding; and the yellow pumpkins lying beneath them, turning up their fair round bellies to the sun, and giving ample prospects of the most luxurious of pies; and anon he passed the fragrant buckwheat fields, breathing the odor of the bee-hive, and as he beheld them, soft anticipations stole over his mind of dainty slapjacks,* well buttered, and garnished with honey or treacle, by the delicate little dimpled hand of Katrina Van Tassel.

Thus feeding his mind with many sweet thoughts and "sugared suppositions," he journeyed along the sides of a range of hills which look out upon some of the goodliest scenes of the mighty Hudson. The sun gradually wheeled his broad disk down into the west. The wide bosom of the Tappan Zee lay motionless and glassy, excepting that here and there a gentle undulation waved and prolonged the blue shadow of the distant mountain. A few amber clouds floated in the sky, without a breath of air to move them. The horizon was of a fine golden tint, changing gradually into a pure apple green, and from that into the deep blue of the mid-heaven. A slanting ray lingered on the woody crests of the precipices that overhung some parts of the river, giving greater depth to the dark-gray and purple of their rocky sides.

A sloop was loitering in the distance, dropping slowly down with the tide, her sail hanging uselessly against the mast; and as the reflection of the sky gleamed along the still water, it seemed as if the vessel was suspended in the air.

It was toward evening that Ichabod arrived at the castle of the Heer Van Tassel, which he found thronged with the pride and flower of the adjacent country. Old farmers, a spare leathern-faced race, in homespun coats and breeches, blue stockings, huge shoes, and magnificent pewter buckles. Their brisk withered little dames, in close crimped caps, long-waisted short-gowns, homespun petti-coats, with scissors and pincushions, and gay calico pockets hanging

---

*Pancakes.

on the outside. Buxom lasses, almost as antiquated as their mothers, excepting where a straw hat, a fine ribbon, or perhaps a white frock, gave symptoms of city innovation. The sons, in short square-skirted coats with rows of stupendous brass buttons, and their hair generally queued in the fashion of the times, especially if they could procure an eel-skin for the purpose, it being esteemed, throughout the country, as a potent nourisher and strengthener of the hair.

Brom Bones, however, was the hero of the scene, having come to the gathering on his favorite steed Daredevil, a creature, like himself, full of mettle and mischief, and which no one but himself could manage. He was, in fact, noted for preferring vicious animals, given to all kinds of tricks, which kept the rider in constant risk of his neck, for he held a tractable well-broken horse as unworthy of a lad of spirit.

Fain would I pause to dwell upon the world of charms that burst upon the enraptured gaze of my hero, as he entered the state parlor of Van Tassel's mansion. Not those of the bevy of buxom lasses, with their luxurious display of red and white; but the ample charms of a genuine Dutch country tea-table, in the sumptuous time of autumn. Such heaped-up platters of cakes of various and almost indescribable kinds, known only to experienced Dutch housewives! There was the doughty dough-nut, the tenderer oly koek,* and the crisp and crumbling cruller; sweet cakes and short cakes, ginger cakes and honey cakes, and the whole family of cakes. And then there were apple pies and peach pies and pumpkin pies; besides slices of ham and smoked beef; and moreover delectable dishes of preserved plums, and peaches, and pears, and quinces; not to mention broiled shad and roasted chickens; together with bowls of milk and cream, all mingled higgledy-piggledy, pretty much as I have enumerated them, with the motherly tea-pot sending up its clouds of vapor from the midst—Heaven bless the mark! I want breath and time to discuss this banquet as it deserves, and am too eager to get on with my story. Happily, Ichabod Crane was not in so great a hurry as his historian, but did ample justice to every dainty.

He was a kind and thankful creature, whoso heart dilated in proportion as his skin was filled with good cheer; and whose spirits

---

*An olykoek is a traditional Dutch fried pastry.

rose with eating as some men's do with drink. He could not help, too, rolling his large eyes round him as he ate, and chuckling with the possibility that he might one day be lord of all this scene of almost unimaginable luxury and splendor. Then, he thought, how soon he'd turn his back upon the old school-house; snap his fingers in the face of Hans Van Ripper, and every other niggardly patron, and kick any itinerant pedagogue out of doors that should dare to call him comrade!

Old Baltus Van Tassel moved about among his guests with a face dilated with content and good humor, round and jolly as the harvest moon. His hospitable attentions were brief, but expressive, being confined to a shake of the hand, a slap on the shoulder, a loud laugh, and a pressing invitation to "fall to, and help themselves."

And now the sound of the music from the common room, or hall, summoned to the dance. The musician was an old grayheaded negro, who had been the itinerant orchestra of the neighborhood for more than half a century. His instrument was as old and battered as himself. The greater part of the time he scraped on two or three strings, accompanying every movement of the bow with a motion of the head; bowing almost to the ground, and stamping with his foot whenever a fresh couple were to start.

Ichabod prided himself upon his dancing as much as upon his vocal powers. Not a limb, not a fibre about him was idle; and to have seen his loosely hung frame in full motion, and clattering about the room, you would have thought Saint Vitus* himself, that blessed patron of the dance, was figuring before you in person. He was the admiration of all the negroes; who, having gathered, of all ages and sizes, from the farm and the neighborhood, stood forming a pyramid of shining black faces at every door and window, gazing with delight at the scene, rolling their white eye-balls, and showing grinning rows of ivory from ear to ear. How could the flogger of urchins be otherwise than animated and joyous? the lady of his heart was his partner in the dance, and smiling graciously in reply to all his amorous oglings; while Brom Bones, sorely smitten with love and jealousy, sat brooding by himself in one corner.

---

*Christian martyr (died c.303); Saint Vitus's dance was a name for chorea, a neurological disease that causes involuntary muscular convulsions.

When the dance was at an end, Ichabod was attracted to a knot of the sager folks, who, with old Van Tassel, sat smoking at one end of the piazza, gossiping over former times, and drawing out long stories about the war.

This neighborhood, at the time of which I am speaking, was one of those highly-favored places which abound with chronicle and great men. The British and American line had run near it during the war;* it had, therefore, been the scene of marauding, and infested with refugees, cow-boys, and all kinds of border chivalry. Just sufficient time had elapsed to enable each storyteller to dress up his tale with a little becoming fiction and, in the indistinctness of his recollection, to make himself the hero of every exploit.

There was the story of Doffue Martling, a large blue-bearded Dutchman, who had nearly taken a British frigate with an old iron nine-pounder from a mud breastwork, only that his gun burst at the sixth discharge. And there was an old gentleman who shall be nameless, being too rich a mynheer to be lightly mentioned, who, in the battle of White-plains, being an excellent master of defence, parried a musket ball with a small sword, insomuch that he absolutely felt it whiz round the blade, and glance off at the hilt: in proof of which, he was ready at any time to show the sword, with the hilt a little bent. There were several more that had been equally great in the field, not one of whom but was persuaded that he had a considerable hand in bringing the war to a happy termination.

But all these were nothing to the tales of ghosts and apparitions that succeeded. The neighborhood is rich in legendary treasures of the kind. Local tales and superstitions thrive best in these sheltered long-settled retreats; but are trampled under foot by the shifting throng that forms the population of most of our country places. Besides, there is no encouragement for ghosts in most of our villages, for they have scarcely had time to finish their first nap, and turn themselves in their graves, before their surviving friends have travelled away from the neighborhood; so that when they turn out at night to walk their rounds, they have no acquaintance left to call upon. This is perhaps the reason why we so seldom hear of ghosts except in our long-established Dutch communities.

---

*The American Revolution.

The immediate cause, however, of the prevalence of supernatural stories in these parts, was doubtless owing to the vicinity of Sleepy Hollow. There was a contagion in the very air that blew from that haunted region; it breathed forth an atmosphere of dreams and fancies infecting all the land. Several of the Sleepy Hollow people were present at Van Tassel's, and, as usual, were doling out their wild and wonderful legends. Many dismal tales were told about funeral trains, and mourning cries and wailings heard and seen about the great tree where the unfortunate Major André* was taken, and which stood in the neighborhood. Some mention was made also of the woman in white, that haunted the dark glen at Raven Rock, and was often heard to shriek on winter nights before a storm, having perished there in the snow. The chief part of the stories, however, turned upon the favorite spectre of Sleepy Hollow, the headless horseman, who had been heard several times of late, patrolling the country; and, it was said, tethered his horse nightly among the graves in the church-yard.

The sequestered situation of this church seems always to have made it a favorite haunt of troubled spirits. It stands on a knoll, surrounded by locust-trees and lofty elms, from among which its decent whitewashed walls shine modestly forth, like Christian purity beaming through the shades of retirement. A gentle slope descends from it to a silver sheet of water, bordered by high trees, between which, peeps may be caught at the blue hills of the Hudson. To look upon its grass-grown yard, where the sunbeams seem to sleep so quietly, one would think that there at least the dead might rest in peace. On one side of the church extends a wide woody dell, along which raves a large brook among broken rocks and trunks of fallen trees. Over a deep black part of the stream, not far from the church, was formerly thrown a wooden bridge; the road that led to it, and the bridge itself, were thickly shaded by overhanging trees, which cast a gloom about it, even in the daytime; but occasioned a fearful darkness at night. This was one of the favorite haunts of the headless horseman; and the place where he was most frequently encountered. The tale was told of old Brouwer, a most heretical disbeliever

---

*British officer (1751–1780) hanged as a spy during the American Revolution.

in ghosts, how he met the horseman returning from his foray into
Sleepy Hollow, and was obliged to get up behind him; how they
galloped over bush and brake, over hill and swamp, until they
reached the bridge; when the horseman suddenly turned into a
skeleton, threw old Brouwer into the brook, and sprang away over
the tree-tops with a clap of thunder.

This story was immediately matched by a thrice marvellous
adventure of Brom Bones, who made light of the galloping Hessian
as an arrant jockey. He affirmed that, on returning one night from
the neighboring village of Sing Sing, he had been overtaken by this
midnight trooper; that he had offered to race with him for a bowl of
punch, and should have won it too, for Daredevil beat the goblin
horse all hollow, but, just as they came to the church bridge, the
Hessian bolted, and vanished in a flash of fire.

All these tales, told in that drowsy undertone with which men
talk in the dark, the countenances of the listeners only now and then
receiving a casual gleam from the glare of a pipe, sank deep in the
mind of Ichabod. He repaid them in kind with large extracts from
his invaluable author, Cotton Mather, and added many marvellous
events that had taken place in his native State of Connecticut, and
fearful sights which he had seen in his nightly walks about Sleepy
Hollow.

The revel now gradually broke up. The old farmers gathered
together their families in their wagons, and were heard for some
time rattling along the hollow roads, and over the distant hills. Some
of the damsels mounted on pillions behind their favorite swains,
and their light-hearted laughter, mingling with the clatter of hoofs,
echoed along the silent woodlands, sounding fainter and fainter
until they gradually died away—and the late scene of noise and
frolic was all silent and deserted. Ichabod only lingered behind,
according to the custom of country lovers, to have a tête-à-tête with
the heiress, fully convinced that he was now on the high road to
success.

What passed at this interview I will not pretend to say, for in fact
I do not know. Something, however, I fear me, must have gone
wrong, for he certainly sallied forth, after no very great interval, with
an air quite desolate and chop-fallen.—Oh these women! these
women! Could that girl have been playing off any of her coquettish

tricks?—Was her encouragement of the poor pedagogue all a mere sham to secure her conquest of his rival?—Heaven only knows, not I!—Let it suffice to say, Ichabod stole forth with the air of one who had been sacking a hen-roost, rather than a fair lady's heart. Without looking to the right or left to notice the scene of rural wealth, on which he had so often gloated, he went straight to the stable, and with several hearty cuffs and kicks, roused his steed most uncourteously from the comfortable quarters in which he was soundly sleeping, dreaming of mountains of corn and oats, and whole valleys of timothy and clover.

It was the very witching time of night that Ichabod, heavy-hearted and crest-fallen, pursued his travel homewards, along the sides of the lofty hills which rise above Tarry Town, and which he had traversed so cheerily in the afternoon. The hour was as dismal as himself. Far below him, the Tappan Zee spread its dusky and in-distinct waste of waters, with here and there the tall mast of a sloop, riding quietly at anchor under the land. In the dead hush of mid-night, he could even hear the barking of the watch dog from the op-posite shore of the Hudson; but it was so vague and faint as only to give an idea of his distance from this faithful companion of man. Now and then, too, the long-drawn crowing of a cock, accidentally awakened, would sound far, far off, from some farmhouse away among the hills—but it was like a dreaming sound in his ear. No signs of life occurred near him, but occasionally the melancholy chirp of a cricket, or perhaps the guttural twang of a bull-frog, from a neighboring marsh, as if sleeping uncomfortably, and turning suddenly in his bed.

All the stories of ghosts and goblins that he had heard in the afternoon, now came crowding upon his recollection. The night grew darker and darker; the stars seemed to sink deeper in the sky, and driving clouds occasionally hid them from his sight. He had never felt so lonely and dismal. He was, moreover, approaching the very place where many of the scenes of the ghost stories had been laid. In the centre of the road stood an enormous tulip-tree, which towered like a giant above all the other trees of the neighborhood, and formed a kind of landmark. Its limbs were gnarled, and fantastic, large enough to form trunks for ordinary trees, twisting down almost to the earth, and rising again into the air. It was connected with the tragical story of the unfortunate André, who had been taken prisoner hard by; and was universally known by the name of Major André's tree. The common people regarded it with a mixture of respect and superstition, partly out of sympathy for the fate of its ill-starred namesake, and partly from the tales of strange sights and doleful lamentations told concerning it.

As Ichabod approached this fearful tree, he began to whistle: he thought his whistle was answered—it was but a blast sweeping sharply through the dry branches. As he approached a little nearer, he thought he saw something white, hanging in the midst of the tree—he paused and ceased whistling; but on looking more narrowly, perceived that it was a place where the tree had been scathed by lightning, and the white wood laid bare. Suddenly he heard a groan—his teeth chattered and his knees smote against the saddle: it was but the rubbing of one huge bough upon another, as they were swayed about by the breeze. He passed the tree in safety, but new perils lay before him.

About two hundred yards from the tree a small brook crossed the road, and ran into a marshy and thickly-wooded glen, known by the name of Wiley's swamp. A few rough logs, laid side by side, served for a bridge over this stream. On that side of the road where the brook entered the wood, a group of oaks and chestnuts, matted thick with wild grapevines, threw a cavernous gloom over it. To pass this bridge was the severest trial. It was at this identical spot that the unfortunate André was captured, and under the covert of those chestnuts and vines were the sturdy yeomen concealed who surprised him. This has ever since been considered a haunted stream, and fearful are the feelings of the schoolboy who has to pass it alone after dark.

As he approached the stream his heart began to thump; he summoned up, however, all his resolution, gave his horse half a score of kicks in the ribs, and attempted to dash briskly across the bridge; but instead of starting forward, the perverse old animal made a lateral movement, and ran broadside against the fence. Ichabod, whose fears increased with the delay, jerked the reins on the other side, and kicked lustily with the contrary foot: it was all in vain; his steed started, it is true, but it was only to plunge to the opposite side of the road into a thicket of brambles and alder bushes. The schoolmaster now bestowed both whip and heel upon the starveling ribs of old Gunpowder, who dashed forward, snuffling and snorting, but came to a stand just by the bridge, with a suddenness that had nearly sent his rider sprawling over his head. Just at this moment a plashy tramp by the side of the bridge caught the sensitive ear of Ichabod. In the dark shadow of the grove, on the margin of the brook, he beheld something huge, misshapen, black and towering. It stirred not, but seemed gathered up in the gloom, like some gigantic monster ready to spring upon the traveller.

The hair of the affrighted pedagogue rose upon his head with terror. What was to be done? To turn and fly was now too late; and besides, what chance was there of escaping ghost or goblin, if such it was, which could ride upon the wings of the wind? Summoning up, therefore, a show of courage, he demanded in stammering accents— "Who are you?" He received no reply. He repeated his demand in a still more agitated voice. Still there was no answer. Once more he cudgelled the sides of the inflexible Gunpowder, and, shutting his eyes, broke forth with involuntary fervor into a psalm tune. Just then the shadowy object of alarm put itself in motion, and, with a scramble and a bound, stood at once in the middle of the road. Though the night was dark and dismal, yet the form of the unknown might now in some degree be ascertained. He appeared to be a horseman of large dimensions, and mounted on a black horse of powerful frame. He made no offer of molestation or sociability, but kept aloof on one side of the road, jogging along on the blind side of old Gunpowder, who had now got over his fright and waywardness.

Ichabod, who had no relish for this strange midnight companion, and bethought himself of the adventure of Brom Bones with the Galloping Hessian, now quickened his steed, in hopes of leaving him behind. The stranger, however, quickened his horse to an equal pace. Ichabod pulled up, and fell into a walk, thinking to lag behind—the other did the same. His heart began to sink within him; he endeavored to resume his psalm tune, but his parched tongue clove to the roof of his mouth, and he could not utter a stave. There was something in the moody and dogged silence of this pertinacious companion, that was mysterious and appalling. It was soon fearfully accounted for. On mounting a rising ground, which brought the figure of his fellow-traveller in relief against the sky, gigantic in height, and muffled in a cloak, Ichabod was horror-struck, on perceiving that he was headless!—but his horror was still more increased, on observing that the head, which should have rested on his shoulders, was carried before him on the pommel of the saddle: his terror rose to desperation; he rained a shower of kicks and blows upon Gunpowder, hoping, by a sudden movement, to give his companion the slip—but the spectre started full jump with him. Away then they dashed, through thick and thin; stones flying, and sparks flashing at every bound. Ichabod's flimsy garments fluttered in the air, as he stretched his long lank body away over his horse's head, in the eagerness of his flight.

They had now reached the road which turns off to Sleepy Hollow; but Gunpowder, who seemed possessed with a demon, instead of keeping up it, made an opposite turn, and plunged headlong down hill to the left. This road leads through a sandy hollow, shaded by trees for about a quarter of a mile, where it crosses the bridge famous in goblin story, and just beyond swells the green knoll on which stands the whitewashed church.

As yet the panic of the steed had given his unskilful rider an apparent advantage in the chase; but just as he had got half way through the hollow, the girths of the saddle gave way, and he felt it slipping from under him.

He seized it by the pommel, and endeavored to hold it firm, but in vain; and had just time to save himself by clasping old Gunpowder round the neck, when the saddle fell to the earth, and he heard it trampled under foot by his pursuer. For a moment the terror of Hans Van Ripper's wrath passed across his mind—for it was his Sunday saddle; but this was no time for petty fears; the goblin was hard on his haunches; and (unskilful rider that he was!) he had much ado to maintain his seat; sometimes slipping on one side, sometimes on another, and sometimes jolted on the high ridge of his horse's back-bone, with a violence that he verily feared would cleave him asunder.

An opening in the trees now cheered him with the hopes that the church bridge was at hand. The wavering reflection of a silver star in the bosom of the brook told him that he was not mistaken. He saw the walls of the church dimly glaring under the trees beyond. He recollected the place where Brom Bones's ghostly competitor had disappeared. "If I can but reach that bridge," thought Ichabod, "I am safe." Just then he heard the black steed panting and blowing close behind him; he even fancied that he felt his hot breath. Another convulsive kick in the ribs, and old Gunpowder sprang upon the bridge; he thundered over the resounding planks; he gained the opposite side; and now Ichabod cast a look behind to see if his pursuer should vanish, according to rule, in a flash of fire and brimstone. Just then he saw the goblin rising in his stirrups, and in the very act of hurling his head at him. Ichabod endeavored to dodge the horrible missile, but too late. It encountered his cranium with a tremendous crash—he was tumbled headlong into the dust, and Gunpowder, the black steed, and the goblin rider, passed by like a whirlwind.

The next morning the old horse was found without his saddle, and with the bridle under his feet, soberly cropping the grass at his master's gate. Ichabod did not make his appearance at breakfast—dinner-hour came, but no Ichabod. The boys assembled at the school-house, and strolled idly about the banks of the brook; but no school-master. Hans Van Ripper now began to feel some uneasiness about the fate of poor Ichabod, and his saddle. An inquiry was set on foot, and after diligent investigation they came upon his traces. In one part of the road leading to the church was found the saddle trampled in the dirt; the tracks of horses' hoofs deeply dented in the road, and evidently at furious speed, were traced to the bridge, beyond which, on the bank of a broad part of the brook, where the water ran deep and black, was found the hat of the unfortunate Ichabod, and close beside it a shattered pumpkin.

The brook was searched, but the body of the schoolmaster was not to be discovered. Hans Van Ripper, as executor of his estate, examined the bundle which contained all his worldly effects. They consisted of two shirts and a half; two stocks for the neck; a pair or two of worsted stockings; an old pair of corduroy small-clothes; a rusty razor; a book of psalm tunes, full of dogs' ears; and a broken pitchpipe. As to the books and furniture of the school-house, they belonged to the community, excepting Cotton Mather's History of Witchcraft, a New England Almanac, and a book of dreams and fortune-telling; in which last was a sheet of foolscap much scribbled and blotted in several fruitless attempts to make a copy of verses in honor of the heiress of Van Tassel. These magic books and the poetic scrawl were forthwith consigned to the flames by Hans Van Ripper; who from that time forward determined to send his children no more to school; observing, that he never knew any good come of this same reading and writing. Whatever money the schoolmaster possessed, and he had received his quarter's pay but a day or two before, he must have had about his person at the time of his disappearance.

The mysterious event caused much speculation at the church on the following Sunday. Knots of gazers and gossips were collected in the churchyard, at the bridge, and at the spot where the hat and pumpkin had been found. The stories of Brouwer, of Bones, and a whole budget of others, were called to mind; and when they had diligently considered them all, and compared them with the symptoms of the present case, they shook their heads, and came to the conclusion that Ichabod had been carried off by the galloping Hessian. As he was a bachelor, and in nobody's debt, nobody troubled his head any more about him. The school was removed to a different quarter of the hollow, and another pedagogue reigned in his stead.

It is true, an old farmer, who had been down to New York on a visit several years after, and from whom this account of the ghostly adventure was received, brought home the intelligence that Ichabod Crane was still alive; that he had left the neighborhood, partly through fear of the goblin and Hans Van Ripper, and partly in mortification at having been suddenly dismissed by the heiress; that he had changed his quarters to a distant part of the country; had kept school and studied law at the same time, had been admitted to the bar, turned politician, electioneered, written for the newspapers, and finally had been made a justice of the Ten Pound Court.* Brom Bones too, who shortly after his rival's disappearance conducted the blooming Katrina in triumph to the altar, was observed to look exceedingly knowing whenever the story of Ichabod was related, and always burst into a hearty laugh at the mention of the pumpkin; which led some to suspect that he knew more about the matter than he chose to tell.

---

*Court of small claims.

The old country wives, however, who are the best judges of these matters, maintain to this day that Ichabod was spirited away by supernatural means; and it is a favorite story often told about the neighborhood round the winter evening fire. The bridge became more than ever an object of superstitious awe, and that may be the reason why the road has been altered of late years, so as to approach the church by the border of the mill-pond. The school-house being deserted, soon fell to decay, and was reported to be haunted by the ghost of the unfortunate pedagogue; and the ploughboy, loitering homeward of a still summer evening, has often fancied his voice at a distance, chanting a melancholy psalm tune among the tranquil solitudes of Sleepy Hollow.

POSTSCRIPT,
Found in the Handwriting of
Mr. Knickerbocker

THE preceding Tale is given, almost in the precise words in which I heard it related at a Corporation meeting of the ancient city of Manhattoes, at which were present many of its sagest and most illustrious burghers. The narrator was a pleasant, shabby, gentlemanly old fellow, in pepper-and-salt clothes, with a sadly humorous face; and one whom I strongly suspected of being poor,—he made such efforts to be entertaining. When his story was concluded, there was much laughter and approbation, particularly from two or three deputy aldermen, who had been asleep a greater part of the time. There was, however, one tall, dry-looking old gentleman, with beetling eyebrows, who maintained a grave and rather severe face throughout: now and then folding his arms, inclining his head, and looking down upon the floor, as if turning a doubt over in his mind. He was one of your wary men, who never laugh, but upon good grounds—when they have reason and the law on their side. When the mirth of the rest of the company had subsided, and silence was restored, he leaned one arm on the elbow of his chair, and, sti the other akimbo, demanded, with a slight but exceedingly sage motion of the head, and contraction of the brow, what was the moral of the story, and what it went to prove?

The story-teller, who was just putting a glass of wine to his lips, as a refreshment after his toils, paused for a moment, looked at his inquirer with an air of infinite deference, and, lowering the glass slowly to the table, observed, that the story was intended most logically to prove:—

"That there is no situation in life but has its advantages and pleasures—provided we will but take a joke as we find it:

"That, therefore, he that runs races with goblin troopers is likely to have rough riding of it.

"Ergo, for a country schoolmaster to be refused the hand of a Dutch heiress, is a certain step to high preferment in the state."

The cautious old gentleman knit his brows tenfold closer after this explanation, being sorely puzzled by the ratiocination of the syllogism; while, methought, the one in pepper-and-salt eyed him with something of a triumphant leer. At length, he observed, that all this was very well, but still he thought the story a little on the extravagant—there were one or two points on which he had his doubts.

"Faith, sir," replied the story-teller, "as to that matter, I don't believe one-half of it myself."

D. K.

L'ENVOY*

Go, little booke, God send thee good passage,
And specially let this be thy prayere,
Unto them all that thee will read or hear,
Where thou art wrong, after their help to call,
Thee to correct in any part or all.

CHAUCER'S *Belle Dame sans Mercie*[†]

In concluding a second volume of the Sketch-Book, the Author cannot but express his deep sense of the indulgence with which his first has been received, and of the liberal disposition that has been evinced to treat him with kindness as a stranger. Even the critics, whatever may be said of them by others, he has found to be a singularly gentle and good-natured race; it is true that each has in turn objected to some one or two articles, and that these individual exceptions, taken in the aggregate, would amount almost to a total condemnation of his work; but then he has been consoled by observing, that what one has particularly censured, another has as particularly praised; and thus, the encomiums[‡] being set off against the objections, he finds his work, upon the whole, commended far beyond its deserts.

He is aware that he runs a risk of forfeiting much of this kind favor by not following the counsel that has been liberally bestowed upon him; for where abundance of valuable advice is given gratis, it may seem a man's own fault if he should go astray. He can only say, in his vindication, that he faithfully determined, for a time, to govern himself in his second volume by the opinions passed upon his first; but he was soon brought to a stand by the contrariety of

---

*Closing the second volume of the London edition [Irving's note].
[†]Long attributed to Chaucer, this poem is in fact a translation by Sir Richard Ros of a poem by the fifteenth-century French writer Alain Chartier.
[‡]Praises.

excellent counsel. One kindly advised him to avoid the ludicrous; another to shun the pathetic; a third assured him that he was tolerable at description, but cautioned him to leave narrative alone; while a fourth declared that he had a very pretty knack at turning a story, and was really entertaining when in a pensive mood, but was grievously mistaken if he imagined himself to possess a spirit of humor.

Thus perplexed by the advice of his friends, who each in turn closed some particular path, but left him all the world beside to range in, he found that to follow all their counsels would, in fact, be to stand still. He remained for a time sadly embarrassed; when, all at once, the thought struck him to ramble on as he had begun; that his work being miscellaneous, and written for different humors, it could not be expected that any one would be pleased with the whole; but that if it should contain something to suit each reader, his end would be completely answered. Few guests sit down to a varied table with an equal appetite for every dish. One has an elegant horror of a roasted pig; another holds a curry or a devil in utter abomination; a third cannot tolerate the ancient flavor of venison and wildfowl; and a fourth, of truly masculine stomach, looks with sovereign contempt on those knick-knacks, here and there dished up for the ladies. Thus each article is condemned in its turn; and yet, amidst this variety of appetites, seldom does a dish go away from the table without being tasted and relished by some one or other of the guests.

With these considerations he ventures to serve up this second volume in the same heterogeneous way with his first; simply requesting the reader, if he should find here and there something to please him, to rest assured that it was written expressly for intelligent readers like himself; but entreating him, should he find any thing to dislike, to tolerate it, as one of those articles which the author has been obliged to write for readers of a less refined taste.

To be serious.—The author is conscious of the numerous faults and imperfections of his work; and well aware how little he is disciplined and accomplished in the arts of authorship. His deficiencies are also increased by a diffidence arising from his peculiar situation. He finds himself writing in a strange land, and appearing before a public which he has been accustomed, from childhood, to regard with the highest feelings of awe and reverence. He is full of solicitude to deserve their approbation, yet finds that very solicitude continually embarrassing his powers, and depriving him of that ease and confidence which are necessary to successful exertion. Still the kindness with which he is treated encourages him to go on, hoping that in time he may acquire a steadier footing; and thus he proceeds, half venturing, half shrinking, surprised at his own good fortune, and wondering at his own temerity.

SELECTIONS FROM

BRACEBRIDGE HALL[1]

The Hall

The ancientest house, and the best for housekeeping, in this county or the next; and though the master of it write but squire, I know no lord like him.

—Merry Beggars*

The reader, if he has perused the volumes of the "Sketch-Book," will probably recollect something of the Bracebridge family, with which I once passed a Christmas. I am now on another visit at the Hall, having been invited to a wedding which is shortly to take place. The Squire's second son, Guy, a fine, spirited young captain in the army, is about to be married to his father's ward, the fair Julia Templeton. A gathering of relations and friends has already commenced, to celebrate the joyful occasion; for the old gentleman is an enemy to quiet, private weddings. "There is nothing," he says, "like launching a young couple gayly, and cheering them from the shore; a good outset is half the voyage."

Before proceeding any farther, I would beg that the Squire might not be confounded with that class of hard-riding, fox-hunting gentlemen, so often described, and, in fact, so nearly extinct in England. I use this rural title partly because it is his universal appellation throughout the neighborhood, and partly because it saves me the frequent repetition of his name, which is one of those rough old English names at which Frenchmen exclaim in despair.

The Squire is, in fact, a lingering specimen of the old English country gentleman; rusticated a little by living almost entirely on his estate, and something of a humorist, as Englishmen are apt to become when they have an opportunity of living in their own way. I like his hobby passing well, however, which is, a bigoted devotion to old English manners and customs; it jumps a little with my own

*From *The Jovial Crew; or, The Merry Beggars* (1641), by English dramatist Richard Brome.

humor, having as yet a lively and unsated curiosity about the ancient and genuine characteristics of my "father-land."

There are some traits about the Squire's family, also, which appear to me to be national. It is one of those old aristocratical families which, I believe, are peculiar to England, and scarcely understood in other countries; that is to say, families of the ancient gentry, who, though destitute of titled rank, maintain a high ancestral pride; who look down upon all nobility of recent creation, and would consider it a sacrifice of dignity to merge the venerable name of their house in a modern title.

The feeling is very much fostered by the importance which they enjoy on their hereditary domains. The family mansion is an old manor-house, standing in a retired and beautiful part of Yorkshire. Its inhabitants have been always regarded, through the surrounding country, as "the great ones of the earth;"* and the little village near the Hall looks up to the Squire with almost feudal homage. An old manor-house, and an old family of this kind, are rarely to be met with at the present day; and it is probably the peculiar humor of the Squire that has retained this secluded specimen of English house-keeping in something like the genuine old style.

I am again quartered in the panelled chamber, in the antique wing of the house. The prospect from my window, however, has quite a different aspect from that which it wore on my winter visit. Though early in the month of April, yet a few warm, sunshiny days have drawn forth the beauties of the spring, which, I think, are always most captivating on their first opening. The parterres of the old-fashioned garden are gay with flowers; and the gardener has brought out his exotics, and placed them along the stone balustrades. The trees are clothed with green buds and tender leaves. When I throw open my jingling casement, I smell the odor of mignonette, and hear the hum of the bees from the flowers against the sunny wall, with the varied song of the throstle, and the cheerful notes of the tuneful little wren.

While sojourning in this stronghold of old fashions, it is my intention to make occasional sketches of the scenes and characters before me. I would have it understood, however, that I am not

---

*See the Bible, Revelations 18:23.

writing a novel, and have nothing of intricate plot nor marvellous adventure to promise the reader. The Hall of which I treat has, for aught I know, neither trap-door, nor sliding-panel, nor donjon-keep;* and indeed appears to have no mystery about it. The family is a worthy, well-meaning family, that, in all probability, will eat and drink, and go to bed, and get up regularly, from one end of my work to the other; and the Squire is so kind-hearted, that I see no likelihood of his throwing any kind of distress in the way of the approaching nuptials. In a word, I cannot foresee a single extraordinary event that is likely to occur in the whole term of my sojourn at the Hall.

I tell this honestly to the reader, lest, when he finds me dallying along, through every-day English scenes, he may hurry ahead, in hopes of meeting with some marvellous adventure further on. I invite him, on the contrary, to ramble gently on with me, as he would saunter out into the fields, stopping occasionally to gather a flower, or listen to a bird, or admire a prospect, without any anxiety to arrive at the end of his career. Should I, however, in the course of my wanderings about this old mansion, see or hear anything curious, that might serve to vary the monotony of this every-day life, I shall not fail to report it for the reader's entertainment:

> For freshest wits I know will soon be wearie,
> Of any book, how grave soe'er it be,
> Except it have odd matter, strange and merrie,
> Well sauc'd with lies, and glared all with glee.†

---

*Fortified inner tower, or dungeon.
†*Mirror for Magistrates* [Irving's note]. See footnote on p. 113.

Story-Telling[2]

A favorite evening pastime at the Hall, and one which the worthy Squire is fond of promoting, is story-telling, "a good old-fashioned fireside amusement," as he terms it. Indeed, I believe he promotes it chiefly because it was one of the choice recreations in those days of yore when ladies and gentlemen were not much in the habit of reading. Be this as it may, he will often, at supper-table, when conversation flags, call on some one or other of the company for a story, as it was formerly the custom to call for a song; and it is edifying to see the exemplary patience, and even satisfaction, with which the good old gentleman will sit and listen to some hackneyed tale that he has heard for at least a hundred times.

In this way one evening the current of anecdotes and stories ran upon mysterious personages that have figured at different times, and filled the world with doubts and conjecture; such as the Wandering Jew, the Man with the Iron Mask, who tormented the curiosity of all Europe; the Invisible Girl, and last, though not least, the Pig-faced Lady.[3]

At length one of the company was called upon who had the most unpromising physiognomy for a story-teller that ever I had seen. He was a thin, pale, weazen-faced man, extremely nervous, who had sat at one corner of the table, shrunk up, as it were, into himself, and almost swallowed up in the cape of his coat, as a turtle in its shell.

The very demand seemed to throw him into a nervous agitation, yet he did not refuse. He emerged his head out of his shell, made a few odd grimaces and gesticulations, before he could get his muscles into order, or his voice under command, and then offered to give some account of a mysterious personage whom he had recently encountered in the course of his travels, and one whom he thought fully entitled of being classed with the Man with the Iron Mask.

I was so much struck with his extraordinary narrative, that I have written it out to the best of my recollection, for the amusement of the reader. I think it has in it all the elements of that mysterious and romantic narrative so greedily sought after at the present day.

The Stout Gentleman[4]

A STAGE-COACH ROMANCE

I'll cross it though it blast me!

Hamlet*

It was a rainy Sunday in the gloomy month of November. I had been detained, in the course of a journey, by a slight indisposition, from which I was recovering; but was still feverish, and obliged to keep within doors all day, in an inn of the small town of Derby. A wet Sunday in a country inn!—whoever has had the luck to experience one can alone judge of my situation. The rain pattered against the casements; the bells tolled for church with a melancholy sound. I went to the windows in quest of something to amuse the eye; but it seemed as if I had been placed completely out of the reach of all amusement. The windows of my bedroom looked out among tiled roofs and stacks of chimneys, while those of my sitting-room commanded a full view of the stable-yard. I know of nothing more calculated to make a man sick of this world than a stable-yard on a rainy day. The place was littered with wet straw that had been kicked about by travellers and stable-boys. In one corner was a stagnant pool of water, surrounding an island of muck; there were several half-drowned fowls crowded together under a cart, among which was a miserable, crestfallen cock, drenched out of all life and spirit; his drooping tail matted, as it were, into a single feather, along which the water trickled from his back; near the cart was a half-dozing cow, chewing the cud, and standing patiently to be rained on, with wreaths of vapor rising from her reeking hide; a walleyed horse, tired of the loneliness of the stable, was poking his spectral head out

---

*From Shakespeare's *Hamlet, Prince of Denmark* (act 1, scene 1).

of a window, with the rain dripping on it from the eaves; an unhappy cur, chained to a dog-house hard by, uttered something, every
now and then, between a bark and a yelp; a drab of a kitchen-wench
tramped backwards and forwards through the yard in pattens, looking as sulky as the weather itself; everything, in short, was comfortless and forlorn, excepting a crew of hardened ducks, assembled like
boon companions round a puddle, and making a riotous noise over
their liquor.

I was lonely and listless, and wanted amusement. My room soon
became insupportable. I abandoned it, and sought what is technically
called the travellers'-room. This is a public room set apart at most
inns for the accommodation of a class of wayfarers called travellers,
or riders; a kind of commercial knights-errant, who are incessantly
scouring the kingdom in gigs, on horseback, or by coach. They are
the only successors that I know of at the present day to the knights-
errant of yore. They lead the same kind of roving, adventurous life,
only changing the lance for a driving-whip, the buckler for a pattern-
card,* and the coat of mail for an upper Benjamin.† Instead of vindi-
cating the charms of peerless beauty, they rove about, spreading the
fame and standing of some substantial tradesman, or manufacturer,
and are ready at any time to bargain in his name; it being the fashion
nowadays to trade, instead of fight, with one another. As the room of
the hostel, in the good old fighting-times, would be hung round at
night with the armor of way-worn warriors, such as coats of mail, fal-
chions, and yawning helmets, so the travellers'-room is garnished
with the harnessing of their successors, with box-coats, whips of all
kinds, spurs, gaiters, and oil-cloth covered hats.

I was in hopes of finding some of these worthies to talk with, but
was disappointed. There were, indeed, two or three in the room; but
I could make nothing of them. One was just finishing his breakfast,
quarrelling with his bread and butter, and huffing the waiter;
another buttoned on a pair of gaiters, with many execrations at
Boots for not having cleaned his shoes well; a third sat drumming on
the table with his fingers and looking at the rain as it streamed down

---

*Card showing samples of their wares.
†Overcoat.

the window-glass; they all appeared infected by the weather, and disappeared, one after the other, without exchanging a word.

I sauntered to the window, and stood gazing at the people, picking their way to church, with petticoats hoisted midleg high, and dripping umbrellas. The bell ceased to toll, and the streets became silent. I then amused myself with watching the daughters of a tradesman opposite; who, being confined to the house for fear of wetting their Sunday finery, played off their charms at the front windows, to fascinate the chance tenants of the inn. They at length were summoned away by a vigilant vinegar-faced mother, and I had nothing further from without to amuse me.

What was I to do to pass away the long-lived day? I was sadly nervous and lonely; and everything about an inn seems calculated to make a dull day ten times duller. Old newspapers, smelling of beer and tobacco-smoke, and which I had already read half a dozen times. Good-for-nothing books, that were worse than rainy weather. I bored myself to death with an old volume of the Lady's Magazine.* I read all the commonplace names of ambitious travellers scrawled on the panes of glass; the eternal families of the Smiths, and the Browns, and the Jacksons, and the Johnsons, and all the other sons; and I deciphered several scraps of fatiguing inn-window poetry which I have met with in all parts of the world.

The day continued lowering and gloomy; the slovenly, ragged, spongy cloud drifted heavily along; there was no variety even in the rain: it was one dull, continued, monotonous patter—patter—patter, excepting that now and then I was enlivened by the idea of a brisk shower, from the rattling of the drops upon a passing umbrella.

It was quite *refreshing* (if I may be allowed a hackneyed phrase of the day) when, in the course of the morning, a horn blew, and a stage-coach whirled through the street, with outside passengers stuck all over it, cowering under cotton umbrellas, and seethed together, and reeking with the steams of wet box-coats and upper Benjamins.

---

*A number of periodicals were published under the title *Ladies Magazine*; Irving probably had in mind the one edited by Oliver Goldsmith from 1759 to 1763.

The sound brought out from their lurking-places a crew of vagabond boys, and vagabond dogs, and the carroty-headed hostler, and that nondescript animal ycleped* Boots, and all the other vagabond race that infest the purlieus of an inn; but the bustle was transient; the coach again whirled on its way; and boy and dog, and hostler and Boots, all slunk back again to their holes; the street again became silent, and the rain continued to rain on. In fact, there was no hope of its clearing up; the barometer pointed to rainy weather; mine hostess's tortoise-shell cat sat by the fire washing her face, and rubbing her paws over her ears; and, on referring to the Almanac, I found a direful prediction stretching from the top of the page to the bottom through the whole month, "expect—much—rain—about—this—time!"

I was dreadfully hipped.† The hours seemed as if they would never creep by. The very ticking of the clock became irksome. At length the stillness of the house was interrupted by the ringing of a bell. Shortly after I heard the voice of a waiter at the bar: "The stout gentleman in No. 13 wants his breakfast. Tea and bread and butter, with ham and eggs; the eggs not to be too much done."

In such a situation as mine, every incident is of importance. Here was a subject of speculation presented to my mind, and ample exercise for my imagination. I am prone to paint pictures to myself, and on this occasion I had some materials to work upon. Had the guest upstairs been mentioned as Mr. Smith, or Mr. Brown, or Mr. Jackson, or Mr. Johnson, or merely as "the gentleman in No. 13," it would have been a perfect blank to me. I should have thought nothing of it; but "The stout gentleman!"—the very name had something in it of the picturesque. It at once gave the size; it embodied the personage to my mind's eye, and my fancy did the rest.

He was stout, or, as some term it, lusty; in all probability, therefore, he was advanced in life, some people expanding as they grow old. By his breakfasting rather late, and in his own room, he must be a man accustomed to live at his ease, and above the necessity of early rising; no doubt a round, rosy, lusty old gentleman.

---

*Middle English for "named."
†Melancholy.

There was another violent ringing. The stout gentleman was impatient for his breakfast. He was evidently a man of importance; "well to do in the world;" accustomed to be promptly waited upon; of a keen appetite and a little cross when hungry; "perhaps," thought I, "he may be some London Alderman; or who knows but he may be a Member of Parliament?"

The breakfast was sent up, and there was a short interval of silence; he was, doubtless, making the tea. Presently there was a violent ringing; and before it could be answered, another ringing still more violent. "Bless me! what a choleric old gentleman!" The waiter came down in a huff. The butter was rancid, the eggs were overdone, the ham was too salt;—the stout gentleman was evidently nice in his eating; one of those who eat and growl, and keep the waiter on the trot, and live in a state militant with the household.

The hostess got into a fume. I should observe that she was a brisk, coquettish woman; a little of a shrew, and something of a slammerkin, but very pretty withal; with a nincompoop for a husband, as shrews are apt to have. She rated the servants roundly for their negligence in sending up so bad a breakfast, but said not a word against the stout gentleman; by which I clearly perceived that he must be a man of consequence, entitled to make a noise and to give trouble at a country inn. Other eggs, and ham, and bread and butter were sent up. They appeared to be more graciously received; at least there was no further complaint.

I had not made many turns about the travellers'-room, when there was another ringing. Shortly afterwards there was a stir and an inquest about the house. The stout gentleman wanted the Times or the Chronicle newspaper.* I set him down, therefore, for a Whig;† or rather, from his being so absolute and lordly where he had a chance, I suspected him of being a Radical. Hunt,‡ I had heard, was a large man; "who knows," thought I, "but it is Hunt himself!"

---

*The *London Times* and the *Morning Chronicle* were the leading British newspapers in early-nineteenth-century England.

†English political party that championed reform, in particular the limiting of royal authority.

‡Henry Hunt (1773–1835), English radical politician; with English journalist William Cobbett (1763–1835), he formed the Radical Reform Association, which advocated for such labor reform laws as a ten-hour day and an end to child labor.

My curiosity began to be awakened. I inquired of the waiter who was this stout gentleman that was making all this stir; but I could get no information: nobody seemed to know his name. The landlords of bustling inns seldom trouble their heads about the names or occupations of their transient guests. The color of a coat, the shape or size of the person, is enough to suggest a travelling name. It is either the tall gentleman, or the short gentleman, or the gentleman in black, or the gentleman in snuff-color; or, as in the present instance, the stout gentleman. A designation of the kind once hit on, answers every purpose, and saves all further inquiry.

Rain—rain—rain! pitiless, ceaseless rain! No such thing as putting a foot out of doors, and no occupation nor amusement within. By and by I heard some one walking overhead. It was in the stout gentleman's room. He evidently was a large man by the heaviness of his tread; and an old man from his wearing such creaking soles. "He is doubtless," thought I, "some rich old square-toes of regular habits, and is now taking exercise after breakfast."

I now read all the advertisements of coaches and hotels that were stuck about the mantelpiece. The Lady's Magazine had become an abomination to me; it was as tedious as the day itself. I wandered out, not knowing what to do, and ascended again to my room. I had not been there long, when there was a squall from a neighboring bedroom. A door opened and slammed violently; a chamber-maid, that I had remarked for having a ruddy, good-humored face, went down stairs in a violent flurry. The stout gentleman had been rude to her!

This sent a whole host of my deductions to the deuce in a moment. This unknown personage could not be an old gentleman; for old gentlemen are not apt to be so obstreperous to chamber-maids. He could not be a young gentleman; for young gentlemen are not apt to inspire such indignation. He must be a middle-aged man, and confounded ugly into the bargain, or the girl would not have taken the matter in such terrible dudgeon.* I confess I was sorely puzzled.

In a few minutes I heard the voice of my landlady. I caught a glance of her as she came tramping up-stairs,—her face glowing, her

---

*Offense.

cap flaring, her tongue wagging the whole way. "She'd have no such doings in her house, she'd warrant. If gentlemen did spend money freely, it was no rule. She'd have no servant-maids of hers treated in that way, when they were about their work, that's what she wouldn't."

As I hate squabbles, particularly with women, and above all with pretty women, I slunk back into my room, and partly closed the door; but my curiosity was too much excited not to listen. The landlady marched intrepidly to the enemy's citadel, and entered it with a storm: the door closed after her. I heard her voice in high windy clamor for a moment or two. Then it gradually subsided, like a gust of wind in a garret; then there was a laugh; then I heard nothing more.

After a little while my landlady came out with an odd smile on her face, adjusting her cap, which was a little on one side. As she went down stairs, I heard the landlord ask her what was the matter; she said, "Nothing at all, only the girl's a fool."—I was more than ever perplexed what to make of this unaccountable personage, who could put a good-natured chamber-maid in a passion, and send away a termagant landlady in smiles. He could not be so old, nor cross, nor ugly either.

I had to go to work at his picture again, and to paint him entirely different. I now set him down for one of those stout gentlemen that are frequently met with swaggering about the doors of country inns. Moist, merry fellows, in Belcher handkerchiefs,* whose bulk is a little assisted by malt-liquors. Men who have seen the world, and been sworn at Highgate; who are used to tavern-life; up to all the tricks of tapsters, and knowing in the ways of sinful publicans. Free-livers on a small scale; who are prodigal within the compass of a guinea: who call all the waiters by name, tousle the maids, gossip with the landlady at the bar, and prose over a pint glass of port, or a glass of negus,† after dinner.

The morning wore away in forming these and similar surmises. As fast as I wove one system of belief, some movement of the

---

*So called after English boxer James Belcher (1781–1811), who often wore a blue handkerchief with white spots. (See William Hazlitt's essay "The Fight.")
†Cocktail of hot water, wine, and lemon juice, sweetened and spiced.

unknown would completely overturn it, and throw all my thoughts again into confusion. Such are the solitary operations of a feverish mind. I was, as I have said, extremely nervous; and the continual meditation on the concerns of this invisible personage began to have its effect:—I was getting a fit of the fidgets.

Dinner-time came. I hoped the stout gentleman might dine in the travellers'-room, and that I might at length get a view of his person; but no—he had dinner served in his own room. What could be the meaning of this solitude and mystery? He could not be a radical; there was something too aristocratical in thus keeping himself apart from the rest of the world, and condemning himself to his own dull company throughout a rainy day. And then, too, he lived too well for a discontented politician. He seemed to expatiate on a variety of dishes, and to sit over his wine like a jolly friend of good living. Indeed, my doubts on this head were soon at an end; for he could not have finished his first bottle before I could faintly hear him humming a tune; and on listening I found it to be "God save the King." 'Twas plain, then, he was no radical, but a faithful subject; one who grew loyal over his bottle, and was ready to stand by king and constitution, when he could stand by nothing else. But who could he be? My conjectures began to run wild. Was he not some personage of distinction travelling incog.?* "God knows!" said I, at my wit's end; "it may be one of the royal family for aught I know, for they are all stout gentlemen!"

The weather continued rainy. The mysterious unknown kept his room, and, as far as I could judge, his chair, for I did not hear him move. In the meantime, as the day advanced, the travellers'-room began to be frequented. Some, who had just arrived, came in buttoned up in box-coats; others came home who had been dispersed about the town; some took their dinners, and some their tea. Had I been in a different mood, I should have found entertainment in studying this peculiar class of men. There were two especially, who were regular wags of the road, and up to all the standing jokes of travellers. They had a thousand sly things to say to the waiting-maid, whom they called Louisa, and Ethelinda, and a dozen other fine

---

*Incognito.

names, changing the name every time, and chuckling amazingly at their own waggery. My mind, however, had been completely engrossed by the stout gentleman. He had kept my fancy in chase during a long day, and it was not now to be diverted from the scent.

The evening gradually wore away. The travellers read the papers two or three times over. Some drew round the fire and told long stories about their horses, about their adventures, their overturns, and breakings-down. They discussed the credit of different merchants and different inns; and the two wags told several choice anecdotes of pretty chamber-maids and kind landladies. All this passed as they were quietly taking what they called their night-caps, that is to say, strong glasses of brandy and water and sugar, or some other mixture of the kind; after which they one after another rang for "Boots" and the chamber-maid, and walked off to bed in old shoes cut down into marvellously uncomfortable slippers.

There was now only one man left: a short-legged, longbodied, plethoric fellow, with a very large, sandy head. He sat by himself, with a glass of port-wine negus, and a spoon; sipping and stirring, and meditating and sipping, until nothing was left but the spoon. He gradually fell asleep bolt upright in his chair, with the empty glass standing before him; and the candle seemed to fall asleep too, for the wick grew long, and black, and cabbaged at the end, and dimmed the little light that remained in the chamber. The gloom that now prevailed was contagious. Around hung the shapeless, and almost spectral, box-coats of departed travellers, long since buried in deep sleep. I only heard the ticking of the clock, with the deep-drawn breathings of the sleeping topers, and the drippings of the rain, drop—drop—drop, from the eaves of the house. The church-bells chimed midnight. All at once the stout gentleman began to walk overhead, pacing slowly backwards and forwards. There was something extremely awful in all this, especially to one in my state of nerves. These ghastly great-coats, these guttural breathings, and the creaking footsteps of this mysterious being. His steps grew fainter and fainter, and at length died away. I could bear it no longer. I was wound up to the desperation of a hero of romance. "Be he who or what he may," said I to myself, "I'll have a sight of him!" I seized a chamber-candle, and hurried up to No. 13. The door stood ajar. I hesitated—I entered: the room was deserted. There stood a large, broad-bottomed elbow-chair at a table, on which was an empty tumbler, and a "Times," newspaper, and the room smelt powerfully of Stilton cheese.

The mysterious stranger had evidently but just retired. I turned off, sorely disappointed, to my room, which had been changed to the front of the house. As I went along the corridor, I saw a large pair of boots, with dirty, waxed tops, standing at the door of a bedchamber. They doubtless belonged to the unknown; but it would not do to disturb so redoubtable a personage in his den: he might discharge a pistol, or something worse, at my head. I went to bed, therefore, and lay awake half the night in a terribly nervous state; and even when I fell asleep, I was still haunted in my dreams by the idea of the stout gentleman and his wax-topped boots.

I slept rather late the next morning, and was awakened by some stir and bustle in the house, which I could not at first comprehend; until getting more awake, I found there was a mail-coach starting from the door. Suddenly there was a cry from below, "The gentleman has forgot his umbrella! Look for the gentleman's umbrella in No. 13!" I heard an immediate scampering of a chambermaid along the passage, and a shrill reply as she ran, "Here it is! here's the gentleman's umbrella!"

The mysterious stranger then was on the point of setting off. This was the only chance I should ever have of knowing him. I sprang out of bed, scrambled to the window, snatched aside the curtains, and just caught a glimpse of the rear of a person getting in at the coach-door. The skirts of a brown coat parted behind, and gave me a full view of the broad disk of a pair of drab breeches. The door closed— "all right!" was the word—the coach whirled off;—and that was all I ever saw of the stout gentleman!

The Historian⁵

Hermione.	Pray you sit by us,
	And tell's a tale.
Mamilius.	Merry or sad shall't be?
Hermione.	As merry as you will.
Mamilius.	A sad tale's best for winter.
	I have one of sprites and goblins.
Hermione.	Let's have that, sir.

Winter's Tale*

A s this is a story-telling age, I have been tempted occasionally to give the reader one of the many tales served up with supper at the Hall. I might, indeed, have furnished a series almost equal in number to the "Arabian Nights";⁶ but some were rather hackneyed and tedious; others I did not feel warranted in betraying into print; and many more were of the old general's relating, and turned principally upon tiger-hunting, elephant-riding, and Seringapatam, enlivened by the wonderful deeds of Tippoo Saib,† and the excellent jokes of Major Pendergast.

I had all along maintained a quiet post at a corner of the table, where I had been able to indulge my humor undisturbed; listening attentively when the story was very good, and dozing a little when it was rather dull, which I consider the perfection of auditorship.

I was roused the other evening from a slight trance, into which I had fallen during one of the general's histories, by a sudden call from the Squire to furnish some entertainment of the kind in my turn. Having been so profound a listener to others, I could not in conscience refuse; but neither my memory nor invention being

---

*From Shakespeare's *The Winter's Tale* (act 2, scene 1).
†Or Tipu Sahib; sultan of Mysore (in southern India), who, aided by the French, fought against British colonization of India; he was defeated by General Wellesley at the city of Seringapatam in 1799.

ready to answer so unexpected a demand, I begged leave to read a manuscript tale from the pen of my fellow-countryman, the late Mr. Diedrich Knickerbocker, the historian of New York. As this ancient chronicler may not be better known to my readers than he was to the company at the Hall, a word or two concerning him may not be amiss, before proceeding to his manuscript.

Diedrich Knickerbocker was a native of New York, a descendant from one of the ancient Dutch families which originally settled that province, and remained there after it was taken possession of by the English in 1664. The descendants of these Dutch families still remain in villages and neighborhoods in various parts of the country, retaining, with singular obstinacy, the dresses, manners, and even language of their ancestors, and forming a very distinct and curious feature in the motley population of the State. In a hamlet whose spire may be seen from New York, rising from above the brow of a hill on the opposite side of the Hudson, many of the old folks, even at the present day, speak English with an accent, and the Dominie preaches in Dutch; and so completely is the hereditary love of quiet and silence maintained, that in one of these drowsy villages, in the middle of a warm summer's day, the buzzing of a stout blue-bottle fly will resound from one end of the place to the other.

With the laudable hereditary feeling thus kept up among these worthy people, did Mr. Knickerbocker undertake to write a history of his native city, comprising the reign of its three Dutch governors during the time that it was yet under the domination of the Hogen-mogens of Holland. In the execution of this design the little Dutch-man has displayed great historical research, and a wonderful consciousness of the dignity of his subject. His work, however, has been so little understood as to be pronounced a mere work of humor, satirizing the follies of the times, both in politics and morals, and giving whimsical views of human nature.

Be this as it may:—among the papers left behind him were several tales of a lighter nature, apparently thrown together from materials gathered during his profound researches for his history, and which he seems to have cast by with neglect, as unworthy of publication. Some of these have fallen into my hands by an accident which it is needless at present to mention; and one of these very stories, with its prelude in the words of Mr. Knickerbocker, I undertook to read, by way of acquitting myself of the debt which I owed to the other story-tellers at the Hall. I subjoin it for such of my readers as are fond of stories.

The Haunted House[7]

FROM THE MSS. OF THE LATE DIEDRICH KNICKERBOCKER

Formerly almost every place had a house of this kind. If a house was seated on some melancholy place, or built in some old romantic manner, or if any particular accident had happened in it, such as murder, sudden death, or the like, to be sure that house had a mark set on it, and was afterwards esteemed the habitation of a ghost.

—BOURNE'S ANTIQUITIES*

In the neighborhood of the ancient city of the Manhattoes[†] there stood, not very many years since, an old mansion, which, when I was a boy, went by the name of the Haunted House. It was one of the very few remains of the architecture of the early Dutch settlers, and must have been a house of some consequence at the time when it was built. It consisted of a centre and two wings, the gable ends of which were shaped like stairs. It was built partly of wood, and partly of small Dutch bricks, such as the worthy colonists brought with them from Holland, before they discovered that bricks could be manufactured elsewhere. The house stood remote from the road, in the centre of a large field, with an avenue of old locust[‡] trees leading up to it, several of which had been shivered by lightning, and two or three blown down. A few apple-trees grew straggling about the field; there were traces also of what had been a kitchen-garden; but the fences were broken down, the vegetables had disappeared, or

---

Antiquitates vulgares (1725), by English historian Henry Bourne; this quotation has not been located.
[†]Manhattan, a borough of New York City.
[‡]Acacias [Irving's note].

had grown wild, and turned to little better than weeds, with here and there a ragged rose-bush, or a tall sunflower shooting up from among the brambles, and hanging its head sorrowfully, as if contemplating the surrounding desolation. Part of the roof of the old house had fallen in, the windows were shattered, the panels of the doors broken, and mended with rough boards, and two rusty weather-cocks at the ends of the house made a great jingling and whistling as they whirled about, but always pointed wrong. The appearance of the whole place was forlorn and desolate at the best of times; but, in unruly weather, the howling of the wind about the crazy old mansion, the screeching of the weather-cocks, and the slamming and banging of a few loose window-shutters, had altogether so wild and dreary an effect, that the neighborhood stood perfectly in awe of the place, and pronounced it the rendezvous of hobgoblins. I recollect the old building well; for many times, when an idle, unlucky urchin, I have prowled round its precinct, with some of my graceless companions, on holiday afternoons, when out on a free-booting cruise among the orchards. There was a tree standing near the house that bore the most beautiful and tempting fruit; but then it was on enchanted ground, for the place was so charmed by frightful stories that we dreaded to approach it. Sometimes we would venture in a body, and get near the Hesperian tree,* keeping an eye upon the old mansion, and darting fearful glances into its shattered windows, when, just as we were about to seize upon our prize, an exclamation from some one of the gang, or an accidental noise, would throw us all into a panic, and we would scamper headlong from the place, nor stop until we had got quite into the road. Then there was sure to be a host of fearful anecdotes told of strange cries and groans, or of some hideous face suddenly seen staring out of one of the windows. By degrees we ceased to venture into these lonely grounds, but would stand at a distance, and throw stones at the building; and there was something fearfully pleasing in the sound as they rattled along the roof, or sometimes struck some jingling fragments of glass out of the windows.

---

*In Greek mythology, the Hesperides were nymphs who guarded a garden with a tree that bore golden apples.

The origin of this house was lost in the obscurity that covers the early period of the province, while under the government of their high mightinesses the states-general. Some reported it to have been a country residence of Wilhelmus Kieft,* commonly called the Testy, one of the Dutch governors of New Amsterdam; others said it had been built by a naval commander who served under Van Tromp,† and who, on being disappointed of preferment, retired from the service in disgust, became a philosopher through sheer spite, and brought over all his wealth to the province, that he might live according to his humor, and despise the world. The reason of its having fallen to decay was likewise a matter of dispute; some said it was in chancery, and had already cost more than its worth in legal expense; but the most current, and, of course, the most probable account, was that it was haunted, and that nobody could live quietly in it. There can, in fact, be very little doubt that this last was the case, there were so many corroborating stories to prove it,—not an old woman in the neighborhood but could furnish at least a score. A grayheaded curmudgeon of a negro who lived hard by had a whole budget of them to tell, many of which had happened to himself. I recollect many a time stopping with my schoolmates, and getting him to relate some. The old crone lived in a hovel, in the midst of a small patch of potatoes and Indian corn, which his master had given him on setting him free. He would come to us, with his hoe in his hand, and as we sat perched, like a row of swallows, on the rail of a fence, in the mellow twilight of a summer evening, would tell us such fearful stories, accompanied by such awful rollings of his white eyes, that we were almost afraid of our own footsteps as we returned home afterwards in the dark.

Poor old Pompey! many years are past since he died, and went to keep company with the ghosts he was so fond of talking about. He was buried in a corner of his own little potato patch; the plough soon passed over his grave, and levelled it with the rest of the field, and nobody thought any more of the grayheaded negro. By singular chance I was strolling in that neighborhood, several years afterwards,

---

*See footnote on p. 424.
†See footnote on p. 402.

when I had grown up to be a young man, and I found a knot of gossips speculating on a skull which had just been turned up by a ploughshare. They of course determined it to be the remains of some one who had been murdered, and they had raked up with it some of the traditionary tales of the haunted house. I knew it at once to be the relic of poor Pompey, but I held my tongue; for I am too considerate of other people's enjoyment even to mar a story of a ghost or a murder. I took care, however, to see the bones of my old friend once more buried in a place where they were not likely to be disturbed. As I sat on the turf and watched the interment, I fell into a long conversation with an old gentleman of the neighborhood, John Josse Vandermoere, a pleasant gossiping man, whose whole life was spent in hearing and telling the news of the province. He recollected old Pompey, and his stories about the Haunted House; but he assured me he could give me one still more strange than any that Pompey had related; and on my expressing a great curiosity to hear it, he sat down beside me on the turf, and told the following tale. I have endeavored to give it as nearly as possible in his words; but it is now many years since, and I am grown old, and my memory is not over-good. I cannot therefore vouch for the language, but I am always scrupulous as to facts.

D. K.

Dolph Heyliger

"I take the town of concord, where I dwell,
All Kilborn be my witness, if I were not
Begot in bashfulness, brought up in shamefacedness.
Let 'un bring a dog but to my vace that can
Zay I have beat 'un, and without a vault;
Or but a cat will swear upon a book,
I have as much as zet a vire her tail,
And I'll give him or her a crown for 'mends."

TALE OF A TUB*

In the early time of the province of New York, while it groaned under the tyranny of the English governor, Lord Cornbury,[†] who carried his cruelties towards the Dutch inhabitants so far as to allow no Dominie, or schoolmaster, to officiate in their language without his special license; about this time there lived in the jolly little old city of the Manhattoes a kind motherly dame, known by the name of Dame Heyliger. She was the widow of a Dutch sea-captain, who died suddenly of a fever, in consequence of working too hard, and eating too heartily, at the time when all the inhabitants turned out in a panic, to fortify the place against the invasion of a small French privateer.[‡] He left her with very little money, and one infant son, the only survivor of several children. The good woman had need of much management to make both ends meet, and keep up a decent appearance. However, as her husband had fallen a victim to his zeal for the public safety, it was universally agreed that "something ought to be done for the widow"; and on the hopes of this

---

*From *A Tale of a Tub* (1633), by English poet Ben Jonson (act 3, scene 1, lines 67–74).
[†]Edward Hyde, Lord Cornbury, royal governor of New York and New Jersey (1703–1708).
[‡]1705 [Irving's note].

"something" she lived tolerably for some years; in the meantime everybody pitied and spoke well of her, and that helped along.

She lived in a small house, in a small street, called Garden Street, very probably from a garden which may have flourished there some time or other. As her necessities every year grew greater, and the talk of the public about doing "something for her" grew less, she had to cast about for some mode of doing something for herself, by way of helping out her slender means, and maintaining her independence, of which she was somewhat tenacious.

Living in a mercantile town, she had caught something of the spirit, and determined to venture a little in the great lottery of commerce. On a sudden, therefore, to the great surprise of the street, there appeared at her window a grand array of gingerbread kings and queens, with their arms stuck akimbo, after the invariable royal manner. There were also several broken tumblers, some filled with sugar-plums, some with marbles; there were, moreover, cakes of various kinds, and barley-sugar, and Holland dolls, and wooden horses, with here and there gilt-covered picture-books, and now and then a skein of thread, or a dangling pound of candles. At the door of the house sat the good old dame's cat, a decent demure-looking personage, who seemed to scan everybody that passed, to criticize their dress, and now and then to stretch her neck, and to look out with sudden curiosity, to see what was going on at the other end of the street; but if by chance any idle vagabond dog came by, and offered to be uncivil—hoity-toity!—how she would bristle up, and growl, and spit, and strike out her paws! she was as indignant as ever was an ancient and ugly spinster on the approach of some graceless profligate.

But though the good woman had to come down to those humble means of subsistence, yet she still kept up a feeling of family pride, being descended from the Vanderspiegels, of Amsterdam; and she had the family arms painted and framed, and hung over her mantelpiece. She was, in truth, much respected by all the poorer people of the place; her house was quite a resort of the old wives of the neighborhood; they would drop in there of a winter's afternoon, as she sat knitting on one side of her fireplace, her cat purring on the other, and the teakettle singing before it; and they would gossip with her until late in the evening. There was always an arm-chair for

Peter de Groodt, sometimes called Long Peter, and sometimes Peter Longlegs, the clerk and sexton of the little Lutheran church, who was her great crony, and indeed the oracle of her fireside. Nay, the Dominie himself did not disdain, now and then, to step in, converse about the state of her mind, and take a glass of her special good cherry-brandy. Indeed, he never failed to call on New-Year's day, and wish her a happy New Year; and the good dame, who was a little vain on some points, always piqued herself on giving him as large a cake as any one in town.

I have said that she had one son. He was the child of her old age; but could hardly be called the comfort, for, of all unlucky urchins, Dolph Heyliger was the most mischievous. Not that the whipster was really vicious; he was only full of fun and frolic, and had that daring, gamesome spirit which is extolled in a rich man's child, but execrated in a poor man's. He was continually getting into scrapes; his mother was incessantly harassed with complaints of some waggish pranks which he had played off; bills were sent in for windows that he had broken; in a word, he had not reached his fourteenth year before he was pronounced, by all the neighborhood, to be a "wicked dog, the wickedest dog in the street!" Nay, one old gentleman, in a claret-colored coat, with a thin red face, and ferret eyes, went so far as to assure Dame Heyliger, that her son would, one day or other, come to the gallows!

Yet, notwithstanding all this, the poor old soul loved her boy. It seemed as though she loved him the better the worse he behaved, and that he grew more in her favor the more he grew out of favor with the world. Mothers are foolish, fond-hearted beings; there's no reasoning them out of their dotage; and, indeed, this poor woman's child was all that was left to love her in this world;—so we must not think it hard that she turned a deaf ear to her good friends, who sought to prove to her that Dolph would come to a halter.

To do the varlet justice, too, he was strongly attached to his parent. He would not willingly have given her pain on any account; and when he had been doing wrong, it was but for him to catch his poor mother's eye fixed wistfully and sorrowfully upon him, to fill his heart with bitterness and contrition. But he was a heedless youngster, and could not, for the life of him, resist any new temptation to fun and mischief. Though quick at his learning, whenever he could be brought to apply himself, he was always prone to be led away by idle company, and would play truant to hunt after birds'-nests, to rob orchards, or to swim in the Hudson.

In this way he grew up, a tall, lubberly* boy; and his mother began to be greatly perplexed what to do with him, or how to put him in a way to do for himself; for he had acquired such an unlucky reputation, that no one seemed willing to employ him.

Many were the consultations that she held with Peter de Groodt, the clerk and sexton, who was her prime counsellor. Peter was as much perplexed as herself, for he had no great opinion of the boy, and thought he would never come to good. He at once advised her to send him to sea: a piece of advice only given in the most desperate cases; but Dame Heyliger would not listen to such an idea; she could not think of letting Dolph go out of her sight. She was sitting one day knitting by her fireside, in great perplexity, when the sexton entered with an air of unusual vivacity and briskness. He had just come from a funeral. It had been that of a boy of Dolph's years, who had been apprentice to a famous German doctor, and had died of a consumption.† It is true, there had been a whisper that the deceased had been brought to his end by being made the subject of the doctor's experiments, on which he was apt to try the effects of a new compound, or a quieting draught. This, however, it is likely, was a mere scandal; at any rate, Peter de Groodt did not think it worth mentioning; though, had we time to philosophize, it would be a curious matter for speculation, why a doctor's family is apt to be so lean and cadaverous, and a butcher's so jolly and rubicund.

Peter de Groodt, as I said before, entered the house of Dame Heyliger with unusual alacrity. A bright idea had popped into his head at the funeral, over which he had chuckled as he shovelled the earth into the grave of the doctor's disciple. It had occurred to him, that, as the situation of the deceased was vacant at the doctor's, it would be the very place for Dolph. The boy had parts, and could pound a pestle, and run an errand with any boy in the town; and what more was wanted in a student?

*Big and clumsy.
†Tuberculosis.

The suggestion of the sage Peter was a vision of glory to the mother. She already saw Dolph, in her mind's eye, with a cane at his nose, a knocker at his door, and an M. D. at the end of his name,— one of the established dignitaries of the town.

The matter, once undertaken, was soon effected; the sexton had some influence with the doctor, they having had much dealing together in the way of their separate professions; and the very next morning he called and conducted the urchin, clad in his Sunday clothes, to undergo the inspection of Dr. Karl Lodovick Knipperhausen.

They found the doctor seated in an elbow-chair, in one corner of his study, or laboratory, with a large volume, in German print, before him. He was a short fat man, with a dark square face, rendered more dark by a black velvet cap. He had a little nobbed nose, not unlike the ace of spades, with a pair of spectacles gleaming on each side of his dusky countenance, like a couple of bow-windows.

Dolph felt struck with awe on entering into the presence of this learned man; and gazed about him with boyish wonder at the furniture of this chamber of knowledge; which appeared to him almost as the den of a magician. In the centre stood a claw-footed table, with pestle and mortar, phials and gallipots,* and a pair of small burnished scales. At one end was a heavy clothes-press, turned into a receptacle for drugs and compounds; against which hung the doctor's hat and cloak, and gold-headed cane, and on the top grinned a human skull. Along the mantelpiece were glass vessels, in which were snakes and lizards, and a human fœtus preserved in spirits. A closet, the doors of which were taken off, contained three whole shelves of books, and some, too, of mighty folio dimensions,— a collection the like of which Dolph had never before beheld. As, however, the library did not take up the whole of the closet, the doctor's thrifty housekeeper had occupied the rest with pots of pickles and preserves; and had hung about the room, among awful implements of the healing art, strings of red pepper and corpulent cucumbers, carefully preserved for seed.

---

*Small covered pots used to hold ointments.

Peter de Groodt and his protegé were received with great gravity and stateliness by the doctor, who was a very wise, dignified little man, and never smiled. He surveyed Dolph from head to foot, above, and under, and through his spectacles, and the poor lad's heart quailed as these great glasses glared on him like two full moons. The doctor heard all that Peter de Groodt had to say in favor of the youthful candidate; and then wetting his thumb with the end of his tongue, he began deliberately to turn over page after page of the great black volume before him. At length, after many hums and haws, and strokings of the chin, and all that hesitation and deliberation with which a wise man proceeds to do what he intended to do from the very first, the doctor agreed to take the lad as a disciple; to give him bed, board, and clothing, and to instruct him in the healing art; in return for which he was to have his services until his twenty-first year.

Behold, then, our hero, all at once transformed from an unlucky urchin running wild about the streets, to a student of medicine, diligently pounding a pestle, under the auspices of the learned Doctor Karl Lodovick Knipperhausen. It was a happy transition for his fond old mother. She was delighted with the idea of her boy's being brought up worthy of his ancestors; and anticipated the day when he would be able to hold up his head with the lawyer, that lived in the large house opposite; or, peradventure, with the Dominie himself.

Doctor Knipperhausen was a native of the Palatinate in Germany; whence, in company with many of his countrymen, he had taken refuge in England, on account of religious persecution. He was one of nearly three thousand Palatines, who came over from England in 1710, under the protection of Governor Hunter.* Where the doctor had studied, how he had acquired his medical knowledge, and where he had received his diploma, it is hard at present to say, for nobody knew at the time; yet it is certain that his profound skill and abstruse knowledge were the talk and wonder of the common people, far and near.

His practice was totally different from that of any other physician,—consisting in mysterious compounds, known only to

---

*Robert Hunter, royal governor of New York and New Jersey (1710–1719); he brought the Palatines (German refugees) to New York to produce naval stores for England.

himself, in the preparing and administering of which, it was said, he always consulted the stars. So high an opinion was entertained of his skill, particularly by the German and Dutch inhabitants, that they always resorted to him in desperate cases. He was one of those infallible doctors that are always effecting sudden and surprising cures, when the patient has been given up by all the regular physicians; unless, as is shrewdly observed, the case has been left too long before it was put into their hands. The doctor's library was the talk and marvel of the neighborhood, I might almost say of the entire burgh. The good people looked with reverence at a man who had read three whole shelves full of books, and some of them, too, as large as a family Bible. There were many disputes among the members of the little Lutheran church, as to which was the wisest man, the doctor or the Dominie. Some of his admirers even went so far as to say, that he knew more than the governor himself,—in a word, it was thought that there was no end to his knowledge!

No sooner was Dolph received into the doctor's family, than he was put in possession of the lodging of his predecessor. It was a garret-room of a steep-roofed Dutch house, where the rain had pattered on the shingles, and the lightning gleamed, and the wind piped through the crannies in stormy weather; and where whole troops of hungry rats, like Don Cossacks,* galloped about, in defiance of traps and ratsbane.

He was soon up to his ears in medical studies, being employed, morning, noon, and night, in rolling pills, filtering tinctures, or pounding the pestle and mortar in one corner of the laboratory; while the doctor would take his seat in another corner, when he had nothing else to do, or expected visitors, and arrayed in his morning-gown and velvet cap, would pore over the contents of some folio volume. It is true, that the regular thumping of Dolph's pestle, or, perhaps, the drowsy buzzing of the summer-flies, would now and then lull the little man into a slumber; but then his spectacles were always wide awake, and studiously regarding the book.

There was another personage in the house, however, to whom Dolph was obliged to pay allegiance. Though a bachelor, and a man

---

*Mercenary soldiers from the Ukraine region.

of such great dignity and importance, the doctor was, like many other wise men, subject to petticoat government. He was completely under the sway of his housekeeper,—a spare, busy, fretting house-wife, in a little, round, quilted German cap, with a huge bunch of keys jingling at the girdle of an exceedingly long waist. Frau Ilsé (or Frow Ilsy, as it was pronounced) had accompanied him in his various migrations from Germany to England, and from England to the province; managing his establishment and himself too: ruling him, it is true, with a gentle hand, but carrying a high hand with all the world beside. How she had acquired such ascendency I do not pretend to say. People, it is true, did talk—but have not people been prone to talk ever since the world began? Who can tell how women generally contrive to get the upperhand? A husband, it is true, may now and then be master in his own house; but who ever knew a bachelor that was not managed by his housekeeper?

Indeed, Frau Ilsy's power was not confined to the doctor's household. She was one of those prying gossips who know every one's business better than they do themselves; and whose all-seeing eyes, and all-telling tongues, are terrors throughout a neighborhood.

Nothing of any moment transpired in the world of scandal of this little burgh, but it was known to Frau Ilsy. She had her crew of cronies, that were perpetually hurrying to her little parlor with some precious bit of news; nay, she would sometimes discuss a whole volume of secret history, as she held the street-door ajar, and gossiped with one of these garrulous cronies in the very teeth of a December blast.

Between the doctor and the housekeeper it may easily be supposed that Dolph had a busy life of it. As Frau Ilsy kept the keys, and literally ruled the roast, it was starvation to offend her, though he found the study of her temper more perplexing even than that of medicine. When not busy in the laboratory, she kept him running hither and thither on her errands; and on Sundays he was obliged to accompany her to and from church, and carry her Bible. Many a time has the poor varlet stood shivering and blowing his fingers, or holding his frostbitten nose, in the church-yard, while Ilsy and her cronies were huddled together, wagging their heads, and tearing some unlucky character to pieces.

With all his advantages, however, Dolph made very slow progress in his art. This was no fault of the doctor's, certainly, for he took unwearied pains with the lad, keeping him close to the pestle and mortar, or on the trot about town with phials and pill-boxes; and if he ever flagged in his industry, which he was rather apt to do, the doctor would fly into a passion, and ask him if he ever expected to learn his profession, unless he applied himself closer to the study. The fact is, he still retained the fondness for sport and mischief that had marked his childhood; the habit, indeed, had strengthened with his years, and gained force from being thwarted and constrained. He daily grew more and more untractable, and lost favor in the eyes both of the doctor and the housekeeper.

In the meantime the doctor went on, waxing wealthy and renowned. He was famous for his skill in managing cases not laid down in the books. He had cured several old women and young girls of witchcraft,—a terrible complaint, and nearly as prevalent in the province in those days as hydrophobia* is at present. He had even restored one strapping country-girl to perfect health, who had gone so far as to vomit crooked pins and needles; which is considered a desperate stage of the malady. It was whispered, also, that he was possessed of the art of preparing love-powders; and many applications had he in consequence from love-sick patients of both sexes. But all these cases formed the mysterious part of his practice, in which, according to the cant phrase, "secrecy and honor might be depended on." Dolph, therefore, was obliged to turn out of the study whenever such consultations occurred, though it is said he learnt more of the secrets of the art at the key-hole than by all the rest of his studies put together.

As the doctor increased in wealth, he began to extend his possessions, and to look forward, like other great men, to the time when he should retire to the repose of a country-seat. For this purpose he had purchased a farm, or, as the Dutch settlers called it, a *bowerie*, a few miles from town. It had been the residence of a wealthy family, that had returned some time since to Holland. A large mansion-house stood in the centre of it, very much out of repair, and which, in consequence of certain reports, had received the appellation of the

---

*Rabies.

Haunted House. Either from these reports, or from its actual dreariness, the doctor found it impossible to get a tenant; and that the place might not fall to ruin before he could reside in it himself, he placed a country boor,* with his family, in one wing, with the privilege of cultivating the farm on shares.

The doctor now felt all the dignity of a landholder rising within him. He had a little of the German pride of territory in his composition, and almost looked upon himself as owner of a principality. He began to complain of the fatigue of business; and was fond of riding out "to look at his estate." His little expeditions to his lands were attended with a bustle and parade that created a sensation throughout the neighborhood. His walleyed horse stood, stamping and whisking off the flies, for a full hour before the house. Then the doctor's saddle-bags would be brought out and adjusted; then, after a little while, his cloak would be rolled up and strapped to the saddle; then his umbrella would be buttoned to the cloak; while, in the meantime, a group of ragged boys, that observant class of beings, would gather before the door. At length the doctor would issue forth, in a pair of jack-boots that reached above his knees, and a cocked hat flapped down in front. As he was a short, fat man, he took some time to mount into the saddle; and when there, he took some time to have the saddle and stirrups properly adjusted, enjoying the wonder and admiration of the urchin crowd. Even after he had set off, he would pause in the middle of the street, or trot back two or three times to give some parting orders; which were answered by the housekeeper from the door, or Dolph from the study, or the black cook from the cellar, or the chambermaid from the garret-window; and there were generally some last words bawled after him, just as he was turning the corner.

The whole neighborhood would be aroused by this pomp and circumstance. The cobbler would leave his last; the barber would thrust out his frizzled head, with a comb sticking in it; a knot would collect at the grocer's door, and the word would be buzzed from one end of the street to the other, "The doctor's riding out to his country-seat!"

These were golden moments for Dolph. No sooner was the doctor out of sight, than pestle and mortar were abandoned; the

---

*Farmer (from the Dutch word *boer*).

laboratory was left to take care of itself, and the student was off on some madcap frolic.

Indeed, it must be confessed, the youngster, as he grew up, seemed in a fair way to fulfil the prediction of the old claret-colored gentleman. He was the ringleader of all holiday sports and midnight gambols; ready for all kinds of mischievous pranks and hair-brained adventures.

There is nothing so troublesome as a hero on a small scale, or, rather, a hero in a small town. Dolph soon became the abhorrence of all drowsy, housekeeping old citizens, who hated noise, and had no relish for waggery. The good dames, too, considered him as little better than a reprobate, gathered their daughters under their wings whenever he approached, and pointed him out as a warning to their sons. No one seemed to hold him in much regard except the wild striplings of the place, who were captivated by his open-hearted, daring manners,—and the negroes, who always looked upon every idle, do-nothing youngster as a kind of gentleman. Even the good Peter de Groodt, who had considered himself a kind of patron of the lad, began to despair of him; and would shake his head dubiously, as he listened to a long complaint from the housekeeper, and sipped a glass of her raspberry brandy.

Still his mother was not to be wearied out of her affection by all the waywardness of her boy; nor disheartened by the stories of his misdeeds, with which her good friends were continually regaling her. She had, it is true, very little of the pleasure which rich people enjoy, in always hearing their children praised; but she considered all this ill-will as a kind of persecution which he suffered, and she liked him the better on that account. She saw him growing up a fine, tall, good-looking youngster, and she looked at him with the secret pride of a mother's heart. It was her great desire that Dolph should appear like a gentleman, and all the money she could save went towards helping out his pocket and his wardrobe. She would look out of the window after him, as he sallied forth in his best array, and her heart would yearn with delight; and once, when Peter de Groodt, struck with the youngster's gallant appearance on a bright Sunday morning, observed, "Well, after all, Dolph does grow a comely fellow!" the tear of pride started into the mother's eye. "Ah, neighbor! neighbor!" exclaimed she, "they may say what they please; poor Dolph will yet hold up his head with the best of them!"

Dolph Heyliger had now nearly attained his one-and-twentieth year, and the term of his medical studies was just expiring; yet it must be confessed that he knew little more of the profession than when he first entered the doctor's doors. This, however, could not be from any want of quickness of parts, for he showed amazing aptness in mastering other branches of knowledge, which he could only have studied at intervals. He was, for instance, a sure marksman, and won all the geese and turkeys at Christmas holidays. He was a bold rider; he was famous for leaping and wrestling; he played tolerably on the fiddle; could swim like a fish; and was the best hand in the whole place at fives and nine-pins.

All these accomplishments, however, procured him no favor in the eyes of the doctor, who grew more and more crabbed and intolerant the nearer the term of apprenticeship approached. Frau Ilsy, too, was forever finding some occasion to raise a windy tempest about his ears, and seldom encountered him about the house without a clatter of the tongue; so that at length the jingling of her keys, as she approached, was to Dolph like the ringing of the prompter's bell, that gives notice of a theatrical thunder-storm. Nothing but the infinite good-humor of the heedless youngster enabled him to bear all this domestic tyranny without open rebellion. It was evident that the doctor and his housekeeper were preparing to beat the poor youth out of the nest, the moment his term should have expired,—a short-hand mode which the doctor had of providing for useless disciples.

Indeed the little man had been rendered more than usually irritable lately in consequence of various cares and vexations which his country estate had brought upon him. The doctor had been repeatedly annoyed by the rumors and tales which prevailed concerning the old mansion, and found it difficult to prevail even upon the country-man and his family to remain there rent-free. Every time he rode out to the farm he was teased by some fresh complaint of strange noises and fearful sights, with which the tenants were disturbed at night; and the doctor would come home fretting and fuming, and vent his spleen upon the whole household. It was indeed a sore grievance that affected him both in pride and purse. He was threatened with an absolute loss of the profits of his property; and then, what a blow to his territorial consequence, to be the landlord of a haunted house!

It was observed, however, that with all his vexation, the doctor never proposed to sleep in the house himself; nay, he could never be prevailed upon to remain on the premises after dark, but made the best of his way for town as soon as the bats began to flit about in the twilight. The fact was, the doctor had a secret belief in ghosts, having passed the early part of his life in a country where they particularly abound; and indeed the story went, that, when a boy, he had once seen the devil upon the Hartz Mountains in Germany.

At length the doctor's vexations on this head were brought to a crisis. One morning as he sat dozing over a volume in his study, he was suddenly startled from his slumbers by the bustling in of the housekeeper.

"Here's a fine to do!" cried she, as she entered the room. "Here's Claus Hopper come in, bag and baggage, from the farm, and swears he'll have nothing more to do with it. The whole family have been frightened out of their wits; for there's such racketing and rummaging about the old house, that they can't sleep quiet in their beds!"

"Donner and blitzen!" cried the doctor, impatiently; "will they never have done chattering about that house? What a pack of fools, to let a few rats and mice frighten them out of good quarters!"

"Nay, nay," said the housekeeper, wagging her head knowingly, and piqued at having a good ghost-story doubted, "there's more in it than rats and mice. All the neighborhood talks about the house; and then such sights as have been seen in it! Peter de Groodt tells me, that the family that sold you the house, and went to Holland, dropped several strange hints about it, and said, 'they wished you joy of your bargain;' and you know yourself there's no getting any family to live in it."

"Peter de Groodt's a ninny—an old woman," said the doctor, peevishly; "I'll warrant he's been filling these people's heads full of stories. It's just like his nonsense about the ghost that haunted the church-belfry, as an excuse for not ringing the bell that cold night when Harmanus Brinkerhoff's house was on fire. Send Claus to me."

Claus Hopper now made his appearance: a simple country lout, full of awe at finding himself in the very study of Dr. Knipperhausen, and too much embarrassed to enter in much detail of the matters that had caused his alarm. He stood twirling his hat in one hand, resting sometimes on one leg, sometimes on the other, looking occasionally at the doctor, and now and then stealing a fearful glance at the death's-head that seemed ogling him from the top of the clothes-press.

The doctor tried every means to persuade him to return to the farm, but all in vain; he maintained a dogged determination on the subject; and at the close of every argument or solicitation would make the same brief, inflexible reply, "*Ich kan nicht, mynheer.*"* The doctor was a "little pot, and soon hot;" his patience was exhausted by these continual vexations about his estate. The stubborn refusal of Claus Hopper seemed to him like flat rebellion; his temper suddenly boiled over, and Claus was glad to make a rapid retreat to escape scalding.

When the bumpkin got to the housekeeper's room, he found Peter de Groodt, and several other true believers, ready to receive him. Here he indemnified himself for the restraint he had suffered in the study, and opened a budget of stories about the haunted house that astonished all his hearers. The housekeeper believed them all, if it was only to spite the doctor for having received her intelligence so uncourteously. Peter de Groodt matched them with many a wonderful legend of the times of the Dutch dynasty, and of the Devil's Stepping-stones; and of the pirate hanged at Gibbet Island, that continued to swing there at night long after the gallows was taken down; and of the ghost of the unfortunate Governor Leisler,† hanged for treason, which haunted the old fort and the government-house. The gossiping knot dispersed, each charged with direful intelligence. The sexton disburdened himself at a vestry meeting that was held that very day, and the black cook forsook her kitchen, and spent half the day at the street-pump, that gossiping-place of servants, dealing forth the news to all that came for water. In a little time the whole town was in a buzz with tales about the haunted house. Some said that Claus Hopper had seen the devil, while others hinted that the house was haunted by the ghosts of some of the patients whom the doctor had physicked out of the

---

*I will not, sir (Dutch and low German).
†Jacob Leisler (c.1640–1691), known for leading Leisler's Rebellion (1689), in which he deposed New York's lieutenant governor, Francis Nicholson, and named himself governor; he was tried and executed after refusing to step down.

world, and that was the reason why he did not venture to live in it himself.

All this put the little doctor in a terrible fume. He threatened vengeance on any one who should affect the value of his property by exciting popular prejudices. He complained loudly of thus being in a manner dispossessed of his territories by mere bugbears; but he secretly determined to have the house exorcised by the Dominie. Great was his relief, therefore, when in the midst of his perplexities, Dolph stepped forward and undertook to garrison the haunted house. The youngster had been listening to all the stories of Claus Hopper and Peter de Groodt: he was fond of adventure, he loved the marvellous, and his imagination had become quite excited by these tales of wonder. Besides, he had led such an uncomfortable life at the doctor's, being subjected to the intolerable thraldom of early hours, that he was delighted at the prospect of having a house to himself, even though it should be a haunted one. His offer was eagerly accepted, and it was determined he should mount guard that very night. His only stipulation was, that the enterprise should be kept secret from his mother; for he knew the poor soul would not sleep a wink if she knew her son was waging war with the powers of darkness.

When night came on he set out on this perilous expedition. The old black cook, his only friend in the household, had provide him with a little mess for supper, and a rush-light;* and she tied round his neck an amulet, given her by an African conjurer, as a charm against evil spirits. Dolph was escorted on his way by the doctor and Peter de Groodt, who had agreed to accompany him to the house, and to see him safe lodged. The night was overcast, and it was very dark when they arrived at the grounds which surrounded the mansion. The sexton led the way with the lantern. As they walked along the avenue of acacias, the fitful light, catching from bush to bush, and tree to tree, often startled the doughty Peter, and made him fall back upon his followers; and the doctor grappled still closer hold of Dolph's arm, observing that the ground was very slippery and uneven. At one time they were nearly put to total rout by a bat, which came flitting about the lantern; and the notes of the insects from the trees,

---

*Candle made of the dried pith of a rush plant dipped in tallow.

and the frogs from a neighboring pond, formed a most drowsy and doleful concert. The front door of the mansion opened with a grating sound, that made the doctor turn pale. They entered a tolerably large hall, such as is common in American country-houses, and which serves for a sitting-room in warm weather. From this they went up a wide staircase, that groaned and creaked as they trod, every step making its particular note, like the key of a harpsichord. This led to another hall on the second story, whence they entered the room where Dolph was to sleep. It was large and scantily furnished; the shutters were closed; but as they were much broken, there was no want of a circulation of air. It appeared to have been that sacred chamber, known among Dutch housewives by the name of "the best bedroom;" which is the best furnished room in the house, but in which scarce anybody is ever permitted to sleep. Its splendor, however, was all at an end. There were a few broken articles of furniture about the room, and in the centre stood a heavy deal table and a large arm-chair both of which had the look of being coeval* with the mansion. The fireplace was wide, and had been faced with Dutch tiles, representing Scripture stories; but some of them had fallen out of their places, and lay scattered about the hearth. The sexton lit the rush-light; and the doctor, looking fearfully about the room, was just exhorting Dolph to be of good cheer, and to pluck up a stout heart, when a noise in the chimney, like voices and struggling, struck a sudden panic into the sexton. He took to his heels with the lantern; the doctor followed hard after him; the stairs groaned and creaked as they hurried down, increasing their agitation and speed by its noise. The front door slammed after them; and Dolph heard them scrabbling down the avenue, till the sound of their feet was lost in the distance. That he did not join in this precipitate retreat might have been owing to his possessing a little more courage than his companions, or perhaps that he had caught a glimpse of the cause of their dismay, in a nest of chimney-swallows, that came tumbling down into the fireplace.

Being now left to himself, he secured the front door by a strong bolt and bar; and having seen that the other entrances were fastened, returned to his desolate chamber. Having made his supper from the

---

*Of the same age.

basket which the good old cook had provided, he locked the chamber-door, and retired to rest on a mattress in one corner. The night was calm and still; and nothing broke upon the profound quiet but the lonely chirping of a cricket from the chimney of a distant chamber. The rush-light, which stood in the centre of the deal table, shed a feeble yellow ray, dimly illumining the chamber, and making uncouth shapes and shadows on the walls, from the clothes which Dolph had thrown over a chair.

With all his boldness of heart, there was something subduing in this desolate scene; and he felt his spirits flag within him, as he lay on his hard bed and gazed about the room. He was turning over in his mind his idle habits, his doubtful prospects, and now and then heaving a heavy sigh as he thought on his poor old mother; for there is nothing like the silence and loneliness of night to bring dark shadows over the brightest mind. By and by he thought he heard a sound as of some one walking below stairs. He listened, and distinctly heard a step on the great staircase. It approached solemnly and slowly, tramp—tramp—tramp! It was evidently the tread of some heavy personage; and yet how could he have got into the house without making a noise? He had examined all the fastenings, and was certain that every entrance was secure. Still the steps advanced, tramp—tramp—tramp! It was evident that the person approaching could not be a robber, the step was too loud and deliberate; a robber would either be stealthy or precipitate. And now the footsteps had ascended the staircase; they were slowly advancing along the passage, resounding through the silent and empty apartments. The very cricket had ceased its melancholy note, and nothing interrupted their awful distinctness. The door, which had been locked on the inside, slowly swung open, as if self-moved. The footsteps entered the room; but no one was to be seen. They passed slowly and audibly across it, tramp—tramp—tramp! but whatever made the sound was invisible. Dolph rubbed his eyes, and stared about him; he could see to every part of the dimly-lighted chamber; all was vacant; yet still he heard those mysterious footsteps, solemnly walking about the chamber. They ceased, and all was dead silence. There was something more appalling in this invisible visitation than there would have been in anything that addressed itself to the eye-sight. It was awfully vague and indefinite. He felt his heart beat against his ribs; a cold sweat broke out upon his forehead; he lay for some time in a state of violent agitation: nothing, however, occurred to increase his alarm. His light gradually burnt down into the socket, and he fell asleep. When he awoke it was broad daylight; the sun was peering through the cracks of the window-shutters, and the birds were merrily singing about the house. The bright cheery day soon put to flight all the terrors of the preceding night. Dolph laughed, or rather tried to laugh, at all that had passed, and endeavored to persuade himself that it was a mere freak of the imagination, conjured up by the stories he had heard; but he was a little puzzled to find the door of his room locked on the inside, notwithstanding that he had positively seen it swing open as the footsteps had entered. He returned to town in a state of considerable perplexity; but he determined to say nothing on the subject, until his doubts were either confirmed or removed by another night's watching. His silence was a grievous disappointment to the gossips who had gathered at the doctor's mansion. They had prepared their minds to hear direful tales, and were almost in a rage at being assured he had nothing to relate.

The next night, then, Dolph repeated his vigil. He now entered the house with some trepidation. He was particular in examining the fastenings of all the doors, and securing them well. He locked the door of his chamber, and placed a chair against it; then having dispatched his supper, he threw himself on his mattress and endeavored to sleep. It was all in vain; a thousand crowding fancies kept him waking. The time slowly dragged on, as if minutes were spinning themselves out into hours. As the night advanced, he grew more and more nervous; and he almost started from his couch when he heard the mysterious footstep again on the staircase. Up it came, as before, solemnly and slowly, tramp—tramp—tramp! It approached along the passage; the door again swung open, as if there had been neither lock nor impediment, and a strange-looking figure stalked into the room. It was an elderly man, large and robust, clothed in the old Flemish fashion. He had on a kind of short cloak, with a garment under it, belted round the waist; trunk-hose, with great bunches or bows at the knees; and a pair of russet boots, very large at top, and standing widely from his legs. His hat was broad and slouched, with a feather trailing over one side. His iron-gray hair hang in thick masses on his neck; and he had a short grizzled beard. He walked slowly round the room, as if examining that all was safe; then, hanging his hat on a peg beside the door, he sat down in the elbow-chair, and, leaning his elbow on the table, fixed his eyes on Dolph with an unmoving and deadening stare.

Dolph was not naturally a coward; but he had been brought up in an implicit belief in ghosts and goblins. A thousand stories came swarming to his mind that he had heard about this building; and as he looked at this strange personage, with his uncouth garb, his pale visage, his grizzly beard, and his fixed, staring, fishlike eye, his teeth began to chatter, his hair to rise on his head, and a cold sweat to break out all over his body. How long he remained in this situation he could not tell, for he was like one fascinated. He could not take his gaze off from the spectre; but lay staring at him, with his whole intellect absorbed in the contemplation. The old man remained seated behind the table, without stirring, or turning an eye, always keeping a dead steady glare upon Dolph. At length the household cock, from a neighboring farm, clapped his wings, and gave a loud cheerful crow that rung over the fields. At the sound the old man slowly rose, and took down his hat from the peg; the door opened, and closed after him; he was heard to go slowly down the staircase, tramp—tramp—tramp!—and when he had got to the bottom, all was again silent. Dolph lay and listened earnestly; counted every footfall; listened, and listened, if the steps should return, until, exhausted by watching and agitation, he fell into a troubled sleep.

Daylight again brought fresh courage and assurance. He would fain have considered all that had passed as a mere dream; yet there stood the chair in which the unknown had seated himself; there was the table on which he had leaned; there was the peg on which he had hung his hat; and there was the door, locked precisely as he himself had locked it, with the chair placed against it. He hastened down-stairs, and examined the doors and windows; all were exactly in the same state in which he had left them, and there was no apparent way by which any being could have entered and left the house, without leaving some trace behind. "Pooh!" said Dolph to himself, "it was all a dream:"—but it would not do; the more he endeavored to shake the scene off from his mind, the more it haunted him.

Though he persisted in a strict silence as to all that he had seen or heard, yet his looks betrayed the uncomfortable night that he had passed. It was evident that there was something wonderful hidden under this mysterious reserve. The doctor took him into the study, locked the door, and sought to have a full and confidential communication; but he could get nothing out of him. Frau Ilsy took him aside into the pantry, but to as little purpose; and Peter de Groodt held him by the button for a full hour, in the church-yard, the very place to get at the bottom of a ghost-story, but came off not a whit wiser than the rest. It is always the case, however, that one truth concealed makes a dozen current lies. It is like a guinea locked up in a bank, that has a dozen paper representatives. Before the day was over, the neighborhood was full of reports. Some said that Dolph Heyliger watched in the haunted house, with pistols loaded with silver bullets; others, that he had a long talk with a spectre without a head; others, that Doctor Knipperhausen and the sexton had been hunted down the Bowery lane, and quite into town, by a legion of ghosts of their customers. Some shook their heads, and thought it a shame the doctor should put Dolph to pass the night alone in that dismal house, where he might be spirited away no one knew whither; while others observed, with a shrug, that if the devil did carry off the youngster, it would be but taking his own.

These rumors at length reached the ears of the good Dame Heyliger, and, as may be supposed, threw her into a terrible alarm. For her son to have opposed himself to danger from living foes, would have been nothing so dreadful in her eyes, as to dare alone the terrors of the haunted house. She hastened to the doctor's, and passed a great part of the day in attempting to dissuade Dolph from repeating his vigil; she told him a score of tales, which her gossiping friends had just related to her, of persons who had been carried off, when watching alone in old ruinous houses. It was all to no effect. Dolph's pride, as well as curiosity, was piqued. He endeavored to calm the apprehensions of his mother, and to assure her that there was no truth in all the rumors she had heard; she looked at him dubiously and shook her head; but finding his determination was not to be shaken, she brought him a little thick Dutch Bible, with brass clasps, to take with him, as a sword wherewith to fight the powers of darkness; and, lest that might not be sufficient, the housekeeper gave him the Heidelberg catechism* by way of dagger.

The next night, therefore, Dolph took up his quarters for the third time in the old mansion. Whether dream or not, the same thing was repeated. Towards midnight, when everything was still, the same sound echoed through the empty halls, tramp—tramp—tramp! The stairs were again ascended; the door again swung open; the old man entered; walked round the room; hung up his hat, and seated himself by the table. The same fear and trembling came over poor Dolph, though not in so violent a degree. He lay in the same way, motionless and fascinated, staring at the figure, which regarded him as before with a dead, fixed, chilling gaze. In this way they remained for a long time, till, by degrees, Dolph's courage began gradually to revive. Whether alive or dead, this being had certainly some object in his visitation; and he recollected to have heard it said, spirits have no power to speak until spoken to. Summoning up resolution, therefore, and making two or three attempts, before he could get his parched tongue in motion, he addressed the unknown in the most solemn form of adjuration, and demanded to know what was the motive of his visit.

No sooner had he finished, than the old man rose, took down his hat, the door opened, and he went out, looking back upon Dolph just as he crossed the threshold, as if expecting him to follow. The youngster did not hesitate an instant. He took the candle in his hand, and the Bible under his arm, and obeyed the tacit invitation. The candle emitted a feeble, uncertain ray, but still he could see the figure before him slowly descend the stairs. He followed trembling. When it had reached the bottom of the stairs, it turned through the hall towards the back door of the mansion. Dolph held the light over the balustrades; but, in his eagerness to catch a sight of the unknown, he flared his feeble taper so suddenly, that it went out. Still there was sufficient light from the pale moonbeams, that fell through a narrow window, to give him an indistinct view of the figure, near the door. He followed, therefore, down stairs, and turned towards the place; but when he arrived there, the unknown had disappeared. The door remained fast barred and bolted; there was

---

*Calvinist manual (1563) used to instruct children in the Christian faith.

no other mode of exit; yet the being, whatever he might be, was gone. He unfastened the door, and looked out into the fields. It was a hazy, moonlight night, so that the eye could distinguish objects at some distance. He thought he saw the unknown in a footpath which led from the door. He was not mistaken; but how had he got out of the house? He did not pause to think, but followed on. The old man proceeded at a measured pace, without looking about him, his footsteps sounding on the hard ground. He passed through the orchard of apple-trees, always keeping the footpath. It led to a well, situated in a little hollow, which had supplied the farm with water. Just at this well Dolph lost sight of him. He rubbed his eyes and looked again; but nothing was to be seen of the unknown. He reached the well, but nobody was there. All the surrounding ground was open and clear; there was no bush nor hiding-place. He looked down the well, and saw, at a great depth, the reflection of the sky in the still water. After remaining here for some time, without seeing or hearing anything more of his mysterious conductor, he returned to the house, full of awe and wonder. He bolted the door, groped his way back to bed, and it was long before he could compose himself to sleep.

His dreams were strange and troubled. He thought he was following the old man along the side of a great river, until they came to a vessel on the point of sailing; and that his conductor led him on board and vanished. He remembered the commander of the vessel, a short swarthy man, with crisped black hair, blind of one eye, and lame of one leg; but the rest of his dream was very confused. Sometimes he was sailing; sometimes on shore; now amidst storms and tempests, and now wandering quietly in unknown streets. The figure of the old man was strangely mingled up with the incidents of the dream, and the whole distinctly wound up by his finding himself on board of the vessel again, returning home, with a great bag of money!

When he woke, the gray, cool light of dawn was streaking the horizon, and the cocks passing the reveille from farm to farm throughout the country. He rose more harassed and perplexed than ever. He was singularly confounded by all that he had seen and dreamt, and began to doubt whether his mind was not affected, and whether all that passing in his thoughts might not be mere feverish fantasy. In his present state of mind, he did not feel disposed to return immediately to the doctor's, and undergo the cross-questioning of the household. He made a scanty breakfast, therefore, on the remains of the last night's provisions, and then wandered out into the fields to meditate on all that had befallen him. Lost in thought, he rambled about, gradually approaching the town, until the morning was far advanced, when he was aroused by a hurry and bustle around him. He found himself near the water's edge, in a throng of people, hurrying to a pier, where was a vessel ready to make sail. He was unconsciously carried along by the impulse of the crowd, and found that it was a sloop, on the point of sailing up the Hudson to Albany. There was much leave-taking, and kissing of old women and children, and great activity in carrying on board baskets of bread and cakes, and provisions of all kinds, notwithstanding the mighty joints of meat that dangled over the stern; for a voyage to Albany was an expedition of great moment in those days. The commander of the sloop was hurrying about, and giving a world of orders, which were not very strictly attended to; one man being busy in lighting his pipe, and another in sharpening his snickersnee.*

The appearance of the commander suddenly caught Dolph's attention. He was short and swarthy, with crisped black hair; blind of one eye and lame of one leg—the very commander that he had seen in his dream! Surprised and aroused, he considered the scene more attentively, and recalled still further traces of his dream: the appearance of the vessel, of the river, and of images, a variety of other objects accorded with the imperfect vaguely rising to recollection.

As he stood musing on these circumstances, the captain suddenly called out to him in Dutch, "Step on board, young man, or you'll be left behind!" he was startled by the summons; he saw that the sloop was cast loose, and was actually moving from the pier; it seemed as if he was actuated by some irresistible impulse; he sprang upon the deck, and the next moment the sloop was hurried off by the wind and tide. Dolph's thoughts and feelings were all in tumult and confusion. He had been strongly worked upon by the events which had recently befallen him, and could not but think there was some connection between his present situation and his last night's dream. He felt as if under supernatural influence; and tried to assure himself

---

*Hunting knife.

with an old and favorite maxim of his, that "one way or other all would turn out for the best." For a moment, the indignation of the doctor at his departure, without leave, passed across his mind, but that was matter of little moment; then he thought of the distress of his mother at his strange disappearance, and the idea gave him a sudden pang; he would have entreated to be put on shore; but he knew with such wind and tide the entreaty would have been in vain. Then the inspiring love of novelty and adventure came rushing in full tide through his bosom; he felt himself launched strangely and suddenly on the world, and under full way to explore the regions of wonder that lay up this mighty river, and beyond those blue mountains which had bounded his horizon since childhood. While he was lost in this whirl of thought, the sails strained to the breeze; the shores seemed to hurry away behind him; and before he perfectly recovered his self-possession, the sloop was ploughing her way past Spiking-devil and Yonkers,* and the tallest chimney of the Manhattoes had faded from his sight.

I have said that a voyage up the Hudson in those days was an undertaking of some moment; indeed, it was as much thought of as a voyage to Europe is at present. The sloops were often many days on the way; the cautious navigators taking in sail when it blew fresh, and coming to anchor at night; and stopping to send the boat ashore for milk for tea; without which it was impossible for the worthy old lady passengers to subsist. And there were the much-talked-of perils of the Tappaan Zee, and the highlands. In short, a prudent Dutch burgher would talk of such a voyage for months, and even years, beforehand; and never undertook it without putting his affairs in order, making his will, and having prayers said for him in the Low Dutch churches.

In the course of such a voyage, therefore, Dolph was satisfied he would have time enough to reflect, and to make up his mind as to what he should do when he arrived at Albany. The captain, with his blind eye, and lame leg, would, it is true, bring his strange dream to mind, and perplex him sadly for a few moments; but of late his life had been made up so much of dreams and realities, his nights and

---

*Landmarks along the Hudson River (subsequent references to such landmarks will not be annotated).

days had been so jumbled together, that he seemed to be moving continually in a delusion. There is always, however, a kind of vagabond consolation in a man's having nothing in this world to lose; with this Dolph comforted his heart, and determined to make the most of the present enjoyment.

In the second day of the voyage they came to the highlands. It was the latter part of a calm, sultry day, that they floated gently with the tide between these stern mountains. There was that perfect quiet which prevails over nature in the languor of summer heat; the turning of a plank, or the accidental falling of an oar on deck, was echoed from the mountain-side, and reverberated along the shores; and if by chance the captain gave a shout of command, there were airy tongues which mocked it from every cliff.

Dolph gazed about him in mute delight and wonder at these scenes of nature's magnificence. To the left the Dunderberg reared its woody precipices, height over height, forest over forest, away into the deep summer sky. To the right, strutted forth the bold promontory of Antony's Nose, with a solitary eagle wheeling about it; while beyond, mountain succeeded to mountain, until they seemed to lock their arms together, and confine this mighty river in their embraces. There was a feeling of quiet luxury in gazing at the broad, green bosoms here and there scooped out among the precipices; or at woodlands high in air, nodding over the edge of some beetling bluff, and their foliage all transparent in the yellow sunshine.

In the midst of his admiration, Dolph remarked a pile of bright, snowy clouds, peering above the western heights. It was succeeded by another, and another, each seemingly pushing onwards its predecessor, and towering, with dazzling brilliancy, in the deep-blue atmosphere; and now muttering peals of thunder were faintly heard rolling behind the mountains. The river, hitherto still and glassy, reflecting pictures of the sky and land, now showed a dark ripple at a distance, as the breeze came creeping up it. The fish-hawks wheeled and screamed, and sought their nests on the high dry trees; the crows flew clamorously to the crevices of the rocks, and all nature seemed conscious of the approaching thunder-gust.

The clouds now rolled in volumes over the mountain-tops; their summits still bright and snowy, but the lower parts of an inky blackness. The rain began to patter down in broad and scattered drops; the wind freshened, and curled up the waves; at length it seemed as if the bellying clouds were torn open by the mountain-tops, and complete torrents of rain came rattling down. The lightning leaped from cloud to cloud, and streamed quivering against the rocks, splitting and rending the stoutest forest-trees. The thunder burst in tremendous explosions; the peals were echoed from mountain to mountain; they crashed upon Dunderberg, and rolled up the long defile of the highlands, each headland making a new echo, until old Bull Hill seemed to bellow back the storm.

For a time the scudding rack and mist, and the sheeted rain, almost hid the landscape from the sight. There was a fearful gloom, illumined still more fearfully by the streams of lightning which glittered among the raindrops. Never had Dolph beheld such an absolute warring of the elements; it seemed as if the storm was tearing and rending its way through this mountain defile, and had brought all the artillery of heaven into action.

The vessel was hurried on by the increasing wind, until she came to where the river makes a sudden bend, the only one in the whole course of its majestic career.* Just as they turned the point, a violent flaw of wind came sweeping down a mountain gully, bending the forest before it, and, in a moment, lashing up the river into white froth and foam. The captain saw the danger, and cried out to lower the sail. Before the order could be obeyed, the flaw struck the sloop, and threw her on her beam ends. Everything now was fright and confusion: the flapping of the sails, the whistling and rushing of the wind, the bawling of the captain and crew, the shrieking of the passengers, all mingled with the rolling and bellowing of the thunder. In the midst of the uproar the sloop righted; at the same time the mainsail shifted, the boom came sweeping the quarter-deck, and Dolph, who was gazing unguardedly at the clouds, found himself, in a moment, floundering in the river.

For once in his life one of his idle accomplishments was of use to him. The many truant hours he had devoted to sporting in the Hudson had made him an expert swimmer; yet with all his strength and skill he found great difficulty in reaching the shore. His

---

*This must have been the bend at West Point [Irving's note].

disappearance from the deck had not been noticed by the crew, who were all occupied by their own danger. The sloop was driven along with inconceivable rapidity. She had hard work to weather a long promontory on the eastern shore, round which the river turned, and which completely shut her from Dolph's view.

It was on a point of the western shore that he landed, and, scrambling up the rocks, threw himself, faint and exhausted, at the foot of a tree. By degrees the thundergust passed over. The clouds rolled away to the east, where they lay piled in feathery masses, tinted with the last rosy rays of the sun. The distant play of the lightning might be seen about the dark bases, and now and then might be heard the faint muttering of the thunder. Dolph rose, and sought about to see if any path led from the shore, but all was savage and trackless. The rocks were piled upon each other; great trunks of trees lay shattered about, as they had been blown down by the strong winds which draw through these mountains, or had fallen through age. The rocks, too, were overhung with wild vines and briers, which completely matted themselves together, and opposed a barrier to all ingress; every movement that he made shook down a shower from the dripping foliage. He attempted to scale one of these almost perpendicular heights; but, though strong and agile, he found it an Herculean* undertaking. Often he was supported merely by crumbling projections of the rock, and sometimes he clung to roots and branches of trees, and hung almost suspended in the air. The wood-pigeon came cleaving his whistling flight by him, and the eagle screamed from the brow of the impending cliff. As he was thus clambering, he was on the point of seizing hold of a shrub to aid his ascent, when something rustled among the leaves, and he saw a snake quivering along like lightning, almost from under his hand. It coiled itself up immediately, in an attitude of defiance, with flattened head, distended jaws, and quickly vibrating tongue, that played like a little flame about its mouth. Dolph's heart turned faint within him, and he had well-nigh let go his hold and tumbled down the precipice. The serpent stood on the defensive but for an instant; and finding there was no attack, glided away into a cleft of the rock.

---

*See footnote on p. 10.

Dolph's eye followed it with fearful intensity, and saw a nest of adders, knotted, and writhing, and hissing in the chasm. He hastened with all speed from so frightful a neighborhood. His imagination, full of this new horror, saw an adder in every curling vine, and heard the tail of a rattlesnake in every dry leaf that rustled.

At length he succeeded in scrambling to the summit of a precipice; but it was covered by a dense forest. Wherever he could gain a lookout between trees, he beheld heights and cliffs, one rising beyond another, until huge mountains overtopped the whole. There were no signs of cultivation; no smoke curling among the trees to indicate a human residence. Everything was wild and solitary. As he was standing on the edge of a precipice overlooking a deep ravine fringed with trees, his feet detached a great fragment of rock; it fell, crashing its way through the tree-tops, down into the chasm. A loud whoop, or rather yell, issued from the bottom of the glen; the moment after there was a report of a gun; and a ball came whistling over his head, cutting the twigs and leaves, and burying itself deep in the bark of a chestnut-tree.

Dolph did not wait for a second shot, but made a precipitate retreat; fearing every moment to hear the enemy in pursuit. He succeeded, however, in returning unmolested to the shore, and determined to penetrate no farther into a country so beset with savage perils.

He sat himself down, dripping, disconsolately, on a stone. What was to be done? where was he to shelter himself? The hour of repose was approaching: the birds were seeking their nests, the bat began to flit about in the twilight, and the night-hawk, soaring high in the heaven, seemed to be calling out the stars. Night gradually closed in, and wrapped everything in gloom; and though it was the latter part of summer, the breeze stealing along the river, and among these dripping forests, was chilly and penetrating, especially to a half-drowned man.

As he sat drooping and despondent in this comfortless condition, he perceived a light gleaming through the trees near the shore, where the winding of the river made a deep bay. It cheered him with the hope of a human habitation, where he might get something to appease the clamorous cravings of his stomach, and what was equally necessary in his shipwrecked condition, a comfortable shelter for the night. With extreme difficulty he made his way toward the light, along ledges of rocks, down which he was in danger of sliding into the river, and over great trunks of fallen trees; some of which had been blown down in the late storm, and lay so thickly together that he had to struggle through their branches. At length he came to the brow of a rock overhanging a small dell, whence the light proceeded. It was from a fire at the foot of a great tree in the midst of a grassy interval or plat among the rocks. The fire cast up a red glare among the gray crags, and impending trees; leaving chasms of deep gloom, that resembled entrances to caverns. A small brook rippled close by, betrayed by the quivering reflection of the flame. There were two figures moving about the fire, and others squatted before it. As they were between him and the light, they were in complete shadow: but one of them happening to move round to the opposite side, Dolph was startled at perceiving, by the glare falling on painted features, and glittering on silver ornaments, that he was an Indian. He now looked more narrowly, and saw guns leaning against a tree, and a dead body lying on the ground. Here was the very foe that had fired at him from the glen. He endeavored to retreat quietly, not caring to intrust himself to these half-human beings in so savage and lonely a place. It was too late: the Indian, with that eagle quickness of eye so remarkable in his race, perceived something stirring among the bushes on the rock: he seized one of the guns that leaned against the tree; one moment more, and Dolph might have had his passion for adventure cured by a bullet. He halloed loudly, with the Indian salutation of friendship; the whole party sprang upon their feet; the salutation was returned, and the straggler was invited to join them at the fire.

On approaching, he found, to his consolation, the party was composed of white men as well as Indians. One, evidently the principal personage, or commander, was seated on a trunk of a tree before the fire. He was a large, stout man, somewhat advanced in life, but hale and hearty. His face was bronzed almost to the color of an Indian's; he had strong but rather jovial features, an aquiline nose, and a mouth shaped like a mastiff's. His face was half thrown in shade by a broad hat, with a buck's tail in it. His gray hair hung short in his neck. He wore a hunting-frock, with Indian leggins, and moccasons, and a tomahawk in the broad wampum-belt* round his waist. As Dolph caught a distinct view of his person and features, something reminded him of the old man of the haunted house. The man before him, however, was different in dress and age; he was more cheery too in aspect, and it was hard to find where the vague resemblance lay; but a resemblance there certainly was. Dolph felt some degree of awe in approaching him; but was assured by a frank, hearty welcome. He was still further encouraged by perceiving that the dead body, which had caused him some alarm, was that of a deer; and his satisfaction was complete in discerning, by savory steams from a kettle, suspended by a hooked stick over the fire, that there was a part cooking for the evening's repast.

He had, in fact, fallen in with a rambling hunting-party, such as often took place in those days among the settlers along the river. The hunter is always hospitable; and nothing makes men more social and unceremonious than meeting in the wilderness. The commander of the party poured out a dram of cheering liquor, which he gave him with a merry leer, to warm his heart; and ordered one of his followers to fetch some garments from a pinnace,† moored in a cove close by, while those in which our hero was dripping might be dried before the fire.

Dolph found, as he had suspected, that the shot from the glen, which had come so near giving him his quietus when on the precipice, was from the party before him. He had nearly crushed one of them by the fragments of rock which he had detached; and the jovial old hunter, in the broad hat and buck-tail, had fired at the place where he saw the bushes move, supposing it to be the sound of some wild animal. He laughed heartily at the blunder, it being what is considered an exceeding good joke among hunters: "but faith, my lad," said he, "if I had but caught a glimpse of you to take sight at, you would have followed the rock. Antony Vander Heyden is seldom known to miss his aim." These last words were at once a clue to Dolph's curiosity: and a few questions let him completely into the character of the man before him, and of his band of woodland

---

*Belt made of strings of beads or shells that were used for money by some Native Americans.

†Small, schooner-rigged boat.

rangers. The commander in the broad hat and hunting-frock was no less a personage than the Heer Antony Vander Heyden, of Albany, of whom Dolph had many a time heard. He was, in fact, the hero of many a story, his singular humors and whimsical habits being matters of wonder to his quiet Dutch neighbors. As he was a man of property, having had a father before him from whom he inherited large tracts of wild land, and whole barrels full of wampum, he could indulge his humors without control. Instead of staying quietly at home, eating and drinking at regular mealtimes, amusing himself by smoking his pipe on the bench before the door, and then turning into a comfortable bed at night, he delighted in all kinds of rough, wild expeditions: never so happy as when on a hunting-party in the wilderness, sleeping under trees or bark sheds, or cruising down the river, or on some woodland lake, fishing and fowling, and living the Lord knows how.

He was a great friend to Indians, and to an Indian mode of life; which he considered true natural liberty and manly enjoyment. When at home he had always several Indian hangers-on who loitered about his house, sleeping like hounds in the sunshine; or preparing hunting and fishing tackle for some new expedition; or shooting at marks with bows and arrows.

Over these vagrant beings Heer Antony had as perfect command as a huntsman over his pack; though they were great nuisances to the regular people of his neighborhood. As he was a rich man, no one ventured to thwart his humors; indeed, his hearty, joyous manner made him universally popular. He would troll a Dutch song as he tramped along the street; hail every one a mile off, and when he entered a house, would slap the good man familiarly on the back, shake him by the hand till he roared, and kiss his wife and daughter before his face,—in short, there was no pride nor ill humor about Heer Antony.

Besides his Indian hangers-on, he had three or four humble friends among the white men, who looked up to him as a patron, and had the run of his kitchen, and the favor of being taken with him occasionally on his expeditions. With a medley of such retainers he was at present on a cruise along the shores of the Hudson, in a pinnace kept for his own recreation. There were two white men with him, dressed partly in the Indian style, with moccasins and hunting-shirts; the rest of his crew consisted of four favorite Indians. They had been prowling about the river, without any definite object, until they found themselves in the highlands; where they had passed two or three days, hunting the deer which still lingered among these mountains.

"It is lucky for you, young man," said Antony Vander Heyden, "that you happened to be knocked overboard to-day, as to-morrow morning we start early on our return homewards; and you might then have looked in vain for a meal among the mountains—but come, lads, stir about! stir about! Let's see what prog* we have for supper; the kettle has boiled long enough; my stomach cries cupboard; and I'll warrant our guest is in no mood to dally with his trencher."

There was a bustle now in the little encampment; one took off the kettle and turned a part of the contents into a huge wooden bowl. Another prepared a flat rock for a table; while a third brought various utensils from the pinnace; Heer Antony himself brought a flask or two of precious liquor from his own private locker; knowing his boon companions too well to trust any of them with the key.

A rude but hearty repast was soon spread; consisting of venison smoking from the kettle, with cold bacon, boiled Indian corn, and mighty loaves of good brown household bread. Never had Dolph made a more delicious repast; and when he had washed it down with two or three draughts from the Heer Antony's flask, and felt the jolly liquor sending its warmth through his veins, and glowing round his very heart, he would not have changed his situation, no, not with the governor of the province.

The Heer Antony, too, grew chirping and joyous; told half a dozen fat stories, at which his white followers laughed immoderately, though the Indians, as usual, maintained an invincible gravity.

"This is your true life, my boy!" said he, slapping Dolph on the shoulder; "a man is never a man till he can defy wind and weather, range woods and wilds, sleep under a tree, and live on bass-wood leaves!"

---

*Provisions.

And then would he sing a stave or two of a Dutch drinking-song, swaying a short swab Dutch bottle in his hand, while his myrmidons* would join in the chorus, until the woods echoed again;—as the good old song has it,

> "They all with a shout made the elements ring
> So soon as the office was o'er,
> To feasting they went, with true merriment,
> And tippled strong liquor gillore."†

In the midst of his joviality, however, Heer Antony did not lose sight of discretion. Though he pushed the bottle without reserve to Dolph, he always took care to help his followers himself, knowing the beings he had to deal with; and was particular in granting but a moderate allowance to the Indians. The repast being ended, the Indians having drunk their liquor, and smoked their pipes, now wrapped themselves in their blankets, stretched themselves on the ground, with their feet to the fire, and soon fell asleep, like so many tired hounds. The rest of the party remained chatting before the fire, which the gloom of the forest, and the dampness of the air from the late storm, rendered extremely grateful and comforting. The conversation gradually moderated from the hilarity of supper-time, and turned upon hunting-adventures, and exploits and perils in the wilderness, many of which were so strange and improbable, that I will not venture to repeat them, lest the veracity of Antony Vander Heyden and his comrades should be brought into question. There were many legendary tales told, also, about the river, and the settlements on its borders; in which valuable kind of lore the Heer Antony seemed deeply versed. As the sturdy bush-beater sat in a twisted root of a tree, that served him for an arm-chair, dealing forth these wild stories, with the fire gleaming on his strongly marked visage, Dolph was again repeatedly perplexed by something that reminded him of the phantom of the haunted house; some vague resemblance not to be fixed upon any precise feature or lineament, but pervading the general air of his countenance and figure.

---

*In Greek mythology, warriors under Achilles' leadership in the Trojan War.
†The song is unidentified.

The circumstance of Dolph's falling overboard led to the relation of divers disasters and singular mishaps that had befallen voyagers on this great river, particularly in the earlier periods of colonial history; most of which the Heer deliberately attributed to supernatural causes. Dolph stared at this suggestion; but the old gentleman assured him it was very currently believed by the settlers along the river, that these highlands were under the dominion of supernatural and mischievous beings, which seemed to have taken some pique against the Dutch colonists in the early time of the settlement. In consequence of this, they have ever taken particular delight in venting their spleen, and indulging their humors, upon the Dutch skippers; bothering them with flaws, head-winds, counter-currents, and all kinds of impediments, insomuch that a Dutch navigator was always obliged to be exceedingly wary and deliberate in his proceedings; to come to anchor at dusk; to drop his peak, or take in sail, whenever he saw a swag-bellied cloud rolling over the mountains; in short, to take so many precautions, that he was often apt to be an incredible time in toiling up the river.

Some, he said, believed these mischievous powers of the air to be the evil spirits conjured up by the Indian wizards, in the early times of the province, to revenge themselves on the strangers who had dispossessed them of their country. They even attributed to their incantations the misadventure which befell the renowned Hendrick Hudson, when he sailed so gallantly up this river in quest of a northwest passage, and, as he thought, ran his ship aground; which they affirm was nothing more nor less than a spell of these same wizards, to prevent his getting to China in this direction.

The greater part, however, Heer Antony observed, accounted for all the extraordinary circumstances attending this river, and the perplexities of the skippers who navigated it, by the old legend of the Storm-ship which haunted Point-no-point. On finding Dolph to be utterly ignorant of this tradition, the Heer stared at him for a moment with surprise, and wondered where he had passed his life, to be uninformed on so important a point of history. To pass away the remainder of the evening, therefore, he undertook the tale, as far as his memory would serve, in the very words in which it had been written out by Mynheer Selyne,* an early poet of the New Netherlandts. Giving, then, a stir to the fire, that sent up its sparks among the trees like a little volcano, he adjusted himself comfortably in his root of a tree, and throwing back his head, and closing his eyes for a few moments, to summon up his recollection, he related the following legend.

---

*Henricus Selyns (1636–1701), pastor of the Reformed Dutch Church of New York (his poems were included in H. C. Murphy's *Anthology of New Netherland*, 1865).

The Storm-Ship

In the golden age of the province of the New Netherlands, when under the sway of Wouter Van Twiller,* otherwise called the Doubter, the people of the Manhattoes were alarmed one sultry afternoon, just about the time of the summer solstice, by a tremendous storm of thunder and lightning. The rain fell in such torrents as absolutely to spatter up and smoke along the ground. It seemed as if the thunder rattled and rolled over the very roofs of the houses; the lightning was seen to play about the church of St. Nicholas, and to strive three times, in vain, to strike its weather-cock. Garret Van Horne's new chimney was split almost from top to bottom; and Doffue Mildeberger was struck speechless from his bald-faced mare, just as he was riding into town. In a word, it was one of those unparalleled storms which only happen once within the memory of that venerable personage known in all towns by the appellation of "the oldest inhabitant."

Great was the terror of the good old women of the Manhattoes. They gathered their children together, and took refuge in the cellars; after having hung a shoe on the iron point of every bedpost, lest it should attract the lightning. At length the storm abated; the thunder sank into a growl, and the setting sun, breaking from under the fringed borders of the clouds, made the broad bosom of the bay to gleam like a sea of molten gold.

The word was given from the fort that a ship was standing up the bay. It passed from mouth to mouth, and street to street, and soon put the little capital in a bustle. The arrival of a ship, in those early times of the settlement, was an event of vast importance to the inhabitants. It brought them news from the old world, from the land of their birth, from which they were so completely severed: to the yearly ship, too, they looked for their supply of luxuries, of finery, of comforts, and almost of necessaries. The good vrouw† could not

---

*See footnote on p. 411.
†Woman (Dutch).

have her new cap nor new gown until the arrival of the ship; the artist waited for it for his tools, the burgomaster for his pipe and his supply of Hollands, the schoolboy for his top and marbles, and the lordly landholder for the bricks with which he was to build his new mansion. Thus every one, rich and poor, great and small, looked out for the arrival of the ship. It was the great yearly event of the town of New Amsterdam; and from one end of the year to the other, the ship—the ship—the ship—was the continual topic of conversation.

The news from the fort, therefore, brought all the populace down to the Battery,* to behold the wished-for sight. It was not exactly the time when she had been expected to arrive, and the circumstance was a matter of some speculation. Many were the groups collected about the Battery. Here and there might be seen a burgomaster, of slow and pompous gravity, giving his opinion with great confidence to a crowd of old women and idle boys. At another place was a knot of old weather-beaten fellows, who had been seamen or fishermen in their times, and were great authorities on such occasions; these gave different opinions, and caused great disputes among their several adherents: but the man most looked up to, and followed and watched by the crowd, was Hans Van Pelt, an old Dutch sea-captain retired from service, the nautical oracle of the place. He reconnoitred the ship through an ancient telescope, covered with tarry canvas, hummed a Dutch tune to himself, and said nothing. A hum, however, from Hans Van Pelt, had always more weight with the public than a speech from another man.

In the meantime the ship became more distinct to the naked eye: she was a stout, round, Dutch-built vessel, with high bow and poop, and bearing Dutch colors. The evening sun gilded her bellying canvas, as she came riding over the long waving billows. The sentinel who had given notice of her approach, declared, that he first got sight of her when she was in the centre of the bay; and that she broke suddenly on his sight, just as if she had come out of the bosom of the black thunder-cloud. The by-standers looked at Hans Van Pelt, to see what he would say to this report: Hans Van Pelt screwed his

---

*Site of the fortifications that guarded the approach to New York's harbor.

mouth closer together, and said nothing; upon which some shook their heads, and others shrugged their shoulders.

The ship was now repeatedly hailed, but made no reply, and passing by the fort, stood on up the Hudson. A gun was brought to bear on her, and, with some difficulty, loaded and fired by Hans Van Pelt, the garrison not being expert in artillery. The shot seemed absolutely to pass through the ship, and to skip along the water on the other side, but no notice was taken of it! What was strange, she had all her sails set, and sailed right against wind and tide, which were both down the river. Upon this Hans Van Pelt, who was likewise harbor-master, ordered his boat, and set off to board her; but after rowing two or three hours, he returned without success. Sometimes he would get within one or two hundred yards of her, and then, in a twinkling, she would be half a mile off. Some said it was because his oarsmen, who were rather pursy and short-winded, stopped every now and then to take breath, and spit on their hands; but this it is probable was a mere scandal. He got near enough, however, to see the crew; who were all dressed in the Dutch style, the officers in doublets and high hats and feathers; not a word was spoken by any one on board; they stood as motionless as so many statues, and the ship seemed as if left to her own government. Thus she kept on, away up the river, lessening and lessening in the evening sunshine, until she faded from sight, like a little white cloud melting away in the summer sky.

The appearance of this ship threw the governor into one of the deepest doubts that ever beset him in the whole course of his administration. Fears were entertained for the security of the infant settlements on the river, lest this might be an enemy's ship in disguise, sent to take possession. The governor called together his council repeatedly to assist him with their conjectures. He sat in his chair of state, built of timber from the sacred forest of the Hague, smoking his long jasmin pipe, and listening to all that his counsellors had to say on a subject about which they knew nothing; but in spite of all the conjecturing of the sagest and oldest heads, the governor still continued to doubt.

Messengers were dispatched to different places on the river; but they returned without any tidings—the ship had made no port. Day after day, and week after week, elapsed, but she never returned down the Hudson. As, however, the council seemed solicitous for intelligence, they had it in abundance. The captains of the sloops seldom arrived without bringing some report of having seen the strange ship at different parts of the river; sometimes near the Pallisadoes, sometimes off Croton Point, and sometimes in the highlands; but she never was reported as having been seen above the highlands. The crews of the sloops, it is true, generally differed among themselves in their accounts of these apparitions; but that may have arisen from the uncertain situations in which they saw her. Sometimes it was by the flashes of the thunder-storm lighting up a pitchy night, and giving glimpses of her careering across Tappaan Zee, or the wide waste of Haverstraw Bay. At one moment she would appear close upon them, as if likely to run them down, and would throw them into great bustle and alarm; but the next flash would show her far off, always sailing against the wind. Sometimes, in quiet moonlight nights, she would be seen under some high bluff of the highlands, all in deep shadow, excepting her topsails glittering in the moonbeams; by the time, however, that the voyagers reached the place, no ship was to be seen; and when they had passed on for some distance, and looked back, behold! there she was again, with her topsails in the moonshine! Her appearance was always just after, or just before, or just in the midst of unruly weather; and she was known among the skippers and voyagers of the Hudson by the name of "the storm-ship."

These reports perplexed the governor and his council more than ever; and it would be endless to repeat the conjectures and opinions uttered on the subject. Some quoted cases in point, of ships seen off the coast of New England, navigated by witches and goblins. Old Hans Van Pelt, who had been more than once to the Dutch colony at the Cape of Good Hope, insisted that this must be the flying Dutchman, which had so long haunted Table Bay; but being unable to make port, had now sought another harbor. Others suggested, that, if it really was a supernatural apparition, as there was every natural reason to believe, it might be Hendrick Hudson, and his crew of the Halfmoon; who, it was well known, had once run aground in the upper part of the river in seeking a northwest passage to China. This opinion had very little weight with the governor, but it passed current out of doors; for indeed it had already been reported, that Hendrick Hudson and his crew haunted the Kaatskill Mountains;* and it appeared very reasonable to suppose, that his ship might infest the river where the enterprise was baffled, or that it might bear the shadowy crew to their periodical revels in the mountain.

Other events occurred to occupy the thoughts and doubts of the sage Wouter and his council, and the storm-ship ceased to be a subject of deliberation at the board. It continued, however, a matter of popular belief and marvellous anecdote through the whole time of the Dutch government, and particularly just before the capture of New Amsterdam, and the subjugation of the province by the English squadron.† About that time the storm-ship was repeatedly seen in the Tappaan Zee, and about Weehawk, and even down as far as Hoboken; and her appearance was supposed to be ominous of the approaching squall in public affairs, and the downfall of Dutch domination.

Since that time we have no authentic accounts of her; though it is said she still haunts the highlands, and cruises about Point-no-point. People who live along the river insist that they sometimes see her in summer moonlight; and that in a deep still midnight they have heard the chant of her crew, as if heaving the lead; but sights and sounds are so deceptive along the mountainous shores, and about the wide bays and long reaches of this great river, that I confess I have very strong doubts upon the subject.

It is certain, nevertheless, that strange things have been seen in these highlands in storms, which are considered as connected with the old story of the ship. The captains of the river craft talk of a little bulbous-bottomed Dutch goblin, in trunk-hose and sugar-loafed hat, with a speaking-trumpet in his hand, which they say keeps about the Dunderberg.‡ They declare that they have heard him, in stormy weather, in the midst of the turmoil, giving orders in Low Dutch for the piping up of a fresh gust of wind, or the rattling off of another thunder-clap. That sometimes he has been seen surrounded by a crew of little imps in broad breeches and short doublets; tumbling head-over-heels in the rack and mist, and playing a thousand

---

*See "Rip Van Winkle" (p. 87).
†See p. 454.
‡*i.e.*, The "Thunder-Mountain," so called from its echoes [Irving's note].

gambols in the air; or buzzing like a swarm of flies about Antony's Nose; and that, at such times, the hurry-scurry of the storm was always greatest. One time a sloop, in passing by the Dunderberg, was overtaken by a thunder-gust, that came scouring round the mountain, and seemed to burst just over the vessel. Though tight and well ballasted, she labored dreadfully, and the water came over the gunwale. All the crew were amazed when it was discovered that there was a little white sugar-loaf hat on the mast-head, known at once to be the hat of the Heer of the Dunderberg. Nobody, however, dared to climb to the mast-head, and get rid of this terrible hat. The sloop continued laboring and rocking, as if she would have rolled her mast overboard, and seemed in continual danger either of upsetting or of running on shore. In this way she drove quite through the highlands, until she had passed Pollopol's Island, where, it is said, the jurisdiction of the Dunderberg potentate ceases. No sooner had she passed this bourn,* than the little hat spun up into the air like a top, whirled up all the clouds into a vortex, and hurried them back to the summit of the Dunderberg; while the sloop righted herself, and sailed on as quietly as if in a mill-pond. Nothing saved her from utter wreck but the fortunate circumstance of having a horse-shoe nailed against the mast,—a wise precaution against evil spirits, since adopted by all the Dutch captains that navigate this haunted river.

There is another story told of this foul-weather urchin, by Skipper Daniel Ouselsticker, of Fishkill, who was never known to tell a lie. He declared, that, in a severe squall, he saw him seated astride of his bowsprit, riding the sloop ashore, full butt against Antony's Nose, and that he was exorcised by Dominie Van Gieson, of Esopus, who happened to be on board, and who sang the hymn of St. Nicholas; whereupon the goblin threw himself up in the air like a ball, and went off in a whirlwind, carrying away with him the nightcap of the Dominie's wife; which was discovered the next Sunday morning hanging on the weather-cock of Esopus churchsteeple, at least forty miles off! Several events of this kind having taken place, the regular skippers of the river, for a long time, did not venture to pass the Dunderberg without lowering their peaks, out of homage to the Heer of the mountain; and it was observed that

---

*Boundary line.

all such as paid this tribute of respect were suffered to pass unmolested.*

"Such," said Antony Vander Heyden, "are a few of the stories written down by Selyne, the poet, concerning the storm-ship,— which he affirms to have brought a crew of mischievous imps into the province, from some old ghost-ridden country of Europe. I could give a host more, if necessary; for all the accidents that so often befall the river craft in the highlands are said to be tricks played off by these imps of the Dunderberg; but I see that you are nodding, so let us turn in for the night."

The moon had just raised her silver horns above the round back of Old Bull Hill, and lit up the gray rocks and shagged forests, and glittered on the waving bosom of the river. The night-dew was falling, and the late gloomy mountains began to soften and put on a gray aërial tint in the dewy light. The hunters stirred the fire, and threw on fresh fuel to qualify the damp of the night-air. They then prepared a bed of branches and dry leaves under a ledge of rocks for Dolph; while Antony Vander Heyden, wrapping himself in a huge coat of skins, stretched himself before the fire. It was some time, however, before Dolph could close his eyes. He lay contemplating the strange scene before him: the wild woods and rocks around; the fire throwing fitful gleams on the faces of the sleeping savages; and

---

*Among the superstitions which prevailed in the colonies, during the early times of the settlements, there seems to have been a singular one about phantom ships. The superstitious fancies of men are always apt to turn upon those objects which concern their daily occupations. The solitary ship, which, from year to year, came like a raven in the wilderness [see the Bible, 1 Kings 17:1–17], bringing to the inhabitants of a settlement the comforts of life from the world from which they were cut off, was apt to be present to their dreams, whether sleeping or waking. The accidental sight from shore of a sail gliding along the horizon in those as yet lonely seas, was apt to be a matter of much talk and speculation. There is mention made in one of the early New England writers of a ship navigated by witches, with a great horse that stood by the mainmast. I have met with another story, somewhere, of a ship that drove on shore, in fair, sunny, tranquil weather, with sails all set, and a table spread in the cabin, as if to regale a number of guests, yet not a living being on board. These phantom ships always sailed in the eye of the wind; or ploughed their way with great velocity, making the smooth sea foam before their bows, when not a breath of air was stirring.

Moore has finely wrought up one of these legends of the sea into a little tale ["Written on Passing Deadman's Island in the Gulf of the St. Lawrence, Late in the Evening, September, 1804," by Irish poet Sir Thomas Moore], which, within a small compass, contains the very essence of this species of supernatural fiction. I allude to his *Spectre Ship, bound to Deadman's Isle* [Irving's note].

the Heer Antony, too, who so singularly, yet vaguely, reminded him of the nightly visitant to the haunted house. Now and then he heard the cry of some wild animal from the forest; or the hooting of the owl; or the notes of the whippoorwill, which seemed to abound among these solitudes; or the splash of a sturgeon, leaping out of the river and falling back full-length on its placid surface. He contrasted all this with his accustomed nest in the garret-room of the doctor's mansion;—where the only sounds at night were the church-clock telling the hour; the drowsy voice of the watchman, drawling out all was well; the deep snoring of the doctor's clubbed nose from below-stairs; or the cautious labors of some carpenter rat gnawing in the wainscot. His thoughts then wandered to his poor old mother: what would she think of his mysterious disappearance—what anxiety and distress would she not suffer? This thought would continually intrude itself to mar his present enjoyment. It brought with it a feeling of pain and compunction, and he fell asleep with the tears yet standing in his eyes.

Were this a mere tale of fancy, here would be a fine opportunity for weaving in strange adventures among these wild mountains, and roving hunters; and, after involving my hero in a variety of perils and difficulties, rescuing him from them all by some miraculous contrivance; but as this is absolutely a true story, I must content myself with simple facts, and keep to probabilities.

At an early hour of the next day, therefore, after a hearty morning's meal, the encampment broke up, and our adventurers embarked in the pinnace of Antony Vander Heyden. There being no wind for the sails, the Indians rowed her gently along, keeping time to a kind of chant of one of the white men. The day was serene and beautiful; the river without a wave; and as the vessel cleft the glassy water, it left a long, undulating track behind. The crows, who had scented the hunters' banquet, were already gathering and hovering in the air, just where a column of thin, blue smoke, rising from among the trees, showed the place of their last night's quarters. As they coasted along the bases of the mountains, the Heer Antony pointed out to Dolph a bald eagle, the sovereign of these regions, who sat perched on a dry tree that projected over the river, and, with eye turned upwards, seemed to be drinking in the splendor of the morning sun. Their approach disturbed the monarch's meditations.

He first spread one wing, and then the other; balanced himself for a moment; and then, quitting his perch with dignified composure, wheeled slowly over their heads. Dolph snatched up a gun, and sent a whistling ball after him, that cut some of the feathers from his wing; the report of the gun leaped sharply from rock to rock, and awakened a thousand echoes; but the monarch of the air sailed calmly on, ascending higher and higher, and wheeling widely as he ascended, soaring up the green bosom of the woody mountain, until he disappeared over the brow of a beetling precipice. Dolph felt in a manner rebuked by this proud tranquillity, and almost reproached himself for having so wantonly insulted this majestic bird. Heer Antony told him, laughing, to remember that he was not yet out of the territories of the lord of the Dunderberg; and an old Indian shook his head, and observed, that there was bad luck in killing an eagle; the hunter, on the contrary, should always leave him a portion of his spoils.

Nothing, however, occurred to molest them on their voyage. They passed pleasantly through magnificent and lonely scenes, until they came to where Pollopol's Island lay, like a floating bower at the extremity of the highlands. Here they landed, until the heat of the day should abate, or a breeze spring up that might supersede the labor of the oar. Some prepared the mid-day meal, while others reposed under the shade of the trees, in luxurious summer indolence, looking drowsily forth upon the beauty of the scene. On the one side were the highlands, vast and cragged, feathered to the top with forests, and throwing their shadows on the glassy water that dimpled at their feet. On the other side was a wide expanse of the river, like a broad lake, with long sunny reaches, and green headlands; and the distant line of Shawangunk mountains waving along a clear horizon, or checkered by a fleecy cloud.

But I forbear to dwell on the particulars of their cruise along the river; this vagrant, amphibious life, careering across silver sheets of water; coasting wild woodland shores; banqueting on shady promontories, with the spreading tree overhead, the river curling its light foam to one's feet, and distant mountain, and rock, and tree, and snowy cloud, and deep-blue sky, all mingling in summer beauty before one; all this, though never cloying in the enjoyment, would be but tedious in narration.

When encamped by the water-side, some of the party would go into the woods and hunt; others would fish: sometimes they would amuse themselves by shooting at a mark, by leaping, by running, by wrestling; and Dolph gained great favor in the eyes of Antony Vander Heyden, by his skill and adroitness in all these exercises; which the Heer considered as the highest of manly accomplishments.

Thus did they coast jollily on, choosing only the pleasant hours for voyaging; sometimes in the cool morning dawn, sometimes in the sober evening twilight, and sometimes when the moonshine spangled the crisp curling waves that whispered along the sides of their little bark. Never had Dolph felt so completely in his element; never had he met with anything so completely to his taste as this wild hap-hazard life. He was the very man to second Antony Vander Heyden in his rambling humors, and gained continually on his affections. The heart of the old bushwhacker yearned toward the young man, who seemed thus growing up in his own likeness; and as they approached to the end of their voyage, he could not help inquiring a little into his history. Dolph frankly told him his course of life, his severe medical studies, his little proficiency, and his very dubious prospects. The Heer was shocked to find that such amazing talents and accomplishments were to be cramped and buried under a doctor's wig. He had a sovereign contempt for the healing art, having never had any other physician than the butcher. He bore a mortal grudge to all kinds of study also, ever since he had been flogged about an unintelligible book when he was a boy. But to think that a young fellow like Dolph, of such wonderful abilities, who could shoot, fish, run, jump, ride, and wrestle, should be obliged to roll pills, and administer juleps for a living—'twas monstrous! He told Dolph never to despair, but to "throw physic to the dogs"; for a young fellow of his prodigious talents could never fail to make his way. "As you seem to have no acquaintance in Albany," said Heer Antony, "you shall go home with me, and remain under my roof until you can look about you; and in the meantime we can take an occasional bout at shooting and fishing, for it is a pity that such talents should lie idle."

Dolph, who was at the mercy of chance, was not hard to be persuaded. Indeed, on turning over matters in his mind, which he did very sagely and deliberately, he could not but think that Antony

Vander Heyden was, "somehow or other," connected with the story of the Haunted House; that the misadventure in the highlands, which had thrown them so strangely together, was, "somehow or other," to work out something good: in short, there is nothing so convenient as this "somehow-or-other" way of accommodating one's self to circumstances; it is the mainstay of a heedless actor, and tardy reasoner, like Dolph Heyliger; and he who can, in this loose, easy way, link foregone evil to anticipated good, possesses a secret of happiness almost equal to the philosopher's stone.*

On their arrival at Albany, the sight of Dolph's companion seemed to cause universal satisfaction. Many were the greetings at the river-side, and the salutations in the streets; the dogs bounded before him; the boys whooped as he passed; everybody seemed to know Antony Vander Heyden. Dolph followed on in silence, admiring the neatness of this worthy burgh; for in those days Albany was in all its glory, and inhabited almost exclusively by the descendants of the original Dutch settlers, not having as yet been discovered and colonized by the restless people of New England. Everything was quiet and orderly; everything was conducted calmly and leisurely; no hurry, no bustle, no struggling and scrambling for existence. The grass grew about the unpaved streets, and relieved the eye by its refreshing verdure. Tall sycamores or pendent willows shaded the houses, with caterpillars swinging, in long silken strings, from their branches; or moths, fluttering about like coxcombs, in joy at their gay transformation. The houses were built in the old Dutch style, with the gable-ends towards the street. The thrifty housewife was seated on a bench before her door, in close-crimped cap, bright-flowered gown, and white apron, busily employed in knitting. The husband smoked his pipe on the opposite bench; and the little pet negro girl, seated on the step at her mistress's feet, was industriously plying her needle. The swallows sported about the eaves, or skimmed along the streets, and brought back some rich booty for their clamorous young; and the little housekeeping wren flew in and out of a Liliputian† house, or an old hat nailed against the wall.

---

*Legendary substance said to change baser metals into gold.
†See footnote on p. 37.

The cows were coming home, lowing through the streets, to be milked at their owner's door; and if, perchance, there were any loiterers, some negro urchin, with a long goad, was gently urging them homewards.

As Dolph's companion passed on, he received a tranquil nod from the burghers, and a friendly word from their wives; all calling him familiarly by the name of Antony; for it was the custom in this stronghold of the patriarchs, where they had all grown up together from childhood, to call each other by the Christian name. The Heer did not pause to have his usual jokes with them, for he was impatient to reach his home. At length they arrived at his mansion. It was of some magnitude, in the Dutch style, with large iron figures on the gables, that gave the date of its erection, and showed that it had been built in the earliest times of the settlement.

The news of Heer Antony's arrival had preceded him, and the whole household was on the look-out. A crew of negroes, large and small, had collected in front of the house to receive him. The old, white-headed ones, who had grown gray in his service, grinned for joy, and made many awkward bows and grimaces, and the little ones capered about his knees. But the most happy being in the household was a little, plump, blooming lass, his only child, and the darling of his heart. She came bounding out of the house; but the sight of a strange young man with her father called up, for a moment, all the bashfulness of a homebred damsel. Dolph gazed at her with wonder and delight; never had he seen, as he thought, anything so comely in the shape of a woman. She was dressed in the good old Dutch taste, with long stays, and full, short petticoats, so admirably adapted to show and set off the female form. Her hair, turned up under a small round cap, displayed the fairness of her forehead; she had fine, blue, laughing eyes, a trim, slender waist, and soft swell—but, in a word, she was a little Dutch divinity; and Dolph, who never stopped half-way in a new impulse, fell desperately in love with her.

Dolph was now ushered into the house with a hearty welcome. In the interior was a mingled display of Heer Antony's taste and habits, and of the opulence of his predecessors. The chambers were furnished with good old mahogany; the beaufets* and cupboards

*Sideboards.

glittered with embossed silver and painted china. Over the parlor fireplace was, as usual, the family coat of arms, painted and framed; above which was a long duck fowling-piece, flanked by an Indian pouch, and a powderhorn. The room was decorated with many Indian articles, such as pipes of peace, tomahawks, scalping-knives, hunting-pouches, and belts of wampum; and there were various kinds of fishing-tackle, and two or three fowling pieces in the corners. The household affairs seemed to be conducted, in some measure, after the master's humors; corrected, perhaps, by a little quiet management of the daughter's. There was a great degree of patriarchal simplicity, and good-humored indulgence. The negroes came into the room without being called, merely to look at their master, and hear of his adventures; they would stand listening at the door until he had finished a story, and then go off on a broad grin, to repeat it in the kitchen. A couple of pet negro children were playing about the floor with the dogs, and sharing with them their bread and butter. All the domestics looked hearty and happy; and when the table was set for the evening repast, the variety and abundance of good household luxuries bore testimony to the open-handed liberality of the Heer, and the notable housewifery of his daughter.

In the evening there dropped in several of the worthies of the place, the Van Rensellaers, and the Gansevoorts, and the Rosebooms,* and others of Antony Vander Heyden's intimates, to hear an account of his expedition; for he was the Sinbad[†] of Albany, and his exploits and adventures were favorite topics of conversation among the inhabitants. While these sat gossiping together about the door of the hall, and telling long twilight stories, Dolph was cosily seated, entertaining the daughter, on a window-bench. He had already got on intimate terms; for those were not times of false reserve and idle ceremony; and, besides, there is something wonderfully propitious to a lover's suit in the delightful dusk of a long summer evening; it gives courage to the most timid tongue, and hides

---

*Wealthy Dutch families whose descendants were recognized as the aristocracy of New York; American author Herman Melville's mother was a Gansevoort.
[†]"Sinbad, the Sailor" is one of the better-known stories from *The Arabian Nights* (see endnote 6 to *Bracebridge Hall*).

the blushes of the bashful. The stars alone twinkled brightly; and now and then a fire-fly streamed his transient light before the window, or, wandering into the room, flew gleaming about the ceiling.

What Dolph whispered in her ear that long summer evening, it is impossible to say; his words were so low and indistinct, that they never reached the ear of the historian. It is probable, however, that they were to the purpose; for he had a natural talent at pleasing the sex, and was never long in company with a petticoat without paying proper court to it. In the meantime the visitors, one by one, departed; Antony Vander Heyden, who had fairly talked himself silent, sat nodding alone in his chair by the door, when he was suddenly aroused by a hearty salute with which Dolph Heyliger had unguardedly rounded off one of his periods, and which echoed through the still chamber like the report of a pistol. The Heer started up, rubbed his eyes, called for lights, and observed that it was high time to go to bed; though, on parting for the night, he squeezed Dolph heartily by the hand, looked kindly in his face, and shook his head knowingly; for the Heer well remembered what he himself had been at the youngster's age.

The chamber in which our hero was lodged was spacious, and panelled with oak. It was furnished with clothes-presses, and mighty chests of drawers, well waxed, and glittering with brass ornaments. These contained ample stock of family linen; for the Dutch housewives had always a laudable pride in showing off their household treasures to strangers.

Dolph's mind, however, was too full to take particular note of the objects around him; yet he could not help continually comparing the free open-hearted cheeriness of this establishment with the starveling, sordid, joyless housekeeping at Doctor Knipperhausen's. Still something marred the enjoyment: the idea that he must take leave of his hearty host, and pretty hostess, and cast himself once more adrift upon the world. To linger here would be folly: he should only get deeper in love; and for a poor varlet, like himself, to aspire to the daughter of the great Heer Vander Heyden—it was madness to think of such a thing! The very kindness that the girl had shown towards him prompted him, on reflection, to hasten his departure; it would be a poor return for the frank hospitality of his host to entangle his daughter's heart in an injudicious attachment.

In a word, Dolph was like many other young reasoners of exceeding good hearts and giddy heads,—who think after they act, and act differently from what they think,—who make excellent determinations overnight, and forget to keep them the next morning.

"This is a fine conclusion, truly, of my voyage," said he, as he almost buried himself in a sumptuous featherbed, and drew the fresh white sheets up to his chin. "Here am I, instead of finding a bag of money to carry home, launched in a strange place, with scarcely a stiver in my pocket; and, what is worse, have jumped ashore up to my very ears in love into the bargain. However," added he, after some pause, stretching himself, and turning himself in bed, "I'm in good quarters for the present, at least; so I'll e'en enjoy the present moment, and let the next take care of itself; I dare say all will work out, 'somehow or other,' for the best."

As he said these words, he reached out his hand to extinguish the candle, when he was suddenly struck with astonishment and dismay, for he thought he beheld the phantom of the haunted house, staring on him from a dusky part of the chamber. A second look reassured him, as he perceived that what he had taken for the spectre was, in fact, nothing but a Flemish portrait, hanging in a shadowy corner, just behind a clothes-press. It was, however, the precise representation of his nightly visitor. The same cloak and belted jerkin, the same grizzled beard and fixed eye, the same broad slouched hat, with a feather hanging over one side. Dolph now called to mind the resemblance he had frequently remarked between his host and the old man of the haunted house; and was fully convinced they were in some way connected, and that some especial destiny had governed his voyage. He lay gazing on the portrait with almost as much awe as he had gazed on the ghostly original, until the shrill houseclock warned him of the lateness of the hour. He put out the light; but remained for a long time turning over these curious circumstances and coincidences in his mind, until he fell asleep. His dreams partook of the nature of his waking thoughts. He fancied that he still lay gazing on the picture, until, by degrees, it became animated; that the figure descended from the wall, and walked out of the room; that he followed it, and found himself by the well to which the old man pointed, smiled on him, and disappeared.

In the morning, when he waked, he found his host standing by his bedside, who gave him a hearty morning's salutation, and asked him how he had slept. Dolph answered cheerily; but took occasion to inquire about the portrait that hung against the wall. "Ah," said Heer Antony, "that's a portrait of old Killian Vander Spiegel, once a burgomaster of Amsterdam, who, on some popular troubles, abandoned Holland, and came over to the province during the government of Peter Stuyvesant.* He was my ancestor by the mother's side, and an old miserly curmudgeon he was. When the English took possession of New Amsterdam, in 1664, he retired into the country. He fell into a melancholy, apprehending that his wealth would be taken from him and he come to beggary. He turned all his property into cash, and used to hide it away. He was for a year or two concealed in various places, fancying himself sought after by the English, to strip him of his wealth; and finally he was found dead in his bed one morning, without any one being able to discover where he had concealed the greater part of his money."

When his host had left the room, Dolph remained for some time lost in thought. His whole mind was occupied by what he had heard. Vander Spiegel was his mother's family name; and he recollected to have heard her speak of this very Killian Vander Spiegel as one of her ancestors. He had heard her say, too, that her father was Killian's rightful heir, only that the old man died without leaving anything to be inherited. It now appeared that Heer Antony was likewise a descendant, and perhaps an heir also, of this poor rich man; and that thus the Heyligers and the Vander Heydens were remotely connected. "What," thought he, "if, after all, this is the interpretation of my dream, that this is the way I am to make my fortune by this voyage to Albany, and that I am to find the old man's hidden wealth in the bottom of that well? But what an odd roundabout mode of communicating the matter! Why the plague could not the old goblin have told me about the well at once, without sending me all the way to Albany, to hear a story that was to send me all the way back again?"

These thoughts passed through his mind while he was dressing. He descended the stairs, full of perplexity, when the bright face of Marie Vander Heyden suddenly beamed in smiles upon him, and seemed to give him a clue to the whole mystery. "After all," thought

*See p. 447.

he, "the old goblin is in the right. If I am to get his wealth, he means that I shall marry his pretty descendant; thus both branches of the family will again be united, and the property go on in the proper channel."

No sooner did this idea enter his head, than it carried conviction with it. He was now all impatience to hurry back and secure the treasure, which, he did not doubt, lay at the bottom of the well, and which he feared every moment might be discovered by some other person. "Who knows," thought he, "but this night-walking old fellow of the haunted house may be in the habit of haunting every visitor, and may give a hint to some shrewder fellow than myself, who will take a shorter cut to the well than by the way of Albany?" He wished a thousand times that the babbling old ghost was laid in the Red Sea, and his rambling portrait with him. He was in a perfect fever to depart. Two or three days elapsed before any opportunity presented for returning down the river. They were ages to Dolph, notwithstanding that he was basking in the smiles of the pretty Marie, and daily getting more and more enamoured.

At length the very sloop from which he had been knocked overboard prepared to make sail. Dolph made an awkward apology to his host for his sudden departure. Antony Vander Heyden was sorely astonished. He had concerted* half a dozen excursions into the wilderness; and his Indians were actually preparing for a grand expedition to one of the lakes. He took Dolph aside, and exerted his eloquence to get him to abandon all thoughts of business and to remain with him, but in vain; and he at length gave up the attempt, observing, "that it was a thousand pities so fine a young man should throw himself away." Heer Antony, however, gave him a hearty shake by the hand at parting, with a favorite fowling-piece, and an invitation to come to his house whenever he revisited Albany. The pretty little Marie said nothing; but as he gave her a farewell kiss, her dimpled cheek turned pale, and a tear stood in her eye.

Dolph sprang lightly on board of the vessel. They hoisted sail; the wind was fair; they soon lost sight of Albany, its green hills and embowered islands. They were wafted gayly past the Kaatskill

---

*That is, planned.

Mountains, whose fairy heights were bright and cloudless. They passed prosperously through the highlands, without any molestation from the Dunderberg goblin and his crew; they swept on across Haverstraw Bay, and by Croton Point, and through the Tappaan Zee, and under the Palisadoes, until, in the afternoon of the third day, they saw the promontory of Hoboken hanging like a cloud in the air; and, shortly after, the roofs of the Manhattoes rising out of the water.

Dolph's first care was to repair to his mother's house; for he was continually goaded by the idea of the uneasiness she must experience on his account. He was puzzling his brains, as he went along, to think how he should account for his absence without betraying the secrets of the haunted house. In the midst of these cogitations he entered the street in which his mother's house was situated, when he was thunderstruck at beholding it a heap of ruins.

There had evidently been a great fire, which had destroyed several large houses, and the humble dwelling of poor Dame Heyliger had been involved in the conflagration. The walls were not so completely destroyed, but that Dolph could distinguish some traces of the scene of his childhood. The fireplace, about which he had often played, still remained, ornamented with Dutch tiles, illustrating passages in Bible history, on which he had many a time gazed with admiration. Among the rubbish lay the wreck of the good dame's elbow-chair, from which she had given him so many a wholesale precept; and hard by it was the family Bible, with brass clasps; now, alas! reduced almost to a cinder.

For a moment Dolph was overcome by this dismal sight, for he was seized with the fear that his mother had perished in the flames. He was relieved, however, from his horrible apprehension by one of the neighbors, who happened to come by and informed him that his mother was yet alive.

The good woman had, indeed, lost everything by this unlooked-for calamity; for the populace had been so intent upon saving the fine furniture of her rich neighbors, that the little tenement, and the little all of poor Dame Heyliger, had been suffered to consume without interruption; nay, had it not been for the gallant assistance of her old crony, Peter de Groodt, the worthy dame and her cat might have shared the fate of their habitation.

As it was, she had been overcome with fright and affliction, and lay ill in body and sick at heart. The public, however, had showed her its wonted kindness. The furniture of her rich neighbors being, as far as possible rescued from the flames; themselves duly and ceremoniously visited and condoled with on the injury of their property, and their ladies commiserated on the agitation of their nerves; the public, at length, began to recollect something about poor Dame Heyliger. She forthwith became again a subject of universal sympathy; everybody pitied her more than ever; and if pity could but have been coined into cash—good Lord! how rich she would have been!

It was now determined, in good earnest, that something ought to be done for her without delay. The Dominie, therefore, put up prayers for her on Sunday, in which all the congregation joined most heartily. Even Cobus Groesbeek, the alderman, and Mynheer Milledollar, the great Dutch merchant, stood up in their pews, and did not spare their voices on the occasion; and it was thought the prayers of such great men could not but have their due weight. Doctor Knipperhausen, too, visited her professionally, and gave her abundance of advice gratis, and was universally lauded for his charity. As to her old friend, Peter de Groodt, he was a poor man, whose pity, and prayers, and advice could be of but little avail, so he gave her all that was in his power—he gave her shelter.

To the humble dwelling of Peter de Groodt, then, did Dolph turn his steps. On his way thither he recalled all the tenderness and kindness of his simple-hearted parent, her indulgence of his errors, her blindness to his faults; and then he bethought himself of his own idle, harum-scarum* life. "I've been a sad scapegrace,"† said Dolph, shaking his head sorrowfully. "I've been a complete sink-pocket,‡ that's the truth of it.—But," added he briskly, and clasping his hands, "only let her live—only let her live—and I will show myself indeed a son!"

As Dolph approached the house he met Peter de Groodt coming out of it. The old man started back aghast, doubting whether it was

---

*Reckless.
†Rascal.
‡One living off others.

not a ghost that stood before him. It being bright daylight, however, Peter soon plucked up heart, satisfied that no ghost dare show his face in such clear sunshine. Dolph now learned from the worthy sexton the consternation and rumor to which his mysterious disappearance had given rise. It had been universally believed that he had been spirited away by those hobgoblin gentry that infested the haunted house; and old Abraham Vandozer, who lived by the great buttonwood-trees, near the three-mile stone, affirmed, that he had heard a terrible noise in the air, as he was going home late at night, which seemed just as if a flock of wild geese were overhead, passing off towards the northward. The haunted house was, in consequence, looked upon with ten times more awe than ever; nobody would venture to pass a night in it for the world, and even the doctor had ceased to make his expeditions to it in the daytime.

It required some preparation before Dolph's return could be made known to his mother, the poor soul having bewailed him as lost; and her spirits having been sorely broken down by a number of comforters, who daily cheered her with stories of ghosts, and of people carried away by the devil. He found her confined to her bed, with the other member of the Heyliger family, the good dame's cat, purring beside her, but sadly singed, and utterly despoiled of those whiskers which were the glory of her physiognomy. The poor woman threw her arms about Dolph's neck. "My boy! my boy! art thou still alive?" For a time she seemed to have forgotten all her losses and troubles in her joy at his return. Even the sage grimalkin* showed indubitable signs of joy at the return of the youngster. She saw, perhaps, that they were a forlorn and undone family, and felt a touch of that kindliness which fellow-sufferers only know. But, in truth, cats are a slandered people; they have more affection in them than the world commonly gives them credit for.

The good dame's eyes glistened as she saw one being at least, besides herself, rejoiced at her son's return. "Tib knows thee! poor dumb beast!" said she, smoothing down the mottled coat of her favorite; then recollecting herself, with a melancholy shake of the head, "Ah, my poor Dolph!" exclaimed she, "thy mother can help

---

*Old female cat.

thee no longer! She can no longer help herself! What will become of thee, my poor boy!"

"Mother," said Dolph, "don't talk in that strain; I've been too long a charge upon you; it's now my part to take care of you in your old days. Come! be of good cheer! you, and I, and Tib will all see better days. I'm here, you see, young, and sound, and hearty; then don't let us despair; I dare say things will all, somehow or other, turn out for the best."

While this scene was going on with the Heyliger family, the news was carried to Doctor Knipperhausen of the safe return of his disciple. The little doctor scarce knew whether to rejoice or be sorry at the tidings. He was happy at having the foul reports which had prevailed concerning his country mansion thus disproved; but he grieved at having his disciple, of whom he had supposed himself fairly disencumbered, thus drifting back, a heavy charge upon his hands. While balancing between these two feelings, he was determined by the counsels of Frau Ilsy, who advised him to take advantage of the truant absence of the youngster, and shut the door upon him forever.

At the hour of bedtime, therefore, when it was supposed the recreant disciple would seek his old quarters, everything was prepared for his reception. Dolph, having talked his mother into a state of tranquillity, sought the mansion of his quondam* master, and raised the knocker with a faltering hand. Scarcely, however, had it given a dubious rap, when the doctor's head, in a red nightcap, popped out of one window, and the housekeeper's, in a white nightcap, out of another. He was now greeted with a tremendous volley of hard names and hard language, mingled with invaluable pieces of advice, such as are seldom ventured to be given excepting to a friend in distress, or a culprit at the bar. In a few moments, not a window in the street but had its particular nightcap, listening to the shrill treble of Frau Ilsy, and the guttural croaking of Dr. Knipperhausen; and the word went from window to window, "Ah! here's Dolph Heyliger come back, and at his old pranks again." In short, poor Dolph found he was likely to get nothing from the doctor but good advice; a commodity so abundant as even to be thrown out of the window; so

---

*Former.

he was fain to beat a retreat, and take up his quarters for the night under the lowly roof of honest Peter de Groodt.

The next morning, bright and early, Dolph was out at the haunted house. Everything looked just as he had left it. The fields were grass-grown and matted, and appeared as if nobody had traversed them since his departure. With palpitating heart he hastened to the well. He looked down into it, and saw that it was of great depth, with water at the bottom. He had provided himself with a strong line, such as the fishermen use on the banks of Newfoundland. At the end was a heavy plummet and a large fish-hook. With this he began to sound the bottom of the well, and to angle about in the water. The water was of some depth; there was also much rubbish, stones from the top having fallen in. Several times his hook got entangled, and he came near breaking his line. Now and then, too, he hauled up mere trash, such as the skull of a horse, an iron hoop, and a shattered iron-bound bucket. He had now been several hours employed without finding anything to repay his trouble, or to encourage him to proceed. He began to think himself a great fool, to be thus decoyed into a wild-goose chase by mere dreams, and was on the point of throwing line and all into the well, and giving up all further angling.

"One more cast of the line," said he, "and that shall be the last." As he sounded, he felt the plummet slip, as it were, through the interstices of loose stones; and as he drew back the line, he felt that the hook had taken hold of something heavy. He had to manage his line with great caution, lest it should be broken by the strain upon it. By degrees the rubbish which lay upon the article he had hooked gave way; he drew it to the surface of the water, and what was his rapture at seeing something like silver glittering at the end of his line! Almost breathless with anxiety, he drew it up to the mouth of the well, surprised at its great weight, and fearing every instant that his hook would slip from its hold, and his prize tumble again to the bottom. At length he landed it safe beside the well. It was a great silver porringer, of an ancient form, richly embossed, and with armorial bearings engraved on its side, similar to those over his mother's mantelpiece. The lid was fastened down by several twists of wire; Dolph loosened them with a trembling hand, and, on lifting the lid, behold! the vessel was filled with broad golden pieces, of a coinage which he had never seen before! It was evident he had lit on the place where Killian Vander Spiegel had concealed his treasure.

Fearful of being seen by some straggler, he cautiously retired, and buried his pot of money in a secret place. He now spread terrible stories about the haunted house, and deterred every one from approaching it, while he made frequent visits to it in stormy days, when no one was stirring in the neighboring fields; though, to tell the truth, he did not care to venture there in the dark. For once in his life he was diligent and industrious, and followed up his new trade of angling with such perseverance and success, that in a little while he had hooked up wealth enough to make him, in those moderate days, a rich burgher for life.

It would be tedious to detail minutely the rest of this story. To tell how he gradually managed to bring his property into use without exciting surprise and inquiry,—how he satisfied all scruples with regard to retaining the property, and at the same time gratified his own feelings by marrying the pretty Marie Vander Heyden,—and how he and Heer Antony had many a merry and roving expedition together.

I must not omit to say, however, that Dolph took his mother home to live with him, and cherished her in her old days. The good dame, too, had the satisfaction of no longer hearing her son made the theme of censure; on the contrary, he grew daily in public esteem; everybody spoke well of him and his wines; and the lordliest burgomaster was never known to decline his invitation to dinner. Dolph often related, at his own table, the wicked pranks which had once been the abhorrence of the town; but they were now considered excellent jokes, and the gravest dignitary was fain to hold his sides when listening to them. No one was more struck with Dolph's increasing merit than his old master the doctor; and so forgiving was Dolph, that he absolutely employed the doctor as his family physician, only taking care that his prescriptions should be always thrown out of the window. His mother had often her junto of old cronies to take a snug cup of tea with her in her comfortable little parlor; and Peter de Groodt, as he sat by the fireside, with one of her grandchildren on his knee, would many a time congratulate her upon her son turning out so great a man; upon which the good old soul would wag her head with exultation, and exclaim, "Ah, neighbor,

neighbor! did I not say that Dolph would one day or other hold up his head with the best of them?"

Thus did Dolph Heyliger go on, cheerily and prosperously, growing merrier as he grew older and wiser, and completely falsifying the old proverb about money got over the devil's back;* for he made good use of his wealth, and became a distinguished citizen, and a valuable member of the community. He was a great promoter of public institutions, such as beef-steak societies and catch-clubs.† He presided at all public dinners, and was the first that introduced turtle from the West Indies. He improved the breed of race-horses and game-cocks, and was so great a patron of modest merit, that any one who could sing a good song, or tell a good story, was sure to find a place at his table.

He was a member, too, of the corporation, made several laws for the protection of game and oysters, and bequeathed to the board a large silver punch-bowl, made out of the identical porringer before mentioned, and which is in the possession of the corporation to this very day.

Finally, he died, in a florid old age, of an apoplexy‡ at a corporation feast, and was buried with great honors in the yard of the little Dutch church in Garden Street, where his tombstone may still be seen with a modest epitaph in Dutch, by his friend Mynheer Justus Benson, an ancient and excellent poet of the province.

The foregoing tale rests on better authority than most tales of the kind, as I have it at second-hand from the lips of Dolph Heyliger himself. He never related it till towards the latter part of his life, and then in great confidence (for he was very discreet), to a few of his particular cronies at his own table, over a supernumerary bowl of punch; and, strange as the hobgoblin parts of the story may seem, there never was a single doubt expressed on the subject by any of his guests. It may not be amiss, before concluding, to observe that, in addition to his other accomplishments, Dolph Heyliger was noted for being the ablest drawer of the long-bow§ in the whole province.

---

*That is, what is got over the devil's back is spent under his belly (squandered).
†Social clubs.
‡Sudden fit of emotion; a stroke.
§That is, the ablest teller of tall tales.

The Author's Farewell[8]

And so, without more circumstance at all,
I hold it fit that we shake hands and part.

HAMLET*

Having taken leave of the Hall and its inmates, and brought the history of my visit to something like a close, there seems to remain nothing further than to make my bow, and exit. It is my foible, however, to get on such companionable terms with my reader in the course of a work, that it really costs me some pain to part with him, and I am apt to keep him by the hand, and have a few farewell words at the end of my last volume.

When I cast an eye back upon the work I am just concluding, I cannot but be sensible how full it must be of errors and imperfections; indeed, how should it be otherwise, writing, as I do, about subjects and scenes with which, as a stranger, I am but partially acquainted? Many will, doubtless, find cause to smile at very obvious blunders which I may have made; and many may, perhaps, be offended at what they may conceive prejudiced representations. Some will think I might have said much more on such subjects as may suit their peculiar tastes; whilst others will think I had done wiser to have left those subjects entirely alone.

It will probably be said, too, by some, that I view England with a partial eye. Perhaps I do; for I can never forget that it is my "fatherland." And yet the circumstances under which I have viewed it have by no means been such as were calculated to produce favorable impressions. For the greater part of the time that I have resided in it, I have lived almost unknowing and unknown; seeking no favors and receiving none;—"a stranger and a sojourner in the land,"† and subject to all the chills and neglects that are the common lot of the stranger.

---

*From Shakespeare's *Hamlet, Prince of Denmark* (act 1, scene 5).
†See the Bible, Genesis 23:4 (King James Version); compare also with the conclusion of Irving's sketch "The Voyage" (p. 57).

When I consider these circumstances, and recollect how often I have taken up my pen, with a mind ill at ease, and spirits much dejected and cast down, I cannot but think I was not likely to err on the favorable side of the picture. The opinions I have given of English character have been the result of much quiet, dispassionate, and varied observation. It is a character not to be hastily studied, for it always puts on a repulsive and ungracious aspect to a stranger. Let those, then, who condemn my representations as too favorable, observe this people as closely and deliberately as I have done, and they will, probably, change their opinion. Of one thing, at any rate, I am certain, that I have spoken honestly and sincerely, from the convictions of my mind and the dictates of my heart. When I first published my former writings, it was with no hope of gaining favor in English eyes, for I little thought they were to become current out of my own country; and had I merely sought popularity among my own countrymen, I should have taken a more direct and obvious way, by gratifying rather than rebuking the angry feelings then prevalent against England.

And here let me acknowledge my warm, my thankful feelings, at the effect produced by one of my trivial lucubrations. I allude to the essay in the "Sketch-Book," on the subject of the literary feuds between England and America. I cannot express the heartfelt delight I have experienced at the unexpected sympathy and approbation with which those remarks have been received on both sides of the Atlantic. I speak this not from any paltry feelings of gratified vanity, for I attribute the effect to no merit of my pen. The paper in question was brief and casual, and the ideas it conveyed were simple and obvious. "It was the cause; it was the cause"* alone. There was a predisposition on the part of my readers to be favorably affected. My countrymen responded in heart to the filial feelings I had avowed in their name towards the parent country; and there was a generous sympathy in every English bosom towards a solitary individual, lifting up his voice in a strange land, to vindicate the injured character of his nation. There are some causes so sacred as to carry with them an irresistible appeal to every virtuous bosom; and he needs but

---

*Allusion to Shakespeare's *Othello, the Moor of Venice* (act 5, scene 2).

little power of eloquence, who defends the honor of his wife, his mother, or his country.

I hail, therefore, the success of that brief paper as showing how much good may be done by a kind word, however feeble, when spoken in season,—as showing how much dormant good feeling actually exists in each country, towards the other, which only wants the slightest spark to kindle it into a genial flame,—as showing, in fact, what I have all along believed and asserted, that the two nations would grow together in esteem and amity, if meddling and malignant spirits would but throw by their mischievous pens, and leave kindred hearts to the kindly impulses of nature.

I once more assert, and I assert it with increased conviction of its truth, that there exists among the great majority of my countrymen a favorable feeling toward England. I repeat this assertion, because I think it a truth that cannot too often be reiterated, and because it has met with some contradiction. Among all the liberal and enlightened minds of my countrymen, among all those which eventually give a tone to national opinion, there exists a cordial desire to be on terms of courtesy and friendship. But at the same time there exists in those very minds a distrust of reciprocal good-will on the part of England. They have been rendered morbidly sensitive by the attacks made upon their country by the English press; and their occasional irritability on this subject has been misinterpreted into a settled and unnatural hostility.

For my part, I consider this jealous sensibility as belonging to generous natures. I should look upon my countrymen as fallen indeed from that independence of spirit which is their birth-gift, as fallen indeed from that pride of character which they inherit from the proud nation from which they sprung, could they tamely sit down under the infliction of contumely and insult. Indeed, the very impatience which they show as to the misrepresentations of the press, proves their respect for English opinion, and their desire for English amity; for there is never jealousy where there is not strong regard.

It is easy to say, that these attacks are all the effusions of worthless scribblers, and treated with silent contempt by the nation; but, alas! the slanders of the scribbler travel abroad, and the silent contempt of the nation is only known at home. With England, then, it remains, as I have formerly asserted, to promote a mutual spirit of conciliation; she has but to hold the language of friendship and respect, and she is secure of the good-will of every American bosom.

In expressing these sentiments, I would utter nothing that should commit the proper spirit of my countrymen. We seek no boon at England's hands: we ask nothing as a favor. Her friendship is not necessary, nor would her hostility be dangerous to our well-being. We ask nothing from abroad that we cannot reciprocate. But with respect to England, we have a warm feeling of the heart, the glow of consanguinity that still lingers in our blood. Interest apart—past differences forgotten—we extend the hand of old relationship. We merely ask, do not estrange us from you; do not destroy the ancient tie of blood; do not let scoffers and slanderers drive a kindred nation from your side: we would fain be friends; do not compel us to be enemies.

There needs no better rallying ground for international amity than that furnished by an eminent English writer. "There is," says he, "a sacred bond between us of blood and of language, which no circumstances can break. Our literature must always be theirs; and though their laws are no longer the same as ours, we have the same Bible, and we address our common Father in the same prayer. Nations are too ready to admit that they have natural enemies; why should they be less willing to believe that they have natural friends?"*

To the magnanimous spirits of both countries must we trust to carry such a natural alliance of affection into full effect. To pens more powerful than mine I leave the noble task of promoting the cause of national amity. To the intelligent and enlightened of my own country I address my parting voice, entreating them to show themselves superior to the petty attacks of the ignorant and the worthless, and still to look with dispassionate and philosophic eye to the moral character of England, as the intellectual source of our rising greatness; while I appeal to every generous-minded Englishman

---

*From an article (said to be by Robert Southey, Esq.) published in the *Quarterly Review*. It is to be lamented that that publication should so often forget the generous text here given [Irving's note]. Robert Southey (1774–1843) was an English poet and man of letters.

from the slanders which disgrace the press, insult the understanding, and belie the magnanimity of his country; and I invite him to look to America as to a kindred nation worthy of its origin; giving, in the healthy vigor of its growth, the best of comments on its parent stock; and reflecting, in the dawning brightness of its fame, the moral effulgence of British glory.

I am sure that such an appeal will not be made in vain. Indeed, I have noticed, for some time past, an essential change in English sentiment with regard to America. In parliament, that fountainhead of public opinion, there seems to be an emulation, on both sides of the house, in holding the language of courtesy and friendship. The same spirit is daily becoming more and more prevalent in good society. There is a growing curiosity concerning my country; a craving desire for correct information, that cannot fail to lead to a favorable understanding. The scoffer, I trust, has had his day; the time of the slanderer is gone by; the ribald jokes, the stale commonplaces, which have so long passed current when America was the theme, are now banished to the ignorant and the vulgar, or only perpetuated by the hireling scribblers and traditional jesters of the press. The intelligent and high-minded now pride themselves upon making America their study.

But however my feelings may be understood or reciprocated on either side of the Atlantic, I utter them without reserve, for I have ever found that to speak frankly is to speak safely. I am not so sanguine as to believe that the two nations are ever to be bound together by any romantic ties of feeling; but I believe that much may be done by keeping alive cordial sentiments, were every well-disposed mind occasionally to throw in a simple word of kindness. If I have, indeed, produced any such effect by my writings, it will be a soothing reflection to me, that for once, in the course of a rather negligent life, I have been useful; that for once, by the casual exercise of a pen which has been in general but too unprofitably employed, I have awakened a chord of sympathy between the land of my fathers and the dear land which gave me birth.

In the spirit of these sentiments I now take my farewell of the paternal soil. With anxious eye do I behold the clouds of doubt and difficulty that lower over it, and earnestly do I hope they may all clear up into serene and settled sunshine. In bidding this last adieu, my heart is filled with fond, yet melancholy emotions; and still I linger, and still, like a child leaving the venerable abodes of his forefathers, I turn to breathe forth a filial benediction: "Peace be within thy walls, oh England! and plenteousness within thy palaces; for my brethren and my companions' sake I will now say, Peace be within thee!"

SELECTIONS FROM

TALES OF A TRAVELLER

To the Reader[1]

Worthy and dear reader!—Hast thou ever been waylaid in the midst of a pleasant tour by some treacherous malady: thy heels tripped up, and thou left to count the tedious minutes as they passed, in the solitude of an inn-chamber? If thou hast, thou wilt be able to pity me. Behold me, interrupted in the course of my journeying up the fair banks of the Rhine, and laid up by indisposition in this old frontier town of Mentz. I have worn out every source of amusement. I know the sound of every clock that strikes, and bell that rings, in the place. I know to a second when to listen for the first tap of the Prussian drum, as it summons the garrison to parade, or at what hour to expect the distant sound of the Austrian military band. All these have grown wearisome to me; and even the well-known step of my doctor, as he slowly paces the corridor, with healing in the creak of his shoes, no longer affords an agreeable interruption to the monotony of my apartment.

For a time I attempted to beguile the weary hours by studying German under the tuition of mine host's pretty little daughter, Katrine; but I soon found even German had not power to charm a languid ear, and that the conjugating of *ich liebe** might be powerless, however rosy the lips which uttered it.

I tried to read, but my mind would not fix itself. I turned over volume after volume, but threw them by with distaste: "Well, then," said I at length, in despair, "if I cannot read a book, I will write one." Never was there a more lucky idea; it at once gave me occupation and amusement. The writing of a book was considered in old times as an enterprise of toil and difficulty, insomuch that the most trifling lucubration was denominated a "work," and the world talked with awe and reverence of "the labors of the learned." These matters are better understood nowadays.

---

*I love (German).

Thanks to the improvements in all kind of manufactures, the art of book-making has been made familiar to the meanest capacity. Everybody is an author. The scribbling of a quarto is the mere pastime of the idle; the young gentleman throws off his brace of duodecimos in the intervals of the sporting-season, and the young lady produces her set of volumes with the same facility that her great-grandmother worked a set of chair-bottoms.

The idea having struck me, therefore, to write a book, the reader will easily perceive that the execution of it was no difficult matter. I rummaged my portfolio, and cast about, in my recollection, for those floating materials which a man naturally collects in travelling; and here I have arranged them in this little work.

As I know this to be a story-telling and a story-reading age, and that the world is fond of being taught by apologue,* I have digested the instruction I would convey into a number of tales. They may not possess the power of amusement which the tales told by many of my contemporaries possess; but then I value myself on the sound moral which each of them contains. This may not be apparent at first, but the reader will be sure to find it out in the end. I am for curing the world by gentle alteratives, not by violent doses; indeed, the patient should never be conscious that he is taking a dose. I have learnt this much from experience under the hands of the worthy Hippocrates[†] of Mentz.

I am not, therefore, for those barefaced tales which carry their moral on the surface, staring one in the face; they are enough to deter the squeamish reader. On the contrary, I have often hid my moral from sight, and disguised it as much as possible by sweets and spices, so that while the simple reader is listening with open mouth to a ghost or a love story, he may have a *bolus*[§] of sound morality popped down his throat, and be never the wiser for the fraud.

As the public is apt to be curious about the sources whence an author draws his stories, doubtless that it may know how far to put faith in them, I would observe, that the Adventure of the German Student, or rather the latter part of it, is founded on an anecdote

---

*Moral fable.
[†]Greek physician (c.460–c.377 B.C.) known as the father of medicine.
[§]Pill.

related to me as existing somewhere in French; and, indeed, I have been told, since writing it, that an ingenious tale has been founded on it by an English writer; but I have never met with either the former or the latter in print. Some of the circumstances in the Adventure of the Mysterious Picture, and in the Story of the Young Italian, are vague recollections of anecdotes related to me some years since; but from what source derived, I do not know. The Adventure of the Young Painter among the banditti is taken almost entirely from an authentic narrative in manuscript.

As to the other tales contained in this work, and indeed to my tales generally, I can make but one observation: I am an old traveller; I have read somewhat, heard and seen more, and dreamt more than all. My brain is filled, therefore, with all kinds of odds and ends. In travelling, these heterogeneous matters have become shaken up in my mind, as the articles are apt to be in an ill-packed travelling-trunk; so that when I attempt to draw forth a fact, I cannot determine whether I have read, heard, or dreamt it; and I am always at a loss to know how much to believe of my own stories.

These matters being premised, fall to, worthy reader, with good appetite; and, above all, with good-humor to what is here set before thee. If the tales I have furnished should prove to be bad, they will at least be found short; so that no one will be wearied long on the same theme. "Variety is charming," as some poet observes.

There is a certain relief in change, even though it be from bad to worse! As I have often found in travelling in a stage-coach, that it is often a comfort to shift one's position, and be bruised in a new place.

Ever thine,

GEOFFREY CRAYON

Dated from the HOTEL DE DARMSTADT,
    ci-devant HOTEL DE PARIS,
        MENTZ, *otherwise called* MAYENCE.

PART FIRST

STRANGE STORIES

BY A NERVOUS GENTLEMAN

I'll tell you more, there was a fish taken,
A monstrous fish, with a sword by 's side, a long sword,
A pike in 's neck, and a gun in's nose, a huge gun,
And letters of mart in 's mouth from the Duke of Florence.
Cleanthes.—This is a monstrous lie.
Tony.—I do confess it.
Do you think I'd tell you truths?

FLETCHER'S *WIFE FOR A MONTH**

The Great Unknown

The following adventures were related to me by the same nervous gentleman who told me the romantic tale of the Stout Gentleman, published in "Bracebridge Hall." It is very singular, that, although I expressly stated that story to have been told

---

*From the 1624 play by English dramatist John Fletcher (act 2, scene 1).

to me, and described the very person who told it, still it has been received as an adventure that happened to myself. Now I protest I never met with any adventure of the kind. I should not have grieved at this, had it not been intimated by the author of "Waverley," in an introduction to his novel of "Peveril of the Peak," that he was himself the stout gentleman alluded to. I have ever since been importuned by questions and letters from gentlemen, and particularly from ladies without number, touching what I had seen of the Great Unknown.*

Now all this is extremely tantalizing. It is like being congratulated on the high prize when one has drawn a blank; for I have just as great a desire as any one of the public to penetrate the mystery of that very singular personage, whose voice fills every corner of the world, without any one being able to tell whence it comes.

My friend, the nervous gentleman, also, who is a man of very shy, retired habits, complains that he has been excessively annoyed in consequence of its getting about in his neighborhood that he is the fortunate personage. Insomuch, that he has become a character of considerable notoriety in two or three country-towns, and has been repeatedly teased to exhibit himself at blue-stocking parties, for no other reason than that of being "the gentleman who has had a glimpse of the author of 'Waverley.'"

Indeed the poor man has grown ten times as nervous as ever since he has discovered, on such good authority, who the stout gentleman was; and will never forgive himself for not having made a more resolute effort to get a full sight of him. He has anxiously endeavored to call up a recollection of what he saw of that portly personage; and has ever since kept a curious eye on all gentlemen of more than ordinary dimensions, whom he has seen getting into stage-coaches. All in vain! The features he had caught a glimpse of seem common to the whole race of stout

---

*The Great Unknown" is a nickname of Scottish author Sir Walter Scott. Scott published *Waverley* (1814), *Peveril of the Peak* (1822), and all of his other novels anonymously until 1827, generating much public speculation as to their authorship; his identity was an open secret by the time Irving published *Tales of a Traveller* (1824).

gentlemen, and the Great Unknown remains as great an unknown as ever.

Having premised these circumstances, I will now let the nervous
gentleman proceed with his stories.

The Hunting-Dinner[2]

I was once at a hunting-dinner, given by a worthy fox-hunting old Baronet, who kept bachelor's hall in jovial style in an ancient rook-haunted family-mansion, in one of the middle counties. He had been a devoted admirer of the fair sex in his younger days; but, having travelled much, studied the sex in various countries with distinguished success, and returned home profoundly instructed, as he supposed, in the ways of woman, and a perfect master of the art of pleasing, had the mortification of being jilted by a little boarding-school girl, who was scarcely versed in the accidence of love.

The Baronet was completely overcome by such an incredible defeat; retired from the world in disgust; put himself under the government of his housekeeper; and took to fox-hunting like a perfect Nimrod.* Whatever poets may say to the contrary, a man will grow out of love as he grows old; and a pack of fox-hounds may chase out of his heart even the memory of a boarding-school goddess. The Baronet was, when I saw him, as merry and mellow an old bachelor as ever followed a hound; and the love he had once felt for one woman had spread itself over the whole sex, so that there was not a pretty face in the whole country round but came in for a share.

The dinner was prolonged till a late hour; for our host having no ladies in his houschold to summon us to the drawing-room, the bottle maintained its true bachelor sway, unrivalled by its potent enemy, the tea-kettle. The old hall in which we dined echoed to bursts of robustious fox-hunting merriment, that made the ancient antlers shake on the walls. By degrees, however, the wine and the wassail† of mine host began to operate upon bodies already a little jaded by the chase. The choice spirits which flashed up at the beginning of the dinner, sparkled for a time, then gradually went out one after another, or only emitted now and then a faint gleam from the

---

*A great hunter; see the Bible, Genesis 10:8–9.
†Liquor, usually a spiced ale or wine.

socket. Some of the briskest talkers, who had given tongue so bravely at the first burst, fell fast asleep; and none kept on their way but certain of those long-winded prosers, who, like short-legged hounds, worry on unnoticed at the bottom of conversation, but are sure to be in at the death. Even these at length subsided into silence; and scarcely anything was heard but the nasal communications of two or three veteran masticators, who having been silent while awake, were indemnifying the company in their sleep.

At length the announcement of tea and coffee in the cedar-parlor roused all hands from this temporary torpor. Every one awoke marvellously renovated, and while sipping the refreshing beverage out of the Baronet's old-fashioned hereditary china, began to think of departing for their several homes. But here a sudden difficulty arose. While we had been prolonging our repast, a heavy winter storm had set in, with snow, rain, and sleet, driven by such bitter blasts of wind, that they threatened to penetrate to the very bone.

"It's all in vain," said our hospitable host, "to think of putting one's head out of doors in such weather. So, gentlemen, I hold you my guests for this night at least, and will have your quarters prepared accordingly."

The unruly weather, which became more and more tempestuous, rendered the hospitable suggestion unanswerable. The only question was, whether such an unexpected accession of company to an already crowded house would not put the housekeeper to her trumps* to accommodate them.

"Pshaw," cried mine host; "did you ever know a bachelor's hall that was not elastic, and able to accommodate twice as many as it could hold?" So, out of a good-humored pique, the housekeeper was summoned to a consultation before us all. The old lady appeared in her gala suit of faded brocade, which rustled with flurry and agitation; for, in spite of our host's bravado, she was a little perplexed. But in a bachelor's house, and with bachelor guests, these matters are readily managed. There is no lady of the house to stand upon squeamish points about lodging gentlemen in odd holes and corners, and exposing the shabby parts of the establishment. A bachelor's housekeeper is used to

---

*That is, to her limits.

shifts and emergencies; so, after much worrying to and fro, and divers consultations about the red-room, and the blue-room, and the chintz-room, and the damask-room, and the little room with the bow-window, the matter was finally arranged.

When all this was done, we were once more summoned to the standing rural amusement of eating. The time that had been consumed in dozing after dinner, and in the refreshment and consultation of the cedar-parlor, was sufficient, in the opinion of the rosy-faced butler, to engender a reasonable appetite for supper. A slight repast had, therefore, been tricked up from the residue of dinner, consisting of a cold sirloin of beef, hashed venison, a devilled leg of a turkey or so, and a few other of those light articles taken by country gentlemen to ensure sound sleep and heavy snoring.

The nap after dinner had brightened up every one's wit; and a great deal of excellent humor was expended upon the perplexities of mine host and his housekeeper, by certain married gentlemen of the company, who considered themselves privileged in joking with a bachelor's establishment. From this the banter turned as to what quarters each would find, on being thus suddenly billeted in so antiquated a mansion.

"By my soul," said an Irish captain of dragoons, one of the most merry and boisterous of the party, "by my soul, but I should not be surprised if some of those good-looking gentlefolks that hang along the walls should walk about the rooms of this stormy night; or if I should find the ghosts of one of those long-waisted ladies turning into my bed in mistake for her grave in the churchyard."

"Do you believe in ghosts, then?" said a thin, hatchet-faced gentleman, with projecting eyes like a lobster.

I had remarked this last personage during dinner-time for one of those incessant questioners, who have a craving, unhealthy appetite in conversation. He never seemed satisfied with the whole of a story; never laughed when others laughed; but always put the joke to the question. He never could enjoy the kernel of the nut, but pestered himself to get more out of the shell. "Do you believe in ghosts, then?" said the inquisitive gentleman.

"Faith, but I do," replied the jovial Irishman. "I was brought up in the fear and belief of them. We had a Benshee in our own family, honey."

"A Benshee, and what's that?" cried the questioner.

"Why, an old lady ghost that tends upon your real Milesian families,* and waits at their window to let them know when some of them are to die."

"A mighty pleasant piece of information!" cried an elderly gentleman with a knowing look, and with a flexible nose, to which he could give a whimsical twist when he wished to be waggish.

"By my soul, but I'd have you to know it's a piece of distinction to be waited on by a Benshee. It's a proof that one has pure blood in one's veins. But i' faith, now we are talking of ghosts, there never was a house or a night better fitted than the present for a ghost adventure. Pray, Sir John, haven't you such a thing as a haunted chamber to put a guest in?"

"Perhaps," said the Baronet, smiling, "I might accommodate you even on that point."

"Oh, I should like it of all things, my jewel. Some dark oaken room, with ugly woe-begone portraits, that stare dismally at one; and about which the housekeeper has a power of delightful stories of love and murder. And then a dim lamp, a table with a rusty sword across it, and a spectre all in white, to draw aside one's curtains at midnight"—

"In truth," said an old gentleman at one end of the table, "you put me in mind of an anecdote"—

"Oh, a ghost-story! a ghost-story!" was vociferated round the board, every one edging his chair a little nearer.

The attention of the whole company was now turned upon the speaker. He was an old gentleman, one side of whose face was no match for the other. The eye-lid drooped and hung down like an unhinged window-shutter. Indeed, the whole side of his head was dilapidated, and seemed like the wing of a house shut up and haunted. I'll warrant that side was well stuffed with ghost-stories.

There was a universal demand for the tale.

"Nay," said the old gentleman, "it's a mere anecdote, and a very commonplace one; but such as it is you shall have it. It is a story that I once heard my uncle tell as having happened to himself. He was a

*Descendants of King Milesius, legendary Celtic invader of Ireland.

man very apt to meet with strange adventures. I have heard him tell of others much more singular."

"What kind of a man was your uncle?" said the questioning gentleman.

"Why, he was rather a dry, shrewd kind of body; a great traveller, and fond of telling his adventures."

"Pray, how old might he have been when that happened?"

"When what happened?" cried the gentleman with the flexible nose, impatiently. "Egad, you have not given anything a chance to happen. Come, never mind our uncle's age; let us have his adventures."

The inquisitive gentleman being for the moment silenced, the old gentleman with the haunted head proceeded.[3]

Adventure of the German Student [4]

O n a stormy night, in the tempestuous times of the French revolution, a young German was returning to his lodgings, at a late hour, across the old part of Paris. The lightning gleamed, and the loud claps of thunder rattled through the lofty narrow streets—but I should first tell you something about this young German.

Gottfried Wolfgang was a young man of good family. He had studied for some time at Göttingen, but being of a visionary and enthusiastic character, he had wandered into those wild and speculative doctrines which have so often bewildered German students. His secluded life, his intense application, and the singular nature of his studies, had an effect on both mind and body. His health was impaired; his imagination diseased. He had been indulging in fanciful speculations on spiritual essences, until, like Swedenborg,* he had an ideal world of his own around him. He took up a notion, I do not know from what cause, that there was an evil influence hanging over him; an evil genius or spirit seeking to ensnare him and ensure his perdition. Such an idea working on his melancholy temperament, produced the most gloomy effects. He became haggard and desponding. His friends discovered the mental malady preying upon him, and determined that the best cure was a change of scene; he was sent, therefore, to finish his studies amid the splendors and gayeties of Paris.

Wolfgang arrived at Paris at the breaking out of the revolution.† The popular delirium at first caught his enthusiastic mind, and he was captivated by the political and philosophical theories of the day: but the scenes of blood which followed shocked his sensitive nature, disgusted him with society and the world, and made him more than ever a recluse. He shut himself up in a solitary apartment in the *Pays*

---

*Emmanuel Swedenborg (1688–1772), Swedish scientist, anatomist, and mystic, whose theory of correspondences influenced the transcendentalist movement in America.
†The French Revolution, which began in 1789.

Latin, the quarter of students. There, in a gloomy street not far from the monastic walls of the Sorbonne,* he pursued his favorite speculations. Sometimes he spent hours together in the great libraries of Paris, those catacombs of departed authors, rummaging among their hoards of dusty and obsolete works in quest of food for his unhealthy appetite. He was, in a manner, a literary ghoul, feeding in the charnel-house of decayed literature.

Wolfgang, though solitary and recluse, was of an ardent temperament, but for a time it operated merely upon his imagination. He was too shy and ignorant of the world to make any advances to the fair, but he was a passionate admirer of female beauty, and in his lonely chamber would often lose himself in reveries on forms and faces which he had seen, and his fancy would deck out images of loveliness far surpassing the reality.

While his mind was in this excited and sublimated state, a dream produced an extraordinary effect upon him. It was of a female face of transcendent beauty. So strong was the impression made, that he dreamt of it again and again. It haunted his thoughts by day, his slumbers by night; in fine, he became passionately enamoured of this shadow of a dream. This lasted so long that it became one of those fixed ideas which haunt the minds of melancholy men, and are at times mistaken for madness.

Such was Gottfried Wolfgang, and such his situation at the time I mentioned. He was returning home late one stormy night, through some of the old and gloomy streets of the *Marais*, the ancient part of Paris. The loud claps of thunder rattled among the high houses of the narrow streets. He came to the Place de Grève, the square where public executions are performed. The lightning quivered about the pinnacles of the ancient Hôtel de Ville, and shed flickering gleams over the open space in front. As Wolfgang was crossing the square, he shrank back with horror at finding himself close by the guillotine. It was the height of the reign of terror, when this dreadful instrument of death stood ever ready, and its scaffold was continually running with the blood of the virtuous and the brave. It had that very day been actively employed in the work of carnage, and there it stood in

*La Sorbonne, the University of Paris.

grim array, amidst a silent and sleeping city, waiting for fresh victims.

Wolfgang's heart sickened within him, and he was turning shuddering from the horrible engine, when he beheld a shadowy form, cowering as it were at the foot of the steps which led up to the scaffold. A succession of vivid flashes of lightning revealed it more distinctly. It was a female figure, dressed in black. She was seated on one of the lower steps of the scaffold, leaning forward, her face hid in her lap; and her long dishevelled tresses hanging to the ground, streaming with the rain which fell in torrents. Wolfgang paused. There was something awful in this solitary monument of woe. The female had the appearance of being above the common order. He knew the times to be full of vicissitude, and that many a fair head, which had once been pillowed on down, now wandered houseless. Perhaps this was some poor mourner whom the dreadful axe had rendered desolate, and who sat here heart-broken on the strand of existence, from which all that was dear to her had been launched into eternity.

He approached, and addressed her in the accents of sympathy. She raised her head and gazed wildly at him. What was his astonishment at beholding, by the bright glare of the lightning, the very face which had haunted him in his dreams. It was pale and disconsolate, but ravishingly beautiful.

Trembling with violent and conflicting emotions, Wolfgang again accosted her. He spoke something of her being exposed at such an hour of the night, and to the fury of such a storm, and offered to conduct her to her friends. She pointed to the guillotine with a gesture of dreadful signification.

"I have no friend on earth!" said she.

"But you have a home," said Wolfgang.

"Yes—in the grave!"

The heart of the student melted at the words.

"If a stranger dare make an offer," said he, "without danger of being misunderstood, I would offer my humble dwelling as a shelter; myself as a devoted friend. I am friendless myself in Paris, and a stranger in the land;* but if my life could be of service, it is at your disposal, and should be sacrificed before harm or indignity should come to you."

---

*Compare with the conclusion of Irving's sketch "The Voyage" (p. 57).

There was an honest earnestness in the young man's manner that had its effect. His foreign accent, too, was in his favor; it showed him not to be a hackneyed inhabitant of Paris. Indeed, there is an eloquence in true enthusiasm that is not to be doubted. The homeless stranger confided herself implicitly to the protection of the student.

He supported her faltering steps across the Pont Neuf, and by the place where the statue of Henry the Fourth had been overthrown by the populace. The storm had abated, and the thunder rumbled at a distance. All Paris was quiet; that great volcano of human passion slumbered for a while, to gather fresh strength for the next day's eruption. The student conducted his charge through the ancient streets of the *Pays Latin*, and by the dusky walls of the Sorbonne, to the great dingy hotel which he inhabited. The old portress who admitted them stared with surprise at the unusual sight of the melancholy Wolfgang with a female companion.

On entering his apartment, the student, for the first time, blushed at the scantiness and indifference of his dwelling. He had but one chamber—an old-fashioned saloon—heavily carved, and fantastically furnished with the remains of former magnificence, for it was one of those hotels in the quarter of the Luxembourg palace, which had once belonged to nobility. It was lumbered with books and papers, and all the usual apparatus of a student, and his bed stood in a recess at one end.

When lights were brought, and Wolfgang had a better opportunity of contemplating the stranger, he was more than ever intoxicated by her beauty. Her face was pale, but of a dazzling fairness, set off by a profusion of raven hair that hung clustering about it. Her eyes were large and brilliant, with a singular expression approaching almost to wildness. As far as her black dress permitted her shape to be seen, it was of perfect symmetry. Her whole appearance was highly striking, though she was dressed in the simplest style. The only thing approaching to an ornament which she wore, was a broad black band round her neck, clasped by diamonds.

The perplexity now commenced with the student how to dispose of the helpless being thus thrown upon his protection. He thought of abandoning his chamber to her, and seeking shelter for himself elsewhere. Still, he was so fascinated by her charms, there seemed to be such a spell upon his thoughts and senses, that he could not tear himself from her presence. Her manner, too, was singular and unaccountable. She spoke no more of the guillotine. Her grief had abated. The attentions of the student had first won her confidence, and then, apparently, her heart. She was evidently an enthusiast like himself, and enthusiasts soon understand each other.

In the infatuation of the moment, Wolfgang avowed his passion for her. He told her the story of his mysterious dream, and how she had possessed his heart before he had even seen her. She was strangely affected by his recital, and acknowledged to have felt an impulse towards him equally unaccountable. It was the time for wild theory and wild actions. Old prejudices and superstitions were done away; everything was under the sway of the "Goddess of Reason." Among other rubbish of the old times, the forms and ceremonies of marriage began to be considered superfluous bonds for honorable minds. Social compacts were the vogue. Wolfgang was too much of a theorist not to be tainted by the liberal doctrines of the day.

"Why should we separate?" said he: "our hearts are united; in the eye of reason and honor we are as one. What need is there of sordid forms to bind high souls together?"

The stranger listened with emotion: she had evidently received illumination at the same school.

"You have no home nor family," continued he: "let me be everything to you, or rather let us be everything to one another. If form is necessary, form shall be observed—there is my hand. I pledge myself to you forever."

"Forever?" said the stranger, solemnly.

"Forever!" replied Wolfgang.

The stranger clasped the hand extended to her: "Then I am yours," murmured she, and sank upon his bosom.

The next morning the student left his bride sleeping, and sallied forth at an early hour to seek more spacious apartments suitable to the change in his situation. When he returned, he found the stranger lying with her head hanging over the bed, and one arm thrown over it. He spoke to her, but received no reply. He advanced to awaken her from her uneasy posture. On taking her hand, it was cold—there was no pulsation—her face was pallid and ghastly. In a word, she was a corpse.

Horrified and frantic, he alarmed the house. A scene of confusion ensued. The police were summoned. As the officer of police entered the room, he started back on beholding the corpse.

"Great heaven!" cried he, "how did this woman come here?"

"Do you know anything about her?" said Wolfgang eagerly.

"Do I?" exclaimed the officer: "she was guillotined yesterday."

He stepped forward; undid the black collar round the neck of the corpse, and the head rolled on the floor!

The student burst into a frenzy. "The fiend! the fiend has gained possession of me!" shrieked he: "I am lost forever."

They tried to soothe him, but in vain. He was possessed with the frightful belief that an evil spirit had reanimated the dead body to ensnare him. He went distracted, and died in a mad-house.

Here the old gentleman with the haunted head finished his narrative.

"And is this really a fact?" said the inquisitive gentleman.

"A fact not to be doubted," replied the other. "I had it from the best authority. The student told it me himself. I saw him in a mad-house in Paris."

Adventure of the Mysterious Picture[5]

As one story of a kind produces another, and as all the company seemed fully engrossed with the subject, and disposed to bring their relatives and ancestors upon the scene, there is no knowing how many more strange adventures we might have heard, had not a corpulent old fox-hunter, who had slept soundly through the whole, now suddenly awakened, with a loud and long-drawn yawn. The sound broke the charm: the ghosts took to flight, as though it had been cock-crowing, and there was a universal move for bed.

"And now for the haunted chamber," said the Irish Captain, taking his candle.

"Ay, who's to be the hero of the night?" said the gentleman with the ruined head.

"That we shall see in the morning," said the old gentleman with the nose: "whoever looks pale and grizzly will have seen the ghost."

"Well, gentlemen," said the Baronet, "there's many a true thing said in jest—in fact, one of you will sleep in the room to-night"——

"What—a haunted room?—a haunted room?—I claim the adventure—and I—and I—and I," said a dozen guests, talking and laughing at the same time.

"No, no," said mine host, "there is a secret about one of my rooms on which I feel disposed to try an experiment: so, gentlemen, none of you shall know who has the haunted chamber until circumstances reveal it. I will not even know it myself, but will leave it to chance and the allotment of the housekeeper. At the same time, if it will be any satisfaction to you, I will observe, for the honor of my paternal mansion, that there's scarcely a chamber in it but is well worthy of being haunted."

We now separated for the night, and each went to his allotted room. Mine was in one wing of the building, and I could not but smile at its resemblance in style to those eventful apartments described in the tales of the supper-table. It was spacious and gloomy, decorated with lamp-black portraits; a bed of ancient damask, with a tester* sufficiently lofty to grace a couch of state, and a number of massive pieces of old-fashioned furniture. I drew a great claw-footed arm-chair before the wide fire-place; stirred up the fire; sat looking into it, and musing upon the odd stories I had heard, until, partly overcome by the fatigue of the day's hunting, and partly by the wine and wassail of mine host, I fell asleep in my chair.

The uneasiness of my position made my slumber troubled, and laid me at the mercy of all kinds of wild and fearful dreams. Now it was that my perfidious dinner and supper rose in rebellion against my peace. I was hag-ridden by a fat saddle of mutton; a plum-pudding weighed like lead upon my conscience; the merry-thought of a capon filled me with horrible suggestions; and a devilled leg of a turkey stalked in all kinds of diabolical shapes through my imagination. In short, I had a violent fit of the nightmare. Some strange, indefinite evil seemed hanging over me which I could not avert; something terrible and loathsome oppressed me which I could not shake off. I was conscious of being asleep, and strove to rouse myself, but every effort redoubled the evil; until gasping, struggling, almost strangling, I suddenly sprang bolt upright in my chair, and awoke.

The light on the mantel-piece had burnt low, and the wick was divided; there was a great winding-sheet made by the dripping wax on the side towards me. The disordered taper emitted a broad flaring flame, and threw a strong light on a painting over the fireplace which I had not hitherto observed. It consisted merely of a head, or rather a face, staring full upon me, with an expression that was startling. It was without a frame, and at the first glance I could hardly persuade myself that it was not a real face thrusting itself out of the dark oaken panel. I sat in my chair gazing at it, and the more I gazed, the more it disquieted me. I had never before been affected in the same way by any painting. The emotions it caused were strange and indefinite. They were something like what I have heard ascribed to the eyes of the basilisk,† or like that mysterious influence in reptiles termed fascination. I passed my hand over my eyes several times, as if seeking instinctively to brush away the illusion—in vain. They instantly reverted to the picture, and its chilling, creeping influence

---

*Canopy over a four-poster bed.
†Mythical reptile whose gaze kills its victims.

over my flesh and blood was redoubled. I looked round the room on other pictures, either to divert my attention, or to see whether the same effect would be produced by them. Some of them were grim enough to produce the effect, if the mere grimness of the painting produced it.—No such thing—my eye passed over them all with perfect indifference, but the moment it reverted to this visage over the fireplace, it was as if an electric shock darted through me. The other pictures were dim and faded, but this one protruded from a plain background in the strongest relief, and with wonderful truth of coloring. The expression was that of agony—the agony of intense bodily pain; but a menace scowled upon the brow, and a few sprinklings of blood added to its ghastliness. Yet it was not all these characteristics; it was some horror of the mind, some inscrutable antipathy awakened by this picture, which harrowed up my feelings.

I tried to persuade myself that this was chimerical, that my brain was confused by the fumes of mine host's good cheer, and in some measure by the odd stories about paintings which had been told at supper. I determined to shake off these vapors of the mind; rose from my chair; walked about the room; snapped my fingers; rallied myself; laughed aloud.—It was a forced laugh, and the echo of it in the old chamber jarred upon my ear.—I walked to the window, and tried to discern the landscape through the glass. It was pitch darkness, and a howling storm without; and as I heard the wind moan among the trees, I caught a reflection of this accursed visage in the pane of glass, as though it were staring through the window at me. Even the reflection of it was thrilling.

How was this vile nervous fit, for such I now persuaded myself it was, to be conquered? I determined to force myself not to look at the painting, but to undress quickly and get into bed.—I began to undress, but in spite of every effort I could not keep myself from stealing a glance every now and then at the picture; and a glance was sufficient to distress me. Even when my back was turned to it, the idea of this strange face behind me, peeping over my shoulder, was insupportable. I threw off my clothes and hurried into bed, but still this visage gazed upon me. I had a full view of it in my bed, and for some time could not take my eyes from it. I had grown nervous to a dismal degree. I put out the light, and tried to force myself to sleep— all in vain. The fire gleaming up a little, threw an uncertain light about the room, leaving, however, the region of the picture in deep shadow. What, thought I, if this be the chamber about which mine host spoke as having a mystery reigning over it? I had taken his words merely as spoken in jest; might they have a real import? I looked around. The faintly lighted apartment had all the qualifications requisite for a haunted chamber. It began in my infected imagination to assume strange appearances—the old portraits turned paler and paler, and blacker and blacker; the streaks of light and shadow thrown among the quaint articles of furniture gave them more singular shapes and characters.—There was a huge dark clothes-press of antique form, gorgeous in brass and lustrous with wax, that began to grow oppressive to me.

"Am I then," thought I, "indeed the hero of the haunted room? Is there really a spell laid upon me, or is this all some contrivance of mine host to raise a laugh at my expense?" The idea of being hag-ridden by my own fancy all night, and then bantered on my haggard looks the next day, was intolerable; but the very idea was sufficient to produce the effect, and to render me still more nervous.—"Pish," said I, "it can be no such thing. How could my worthy host imagine that I, or any man, would be so worried by a mere picture? It is my own diseased imagination that torments me."

I turned in bed, and shifted from side to side, to try to fall asleep; but all in vain; when one cannot get asleep by lying quiet, it is seldom that tossing about will effect the purpose. The fire gradually went out, and left the room in total darkness. Still I had the idea of that inexplicable countenance gazing and keeping watch upon me through the gloom—nay, what was worse, the very darkness seemed to magnify its terrors. It was like having an unseen enemy hanging about one in the night. Instead of having one picture now to worry me, I had a hundred. I fancied it in every direction—"There it is," thought I, "and there! and there! with its horrible and mysterious expression still gazing and gazing on me! No—if I must suffer the strange and dismal influence, it were better face a single foe than thus be haunted by a thousand images of it."

Whoever has been in a state of nervous agitation, must know that the longer it continues the more uncontrollable it grows. The very air of the chamber seemed at length infected by the baleful presence of this picture. I fancied it hovering over me. I almost felt the fearful visage from the wall approaching my face—it seemed breathing upon me. "This is not to be borne," said I, at length, springing out of bed: "I can stand this no longer—I shall only tumble and toss about here all night; make a very spectre of myself, and become the hero of the haunted chamber in good earnest. Whatever be the ill consequences, I'll quit this cursed room and seek a night's rest elsewhere—they can but laugh at me, at all events, and they'll be sure to have the laugh upon me if I pass a sleepless night, and show them a haggard and woe-begone visage in the morning."

All this was half-muttered to myself as I hastily slipped on my clothes, which having done, I groped my way out of the room and down-stairs to the drawing-room. Here, after tumbling over two or three pieces of furniture, I made out to reach a sofa, and stretching myself upon it, determined to bivouac there for the night. The moment I found myself out of the neighborhood of that strange picture, it seemed as if the charm were broken. All its influence was at an end. I felt assured that it was confined to its own dreary chamber, for I had, with a sort of instinctive caution, turned the key when I closed the door. I soon calmed down, therefore, into a state of tranquillity; from that into a drowsiness, and finally into a deep sleep; out of which I did not awake until the housemaid, with her besom* and her matin-song, came to put the room in order. She stared at finding me stretched upon the sofa, but I presume circumstances of the kind were not uncommon after hunting-dinners in her master's bachelor establishment, for she went on with her song and her work, and took no further heed of me.

I had an unconquerable repugnance to return to my chamber; so I found my way to the butler's quarters, made my toilet in the best way circumstances would permit, and was among the first to appear at the breakfast-table. Our breakfast was a substantial fox-hunter's repast, and the company generally assembled at it. When ample justice had been done to the tea, coffee, cold meats, and humming ale, for all these were furnished in abundance, according to the tastes of the different guests, the conversation began to break out with all the liveliness and freshness of morning mirth.

---

*Broom.

"But who is the hero of the haunted chamber—who has seen the ghost last night?" said the inquisitive gentleman, rolling his lobster-eyes about the table.

The question set every tongue in motion; a vast deal of bantering, criticizing of countenances, of mutual accusation and retort took place. Some had drunk deep, and some were unshaven, so that there were suspicious faces enough in the assembly. I alone could not enter with ease and vivacity into the joke—I felt tongue-tied, embarrassed. A recollection of what I had seen and felt the preceding night still haunted my mind. It seemed as if the mysterious picture still held a thrall upon me. I thought also that our host's eye was turned on me with an air of curiosity. In short, I was conscious that I was the hero of the night, and felt as if every one might read it in my looks. The joke, however, passed over, and no suspicion seemed to attach to me. I was just congratulating myself on my escape, when a servant came in saying, that the gentleman who had slept on the sofa in the drawing-room had left his watch under one of the pillows. My repeater was in his hand.

"What!" said the inquisitive gentleman, "did any gentleman sleep on the sofa?"

"Soho! soho! a hare—a hare!" cried the old gentleman with the flexible nose.

I could not avoid acknowledging the watch, and was rising in great confusion, when a boisterous old squire who sat beside me exclaimed, slapping me on the shoulder, " 'Sblood, lad, thou art the man as has seen the ghost!"

The attention of the company was immediately turned on me: if my face had been pale the moment before, it now glowed almost to burning. I tried to laugh, but could only make a grimace, and found the muscles of my face twitching at sixes and sevens,* and totally out of all control.

It takes but little to raise a laugh among a set of fox-hunters; there was a world of merriment and joking on the subject, and as I never relished a joke overmuch when it was at my own expense, I began to feel a little nettled. I tried to look cool and calm, and to restrain my

---

*In confusion.

pique; but the coolness and calmness of a man in a passion are confounded treacherous.

"Gentlemen," said I, with a slight cocking of the chin and a bad attempt at a smile, "this is all very pleasant—ha! ha!—very pleasant—but I'd have you know, I am as little superstitious as any of you—ha! ha!—and as to anything like timidity—you may smile, gentlemen, but I trust there's no one here means to insinuate, that— as to a room's being haunted—I repeat, gentlemen (growing a little warm at seeing a cursed grin breaking out round me), as to a room's being haunted, I have as little faith in such silly stories as any one. But, since you put the matter home to me, I will say that I have met with something in my room strange and inexplicable to me. (A shout of laughter.) Gentlemen, I am serious; I know well what I am saying; I am calm, gentlemen, (striking my fist upon the table), by Heaven I am calm. I am neither trifling, nor do I wish to be trifled with. (The laughter of the company suppressed, and with ludicrous attempts at gravity.) There is a picture in the room in which I was put last night, that has had an effect upon me the most singular and incomprehensible."

"A picture?" said the old gentleman with the haunted head. "A picture!" cried the narrator with the nose. "A picture! a picture!" echoed several voices. Here there was an ungovernable peal of laughter. I could not contain myself. I started up from my seat; looked round on the company with fiery indignation; thrust both of my hands into my pockets, and strode up to one of the windows as though I would have walked through it. I stopped short, looked out upon the landscape without distinguishing a feature of it, and felt my gorge rising almost to suffocation.

Mine host saw it was time to interfere. He had maintained an air of gravity through the whole of the scene; and now stepped forth, as if to shelter me from the overwhelming merriment of my companions.

"Gentlemen," said he, "I dislike to spoil sport, but you have had your laugh, and the joke of the haunted chamber has been enjoyed. I must now take the part of my guest. I must not only vindicate him from your pleasantries, but I must reconcile him to himself, for I suspect he is a little out of humor with his own feelings; and, above all, I must crave his pardon for having made him the subject of a kind of experiment. Yes, gentlemen, there is something strange and peculiar in the chamber to which our friend was shown last night; there is a picture in my house which possesses a singular and mysterious influence, and with which there is connected a very curious story. It is a picture to which I attach a value from a variety of circumstances; and though I have often been tempted to destroy it, from the odd and uncomfortable sensations which it produces in every one that beholds it, yet I have never been able to prevail upon myself to make the sacrifice. It is a picture I never like to look upon myself, and which is held in awe by all my servants. I have therefore banished it to a room but rarely used, and should have had it covered last night, had not the nature of our conversation, and the whimsical talk about a haunted chamber, tempted me to let it remain, by way of experiment, to see whether a stranger, totally unacquainted with its story, would be affected by it."

The words of the Baronet had turned every thought into a different channel. All were anxious to hear the story of the mysterious picture; and, for myself, so strangely were my feelings interested, that I forgot to feel piqued at the experiment my host had made upon my nerves, and joined eagerly in the general entreaty. As the morning was stormy, and denied all egress, my host was glad of any means of entertaining his company; so, drawing his arm-chair towards the fire, he began.

Adventure of the Mysterious Stranger[6]

Many years since, when I was a young man, and had just left Oxford, I was sent on the grand tour to finish my education. I believe my parents had tried in vain to inoculate me with wisdom; so they sent me to mingle with society, in hopes that I might take it the natural way. Such, at least, appears the reason for which nine-tenths of our youngsters are sent abroad. In the course of my tour I remained some time at Venice. The romantic character of that place delighted me; I was very much amused by the air of adventure and intrigue prevalent in this region of masks* and gondolas; and I was exceedingly smitten by a pair of languishing black eyes, that played upon my heart from under an Italian mantle; so I persuaded myself that I was lingering at Venice to study men and manners; at least I persuaded my friends so, and that answered all my purposes.

I was a little prone to be struck by peculiarities in character and conduct, and my imagination was so full of romantic associations with Italy that I was always on the look-out for adventure. Everything chimed in with such a humor in this old mermaid of a city. My suite of apartments were in a proud, melancholy palace on the grand canal, formerly the residence of a magnifico, and sumptuous with the traces of decayed grandeur. My gondolier was one of the shrewdest of his class, active, merry, intelligent, and, like his brethren, secret as the grave; that is to say, secret to all the world except his master. I had not had him a week before he put me behind all the curtains in Venice. I liked the silence and mystery of the place, and when I sometimes saw from my window a black gondola gliding mysteriously along in the dusk of the evening, with nothing visible but its little glimmering lantern, I would jump into my own zende-letta, and give a signal for pursuit— "But I am running away from my subject with the recollection of youthful follies," said the Baronet, checking himself. "Let us come to the point."

---

*Venice is the site of an annual carnival in which participants dress in masquerade.

Among my familiar resorts was a casino under the arcades on one side of the grand square of St. Mark. Here I used frequently to lounge and take my ice, on those warm summer-nights, when in Italy everybody lives abroad until morning. I was seated here one evening, when a group of Italians took their seat at a table on the opposite side of the saloon. Their conversation was gay and animated, and carried on with Italian vivacity and gesticulation. I remarked among them one young man, however, who appeared to take no share, and find no enjoyment in the conversation, though he seemed to force himself to attend to it. He was tall and slender, and of extremely prepossessing appearance. His features were fine, though emaciated. He had a profusion of black glossy hair, that curled lightly about his head, and contrasted with the extreme paleness of his countenance. His brow was haggard; deep furrows seemed to have been ploughed into his visage by care, not by age, for he was evidently in the prime of youth. His eye was full of expression and fire, but wild and unsteady. He seemed to be tormented by some strange fancy or apprehension. In spite of every effort to fix his attention on the conversation of his companions, I noticed that every now and then he would turn his head slowly round, give a glance over his shoulder, and then withdraw it with a sudden jerk, as if something painful met his eye. This was repeated at intervals of about a minute, and he appeared hardly to have recovered from one shock, before I saw him slowly preparing to encounter another.

After sitting some time in the casino, the party paid for the refreshment they had taken, and departed. The young man was the last to leave the saloon, and I remarked him glancing behind him in the same way, just as he passed out of the door. I could not resist the impulse to rise and follow him; for I was at an age when a romantic feeling of curiosity is easily awakened. The party walked slowly down the arcades, talking and laughing as they went. They crossed the Piazzetta, but paused in the middle of it to enjoy the scene. It was one of those moonlight nights, so brilliant and clear in the pure atmosphere of Italy. The moonbeams streamed on the tall tower of St. Mark, and lighted up the magnificent front and swelling domes of the cathedral. The party expressed their delight in animated terms. I kept my eye upon the young man. He alone seemed abstracted and self-occupied. I noticed the same singular and, as it were, furtive glance over the shoulder, which had attracted my attention in the casino. The party moved on, and I followed; they passed along the walk called the Broglio, turned the corner of the Ducal Palace, and getting into the gondola, glided swiftly away.

The countenance and conduct of this young man dwelt upon my mind, and interested me exceedingly. I met him a day or two afterwards in a gallery of paintings. He was evidently a connoisseur, for he always singled out the most masterly productions, and a few remarks drawn from him by his companions showed an intimate acquaintance with the art. His own taste, however, ran on singular extremes. On Salvator Rosa,* in his most savage and solitary scenes; on Raphael, Titian, and Correggio,† in their softest delineations of female beauty; on these he would occasionally gaze with transient enthusiasm. But this seemed only a momentary forgetfulness. Still would recur that cautious glance behind, and always quickly withdrawn, as though something terrible met his view.

I encountered him frequently afterwards at the theatre, at balls, at concerts; at promenades in the gardens of San Georgio; at the grotesque exhibitions in the square of St. Mark; among the throng of merchants on the exchange by the Rialto. He seemed, in fact, to seek crowds; to hunt after bustle and amusement; yet never to take any interest in either the business or the gayety of the scene. Ever an air of painful thought, of wretched abstraction; and ever that strange and recurring movement of glancing fearfully over the shoulder. I did not know at first but this might be caused by apprehension of arrest; or, perhaps, from dread of assassination. But if so, why should he go thus continually abroad? why expose himself at all times and in all places?

I became anxious to know this stranger. I was drawn to him by that romantic sympathy which sometimes draws young men towards each other. His melancholy threw a charm about him, no doubt heightened by the touching expression of his countenance, and the manly graces of his person; for manly beauty has its effect

---

*Italian painter and poet (1615–1673), whose work was admired by members of the picturesque school (see endnote 4 to *The Sketch-Book*).
†Raphael (1483–1520), Titian (c.1485–1576), and Correggio (1490?–1534) were painters of the Italian High Renaissance.

even upon men. I had an Englishman's habitual diffidence and awkwardness to contend with; but from frequently meeting him in the casinos, I gradually edged myself into his acquaintance. I had no reserve on his part to contend with. He seemed, on the contrary, to court society; and, in fact, to seek any thing rather than be alone.

When he found that I really took an interest in him, he threw himself entirely on my friendship. He clung to me like a drowning man. He would walk with me for hours up and down the place of St. Mark—or would sit, until night was far advanced, in my apartments. He took rooms under the same roof with me; and his constant request was that I would permit him, when it did not incommode me, to sit by me in my saloon. It was not that he seemed to take a particular delight in my conversation, but rather that he craved the vicinity of a human being; and, above all, of a being that sympathized with him. "I have often heard," said he, "of the sincerity of Englishmen—thank God I have one at length for a friend!"

Yet he never seemed disposed to avail himself of my sympathy other than by mere companionship. He never sought to unbosom himself to me: there appeared to be a settled corroding anguish in his bosom that neither could be soothed "by silence nor by speaking."

A devouring melancholy preyed upon his heart, and seemed to be drying up the very blood in his veins. It was not a soft melancholy, the disease of the affections, but a parching, withering agony. I could see at times that his mouth was dry and feverish; he panted rather than breathed; his eyes were bloodshot; his cheeks pale and livid; with now and then faint streaks of red athwart them, baleful gleams of the fire that was consuming his heart. As my arm was within his, I felt him press it at times with a convulsive motion to his side; his hands would clinch themselves involuntarily, and a kind of shudder would run through his frame.

I reasoned with him about his melancholy, sought to draw from him the cause; he shrunk from all confiding: "Do not seek to know it," said he, "you could not relieve it if you knew it; you would not even seek to relieve it. On the contrary, I should lose your sympathy, and that," said he, pressing my hand convulsively, "that I feel has become too dear to me to risk."

I endeavored to awaken hope within him. He was young; life had a thousand pleasures in store for him; there was a healthy reaction in the youthful heart; it medicines all its own wounds; "Come, come," said I, "there is no grief so great that youth cannot outgrow it."—"No! no!" said he, clinching his teeth, and striking repeatedly, with the energy of despair, on his bosom,—"it is here! here! deep-rooted; draining my heart's blood. It grows and grows, while my heart withers and withers. I have a dreadful monitor that gives me no repose—that follows me step by step—and will follow me step by step, until it pushes me into my grave!"

As he said this he involuntarily gave one of those fearful glances over his shoulder, and shrunk back with more than usual horror. I could not resist the temptation to allude to this movement, which I supposed to be some mere malady of the nerves. The moment I mentioned it, his face became crimsoned and convulsed; he grasped me by both hands—

"For God's sake," exclaimed he, with a piercing voice, "never allude to that again.—Let us avoid this subject, my friend; you cannot relieve me, indeed you cannot relieve me, but you may add to the torments I suffer.—At some future day you shall know all."

I never resumed the subject; for however much my curiosity might be roused, I felt too true a compassion for his sufferings to increase them by my intrusion. I sought various ways to divert his mind, and to arouse him from the constant meditations in which he was plunged. He saw my efforts, and seconded them as far as in his power, for there was nothing moody or wayward in his nature. On the contrary, there was something frank, generous, unassuming, in his whole deportment. All the sentiments he uttered were noble and lofty. He claimed no indulgence, asked no toleration, but seemed content to carry his load of misery in silence, and only sought to carry it by my side. There was a mute beseeching manner about him, as if he craved companionship as a charitable boon; and a tacit thankfulness in his looks, as if he felt grateful to me for not repulsing him.

I felt this melancholy to be infectious. It stole over my spirits; interfered with all my gay pursuits, and gradually saddened my life; yet I could not prevail upon myself to shake off a being who seemed to hang upon me for support. In truth, the generous traits of char-acter which beamed through all his gloom penetrated to my heart. His bounty was lavish and open-handed; his charity melting and spontaneous; not confined to mere donations, which humiliate as much as they relieve. The tone of his voice, the beam of his eye, enhanced every gift, and surprised the poor suppliant with that rarest and sweetest of charities, the charity not merely of the hand, but of the heart. Indeed his liberality seemed to have something in it of self-abasement and expiation. He, in a manner, humbled himself before the mendicant. "What right have I to ease and affluence"— would he murmur to himself—"when innocence wanders in misery and rags?"

The carnival-time arrived. I hoped the gay scenes then presented might have some cheering effect. I mingled with him in the motley throng that crowded the place of St. Mark. We frequented operas, masquerades, balls—all in vain. The evil kept growing on him. He became more and more haggard and agitated. Often, after we had returned from one of these scenes of revelry, I have entered his room and found him lying on his face on the sofa; his hands clinched in his fine hair, and his whole countenance bearing traces, of the convulsions of his mind.

The carnival passed away; the time of Lent succeeded; passion-week arrived; we attended one evening a solemn service in one of the churches, in the course of which a grand piece of vocal and instrumental music was performed relating to the death of our Saviour.

I had remarked that he was always powerfully affected by music; on this occasion he was so in an extraordinary degree. As the pealing notes swelled through the lofty aisles, he seemed to kindle with fervor; his eyes rolled upwards, until nothing but the whites were visible; his hands were clasped together, until the fingers were deeply imprinted in the flesh. When the music expressed the dying agony, his face gradually sank upon his knees; and at the touching words resounding through the church, "*Gesu mori*,"* sobs burst from him uncontrolled—I had never seen him weep before. His had always been agony rather than sorrow. I augured well from the circumstance, and let him weep on uninterrupted. When the service was ended, we left the church. He hung on my arm as we walked

---

*Jesus is dead (Latin).

homewards with something of a softer and more subdued manner, instead of that nervous agitation I had been accustomed to witness. He alluded to the service we had heard. "Music," said he, "is indeed the voice of heaven; never before have I felt more impressed by the story of the atonement of our Saviour.—Yes, my friend," said he, clasping his hands with a kind of transport, "I know that my Redeemer liveth!"

We parted for the night. His room was not far from mine, and I heard him for some time busied in it. I fell asleep, but was awakened before daylight. The young man stood by my bedside, dressed for travelling. He held a sealed packet and a large parcel in his hand, which he laid on the table.

"Farewell, my friend," said he, "I am about to set forth on a long journey; but, before I go, I leave with you these remembrances. In this packet you will find the particulars of my story. When you read them I shall be far away; do not remember me with aversion.— You have been indeed a friend to me.—You have poured oil into a broken heart, but you could not heal it. Farewell! let me kiss your hand—I am unworthy to embrace you." He sank on his knees, seized my hand in despite of my efforts to the contrary, and covered it with kisses. I was so surprised by all the scene, that I had not been able to say a word.—"But we shall meet again," said I, hastily, as I saw him hurrying towards the door. "Never, never, in this world!" said he, solemnly.—He sprang once more to my bedside—seized my hand, pressed it to his heart and to his lips, and rushed out of the room.

Here the Baronet paused. He seemed lost in thought, and sat looking upon the floor, and drumming with his fingers on the arm of his chair.

"And did this mysterious personage return?" said the inquisitive gentleman.

"Never!" replied the Baronet, with a pensive shake of the head,— "I never saw him again."

"And pray what has all this to do with the picture?" inquired the old gentleman with the nose.

"True," said the questioner; "is it the portrait of that crack-brained Italian?"

"No," said the Baronet, dryly, not half liking the appellation given to his hero; "but this picture was enclosed in the parcel he left with me. The sealed packet contained its explanation. There was a request on the outside that I would not open it until six months had elapsed. I kept my promise in spite of my curiosity. I have a translation of it by me, and had meant to read it, by way of accounting for the mystery of the chamber; but I fear I have already detained the company too long."

Here there was a general wish expressed to have the manuscript read, particularly on the part of the inquisitive gentleman; so the worthy Baronet drew out a fairly-written manuscript, and, wiping his spectacles, read aloud the following story.—

The Story of the Young Italian[7]

Iwas born at Naples. My parents, though of noble rank, were limited in fortune, or rather, my father was ostentatious beyond his means, and expended so much on his palace, his equipage, and his retinue, that he was continually straitened in his pecuniary circumstances. I was a younger son, and looked upon with indifference by my father, who, from a principle of family-pride, wished to leave all his property to my elder brother. I showed, when quite a child, an extreme sensibility. Everything affected me violently. While yet an infant in my mother's arms, and before I had learned to talk, I could be wrought upon to a wonderful degree of anguish or delight by the power of music. As I grew older, my feelings remained equally acute, and I was easily transported into paroxysms of pleasure or rage. It was the amusement of my relations and of the domestics to play upon this irritable temperament. I was moved to tears, tickled to laughter, provoked to fury, for the entertainment of company, who were amused by such a tempest of mighty passion in a pigmy frame;—they little thought, or perhaps little heeded the dangerous sensibilities they were fostering. I thus became a little creature of passion before reason was developed. In a short time I grew too old to be a plaything, and then I became a torment. The tricks and passions I had been teased into became irksome, and I was disliked by my teachers for the very lessons they had taught me. My mother died; and my power as a spoiled child was at an end. There was no longer any necessity to humor or tolerate me, for there was nothing to be gained by it, as I was no favorite of my father. I therefore experienced the fate of a spoiled child in such a situation, and was neglected, or noticed only to be crossed and contradicted. Such was the early treatment of a heart which, if I can judge of it at all, was naturally disposed to the extremes of tenderness and affection.

My father, as I have already said, never liked me—in fact, he never understood me; he looked upon me as wilful and wayward, as deficient in natural affection. It was the stateliness of his own manner, the loftiness and grandeur of his own look, which had repelled me from his arms. I always pictured him to myself as I had seen him, clad in his senatorial robes, rustling with pomp and pride. The magnificence of his person daunted my young imagination. I could never approach him with the confiding affection of a child.

My father's feelings were wrapt up in my elder brother. He was to be the inheritor of the family-title and the family-dignity, and everything was sacrificed to him—I, as well as everything else. It was determined to devote me to the Church, that so my humors and myself might be removed out of the way, either of tasking my father's time and trouble, or interfering with the interests of my brother. At an early age, therefore, before my mind had dawned upon the world and its delights, or known anything of it beyond the precincts of my father's palace, I was sent to a convent, the superior of which was my uncle, and was confided entirely to his care.

My uncle was a man totally estranged from the world: he had never relished, for he had never tasted its pleasures; and he regarded rigid self-denial as the great basis of Christian virtue. He considered every one's temperament like his own; or at least he made them conform to it. His character and habits had an influence over the fraternity of which he was superior: a more gloomy, saturnine set of beings were never assembled together. The convent, too, was calculated to awaken sad and solitary thoughts. It was situated in a gloomy gorge of those mountains away south of Vesuvius. All distant views were shut out by sterile volcanic heights. A mountain-stream raved beneath its walls, and eagles screamed about its turrets.

I had been sent to this place at so tender an age as soon to lose all distinct recollection of the scenes I had left behind. As my mind expanded, therefore, it formed its idea of the world from the convent and its vicinity, and a dreary world it appeared to me. An early tinge of melancholy was thus infused into my character; and the dismal stories of the monks, about devils and evil spirits, with which they affrighted my young imagination, gave me a tendency to superstition which I could never effectually shake off. They took the same delight to work upon my ardent feelings, that had been so mischievously executed by my father's household. I can recollect the horrors with which they fed my heated fancy during an eruption of Vesuvius. We were distant from that volcano, with mountains between us;

but its convulsive throes shook the solid foundations of nature. Earthquakes threatened to topple down our convent-towers. A lurid, baleful light hung in the heavens at night, and showers of ashes, borne by the wind, fell in our narrow valley. The monks talked of the earth being honeycombed beneath us; of streams of molten lava raging through its veins; of caverns of sulphurous flames roaring in the centre, the abodes of demons and the damned; of fiery gulfs ready to yawn beneath our feet. All these tales were told to the doleful accompaniment of the mountain's thunders, whose low bellowing made the walls of our convent vibrate.

One of the monks had been a painter, but had retired from the world, and embraced this dismal life in expiation of some crime. He was a melancholy man, who pursued his art in the solitude of his cell, but made it a source of penance to him. His employment was to portray, either on canvas or in waxen models, the human face and human form, in the agonies of death, and in all the stages of dissolution and decay. The fearful mysteries of the charnel-house were unfolded in his labors; the loathsome banquet of the beetle and the worm. I turn with shuddering even from the recollection of his works; yet, at the time, my strong but ill-directed imagination seized with ardor upon his instructions in his art. Anything was a variety from the dry studies and monotonous duties of the cloister. In a little while I became expert with my pencil, and my gloomy productions were thought worthy of decorating some of the altars of the chapel.

In this dismal way was a creature of feeling and fancy brought up. Everything genial and amiable in my nature was repressed, and nothing brought out but what was unprofitable and ungracious. I was ardent in my temperament; quick, mercurial, impetuous, formed to be a creature all love and adoration; but a leaden hand was laid on all my finer qualities. I was taught nothing but fear and hatred. I hated my uncle. I hated the monks. I hated the convent in which I was immured. I hated the world; and I almost hated myself for being, as I supposed, so hating and hateful an animal.

When I had nearly attained the age of sixteen, I was suffered, on one occasion, to accompany one of the brethren on a mission to a distant part of the country. We soon left behind us the gloomy valley in which I had been pent up for so many years, and after a short journey among the mountains, emerged upon the voluptuous landscape that spreads itself about the Bay of Naples. Heavens! how transported was I, when I stretched my gaze over a vast reach of delicious sunny country, gay with groves and vineyards: with Vesuvius rearing its forked summit to my right; the blue Mediterranean to my left, with its enchanting coast, studded with shining towns and sumptuous villas; and Naples, my native Naples, gleaming far, far in the distance.

Good God! was this the lovely world from which I had been excluded! I had reached that age when the sensibilities are in all their bloom and freshness. Mine had been checked and chilled. They now burst forth with the suddenness of a retarded spring-time. My heart, hitherto unnaturally shrunk up, expanded into a riot of vague but delicious emotions. The beauty of nature intoxicated—bewildered me. The song of the peasants; their cheerful looks; their happy avocations; the picturesque gayety of their dresses; their rustic music; their dances; all broke upon me like witchcraft. My soul responded to the music, my heart danced in my bosom. All the men appeared amiable, all the women lovely.

I returned to the convent; that is to say, my body returned, but my heart and soul never entered there again. I could not forget this glimpse of a beautiful and a happy world—a world so suited to my natural character. I had felt so happy while in it; so different a being from what I felt myself when in the convent—that tomb of the living. I contrasted the countenances of the beings I had seen, full of fire and freshness and enjoyment, with the pallid, leaden, lack-lustre visages of the monks: the dance with the droning chant of the chapel. I had before found the exercises of the cloister wearisome, they now became intolerable. The dull round of duties wore away my spirit; my nerves became irritated by the fretful tinkling of the convent-bell, evermore dinging among the mountain-echoes, evermore calling me from my repose at night, my pencil by day, to attend to some tedious and mechanical ceremony of devotion.

I was not of a nature to meditate long without putting my thoughts into action. My spirit had been suddenly aroused, and was now all awake within me. I watched an opportunity, fled from the convent, and made my way on foot to Naples. As I entered its gay and crowded streets, and beheld the variety and stir of life around me, the luxury of palaces, the splendor of equipages, and the pantomimic animation of the motley populace, I seemed as if awakened to a world of enchantment, and solemnly vowed that nothing should force me back to the monotony of the cloister.

I had to inquire my way to my father's palace, for I had been so young on leaving it that I knew not its situation. I found some difficulty in getting admitted to my father's presence; for the domestics scarcely knew that there was such a being as myself in existence, and my monastic dress did not operate in my favor. Even my father entertained no recollection of my person. I told him my name, threw myself at his feet, implored his forgiveness, and entreated that I might not be sent back to the convent.

He received me with the condescension of a patron, rather than the fondness of a parent; listened patiently, but coldly, to my tale of monastic grievances and disgusts, and promised to think what else could be done for me. This coldness blighted and drove back all the frank affection of my nature, that was ready to spring forth at the least warmth of parental kindness. All my early feelings towards my father revived. I again looked up to him as the stately magnificent being that had daunted my childish imagination, and felt as if I had no pretensions to his sympathies. My brother engrossed all his care and love; he inherited his nature, and carried himself towards me with a protecting rather than a fraternal air. It wounded my pride, which was great. I could brook condescension from my father, for I looked up to him with awe, as a superior being; but I could not brook patronage from a brother, who I felt was intellectually my inferior. The servants perceived that I was an unwelcome intruder in the paternal mansion, and, menial-like, they treated me with neglect. Thus baffled at every point, my affections outraged wherever they would attach themselves, I became sullen, silent, and desponding. My feelings, driven back upon myself, entered and preyed upon my own heart. I remained for some days an unwelcome guest rather than a restored son in my father's house. I was doomed never to be properly known there. I was made, by wrong treatment, strange even to myself, and they judged of me from my strangeness.

I was startled one day at the sight of one of the monks of my convent gliding out of my father's room. He saw me, but pretended not to notice me, and this very hypocrisy made me suspect something.

I had become sore and susceptible in my feelings, everything inflicted a wound on them. In this state of mind, I was treated with marked disrespect by a pampered minion, the favorite servant of my father. All the pride and passion of my nature rose in an instant, and I struck him to the earth. My father was passing by; he stopped not to inquire the reason, nor indeed could he read the long course of mental sufferings which were the real cause. He rebuked me with anger and scorn; summoning all the haughtiness of his nature and grandeur of his look to give weight to the contumely with which he treated me. I felt that I had not deserved it. I felt that I was not appreciated. I felt that I had that within me which merited better treatment. My heart swelled against a father's injustice. I broke through my habitual awe of him—I replied to him with impatience. My hot spirit flushed in my cheek and kindled in my eye; but my sensitive heart swelled as quickly and before I had half vented my passion, I felt it suffocated and quenched in my tears. My father was astonished and incensed at this turning of the worm,* and ordered me to my chamber. I retired in silence, choking with contending emotions.

I had not been long there when I overheard voices in an adjoining apartment. It was a consultation between my father and the monk, about the means of getting me back quietly to the convent. My resolution was taken. I had no longer a home nor a father. That very night I left the paternal roof. I got on board a vessel about making sail from the harbor, and abandoned myself to the wide world. No matter to what port she steered; any part of so beautiful a world was better than my convent. No matter where I was cast by fortune; any place would be more a home to me than the home I had left behind. The vessel was bound to Genoa. We arrived there after a voyage of a few days.

As I entered the harbor between the moles† which embrace it, and beheld the amphitheatre of palaces, and churches, and splendid gardens, rising one above another, I felt at once its title to the appellation of Genoa the Superb. I landed on the mole an utter stranger, without knowing what to do, or whither to direct my steps.

---

*Proverbial for "sudden reversal."
†Breakwater piers.

No matter: I was released from the thraldom of the convent and the humiliations of home. When I traversed the Strada Balbi and the Strada Nuova, those streets of palaces, and gazed at the wonders of architecture around me; when I wandered at close of day amid a gay throng of the brilliant and the beautiful, through the green alleys of the Acquaverde, or among the colonnades and terraces of the magnificent Doria gardens; I thought it impossible to be ever otherwise than happy in Genoa. A few days sufficed to show me my mistake. My scanty purse was exhausted, and for the first time in my life I experienced the sordid distress of penury. I had never known the want of money, and had never adverted to the possibility of such an evil. I was ignorant of the world and all its ways; and when first the idea of destitution came over my mind, its effect was withering. I was wandering penniless through the streets which no longer delighted my eyes, when chance led my steps into the magnificent church of the Annunciata.

A celebrated painter of the day was at that moment superintending the placing of one of his pictures over an altar. The proficiency which I had acquired in his art during my residence in the convent, had made me an enthusiastic amateur. I was struck, at the first glance, with the painting. It was the face of a Madonna. So innocent, so lovely, such a divine expression of maternal tenderness! I lost, for the moment, all recollection of myself in the enthusiasm of my art. I clasped my hands together, and uttered an ejaculation of delight. The painter perceived my emotion. He was flattered and gratified by it. My air and manner pleased him, and he accosted me. I felt too much the want of friendship to repel the advances of a stranger; and there was something in this one so benevolent and winning, that in a moment he gained my confidence.

I told him my story and my situation, concealing only my name and rank. He appeared strongly interested by my recital, invited me to his house, and from that time I became his favorite pupil. He thought he perceived in me extraordinary talents for the art, and his encomiums awakened all my ardor. What a blissful period of my existence was it that I passed beneath his roof! Another being seemed created within me; or rather, all that was amiable and excellent was drawn out. I was as recluse as ever I had been at the convent, but how different was my seclusion! My time was spent in storing my mind with lofty and poetical ideas; in meditating on all that was striking and noble in history and fiction; in studying and tracing all that was sublime and beautiful in nature. I was always a visionary, imaginative being, but now my reveries and imaginings all elevated me to rapture. I looked up to my master as to a benevolent genius that had opened to me a region of enchantment. He was not a native of Genoa, but had been drawn thither by the solicitations of several of the nobility, and had resided there but a few years, for the completion of certain works. His health was delicate, and he had to confide much of the filling up of his designs to the pencils of his scholars. He considered me as particularly happy in delineating the human countenance; in seizing upon characteristic though fleeting expressions, and fixing them powerfully upon my canvas. I was employed continually, therefore, in sketching faces, and often, when some particular grace or beauty of expression was wanted in a countenance, it was intrusted to my pencil. My benefactor was fond of bringing me forward; and partly, perhaps, through my actual skill, and partly through his partial praises, I began to be noted for the expressions of my countenances.

Among the various works which he had undertaken, was an historical piece for one of the palaces of Genoa, in which were to be introduced the likenesses of several of the family. Among these was one intrusted to my pencil. It was that of a young girl, as yet in a convent for her education. She came out for the purpose of sitting for the picture. I first saw her in an apartment of one of the sumptuous palaces of Genoa. She stood before a casement that looked out upon the bay; a stream of vernal sunshine fell upon her, and shed a kind of glory round her, as it lit up the rich crimson chamber. She was but sixteen years of age—and oh, how lovely! The scene broke upon me like a mere vision of spring and youth and beauty. I could have fallen down and worshipped her. She was like one of those fictions of poets and painters, when they would express the *beau ideal* that haunts their minds with shapes of indescribable perfection. I was permitted to watch her countenance in various positions, and I fondly protracted the study that was undoing me. The more I gazed on her, the more I became enamoured; there was something almost painful in my intense admiration. I was but nineteen years of age, shy, diffident, and inexperienced. I was treated with attention by her mother;

for my youth and my enthusiasm in my art had won favor for me; and I am inclined to think something in my air and manner inspired interest and respect. Still the kindness with which I was treated could not dispel the embarrassment into which my own imagination threw me when in presence of this lovely being. It elevated her into something almost more than mortal. She seemed too exquisite for earthly use; too delicate and exalted for human attainment. As I sat tracing her charms on my canvas, with my eyes occasionally riveted on her features, I drank in delicious poison that made me giddy. My heart alternately gushed with tenderness, and ached with despair. Now I became more than ever sensible of the violent fires that had lain dormant at the bottom of my soul. You who were born in a more temperate climate, and under a cooler sky, have little idea of the violence of passion in our southern bosoms.

A few days finished my task. Bianca returned to her convent, but her image remained indelibly impressed upon my heart. It dwelt in my imagination; it became my pervading idea of beauty. It had an effect even upon my pencil. I became noted for my felicity in depicting female loveliness: it was but because I multiplied the image of Bianca. I soothed and yet fed my fancy by introducing her in all the productions of my master. I have stood, with delight, in one of the chapels of the Annunciata, and heard the crowd extol the seraphic beauty of a saint which I had painted. I have seen them bow down in adoration before the painting; they were bowing before the loveliness of Bianca.

I existed in this kind of dream, I might almost say delirium, for upwards of a year. Such is the tenacity of my imagination, that the image formed in it continued in all its power and freshness. Indeed, I was a solitary, meditative being, much given to reverie, and apt to foster ideas which had once taken strong possession of me. I was roused from this fond, melancholy, delicious dream by the death of my worthy benefactor. I cannot describe the pangs his death occasioned me. It left me alone, and almost broken-hearted. He bequeathed to me his little property, which, from the liberality of his disposition, and his expensive style of living, was indeed but small; and he most particularly recommended me, in dying, to the protection of a nobleman who had been his patron.

The latter was a man who passed for munificent. He was a lover and an encourager of the arts, and evidently wished to be thought so. He fancied he saw in me indications of future excellence; my pencil had already attracted attention; he took me at once under his protection. Seeing that I was overwhelmed with grief, and incapable of exerting myself in the mansion of my late benefactor, he invited me to sojourn for a time at a villa which he possessed on the border of the sea, in the picturesque neighborhood of Sestri di Ponente.

I found at the villa the count's only son, Filippo. He was nearly of my age; prepossessing in his appearance, and fascinating in his manners, he attached himself to me, and seemed to court my good opinion. I thought there was something of profession in his kindness, and of caprice in his disposition; but I had nothing else near me to attach myself to, and my heart felt the need of something to repose upon. His education had been neglected; he looked upon me as his superior in mental powers and acquirements, and tacitly acknowledged my superiority. I felt that I was his equal in birth, and that gave independence to my manners, which had its effect. The caprice and tyranny I saw sometimes exercised on others, over whom he had power, were never manifested towards me. We became intimate friends and frequent companions. Still I loved to be alone, and to indulge in the reveries of my own imagination among the scenery by which I was surrounded. The villa commanded a wide view of the Mediterranean, and of the picturesque Ligurian coast. It stood alone in the midst of ornamented grounds, finely decorated with statues and fountains, and laid out in groves and alleys and shady lawns. Everything was assembled here that could gratify the taste, or agreeably occupy the mind. Soothed by the tranquillity of this elegant retreat, the turbulence of my feelings gradually subsided, and blending with the romantic spell which still reigned over my imagination, produced a soft, voluptuous melancholy.

I had not been long under the roof of the count, when our solitude was enlivened by another inhabitant. It was a daughter of a relative of the count, who had lately died in reduced circumstances, bequeathing this only child to his protection. I had heard much of her beauty from Filippo, but my fancy had become so engrossed by one idea of beauty, as not to admit of any other. We were in the central saloon of the villa when she arrived. She was still in mourning, and approached, leaning on the count's arm. As they ascended the marble portico, I was struck by the elegance of her figure and movement, by the grace with which the *mezzaro*, the bewitching veil of Genoa, was folded about her slender form. They entered. Heavens! what was my surprise when I beheld Bianca before me! It was herself; pale with grief, but still more matured in loveliness than when I had last beheld her. The time that had elapsed had developed the graces of her person, and the sorrow she had undergone had diffused over her countenance an irresistible tenderness.

She blushed and trembled at seeing me, and tears rushed into her eyes, for she remembered in whose company she had been accustomed to behold me. For my part, I cannot express what were my emotions. By degrees I overcame the extreme shyness that had formerly paralyzed me in her presence. We were drawn together by sympathy of situation. We had each lost our best friend in the world; we were each, in some measure, thrown upon the kindness of others. When I came to know her intellectually, all my ideal picturings of her were confirmed. Her newness to the world, her delightful susceptibility to everything beautiful and agreeable in nature, reminded me of my own emotions when first I escaped from the convent. Her rectitude of thinking delighted my judgment; the sweetness of her nature wrapped itself round my heart; and then her young, and tender, and budding loveliness, sent a delicious madness to my brain.

I gazed upon her with a kind of idolatry, as something more than mortal; and I felt humiliated at the idea of my comparative unworthiness. Yet she was mortal; and one of mortality's most susceptible and loving compounds;—for she loved me!

How first I discovered the transporting truth I cannot recollect. I believe it stole upon me by degrees as a wonder past hope or belief. We were both at such a tender and loving age; in constant intercourse with each other; mingling in the same elegant pursuits,—for music, poetry, and painting were our mutual delights; and we were almost separated from society among lovely and romantic scenery. Is it strange that two young hearts, thus brought together, should readily twine round each other?

Oh, gods! what a dream—a transient dream of unalloyed delight, then passed over my soul! Then it was that the world around me was indeed a paradise; for I had woman—lovely, delicious woman, to share it with me! How often have I rambled along the picturesque shores of Sestri, or climbed its wild mountains, with the coast gemmed with villas, and the blue sea far below me, and the slender Faro of Genoa on its romantic promontory in the distance; and as I sustained the faltering steps of Bianca, have thought there could no unhappiness enter into so beautiful a world! How often have we listened together to the nightingale, as it poured forth its rich notes among the moonlight bowers of the garden, and have wondered that poets could ever have fancied anything melancholy in its song! Why, oh why is this budding season of life and tenderness so transient! why is this rosy cloud of love, that sheds such a glow over the morning of our days, so prone to brew up into the whirlwind and the storm!

I was the first to awaken from this blissful delirium of the affections. I had gained Bianca's heart, what was I to do with it? I had no wealth nor prospect to entitle me to her hand; was I to take advantage of her ignorance of the world, of her confiding affection, and draw her down to my own poverty? Was this requiting the hospitality of the count? was this requiting the love of Bianca?

Now first I began to feel that even successful love may have its bitterness. A corroding care gathered about my heart. I moved about the palace like a guilty being. I felt as if I had abused its hospitality, as if I were a thief within its walls. I could no longer look with unembarrassed mien in the countenance of the count. I accused myself of perfidy to him, and I thought he read it in my looks, and began to distrust and despise me. His manner had always been ostentatious and condescending; it now appeared cold and haughty. Filippo, too, became reserved and distant; or at least I suspected him to be so. Heavens! was this the mere coinage of my brain? Was I to become suspicious of all the world? a poor, surmising wretch; watching looks and gestures; and torturing myself with misconstructions? Or, if true, was I to remain beneath a roof where I was merely tolerated, and linger there on sufferance? "This is not to be endured!" exclaimed I: "I will tear myself from this state of self-abasement—I will break through this fascination and fly—Fly!—Whither? from the world? for where is the world when I leave Bianca behind me?"

My spirit was naturally proud, and swelled within me at the idea of being looked upon with contumely. Many times I was on the point of declaring my family and rank, and asserting my equality in the presence of Bianca, when I thought her relations assumed an air of superiority. But the feeling was transient. I considered myself discarded and condemned by my family; and had solemnly vowed never to own relationship to them until they themselves should claim it.

The struggle of my mind preyed upon my happiness and my health. It seemed as if the uncertainty of being loved would be less intolerable than thus to be assured of it, and yet not dare to enjoy the conviction. I was no longer the enraptured admirer of Bianca; I no longer hung in ecstasy on the tones of her voice, nor drank in with insatiate gaze the beauty of her countenance. Her very smiles ceased to delight me, for I felt culpable in having won them.

She could not but be sensible of the change in me, and inquired the cause with her usual frankness and simplicity. I could not evade the inquiry, for my heart was full to aching. I told her all the conflict of my soul; my devouring passion, my bitter self-upbraiding. "Yes," said I, "I am unworthy of you. I am an offcast from my family—a wanderer—a nameless, homeless wanderer—with nothing but poverty for my portion; and yet I have dared to love you—have dared to aspire to your love."

My agitation moved her to tears, but she saw nothing in my situation so hopeless as I had depicted it. Brought up in a convent, she knew nothing of the world—its wants—its cares: and indeed what woman is a worldly casuist* in the matters of the heart? Nay, more, she kindled into sweet enthusiasm when she spoke of my fortunes and myself. We had dwelt together on the works of the famous masters. I related to her their histories; the high reputation, the influence, the magnificence to which they had attained. The companions of princes, the favorites of kings, the pride and boast of nations. All this she applied to me. Her love saw nothing in all their great productions that I was not able to achieve; and when I beheld the lovely creature glow with fervor, and her whole countenance radiant with visions of my glory, I was snatched up for the moment into the heaven of her own imagination.

I am dwelling too long upon this part of my story; yet I cannot help lingering over a period of my life on which, with all its cares

---

*Person who resolves problems of conscience with often specious reasoning.

and conflicts, I look back with fondness, for as yet my soul was unstained by a crime. I do not know what might have been the result of this struggle between pride, delicacy, and passion, had I not read in a Neapolitan gazette an account of the sudden death of my brother. It was accompanied by an earnest inquiry for intelligence concerning me, and a prayer, should this meet my eye, that I would hasten to Naples to comfort an infirm and afflicted father.

I was naturally of an affectionate disposition, but my brother had never been as a brother to me. I had long considered myself as disconnected from him, and his death caused me but little emotion. The thoughts of my father, infirm and suffering, touched me, however, to the quick; and when I thought of him, that lofty, magnificent being, now bowed down and desolate, and suing to me for comfort, all my resentment for past neglect was subdued, and a glow of filial affection was awakened within me.

The predominant feeling, however, that overpowered all others, was transport at the sudden change in my whole fortunes. A home, a name, rank, wealth, awaited me; and love painted a still more rapturous prospect in the distance. I hastened to Bianca, and threw myself at her feet. "Oh, Bianca!" exclaimed I, "at length I can claim you for my own. I am no longer a nameless adventurer, a neglected, rejected outcast. Look—read—behold the tidings that restore me to my name and to myself!"

I will not dwell on the scene that ensued. Bianca rejoiced in the reverse of my situation, because she saw it lightened my heart of a load of care; for her own part, she had loved me for myself, and had never doubted that my own merits would command both fame and fortune.

I now felt all my native pride buoyant within me. I no longer walked with my eyes bent to the dust; hope elevated them to the skies—my soul was lit up with fresh fires, and beamed from my countenance.

I wished to impart the change in my circumstances to the count; to let him know who and what I was—and to make formal proposals for the hand of Bianca; but he was absent on a distant estate. I opened my whole soul to Filippo. Now first I told him of my passion, of the doubts and fears that had distracted me, and of the tidings that had suddenly dispelled them. He overwhelmed me with congratulations, and with the warmest expressions of sympathy; I embraced him in the fulness of my heart;—I felt compunctions for having suspected him of coldness, and asked his forgiveness for ever having doubted his friendship.

Nothing is so warm and enthusiastic as a sudden expansion of the heart between young men. Filippo entered into our concerns with the most eager interest. He was our confidant and counsellor. It was determined that I should hasten at once to Naples, to reëstablish myself in my father's affections, and my paternal home; and the moment the reconciliation was effected, and my father's consent insured, I should return and demand Bianca of the count. Filippo engaged to secure his father's acquiescence; indeed he undertook to watch over our interest, and to be the channel through which we might correspond.

My parting with Bianca was tender—delicious—agonizing. It was in a little pavilion of the garden which had been one of our favorite resorts. How often and often did I return to have one more adieu, to have her look once more on me in speechless emotion; to enjoy once more the rapturous sight of those tears streaming down her lovely cheeks; to seize once more on that delicate hand, the frankly accorded pledge of love, and cover it with tears and kisses? Heavens! there is a delight even in the parting agony of two lovers, worth a thousand tame pleasures of the world. I have her at this moment before my eyes, at the window of the pavilion, putting aside the vines which clustered about the casement, her form beaming forth in virgin light, her countenance all tears and smiles, sending a thousand and a thousand adieus after me, as hesitating, in a delirium of fondness and agitation, I faltered my way down the avenue.

As the bark bore me out of the harbor of Genoa, how eagerly my eye stretched along the coast of Sestri till it discovered the villa gleaming from among the trees at the foot of the mountain. As long as day lasted I gazed and gazed upon it, till it lessened and lessened to a mere white speck in the distance; and still my intense and fixed gaze discerned it, when all other objects of the coast had blended into indistinct confusion, or were lost in the evening gloom.

On arriving at Naples, I hastened to my paternal home. My heart yearned for the long-withheld blessing of a father's love. As I entered the proud portal of the ancestral palace, my emotions were so great that I could not speak. No one knew me, the servants gazed at me with curiosity and surprise. A few years of intellectual elevation and development had made a prodigious change in the poor fugitive stripling from the convent. Still, that no one should know me in my rightful home was overpowering. I felt like the prodigal son returned.* I was a stranger in the house of my father. I burst into tears and wept aloud. When I made myself known, however, all was changed. I, who had once been almost repulsed from its walls, and forced to fly as an exile, was welcomed back with acclamation, with servility. One of the servants hastened to prepare my father for my reception; my eagerness to receive the paternal embrace was so great that I could not await his return, but hurried after him. What a spectacle met my eyes as I entered the chamber! My father, whom I had left in the pride of vigorous age, whose noble and majestic bearing had so awed my young imagination, was bowed down and withered into decrepitude. A paralysis had ravaged his stately form, and left it a shaking ruin. He sat propped up in his chair, with pale, relaxed visage, and glassy, wandering eye. His intellect had evidently shared in the ravages of his frame. The servant was endeavoring to make him comprehend that a visitor was at hand. I tottered up to him, and sank at his feet. All his past coldness and neglect were forgotten in his present sufferings. I remembered only that he was my parent, and that I had deserted him. I clasped his knee: my voice was almost filled with convulsive sobs. "Pardon—pardon! oh! my father!" was all that I could utter. His apprehension seemed slowly to return to him. He gazed at me for some moments with a vague, inquiring look; a convulsive tremor quivered about his lips; he feebly extended a shaking hand; laid it upon my head, and burst into an infantine flow of tears.

From that moment he would scarcely spare me from his sight. I appeared the only object that his heart responded to in the world; all else was as a blank to him. He had almost lost the power of speech, and the reasoning faculty seemed at an end. He was mute and passive, excepting that fits of childlike weeping would sometimes come over him without any immediate cause. If I left the room at any time, his eye was incessantly fixed on the door till my return, and on my entrance there was another gush of tears.

---

*See the Bible, Luke 15:11–32.

To talk with him of all my concerns, in this ruined state of mind, would have been worse than useless; to have left him for ever so short a time would have been cruel, unnatural. Here then was a new trial for my affections. I wrote to Bianca an account of my return, and of my actual situation, painting in colors vivid, for they were true, the torments I suffered at our being thus separated; for the youthful lover every day of absence is an age of love lost. I enclosed the letter in one to Filippo, who was the channel of our correspondence. I received a reply from him full of friendship and sympathy; from Bianca, full of assurances of affection and constancy. Week after week, month after month elapsed, without making any change in my circumstances. The vital flame which had seemed nearly extinct when first I met my father, kept fluttering on without any apparent diminution. I watched him constantly, faithfully, I had almost said patiently. I knew that his death alone would set me free—yet I never at any moment wished it. I felt too glad to be able to make any atonement for past disobedience; and denied, as I had been, all endearments of relationship in my early days, my heart yearned towards a father, who in his age and helplessness had thrown himself entirely on me for comfort.

My passion for Bianca gained daily more force from absence: by constant meditation it wore itself a deeper and deeper channel. I made no new friends nor acquaintances; sought none of the pleasures of Naples, which my rank and fortune threw open to me. Mine was a heart that confined itself to few objects, but dwelt upon them with the intenser passion. To sit by my father, administer to his wants, and to meditate on Bianca in the silence of his chamber, was my constant habit. Sometimes I amused myself with my pencil, in portraying the image ever present to my imagination. I transferred to canvas every look and smile of hers that dwelt in my heart. I showed them to my father, in hopes of awakening an interest in his bosom for the mere shadow of my love; but he was too far sunk in intellect to take any notice of them. When I received a letter from Bianca, it was a new source of solitary luxury. Her letters, it is true, were less and less frequent, but they were always full of assurances of unabated affection. They breathed not the frank and innocent warmth with which she expressed herself in conversation, but I accounted for it from the embarrassment which inexperienced minds have often to express themselves upon paper. Filippo assured me of her unaltered constancy. They both lamented, in the strongest terms, our continued separation, though they did justice to the filial piety that kept me by my father's side.

Nearly two years elapsed in this protracted exile. To me they were so many ages. Ardent and impetuous by nature, I scarcely know how I should have supported so long an absence, had I not felt assured that the faith of Bianca was equal to my own. At length my father died. Life went from him almost imperceptibly. I hung over him in mute affliction, and watched the expiring spasms of nature. His last faltering accents whispered repeatedly a blessing on me. Alas! how has it been fulfilled!

When I had paid due honors to his remains, and laid them in the tomb of our ancestors, I arranged briefly my affairs, put them in a posture to be easily at my command from a distance, and embarked once more with a bounding heart for Genoa.

Our voyage was propitious, and oh! what was my rapture, when first, in the dawn of morning, I saw the shadowy summits of the Apennines rising almost like clouds above the horizon! The sweet breath of summer just moved us over the long wavering billows that were rolling us on towards Genoa. By degrees the coast of Sestri rose like a creation of enchantment from the silver bosom of the deep. I beheld the line of villages and palaces studding its borders. My eye reverted to a well-known point, and at length, from the confusion of distant objects, it singled out the villa which contained Bianca. It was a mere speck in the landscape, but glimmering from afar, the polar star of my heart.

Again I gazed at it for a livelong summer's day, but oh! how different the emotions between departure and return. It now kept growing and growing, instead of lessening and lessening on my sight. My heart seemed to dilate with it. I looked at it through a telescope. I gradually defined one feature after another. The balconies of the central saloon where first I met Bianca beneath its roof; the terrace where we so often had passed the delightful summer evenings; the awning which shaded her chamber-window; I almost fancied I saw her form beneath it. Could she but know her lover was in the bark whose white sail now gleamed on the sunny bosom of the sea! My fond impatience increased as we neared the coast;

the ship seemed to lag lazily over the billows; I could almost have sprang into the sea, and swam to the desired shore.

The shadows of evening gradually shrouded the scene; but the moon arose in all her fulness and beauty, and shed the tender light so dear to lovers, over the romantic coast of Sestri. My soul was bathed in unutterable tenderness. I anticipated the heavenly evenings I should pass in once more wandering with Bianca by the light of that blessed moon.

It was late at night before we entered the harbor. As early next morning as I could get released from the formalities of landing, I threw myself on horseback, and hastened to the villa. As I galloped round the rocky promontory on which stands the Faro, and saw the coast of Sestri opening upon me, a thousand anxieties and doubts suddenly sprang up in my bosom. There is something fearful in returning to those we love, while yet uncertain what ills or changes absence may have effected. The turbulence of my agitation shook my very frame. I spurred my horse to redoubled speed; he was covered with foam when we both arrived panting at the gateway that opened to the grounds around the villa. I left my horse at a cottage, and walked through the grounds, that I might regain tranquillity for the approaching interview. I chid myself for having suffered mere doubts and surmises thus suddenly to overcome me; but I was always prone to be carried away by gusts of the feelings.

On entering the garden, everything bore the same look as when I had left it; and this unchanged aspect of things reassured me. There were the alleys in which I had so often walked with Bianca, as we listened to the song of the nightingale; the same shades under which we had so often sat during the noontide heat. There were the same flowers of which she was so fond; and which appeared still to be under the ministry of her hand. Everything looked and breathed of Bianca; hope and joy flushed in my bosom at every step. I passed a little arbor, in which we had often sat and read together;—a book and glove lay on the bench;—it was Bianca's glove; it was a volume of the "Metastasio"* I had given her. The glove lay in my favorite passage. I clasped them to my heart with rapture. "All is safe!" exclaimed I; "she loves me, she is still my own!"

---

*Pietro Metastasio (1698–1782), Italian poet and librettist.

I bounded lightly along the avenue, down which I had faltered slowly at my departure. I beheld her favorite pavilion, which had witnessed our parting-scene. The window was open, with the same vine clambering about it, precisely as when she waved and wept me an adieu. O how transporting was the contrast in my situation! As I passed near the pavilion, I heard the tones of a female voice: they thrilled through me with an appeal to my heart not to be mistaken. Before I could think, I *felt* they were Bianca's. For an instant I paused, overpowered with agitation. I feared to break so suddenly upon her. I softly ascended the steps of the pavilion. The door was open. I saw Bianca seated at a table; her back was towards me, she was warbling a soft melancholy air, and was occupied in drawing. A glance sufficed to show me that she was copying one of my own paintings. I gazed on her for a moment in a delicious tumult of emotions. She paused in her singing: a heavy sigh, almost a sob, followed. I could no longer contain myself. "Bianca!" exclaimed I, in a half-smothered voice. She started at the sound, brushed back the ringlets that hung clustering about her face, darted a glance at me, uttered a piercing shriek, and would have fallen to the earth, had I not caught her in my arms.

"Bianca! my own Bianca!" exclaimed I, folding her to my bosom, my voice stifled in sobs of convulsive joy. She lay in my arms without sense or motion. Alarmed at the effects of my precipitation, I scarce knew what to do. I tried by a thousand endearing words to call her back to consciousness. She slowly recovered, and half opened her eyes.—"Where am I?" murmured she faintly. "Here!" exclaimed I, pressing her to my bosom, "here—close to the heart that adores you—in the arms of your faithful Ottavio!" "Oh no! no! no!" shrieked she, starting into sudden life and terror,—"away! away! leave me! leave me!"

She tore herself from my arms; rushed to a corner of the saloon, and covered her face with her hands, as if the very sight of me were baleful. I was thunderstruck. I could not believe my senses. I followed her, trembling—confounded. I endeavored to take her hand; but she shrunk from my very touch with horror.

"Good heavens, Bianca!" exclaimed I, "what is the meaning of this? Is this my reception after so long an absence? Is this the love you professed for me?"

At the mention of love, a shuddering ran through her. She turned to me a face wild with anguish: "No more of that—no more of that!" gasped she: "talk not to me of love—I—I—am married!"

I reeled as if I had received a mortal blow—a sickness struck to my very heart. I caught at a window-frame for support. For a moment or two everything was chaos around me. When I recovered, I beheld Bianca lying on a sofa, her face buried in the pillow, and sobbing convulsively. Indignation for her fickleness for a moment overpowered every other feeling.

"Faithless! perjured!" cried I, striding across the room. But another glance at that beautiful being in distress checked all my wrath. Anger could not dwell together with her idea in my soul.

"Oh! Bianca," exclaimed I, in anguish, "could I have dreamt of this? Could I have suspected you would have been false to me?"

She raised her face all streaming with tears, all disordered with emotion, and gave me one appealing look. "False to you?—They told me you were dead!"

"What," said I, "in spite of our constant correspondence?"

She gazed wildly at me: "Correspondence? what correspondence!"

"Have you not repeatedly received and replied to my letters?"

She clasped her hands with solemnity and fervor. "As I hope for mercy—never!"

A horrible surmise shot through my brain. "Who told you I was dead?"

"It was reported that the ship in which you embarked for Naples perished at sea."

"But who told you the report?"

She paused for an instant, and trembled;—"Filippo!"

"May the God of heaven curse him!" cried I, extending my clinched fists aloft.

"Oh do not curse him, do not curse him!" exclaimed she, "he is—he is—my husband!"

This was all that was wanting to unfold the perfidy that had been practised upon me. My blood boiled like liquid fire in my veins. I gasped with rage too great for utterance—I remained for a time bewildered by the whirl of horrible thoughts that rushed through my mind. The poor victim of deception before me thought it was with her I was incensed. She faintly murmured forth her exculpation. I will not dwell upon it. I saw in it more than she meant to reveal. I saw with a glance how both of us had been betrayed.

" 'Tis well," muttered I to myself in smothered accents of concentrated fury. "He shall render an account of all this."

Bianca overheard me. New terror flashed in her countenance. "For mercy's sake, do not meet him!—say nothing of what has passed—for my sake say nothing to him—I only shall be the sufferer!"

A new suspicion darted across my mind.—"What!" exclaimed I, "do you then *fear* him? is he *unkind* to you? Tell me," reiterated I, grasping her hand, and looking her eagerly in the face, "tell me— *dares* he to use you harshly?"

"No! no! no!" cried she, faltering and embarrassed; but the glance at her face had told volumes. I saw in her pallid and wasted features, in the prompt terror and subdued agony of her eye, a whole history of a mind broken down by tyranny. Great God! and was this beauteous flower snatched from me to be thus trampled upon? The idea roused me to madness. I clinched my teeth and hands; I foamed at the mouth; every passion seemed to have resolved itself into the fury that like a lava boiled within my heart. Bianca shrunk from me in speechless affright. As I strode by the window, my eye darted down the alley. Fatal moment! I beheld Filippo at a distance! my brain was in delirium—I sprang from the pavilion, and was before him with the quickness of lightning. He saw me as I came rushing upon him—he turned pale, looked wildly to right and left, as if he would have fled, and trembling, drew his sword.

"Wretch!" cried I, "well may you draw your weapon!"

I spoke not another word—I snatched forth a stiletto, put by the sword which trembled in his hand, and buried my poniard in his bosom. He fell with the blow, but my rage was unsated. I sprang upon him with the bloodthirsty feeling of a tiger; redoubled my blows; mangled him in my frenzy, grasped him by the throat, until, with reiterated wounds and strangling convulsions, he expired in my grasp. I remained glaring on the countenance, horrible in death, that seemed to stare back with its protruded eyes upon me. Piercing shrieks roused me from my delirium. I looked round and beheld Bianca flying distractedly towards us. My brain whirled—I waited not to meet her; but fled from the scene of horror. I fled forth from the garden like another Cain,*—a hell within my bosom, and a curse upon my head. I fled without knowing whither, almost without knowing why. My only idea was to get farther and farther from the horrors I had left behind; as if I could throw space between myself and my conscience. I fled to the Apennines, and wandered for days and days among their savage heights. How I existed, I cannot tell; what rocks and precipices I braved, and how I braved them, I know not. I kept on and on, trying to out-travel the curse that clung to me. Alas! the shrieks of Bianca rung forever in my ears. The horrible countenance of my victim was forever before my eyes. The blood of Filippo cried to me from the ground. Rocks, trees, and torrents, all resounded with my crime. Then it was I felt how much more insupportable is the anguish of remorse than every other mental pang. Oh! could I but have cast off this crime that festered in my heart—could I but have regained the innocence that reigned in my breast as I entered the garden at Sestri—could I have but restored my victim to life, I felt as if I could look on with transport, even though Bianca were in his arms.

By degrees this frenzied fever of remorse settled into a permanent malady of the mind—into one of the most horrible that ever poor wretch was cursed with. Wherever I went, the countenance of him I had slain appeared to follow me. Whenever I turned my head, I beheld it behind me, hideous with the contortions of the dying moment. I have tried in every way to escape from this horrible phantom, but in vain. I know not whether it be an illusion of the mind, the consequence of my dismal education at the convent, or whether a phantom really sent by Heaven to punish me, but there it ever is—at all times—in all places. Nor has time nor habit had any effect in familiarizing me with its terrors. I have travelled from place to place—plunged into amusements—tried dissipation and distraction of every kind—all—all in vain. I once had recourse to my pencil, as a desperate experiment. I painted an exact resemblance of this phantom-face. I placed it before me, in hopes that by constantly contemplating the copy, I might diminish the effect of the original. But I only doubled instead of diminishing the misery. Such is

---

*See the Bible, Genesis 4:3–17.

the curse that has clung to my footsteps—that has made my life a burden, but the thought of death terrible. God knows what I have suffered—what days and days, and nights and nights of sleepless torment—what a never-dying worm has preyed upon my heart— what an unquenchable fire has burned within my brain! He knows the wrongs that wrought upon my poor weak nature; that converted the tenderest of affections into the deadliest of fury. He knows best whether a frail erring creature has expiated by long-enduring torture and measureless remorse the crime of a moment of madness. Often, often have I prostrated myself in the dust, and implored that he would give me a sign of his forgiveness, and let me die——

Thus far had I written some time since. I had meant to leave this record of misery and crime with you, to be read when I should be no more.

My prayer to Heaven has at length been heard. You were witness to my emotions last evening at the church, when the vaulted temple resounded with the words of atonement and redemption. I heard a voice speaking to me from the midst of the music; I heard it rising above the pealing of the organ and the voices of the choir—it spoke to me in tones of celestial melody—it promised mercy and forgiveness, but demanded from me full expiation. I go to make it. To-morrow I shall be on my way to Genoa, to surrender myself to justice. You who have pitied my sufferings, who have poured the balm of sympathy into my wounds, do not shrink from my memory with abhorrence now that you know my story. Recollect, that when you read of my crime I shall have atoned for it with my blood!

When the Baronet had finished, there was a universal desire expressed to see the painting of this frightful visage. After much entreaty the Baronet consented, on condition that they should only visit it one by one. He called his housekeeper, and gave her charge to conduct the gentlemen, singly, to the chamber. They all returned varying in their stories: some affected in one way, some in another; some more, some less; but all agreeing that there was a certain something about the painting that had a very odd effect upon the feelings.

I stood in a deep bow-window with the Baronet, and could not help expressing my wonder. "After all," said I, "there are certain mysteries in our nature, certain inscrutable impulses and influences, which warrant one in being superstitious. Who can account for so many persons of different characters being thus strangely affected by a mere painting?"

"And especially when not one of them has seen it!" said the Baronet, with a smile.

"How!" exclaimed I, "not seen it?"

"Not one of them!" replied he, laying his finger on his lips, in sign of secrecy. "I saw that some of them were in a bantering vein, and did not choose that the memento of the poor Italian should be made a jest of. So I gave the housekeeper a hint to show them all to a different chamber!"

Thus end the stories of the Nervous Gentleman.

PART FOURTH

THE MONEY-DIGGERS

FOUND AMONG THE PAPERS OF THE
LATE DIEDRICH KNICKERBOCKER

"Now I remember those old women's words,
Who in my youth would tell me winter's tales:
And speak of sprites and ghosts that glide by night
About the place where treasure hath been hid."

MARLOW'S *Jew of Malta**

Hell-Gate

About six miles from the renowned city of the Manhattoes, in that Sound or arm of the sea which passes between the mainland and Nassau, or Long Island, there is a narrow strait, where the current is violently compressed between shouldering promontories, and horribly perplexed by rocks and shoals. Being, at the best of times, a very violent, impetuous current, it takes these impediments in mighty dudgeon; boiling in whirlpools; brawling and fretting in ripples; raging and roaring in rapids and breakers; and, in short, indulging in all kinds of wrong-headed

---

*From *The Jew of Malta* (c.1589), by English dramatist Christopher Marlowe (act 2, scene 1).

paroxysms. At such times, woe to any unlucky vessel that ventures within its clutches.[8]

This termagant humor, however, prevails only at certain times of tide. At low water, for instance, it is as pacific a stream as you would wish to see; but as the tide rises, it begins to fret; at half-tide it roars with might and main, like a bull bellowing for more drink; but when the tide is full, it relapses into quiet, and, for a time, sleeps as soundly as an alderman after dinner. In fact, it may be compared to a quarrelsome toper,* who is a peaceable fellow enough when he has no liquor at all, or when he has a skinfull; but who, when half-seas-over, plays the very devil.

This mighty, blustering, bullying, hard-drinking little strait was a place of great danger and perplexity to the Dutch navigators of ancient days; hectoring their tub-built barks in a most unruly style; whirling them about in a manner to make any but a Dutchman giddy, and not unfrequently stranding them upon rocks and reefs, as it did the famous squadron of Oloffe the Dreamer,† when seeking a place to found the city of the Manhattoes. Whereupon, out of sheer spleen, they denominated it *Helle-Gat*, and solemnly gave it over to the devil. This appellation has since been aptly rendered into English by the name of Hell-gate, and into nonsense by the name of *Hurl-gate*, according to certain foreign intruders, who neither understood Dutch nor English,—may St. Nicholas confound them!

This strait of Hell-gate was a place of great awe and perilous enterprise to me in my boyhood, having been much of a navigator on those small seas, and having more than once run the risk of shipwreck and drowning in the course of certain holiday voyages, to which, in common with other Dutch urchins, I was rather prone. Indeed, partly from the name, and partly from various strange circumstances connected with it, this place had far more terrors in the eyes of my truant companions and myself than had Scylla and Charybdis‡ for the navigators of yore.

---

*Drunkard.

†See p. 403.

‡In book 12 of Homer's *Odyssey*, the names given to a sea monster and a whirlpool that guard either side of a hazardous strait through which Odysseus must steer his ship.

In the midst of this strait, and hard by a group of rocks called the Hen and Chickens, there lay the wreck of a vessel which had been entangled in the whirlpools and stranded during a storm. There was a wild story told to us of this being the wreck of a pirate, and some tale of bloody murder which I cannot now recollect, but which made us regard it with great awe, and keep far from it in our cruisings. Indeed, the desolate look of the forlorn hulk, and the fearful place where it lay rotting, were enough to awaken strange notions. A row of timber-heads, blackened by time, just peered above the surface at high water; but at low tide a considerable part of the hull was bare, and its great ribs or timbers, partly stripped of their planks, and dripping with seaweeds, looked like the huge skeleton of some sea-monster. There was also the stump of a mast, with a few ropes and blocks swinging about and whistling in the wind, while the sea-gull wheeled and screamed around the melancholy carcass. I have a faint recollection of some hobgoblin tale of sailors' ghosts being seen about this wreck at night, with bare skulls, and blue lights in their sockets instead of eyes, but I have forgotten all the particulars.

In fact, the whole of this neighborhood was like the straits of Pelorus* of yore, a region of fable and romance to me. From the strait to the Manhattoes, the borders of the Sound are greatly diversified, being broken and indented by rocky nooks, overhung with trees, which give them a wild and romantic look. In the time of my boyhood, they abounded with traditions about pirates, ghosts, smugglers, and buried money, which had a wonderful effect upon the young minds of my companions and myself.

As I grew to more mature years, I made diligent research after the truth of these strange traditions; for I have always been a curious investigator of the valuable but obscure branches of the history of my native province. I found infinite difficulty, however, in arriving at any precise information. In seeking to dig up one fact, it is incredible the number of fables that I unearthed. I will say nothing of the devil's stepping-stones, by which the arch-fiend made his retreat from Connecticut to Long Island, across the Sound; seeing the subject is likely to be learnedly treated by a worthy friend and contemporary

---

*Or Strait of Messina; channel dividing Sicily and Italy.

historian whom I have furnished with particulars thereof.* Neither will I say anything of the black man in the three-cornered hat, seated in the stern of a jolly-boat, who used to be seen about Hell-gate in stormy weather, and who went by the name of the pirate's *spuke*, (i. e. pirate's ghost) and whom, it is said, old Governor Stuyvesant[†] once shot with a silver bullet; because I never could meet with any person of stanch credibility who professed to have seen this spectrum, unless it were the widow of Manus Conklen, the blacksmith, of Frogsneck;[‡] but then, poor woman, she was a little purblind, and might have been mistaken; though they say she saw farther than other folks in the dark.

All this, however, was but little satisfactory in regard to the tales of pirates and their buried money, about which I was most curious; and the following is all that I could, for a long time, collect, that had anything like an air of authenticity.

---

*For a very interesting and authentic account of the devil and his stepping-stones, see the valuable Memoir read before the New York Historical Society, since the death of Mr. Knickerbocker, by his friend, an eminent jurist of the place [Irving's note]. Mr. Knickerbocker's "friend" is a reference to Egbert Benson, who presented his memoir to the New York Historical Society in 1816; see *Collections of the New York Historical Society*, second series (1848), vol. 2, pp. 28–148.

[†]See p. 447.

[‡]That is, Throg's Neck, a cape on Long Island Sound in Bronx County, New York.

Kidd the Pirate[9]

In old times, just after the territory of the New Netherlands had been wrested from the hands of their High Mightinesses, the Lords States-General of Holland, by King Charles the Second,* and while it was as yet in an unquiet state, the province was a great resort of random adventurers, loose livers, and all that class of haphazard fellows who live by their wits, and dislike the old-fashioned restraint of law and gospel. Among these, the foremost were the buccaneers. These were rovers of the deep, who perhaps in time of war had been educated in those schools of piracy, the privateers; but having once tasted the sweets of plunder, had ever retained a hankering after it. There is but a slight step from the privateersman to the pirate; both fight for the love of plunder; only that the latter is the bravest, as he dares both the enemy and the gallows.

But in whatever school they had been taught, the buccaneers that kept about the English colonies were daring fellows, and made sad work in times of peace among the Spanish settlements and Spanish merchantmen. The easy access to the harbor of the Manhattoes, the number of hiding-places about its waters, and the laxity of its scarcely organized government, made it a great rendezvous of the pirates; where they might dispose of their booty, and concert new depredations. As they brought home with them wealthy lading of all kinds, the luxuries of the tropics, and the sumptuous spoils of the Spanish provinces, and disposed of them with the proverbial carelessness of freebooters, they were welcome visitors to the thrifty traders of the Manhattoes. Crews of these desperadoes, therefore, the runagates of every country and every clime, might be seen swaggering in open day about the streets of the little burgh, elbowing its quiet mynheers; trafficking away their rich outlandish plunder at

---

*King Charles II of Great Britain and Ireland seized the Dutch colony of New Netherland in 1664; the colony was renamed New York when Charles granted it to his brother James, duke of York.

half or quarter price to the wary merchant; and then squandering their prize-money in taverns, drinking, gambling, singing, swearing, shouting, and astounding the neighborhood with midnight brawl and ruffian revelry.

At length these excesses rose to such a height as to become a scandal to the provinces, and to call loudly for the interposition of government. Measures were accordingly taken to put a stop to the widely extended evil, and to ferret this vermin brood out of the colonies.

Among the agents employed to execute this purpose was the notorious Captain Kidd.* He had long been an equivocal character; one of those nondescript animals of the ocean that are neither fish, flesh, nor fowl. He was somewhat of a trader, something more of a smuggler, with a considerable dash of the picaroon.† He had traded for many years among the pirates, in a little rakish mosquito-built vessel, that could run into all kinds of waters. He knew all their haunts and lurking-places; was always hooking about on mysterious voyages, and was as busy as a Mother Cary's chicken‡ in a storm.

This nondescript personage was pitched upon by government as the very man to hunt the pirates by sea, upon the good old maxim of "setting a rogue to catch a rogue"; or as otters are sometimes used to catch their cousins-german, the fish.

Kidd accordingly sailed for New York, in 1695, in a gallant vessel called the Adventure Galley, well armed and duly commissioned. On arriving at his old haunts, however, he shipped his crew on new terms; enlisted a number of his old comrades, lads of the knife and the pistol; and then set sail for the East. Instead of cruising against pirates, he turned pirate himself; steered to the Madeiras, to Bonavista, and Madagascar, and cruised about the entrance of the Red Sea. Here, among other maritime robberies, he captured a rich Quedah§ merchantman, manned by Moors, though commanded by an Englishman. Kidd would fain have passed this off for a worthy

---

*William "Captain" Kidd (c.1645–1701), Scottish privateer turned pirate.
†Pirate.
‡That is, a storm-petrel, a seabird that lives its life far out at sea.
§Or Kedah, a Malaysian state.

exploit, as being a kind of crusade against the infidels; but government had long since lost all relish for such Christian triumphs.

After roaming the seas, trafficking his prizes, and changing from ship to ship, Kidd had the hardihood to return to Boston, laden with booty, with a crew of swaggering companions at his heels.

Times, however, were changed. The buccaneers could no longer show a whisker in the colonies with impunity. The new Governor, Lord Bellamont,* had signalized himself by his zeal in extirpating these offenders; and was doubly exasperated against Kidd, having been instrumental in appointing him to the trust which he had betrayed. No sooner, therefore, did he show himself in Boston, than the alarm was given of his reappearance, and measures were taken to arrest this cutpurse of the ocean. The daring character which Kidd had acquired, however, and the desperate fellows who followed like bull-dogs at his heels, caused a little delay in his arrest. He took advantage of this, it is said, to bury the greater part of his treasures, and then carried a high head about the streets of Boston. He even attempted to defend himself when arrested, but was secured and thrown into prison, with his followers. Such was the formidable character of this pirate and his crew, that it was thought advisable to dispatch a frigate to bring them to England. Great exertions were made to screen him from justice, but in vain; he and his comrades were tried, condemned, and hanged at Execution Dock in London. Kidd died hard, for the rope with which he was first tied up broke with his weight, and he tumbled to the ground. He was tied up a second time, and more effectually hence came, doubtless, the story of Kidd's having a charmed life, and that he had to be twice hanged.

Such is the main outline of Kidd's history; but it has given birth to an innumerable progeny of traditions. The report of his having buried great treasures of gold and jewels before his arrest, set the brains of all the good people along the coast in a ferment. There were rumors on rumors of great sums of money found here and there, sometimes in one part of the country, sometimes in another; of coins with Moorish inscriptions, doubtless the spoils of his

---

*Richard Coote, earl of Bellamont, colonial governor of New York, Massachusetts, and New Hampshire (1695–1701).

eastern prizes, but which the common people looked upon with superstitious awe, regarding the Moorish letters as diabolical or magical characters.

Some reported the treasure to have been buried in solitary, unsettled places, about Plymouth and Cape Cod; but by degrees various other parts, not only on the eastern coast, but along the shores of the Sound and even of Manhattan and Long Island, were gilded by these rumors. In fact, the rigorous measures of Lord Bellamont spread sudden consternation among the buccaneers in every part of the provinces: they secreted their money and jewels in lonely out-of-the-way places about the wild shores of the rivers and sea-coast, and dispersed themselves over the face of the country. The hand of justice prevented many of them from ever returning to regain their buried treasures, which remained, and remain probably to this day, objects of enterprise for the money-digger.

This is the cause of those frequent reports of trees and rocks bearing mysterious marks, supposed to indicate the spots where treasures lay hidden; and many have been the ransackings after the pirate's booty. In all the stories which once abounded of these enterprises the devil played a conspicuous part. Either he was con- ciliated by ceremonies and invocations, or some solemn compact was made with him. Still he was ever prone to play the money- diggers some slippery trick. Some would dig so far as to come to an iron chest, when some baffling circumstance was sure to take place. Either the earth would fall in and fill up the pit, or some direful noise or apparition would frighten the party from the place: some- times the devil himself would appear, and bear off the prize when within their very grasp; and if they revisited the place the next day, not a trace would be found of their labors of the preceding night.

All these rumors, however, were extremely vague, and for a long time tantalized, without gratifying, my curiosity. There is nothing in this world so hard to get at as truth, and there is nothing in this world but truth that I care for. I sought among all my favorite sources of authentic information, the oldest inhabitants, and partic- ularly the old Dutch wives of the province; but though I flatter my- self that I am better versed than most men in the curious history of my native province, yet for a long time my inquiries were unattended with any substantial result.

At length it happened that, one calm day in the latter part of summer, I was relaxing myself from the toils of severe study, by a day's amusement in fishing in those waters which had been the favorite resort of my boyhood. I was in company with several worthy burghers of my native city, among whom were more than one illustrious member of the corporation, whose names, did I dare to mention them, would do honor to my humble page. Our sport was indifferent. The fish did not bite freely, and we frequently changed our fishing-ground without bettering our luck. We were at length anchored close under a ledge of rocky coast, on the eastern side of the island of Manhatta. It was a still, warm day. The stream whirled and dimpled by us, without a wave or even a ripple; and everything was so calm and quiet, that it was almost startling when the king-fisher would pitch himself from the branch of some high tree, and after suspending himself for a moment in the air, to take his aim, would souse* into the smooth water after his prey. While we were lolling in our boat, half drowsy with the warm stillness of the day, and the dulness of our sport, one of our party, a worthy alderman, was overtaken by a slumber, and, as he dozed, suffered the sinker of his drop-line to lie upon the bottom of the river. On waking, he found he had caught something of importance from the weight. On drawing it to the surface, we were much surprised to find it a long pistol of very curious and outlandish fashion, which, from its rusted condition, and its stock being worm-eaten and covered with barnacles, appeared to have lain a long time under water. The unexpected appearance of this document of warfare occasioned much speculation among my pacific companions. One supposed it to have fallen there during the revolutionary war; another, from the peculiarity of its fashion, attributed it to the voyagers in the earliest days of the settlement; perchance to the renowned Adriaen Block[†] who explored the Sound, and discovered Block Island, since so noted for its cheese. But a third, after regarding it for some time, pronounced it to be of veritable Spanish workmanship.

---

*Dive.

[†]European explorer known for mapping the coastal region of New York and Connecticut (c.1614).

"I'll warrant," said he, "if this pistol could talk, it would tell strange stories of hard fights among the Spanish Dons. I've no doubt but it is a relic of the buccaneers of old times,—who knows but it belonged to Kidd himself?"

"Ah! that Kidd was a resolute fellow," cried an old iron-faced Cape-Cod whaler.—"There's a fine old song about him, all to the tune of—

> My name is Captain Kidd,
> As I sailed, as I sailed;—

and then it tells about how he gained the devil's good graces by burying the Bible:—

> I'd a Bible in my hand,
>   As I sailed, as I sailed,
> And I sunk it in the sand,
>   As I sailed.—

"Odsfish, if I thought this pistol had belonged to Kidd, I should set great store by it, for curiosity's sake By the way, I recollect a story about a fellow who once dug up Kidd's buried money, which was written by a neighbor of mine, and which I learnt by heart. As the fish don't bite just now, I'll tell it to you, by way of passing away the time."—And so saying, he gave us the following narration.

The Devil and Tom Walker[10]

A few miles from Boston in Massachusetts, there is a deep inlet, winding several miles into the interior of the country from Charles Bay, and terminating in a thickly-wooded swamp or morass. On one side of this inlet is a beautiful dark grove; on the opposite side the land rises abruptly from the water's edge into a high ridge, on which grow a few scattered oaks of great age and immense size. Under one of these gigantic trees, according to old stories, there was a great amount of treasure buried by Kidd the pirate. The inlet allowed a facility to bring the money in a boat secretly and at night to the very foot of the hill; the elevation of the place permitted a good lookout to be kept that no one was at hand; while the remarkable trees formed good landmarks by which the place might easily be found again. The old stories add, moreover, that the devil presided at the hiding of the money, and took it under his guardianship; but this, it is well known, he always does with buried treasure, particularly when it has been ill-gotten. Be that as it may, Kidd never returned to recover his wealth; being shortly after seized at Boston, sent out to England, and there hanged for a pirate.

About the year 1727, just at the time that earthquakes were prevalent in New England, and shook many tall sinners down upon their knees, there lived near this place a meagre, miserly fellow, of the name of Tom Walker. He had a wife as miserly as himself: they were so miserly that they even conspired to cheat each other. Whatever the woman could lay hands on, she hid away; a hen could not cackle but she was on the alert to secure the new-laid egg. Her husband was continually prying about to detect her secret hoards, and many and fierce were the conflicts that took place about what ought to have been common property. They lived in a forlorn-looking house that stood alone, and had an air of starvation. A few straggling savin-trees, emblems of sterility, grew near it; no smoke ever curled from its chimney; no traveller stopped at its door. A miserable horse, whose ribs were as articulate as the bars of a gridiron, stalked about a field, where a thin carpet of moss, scarcely covering the ragged beds of pudding-stone, tantalized and balked his hunger; and sometimes he would lean his head over the fence, look piteously at the passer-by, and seem to petition deliverance from this land of famine.

The house and its inmates had altogether a bad name. Tom's wife was a tall termagant, fierce of temper, loud of tongue, and strong of arm. Her voice was often heard in wordy warfare with her husband; and his face sometimes showed signs that their conflicts were not confined to words. No one ventured, however, to interfere between them. The lonely wayfarer shrunk within himself at the horrid clamor and clapper-clawing; eyed the den of discord askance; and hurried on his way, rejoicing, if a bachelor, in his celibacy.

One day that Tom Walker had been to a distant part of the neighborhood, he took what he considered a short cut homeward, through the swamp. Like most short cuts, it was an ill-chosen route. The swamp was thickly grown with great gloomy pines and hemlocks, some of them ninety feet high, which made it dark at noonday, and a retreat for all the owls of the neighborhood. It was full of pits and quagmires, partly covered with weeds and mosses, where the green surface often betrayed the traveller into a gulf of black, smothering mud: there were also dark and stagnant pools, the abodes of the tadpole, the bull-frog, and the water-snake; where the trunks of pines and hemlocks lay half-drowned, half-rotting, looking like alligators sleeping in the mire.

Tom had long been picking his way cautiously through this treacherous forest; stepping from tuft to tuft of rushes and roots, which afforded precarious foothold among deep sloughs; or pacing carefully, like a cat, along the prostrate trunks of trees; startled now and then by the sudden screaming of the bittern, or the quacking of a wild duck rising on the wing from some solitary pool. At length he arrived at a firm piece of ground, which ran out like a peninsula into the deep bosom of the swamp. It had been one of the strongholds of the Indians during their wars with the first colonists. Here they had thrown up a kind of fort, which they had looked upon as almost impregnable, and had used as a place of refuge for their squaws and children. Nothing remained of the old Indian fort but a few embankments, gradually sinking to the level of the surrounding earth, and already overgrown in part by oaks and other forest trees, the foliage of which formed a contrast to the dark pines and hemlocks of the swamp.

It was late in the dusk of evening when Tom Walker reached the old fort, and he paused there awhile to rest himself. Any one but he would have felt unwilling to linger in this lonely, melancholy place, for the common people had a bad opinion of it, from the stories handed down from the time of the Indian wars; when it was asserted that the savages held incantations here, and made sacrifices to the evil spirit.

Tom Walker, however, was not a man to be troubled with any fears of the kind. He reposed himself for some time on the trunk of a fallen hemlock, listening to the boding cry of the tree-toad, and delving with his walking-staff into a mound of black mould at his feet. As he turned up the soil unconsciously, his staff struck against something hard. He raked it out of the vegetable mould, and lo! a cloven skull, with an Indian tomahawk buried deep in it, lay before him. The rust on the weapon showed the time that had elapsed since this death-blow had been given. It was a dreary memento of the fierce struggle that had taken place in this last foothold of the Indian warriors.

"Humph!" said Tom Walker, as he gave it a kick to shake the dirt from it.

"Let that skull alone!" said a gruff voice. Tom lifted up his eyes, and beheld a great black man seated directly opposite him, on the stump of a tree. He was exceedingly surprised, having neither heard nor seen any one approach; and he was still more perplexed on observing, as well as the gathering gloom would permit, that the stranger was neither negro nor Indian. It is true he was dressed in a rude half Indian garb, and had a red belt or sash swathed round his body; but his face was neither black nor copper-color, but swarthy and dingy, and begrimed with soot, as if he had been accustomed to toil among fires and forges. He had a shock of coarse black hair, that stood out from his head in all directions, and bore an axe on his shoulder.

He scowled for a moment at Tom with a pair of great red eyes.

"What are you doing on my grounds?" said the black man, with a hoarse growling voice.

"Your grounds!" said Tom, with a sneer, "no more your grounds than mine; they belong to Deacon Peabody."

"Deacon Peabody be d——d," said the stranger, "as I flatter myself he will be, if he does not look more to his own sins and less to those of his neighbors. Look yonder, and see how Deacon Peabody is faring."

Tom looked in the direction that the stranger pointed and beheld one of the great trees, fair and flourishing without, but rotten at the core, and saw that it had been nearly hewn through, so that the first high wind was likely to blow it down. On the bark of the tree was scored the name of Deacon Peabody, an eminent man, who had waxed wealthy by driving shrewd bargains with the Indians. He now looked around, and found most of the tall trees marked with the name of some great man of the colony, and all more or less scored by the axe. The one on which he had been seated, and which had evidently just been hewn down, bore the name of Crowninshield; and he recollected a mighty rich man of that name, who made a vulgar display of wealth, which it was whispered he had acquired by buccaneering.

"He's just ready for burning!" said the black man with a growl of triumph. "You see I am likely to have a good stock of firewood for winter."

"But what right have you," said Tom, "to cut down Deacon Peabody's timber?"

"The right of a prior claim," said the other. "This woodland belonged to me long before one of your white-faced race put foot upon the soil."

"And pray, who are you, if I may be so bold?" said Tom.

"Oh, I go by various names. I am the wild huntsman in some countries; the black miner in others. In this neighborhood I am known by the name of the black woodsman. I am he to whom the red men consecrated this spot, and in honor of whom they now and then roasted a white man, by way of sweet-smelling sacrifice. Since the red men have been exterminated by you white savages, I amuse myself by presiding at the persecutions of Quakers and Anabaptists; I am the great patron and prompter of slave-dealers, and the grandmaster of the Salem witches."

"The upshot of all which is, that, if I mistake not," said Tom, sturdily, "you are he commonly called Old Scratch."

"The same, at your service!" replied the black man, with a half civil nod.

Such was the opening of this interview, according to the old story; though it has almost too familiar an air to be credited.

One would think that to meet with such a singular personage, in this wild, lonely place, would have shaken any man's nerves; but Tom was a hard-minded fellow, not easily daunted, and he had lived so long with a termagant wife, that he did not even fear the devil.

It is said that after this commencement they had a long and earnest conversation together, as Tom returned homeward. The black man told him of great sums of money buried by Kidd the pirate, under the oak-trees on the high ridge, not far from the morass. All these were under his command, and protected by his power, so that none could find them but such as propitiated his favor. These he offered to place within Tom Walker's reach, having conceived an especial kindness for him; but they were to be had only on certain conditions. What these conditions were may be easily surmised, though Tom never disclosed them publicly. They must have been very hard, for he required time to think of them, and he was not a man to stick at trifles when money was in view. When they had reached the edge of the swamp, the stranger paused. "What proof have I that all you have been telling me is true?" said Tom. "There's my signature," said the black man, pressing his finger on Tom's forehead. So saying, he turned off among the thickets of the swamp, and seemed, as Tom said, to go down, down, down, into the earth, until nothing but his head and shoulders could be seen, and so on, until he totally disappeared.

When Tom reached home, he found the black print of a finger burnt, as it were, into his forehead, which nothing could obliterate.

The first news his wife had to tell him was the sudden death of Absalom Crowninshield, the rich buccaneer. It was announced in the papers with the usual flourish, that "A great man had fallen in Israel."

Tom recollected the tree which his black friend had just hewn down, and which was ready for burning. "Let the freebooter roast," said Tom, "who cares!" He now felt convinced that all he had heard and seen was no illusion.

He was not prone to let his wife into his confidence; but as this was an uneasy secret, he willingly shared it with her. All her avarice was awakened at the mention of hidden gold, and she urged her husband to comply with the black man's terms, and secure what would make them wealthy for life. However Tom might have felt disposed to sell himself to the Devil, he was determined not to do so to oblige his wife; so he flatly refused, out of the mere spirit of contradiction. Many and bitter were the quarrels they had on the subject; but the more she talked, the more resolute was Tom not to be damned to please her.

At length she determined to drive the bargain on her own account, and if she succeeded, to keep all the gain to herself. Being of the same fearless temper as her husband, she set off for the old Indian fort towards the close of a summer's day. She was many hours absent. When she came back, she was reserved and sullen in her replies. She spoke something of a black man, whom she had met about twilight hewing at the root of a tall tree. He was sulky, however, and would not come to terms: she was to go again with a propitiatory offering, but what it was she forbore to say.

The next evening she set off again for the swamp, with her apron heavily laden. Tom waited and waited for her, but in vain; midnight came, but she did not make her appearance: morning, noon, night returned, but still she did not come. Tom now grew uneasy for her safety, especially as he found she had carried off in her apron the silver tea-pot and spoons, and every portable article of value. Another night elapsed, another morning came; but no wife. In a word, she was never heard of more.

What was her real fate nobody knows, in consequence of so many pretending to know. It is one of those facts which have become confounded by a variety of historians. Some asserted that she lost her way among the tangled mazes of the swamp, and sank into some pit or slough; others, more uncharitable, hinted that she had eloped with the household booty, and made off to some other province; while others surmised that the tempter had decoyed her into a dismal quagmire, on the top of which her hat was found lying. In confirmation of this, it was said a great black man, with an axe on his shoulder, was seen late that very evening coming out of the swamp, carrying a bundle tied in a check apron, with an air of surly triumph.

The most current and probable story, however, observes, that Tom Walker grew so anxious about the fate of his wife and his property, that he set out at length to seek them both at the Indian fort. During a long summer's afternoon he searched about the gloomy place, but no wife was to be seen. He called her name repeatedly, but she was nowhere to be heard. The bittern alone responded to his voice, as he flew screaming by; or the bull-frog croaked dolefully from a neighboring pool. At length, it is said, just in the brown hour of twilight, when the owls began to hoot, and the bats to flit about, his attention was attracted by the clamor of carrion crows hovering about a cypress-tree. He looked up, and beheld a bundle tied in a check apron, and hanging in the branches of the tree, with a great vulture perched hard by, as if keeping watch upon it. He leaped with joy; for he recognized his wife's apron, and supposed it to contain the household valuables.

"Let us get hold of the property," said he, consolingly to himself, "and we will endeavor to do without the woman."

As he scrambled up the tree, the vulture spread its wide wings, and sailed off, screaming, into the deep shadows of the forest. Tom seized the checked apron, but, woful sight! found nothing but a heart and liver tied up in it!

Such, according to this most authentic old story, was all that was to be found of Tom's wife. She had probably attempted to deal with the black man as she had been accustomed to deal with her husband; but though a female scold is generally considered a match for the devil, yet in this instance she appears to have had the worst of it. She must have died game, however; for it is said Tom noticed many prints of cloven feet deeply stamped about the tree, and found handfuls of hair, that looked as if they had been plucked from the coarse black shock of the woodman. Tom knew his wife's prowess by experience. He shrugged his shoulders, as he looked at the signs of a fierce clapper-clawing. "Egad," said he to himself, "Old Scratch must have had a tough time of it!"

Tom consoled himself for the loss of his property, with the loss of his wife, for he was a man of fortitude. He even felt something like gratitude towards the black woodman, who, he considered, had done him a kindness. He sought, therefore, to cultivate a further acquaintance with him, but for some time without success; the old black-legs played shy, for whatever people may think, he is not always to be had for calling for: he knows how to play his cards when pretty sure of his game.

At length, it is said, when delay had whetted Tom's eagerness to the quick, and prepared him to agree to anything rather than not gain the promised treasure, he met the black man one evening in his usual woodman's dress, with his axe on his shoulder, sauntering along the swamp, and humming a tune. He affected to receive Tom's advances with great indifference, made brief replies, and went on humming his tune.

By degrees, however, Tom brought him to business, and they began to haggle about the terms on which the former was to have the pirate's treasure. There was one condition which need not be mentioned, being generally understood in all cases where the devil grants favors; but there were others about which, though of less importance, he was inflexibly obstinate. He insisted that the money found through his means should be employed in his service. He proposed, therefore, that Tom should employ it in the black traffic; that is to say, that he should fit out a slave-ship. This, however, Tom resolutely refused: he was bad enough in all conscience; but the devil himself could not tempt him to turn slave-trader.

Finding Tom so squeamish on this point, he did not insist upon it, but proposed, instead, that he should turn usurer;* the devil being extremely anxious for the increase of usurers, looking upon them as his peculiar people.

To this no objections were made, for it was just to Tom's taste.

"You shall open a broker's shop in Boston next month," said the black man.

"I'll do it to-morrow, if you wish," said Tom Walker.

"You shall lend money at two per cent. a month."

"Egad, I'll charge four!" replied Tom Walker.

"You shall extort bonds, foreclose mortgages, drive the merchants to bankruptcy"——

"I'll drive them to the d——l," cried Tom Walker.

"You are the usurer for my money!" said black-legs with delight. "When will you want the rhino?"†

"This very night."

"Done!" said the devil.

"Done!" said Tom Walker.—So they shook hands and struck a bargain.

---

*Moneylender who charges exorbitantly high interest.
†Slang for "money."

A few days' time saw Tom Walker seated behind his desk in a counting-house in Boston.

His reputation for a ready-moneyed man, who would lend money out for a good consideration, soon spread abroad. Everybody remembers the time of Governor Belcher,* when money was particularly scarce. It was a time of paper credit. The country had been deluged with government bills, the famous Land Bank had been established; there had been a rage for speculating; the people had run mad with schemes for new settlements; for building cities in the wilderness; land-jobbers went about with maps of grants, and townships, and Eldorados,† lying nobody knew where, but which everybody was ready to purchase. In a word, the great speculating fever which breaks out every now and then in the country, had raged to an alarming degree, and everybody was dreaming of making sudden fortunes from nothing. As usual the fever had subsided; the dream had gone off, and the imaginary fortunes with it; the patients were left in doleful plight, and the whole country resounded with the consequent cry of "hard times."

At this propitious time of public distress did Tom Walker set up as usurer in Boston. His door was soon thronged by customers. The needy and adventurous; the gambling speculator; the dreaming land-jobber; the thriftless tradesman; the merchant with cracked credit; in short, every one driven to raise money by desperate means and desperate sacrifices, hurried to Tom Walker.

Thus Tom was the universal friend of the needy, and acted like a "friend in need"; that is to say, he always exacted good pay and good security. In proportion to the distress of the applicant was the hardness of his terms. He accumulated bonds and mortgages; gradually squeezed his customers closer and closer: and sent them at length, dry as a sponge, from his door.

In this way he made money hand over hand; became a rich and mighty man, and exalted his cocked hat upon 'Change.‡ He built

---

*Jonathan Belcher, colonial governor of Massachusetts and New Hampshire (1730–1741); he was voted out of office because of his efforts to break up the Land Bank, a joint-stock company formed by merchants after the colony was forbidden to issue paper money.
†See footnote on p. 93.
‡The stock exchange.

himself, as usual, a vast house, out of ostentation; but left the greater part of it unfinished and unfurnished, out of parsimony. He even set up a carriage in the fulness of his vainglory, though he nearly starved the horses which drew it; and as the ungreased wheels groaned and screeched on the axletrees, you would have thought you heard the souls of the poor debtors he was squeezing.

As Tom waxed old, however, he grew thoughtful. Having secured the good things of this world, he began to feel anxious about those of the next. He thought with regret on the bargain he had made with his black friend, and set his wits to work to cheat him out of the conditions. He became, therefore, all of a sudden, a violent church-goer. He prayed loudly and strenuously, as if heaven were to be taken by force of lungs. Indeed, one might always tell when he had sinned most during the week, by the clamor of his Sunday devotion. The quiet Christians who had been modestly and steadfastly travelling Zionward,* were struck with self-reproach at seeing themselves so suddenly outstripped in their career by this new-made convert. Tom was as rigid in religious as in money matters; he was a stern supervisor and censurer of his neighbors, and seemed to think every sin entered up to their account became a credit on his own side of the page. He even talked of the expediency of reviving the persecution of Quakers and Anabaptists. In a word, Tom's zeal became as notorious as his riches.

Still, in spite of all this strenuous attention to forms, Tom had a lurking dread that the devil, after all, would have his due. That he might not be taken unawares, therefore, it is said he always carried a small Bible in his coat-pocket. He had also a great folio Bible on his counting-house desk, and would frequently be found reading it when people called on business; on such occasions he would lay his green spectacles in the book, to mark the place, while he turned round to drive some usurious bargain.

Some say that Tom grew a little crack-brained in his old days, and that, fancying his end approaching, he had his horse new shod, saddled and bridled, and buried with his feet uppermost; because he supposed that at the last day the world would be turned upside

---

*Heavenward.

down; in which case he should find his horse standing ready for mounting, and he was determined at the worst to give his old friend a run for it. This, however, is probably a mere old wives' fable. If he really did take such a precaution, it was totally superfluous; at least so says the authentic old legend; which closes his story in the following manner.

One hot summer afternoon in the dog-days, just as a terrible black thunder-gust was coming up, Tom sat in his counting-house, in his white linen cap and India silk morning-gown. He was on the point of foreclosing a mortgage, by which he would complete the ruin of an unlucky land-speculator for whom he had professed the greatest friendship. The poor land-jobber begged him to grant a few months' indulgence. Tom had grown testy and irritated, and refused another day.

"My family will be ruined, and brought upon the parish," said the land-jobber. "Charity begins at home," replied Tom; "I must take care of myself in these hard times."

"You have made so much money out of me," said the speculator.

Tom lost his patience and his piety. "The devil take me," said he, "if I have made a farthing!"

Just then there were three loud knocks at the street-door. He stepped out to see who was there. A black man was holding a black horse, which neighed and stamped with impatience.

"Tom, you're come for," said the black fellow, gruffly. Tom shrank back, but too late. He had left his little Bible at the bottom of his coat-pocket, and his big Bible on the desk buried under the mortgage he was about to foreclose: never was sinner taken more unawares. The black man whisked him like a child into the saddle, gave the horse the lash, and away he galloped, with Tom on his back, in the midst of the thunder-storm. The clerks stuck their pens behind their ears, and stared after him from the windows. Away went Tom Walker, dashing down the streets; his white cap bobbing up and down; his morning-gown fluttering in the wind, and his steed striking fire out of the pavement at every bound. When the clerks turned to look for the black man, he had disappeared.

Tom Walker never returned to foreclose the mortgage. A countryman, who lived on the border of the swamp, reported that in the height of the thunder-gust he had heard a great clattering of hoofs and a howling along the road, and running to the window caught sight of a figure, such as I have described, on a horse that galloped like mad across the fields, over the hills, and down into the black hemlock swamp towards the old Indian fort; and that shortly after a thunder-bolt falling in that direction seemed to set the whole forest in a blaze.

The good people of Boston shook their heads and shrugged their shoulders, but had been so much accustomed to witches and goblins, and tricks of the devil, in all kinds of shapes, from the first settlement of the colony, that they were not so much horror-struck as might have been expected. Trustees were appointed to take charge of Tom's effects. There was nothing, however, to administer upon. On searching his coffers, all his bonds and mortgages were found reduced to cinders. In place of gold and silver, his iron chest was filled with chips and shavings; two skeletons lay in his stable instead of his half-starved horses, and the very next day his great house took fire and was burnt to the ground.

Such was the end of Tom Walker and his ill-gotten wealth. Let all griping money-brokers lay this story to heart. The truth of it is not to be doubted. The very hole under the oak-trees, whence he dug Kidd's money, is to be seen to this day; and the neighboring swamp and old Indian fort are often haunted in stormy nights by a figure on horseback, in morning-gown and white cap, which is doubtless the troubled spirit of the usurer. In fact, the story has resolved itself into a proverb, and is the origin of that popular saying, so prevalent throughout New England, of "The Devil and Tom Walker."

SELECTIONS FROM

A History of New York

[1844 revised edition]

The Author's Apology

T he following work,[1] in which, at the outset, nothing more was contemplated than a temporary *jeu d'esprit*,* was commenced in company with my brother, the late Peter Irving, Esq. Our idea was, to parody a small handbook which had recently appeared, entitled "A Picture of New York." Like that, our work was to begin with an historical sketch; to be followed by notices of the customs, manners, and institutions of the city; written in a serio-comic vein, and treating local errors, follies, and abuses with good-humored satire.

To burlesque the pedantic lore displayed in certain American works, our historical sketch was to commence with the creation of the world; and we laid all kinds of works under contribution for trite citations, relevant, or irrelevant, to give it the proper air of learned research. Before this crude mass of mock erudition could be digested into form, my brother departed for Europe, and I was left to prosecute the enterprise alone.

I now altered the plan of the work. Discarding all idea of a parody on the "Picture of New York," I determined that what had been origi-nally intended as an introductory sketch, should comprise the whole work, and form a comic history of the city. I accordingly moulded the mass of citations and disquisitions into introductory chapters, forming the first book; but it soon became evident to me, that, like Robinson Crusoe with his boat, I had begun on too large a scale, and that, to launch my history successfully, I must reduce its proportions.† I accordingly resolved to confine it to the period of the Dutch domination, which, in its rise, progress, and decline, pre-sented that unity of subject required by classic rule. It was a period,

---

*Game of wit (French).
†In chapter 16 of *Robinson Crusoe* (1719), by English novelist Daniel Defoe, Crusoe makes a dugout canoe from an enormous cedar only to discover it is too large for him to move.

also, at that time almost a *terra incognita** in history. In fact, I was
surprised to find how few of my fellow-citizens were aware that
New York had ever been called New Amsterdam, or had heard of
the names of its early Dutch governors, or cared a straw about their
ancient Dutch progenitors.

This, then, broke upon me as the poetic age of our city; poetic from
its very obscurity; and open, like the early and obscure days of ancient
Rome, to all the embellishments of heroic fiction. I hailed my native
city, as fortunate above all other American cities, in having an antiquity
thus extending back into the regions of doubt and fable; neither did I
conceive I was committing any grievous historical sin in helping out
the few facts I could collect in this remote and forgotten region with
figments of my own brain, or in giving characteristic attributes to the
few names connected with it which I might dig up from oblivion.

In this, doubtless, I reasoned like a young and inexperienced
writer, besotted with his own fancies; and my presumptuous tres-
passes into this sacred, though neglected region of history have met
with deserved rebuke from men of soberer minds. It is too late, however, to recall the shaft thus rashly launched. To any one whose sense
of fitness it may wound, I can only say with Hamlet,—

> Let my disclaiming from a purposed evil
> Free me so far in your most generous thoughts,
> That I have shot my arrow o'er the house,
> And hurt my brother.[†]

I will say this in further apology for my work: that, if it has taken
an unwarrantable liberty with our early provincial history, it has at
least turned attention to that history and provoked research. It is
only since this work appeared that the forgotten archives of the
province have been rummaged, and the facts and personages of the
olden time rescued from the dust of oblivion, and elevated into
whatever importance they may virtually possess.

The main object of my work, in fact, had a bearing wide from the
sober aim of history; but one which, I trust, will meet with some
indulgence from poetic minds. It was to embody the traditions of

---

*Unexplored region.
[†]From Shakespeare's *Hamlet, Prince of Denmark* (act 5, scene 2).

our city in an amusing form; to illustrate its local humors, customs, and peculiarities; to clothe home scenes and places and familiar names with those imaginative and whimsical associations so seldom met with in our new country, but which live like charms and spells about the cities of the old world, binding the heart of the native inhabitant to his home.

In this I have reason to believe I have in some measure succeeded. Before the appearance of my work the popular traditions of our city were unrecorded; the peculiar and racy customs and usages derived from our Dutch progenitors were unnoticed or regarded with indifference, or adverted to with a sneer. Now they form a convivial currency, and are brought forward on all occasions; they link our whole community together in good-humor and good fellowship; they are the rallying points of home feeling, the seasoning of our civic festivities, the staple of local tales and local pleasantries, and are so harped upon by our writers of popular fiction, that I find myself almost crowded off the legendary ground which I was the first to explore, by the host who have followed in my footsteps.

I dwell on this head, because, at the first appearance of my work, its aim and drift were misapprehended by some of the descendants of the Dutch worthies; and because I understand that now and then one may still be found to regard it with a captious* eye. The far greater part, however, I have reason to flatter myself, receive my good-humored picturings in the same temper in which they were executed; and when I find, after a lapse of nearly forty years, this hap-hazard production of my youth still cherished among them,— when I find its very name become a "household word" and used to give the home stamp to everything recommended for popular acceptation, such as Knickerbocker societies, Knickerbocker insurance companies, Knickerbocker steamboats, Knickerbocker omnibuses, Knickerbocker bread, and Knickerbocker ice,—and when I find New Yorkers of Dutch descent priding themselves upon being "genuine Knickerbockers,"—I please myself with the persuasion that I have struck the right chord; that my dealings with the good old Dutch times, and the customs and usages derived from them, are

---

*Highly critical.

in harmony with the feelings and humors of my townsmen; that I have opened a vein of pleasant associations and quaint characteristics peculiar to my native place, and which its inhabitants will not willingly suffer to pass away; and that, though other histories of New York may appear of higher claims to learned acceptation, and may take their dignified and appropriate rank in the family library, Knickerbocker's history will still be received with good-humored indulgence, and be thumbed and chuckled over by the family fireside.

W.I.

SUNNYSIDE, 1848

Notices[2]

WHICH APPEARED IN THE NEWSPAPERS
PREVIOUS TO THE PUBLICATION OF
THIS WORK

From the Evening Post of October 26, 1809
DISTRESSING

Left his lodgings, some time since, and has not since been heard of, a small elderly gentleman, dressed in an old black coat and cocked hat, by the name of *Knickerbocker*. As there are some reasons for believing he is not entirely in his right mind, and as great anxiety is entertained about him, any information concerning him left either at the Columbian Hotel, Mulberry Street, or at the office of this paper, will be thankfully received.

P. S. Printers of newspapers would be aiding the cause of humanity in giving an insertion to the above.

From the same, November 6, 1809

To the Editor of the Evening Post:

Sir,—Having read in your paper of the 26th October last, a paragraph respecting an old gentleman by the name of *Knickerbocker*, who was missing from his lodgings; if it would be any relief to his friends, or furnish them with any clue to discover where he is, you may inform them that a person answering the description given, was seen by the passengers of the Albany stage, early in the morning, about four or five weeks since, resting himself by the side of the road, a little above King's Bridge. He had in his hand a small bundle, tied in a red bandana handkerchief; he appeared to be travelling northward, and was very much fatigued and exhausted.

A TRAVELLER.

From the same, November 16, 1809

To the Editor of the Evening Post:

SIR,—You have been good enough to publish in your paper a paragraph about Mr. *Diedrich Knickerbocker*, who was missing so strangely some time since. Nothing satisfactory has been heard of the old gentleman since; but *a very curious kind of a written book* has been found in his room, in his own handwriting. Now I wish you to notice him, if he is still alive, that if he does not return and pay off his bill for boarding and lodging, I shall have to dispose of his book to satisfy me for the same.

I am, sir, your humble servant,

SETH HANDASIDE,
Landlord of the Independent Columbian Hotel,
Mulberry Street

From the same, November 28, 1809

LITERARY NOTICE
INSKEEP & BRADFORD have in press, and will shortly publish,
A HISTORY OF NEW YORK,
In two volumes, duodecimo. Price Three Dollars.
Containing an account of its discovery and settlement, with its internal policies, manners, customs, wars, &c., &c., under the Dutch government, furnishing many curious and interesting particulars never before published, and which are gathered from various manuscript and other authenticated sources, the whole being interspersed with philosophical speculations and moral precepts.

This work was found in the chamber of Mr. Diedrich Knickerbocker, the old gentleman whose sudden and mysterious disappearance has been noticed. It is published in order to discharge certain debts he has left behind.

From the American Citizen, December 6, 1809

Is this day published
By INSKEEP & BRADFORD, No. 128 Broadway.
A HISTORY OF NEW YORK,
&c., &c.
(Containing same as above.)

Account of the Author

It was some time, if I recollect right, in the early part of the autumn of 1808, that a stranger applied for lodgings at the Independent Columbian Hotel in Mulberry Street, of which I am landlord. He was a small, brisk-looking old gentleman, dressed in a rusty black coat, a pair of olive velvet breeches, and a small cocked hat. He had a few gray hairs plaited and clubbed behind, and his beard seemed to be of some eight-and-forty hours' growth. The only piece of finery which he bore about him was a bright pair of square silver shoe-buckles; and all his baggage was contained in a pair of saddle-bags, which he carried under his arm. His whole appearance was something out of the common run; and my wife, who is a very shrewd body, at once set him down for some eminent country schoolmaster.

As the Independent Columbian Hotel is a very small house, I was a little puzzled at first where to put him; but my wife, who seemed taken with his looks, would needs put him in her best chamber, which is genteelly set off with the profiles of the whole family, done in black, by those two great painters, Jarvis and Wood;* and commands a very pleasant view of the new grounds on the Collect, together with the rear of the Poor-House and Bridewell, and a full front of the Hospital; so that it is the cheerfullest room in the whole house.

During the whole time that he stayed with us, we found him a very worthy good sort of an old gentleman, though a little queer in his ways. He would keep in his room for days together, and if any of the children cried, or made a noise about his door, he would bounce out in a great passion, with his hands full of papers, and say something about "deranging his ideas"; which made my wife believe sometimes that he was not altogether *compos*.† Indeed, there was

---

*John Wesley Jarvis (1781–1839) and Joseph Wood (1778?–1832?), New York artists famous for their silhouettes and miniatures; Jarvis painted Irving's portrait in 1809.
†From the Latin *compos mentis* ("in good mental health").

more than one reason to make her think so, for his room was always covered with scraps of paper and old mouldy books, laying about at sixes and sevens, which he would never let anybody touch; for he said he had laid them all away in their proper places, so that he might know where to find them; though for that matter, he was half his time worrying about the house in search of some book or writing which he had carefully put out of the way. I shall never forget what a pother he once made, because my wife cleaned out his room when his back was turned, and put everything to rights; for he swore he would never be able to get his papers in order again in a twelve-month. Upon this, my wife ventured to ask him what he did with so many books and papers; and he told her that he was "seeking for immortality"; which made her think more than ever that the poor old gentleman's head was a little cracked.

He was a very inquisitive body, and when not in his room, was continually poking about town, hearing all the news, and prying into everything that was going on: this was particularly the case about election time, when he did nothing but bustle about from poll to poll, attending all ward meetings, and committee rooms; though I could never find that he took part with either side of the question. On the contrary, he would come home and rail at both parties with great wrath,—and plainly proved one day, to the satisfaction of my wife and three old ladies who were drinking tea with her, that the two parties were like two rogues, each tugging at a skirt of the nation; and that in the end they would tear the very coat off its back, and expose its nakedness. Indeed, he was an oracle among the neighbors, who would collect around him to hear him talk of an afternoon, as he smoked his pipe on the bench before the door; and I really believe he would have brought over the whole neighborhood to his own side of the question, if they could ever have found out what it was.

He was very much given to argue, or, as he called it, *philosophize*, about the most trifling matter; and to do him justice, I never knew anybody that was a match for him, except it was a grave-looking old gentleman who called now and then to see him, and often posed him in an argument. But this is nothing surprising, as I have since found out this stranger is the city librarian; who, of course, must be a man of great learning: and I have my doubts if he had not some hand in the following history.

As our lodger had been a long time with us, and we had never received any pay, my wife began to be somewhat uneasy, and curious to find out who and what he was. She accordingly made bold to put the question to his friend, the librarian, who replied in his dry way that he was one of the *literati*,* which she supposed to mean some new party in politics. I scorn to push a lodger for his pay; so I let day after day pass on without dunning[†] the old gentleman for a farthing: but my wife, who always takes these matters on herself, and is, as I said, a shrewd kind of a woman, at last got out of patience, and hinted that she thought it high time "some people should have a sight of some people's money." To which the old gentleman replied, in a mighty touchy manner, that she need not make herself uneasy, for that he had a treasure there (pointing to his saddle-bags), worth her whole house put together. This was the only answer we could ever get from him; and as my wife, by some of those odd ways in which women find out everything, learnt that he was of very great connections, being related to the Knickerbockers of Scaghtikoke, and cousin-german to the congressman of that name, she did not like to treat him uncivilly. What is more, she even offered, merely by way of making things easy, to let him live scot-free, if he would teach the children their letters; and to try her best and get her neighbors to send their children also: but the old gentleman took it in such dudgeon, and seemed so affronted at being taken for a schoolmaster, that she never dared to speak on the subject again.

About two months ago, he went out of a morning, with a bundle in his hand, and has never been heard of since. All kinds of inquiries were made after him, but in vain. I wrote to his relations at Scaghtikoke, but they sent for answer, that he had not been there since the year before last, when he had a great dispute with the congressman about politics, and left the place in a huff, and they had neither heard nor seen anything of him from that time to this. I must own I felt very much worried about the poor old gentleman, for I thought something bad must have happened to him, that he should be missing so long, and never return to pay his bill. I therefore advertised him in the newspapers, and though my melancholy

---

*Men of letters.
†Collecting on a debt.

advertisement was published by several humane printers, yet I have never been able to learn anything satisfactory about him.

My wife now said it was high time to take care of ourselves, and see if he had left anything behind in his room, that would pay us for his board and lodging. We found nothing, however, but some old books and musty writings, and his saddle-bags; which, being opened in the presence of the librarian, contained only a few articles of worn-out clothes, and a large bundle of blotted paper. On looking over this, the librarian told us he had no doubt it was the treasure which the old gentleman had spoken about; as it proved to be a most excellent and faithful HISTORY OF NEW YORK, which he advised us by all means to publish, assuring us that it would be so eagerly bought up by a discerning public, that he had no doubt it would be enough to pay our arrears ten times over. Upon this we got a very learned schoolmaster, who teaches our children, to prepare it for the press, which he accordingly has done; and has, moreover, added to it a number of valuable notes of his own.

This, therefore, is a true statement of my reasons for having this work printed, without waiting for the consent of the author; and I here declare, that, if he ever returns, (though I much fear some unhappy accident has befallen him), I stand ready to account with him like a true and honest man. Which is all at present,

From the public's humble servant,

SETH HANDASIDE
Independent Columbian Hotel, New York.

The foregoing account of the author was prefixed to the first edition of this work. Shortly after its publication, a letter was received from him, by Mr. Handaside, dated at a small Dutch village on the banks of the Hudson, whither he had travelled for the purpose of inspecting certain ancient records. As this was one of those few and happy villages into which newspapers never find their way, it is not a matter of surprise that Mr. Knickerbocker should never have seen the numerous advertisements that were made concerning him, and that he should learn of the publication of his history by mere accident.

He expressed much concern at its premature appearance, as thereby he was prevented from making several important corrections and alterations, as well as from profiting by many curious hints

which he had collected during his travels along the shores of the
Tappan Sea, and his sojourn at Haverstraw and Esopus.

Finding that there was no longer any immediate necessity for his
return to New York, he extended his journey up to the residence of
his relations at Scaghtikoke. On his way thither he stopped for some
days at Albany, for which city he is known to have entertained a great
partiality. He found it, however, considerably altered, and was much
concerned at the inroads and improvements which the Yankees were
making, and the consequent decline of the good old Dutch manners. Indeed, he was informed that these intruders were making sad
innovations in all parts of the State; where they had given great trouble and vexation to the regular Dutch settlers by the introduction
of turnpike-gates, and country school-houses. It is said, also, that
Mr. Knickerbocker shook his head sorrowfully at noticing the gradual
decay of the great Vander Heyden palace; but was highly indignant
at finding that the ancient Dutch church, which stood in the middle
of the street, had been pulled down since his last visit.

The fame of Mr. Knickerbocker's history having reached even to
Albany, he received much flattering attention from its worthy
burghers, some of whom, however, pointed out two or three very
great errors he had fallen into, particularly that of suspending a
lump of sugar over the Albany tea-tables, which, they assured him,
had been discontinued for some years past. Several families, moreover,
were somewhat piqued that their ancestors had not been mentioned
in his work, and showed great jealousy of their neighbors who
had thus been distinguished; while the latter, it must be confessed,
plumed themselves vastly thereupon; considering these recordings
in the light of letters-patent of nobility, establishing their claims to
ancestry,—which, in this republican country, is a matter of no little
solicitude and vainglory.

It is also said, that he enjoyed high favor and countenance from
the governor, who once asked him to dinner, and was seen two or
three times to shake hands with him, when they met in the streets;
which certainly was going great lengths, considering that they differed in politics. Indeed, certain of the governor's confidential
friends, to whom he could venture to speak his mind freely on such
matters, have assured us, that he privately entertained a considerable
good will for our author,—nay, he even once went so far as to

declare, and that openly too, and at his own table, just after dinner, that "Knickerbocker was a very well-meaning sort of an old gentleman, and no fool." From all which many have been led to suppose that, had our author been of different politics, and written for the newspapers instead of wasting his talents on histories, he might have risen to some post of honor and profit,—peradventure, to be a notary-public, or even a justice in the ten-pound court.

Beside the honors and civilities already mentioned, he was much caressed by the *literati* of Albany; particularly by Mr. John Cook, who entertained him very hospitably at his circulating library and reading-room, where they used to drink Spa water, and talk about the ancients. He found Mr. Cook a man after his own heart,—of great literary research, and a curious collector of books. At parting, the latter, in testimony of friendship, made him a present of the two oldest works in his collection; which were the earliest edition of the Heidelberg Catechism,* and Adrian Vander Donck's[†] famous account of the New Netherlands: by the last of which, Mr. Knickerbocker profited greatly in his second edition.

Having passed some time very agreeably at Albany, our author proceeded to Scaghtikoke, where, it is but justice to say, he was received with open arms, and treated with wonderful loving-kindness. He was much looked up to by the family, being the first historian of the name; and was considered almost as great a man as his cousin the congressman,—with whom, by the by, he became perfectly reconciled, and contracted a strong friendship.

In spite, however, of the kindness of his relations and their great attention to his comforts, the old gentleman soon became restless and discontented. His history being published, he had no longer any business to occupy his thoughts, or any scheme to excite his hopes and anticipations. This, to a busy mind like his, was a truly deplorable situation; and, had he not been a man of inflexible morals and regular habits, there would have been great danger of his taking to politics, or drinking,—both which pernicious vices we daily see men driven to by mere spleen and idleness.

---

*See footnote on p. 240.
[†]See footnote on p. 87.

It is true, he sometimes employed himself in preparing a second edition of his history, wherein he endeavored to correct and improve many passages with which he was dissatisfied, and to rectify some mistakes that had crept into it; for he was particularly anxious that his work should be noted for its authenticity; which, indeed, is the very life and soul of history. But the glow of composition had departed,—he had to leave many places untouched, which he would fain have altered; and even where he did make alterations, he seemed always in doubt whether they were for the better or the worse.

After a residence of some time at Scaghtikoke, he began to feel a strong desire to return to New York, which he ever regarded with the warmest affection; not merely because it was his native city, but because he really considered it the very best city in the whole world. On his return, he entered into the full enjoyment of the advantages of a literary reputation. He was continually importuned to write advertisements, petitions, handbills, and productions of similar import; and, although he never meddled with the public papers, yet had he the credit of writing innumerable essays, and smart things, that appeared on all subjects, and all sides of the question; in all which he was clearly detected "by his style."*

He contracted, moreover, a considerable debt at the post-office, in consequence of the numerous letters he received from authors and printers soliciting his subscription, and he was applied to by every charitable society for yearly donations, which he gave very cheerfully, considering these applications as so many compliments. He was once invited to a great corporation dinner; and was even twice summoned to attend as a juryman at the court of quarter sessions. Indeed, so renowned did he become, that he could no longer pry about, as formerly, in all holes and corners of the city, according to the bent of his humor, unnoticed and uninterrupted; but several times when he has been sauntering the streets, on his usual rambles of observation, equipped with his cane and cocked hat, the little boys at play have been known to cry, "There goes Diedrich!"—at which the old gentleman seemed not a little pleased, looking upon these salutations in the light of the praise of posterity.

---

*Irving indulges here in a moment of self-portraiture; critics often praised Irving for his style.

In a word, if we take into consideration all these various honors and distinctions, together with an exuberant eulogium passed on him in the Port Folio,*—(with which, we are told, the old gentleman was so much overpowered, that he was sick for two or three days),— it must be confessed, that few authors have ever lived to receive such illustrious rewards, or have so completely enjoyed in advance their own immortality.

After his return from Scaghtikoke, Mr. Knickerbocker took up his residence at a little rural retreat, which the Stuyvesants had granted him on the family domain, in gratitude for his honorable mention of their ancestor. It was pleasantly situated on the borders of one of the salt marshes beyond Corlear's Hook; subject, indeed, to be occasionally overflowed, and much infested, in the summer time, with mosquitoes; but otherwise very agreeable, producing abundant crops of salt grass and bulrushes.

Here, we are sorry to say, the good old gentleman fell dangerously ill of a fever, occasioned by the neighboring marshes. When he found his end approaching, he disposed of his worldly affairs, leaving the bulk of his fortune to the New York Historical Society; his Heidelberg Catechism, and Vander Donck's work to the city library; and his saddle-bags to Mr. Hanaside. He forgave all his enemies,— that is to say, all who bore any enmity towards him; for as to himself, he declared he died in good will with all the world. And, after dictating several kind messages to his relations at Scaghtikoke, as well as to certain of our most substantial Dutch citizens, he expired in the arms of his friend the librarian.

His remains were interred, according to his own request, in St. Mark's churchyard, close by the bones of his favorite hero, Peter Stuyvesant; and it is rumored, that the Historical Society have it in mind to erect a wooden monument to his memory in the Bowling Green.

---

*The Philadelphia *Port Folio*, a weekly edited by Joseph Dennie, favorably reviewed Irving's *A History of New York* in October 1812.

To the Public

To rescue from oblivion the memory of former incidents, and to render a just tribute of renown to the many great and wonderful transactions of our Dutch progenitors, Diedrich Knickerbocker, native of the city of New York, produces this historical essay."* Like the great Father of History, whose words I have just quoted, I treat of times long past, over which the twilight of uncertainty had already thrown its shadows, and the night of forgetfulness was about to descend forever. With great solicitude had I long beheld the early history of this venerable and ancient city gradually slipping from our grasp, trembling on the lips of narrative old age, and day by day dropping piecemeal into the tomb. In a little while, thought I, and those reverend Dutch burghers, who serve as the tottering monuments of good old times, will be gathered to their fathers; their children, engrossed by the empty pleasures or insignificant transactions of the present age, will neglect to treasure up the recollections of the past, and posterity will search in vain for memorials of the days of the Patriarchs. The origin of our city will be buried in eternal oblivion, and even the names and achievements of Wouter Van Twiller, William Kieft, and Peter Stuyvesant,[†] be enveloped in doubt and fiction, like those of Romulus and Remus, of Charlemagne, King Arthur, Rinaldo, and Godfrey of Bologne.[‡]

Determined, therefore, to avert if possible this threatened misfortune, I industriously set myself to work, to gather together all the

---

*Beloe's Herodotus [Irving's note]. *The History of Herodotus*, by William Beloe (London, 1791).

[†]For notes on Wouter Van Twiller, William Kieft, and Peter Stuyvesant, see footnotes on pp. 411, 424, and 447, respectively.

[‡]Romulus and Remus: mythical founders of Rome; Charlemagne (742?–814): Carolingian king of the Franks, whose exploits are recounted in the French medieval epic *Chanson de Roland*; King Arthur: legendary Celtic warrior whose Knights of the Round Table are the subject of numerous medieval epics, including Sir Thomas Malory's *Morte d'Arthur*; Rinaldo: title character of a chivalric poem (1562) by Italian poet Torquato Tasso; Godfrey of Bologne, or Godfrey of Bouillon (c.1058–1100): leader of the First Crusade, who was crowned king of Jerusalem in 1099.

fragments of our infant history which still existed, and like my reverend prototype, Herodotus, where no written records could be found, I have endeavored to continue the chain of history by well-authenticated traditions.

In this arduous undertaking, which has been the whole business of a long and solitary life, it is incredible the number of learned authors I have consulted; and all but to little purpose. Strange as it may seem, though such multitudes of excellent works have been written about this country, there are none extant which gave any full and satisfactory account of the early history of New York, or of its three first Dutch governors. I have, however, gained much valuable and curious matter, from an elaborate manuscript written in exceeding pure and classic Low Dutch, excepting a few errors in orthography, which was found in the archives of the Stuyvesant family.* Many legends, letters, and other documents have I likewise gleaned, in my researches among the family chests and lumber-garrets of our respectable Dutch citizens; and I have gathered a host of well-authenticated traditions from divers excellent old ladies of my acquaintance, who requested that their names might not be mentioned. Nor must I neglect to acknowledge how greatly I have been assisted by that admirable and praiseworthy institution, the NEW YORK HISTORICAL SOCIETY, to which I here publicly return my sincere acknowledgments.

In the conduct of this inestimable work I have adopted no individual model; but, on the contrary, have simply contented myself with combining and concentrating the excellences of the most approved ancient historians. Like Xenophon, I have maintained the utmost impartiality, and the strictest adherence to truth throughout my history. I have enriched it after the manner of Sallust, with various characters of ancient worthies, drawn at full length, and faithfully colored. I have seasoned it with profound political speculations like Thucydides, sweetened it with the graces of sentiment like Tacitus, and infused into the whole the dignity, the grandeur, and magnificence of Livy.

I am aware that I shall incur the censure of numerous very learned and judicious critics, for indulging too frequently in the

---

‡This manuscript is an invention of Irving's.

bold excursive manner of my favorite Herodotus. And to be candid, I have found it impossible always to resist the allurements of those pleasing episodes which like flowery banks and fragrant bowers, beset the dusty road of the historian, and entice him to turn aside, and refresh himself from his wayfaring. But I trust it will be found that I have always resumed my staff, and addressed myself to my weary journey with renovated spirits, so that both my readers and myself have been benefited by the relaxation.

Indeed, though it has been my constant wish and uniform endeavor to rival Polybius* himself, in observing the requisite unity of history, yet the loose and unconnected manner in which many of the facts herein recorded have come to hand, rendered such an attempt extremely difficult. This difficulty was likewise increased by one of the grand objects contemplated in my work, which was to trace the rise of sundry customs and institutions in this best of cities, and to compare them, when in the germ of infancy, with what they are in the present old age of knowledge and improvement.

But the chief merit on which I value myself, and found my hopes for future regard, is that faithful veracity with which I have compiled this invaluable little work; carefully winnowing away the chaff of hypothesis, and discarding the tares of fable, which are too apt to spring up and choke the seeds of truth and wholesome knowledge. Had I been anxious to captivate the superficial throng, who skim like swallows over the surface of literature; or had I been anxious to commend my writings to the pampered palates of literary epicures, I might have availed myself of the obscurity that overshadows the infant years of our city, to introduce a thousand pleasing fictions. But I have scrupulously discarded many a pithy tale and marvellous adventure, whereby the drowsy ear of summer indolence might be enthralled; jealously maintaining that fidelity, gravity, and dignity, which should ever distinguish the historian. "For a writer of this class," observes an elegant critic, "must sustain the character of a wise man, writing for the instruction of posterity; one who has studied

---

*Xenophon (c.430–c.355 B.C.), Gaius Sallustius Crispus (or Sallust, c.86–c.34 B.C.), Thucydides (c.460–c.400 B.C.), Tacitus (A.D. c.55–c.117), Livy (59 B.C.–A.D. 17), and Polybius (c.203–c.120 B.C.) were all historians of ancient Greece and Rome.

to inform himself well, who has pondered his subject with care, and addresses himself to our judgment, rather than to our imagination."*

Thrice happy, therefore, is this our renowned city in having incidents worthy of swelling the theme of history; and doubly thrice happy is it in having such an historian as myself to relate them. For after all, gentle reader, cities *of themselves*, and, in fact, empires *of themselves*, are nothing without an historian. It is the patient narrator who records their prosperity as they rise,—who blazons forth the splendor of their noon-tide meridian,—who props their feeble memorials as they totter to decay,—who gathers together their scattered fragments as they rot,—and who piously, at length, collects their ashes into the mausoleum of his work and rears a monument that will transmit their renown to all succeeding ages.

What has been the fate of many fair cities of antiquity, whose nameless ruins encumber the plains of Europe and Asia, and awaken the fruitless inquiry of the traveller? They have sunk into dust and silence,—they have perished from remembrance for want of an historian! The philanthropist may weep over their desolation,—the poet may wander among their mouldering arches and broken columns, and indulge the visionary flights of his fancy,—but, alas! alas! the modern historian, whose pen, like my own, is doomed to confine itself to dull matter-of-fact, seeks in vain among their oblivious remains for some memorial that may tell the instructive tale of their glory and their ruin.

"Wars, conflagrations, deluges," says Aristotle, "destroy nations, and with them all their monuments, their discoveries, and their vanities. The torch of science has more than once been extinguished and rekindled;—a few individuals, who have escaped by accident, reunite the thread of generations."†

The same sad misfortune which has happened to so many ancient cities will happen again, and from the same sad cause, to nine tenths of those which now flourish on the face of the globe. With most of them the time for recording their early history is gone by; their origin, their foundation, together with the eventful period

*Quotation from *Lectures on Rhetoric and Belles Lettres* (1783), by Scottish clergyman Hugh Blair.
†The quote is unlocated.

of their youth, are forever buried in the rubbish of years; and the same would have been the case with this fair portion of the earth, if I had not snatched it from obscurity in the very nick of time, at the moment that those matters herein recorded were about entering into the wide-spread, insatiable maw of oblivion,—if I had not dragged them out, as it were, by the very locks, just as the monster's adamantine fangs were closing upon them forever! And here have I, as before observed, carefully collected, collated, and arranged them, scrip and scrap, "*punt en punt, gat en gat,*"* and commenced in this little work a history, to serve as a foundation on which other historians may hereafter raise a noble super-structure, swelling in process of time, until *Knickerbocker's New York* may be equally voluminous with *Gibbon's Rome,*† or *Hume and Smollett's England!*‡

And now indulge me for a moment, while I lay down my pen, skip to some little eminence at the distance of two or three hundred years ahead; and, casting back a bird's-eye glance over the waste of years that is to roll between, discover myself—little I—at this moment the progenitor, prototype, and precursor of them all, posted at the head of this host of literary worthies, with my book under my arm, and New York on my back, pressing forward, like a gallant commander, to honor and immortality.

Such are the vainglorious imaginings that will now and then enter into the brain of the author,—that irradiate, as with celestial light, his solitary chamber, cheering his weary spirits, and animating him to persevere in his labors. And I have freely given utterance to these rhapsodies whenever they have occurred; not, I trust, from an unusual spirit of egotism, but merely that the reader may for once have an idea how an author thinks and feels while he is writing,—a kind of knowledge very rare and curious, and much to be desired.

---

*A bad pun in Dutch: "point by point, rump by rump."
†*The History of the Decline and Fall of the Roman Empire,* by English historian Edward Gibbon (6 vols., 1776–1788).
‡In fact, two separate histories sometimes printed together by later publishers: *The History of England from the Invasion of Julius Caesar to the Revolution in 1688,* by Scottish historian David Hume (1754–1762), and *History of England from the Revolution in 1688 to the Death of George III, Designed as a Continuation of Mr. Hume's History,* by Scottish author Tobias Smollett (1757–1758).

BOOK II

Treating of the First Settlement of the Province of Nieuw Nederlandts

Chapter I

IN WHICH ARE CONTAINED DIVERS REASONS WHY
A MAN SHOULD NOT WRITE IN A HURRY; ALSO, OF
MASTER HENDRICK HUDSON, HIS DISCOVERY OF
A STRANGE COUNTRY,—AND HOW HE WAS
MAGNIFICENTLY REWARDED BY THE MUNIFICENCE
OF THEIR HIGH MIGHTINESSES

My great-grandfather, by the mother's side, Hermanus Van Clattercop, when employed to build the large stone church at Rotterdam, which stands about three hundred yards to your left after you turn off from the Boomkeys, and which is so conveniently constructed, that all the zealous Christians of Rotterdam prefer sleeping through a sermon there to any other church in the city,—my great-grandfather, I say, when employed to build that famous church, did in the first place send to Delft for a box of long pipes; then having purchased a new spitting-box and a hundred-weight of the best Virginia, he sat himself down, and did nothing for the space of three months but smoke most laboriously. Then did he spend full three months more in trudging on foot, and voyaging in trekschuit, from Rotterdam to Amsterdam—to Delft— to Haerlem—to Leyden—to the Hague, knocking his head and breaking his pipe against every church in his road. Then did he advance gradually nearer and nearer to Rotterdam, until he came in full sight of the identical spot whereon the church was to be built. Then did he spend three months longer in walking round it and round it, contemplating it, first from one point of view, and then from another,—now would he be paddled by it on the canal,—now would he peep at it through a telescope from the other side of the Meuse, and now would he take a bird's-eye glance at it from the top of one of those gigantic windmills which protect the gates of the city. The good folks of the place were on the tiptoe of expectation and impatience;—notwithstanding all the turmoil of my great-grandfather, not a symptom of the church was yet to be seen; they even began to fear it would never be brought into the world, but that its great projector would lie down and die in labor of the mighty plan he had conceived. At length, having occupied twelve good months in puffing and paddling, and talking and walking,—having travelled over all Holland, and even taken a peep into France and Germany,—having smoked five hundred and ninety-nine pipes, and three hundred-weight of the best Virginia tobacco,—my great-grandfather gathered together all that knowing and industrious class of citizens who prefer attending to anybody's business sooner than their own, and having pulled off his coat and five pair of breeches, he advanced sturdily up and laid the corner-stone of the church, in presence of the whole multitude—just at the commencement of the thirteenth month.

In a similar manner, and with the example of my worthy ancestor full before my eyes, have I proceeded in writing this most authentic history. The honest Rotterdamers no doubt thought my great-grandfather was doing nothing at all to the purpose, while he was making such a world of prefatory bustle about the building of his church—and many of the ingenious inhabitants of this fair city will unquestionably suppose that all the preliminary chapters, with the discovery, population, and final settlement of America, were totally irrelevant and superfluous,—and that the main business, the history of New York, is not a jot more advanced than if I had never taken up my pen. Never were wise people more mistaken in their conjectures: in consequence of going to work slowly and deliberately, the church came out of my grandfather's hands one of the most sumptuous, goodly, and glorious edifices in the known world,—excepting that, like our magnificent capitol, at Washington,* it was begun on so grand a scale that the good folks could not afford to finish more than the wing of it. So, likewise, I trust, if ever I am able to finish this work on the plan I have commenced, (of which, in simple truth, I sometimes have my doubts,) it will be found that I have pursued the latest rules of my art, as exemplified in the writings of all the great American historians, and wrought a very large history out of a small subject,—which, nowadays, is considered one of the great triumphs of historic skill. To proceed, then, with the thread of my story.

In the ever-memorable year of our Lord, 1609, on a Saturday morning, the five-and-twentieth day of March, old style, did that "worthy and irrecoverable discoverer, (as he has justly been called), Master Henry Hudson,"† set sail from Holland in a stout vessel called the Half-Moon, being employed by the Dutch East India Company, to seek a northwest passage to China.

Henry (or, as the Dutch historians call him, Hendrick) Hudson was a seafaring man of renown, who had learned to smoke tobacco under Sir Walter Raleigh,‡ and is said to have been the first to introduce it into Holland, which gained him much popularity in that country, and caused him to find great favor in the eyes of their High Mightinesses, the Lords States General, and also of the honorable West India Company. He was a short, square, brawny old gentleman, with a double chin, a mastiff mouth, and a broad copper nose, which was supposed in those days to have acquired its fiery hue from the constant neighborhood of his tobacco-pipe.

---

*The architectural plan for Washington, D.C., drafted by French-born American architect Pierre Charles L'Enfant in 1791, took decades to complete.
†See endnote 9 to *The Sketch-Book*.
‡Sir Walter Raleigh (1554?–1618), English explorer who sought to establish a colony at Roanoke Island, North Carolina, between 1584 and 1589.

He wore a true Andrea Ferrara,* tucked in a leathern belt, and a commodore's cocked hat on one side of his head. He was remarkable for always jerking up his breeches when he gave out his orders, and his voice sounded not unlike the brattling of a tin trumpet,—owing to the number of hard northwesters which he had swallowed in the course of his seafaring.

Such was Hendrick Hudson, of whom we have heard so much, and know so little; and I have been thus particular in his description for the benefit of modern painters and statuaries, that they may represent him as he was,—and not, according to their common custom with modern heroes, make him look like Cæsar, or Marcus Aurelius, or the Apollo of Belvidere.[†]

As chief mate and favorite companion, the commodore chose master Robert Juet,[‡] of Limehouse, in England. By some his name has been spelled *Chewit,* and ascribed to the circumstances of his having been the first man that ever chewed tobacco; but this I believe to be a mere flippancy; more especially as certain of his progeny are living at this day, who write their names Juet. He was an old comrade and early schoolmate of the great Hudson, with whom he had often played truant and sailed chip boats in a neighboring pond, when they were little boys: from whence it is said that the commodore first derived his bias towards a seafaring life. Certain it is that the old people about Limehouse declared Robert Juet to be an unlucky urchin, prone to mischief, that would one day or other come to the gallows.

He grew up, as boys of that kind often grow up, a rambling, heedless varlet, tossed about in all quarters of the world,—meeting with more perils and wonders than did Sinbad the Sailor,[§] without growing

---

*Broadsword bearing the mark of the famed craftsmen of the Italian house of Ferrara.

[†](Gaius) Julius Caesar (100?–44 B.C.): Roman general and statesman; Marcus Aurelius (A.D. 21–180): Roman emperor and stoic philosopher; Apollo of Belvidere, or Apollo Belvedere: Roman copy of the famous statue of the Greek god Apollo attributed to Leochares (fourth century B.C.), named after the Belvedere Court in Vatican City, where it once stood.

[‡]Robert Juet (died c.1611) was a crewman on Henry Hudson's expedition into Hudson Bay and was set adrift with Hudson after the crew's mutiny (see endnote 9 to *The Sketch-Book*); Juet's journal was included in *Purchas, His Pilgrimes* (1625), travel literature compiled by English clergyman Samuel Purchas.

[§]See footnote on p. 267.

a whit more wise, prudent, or ill-natured. Under every misfortune, he comforted himself with a quid of tobacco, and the truly philosophic maxim, that "it will be all the same thing a hundred years hence." He was skilled in the art of carving anchors and true lover's knots on the bulk-heads and quarter-railings, and was considered a great wit on board ship, in consequence of his playing pranks on everybody around, and now and then even making a wry face at old Hendrick, when his back was turned.

To this universal genius are we indebted for many particulars concerning this voyage; of which he wrote a history, at the request of the commodore, who had an unconquerable aversion to writing himself, from having received so many floggings about it when at school. To supply the deficiencies of master Juet's journal, which is written with true log-book brevity, I have availed myself of divers family traditions, handed down from my great-great-grandfather, who accompanied the expedition in the capacity of cabin-boy.

From all that I can learn, few incidents worthy of remark happened in the voyage; and it mortifies me exceedingly that I have to admit so noted an expedition into my work, without making any more of it.

Suffice it to say, the voyage was prosperous and tranquil; the crew, being a patient people, much given to slumber and vacuity, and but little troubled with the disease of thinking,—a malady of the mind, which is the sure breeder of discontent. Hudson had laid in abundance of gin and sourkrout, and every man was allowed to sleep quietly at his post unless the wind blew. True it is, some slight disaffection was shown on two or three occasions, at certain unreasonable conduct of Commodore Hudson. Thus, for instance, he forbore to shorten sail when the wind was light, and the weather serene, which was considered among the most experienced Dutch seamen as certain *weather-breeders*, or prognostics that the weather would change for the worse. He acted, moreover, in direct contradiction to that ancient and sage rule of the Dutch navigators, who always took in sail at night, put the helm a-port, and turned in,—by which precaution they had a good night's rest, were sure of knowing where they were the next morning, and stood but little chance of running down a continent in the dark. He likewise prohibited the seamen from wearing more than five jackets and six pair of breeches, under pretence of rendering them more alert; and no man was permitted to go aloft and hand in sails with a pipe in his mouth, as is the invariable Dutch custom at the present day. All these grievances, though they might ruffle for a moment the constitutional tranquillity of the honest Dutch tars, made but transient impression;—they ate hugely, drank profusely, and slept immeasurably; and being under the especial guidance of Providence, the ship was safely conducted to the coast of America; where, after sundry unimportant touchings and standings off and on, she at length, on the fourth day of September, entered that majestic bay which at this day expands its ample bosom before the city of New York, and which had never before been visited by any European.*

It has been traditionary in our family, that when the great navigator was first blessed with a view of this enchanting island, he was observed, for the first and only time in his life, to exhibit strong

---

*True it is—and I am not ignorant of the fact—that in a certain apocryphal book of voyages, compiled by one Hakluyt, [Richard Hakluyt (1552?–1616), English geographer whose *The Principall Navigations, Voiages and Discoveries of the English Nation* (1589) gave some of the first European accounts of the New World] is to be found a letter written to Francis the First, by one Giovanne, or John Verazzani, [Or Giovanni da Verrazzano (1485–1528), Italian navigator who explored the New World for the French] on which some writers are inclined to found a belief that this delightful bay had been visited nearly a century previous to the voyage of the enterprising Hudson. Now this (albeit it has met with the countenance of certain very judicious and learned men) I hold in utter disbelief, [worthless] and that for various good and substantial reasons: *First*, Because on strict examination it will be found, that the description given by this Verazzani applies about as well to the bay of New York as it does to my nightcap. *Secondly*, Because that this John Verazzani, for whom I already begin to feel a most bitter enmity, is a native of Florence; and everybody knows the crafty wiles of these losel Florentines, by which they filched away the laurels from the brows of the immortal Colon (vulgarly called Columbus), and bestowed them on their officious townsman, Amerigo Vespucci; [Italian-Spanish explorer (1454–1512) of the New World] and I make no doubt they are equally ready to rob the illustrious Hudson of the credit of discovering this beautiful island, adorned by the city of New York, and placing it beside their usurped discovery of South America. And, *thirdly*, I award my decision in favor of the pretensions of Hendrick Hudson, inasmuch as his expedition sailed from Holland, being truly and absolutely a Dutch enterprise;—and though all the proofs in the world were introduced on the other side, I would set them at naught, as undeserving my attention. If these three reasons be not sufficient to satisfy every burgher of this ancient city, all I can say is, they are degenerate descendants from their venerable Dutch ancestors, and totally unworthy the trouble of convincing. Thus, therefore, the title of Hendrick Hudson to his renowned discovery is fully vindicated.

symptoms of astonishment and admiration. He is said to have turned to master Juet, and uttered these remarkable words, while he pointed towards this paradise of the new world,—"See! there!"—and thereupon, as was always his way when he was uncommonly pleased, he did puff out such clouds of dense tobacco-smoke, that in one minute the vessel was out of sight of land, and master Juet was fain to wait until the winds dispersed this impenetrable fog.

It was indeed,—as my great-grandfather used to say,—though in truth I never heard him, for he died, as might be expected, before I was born,—"It was indeed a spot on which the eye might have revelled forever, in ever new and never-ending beauties." The island of Manhattan spread wide before them, like some sweet vision of fancy, or some fair creation of industrious magic. Its hills of smiling green swelled gently one above another, crowned with lofty trees of luxuriant growth; some pointing their tapering foliage towards the clouds, which were gloriously transparent; and others loaded with a verdant burden of clambering vines, bowing their branches to the earth, that was covered with flowers. On the gentle declivities of the hills were scattered in gay profusion, the dog-wood, the sumach, and the wild brier, whose scarlet berries and white blossoms glowed brightly among the deep green of the surrounding foliage; and here and there a curling column of smoke, rising from the little glens that opened along the shore, seemed to promise the weary voyagers a welcome at the hands of their fellow-creatures. As they stood gazing with entranced attention on the scene before them, a red man, crowned with feathers, issued from one of these glens, and after contemplating in wonder the gallant ship, as she sat like a stately swan swimming on a silver lake, sounded the war-whoop, and bounded into the woods like a wild deer, to the utter astonishment of the phlegmatic Dutchmen, who had never heard such a noise, or witnessed such a caper in their whole lives.

Of the transactions of our adventurers with the savages, and how the latter smoked copper pipes, and ate dried currants; how they brought great store of tobacco and oysters; how they shot one of the ship's crew, and how he was buried, I shall say nothing; being that I consider them unimportant to my history. After tarrying a few days in the bay, in order to refresh themselves after their seafaring, our voyagers weighed anchor, to explore a mighty river which emptied

into the bay. This river, it is said, was known among the savages by
the name of the *Shatemuck*; though we are assured in an excellent
little history published in 1674, by John Josselyn, Gent.,* that it was
called the *Mohegan*,† and master Richard Bloome,‡ who wrote some
time afterwards, asserts the same,—so that I very much incline in
favor of the opinion of these two honest gentlemen. Be this as it may,
up this river did the adventurous Hendrick proceed, little doubting
but it would turn out to be the much looked-for passage to China!

The journal goes on to make mention of divers interviews between the crew and the natives, in the voyage up the river; but as
they would be impertinent to my history, I shall pass over them in
silence, except the following dry joke, played off by the old commodore and his school-fellow, Robert Juet, which does such vast
credit to their experimental philosophy, that I cannot refrain from
inserting it. "Our master and his mate determined to try some of the
chiefe men of the countrey, whether they had any treacherie in
them. So they tooke them downe into the cabin, and gave them so
much wine and aqua vitæ, that they were all merrie; and one of
them had his wife with him, which sate so modestly, as any of our
countrey women would do in a strange place. In the end, one of
them was drunke, which had been aborde of our ship all the time
that we had been there, and that was strange to them, for they could
not tell how to take it."§

Having satisfied himself by this ingenious experiment, that the
natives were an honest, social race of jolly roysters, who had no ob-
jection to a drinking-bout and were very merry in their cups, the old
commodore chuckled hugely to himself, and thrusting a double
quid of tobacco in his cheek, directed master Juet to have it carefully
recorded, for the satisfaction of all the natural philosophers of the
university of Leyden,—which done, he proceeded on his voyage,

---

*John Josselyn (flourished 1638–1675) published two histories in 1674: *An Account
of Two Voyages to New England* and *Chronological Observations of America*.
†This river is likewise laid down in Ogilvy's map as Manhattan—Noordt—
Montaigne and Mauritius river [Irving's note]. See *America*, by John Ogilby
(London, 1671).
‡Richard Blome, author of *The Present State of His Majesties Isles and Territories in
America* (London, 1687).
§Juet's Journ. Purch. Pil. [Irving's note]. See footnote on p. 391.

with great self-complacency. After sailing, however, above an hundred miles up the river, he found the watery world around him began to grow more shallow and confined, the current more rapid, and perfectly fresh,—phenomena not uncommon in the ascent of rivers, but which puzzled the honest Dutchmen prodigiously. A consultation was therefore called, and having deliberated full six hours, they were brought to a determination by the ship's running aground,—whereupon they unanimously concluded, that there was but little chance of getting to China in this direction. A boat, however, was despatched to explore higher up the river, which, on its return, confirmed the opinion; upon this the ship was warped off and put about, with great difficulty, being, like most of her sex, exceedingly hard to govern; and the adventurous Hudson, according to the account of my great-great-grandfather, returned down the river—with a prodigious flea in his ear!

Being satisfied that there was little likelihood of getting to China, unless, like the blind man, he returned from whence he set out, and took a fresh start, he forthwith recrossed the sea to Holland, where he was received with great welcome by the honorable East India Company, who were very much rejoiced to see him come back safe—with their ship; and at a large and respectable meeting of the first merchants and burgomasters of Amsterdam, it was unanimously determined, that, as a munificent reward for the eminent services he had performed, and the important discovery he had made, the great river Mohegan should be called after his name!—and it continues to be called Hudson river unto this very day.

Chapter II

CONTAINING AN ACCOUNT OF A MIGHTY ARK
WHICH FLOATED, UNDER THE PROTECTION OF
ST. NICHOLAS, FROM HOLLAND TO GIBBET ISLAND,—
THE DESCENT OF THE STRANGE ANIMALS
THEREFROM,—A GREAT VICTORY, AND A
DESCRIPTION OF THE ANCIENT
VILLAGE OF COMMUNIPAW

The delectable accounts given by the great Hudson, and master Juet, of the country they had discovered, excited not a little talk and speculation among the good people of Holland. Letters-patent were granted by government to an association of merchants, called the West India Company, for the exclusive trade on Hudson river, on which they erected a trading-house, called Fort Aurania, or Orange, from whence did spring the great city of Albany. But I forbear to dwell on the various commercial and colonizing enterprises which took place,— among which was that of Mynheer Adrian Block,* who discovered and gave a name to Block Island, since famous for its cheese,— and shall barely confine myself to that which gave birth to this renowned city.

It was some three or four years after the return of the immortal Hendrick, that a crew of honest, Low-Dutch colonists set sail from the city of Amsterdam for the shores of America. It is an irreparable loss to history, and a great proof of the darkness of the age, and the lamentable neglect of the noble art of book-making, since so

*See footnote on p. 353.

industriously cultivated by knowing sea-captains, and learned supercargoes, that an expedition so interesting and important in its results should be passed over in utter silence. To my great-great-grandfather am I again indebted for the few facts I am enabled to give concerning it,—he having once more embarked for this country, with a full determination, as he said, of ending his days here, and of begetting a race of Knickerbockers that should rise to be great men in the land.

The ship in which these illustrious adventurers set sail was called the *Goede Vrouw*, or good woman, in compliment to the wife of the President of the West India Company, who was allowed by every-body (except her husband) to be a sweet-tempered lady—when not in liquor. It was in truth a most gallant vessel, of the most approved Dutch construction, and made by the ablest ship-carpenters of Amsterdam, who, it is well known, always model their ships after the fair forms of their countrywomen. Accordingly it had one hundred feet in the beam, one hundred feet in the keel, and one hundred feet from the bottom of the stern-post to the tafferel. Like the beauteous model, who was declared to be the greatest belle in Amsterdam, it was full in the bows, with a pair of enormous cat-heads, a copper bottom, and withal a most prodigious poop!

The architect, who was somewhat of a religious man, far from decorating the ship with pagan idols, such as Jupiter, Neptune, or Hercules,* (which heathenish abominations, I have no doubt, occasion the misfortunes and shipwreck of many a noble vessel),— he, I say on the contrary, did laudably erect for a head, a goodly image of St. Nicholas, equipped with a low, broad-brimmed hat, a huge pair of Flemish trunk-hose, and a pipe that reached to the end of the bowsprit. Thus gallantly furnished, the stanch ship floated sideways, like a majestic goose, out of the harbor of the great city of Amsterdam, and all the bells, that were not otherwise engaged, rang a triple bob-major on the joyful occasion.

My great-great-grandfather remarks, that the voyage was uncommonly prosperous, for, being under the especial care of the

---

*Figures of classical mythology: Jupiter, supreme ruler of the Roman gods; Neptune, Roman god of the sea; and the hero Hercules, who possessed remarkable strength and the courage to accomplish any task.

ever-revered St. Nicholas,* the Goede Vrouw seemed to be endowed with qualities unknown to common vessels. Thus she made as much leeway as headway, could get along very nearly as fast with the wind ahead as when it was a-poop,—and was particularly great in a calm; in consequence of which singular advantages she made out to accomplish her voyage in a very few months, and came to anchor at the mouth of the Hudson, a little to the east of Gibbet Island.

Here, lifting up their eyes, they beheld, on what is at present called the Jersey shore, a small Indian village, pleasantly embowered in a grove of spreading elms, and the natives all collected on the beach, gazing in stupid admiration at the Goede Vrouw. A boat was immediately despatched to enter into a treaty with them, and approaching the shore, hailed them through a trumpet, in the most friendly terms; but so horribly confounded were these poor savages at the tremendous and uncouth sound of the Low-Dutch language, that they one and all took to their heels, and scampered over the Bergen hills; nor did they stop until they had buried themselves, head and ears, in the marshes on the other side, where they all miserably perished to a man;—and their bones, being collected and decently covered by the Tammany Society[†] of that day, formed that singular mound called RATTLESNAKE HILL, which rises out of the centre of the salt marshes a little to the east of the Newark Causeway.

Animated by this unlooked-for victory, our valiant heroes sprang ashore in triumph, took possession of the soil as conquerors, in the name of their High Mightinesses the Lords States General; and, marching fearlessly forward, carried the village of COMMUNIPAW by storm, notwithstanding that it was vigorously defended by some half a score of old squaws and pappooses. On looking about them they were so transported with the excellencies of the place, that they had very little doubt the blessed St. Nicholas had guided them thither, as the very spot whereon to settle their colony. The softness of the soil was wonderfully adapted to the driving of piles; the swamps and marshes around them afforded ample opportunities for the

---

*The imagery and customs associated with St. Nicholas in Irving's *A History of New York* contributed to the spread of the Santa Claus tradition in American culture.
[†]Fraternal organization in New York City founded in 1786; it became the political machine of the Democratic Party in the early decades of the nineteenth century.

constructing of dykes and dams; the shallowness of the shore was peculiarly favorable to the building of docks;—in a word, this spot abounded with all the requisites for the foundation of a great Dutch city. On making a faithful report, therefore, to the crew of the Goede Vrouw, they one and all determined that this was the destined end of their voyage. Accordingly they descended from the Goede Vrouw, men, women, and children, in goodly groups, as did the animals of yore from the ark,* and formed themselves into a thriving settlement, which they called by the Indian name COMMUNIPAW.

As all the world is doubtless perfectly acquainted with Communipaw, it may seem somewhat superfluous to treat of it in the present work; but my readers will please to recollect, notwithstanding it is my chief desire to satisfy the present age, yet I write likewise for posterity, and have to consult the understanding and curiosity of some half a score of centuries yet to come, by which time, perhaps, were it not for this invaluable history, the great Communipaw, like Babylon, Carthage, Nineveh,† and other great cities, might be perfectly extinct,—sunk and forgotten in its own mud,—its inhabitants turned into oysters,‡ and even its situation a fertile subject of learned controversy and hard-headed investigation among indefatigable historians. Let me then piously rescue from oblivion the humble relics of a place, which was the egg from whence was hatched the mighty city of New York!

Communipaw is at present but a small village, pleasantly situated, among rural scenery, on that beauteous part of the Jersey shore which was known in ancient legends by the name of Pavonia,§ and commands a grand prospect of the superb bay of New York. It is within but half an hour's sail of the latter place, provided you have a fair wind, and may be distinctly seen from the city. Nay, it is a well-known fact, which I can testify from my own experience, that on a clear, still summer evening, you may hear, from the Battery of

---

*Noah's ark; see the Bible, Genesis 6–8.
†Razed cities of antiquity.
‡Men by inaction degenerate into oysters.—Kaimes [Irving's note]. Possibly a quote by Henry Home, Lord Kames, Scottish lawyer and philosopher best known for his *Elements of Criticism* (3 vols., 1762).
§Pavonia, in the ancient maps, is given to a tract of country extending from about Hoboken to Amboy [Irving's note].

New York, the obstreperous peals of broad-mouthed laughter of the Dutch negroes at Communipaw, who, like most other negroes, are famous for their risible powers. This is peculiarly the case on Sunday evenings, when, it is remarked by an ingenious and observant philosopher, who has made great discoveries in the neighborhood of this city, that they always laugh loudest, which he attributes to the circumstance of their having their holiday clothes on.

These negroes, in fact, like the monks of the dark ages, engross all the knowledge of the place, and being infinitely more adventurous and more knowing than their masters, carry on all the foreign trade; making frequent voyages to town in canoes loaded with oysters, buttermilk, and cabbages. They are great astrologers, predicting the different changes of weather almost as accurately as an almanac; they are moreover exquisite performers on three-stringed fiddles; in whistling they almost boast the far-famed powers of Orpheus's lyre,* for not a horse or an ox in the place, when at the plough or before the wagon, will budge a foot until he hears the well-known whistle of his black driver and companion.—And from their amazing skill at casting up accounts upon their fingers, they are regarded with as much veneration as were the disciples of Pythagoras[†] of yore, when initiated into the sacred quaternary of numbers.

As to the honest burghers of Communipaw, like wise men and sound philosophers, they never look beyond their pipes, nor trouble their heads about any affairs out of their immediate neighborhood; so that they live in profound and enviable ignorance of all the troubles, anxieties, and revolutions of this distracted planet. I am even told that many among them do verily believe that Holland, of which they have heard so much from tradition, is situated somewhere on Long Island,—that *Spiking-devil* and *the Narrows* are the two ends of the world,—that the country is still under the dominion of their High Mightinesses,—and that the city of New York still goes by the name of Nieuw Amsterdam. They meet every Saturday afternoon at the only tavern in the place, which bears as a sign a square-headed likeness of the Prince of Orange, where they smoke a

---

*The lyre of Orpheus, a celebrated musician of Greek myth, could charm all creatures.
[†]Greek philosopher and mathematician (c.580–c.500 B.C.) who believed that all knowledge could be reduced to numerical relationships.

silent pipe, by way of promoting social conviviality, and invariably drink a mug of cider to the success of Admiral Van Tromp,* who they imagine is still sweeping the British channel, with a broom at his mast-head.[†]

Communipaw, in short, is one of the numerous little villages in the vicinity of this most beautiful of cities, which are so many strongholds and fastnesses, whither the primitive manners of our Dutch forefathers have retreated, and where they are cherished with devout and scrupulous strictness. The dress of the original settlers is handed down inviolate, from father to son: the identical broad-brimmed hat, broad-skirted coat, and broad-bottomed breeches, continue from generation to generation; and several gigantic knee-buckles of massy silver are still in wear, that made gallant display in the days of the patriarchs of Communipaw. The language likewise continues unadulterated by barbarous innovations; and so critically correct is the village schoolmaster in his dialect, that his reading of a Low-Dutch psalm has much the same effect on the nerves as the filing of a handsaw.

---

*Hereditary title of the ruler of the Dutch empire from 1572 to 1795.
[†]After defeating British admiral Robert Blake in 1652, Dutch admiral Maarten Harpertszoon Tromp sailed up and down the English Channel with a broom tied to his masthead as a sign that he would sweep the British navy from the seas.

Chapter VII

HOW THE PEOPLE OF PAVONIA MIGRATED FROM COMMUNIPAW TO THE ISLAND OF MANNA-HATA— AND HOW OLOFFE THE DREAMER PROVED HIMSELF A GREAT LAND-SPECULATOR

It having been solemnly resolved that the seat of empire should be removed from the green shores of Pavonia to the pleasant island of Manna-hata, everybody was anxious to embark under the standard of Oloffe the Dreamer,* and to be among the first sharers of the promised land. A day was appointed for the grand migration, and on that day little Communipaw was in a buzz and a bustle like a hive in swarming-time. Houses were turned inside out and stripped of the venerable furniture which had come from Holland; all the community, great and small, black and white, man, woman, and child, was in commotion, forming lines from the houses to the water-side, like lines of ants from an ant-hill; everybody laden with some article of household furniture; while busy housewives plied backwards and forwards along the lines, helping everything forward by the nimbleness of their tongues.

By degrees a fleet of boats and canoes were piled up with all kinds of household articles: ponderous tables; chests of drawers resplendent with brass ornament's; quaint corner-cupboards; beds and bedsteads; with any quantity of pots, kettles, frying-pans, and Dutch ovens. In each boat embarked a whole family, from the robustious burgher down to the cats and dogs and little negroes. In this way they set off

---

*Oloff Van Cortlandt (1600–1684), one of the founders of the Dutch colony at Manhattan.

across the mouth of the Hudson, under the guidance of Oloffe the Dreamer, who hoisted his standard on the leading boat.

This memorable migration took place on the first of May, and was long cited in tradition as the *grand moving*. The anniversary of it was piously observed among the "sons of the pilgrims of Communipaw," by turning their houses topsy-turvy and carrying all the furniture through the streets, in emblem of the swarming of the parent-hive; and this is the real origin of the universal agitation and "moving" by which this most restless of cities is literally turned out of doors on every May-day.

As the little squadron from Communipaw drew near to the shores of Manna-hata, a sachem, at the head of a band of warriors, appeared to oppose their landing. Some of the most zealous of the pilgrims were for chastising this insolence with powder and ball, according to the approved mode of discoverers; but the sage Oloffe gave them the significant sign of St. Nicholas, laying his finger beside his nose and winking hard with one eye; whereupon his followers perceived that there was something sagacious in the wind. He now addressed the Indians in the blandest terms; and made such tempting display of beads, hawks'-bells, and red blankets, that he was soon permitted to land, and a great land-speculation ensued. And here, let me give the true story of the original purchase of the site of this renowned city, about which so much has been said and written. Some affirm that the first cost was but sixty guilders. The learned Dominie Heckwelder records a tradition* that the Dutch discoverers bargained for only so much land as the hide of a bullock would cover; but that they cut the hide in strips no thicker than a child's finger, so as to take in a large portion of land, and to take in the Indians into the bargain. This, however, is an old fable which the worthy Dominie may have borrowed from antiquity. The true version is, that Oloffe Van Kortlandt bargained for just so much land as a man could cover with his nether garments. The terms being concluded, he produced his friend Mynheer Ten Broeck as the man

---

*MSS. of the Rev. John Heckwelder; New York Historical Society [Irving's note]. John Heckwelder (1743–1823) was a Moravian missionary to the Native American tribes in the Ohio River Valley. He transcribed an account of the Dutch settlement of Manhattan from elders of the Delaware and Mohegan tribes. See the New York Historical Society Collections, second series, vol. 1 (1841), pages 71–74.

whose breeches were to be used in measurement. The simple savages, whose ideas of a man's nether garments had never expanded beyond the dimensions of a breech-clout, stared with astonishment and dismay as they beheld this bulbous-bottomed burgher peeled like an onion, and breeches after breeches spread forth over the land until they covered the actual site of this venerable city.

This is the true history of the adroit bargain by which the island of Manhattan was bought for sixty guilders; and in corroboration of it I will add, that Mynheer Ten Breeches, for his services on this memorable occasion, was elevated to the office of land-measurer; which he ever afterwards exercised in the colony.

Chapter IX

HOW THE CITY OF NEW AMSTERDAM WAXED GREAT
UNDER THE PROTECTION OF
ST. NICHOLAS AND THE ABSENCE OF
LAWS AND STATUTES—HOW OLOFFE THE DREAMER
BEGAN TO DREAM OF AN EXTENSION OF EMPIRE,
AND OF THE
EFFECT OF HIS DREAMS

There is something exceedingly delusive in thus looking back through the long vista of departed years, and catching a glimpse of the fairy realms of antiquity. Like a landscape melting into distance, they receive a thousand charms from their very obscurity, and the fancy delights to fill up their outlines with graces and excellences of its own creation. Thus loom on my imagination those happier days of our city, when as yet New Amsterdam was a mere pastoral town, shrouded in groves of sycamores and willows, and surrounded by trackless forests and wide-spreading waters, that seemed to shut out all the cares and vanities of a wicked world.

In those days did this embryo city present the rare and noble spectacle of a community governed without laws; and thus being left to its own course, and the fostering care of Providence, increased as rapidly as though it had been burdened with a dozen panniers full of those sage laws usually heaped on the backs of young cities—in order to make them grow. And in this particular I greatly admire the wisdom and sound knowledge of human nature, displayed by the sage Oloffe the Dreamer and his fellow-legislators. For my part, I have not so bad an opinion of mankind as many of my brother philosophers. I do not think poor human nature so sorry a piece of workmanship as they would make it out to be; and as far as I have observed, I am fully satisfied that man, if left to himself, would about as readily go right as wrong. It is only this eternally sounding in his ears that it is his duty to go right, which makes him go the very reverse. The noble independence of his nature revolts at this intolerable tyranny of law, and the perpetual interference of officious morality, which are ever besetting his path with finger-posts and directions to "keep to the right, as the law directs"; and like a spirited urchin, he turns directly contrary, and gallops through mud and mire, over hedges and ditches, merely to show that he is a lad of spirit, and out of his leading-strings. And these opinions are amply substantiated by what I have above said of our worthy ancestors; who never being be-preached and be-lectured, and guided and governed by statutes and laws and by-laws, as are their more enlightened descendants, did one and all demean themselves honestly and peaceably, out of pure ignorance, or, in other words, because they knew no better.

Nor must I omit to record one of the earliest measures of this infant settlement, inasmuch as it shows the piety of our forefathers, and that, like good Christians, they were always ready to serve God, after they had first served themselves. Thus, having quietly settled themselves down, and provided for their own comfort, they bethought themselves of testifying their gratitude to the great and good St. Nicholas, for his protecting care, in guiding them to this delectable abode. To this end they built a fair and goodly chapel within the fort, which they consecrated to his name; whereupon he immediately took the town of New Amsterdam under his peculiar patronage, and he has ever since been, and I devoutly hope will ever be, the tutelar saint of this excellent city.

At this early period was instituted that pious ceremony, still religiously observed in all our ancient families of the right breed, of hanging up a stocking in the chimney on St. Nicholas eve; which stocking is always found in the morning miraculously filled; for the good St. Nicholas has ever been a great giver of gifts, particularly to children.

I am moreover told that there is a little legendary book, somewhere extant, written in Low Dutch, which says, that the image of this renowned saint, which whilom graced the bowsprit of the Goede Vrouw, was elevated in front of this chapel, in the centre of what in modern days is called the Bowling Green,—on the very spot, in fact, where he appeared in vision to Oloffe the Dreamer. And the legend further treats of divers miracles wrought by the mighty pipe which the saint held in his mouth, a whiff of which was a sovereign cure for indigestion,—an invaluable relic in this colony of brave trencher-men. As, however, in spite of the most diligent search, I cannot lay my hands upon this little book, I must confess that I entertain considerable doubt on the subject.

Thus benignly fostered by the good St. Nicholas, the infant city thrived apace. Hordes of painted savages, it is true, still lurked about the unsettled parts of the island. The hunter still pitched his bower of skins and bark beside the rills that ran through the cool and shady glens, while here and there might be seen, on some sunny knoll, a group of Indian wigwams, whose smoke arose above the neighboring trees, and floated in the transparent atmosphere. A mutual good-will, however, existed between these wandering beings and the burghers of New Amsterdam. Our benevolent forefathers endeavored as much as possible to ameliorate their situation, by giving them gin, rum, and glass beads, in exchange for their peltries; for it seems the kind-hearted Dutchmen had conceived a great friendship for their savage neighbors, on account of their being pleasant men to trade with, and little skilled in the art of making a bargain.

Now and then a crew of these half-human sons of the forest would make their appearance in the streets of New Amsterdam, fantastically painted and decorated with beads and flaunting feathers, sauntering about with an air of listless indifference,—sometimes in the marketplace, instructing the little Dutch boys in the use of the bow and arrow,—at other times, inflamed with liquor, swaggering and whooping and yelling about the town like so many fiends, to the great dismay of all the good wives, who would hurry their children into the house, fasten the doors, and throw water upon the enemy from the garret windows. It is worthy of mention here, that our fore-fathers were very particular in holding up these wild men as excel-lent domestic examples—and for reasons that may be gathered from the history of master Ogilby, who tells us, that "for the least offence the bridegroom soundly beats his wife and turns her out of doors, and marries another, insomuch that some of them have every year a new wife."* Whether this awful example had any influence or not, history does not mention; but it is certain that our grandmothers were miracles of fidelity and obedience.

True it is, that the good understanding between our ancestors and their savage neighbors was liable to occasional interruptions, and I have heard my grandmother, who was a very wise old woman, and well versed in the history of these parts, tell a long story of a winter's evening, about a battle between the New Amsterdammers and the Indians, which was known by the name of the *Peach War*, and which took place near a peach orchard, in a dark glen, which for a long while went by the name of Murderer's Valley.

The legend of this sylvan war was long current among the nurses, old wives, and other ancient chroniclers of the place; but time and improvement have almost obliterated both the tradition and the scene of battle; for what was once the blood-stained valley is now in the centre of this populous city, and known by the name of *Dey Street*.

I know not whether it was to this "Peach war," and the acquisitions of Indian land which may have grown out of it, that we may ascribe the first seeds of the spirit of "annexation" which now began to manifest themselves. Hitherto the ambition of the worthy burghers had been confined to the lovely island of Manna-hata; and Spiten Devil on the Hudson, and Hell-gate on the Sound, were to them the pillars of Hercules,† the *ne plus ultra*‡ of human enterprise. Shortly after the Peach war, however, a restless spirit was observed among the New Amsterdammers, who began to cast wistful looks upon the wild lands of their Indian neighbors; for, somehow or other, wild Indian land always looks greener in the eyes of settlers than the land they occupy. It is hinted that Oloffe the Dreamer encouraged these notions; having, as has been shown, the inherent spirit of a land speculator, which had been wonderfully quickened and expanded since he had become a landholder. Many of the

---

*See footnote on p. 395.
†That is, the ends of the earth, after the ancient name for the two promontories at the eastern end of the Straits of Gibraltar, where the Mediterranean Sea meets the Atlantic.
‡The utmost limit (Latin).

common people, who had never before owned a foot of land, now began to be discontented with the town lots which had fallen to their shares; others, who had snug farms and tobacco-plantations, found they had not sufficient elbow-room, and began to question the rights of the Indians to the vast regions they pretended to hold— while the good Oloffe indulged in magnificent dreams of foreign conquest and great patroonships in the wilderness.

The result of these dreams were certain exploring expeditions, sent forth in various directions, to "sow the seeds of empire," as it was said. The earliest of these were conducted by Hans Reinier Oothout, an old navigator, famous for the sharpness of his vision, who could see land when it was quite out of sight to ordinary mortals, and who had a spy-glass covered with a bit of tarpauling, with which he could spy up the crookedest river quite to its head-waters. He was accompanied by Mynheer Ten Breeches, as land-measurer, in case of any dispute with the Indians.

What was the consequence of these exploring expeditions? In a little while we find a frontier post or trading-house called Fort Nassau, established far to the south on Delaware River; another, called Fort Goed Hoep (or Good Hope), on the Varsche, or Fresh, or Connecticut River, and another, called Fort Aurania (now Albany), away up the Hudson River; while the boundaries of the province kept extending on every side, nobody knew whither, far into the regions of Terra Incognita.

Of the boundary feuds and troubles which the ambitious little province brought upon itself by these indefinite expansions of its territory, we shall treat at large in the after-pages of this eventful history; sufficient for the present is it to say that the swelling importance of the New Netherlands awakened the attention of the mother-country, who, finding it likely to yield much revenue and no trouble, began to take that interest in its welfare which knowing people evince for rich relations.

But as this opens a new era in the fortunes of New Amsterdam, I will here put an end to this second book of my history, and will treat of the maternal policy of the mother-country in my next.

BOOK III

In Which is Recorded the Golden Reign of Wouter Van Twiller*

Chapter I

OF THE RENOWNED WOUTER VAN TWILLER,
HIS UNPARALLELED VIRTUES   AS LIKEWISE
HIS UNUTTERABLE WISDOM IN THE
LAW-CASE OF WANDLE SCHOONHOVEN AND BARENT
BLEECKER—AND THE GREAT ADMIRATION OF THE
PUBLIC THEREAT

Grievous and very much to be commiserated is the task of the feeling historian, who writes the history of his native land. If it fall to his lot to be the recorder of calamity or crime, the mournful page is watered with his tears; nor can he recall the most

---

*Second Dutch director-general of New Netherland (1632–1637).

prosperous and blissful era, without a melancholy sigh at the reflection that it has passed away forever! I know not whether it be owing to an immoderate love for the simplicity of former times, or to that certain tenderness of heart incident to all sentimental historians; but I candidly confess that I cannot look back on the happier days of our city, which I now describe, without great dejection of spirit. With faltering hand do I withdraw the curtain of oblivion, that veils the modest merit of our venerable ancestors, and as their figures rise to my mental vision, humble myself before their mighty shades.

Such are my feelings when I revisit the family mansion of the Knickerbockers, and spend a lonely hour in the chamber where hang the portraits of my forefathers, shrouded in dust, like the forms they represent. With pious reverence do I gaze on the countenances of those renowned burghers, who have preceded me in the steady march of existence,—whose sober and temperate blood now meanders through my veins, flowing slower and slower in its feeble conduits, until its current shall soon be stopped forever!

These, I say to myself, are but frail memorials of the mighty men who flourished in the days of the patriarchs; but who, alas, have long since mouldered in that tomb towards which my steps are insensibly and irresistibly hastening! As I pace the darkened chamber and lose myself in melancholy musings, the shadowy images around me almost seem to steal once more into existence,—their countenances to assume the animation of life,—their eyes to pursue me in every movement! Carried away by the delusions of fancy, I almost imagine myself surrounded by the shades of the departed, and holding sweet converse with the worthies of antiquity! Ah, hapless Diedrich! born in a degenerate age, abandoned to the buffetings of fortune,— a stranger and a weary pilgrim in thy native land,—blest with no weeping wife, nor family of helpless children, but doomed to wander neglected through those crowded streets, and elbowed by foreign upstarts from those fair abodes where once thine ancestors held sovereign empire!

Let me not, however, lose the historian in the man, nor suffer the doting recollections of age to overcome me, while dwelling with fond garrulity on the virtuous days of the patriarchs,—on those sweet days of simplicity and ease, which never more will dawn on the lovely island of Manna-hata.

These melancholy reflections have been forced from me by the growing wealth and importance of New Amsterdam, which, I plainly perceive, are to involve it in all kinds of perils and disasters. Already, as I observed at the close of my last book, they had awakened the attentions of the mother-country. The usual mark of protection shown by mother-countries to wealthy colonies was forthwith manifested; a governor being sent out to rule over the province, and squeeze out of it as much revenue as possible. The arrival of a governor of course put an end to the protectorate of Oloffe the Dreamer. He appears, however, to have dreamt to some purpose during his sway, as we find him afterwards living as a patroon on a great landed estate on the banks of the Hudson; having virtually forfeited all right to his ancient appellation of Kortlandt or Lackland.

It was in the year of our Lord 1629 that Mynheer Wouter Van Twiller was appointed governor of the province of Nieuw Nederlandts, under the commission and control of their High Mightinesses the Lords States General of the United Netherlands, and the privileged West India Company.

This renowned old gentleman arrived at New Amsterdam in the merry month of June, the sweetest month in all the year; when dan Apollo* seems to dance up the transparent firmament,—when the robin, the thrush, and a thousand other wanton songsters, make the woods to resound with amorous ditties, and the luxurious little boblincon revels among the clover-blossoms of the meadows,—all which happy coincidence persuaded the old dames of New Amsterdam, who were skilled in the art of foretelling events, that this was to be a happy and prosperous administration.

The renowned Wouter (or Walter) Van Twiller was descended from a long line of Dutch burgomasters, who had successively dozed away their lives, and grown fat upon the bench of magistracy in Rotterdam; and who had comported themselves with such singular wisdom and propriety, that they were never either heard or talked of—which, next to being universally applauded, should be the object of ambition of all magistrates and rulers. There are two opposite ways by which some men make a figure in the world: one, by talking faster than they think, and the other, by holding their tongues and not

---

*That is, the sun; after Phoebus Apollo, the god of light in Greek mythology.

thinking at all. By the first, many a smatterer acquires the reputation of a man of quick parts; by the other, many a dunderpate, like the owl, the stupidest of birds, comes to be considered the very type of wisdom. This, by the way, is a casual remark, which I would not, for the universe, have it thought I apply to Governor Van Twiller. It is true he was a man shut up within himself, like an oyster, and rarely spoke, except in monosyllables; but then it was allowed he seldom said a foolish thing. So invincible was his gravity that he was never known to laugh or even to smile through the whole course of a long and prosperous life. Nay, if a joke were uttered in his presence, that set light-minded hearers in a roar, it was observed to throw him into a state of perplexity. Sometimes he would deign to inquire into the matter, and when, after much explanation, the joke was made as plain as a pike-staff, he would continue to smoke his pipe in silence, and at length, knocking out the ashes, would exclaim, "Well! I see nothing in all that to laugh about."

With all his reflective habits, he never made up his mind on a subject. His adherents accounted for this by the astonishing magnitude of his ideas. He conceived every subject on so grand a scale that he had not room in his head to turn it over and examine both sides of it. Certain it is, that, if any matter were propounded to him on which ordinary mortals would rashly determine at first glance, he would put on a vague, mysterious look, shake his capacious head, smoke some time in profound silence, and at length observe, that "he had his doubts about the matter"; which gained him the reputation of a man slow of belief and not easily imposed upon. What is more, it gained him a lasting name; for to this habit of the mind has been attributed his surname of Twiller; which is said to be a corruption of the original Twijfler, or, in plain English, *Doubter*.

The person of this illustrious old gentleman was formed and proportioned, as though it had been moulded by the hands of some cunning Dutch statuary, as a model of majesty and lordly grandeur. He was exactly five feet six inches in height, and six feet five inches in circumference. His head was a perfect sphere, and of such stupendous dimensions, that Dame Nature, with all her sex's ingenuity, would have been puzzled to construct a neck capable of supporting it; wherefore she wisely declined the attempt, and settled it firmly on the top of his backbone, just between the shoulders. His body was oblong and particularly capacious at bottom; which was wisely ordered by Providence, seeing that he was a man of sedentary habits, and very averse to the idle labor of walking. His legs were short, but sturdy in proportion to the weight they had to sustain; so that when erect he had not a little the appearance of a beer-barrel on skids. His face, that infallible index of the mind, presented a vast expanse, unfurrowed by any of those lines and angles which disfigure the human countenance with what is termed expression. Two small grey eyes twinkled feebly in the midst, like two stars of lesser magnitude in a hazy firmament, and his full-fed cheeks, which seemed to have taken toll of everything that went into his mouth, were curiously mottled and streaked with dusky red, like a spitzenberg apple.

His habits were as regular as his person. He daily took his four stated meals, appropriating exactly an hour to each; he smoked and doubted eight hours, and he slept the remaining twelve of the four-and-twenty. Such was the renowned Wouter Van Twiller,— true philosopher, for his mind was either elevated above, or tranquilly settled below, the cares and perplexities of this world. He had lived in it for years, without feeling the least curiosity to know whether the sun revolved round it, or it round the sun; and he had watched, for at least half a century, the smoke curling from his pipe to the ceiling, without once troubling his head with any of those numerous theories by which a philosopher would have perplexed his brain, in accounting for its rising above the surrounding atmosphere.

In his council he presided with great state and solemnity. He sat in a huge chair of solid oak, hewn in the celebrated forest of the Hague, fabricated by an experienced timmerman of Amsterdam, and curiously carved about the arms and feet, into exact imitations of gigantic eagle's claws. Instead of a sceptre, he swayed a long Turkish pipe, wrought with jasmin and amber, which had been presented to a stadtholder of Holland at the conclusion of a treaty with one of the petty Barbary powers.* In this stately chair would he sit, and this magnificent pipe would he smoke, shaking his right knee with a

---

*See endnote 2 to *Salmagundi*.

constant motion, and fixing his eye for hours together upon a little print of Amsterdam, which hung in a black frame against the opposite wall of the council-chamber. Nay, it has even been said, that when any deliberation of extraordinary length and intricacy was on the carpet, the renowned Wouter would shut his eyes for full two hours at a time, that he might not be disturbed by external objects; and at such times the internal commotion of his mind was evinced by certain regular guttural sounds, which his admirers declared were merely the noise of conflict, made by his contending doubts and opinions.

It is with infinite difficulty I have been enabled to collect these biographical anecdotes of the great man under consideration. The facts respecting him were so scattered and vague, and divers of them so questionable in point of authenticity, that I have had to give up the search after many, and decline the admission of still more, which would have tended to heighten the coloring of his portrait.

I have been the more anxious to delineate fully the person and habits of Wouter Van Twiller, from the consideration that he was not only the first, but also the best governor that ever presided over this ancient and respectable province; and so tranquil and benevolent was his reign, that I do not find throughout the whole of it a single instance of any offender being brought to punishment,—a most indubitable sign of a merciful governor, and a case unparalleled, excepting in the reign of the illustrious King Log,* from whom, it is hinted, the renowned Van Twiller was a lineal descendant.

The very outset of the career of this excellent magistrate was distinguished by an example of legal acumen, that gave flattering presage of a wise and equitable administration. The morning after he had been installed in office, and at the moment that he was making his breakfast from a prodigious earthen dish, filled with milk and Indian pudding, he was interrupted by the appearance of Wandle Schoonhoven, a very important old burgher of New Amsterdam, who complained bitterly of one Barent Bleecker, inasmuch as he

---

*In Aesop's fable "The Frogs Desiring a King," Jove (Zeus) throws down a log in answer to the frogs' prayer for a great ruler; when the frogs become dissatisfied, he sends them a stork, which devours them. The lesson is that a ruler who does nothing is preferable to a tyrant.

refused to come to a settlement of accounts, seeing that there was a heavy balance in favor of the said Wandle. Governor Van Twiller, as I have already observed, was a man of few words; he was likewise a mortal enemy to multiplying writings—or being disturbed at his breakfast. Having listened attentively to the statement of Wandle Schoonhoven, giving an occasional grunt, as he shovelled a spoonful of Indian pudding into his mouth,—either as a sign that he relished the dish, or comprehended the story,—he called unto him his constable, and pulling out of his breeches-pocket a huge jack-knife, dispatched it after the defendant as a summons, accompanied by his tobacco-box as a warrant.

This summary process was as effectual in those simple days as was the seal-ring of the great Haroun Alraschid* among the true believers. The two parties being confronted before him, each produced a book of accounts, written in a language and character that would have puzzled any but a High-Dutch commentator, or a learned decipherer of Egyptian obelisks. The sage Wouter took them one after the other, and having poised them in his hands, and attentively counted over the number of leaves, fell straightway into a very great doubt, and smoked for half an hour without saying a word; at length, laying his finger beside his nose, and shutting his eyes for a moment, with the air of a man who has just caught a subtle idea by the tail, he slowly took his pipe from his mouth, puffed forth a column of tobacco-smoke, and with marvellous gravity and solemnity pronounced, that, having carefully counted over the leaves and weighed the books, it was found, that one was just as thick and as heavy as the other: therefore, it was the final opinion of the court that the accounts were equally balanced: therefore, Wandle should give Barent a receipt, and Barent should give Wandle a receipt, and the constable should pay the costs.

This decision, being straightway made known, diffused general joy throughout New Amsterdam, for the people immediately perceived that they had a very wise and equitable magistrate to rule over them. But its happiest effect was, that not another lawsuit took place throughout the whole of his administration; and the office of constable fell into such decay, that there was not one of those losel

---

*Caliph in the *Arabian Nights* tale "Abou Hassan, or the Sleeper Awakened."

scouts known in the province for many years. I am the more particular in dwelling on this transaction, not only because I deem it one of the most sage and righteous judgments on record, and well worthy the attention of modern magistrates, but because it was a miraculous event in the history of the renowned Wouter—being the only time he was ever known to come to a decision in the whole course of his life.

Chapter IV

CONTAINING FURTHER PARTICULARS OF THE GOLDEN
AGE, AND WHAT CONSTITUTED A FINE LADY AND
GENTLEMAN IN THE DAYS OF WALTER THE DOUBTER

In this dulcet period of my history, when the beauteous island of
Manna-hata presented a scene, the very counterpart of those
glowing pictures drawn of the golden reign of Saturn,* there
was, as I have before observed, a happy ignorance, an honest
simplicity prevalent among its inhabitants, which, were I even able
to depict, would be but little understood by the degenerate age
for which I am doomed to write. Even the female sex, those arch
innovators upon the tranquillity, the honesty, and gray-beard customs
of society, seemed for a while to conduct themselves with incredible
sobriety and comeliness.

Their hair, untortured by the abominations of art, was scrupulously pomatumed back from their foreheads with a candle, and
covered with a little cap of quilted calico, which fitted exactly to their
heads. Their petticoats of linsey-woolsey were striped with a variety
of gorgeous dyes,—though I must confess these gallant garments
were rather short, scarce reaching below the knee; but then they
made up in the number, which generally equalled that of the gentleman's small-clothes; and what is still more praiseworthy, they were
all of their own manufacture,—of which circumstance, as may well
be supposed, they were not a little vain.

These were the honest days in which every woman staid at home,
read the Bible, and wore pockets,—ay, and that too of a goodly size,

---

*In Roman mythology, after Jupiter defeated the Titans, the Titan ruler Saturn fled
Mount Olympus, settled in Rome, and founded a community in which all people
were equal and harvests were plentiful.

fashioned with patchwork into many curious devices, and ostenta-tiously worn on the outside. These, in fact, were convenient receptacles, where all good housewives carefully stored away such things as they wished to have at hand; by which means they often came to be incredibly crammed; and I remember there was a story current, when I was a boy, that the lady of Wouter Van Twiller once had occasion to empty her right pocket in search of a wooden ladle, when the contents filled a couple of corn-baskets, and the utensil was discovered lying among some rubbish in one corner;—but we must not give too much faith to all these stories, the anecdotes of those remote periods being very subject to exaggeration.

Besides these notable pockets, they likewise wore scissors and pin-cushions suspended from their girdles by red ribands, or, among the more opulent and showy classes, by brass, and even silver chains,—indubitable tokens of thrifty housewives and industrious spinsters. I cannot say much in vindication of the shortness of the petticoats; it doubtless was introduced for the purpose of giving the stockings a chance to be seen, which were generally of blue worsted, with magnificent red clocks,—or, perhaps, to display a well-turned ankle, and a neat, though serviceable foot, set off by a high-heeled leathern shoe, with a large and splendid silver buckle. Thus we find that the gentle sex in all ages have shown the same disposition to infringe a little upon the laws of decorum, in order to betray a lurking beauty, or gratify an innocent love of finery.

From the sketch here given, it will be seen that our good grand-mothers differed considerably in their ideas of a fine figure from their scantily dressed descendants of the present day. A fine lady, in those times, waddled under more clothes, even on a fair summer's day, than would have clad the whole bevy of a modern ball-room. Nor were they the less admired by the gentlemen in consequence thereof. On the contrary, the greatness of a lover's passion seemed to increase in proportion to the magnitude of its object,—and a voluminous damsel, arrayed in a dozen of petticoats, was declared by a Low-Dutch sonneteer of the province to be radiant as a sun-flower, and luxuriant as a full-blown cabbage. Certain it is, that in those days the heart of a lover could not contain more than one lady at a time; whereas the heart of a modern gallant has often room enough to accommodate half a dozen. The reason of which I conclude to be, that either the hearts of the gentlemen have grown larger, or the persons of the ladies smaller: this, however, is a question for physiologists to determine.

But there was a secret charm in these petticoats, which, no doubt, entered into the consideration of the prudent gallants. The wardrobe of a lady was in those days her only fortune; and she who had a good stock of petticoats and stockings was as absolutely an heiress as is a Kamtchatka* damsel with a store of bear-skins, or a Lapland† belle with a plenty of reindeer. The ladies, therefore, were very anxious to display these powerful attractions to the greatest advantage; and the best rooms in the house, instead of being adorned with caricatures of dame Nature, in water-colors and needle-work, were always hung round with abundance of homespun garments, the manufacture and the property of the females,— a piece of laudable ostentation that still prevails among the heiresses of our Dutch villages.

The gentlemen, in fact, who figured in the circles of the gay world in these ancient times, corresponded, in most particulars, with the beauteous damsels whose smiles they were ambitious to deserve. True it is, their merits would make but a very inconsiderable impression upon the heart of a modern fair: they neither drove their curricles,‡ nor sported their tandems, for as yet those gaudy vehicles were not even dreamt of; neither did they distinguish themselves by their brilliancy at the table, and their consequent rencontres with watchmen, for our forefathers were of too pacific a disposition to need those guardians of the night, every soul throughout the town being sound asleep before nine o'clock. Neither did they establish their claims to gentility at the expense of their tailors, for as yet those offenders against the pockets of society, and the tranquillity of all aspiring young gentlemen, were unknown in New Amsterdam; every good housewife made the clothes of her husband and family,

---

*Peninsula off Russia's eastern Siberian coast.
†Northern region of Scandinavia and northwestern Russia.
‡Two-wheeled, horse-drawn carriages.

and even the goede vrouw of Van Twiller himself thought it no disparagement to cut out her husband's linsey-woolsey galligaskins.*

Not but what there were some two or three youngsters who manifested the first dawning of what is called fire and spirit; who held all labor in contempt; skulked about docks and market-places; loitered in the sunshine; squandered what little money they could procure at hustlecap and chuck-farthing;† swore, boxed, fought cocks, and raced their neighbors' horses; in short, who promised to be the wonder, the talk, and abomination of the town, had not their stylish career been unfortunately cut short by an affair of honor with a whipping-post.

Far other, however, was the truly fashionable gentleman of those days: his dress, which served for both morning and evening, street and drawing-room, was a linsey-woolsey coat, made, perhaps, by the fair hands of the mistress of his affections, and gallantly bedecked with abundance of large brass buttons; half a score of breeches heightened the proportions of his figure; his shoes were decorated by enormous copper buckles; a low-crowned broad-rimmed hat overshadowed his burly visage; and his hair dangled down his back in a prodigious queue of eel-skin.

Thus equipped, he would manfully sally forth, with pipe in mouth, to besiege some fair damsel's obdurate heart,—not such a pipe, good reader, as that which Acis did sweetly tune in praise of his Galatea,‡ but one of true Delft manufacture, and furnished with a charge of fragrant tobacco. With this would he resolutely set himself down before the fortress, and rarely failed, in the process of time, to smoke the fair enemy into a surrender, upon honorable terms.

Such was the happy reign of Wouter Van Twiller, celebrated in many a long-forgotten song as the real golden age, the rest being nothing but counterfeit copper-washed coin. In that delightful period, a sweet and holy calm reigned over the whole province. The burgomaster

---

*Loose trousers or hose leggings.

†That is, gambling.

‡In Greek mythology, the prince Acis falls in love with Galatea, a sea nymph, and is murdered by the jealous Cyclops Polyphemus; Irving most likely has in mind the libretto of Georg Friedrich Handel's opera *Acis and Galatea* (c.1718).

smoked his pipe in peace; the substantial solace of his domestic cares, after her daily toils were done, sat soberly at the door, with her arms crossed over her apron of snowy white, without being insulted with ribald streetwalkers or vagabond boys,—those unlucky urchins who do so infest our streets, displaying, under the roses of youth, the thorns and briers of iniquity. Then it was that the lover with ten breeches, and the damsel with petticoats of half a score, indulged in all the innocent endearments of virtuous love, without fear and without reproach; for what had that virtue to fear, which was defended by a shield of good linsey-woolseys, equal at least to the seven bull-hides of the invincible Ajax?*

Ah, blissful and never to be forgotten age! when everything was better than it has ever been since, or ever will be again,—when Buttermilk Channel was quite dry at low water,—when the shad in the Hudson were all salmon,—and when the moon shone with a pure and resplendent whiteness, instead of that melancholy yellow light which is the consequence of her sickening at the abominations she every night witnesses in this degenerate city!

Happy would it have been for New Amsterdam could it always have existed in this state of blissful ignorance and lowly simplicity; but, alas! the days of childhood are too sweet to last! Cities, like men, grow out of them in time, and are doomed alike to grow into the bustle, the cares, and miseries of the world. Let no man congratulate himself, when he beholds the child of his bosom or the city of his birth increasing in magnitude and importance,—let the history of his own life teach him the dangers of the one, and this excellent little history of Manna-hata convince him of the calamities of the other.

---

*In book 7 of Homer's *Iliad*, the hero Ajax's brass shield is described as being covered with seven folds of a bull's hide.

BOOK IV

Containing the Chronicles of the Reign of William the Testy*

Chapter I

SHOWING THE NATURE OF HISTORY IN GENERAL;
CONTAINING FARTHERMORE THE UNIVERSAL
ACQUIREMENTS OF WILLIAM THE TESTY, AND HOW A
MAN MAY LEARN SO MUCH AS TO RENDER HIMSELF
GOOD FOR NOTHING

When the lofty Thucydides is about to enter upon his description of the plague that desolated Athens, one of his modern commentators assures the reader, that the history is now going to be exceeding solemn, serious, and pathetic, and

---

*That is, Willem Kieft, third Dutch director-general of New Netherland (1638–1646).

hints, with that air of chuckling gratulation with which a good dame draws forth a choice morsel from a cupboard to regale a favorite, that this plague will give his history a most agreeable variety.

In like manner did my heart leap within me, when I came to the dolorous dilemma of Fort Goed Hoop, which I at once perceived to be the forerunner of a series of great events and entertaining disasters. Such are the true subjects for the historic pen. For what is history, in fact, but a kind of Newgate calendar,* a register of the crimes and miseries that man has inflicted on his fellowman? It is a huge libel on human nature, to which we industriously add page after page, volume after volume, as if we were building up a monument to the honor, rather than the infamy of our species. If we turn over the pages of these chronicles that man has written of himself, what are the characters dignified by the appellation of great, and held up to the admiration of posterity? Tyrants, robbers, conquerors, renowned only for the magnitude of their misdeeds, and the stupendous wrongs and miseries they have inflicted on mankind,—warriors, who have hired themselves to the trade of blood, not from motives of virtuous patriotism, or to protect the injured and defenceless, but merely to gain the vaunted glory of being adroit and successful in massacring their fellow-beings! What are the great events that constitute a glorious era?—The fall of empires; the desolation of happy countries; splendid cities smoking in their ruins; the proudest works of art tumbled in the dust; the shrieks and groans of whole nations ascending unto heaven!

It is thus the historian may be said to thrive on the miseries of mankind, like birds of prey which hover over the field of battle to fatten on the mighty dead. It was observed by a great projector of inland lock-navigation, that rivers, lakes, and oceans were only formed to feed canals. In like manner I am tempted to believe that plots, conspiracies, wars, victories, and massacres are ordained by Providence only as food for the historian.

---

*Named after London's Newgate Prison, *The Newgate Calendar; or, Malefactor's Bloody Register* (first published 1774) contained narrative accounts of notorious crimes.

It is a source of great delight to the philosopher, in studying the wonderful economy of nature, to trace the mutual dependencies of things, how they are created reciprocally for each other, and how the most noxious and apparently unnecessary animal has its uses. Thus those swarms of flies, which are so often execrated as useless vermin, are created for the sustenance of spiders; and spiders, on the other hand, are evidently made to devour flies. So those heroes, who have been such scourges to the world, were bounteously provided as themes for the poet and historian, while the poet and the historian were destined to record the achievements of heroes!

These, and many similar reflections, naturally arose in my mind as I took up my pen to commence the reign of William Kieft: for now the stream of our history, which hitherto has rolled in a tranquil current, is about to depart forever from its peaceful haunts, and brawl through many a turbulent and rugged scene.

As some sleek ox, sunk in the rich repose of a clover-field, dozing and chewing the cud, will bear repeated blows before it raises itself, so the province of Nieuw Nederlandts, having waxed fat under the drowsy reign of the Doubter, needed cuffs and kicks to rouse it into action. The reader will now witness the manner in which a peaceful community advances towards a state of war; which is apt to be like the approach of a horse to a drum, with much prancing and little progress, and too often with the wrong end foremost.

Wilhelmus Kieft, who in 1634 ascended the gubernatorial chair (to borrow a favorite though clumsy appellation of modern phraseologists), was of a lofty descent, his father being inspector of windmills in the ancient town of Saardam; and our hero, we are told, when a boy, made very curious investigations into the nature and operation of these machines, which was one reason why he afterwards came to be so ingenious a governor. His name, according to the most authentic etymologists, was a corruption of Kyver, that is to say, a *wrangler* or *scolder*, and expressed the characteristic of his family, which, for nearly two centuries, had kept the windy town of Saardam in hot water, and produced more tartars and brimstones than any ten families in the place; and so truly did he inherit this family peculiarity, that he had not been a year in the government of the province, before he was universally denominated William the Testy. His appearance answered to his name. He was a brisk, wiry, waspish little old gentleman; such a one as may now and then be seen stumping about our city in a broad-skirted coat with huge buttons, a cocked hat stuck on the back of his head, and a cane as high as his chin. His face was broad, but his features were sharp; his cheeks were scorched into a dusky red by two fiery little gray eyes; his nose turned up, and the corners of his mouth turned down, pretty much like the muzzle of an irritable pug-dog.

I have heard it observed by a profound adept in human physiology, that if a woman waxes fat with the progress of years, her tenure of life is somewhat precarious, but if haply she withers as she grows old, she lives forever. Such promised to be the case with William the Testy, who grew tough in proportion as he dried. He had withered, in fact, not through the process of years, but through the tropical fervor of his soul, which burnt like a vehement rush-light in his bosom, inciting him to incessant broils and bickerings. Ancient traditions speak much of his learning, and of the gallant inroads he had made into the dead languages, in which he had made captive a host of Greek nouns and Latin verbs, and brought off rich booty in ancient saws and apothegms, which he was wont to parade in his public harangues, as a triumphant general of yore his *spolia opima*.* Of metaphysics he knew enough to confound all hearers and himself into the bargain. In logic, he knew the whole family of syllogisms and dilemmas, and was so proud of his skill that he never suffered even a self-evident fact to pass unargued. It was observed, however, that he seldom got into an argument without getting into a perplexity, and then into a passion with his adversary for not being convinced gratis.

He had, moreover, skirmished smartly on the frontiers of several of the sciences, was fond of experimental philosophy, and prided himself upon inventions of all kinds. His abode, which he had fixed at a Boweric or country-seat at a short distance from the city, just at what is now called Dutch Street, soon abounded with proofs of his ingenuity: patent smoke-jacks that required a horse to work them; Dutch ovens that roasted meat without fire; carts that went before the horses; weather-cocks that turned against the wind; and other wrong-headed contrivances that astonished and confounded all

*Spoils of war (Latin).

beholders. The house, too, was beset with paralytic cats and dogs, the subjects of his experimental philosophy; and the yelling and yelping of the latter unhappy victims of science, while aiding in the pursuit of knowledge, soon gained for the place the name of "Dog's Misery," by which it continues to be known even at the present day.

It is in knowledge as in swimming: he who flounders and splashes on the surface makes more noise, and attracts more attention, than the pearl-diver who quietly dives in quest of treasures to the bottom. The vast acquirements of the new governor were the theme of marvel among the simple burghers of New Amsterdam; he figured about the place as learned a man as a Bonze at Pekin,* who has mastered one half of the Chinese alphabet, and was unanimously pronounced a "universal genius!"

I have known in my time many a genius of this stamp; but, to speak my mind freely, I never knew one who, for the ordinary purposes of life, was worth his weight in straw. In this respect, a little sound judgment and plain common sense is worth all the sparkling genius that ever wrote poetry or invented theories. Let us see how the universal acquirements of William the Testy aided him in the affairs of government.

---

*Buddhist monk at Peking (modern-day Beijing, China).

Chapter II

HOW WILLIAM THE TESTY UNDERTOOK TO
CONQUER BY PROCLAMATION—HOW HE
WAS A GREAT MAN ABROAD, BUT A LITTLE MAN
IN HIS OWN HOUSE

No sooner had this bustling little potentate been blown by a whiff of fortune into the seat of government than he called his council together to make them a speech on the state of affairs. Caius Gracchus,* it is said, when he harangued the Roman populace, modulated his tone by an oratorical flute or pitch-pipe; Wilhelmus Kieft, not having such an instrument at hand, availed himself of that musical organ or trump which nature has implanted in the midst of a man's face: in other words, he preluded his address by a sonorous blast of the nose,—a preliminary flourish much in vogue among public orators.

He then commenced by expressing his humble sense of his utter unworthiness of the high post to which he had been appointed; which made some of the simple burghers wonder why he undertook it, not knowing that it is a point of etiquette with a public orator never to enter upon office without declaring himself unworthy to cross the threshold. He then proceeded in a manner highly classic and erudite to speak of government generally, and of the governments of ancient Greece in particular, together with the wars of Rome and Carthage, and the rise and fall of sundry outlandish empires which the worthy burghers had never read nor heard of. Having thus, after

---

*Roman aristocrat and tribune (153?–121 B.C.) who sponsored agrarian reforms that were considered radical by the Senate; he was assassinated, in part because his unorthodox political tactics angered his opponents.

the manner of your learned orator, treated of things in general, he came, by a natural, roundabout transition, to the matter in hand, namely, the daring aggressions of the Yankees.

As my readers are well aware of the advantage a potentate has of handling his enemies as he pleases in his speeches and bulletins, where he has the talk all on his own side, they may rest assured that William the Testy did not let such an opportunity escape of giving the Yankees what is called "a taste of his quality." In speaking of their inroads into the territories of their High Mightinesses, he compared them to the Gauls who desolated Rome, the Goths and Vandals* who overran the fairest plains of Europe; but when he came to speak of the unparalleled audacity with which they of Weathersfield had advanced their patches up to the very walls of Fort Goed Hoop, and threatened to smother the garrison in onions, tears of rage started into his eyes, as though he nosed the very offence in question.

Having thus wrought up his tale to a climax, he assumed a most belligerent look, and assured the council that he had devised an instrument, potent in its effects, and which he trusted would soon drive the Yankees from the land. So saying, he thrust his hand into one of the deep pockets of his broad-skirted coat and drew forth, not an infernal machine, but an instrument in writing, which he laid with great emphasis upon the table.

The burghers gazed at it for a time in silent awe, as a wary house-wife does at a gun, fearful it may go off half-cocked. The document in question had a sinister look, it is true; it was crabbed in text, and from a broad red ribbon dangled the great seal of the province, about the size of a buckwheat pancake. Still, after all, it was but an instrument in writing. Herein, however, existed the wonder of the invention. The document in question was a PROCLAMATION, ordering the Yankees to depart instantly from the territories of their High Mightinesses, under pain of suffering all the forfeitures and punishments in such case made and provided. In was on the moral effect of this formidable instrument that Wilhelmus Kieft calculated, pledging his valor as a governor that, once fulminated against the Yankees, it would, in less than two months, drive every mother's son of them across the borders.

---

*The Gauls, Goths, and Vandals were ancient European peoples who harried the Roman Empire from c.300 to c.455 B.C.

The council broke up in perfect wonder; and nothing was talked of for some time among the old men and women of New Amsterdam but the vast genius of the governor, and his new and cheap mode of fighting by proclamation.

As to Wilhelmus Kieft, having dispatched his proclamation to the frontiers, he put on his cocked hat and corduroy small-clothes, and mounting a tall raw-boned charger, trotted out to his rural retreat of Dog's Misery. Here, like the good Numa,* he reposed from the toils of state, taking lessons in government, not from the nymph Egeria, but from the honored wife of his bosom; who was one of that class of females sent upon the earth a little after the flood, as a punishment for the sins of mankind, and commonly known by the appellation of *knowing women*. In fact, my duty as an historian obliges me to make known a circumstance which was a great secret at the time, and consequently was not a subject of scandal at more than half the tea-tables in New Amsterdam, but which, like many other great secrets, has leaked out in the lapse of years,—and this was, that Wilhelmus the Testy, though one of the most potent little men that ever breathed, yet submitted at home to a species of government, neither laid down in Aristotle nor Plato, in short, it partook of the nature of a pure, unmixed tyranny, and is familiarly denominated *petticoat government*;†—an absolute sway, which, although exceedingly common in these modern days, was very rare among the ancients, if we may judge from the rout made about the domestic economy of honest Socrates; which is the only ancient case on record.

The great Kieft, however, warded off all the sneers and sarcasms of his particular friends, who are ever ready to joke with a man on sore points of the kind, by alleging that it was a government of his own election, to which he submitted through choice, adding at the same time a profound maxim which he had found in an ancient author, that "he who would aspire to *govern*, should first learn to *obey*."

---

*Numa Pompilius, legendary king of Rome who succeeded Romulus and ruled with the help of the nymph Egeria.

†Xanthippe, the wife of Greek philosopher Socrates (c.470–399 B.C.), is infamous for having been shrewish and scolding; compare her with Dame Van Winkle (see pp. 74 and 88).

Chapter III

IN WHICH ARE RECORDED THE
SAGE PROJECTS OF A RULER OF
UNIVERSAL GENIUS—THE ART OF
FIGHTING BY PROCLAMATION—AND
HOW THAT THE VALIANT JACOBUS
VAN CURLET CAME TO BE FOULLY
DISHONORED AT FORT GOED HOOP

Never was a more comprehensive, a more expeditious, or, what is still better, a more economical measure devised, than this of defeating the Yankees by proclamation,—an expedient, likewise, so gentle and humane, there were ten chances to one in favor of its succeeding; but then there was one chance to ten that it would not succeed,—as the ill-natured fates would have it, that single chance carried the day! The proclamation was perfect in all its parts, well constructed, well written, well sealed, and well published; all that was wanting to insure its effect was, that the Yankees should stand in awe of it; but, provoking to relate, they treated it with the most absolute contempt, applied it to an unseemly purpose; and thus did the first warlike proclamation come to a shameful end,—a fate which I am credibly informed has befallen but too many of its successors.

So far from abandoning the country, those varlets continued their encroachments, squatting along the green banks of the Varsche river, and founding Hartford, Stamford, New Haven, and other border-towns. I have already shown how the onion patches of Pyquag were an eye-sore to Jacobus Van Curlet and his garrison; but now these moss-troopers increased in their atrocities, kidnapping hogs, impounding horses, and sometimes grievously rib-roasting their owners. Our worthy forefathers could scarcely stir abroad without danger of being out-jockeyed in horse-flesh, or taken in in bargaining; while, in their absence, some daring Yankee peddler would penetrate to their household, and nearly ruin the good housewives with tin ware and wooden bowls.*

I am well aware of the perils which environ me in this part of my history. While raking with curious hand but pious heart, among the mouldering remains of former days, anxious to draw therefrom the honey of wisdom, I may fare somewhat like that valiant worthy, Samson,† who, in meddling with the carcass of a dead lion, drew a swarm of bees about his ears. Thus, while narrating the many misdeeds of the Yanokie or Yankee race, it is ten chances to one but I offend the morbid sensibilities of certain of their unreasonable descendants, who may fly out and raise such a buzzing about this

---

*The following cases in point appear in Hazard's Collection of State Papers.

"In the meantime, they of Hartford have not onely usurped and taken in the lands of Connecticott, although unrighteously and against the lawes of nations but have hindered our nation in sowing theire own purchased broken up lands, but have also sowed them with corne in the night, which the Nederlanders had broken up and intended to sowe: and have beaten the servants of the high and mighty the honored companie, which were laboring upon theire master's lands, from theire lands, with sticks and plow staves in hostile manner laming, and among the rest, struck Ever Duckings [Evert Duyckink] a hole in his head, with a stick, so that the bloode ran downe very strongly downe upon his body."

"Those of Hartford sold a hogg, that belonged to the honored companie, under pretence that it had eaten of theire grounde grass, when they had not any foot of inheritance. They proffered the hogg for 5s. if the commissioners would have given 5s. for damage; which the commissioners denied, because noe man's own hogg (as men used to say) can trespass upon his owne master's grounde."

The copy in brackets is by Washington Irving. "Hazard's Collection of State Papers" refers to *Historical Collections* (1792–1794), by Ebenezer Hazard, an American public official and historian. Irving's bracketed text probably refers to Evert Duyckinck (c.1620–c.1700), a painter and glazier, known for his stained glass windows; Irving may have included this detail in homage to New York editor and biographer Evert Duyckinck (1816–1878), who published an edition of *Salmagundi* in 1860.

†Samson was a biblical judge of Israel who, according to an angel's prophesy, would be invincible as long as his hair was never cut; the reference here is to his taking honey from a swarm of bees in the carcass of a lion he had slain (see the Bible, Judges 14:8).

unlucky head of mine, that I shall need the tough hide of an Achilles,* or an Orlando Furioso,† to protect me from their stings.

Should such be the case, I should deeply and sincerely lament,— not my misfortune in giving offence, but the wrong-headed perverseness of an ill-natured generation, in taking offence at anything I say. That their ancestors did use my ancestors ill is true, and I am very sorry for it. I would, with all my heart, the fact were otherwise; but as I am recording the sacred events of history, I'd not bate one nail's breadth of the honest truth, though I were sure the whole edition of my work would be bought up and burnt by the common hangman of Connecticut. And in sooth, now that these testy gentlemen have drawn me out, I will make bold to go farther, and observe that this is one of the grand purposes for which we impartial historians are sent into the world,—to redress wrongs and render justice on the heads of the guilty. So that, though a powerful nation may wrong its neighbors with temporary impunity, yet sooner or later an historian springs up, who wreaks ample chastisement on it in return.

Thus these moss-troopers of the east little thought, I'll warrant it, while they were harassing the inoffensive province of Nieuw Nederlandts, and driving its unhappy governor to his wit's end, that an historian would ever arise, and give them their own, with interest. Since, then, I am but performing my bounden duty as an historian, in avenging the wrongs of our revered ancestors, I shall make no further apology; and, indeed, when it is considered that I have all these ancient borderers of the east in my power, and at the mercy of my pen, I trust that it will be admitted I conduct myself with great humanity and moderation.

It was long before William the Testy could be persuaded that his much-vaunted war-measure was ineffectual; on the contrary, he flew in a passion whenever it was doubted, swearing that, though slow in operation, yet when it once began to work, it would soon purge the land of these invaders. When convinced, at length, of the

---

*In Greek mythology, a hero of the Trojan War; his mother dipped him in the River Styx, thereby making him invulnerable except at the heel by which she held him.
†Title character of a medieval romance (1516, 1532) by Italian poet Ludovico Ariosto.

truth, like a shrewd physician he attributed the failure to the quantity, not the quality of the medicine, and resolved to double the dose. He fulminated, therefore, a second proclamation, more vehement than the first, forbidding all intercourse with these Yankee intruders, ordering the Dutch burghers on the frontiers to buy none of their pacing horses, measly pork, apple-sweetmeats, Weathersfield onions, or wooden bowls, and to furnish them with no supplies of gin, gingerbread, or sourkrout.

Another interval elapsed, during which the last proclamation was as little regarded as the first; and the non-intercourse was especially set at naught by the young folks of both sexes, if we may judge by the active bundling which took place along the borders.

At length, one day the inhabitants of New Amsterdam were aroused by a furious barking of dogs, great and small, and beheld, to their surprise, the whole garrison of Fort Goed Hoop straggling into town all tattered and wayworn, with Jacobus Van Curlet* at their head, bringing the melancholy intelligence of the capture of Fort Goed Hoop by the Yankees.

The fate of this important fortress is an impressive warning to all military commanders. It was neither carried by storm nor famine; nor was it undermined; nor bombarded; nor set on fire by red-hot shot; but was taken by a stratagem no less singular than effectual, and which can never fail of success, whenever an opportunity occurs of putting it in practice.

It seems that the Yankees had received intelligence that the garrison of Jacobus Van Curlet had been reduced nearly one eighth by the death of two of his most corpulent soldiers, who had overeaten themselves on fat salmon caught in the Varsche river. A secret expedition was immediately set on foot to surprise the fortress. The crafty enemy, knowing the habits of the garrison to sleep soundly after they had eaten their dinners and smoked their pipes, stole upon them at the noontide of a sultry summer's day, and surprised them in the midst of their slumbers.

---

*Jacobus Van Curlet (also given as Van Curler), Dutch merchant who established the House of Hope, a trading post on the Connecticut River at the site where Hartford now stands.

In an instant the flag of their High Mightinesses was lowered, and the Yankee standard elevated in its stead, being a dried codfish, by way of a spread eagle. A strong garrison was appointed, of long-sided, hard-fisted Yankees, with Weathersfield onions for cockades and feathers. As to Jacobus Van Curlet and his men, they were seized by the nape of the neck, conducted to the gate, and one by one dismissed by a kick in the crupper, as Charles XII dismissed the heavy-bottomed Russians at the battle of Narva;[*] Jacobus Van Curlet receiving two kicks in consideration of his official dignity.

---

[*]At the battle of Narva (November 20, 1700), King Charles XII of Sweden defeated a Russian army that outnumbered his forces by nearly five to one.

Chapter IV

CONTAINING THE FEARFUL WRATH OF
WILLIAM THE TESTY, AND THE ALARM OF
NEW AMSTERDAM—HOW THE GOVERNOR DID
STRONGLY FORTIFY THE CITY—OF THE RISE OF
ANTONY THE TRUMPETER, AND THE WINDY
ADDITION TO THE ARMORIAL BEARINGS OF
NEW AMSTERDAM

Language cannot express the awful ire of William the Testy on hearing of the catastrophe at Fort Goed Hoop. For three good hours his rage was too great for words, or rather the words were too great for him (being a very small man), and he was nearly choked by the misshapen, nine-cornered Dutch oaths and epithets which crowded at once into his gullet. At length his words found vent, and for three days he kept up a constant discharge, anathematizing the Yankees, man, woman, and child, for a set of dieven, schobbejacken, deugenieten, twistzoekeren, blaes-kaken, loosenschalken, kakken-bedden, and a thousand other names, of which, unfortunately for posterity, history does not make mention. Finally, he swore that he would have nothing more to do with such a squatting, bundling, guessing, questioning, swapping, pumpkin-eating, molasses-daubing, shingle-splitting, cider-watering, horse-jockeying, notion-peddling crew; that they might stay at Fort Goed Hoop and rot, before he would dirty his hands by attempting to drive them away: in proof of which he ordered the new-raised troops to be marched forthwith into winter-quarters, although it was not as yet quite midsummer. Great despondency now fell upon the city of New Amsterdam. It was feared that the conquerors of Fort Goed Hoop, flushed with victory and apple-brandy, might march on to the capital, take it by storm, and annex the whole province to Connecticut. The name of Yankee became as terrible among the Nieuw Nederlanders as was that of Gaul among the ancient Romans; insomuch that the good wives of the Manhattoes used it as a bugbear wherewith to frighten their unruly children.

Everybody clamored around the governor, imploring him to put the city in a complete posture of defence; and he listened to their clamors. Nobody could accuse William the Testy of being idle in time of danger, or at any other time. He was never idle, but then he was often busy to very little purpose. When a youngling, he had been impressed with the words of Solomon, "Go to the ant, thou sluggard, observe her ways and be wise;"* in conformity to which he had ever been of a restless, ant-like turn, hurrying hither and thither, nobody knew why or wherefore, busying himself about small matters with an air of great importance and anxiety, and toiling at a grain of mustard-seed in the full conviction that he was moving a mountain. In the present instance, he called in all his inventive powers to his aid, and was continually pondering over plans, making diagrams, and worrying about with a troop of workmen and projectors at his heels. At length, after a world of consultation and contrivance, his plans of defence ended in rearing a great flag-staff in the centre of the fort, and perching a wind-mill on each bastion.

These warlike preparations in some measure allayed the public alarm, especially after an additional means of securing the safety of the city had been suggested by the governor's lady. It has already been hinted in this most authentic history, that in the domestic establishment of William the Testy "the gray mare was the better horse"; in other words, that his wife "ruled the roast," and in governing the governor, governed the province, which might thus be said to be under petticoat government.

Now it came to pass, that about this time there lived in the Manhattoes a jolly, robustious trumpeter, named Antony Van Corlear, famous for his long wind; and who, as the story goes, could twang so potently upon his instrument, that the effect upon all within

---

*See the Bible, Proverbs 6:6.

hearing was like that ascribed to the Scotch bagpipe when it sings right lustily i' the nose.

This sounder of brass was moreover a lusty bachelor, with a pleasant, burly visage, a long nose, and huge whiskers. He had his little *bowerie*, or retreat, in the country, where he led a roistering life, giving dances to the wives and daughters of the burghers of the Manhattoes, insomuch that he became a prodigious favorite with all the women, young and old. He is said to have been the first to collect that famous toll levied on the fair sex at Kissing Bridge, on the highway to Hellgate.*

To this sturdy bachelor the eyes of all the women were turned in this time of darkness and peril, as the very man to second and carry out the plans of defence of the governor. A kind of petticoat council was forthwith held at the government house, at which the governor's lady presided; and this lady, as has been hinted, being all potent with the governor, the result of these councils was the elevation of Antony the Trumpeter to the post of commandant of wind-mills and champion of New Amsterdam.

The city being thus fortified and garrisoned, it would have done one's heart good to see the governor snapping his fingers and fidgeting with delight, as the trumpeter strutted up and down the ramparts, twanging defiance to the whole Yankee race, as does a modern editor to all the principalities and powers on the other side of the Atlantic. In the hands of Antony Van Corlear this windy instrument appeared to him as potent as the horn of the paladin Astolpho,† or even the more classic horn of Alecto;‡ nay, he had almost the temerity to compare it with the rams' horns celebrated in holy writ, at the very sound of which the walls of Jericho fell down.§

---

*The bridge here mentioned by Mr. Knickerbocker still exists; but it is said that the toll is seldom collected nowadays, excepting on sleighing parties, by the descendants of the patriarchs, who still preserve the traditions of the city.

†Cousin of Roland in Ariosto's *Orlando Furioso* (see p. 434).

‡In Greek mythology, Alecto (meaning "unceasing pursuit") is one of the Erinyes, or Furies, who pursue evil-doers; she is sometimes figured blowing a horn to call the other Furies to the chase.

§In the Bible (Joshua 6), the Israelites blow seven rams' horns to bring down the walls of Jericho.

Be all this as it may, the apprehensions of hostilities from the east gradually died away. The Yankees made no further invasion; nay, they declared they had only taken possession of Fort Goed Hoop as being erected within their territories. So far from manifesting hostility, they continued to throng to New Amsterdam with the most innocent countenances imaginable, filling the market with their notions, being as ready to trade with the Nederlanders as ever, and not a whit more prone to get to the windward of them in a bargain.

The old wives of the Manhattoes, who took tea with the governor's lady, attributed all this affected moderation to the awe inspired by the military preparations of the governor, and the windy prowess of Antony the Trumpeter.

There were not wanting illiberal minds, however, who sneered at the governor for thinking to defend his city as he governed it, by mere wind; but William Kieft was not to be jeered out of his windmills: he had seen them perched upon the ramparts of his native city of Saardam, and was persuaded they were connected with the great science of defence; nay, so much piqued was he by having them made a matter of ridicule, that he introduced them into the arms of the city, where they remain to this day, quartered with the ancient beaver of the Manhattoes, an emblem and memento of his policy.

I must not omit to mention that certain wise old burghers of the Manhattoes, skilful in expounding signs and mysteries, after events have come to pass, consider this early intrusion of the wind-mill into the escutcheon of our city, which before had been wholly occupied by the beaver, as portentous of its after fortune, when the quiet Dutchman would be elbowed aside by the enterprising Yankee, and patient industry overtopped by windy speculation.

Chapter VII

GROWING DISCONTENTS OF NEW AMSTERDAM UNDER THE GOVERNMENT OF WILLIAM THE TESTY

It has been remarked by the observant writer of the Stuyvesant manuscript,* that under the administration of William Kieft the disposition of the inhabitants of New Amsterdam experienced an essential change, so that they became very meddlesome and factious. The unfortunate propensity of the little governor to experiment and innovation, and the frequent exacerbations of his temper, kept his council in a continual worry; and the council being to the people at large what yeast or leaven is to a batch, they threw the whole community in a ferment; and the people at large being to the city what the mind is to the body, the unhappy commotions they underwent operated most disastrously upon New Amsterdam,—insomuch that, in certain of their paroxysms of consternation and perplexity, they begat several of the most crooked, distorted, and abominable streets, lanes, and alleys, with which this metropolis is disfigured.

The fact was, that about this time the community, like Balaam's ass,† began to grow more enlightened than its rider, and to show a disposition for what is called "self-government." This restive propensity was first evinced in certain popular meetings, in which the burghers of New Amsterdam met to talk and smoke over the complicated affairs of the province, gradually obfuscating themselves with politics and tobacco-smoke. Hither resorted those idlers and squires of low degree who hang loose on society and are

---

*See p. 384.
†See the Bible, Numbers 22:21–35.

blown about by every wind of doctrine. Cobblers abandoned their stalls to give lessons on political economy; blacksmiths suffered their fires to go out while they stirred up the fires of faction; and even tailors, though said to be the ninth parts of humanity, neglected their own measures to criticize the measures of government.

Strange! that the science of government, which seems to be so generally understood, should invariably be denied to the only one called upon to exercise it. Not one of the politicians in question, but, take his word for it, could have administered affairs ten times better than William the Testy.

Under the instructions of these political oracles the good people of New Amsterdam soon became exceedingly enlightened, and, as a matter of course, exceedingly discontented. They gradually found out the fearful error in which they had indulged, of thinking themselves the happiest people in creation, and were convinced that, all circumstances to the contrary notwithstanding, they were a very unhappy, deluded, and consequently ruined people!

We are naturally prone to discontent, and avaricious after imaginary causes of lamentation. Like lubberly monks we belabor our own shoulders, and take a vast satisfaction in the music of our own groans. Nor is this said by way of paradox; daily experience shows the truth of these observations. It is almost impossible to elevate the spirits of a man groaning under ideal calamities; but nothing is easier than to render him wretched, though on the pinnacle of felicity; as it would be an Herculean* task to hoist a man to the top of a steeple, though the merest child could topple him off thence.

I must not omit to mention that these popular meetings were generally held at some noted tavern, these public edifices possessing what in modern times are thought the true fountains of political inspiration. The ancient Greeks deliberated upon a matter when drunk, and reconsidered it when sober. Mob-politicians in modern times dislike to have two minds upon a subject, so they both deliberate and act when drunk; by this means a world of delay is spared; and as it is universally allowed that a man when drunk sees double, it follows conclusively that he sees twice as well as his sober neighbors.

---

*See footnote on p. 10.

Chapter VIII

OF THE EDICT OF WILLIAM THE TESTY AGAINST TOBACCO—OF THE PIPE-PLOT, AND THE RISE OF FEUDS AND PARTIES

Wilhelmus Kieft, as has already been observed, was a great legislator on a small scale, and had a microscopic eye in public affairs. He had been greatly annoyed by the factious meeting of the good people of New Amsterdam, but, observing that on these occasions the pipe was ever in their mouth, he began to think that the pipe was at the bottom of the affair, and that there was some mysterious affinity between politics and tobacco-smoke. Determined to strike at the root of the evil, he began forthwith to rail at tobacco, as a noxious, nauseous weed, filthy in all its uses; and as to smoking, he denounced it as a heavy tax upon the public pocket,—a vast consumer of time, a great encourager of idleness, and a deadly bane to the prosperity and morals of the people. Finally he issued an edict, prohibiting the smoking of tobacco throughout the New Netherlands. Ill-fated Kieft! Had he lived in the present age and attempted to check the unbounded license of the press, he could not have struck more sorely upon the sensibilities of the million. The pipe, in fact, was the great organ of reflection and deliberation of the New Netherlander. It was his constant companion and solace: was he gay, he smoked; was he sad, he smoked; his pipe was never out of his mouth; it was a part of his physiognomy; without it his best friends would not know him. Take away his pipe? You might as well take away his nose!

The immediate effect of the edict of William the Testy was a popular commotion. A vast multitude, armed with pipes and tobacco-boxes, and an immense supply of ammunition, sat themselves down before the governor's house, and fell to smoking with tremendous violence.

The testy William issued forth like a wrathful spider, demanding the reason of this lawless fumigation. The sturdy rioters replied by lolling back in their seats, and puffing away with redoubled fury, raising such a murky cloud that the governor was fain to take refuge in the interior of his castle.

A long negotiation ensued through the medium of Antony the Trumpeter. The governor was at first wrathful and unyielding, but was gradually smoked into terms. He concluded by permitting the smoking of tobacco, but he abolished the fair long pipes used in the days of Wouter Van Twiller, denoting ease, tranquillity, and sobriety of deportment; these he condemned as incompatible with the despatch of business, in place whereof he substituted little captious short pipes, two inches in length, which, he observed, could be stuck in one corner of the mouth, or twisted in the hat-band, and would never be in the way. Thus ended this alarming insurrection, which was long known by the name of The Pipe-Plot, and which, it has been somewhat quaintly observed, did end, like most plots and seditions, in mere smoke.

But mark, oh, reader! the deplorable evils which did afterwards result. The smoke of these villanous little pipes, continually ascending in a cloud about the nose, penetrated into and befogged the cerebellum, dried up all the kindly moisture of the brain, and rendered the people who use them as vaporish and testy as the governor himself. Nay, what is worse, from being goodly, burly, sleek-conditioned men, they became, like our Dutch yeomanry who smoke short pipes, a lantern-jawed, smoke-dried, leathern-hided race.

Nor was this all. From this fatal schism in tobacco-pipes we may date the rise of parties in the Nieuw Nederlands. The rich and self-important burghers who had made their fortunes, and could afford to be lazy, adhered to the ancient fashion, and formed a kind of aristocracy known as the *Long Pipes*; while the lower order, adopting the reform of William Kieft as more convenient in their handicraft employments, were branded with the plebeian name of *Short Pipes*.

A third party sprang up, headed by the descendants of Robert Chewit, the companion of the great Hudson. These discarded pipes altogether and took to chewing tobacco; hence they were called *Quids*,—an appellation since given to those political mongrels, which sometimes spring up between two great parties, as a mule is produced between a horse and an ass.

And here I would note the great benefit of party distinctions in saving the people at large the trouble of thinking. Hesiod* divides mankind into three classes,—those who think for themselves, those who think as others think, and those who do not think at all. The second class comprises the great mass of society; for most people require a set creed and a file-leader. Hence the origin of party: which means a large body of people, some few of whom think, and all the rest talk. The former take the lead and discipline the latter; prescribing what they must say, what they must approve, what they must hoot at, whom they must support, but, above all, whom they must hate; for no one can be a right good partisan, who is not a thorough-going hater.

The enlightened inhabitants of the Manhattoes, therefore, being divided into parties, were enabled to hate each other with great accuracy. And now the great business of politics went bravely on, the long pipes and short pipes assembling in separate beer-houses, and smoking at each other with implacable vehemence, to the great support of the State and profit of the tavern-keepers. Some, indeed, went so far as to bespatter their adversaries with those odoriferous little words which smell so strong in the Dutch language, believing, like true politicians, that they served their party, and glorified themselves in proportion as they bewrayed their neighbors. But, however they might differ among themselves, all parties agreed in abusing the governor, seeing that he was not a governor of their choice, but appointed by others to rule over them.

Unhappy William Kieft! exclaims the sage writer of the Stuyvesant manuscript, doomed to contend with enemies too knowing to be entrapped, and to reign over a people too wise to be governed. All his foreign expeditions were baffled and set at naught by the all-pervading Yankees; all his home measures were canvassed and condemned by "numerous and respectable meetings" of pot-house politicians.

In the multitude of counsellors, we are told, there is safety; but the multitude of counsellors was a continual source of perplexity to William Kieft. With a temperament as hot as an old radish, and a mind subject to perpetual whirlwinds and tornadoes, he never failed

---

*Greek poet (eighth century B.C.?), author of *Works and Days* and *Theogony*.

to get into a passion with every one who undertook to advise him.
I have observed, however, that your passionate little men, like small
boats with large sails, are easily upset or blown out of their course;
so was it with William the Testy, who was prone to be carried away
by the last piece of advice blown into his ear. The consequence was,
that, though a projector of the first class, yet by continually changing
his projects he gave none a fair trial; and by endeavoring to do everything, he in sober truth did nothing.

In the mean time, the sovereign people got into the saddle,
showed themselves, as usual, unmerciful riders; spurring on the little
governor with harangues and petitions, and thwarting him with
memorials and reproaches, in much the same way as holiday
apprentices manage an unlucky devil of a hack-horse,—so that
Wilhelmus Kieft was kept at a worry or a gallop throughout the
whole of his administration.

BOOK V

CONTAINING THE FIRST PART OF THE REIGN OF PETER STUYVESANT,[*] AND HIS TROUBLES WITH THE AMPHICTYONIC COUNCIL

Chapter I

IN WHICH THE DEATH OF A GREAT MAN IS SHOWN TO BE NO VERY INCONSOLABLE MATTER OF SORROW—AND HOW PETER STUYVESANT ACQUIRED A GREAT NAME FROM THE UNCOMMON STRENGTH OF HIS HEAD

To a profound philosopher like myself, who am apt to see clear through a subject, where the penetration of ordinary people extends but halfway, there is no fact more simple and manifest

---

*Last Dutch director-general of New Netherland (1646–1664).

than that the death of a great man is a matter of very little importance. Much as we may think of ourselves, and much as we may excite the empty plaudits of the million, it is certain that the greatest among us do actually fill but an exceeding small space in the world; and it is equally certain, that even that small space is quickly supplied when we leave it vacant. "Of what consequence is it," said Pliny,* "that individuals appear, or make their exit? the world is a theatre whose scenes and actors are continually changing." Never did philosopher speak more correctly; and I only wonder that so wise a remark could have existed so many ages, and mankind not have laid it more to heart. Sage follows on in the footsteps of sage; one hero just steps out of his triumphal car, to make way for the hero who comes after him; and of the proudest monarch it is merely said, that "he slept with his fathers, and his successor reigned in his stead."

The world, to tell the private truth, cares but little for their loss, and if left to itself would soon forget to grieve; and though a nation has often been figuratively drowned in tears on the death of a great man, yet it is ten to one if an individual tear has been shed on the occasion, excepting from the forlorn pen of some hungry author. It is the historian, the biographer, and the poet, who have the whole burden of grief to sustain,—who—kind souls!—like undertakers in England, act the part of chief mourners,—who inflate a nation with sighs it never heaved, and deluge it with tears it never dreamt of shedding. Thus, while the patriotic author is weeping and howling, in prose, in blank verse, and in rhyme, and collecting the drops of public sorrow into his volume, as into a lachrymal vase,† it is more than probable his fellow-citizens are eating and drinking, fiddling and dancing, as utterly ignorant of the bitter lamentations made in their name as are those men of straw, John Doe and Richard Roe,§ of the plaintiffs for whom they are generously pleased to become sureties.

The most glorious hero that ever desolated nations might have mouldered into oblivion among the rubbish of his own monument,

---

*Probably Gaius Plinius Secundus, or Pliny the Elder (A.D. c.23–79), known for his stoic philosophy; but the quotation is unlocated.

†Vase for collecting tears; in ancient Roman tradition, tombs of the well-to-do held vases that supposedly contained the tears of their grieving relatives.

§Common names for anonymous or unidentified persons.

did not some historian take him into favor, and benevolently transmit his name to posterity; and much as the valiant William Kieft worried, and bustled, and turmoiled, while he had the destinies of a whole colony in his hand, I question seriously whether he will not be obliged to this authentic history for all his future celebrity.

His exit occasioned no convulsion in the city of New Amsterdam nor its vicinity: the earth trembled not, neither did any stars shoot from their spheres; the heavens were not shrouded in black, as poets would fain persuade us they have been, on the death of a hero; the rocks (hard-hearted varlets!) melted not into tears, nor did the trees hang their heads in silent sorrow; and as to the sun, he lay abed the next night just as long, and showed as jolly a face when he rose as he ever did on the same day of the month in any year, either before or since. The good people of New Amsterdam, one and all, declared that he had been a very busy, active, bustling little governor; that he was "the father of his country"; that he was "the noblest work of God"; that "he was a man, take him for all in all, they ne'er should look upon his like again"; together with sundry other civil and affectionate speeches regularly said on the death of all great men: after which they smoked their pipes, thought no more about him, and Peter Stuyvesant succeeded to his station.

Peter Stuyvesant was the last, and, like the renowned Wouter Van Twiller, the best of our ancient Dutch governors. Wouter having surpassed all who preceded him, and Peter, or Piet, as he was sociably called by the old Dutch burghers, who were ever prone to familiarize names, having never been equalled by any successor. He was in fact the very man fitted by nature to retrieve the desperate fortunes of her beloved province, had not the fates, those most potent and unrelenting of all ancient spinsters, destined them to inextricable confusion.

To say merely that he was a hero, would be doing him great injustice: he was in truth a combination of heroes; for he was of a sturdy, raw-boned make, like Ajax Telamon,* with a pair of round shoulders that Hercules would have given his hide for (meaning his lion's hide) when he undertook to ease old Atlas of his load. He was, moreover, as Plutarch describes Coriolanus, not only terrible for the

---

*In Homer's *Iliad*, Ajax was the strongest among the Greeks after Achilles.

force of his arm, but likewise of his voice, which sounded as though it came out of a barrel; and, like the self-same warrior, he possessed a sovereign contempt for the sovereign people, and an iron aspect, which was enough of itself to make the very bowels of his adversaries quake with terror and dismay. All this martial excellency of appearance was inexpressibly heightened by an accidental advantage, with which I am surprised that neither Homer nor Virgil* have graced any of their heroes. This was nothing less than a wooden leg, which was the only prize he had gained in bravely fighting the battles of his country, but of which he was so proud, that he was often heard to declare he valued it more than all his other limbs put together; indeed so highly did he esteem it, that he had it gallantly enchased and relieved with silver devices, which caused it to be related in divers histories and legends that he wore a silver leg.†

Like that choleric warrior Achilles, he was somewhat subject to extempore bursts of passion, which were rather unpleasant to his favorites and attendants, whose perceptions he was apt to quicken, after the manner of his illustrious imitator, Peter the Great,‡ by anointing their shoulders with his walking-staff.

Though I cannot find that he had read Plato, or Aristotle, or Hobbes, or Bacon, or Algernon Sydney, or Tom Paine,§ yet did he sometimes manifest a shrewdness and sagacity in his measures, that one would hardly expect from a man who did not know Greek, and had never studied the ancients. True it is, and I confess it with

---

Homer (c.700 B.C.): Greek poet to whom the *Iliad* and the *Odyssey* are attributed; *Virgil* (70–19 B.C.): Roman poet whose *Aeneid* was a national epic of Roman civilization.

†See the histories of Masters Josselyn and Blome [Irving's note].

‡Czar of Russia (1682–1725) who modernized the government and moved the capital to St. Petersburg.

§The Greek philosopher Plato (427?–347 B.C.) is known for his *Dialogues* and *Republic*. Aristotle (384–322 B.C.) was another Greek philosopher who studied under and succeeded Plato. In *Leviathan* (1651), British philosopher and political scientist Thomas Hobbes argues against the separation of church and state. British statesman and philosopher Francis Bacon (1561–1626) is known as the father of the modern scientific method. English politician Algernon Sydney (1622–1683) opposed Charles II in the English Civil War and was executed for participating in the Rye House Plot; his *Discourses Concerning Government* (1698) were widely read in the colonies. Thomas Paine (1737–1809) was a British-American political philosopher; his pamphlet *Common Sense* justified the American Revolution.

sorrow, that he had an unreasonable aversion to experiments, and was fond of governing his province after the simplest manner; but then he contrived to keep it in better order than did the erudite Kieft, though he had all the philosophers, ancient and modern, to assist and perplex him. I must likewise own that he made but very few laws; but then, again, he took care that those few were rigidly and impartially enforced; and I do not know but justice, on the whole, was as well administered as if there had been volumes of sage acts and statutes yearly made, and daily neglected and forgotten.

He was, in fact, the very reverse of his predecessors being neither tranquil and inert, like Walter the Doubter, nor restless and fidgeting, like William the Testy,—but a man, or rather a governor, of such uncommon activity and decision of mind, that he never sought nor accepted the advice of others,—depending bravely upon his single head, as would a hero of yore upon his single arm, to carry him through all difficulties and dangers. To tell the simple truth, he wanted nothing more to complete him as a statesman than to think always right; for no one can say but that he always acted as he thought. He was never a man to flinch when he found himself in a scrape, but to dash forward through thick and thin, trusting, by hook or by crook, to make all things straight in the end. In a word, he possessed, in an eminent degree, that great quality in a statesman, called perseverance by the polite, but nicknamed obstinacy by the vulgar,—a wonderful salve for official blunders, since he who perseveres in error without flinching gets the credit of boldness and consistency, while he who wavers in seeking to do what is right gets stigmatized as a trimmer. This much is certain; and it is a maxim well worthy the attention of all legislators, great and small, who stand shaking in the wind, irresolute which way to steer, that a ruler who follows his own will pleases himself, while he who seeks to satisfy the wishes and whims of others runs great risk of pleasing nobody. There is nothing, too, like putting down one's foot resolutely when in doubt, and letting things take their course. The clock that stands still points right twice in the four-and-twenty hours, while others may keep going continually and be continually going wrong.

Nor did this magnanimous quality escape the discernment of the good people of Nieuw Nederlands; on the contrary, so much were they struck with the independent will and vigorous resolution displayed on all occasions by their new governor, that they universally called him Hard-Koppig Piet, or Peter the Headstrong,—a great compliment to the strength of his understanding.

If, from all that I have said, thou dost not gather, worthy reader, that Peter Stuyvesant was a tough, sturdy, valiant, weather-beaten, mettlesome, obstinate, leathern-sided, lion-hearted, generous-spirited old governor, either I have written to but little purpose, or thou art very dull at drawing conclusions.

This most excellent governor commenced his administration on the 29th of May, 1647,—a remarkably stormy day, distinguished in all the almanacs of the time which have come down to us by the name of *Windy Friday*. As he was very jealous of his personal and official dignity, he was inaugurated into office with great ceremony,—the goodly oaken chair of the renowned Wouter Van Twiller being carefully preserved for such occasions, in like manner as the chair and stone were reverentially preserved at Schone, in Scotland,* for the coronation of the Caledonian monarchs.

I must not omit to mention that the tempestuous state of the elements, together with its being that unlucky day of the week termed "hanging-day," did not fail to excite much grave speculation and divers very reasonable apprehensions among the more ancient and enlightened inhabitants; and several of the sager sex, who were reputed to be not a little skilled in the mystery of astrology and fortune-telling, did declare outright that they were omens of a disastrous administration;—an event that came to be lamentably verified, and which proves beyond dispute the wisdom of attending to those preternatural intimations furnished by dreams and visions, the flying of birds, falling of stones, and cackling of geese, on which the sages and rulers of ancient times placed such reliance; or to those shooting of stars, eclipses of the moon, howlings of dogs, and flarings of candles, carefully noted and interpreted by the oracular sibyls† of our day,—who, in my humble opinion, are the

---

*After eliminating the seven remaining earls of Caledonia, Kenneth I (c.843) had himself declared king of Scotland at the ancient stone of destiny in the Pictish monastery of Scone.

†Prophetesses.

legitimate inheritors and preservers of the ancient science of divination. This much is certain, that Governor Stuyvesant succeeded to the chair of state at a turbulent period; when foes thronged and threatened from without; when anarchy and stiff-necked opposition reigned rampant within; when the authority of their High Mightinesses the Lords States General, though supported by economy and defended by speeches, protests, and proclamations, yet tottered to its very centre; and when the great city of New Amsterdam, though fortified by flag-staffs, trumpeters, and windmills, seemed, like some fair lady of easy virtue, to lie open to attack, and ready to yield to the first invader.

BOOK VII

CONTAINING THE THIRD PART OF
THE REIGN OF PETER THE
HEADSTRONG—HIS TROUBLES
WITH THE BRITISH NATION, AND
THE DECLINE AND FALL OF THE
DUTCH DYNASTY

Chapter XI

HOW PETER STUYVESANT DEFENDED THE CITY
OF NEW AMSTERDAM FOR SEVERAL DAYS, BY
DINT OF THE STRENGTH OF HIS HEAD

There is something exceedingly sublime and melancholy in the
spectacle which the present crisis of our history presents. An
illustrious and venerable little city,—the metropolis of a vast
extent of uninhabited country,—garrisoned by a doughty host of
orators, chairmen, committee-men, burgomasters, schepens, and
old women,—governed by a determined and strong-headed

warrior, and fortified by mud batteries, palisadoes, and resolu-tions,—blockaded by sea, beleaguered by land, and threatened with direful desolation from without, while its very vitals are torn with internal faction and commotion! Never did historic pen record a page of more complicated distress, unless it be the strife that distracted the Israelites, during the siege of Jerusalem,—where dis-cordant parties were cutting each other's throats, at the moment when the victorious legions of Titus* had toppled down their bulwarks, and were carrying fire and sword into the very *sanctum sanctorum* of the temple.

Governor Stuyvesant having triumphantly put his grand council to the rout, and delivered himself from a multitude of impertinent advisers, dispatched a categorical reply to the commanders of the in-vading squadron; wherein he asserted the right and title of their High Mightinesses the Lords States General to the province of New Netherlands, and trusting in the righteousness of his cause, set the whole British nation at defiance!

My anxiety to extricate my readers and myself from these disas-trous scenes prevents me from giving the whole of this gallant letter, which concluded in these manly and affectionate terms:—

"As touching the threats in your conclusion, we have nothing to answer, only that we fear nothing but what God (who is as just as merciful) shall lay upon us; all things being in his gracious disposal, and we may as well be preserved by him with small forces as by a great army; which makes us to wish you all happiness and prosper-ity, and recommend you to his protection. My lords, your thrice humble and affectionate servant and friend,

P. STUYVESANT"

Thus having thrown his gauntlet, the brave Peter stuck a pair of horse-pistols in his belt, girded an immense powder-horn on his side,—thrust his sound leg into a Hessian boot, and clapping his fierce little war-hat on the top of his head,—paraded up and down in front of his house, determined to defend his beloved city to the last.

---

*Titus Flavius Sabinus Vespasianus (A.D. 39–81), Roman emperor whose legions captured and destroyed Jerusalem in A.D. 70.

While all these struggles and dissensions were prevailing in the unhappy city of New Amsterdam, and while its worthy but ill-starred governor was framing the above-quoted letter, the English commanders did not remain idle. They had agents secretly employed to foment the fears and clamors of the populace; and moreover circulated far and wide, through the adjacent country, a proclamation, repeating the terms they had already held out in their summons to surrender, at the same time beguiling the simple Nederlanders with the most crafty and conciliating professions. They promised that every man who voluntarily submitted to the authority of his British Majesty should retain peaceful possession of his house, his vrouw, and his cabbage-garden. That he should be suffered to smoke his pipe, speak Dutch, wear as many breeches as he pleased, and import bricks, tiles, and stone jugs from Holland, instead of manufacturing them on the spot. That he should on no account be compelled to learn the English language, nor eat codfish on Saturdays, nor keep accounts in any other way than by casting them up on his fingers, and chalking them down upon the crown of his hat; as is observed among the Dutch yeomanry at the present day. That every man should be allowed quietly to inherit his father's hat, coat, shoe-buckles, pipe, and every other personal appendage; and that no man should be obliged to conform to any improvements, inventions, or any other modern innovations; but, on the contrary, should be permitted to build his house, follow his trade, manage his farm, rear his hogs, and educate his children, precisely as his ancestors had done before him from time immemorial. Finally, that he should have all the benefits of free trade, and should not be required to acknowledge any other saint in the calendar than St. Nicholas, who should thenceforward, as before, be considered the tutelar saint of the city.

These terms, as may be supposed, appeared very satisfactory to the people, who had a great disposition to enjoy their property unmolested, and a most singular aversion to engage in a contest, where they could gain little more than honor and broken heads,—the first of which they held in philosophic indifference, the latter in utter detestation. By these insidious means, therefore, did the English succeed in alienating the confidence and affections of the populace from their gallant old governor, whom they considered as obstinately bent upon running them into hideous misadventures; and did not hesitate to speak their minds freely, and abuse him most heartily—behind his back.

Like as a mighty grampus* when assailed and buffeted by roaring waves and brawling surges, still keeps on an undeviating course, rising above the boisterous billows, spouting and blowing as he emerges,—so did the inflexible Peter pursue, unwavering, his determined career, and rise, contemptuous, above the clamors of the rabble.

But when the British warriors found that he set their power at defiance, they dispatched recruiting officers to Jamaica, and Jericho, and Nineveh, and Quag, and Patchog, and all those towns on Long Island which had been subdued of yore by Stoffel Brinkerhoff; stirring up the progeny of Preserved Fish, and Determined Cock, and those other New-England squatters, to assail the city of New Amsterdam by land, while the hostile ships prepared for an assault by water.

The streets of New Amsterdam now presented a scene of wild dismay and consternation. In vain did Peter Stuyvesant order the citizens to arm and assemble on the Battery. Blank terror reigned over the community. The whole party of Short Pipes in the course of a single night had changed into arrant old women—a metamorphosis only to be paralleled by the prodigies recorded by Livy[†] as having happened at Rome at the approach of Hannibal, when statues sweated in pure affright, goats were converted into sheep, and cocks, turning into hens, ran cackling about the street.

Thus baffled in all attempts to put the city in a state of defence, blockaded from without, tormented from within, and menaced with a Yankee invasion, even the stiff-necked will of Peter Stuyvesant for once gave way, and in spite of his mighty heart, which swelled in his throat until it nearly choked him, he consented to a treaty of surrender.

Words cannot express the transports of the populace, on receiving this intelligence; had they obtained a conquest over their enemies, they could not have indulged greater delight. The streets resounded with their congratulations,—they extolled their governor as the father and deliverer of his country,—they crowded to his

---

*Whale.

[†]Livy (59 B.C.–A.D. 17) was a Roman historian; Hannibal (247–183? B.C.) was a general of Carthage who fought numerous battles against the Roman Empire.

house to testify their gratitude, and were ten times more noisy in their plaudits than when he returned, with victory perched upon his beaver, from the glorious capture of Fort Christina.* But the indignant Peter shut his doors and windows, and took refuge in the innermost recesses of his mansion, that he might not hear the ignoble rejoicings of the rabble.

Commissioners were now appointed on both sides, and a capitulation was speedily arranged; all that was wanting to ratify it was that it should be signed by the governor. When the commissioners waited upon him for this purpose, they were received with grim and bitter courtesy. His warlike accoutrements were laid aside,—an old Indian night-gown was wrapped about his rugged limbs, a red night-cap overshadowed his frowning brow, an iron-gray beard of three days' growth gave additional grimness to his visage. Thrice did he seize a worn-out stump of a pen, and essay to sign the loathsome paper,—thrice did he clinch his teeth, and make a horrible countenance, as though a dose of rhubarb, senna, and ipecacuanha[†] had been offered to his lips; at length, dashing it from him, he seized his brass-hilted sword, and jerking it from the scabbard, swore by St. Nicholas, to sooner die than yield to any power under heaven.

For two whole days did he persist in this magnanimous resolution, during which his house was besieged by the rabble, and menaces and clamorous revilings exhausted to no purpose. And now another course was adopted to soothe, if possible, his mighty ire. A procession was formed by the burgomasters and schepens, followed by the populace, to bear the capitulation in state to the governor's dwelling. They found the castle strongly barricadoed, and the old hero in full regimentals, with his cocked hat on his head, posted with a blunderbuss at the garret-window.

There was something in this formidable position that struck even the ignoble vulgar with awe and admiration. The brawling multitude could not but reflect with self-abasement upon their own pusillanimous conduct, when they beheld their hardy but deserted

---

*Swedish settlement on the Delaware River; it was captured by the Dutch under Stuyvesant in 1655.
[†]Herbal remedy used to induce vomiting.

old governor, thus faithful to his post, like a forlorn hope, and fully prepared to defend his ungrateful city to the last. These compunctions, however, were soon overwhelmed by the recurring tide of public apprehension. The populace arranged themselves before the house, taking off their hats with most respectful humility; Burgomaster Roerback, who was of that popular class of orators described by Sallust* as being "talkative rather than eloquent," stepped forth and addressed the governor in a speech of three hours' length, detailing, in the most pathetic terms, the calamitous situation of the province, and urging him in a constant repetition of the same arguments and words to sign the capitulation.

The mighty Peter eyed him from his garret-window in grim silence,—now and then his eye would glance over the surrounding rabble, and an indignant grin, like that of an angry mastiff, would mark his iron visage. But though a man of most undaunted mettle,— though he had a heart as big as an ox, and a head that would have set adamant to scorn,—yet after all he was a mere mortal. Wearied out by these repeated oppositions, and this eternal haranguing, and perceiving that unless he complied, the inhabitants would follow their own inclination, or rather their fears, without waiting for his consent, or, what was still worse, the Yankees would have time to pour in their forces and claim a share in the conquest, he testily ordered them to hand up the paper. It was accordingly hoisted to him on the end of a pole; and having scrawled his name at the bottom of it, he anathematized them all for a set of cowardly, mutinous, degenerate poltroons, threw the capitulation at their heads, slammed down the window, and was heard stumping down-stairs with vehement indignation. The rabble incontinently took to their heels; even the burgomasters were not slow in evacuating the premises, fearing lest the sturdy Peter might issue from his den, and greet them with some unwelcome testimonial of his displeasure.

Within three hours after the surrender, a legion of British beef-fed warriors poured into New Amsterdam, taking possession of the fort and batteries. And now might be heard, from all quarters, the sound of hammers made by the old Dutch burghers, in nailing up their

---

*Roman historian Gaius Sallustius Crispus (or Sallust, c.86–c.34 B.C.).

doors and windows, to protect their vrouws from these fierce barbarians, whom they contemplated in silent sullenness from the garret-windows as they paraded through the streets.

Thus did Colonel Richard Nichols, the commander of the British forces, enter into quiet possession of the conquered realm as *locum tenens** for the Duke of York. The victory was attended with no other outrage than that of changing the name of the province and its metropolis, which thenceforth were denominated NEW YORK, and so have continued to be called unto the present day. The inhabitants, according to treaty, were allowed to maintain quiet possession of their property; but so inveterately did they retain their abhorrence of the British nation, that in a private meeting of the leading citizens it was unanimously determined never to ask any of their conquerors to dinner.

NOTE.—Modern historians assert that when the New Netherlands were thus overrun by the British, as Spain in ancient days by the Saracens,[†] a resolute band refused to bend the neck to the invader. Led by one Garret Van Horne, a valorous and gigantic Dutchman, they crossed the bay and buried themselves among the marshes and cabbage-gardens of Communipaw; as did Pelayo[‡] and his followers among the mountains of Asturias. Here their descendants have remained ever since, keeping themselves apart, like seed-corn, to re-people the city with the genuine breed whenever it shall be effectually recovered from its intruders. It is said the genuine descendants of the Nederlanders who inhabit New York, still look with longing eyes to the green marshes of ancient Pavonia, as did the conquered Spaniards of yore to the stern mountains of Asturias, considering these the regions whence deliverance is to come.

---

*Substitute or proxy.
†Here referring to Moorish invaders of medieval Spain.
‡The first Asturian king, who began the reconquest of Spain from the Saracens.

Chapter XII

CONTAINING THE DIGNIFIED RETIREMENT,
AND MORTAL SURRENDER OF PETER
THE HEADSTRONG

Thus, then, have I concluded this great historical enterprise; but before I lay aside my weary pen, there yet remains to be performed one pious duty. If among the variety of readers who may peruse this book, there should haply be found any of those souls of true nobility, which glow with celestial fire as the history of the generous and the brave, they will doubtless be anxious to know the fate of the gallant Peter Stuyvesant. To gratify one such sterling heart of gold I would go more lengths than to instruct the cold-blooded curiosity of a whole fraternity of philosophers.

No sooner had that high-mettled cavalier signed the articles of capitulation, than, determined not to witness the humiliation of his favorite city, he turned his back on its walls and made a growling retreat to his *bouwery*, or country-seat, which was situated about two miles off; where he passed the remainder of his days in patriarchal retirement. There he enjoyed that tranquillity of mind which he had never known amid the distracting cares of government; and tasted the sweets of absolute and uncontrolled authority, which his factious subjects had so often dashed with the bitterness of opposition.

No persuasions could ever induce him to revisit the city; on the contrary, he would always have his great arm-chair placed with its back to the windows which looked in that direction, until a thick grove of trees planted by his own hand grew up and formed a screen that effectually excluded it from the prospect. He railed continually at the degenerate innovations and improvements introduced by the conquerors; forbade a word of their detested language to be spoken in his family,—a prohibition readily obeyed, since none of the household could speak anything but Dutch,—and even ordered a fine avenue to be cut down in front of his house because it consisted of English cherry-trees.

The same incessant vigilance, which blazed forth when he had a vast province under his care, now showed itself with equal vigor, though in narrower limits. He patrolled with unceasing watchfulness the boundaries of his little territory; repelled every encroachment with intrepid promptness; punished every vagrant depredation upon his orchard or his farm-yard with inflexible severity; and conducted every stray hog or cow in triumph to the pound. But to the indigent neighbor, the friendless stranger, or the weary wanderer, his spacious doors were ever open, and his capacious fireplace, that emblem of his own warm and generous heart, had always a corner to receive and cherish them. There was an exception to this, I must confess, in case the ill-starred applicant were an Englishman or a Yankee; to whom, though he might extend the hand of assistance, he could never be brought to yield the rites of hospitality. Nay, if peradventure some straggling merchant of the East should stop at his door, with his cart-load of tin ware or wooden bowls, the fiery Peter would issue forth like a giant from his castle, and make such a furious clattering among his pots and kettles, that the vender of "*notions*"* was fain to betake himself to instant flight.

His suit of regimentals, worn threadbare by the brush, were carefully hung up in the state bed-chamber, and regularly aired the first fair day of every month; and his cocked hat and trusty sword were suspended in grim repose over the parlor mantelpiece, forming supporters to a full-length portrait of the renowned Admiral Van Tromp.[†] In his domestic empire he maintained strict discipline and a well-organized despotic government; but though his own will was the supreme law, yet the good of his subjects was his constant object. He watched over, not merely their immediate comforts, but their morals, and their ultimate welfare; for he gave them abundance of excellent admonition, nor could any of them complain, that, when occasion required, he was by any means niggardly in bestowing wholesome correction.

---

*Home remedies.
[†]See footnote on p. 402.

The good old Dutch festivals, those periodical demonstrations of an overflowing heart and a thankful spirit, which are falling into sad disuse among my fellow-citizens, were faithfully observed in the mansion of Governor Stuyvesant. New-Year was truly a day of open-handed liberality, of jocund revelry, and warm-hearted congratulation, when the bosom swelled with genial good-fellowship, and the plenteous table was attended with an unceremonious freedom, and honest broad-mouthed merriment, unknown in these days of degeneracy and refinement. Paas and Pinxter* were scrupulously observed throughout his dominions; nor was the day of St. Nicholas suffered to pass by, without making presents, hanging the stocking in the chimney, and complying with all its other ceremonies.

Once a year, on the first day of April, he used to array himself in full regimentals, being the anniversary of his triumphal entry into New Amsterdam, after the conquest of New Sweden. This was always a kind of saturnalia among the domestics, when they considered themselves at liberty, in some measure, to say and do what they pleased; for on this day their master was always observed to unbend, and become exceeding pleasant and jocose, sending the old gray-headed negroes on April-fool's errands for pigeon's milk; not one of whom but allowed himself to be taken in, and humored his old master's jokes, as became a faithful and well-disciplined dependant. Thus did he reign, happily and peacefully on his own land—injuring no man—envying no man—molested by no outward strifes—perplexed by no internal commotions;—and the mighty monarchs of the earth, who were vainly seeking to maintain peace, and promote the welfare of mankind, by war and desolation, would have done well to have made a voyage to the little island of Manna-hata, and learned a lesson in government from the domestic economy of Peter Stuyvesant.

In process of time, however, the old governor, like all other children of mortality, began to exhibit evident tokens of decay. Like an aged oak, which, though it long has braved the fury of the elements, and still retains its gigantic proportions, begins to shake and groan with every blast—so was it with the gallant Peter; for though

---

*Dutch common names for the festivals of Easter and Whitsunday (Pentecost).

he still bore the port and semblance of what he was in the days of his hardihood and chivalry, yet did age and infirmity begin to sap the vigor of his frame,—but his heart, that unconquerable citadel, still triumphed unsubdued. With matchless avidity would he listen to every article of intelligence concerning the battles between the English and Dutch,—still would his pulse beat high whenever he heard of the victories of De Ruyter,* and his countenance lower, and his eyebrows knit, when fortune turned in favor of the English. At length, as on a certain day he had just smoked his fifth pipe, and was napping after dinner, in his arm-chair, conquering the whole British nation in his dreams, he was suddenly aroused by a ringing of bells, rattling of drums, and roaring of cannon, that put all his blood in a ferment. But when he learnt that these rejoicings were in honor of a great victory obtained by the combined English and French fleets over the brave De Ruyter, and the younger Van Tromp, it went so much to his heart, that he took to his bed, and in less than three days was brought to death's door, by a violent cholera morbus! Even in this extremity he still displayed the unconquerable spirit of Peter *the Headstrong*; holding out to the last gasp, with inflexible obstinacy, against a whole army of old women who were bent upon driving the enemy out of his bowels, in the true Dutch mode of defence, by inundation.

While he thus lay, lingering on the verge of dissolution, news was brought him that the brave De Ruyter had made good his retreat, with little loss, and meant once more to meet the enemy in battle. The closing eye of the old warrior kindled with martial fire at the words,—he partly raised himself in bed,—clinched his withered hand, as if he felt within his gripe that sword which waved in triumph before the walls of Fort Christina, and giving a grim smile of exultation, sank back upon his pillow, and expired.

Thus died Peter Stuyvesant,—a valiant soldier—a loyal subject—an upright governor, and an honest Dutchman,—who wanted only a few empires to desolate, to have been immortalized as a hero!

---

*Michiel de Ruyter, Dutch admiral who, in the second Dutch War, defeated the English in the naval encounter known as the Four Days' Battle (June 11–14, 1666); he was defeated in turn by the British at the St. James Day Fight (July 25, 1666).

His funeral obsequies were celebrated with the utmost grandeur and solemnity. The town was perfectly emptied of its inhabitants, who crowded in throngs to pay the last sad honors to their good old governor. All his sterling qualities rushed in full tide upon their recollection, while the memory of his foibles and his faults had expired with him. The ancient burghers contended who should have the privilege of bearing the pall; the populace strove who should walk nearest to the bier; and the melancholy procession was closed by a number of gray-headed negroes, who had wintered and summered in the household of their departed master for the greater part of a century.

With sad and gloomy countenances, the multitude gathered round the grave. They dwelt with mournful hearts on the sturdy virtues, the signal services, and the gallant exploits of the brave old worthy. They recalled, with secret upbraidings, their own factious oppositions to his government; and many an ancient burgher, whose phlegmatic features had never been known to relax, nor his eyes to moisten, was now observed to puff a pensive pipe, and the big drop to steal down his cheek, while he muttered, with affectionate accent, and melancholy shake of the head—"Well, den!—Hardkoppig Peter ben gone at last!"

His remains were deposited in the family vault, under a chapel which he had piously erected on his estate, and dedicated to St. Nicholas,—and which stood on the identical spot at present occupied by St. Mark's church, where his tombstone is still to be seen. His estate, or *bouwery*, as it was called, has ever continued in the possession of his descendants, who, by the uniform integrity of their conduct, and their strict adherence to the customs and manners that prevailed in the "*good old times*," have proved themselves worthy of their illustrious ancestor. Many a time and oft has the farm been haunted at night by enterprising money-diggers, in quest of pots of gold, said to have been buried by the old governor, though I cannot learn that any of them have ever been enriched by their researches; and who is there, among my native-born fellow-citizens, that does not remember when, in the mischievous days of his boyhood, he conceived it a great exploit to rob "Stuyvesant's orchard" on a holiday afternoon?

At this stronghold of the family may still be seen certain memorials of the immortal Peter. His full-length portrait frowns in martial terrors from the parlor-wall; his cocked hat and sword still hang up in the best bedroom; his brimstone-colored breeches were for a long while suspended in the hall, until some years since they occasioned a dispute between a new-married couple; and his silver-mounted wooden leg is still treasured up in the store-room, as an invaluable relique.

Endnotes

Letters of Jonathan Oldstyle, Gent.

1. (p. 7) *Letters of Jonathan Oldstyle, Gent.*: Irving's first publication, *Letters of Jonathan Oldstyle, Gent.*, appeared serially in the New York *Morning Chronicle* from November 15, 1802, to April 23, 1803. The *Chronicle* was a pro-Burrite paper edited by Irving's brother Peter. (The Burrites were a faction of the Democratic-Republican party led by Aaron Burr [1756–1836], the prominent New York politician who became Thomas Jefferson's vice president following the election of 1800.) The first two of the nine letters are included in this edition because they exemplify Irving's early efforts to establish a satiric narrative voice. Although he was only nineteen at the time, Irving assumed the narrative persona of an elderly bachelor critical of "the degeneracy of the present times" (p. 13). In his nostalgia for an idyllic past, Oldstyle anticipates Irving's better-known narrators Diedrich Knickerbocker (*A History of New York*) and Geoffrey Crayon (*The Sketch-Book of Geoffrey Crayon, Gent.*). These letters also reflect the cultural instability of the post-Revolutionary period, in which social values and political opinions seemed to change as quickly as fashion—"they fly from one extreme to the other" (p. 9).

2. (p. 11) *There is nothing that seems more strange and preposterous to me than the manner in which modern marriages are conducted*: Oldstyle's comments on courtship and marriage can be usefully compared with the romantic characterization of marriage in Irving's sketch "The Wife" (p. 65) and with the satire on courtship in "The Legend of Sleepy Hollow" (p. 162). The attitude toward marriage in Irving's writings is often conflicted, and his female characters are either idealized beauties or shrewish wives.

Salmagundi

1. (p. 15) *Salmagundi*: *Salmagundi; or, The Whim-Whams and Opinions of Launcelot Langstaff, Esq. & Others* was a series of twenty pamphlets jointly written by Irving, his brother William, and their friend James Kirke

Paulding and published over the course of a year, from January 24, 1807, to January 25, 1808. This selection includes the introductory remarks from the first number, the "Letters from Mustapha" from nos. III, VII, and XI, and the authors' farewell in the final number. Of the three Mustapha letters, Bruce I. Granger and Martha Hartzog—the editors who prepared the modern scholarly edition of *Salmagundi* for *The Complete Works of Washington Irving*, vol. 6 (Boston: Twayne Publishers, 1977; see "For Further Reading")—definitively attribute to Irving only the one written for no. XI. The two others have been included in this edition to give readers a more complete sense of how the Mustapha series is a satire on America's evolving democratic process. Besides these obvious political satires, the pages of *Salmagundi* lampoon a range of subjects in an effort "to do justice to this queer, odd, rantipole city, and to this whimsical country" (p. 44).

2. (p. 21) *Several Tripolitan prisoners . . . were brought to New York, . . . restore them to their own country.—Paris Ed. [Irving's note]*: Irving refers here to the long-standing conflict between the United States and the Barbary states—northern Africa's Tripolitania, Tunisia, Algeria, and Morocco— whose main port was Tripoli (now the capital of Libya). Tripoli served as the home base of the Barbary pirates, who targeted trade routes along the coast of northern Africa. In the First Barbary War, also known as the Tripolitan War (1801–1805), commander William Bainbridge was captured while trying to enforce a blockade of the harbor at Tripoli. The war serves as the historical backdrop for Irving's satirical treatment of American politics in the "Letters from Mustapha."

3. (p. 21) *who understands all languages, not excepting that manufactured by Psalmanazar*: The reference is to George Psalmanazar (1679?–1763), an English literary imposter whose real name is not known. He published *An Historical and Geographical Description of Formosa* (1704) and invented and taught to students at Oxford University a fictional "Formosan" language. His ruse was discovered in 1706, and he was forced to publicly acknowledge the fraud. Irving likely knew his posthumously published *Memoirs of—, Commonly Known by the Name George Psalmanazar* (1764). Psalmanazar may have provided the example Irving followed when he staged the literary hoax of Diedrich Knickerbocker's disappearance to advertise the publication of *A History of New York* (see the Introduction, p. xxiii).

4. (p. 24) *The present bashaw*: "Bashaw," or "pasha," is a Turkish term that refers to a man of high rank. The reference here is to Thomas Jefferson, third president of the United States (1801–1809). The "Letters of Mustapha" are consistently critical of Jefferson and his administration, lampooning his involvement in the Tripolitan War, presenting him as a disengaged dilettante, and satirizing his rejection of the Bible on scientific grounds (see pp. 28–29). A supporter of the Federalists (advocates of a strong federal government), Irving was sympathetic to those who thought the Jeffersonian Republicans were reducing the government to a "mobocracy" (see pp. 26–27).

5. (p. 26) *No. VII.—Saturday, April 4, 1807*: In this second "Letter from Mustapha," the authors of *Salmagundi* coin a new term to describe America's political system. Because of the seemingly endless debates characteristic of the democratic process, they describe it as a "*logocracy*, or government of words" (p. 27). The extent to which public opinion can be influenced by the press is a theme Irving returned to in his sketch "English Writers on America": "Over no nation does the press hold a more absolute control than over the people of America" (p. 95).

6. (p. 43) *In compliance with . . .* : The subsequent paragraphs are the editors' farewell to their readership in the final number of *Salmagundi*. Paulding and the Irvings decided to end the series after their publisher, David Longworth, took out copyright in his name and raised the price to one shilling.

The Sketch-Book

1. (p. 47) *The Sketch-Book*: *The Sketch-Book of Geoffrey Crayon, Gent.* was published consecutively in the United States and England. The first American edition appeared in seven paperbound numbers between June 23, 1819, and September 13, 1820. When several sketches from the early numbers were reprinted in British newspapers, Irving, fearing that a pirated edition would be published in England, arranged for a volume of the first four numbers to be published in London. He later arranged for the publication of a revised English edition that included the two Native American sketches "Traits of Indian Character" and "Philip of Pokanoket" and also the concluding "L'Envoy." The publication history of *The Sketch-Book* is of interest because it shows Irving's efforts to negotiate the transatlantic audience that American writers had to confront in the early decades of the nineteenth century. The first American edition began with the following "Prospectus":

> The following writings are published on experiment; should they please they may be followed by others. The writer will have to contend with some disadvantages. He is unsettled in his abode, subject to interruptions, and has his share of cares and vicissitudes. He cannot therefore promise a regular plan, nor regular periods of publication. Should he be encouraged to proceed, much time may elapse between the appearance of his numbers; and their size must depend on the materials he has on hand. His writings will partake of the fluctuations of his own thoughts and feelings; sometimes treating of scenes before him; sometimes of others purely imaginary, and sometimes wandering back with his recollections to his native country. He will not be able to give them that tranquil attention necessary to finished composition, and as they must be transmitted across the Atlantic for publication, he must trust to others to correct the frequent errors of the press. Should his writings, however, with all their imperfections, be well received, he cannot conceal that it would be a source of the purest gratification, for though he does not aspire to those high honours that are the rewards of loftier intellects; yet it is the dearest wish of his heart to have a secure, and cherished, though humble, corner in the good opinions and kind feelings of his countrymen.
>
> London, 1819

The first English edition began with the following "Advertisement":

> The following desultory papers are part of a series written in this country, but published in America. The author is aware of the austerity with which the writings of his countrymen have hitherto been treated by British critics: he is conscious, too, that much of the contents of his papers can be interesting only in the eyes of his American readers. It was not his intention, therefore, to have them reprinted in this country. He has, however, observed several of them from time to time inserted in periodical works of merit, and has understood that it was probable they would be republished in a collective form. He has been induced, therefore, to revise and

bring them forward himself, that they may at least come correctly before the public. Should they be deemed of sufficient importance to attract the attention of critics, he solicits for them that courtesy and candour which a stranger has some right to claim, who presents himself at the threshold of a hospitable nation.

February, 1820

The selections from *The Sketch-Book* included in this edition are meant to exhibit Irving's conscious efforts to appeal to both British and American readers.

2. (p. 49) *The Author's Account of Himself*: In "The Author's Account of Himself" Irving identifies Great Britain (and, by extension, "Old Europe") as a repository of history and cultural traditions—the raw materials of fiction that American writers lacked. Although an American "never need . . . look beyond his own country for the sublime and beautiful of natural scenery," he must turn to Europe for "the charms of storied and poetical association . . . the masterpieces of art, the refinements of highly-cultivated society, the quaint peculiarities of ancient and local custom" (p. 50). In his stories set in Sleepy Hollow and in his use of the Dutch colonial history of New York, Irving works to construct a comparable set of "storied and poetical associations" for America.

3. (p. 50) *for I had read in the works of various philosophers, that all animals degenerated in America, and man among the number*: Irving alludes to a theory propounded by a number of British and European scholars, most notably the French naturalist Georges-Louis Leclerc, comte du Buffon (1707–1788). Buffon's account of the "degenerate" form of plant and animal specimens taken from the North American continent was refuted by Thomas Jefferson in *Notes on the State of Virginia* (1785).

4. (p. 51) *humble lovers of the picturesque*: The picturesque was a well-defined school of aesthetics that was part of the romantic reaction against neoclassical formalism. Its principles were outlined and promoted by English writer William Gilpin (1724–1804), English landscape designer Sir Uvedale Price (1747–1829), and English classical scholar Sir Richard Payne Knight (1750–1824), among others. Irving was close friends with a number of painters associated with the picturesque movement, including Washington Allston (1779–1843), Gilbert Stuart Newton (1794–1835), and C. R. Leslie (1794–1859); Leslie is featured in Irving's sketch "The Wife" (although it is Allston upon whom the details of the story are based).

5. (p. 52) *The Voyage*: Crossing the Atlantic from Europe to America often symbolized the erasure of one's ties to the "Old World" in exchange for the opportunity to recreate oneself in the New. In "The Voyage," Irving reverses this process and renders it ironic. He realizes that the Atlantic "interposes a gulf, not merely imaginary, but real, between us and our homes" (p. 53). At the same time, despite the fact that he is traveling back to the home of his forefathers, on his arrival he feels himself to be "a stranger in the land" (p. 57). Irving's presentation of Geoffrey Crayon as enduring a self-imposed exile anticipates a tradition in American literature of characters who define their individuality in terms of the loss, or the absence, of cultural belonging (see the Introduction, p. xxv).

6. (p. 58) *Roscoe*: William Roscoe (1753–1831) was an English historian and author whose principal historical work was *The Life of Lorenzo de' Medici* (1795). In this sketch Irving presents Roscoe as an exemplary model for American writers because of how he "effected [in his life a] union of commerce and the intellectual pursuits, [and] . . . practically proved how beautifully they may be brought to harmonize, and to benefit each other" (pp. 60–61).

7. (p. 65) *The Wife*: In this sketch Irving presents marriage as a romantic ideal. Crayon characterizes a wife as "a ministering angel" in the "dark hour of adversity" (p. 68), a stark contrast with the "terrible virago" Dame Van Winkle, in the subsequent sketch (p. 78).

8. (p. 72) *Rip Van Winkle*: One of Irving's best known stories, "Rip Van Winkle" marks the first time Irving reintroduced Diedrich Knickerbocker, the fictional compiler of *A History of New York* (1809). "Rip Van Winkle" can be read as an historical allegory that prepares the way for American literature by lengthening a reader's sense of history through a deliberate forgetting of the American Revolution (see the Introduction, pp. xviii–xx).

9. (p. 87) *Hendrick Hudson*: English explorer Henry Hudson (1565?–1611?) discovered the Hudson River while searching for a Northwest Passage to India. In 1610 he led an expedition into Hudson Bay, Canada; the voyage ended in mutiny in 1611, when Hudson, his son, and seven crew members were set adrift in an open boat and never seen again.

10. (p. 89) *a little German superstition about the Emperor Frederick* der Rothbart, *and the Kypphaüser mountain*: The Kyffhäuser is a mountain located in central Germany. According to German legend, Frederick I—German king (1152–1190) and Holy Roman Emperor (1155–1190), also known as Frederick Barbarossa or Rothbart (respectively, Italian and German for "Redbeard")—sleeps in a cave there, awakening every hundred years to see if his country needs his leadership. In "Rip Van Winkle," Irving creates a similar legend for Henry Hudson (see p. 87).

11. (p. 91) *English Writers on America*: In this sketch, Irving responds to condemnations of American culture in the British press, dismissing such criticism as little more than "cobwebs woven round the limbs of an infant giant" (p. 94). But while he proclaims the "national power and glory" of America (p. 94), Irving also writes to appease his British readers, insisting that there is still a "kindred tie" between the nations (p. 97). He concludes by instructing his American readers to view English cultural history as "a perpetual volume of reference" because "the spirit of her constitution [and] . . . the manners of her people are . . . all congenial to the American character" (p. 99).

12. (p. 100) *The Art of Book-Making:* This sketch continues the theme introduced in "English Writers on America" insofar as it suggests that all authors possess a "pilfering disposition" that leads them to borrow their ideas and even their style from earlier writers (p. 102). Irving is casting a sly wink here at his own method of borrowing: Because he does not have "a card of admission" to the library, he is "convicted of being an arrant poacher" (p. 106). This is also a veiled allusion that associates Irving with William Shakespeare, who, according to legend, was arrested for poaching deer from the estate of Sir Thomas Lucy. Shakespeare was also known to have borrowed extensively from sources such as *Chronicles of England, Scotland, and Ireland* (1577), by English chronicler Raphael Holinshed.

13. (p. 107) *The Mutability of Literature*: In "The Mutability of Literature" Irving continues to engage the problem that the English literary tradition poses for American writers. Crayon's conversation with a dusty old quarto shows the vast majority of English books to be lost in obscurity. The only way to stave off such neglect is to "root [oneself] in the unchanging principles of human nature," as Shakespeare did (p. 115). American writers can achieve the greatness of a Shakespeare so long as they "write from the heart" (p. 116). Herman Melville took up this idea of an American Shakespeare in his review of Nathaniel Hawthorne's 1846 collection of short stories *Mosses from an*

Old Manse. (The review, "Hawthorne and His Mosses," appeared in *The Literary World* in August 1850.)

14. (p. 112) *"afterwards, also, by deligent travell of Geffry Chaucer and of John Gowre . . . their great praise and immortal commendation" [Irving's note]*: This is a quotation from Holinshed's *Chronicles of England, Scotland, and Ireland* (see note 12, above), which Shakespeare and other Elizabethan dramatists used as a source for several of their works. In this passage, Holinshed traces the development of the literary style of Elizabethan England. He lists: Geoffrey Chaucer (c.1340–1400), English poet and author of *The Canterbury Tales*; John Gower (1330?–1408), English poet and a friend of Chaucer; Richard II (1367–1400), king of England; John Scogan (c.1480), court jester to Edward IV, although there may be some confusion here with Henry Scogan (1361–1407), a poet and a friend of Chaucer; John Lydgate (1370?–1449?), English author and translator who is credited with keeping the Chaucerian poetic tradition alive; Elizabeth I (1533–1603), queen of England during the height of the Renaissance; John Jewel (1522–1571), bishop of Sarum (Salisbury) and author of *Apologia ecclesiae Anglicanae* (1562; *An Apology of the Church of England*); and John Foxe (1516–1587), English clergyman and author of *Book of Martyrs* (1559).

15. (p. 118) *The Inn Kitchen*: "The Inn Kitchen" provides the frame-narrative for the subsequent story, "The Spectre Bridegroom"; this is a narrative technique Irving used extensively in *Bracebridge Hall* (1822) and *Tales of a Traveller* (1824).

16. (p. 120) *The Spectre Bridegroom*: "The Spectre Bridegroom" shows the influence of German folklore and Gothic romanticism on Irving's stories, subjects he studied with the encouragement of Scottish author Sir Walter Scott (1771–1832), whom he met during the summer of 1817 (see the Introduction, p. xxiv).

17. (p. 135) *Traits of Indian Character*: In "Traits of Indian Character," Irving participates in the construction of the myth of "the noble savage," a figure to be used in the development of a uniquely American literary culture. He presents the Native American warriors as figures comparable to the "knights-errant" of Arthurian legend (p. 142), and predicts that "if . . . some dubious memorial of them should survive, it may be in the romantic dreams of the poet, to people in imagination his glades and groves, like the fauns and satyrs and sylvan deities of antiquity" (p. 145). Although Irving may have had in mind poetry such as "Gertrude of Wyoming" (1809), by British poet Thomas Campbell, the heroic type he describes (p. 142) was perhaps most

fully realized by James Fenimore Cooper in his depiction of Chingachgook, the Mohican warrior and companion of Natty Bumppo in *The Leatherstocking Tales* (1823–1841).

18. (p. 146) *Philip of Pokanoket*: Philip of Pokanoket (1639?–1676), also known as King Philip, was chief of the Wampanoag tribe and the son of Massasoit, who signed a treaty with the Pilgrims at Plymouth in 1621. In this sketch, Irving continues the theme of "Traits of Indian Character," presenting Philip as a figure representative of the classical ideal of heroic virtue. The character traits Irving attributes to Philip are those of American individualism as represented in the mythic figure of the frontiersman inspired by the likes of Daniel Boone and Davy Crocket. That Irving imagines these character traits to be attributes of American national identity is suggested in his conclusion to the sketch, which presents King Philip as "a patriot attached to his native soil" with "an untamable love of natural liberty" (p. 161).

19. (p. 162) *The Legend of Sleepy Hollow*: Along with "Rip Van Winkle," this is one of Irving's best-known stories. However, it is the setting, rather than the competition between Ichabod Crane and Brom Bones for the hand of Katrina Van Tassel, that makes this story important. Irving describes Sleepy Hollow as a timeless space for romantic fiction, "a retreat, whither I might steal from the world and its distractions, and dream quietly away the remnant of a troubled life" (p. 163).

Bracebridge Hall

1. (p. 197) *Bracebridge Hall*: Published in 1822, *Bracebridge Hall* is the immediate successor of *The Sketch-Book* and in some ways a continuation of it. *The Sketch-Book* contains a series of sketches (not included in this edition) describing the Christmas festivities at Bracebridge Hall, a fictional English manor based on Irving's visit to Aston Hall in Birmingham and on the hospitality he enjoyed at Abbotsford, in Scotland, while staying with Sir Walter Scott. This section of *The Sketch-Book* was popular with his English audience, and in a conscious effort to appeal to that readership, Irving took Bracebridge Hall as the setting for his second book of sketches and stories.

2. (p. 202) *Story-Telling*: This sketch serves as the frame-narrative (see note 15 above) for "The Stout Gentleman," which follows. The narrator Irving introduces here, "a thin, pale, weazen-faced man, extremely nervous" (p. 202), is one he later uses to narrate the first part of *Tales of a Traveller* (1824), "Strange Stories By a Nervous Gentleman."

3. (p. 202) *the current of anecdotes and stories . . . that have . . . filled the world with doubts and conjecture; such as the Wandering Jew, the Man with the Iron Mask, . . . the Invisible Girl, and . . . the Pig-faced Lady*: This is a list of legendary stories. In medieval myth, the Wandering Jew is an Israelite who mocks Christ at the crucifixion and is cursed to wander the earth alone until the Day of Judgment. The mysterious, unidentified French prisoner known as the "Man with the Iron Mask" was imprisoned from 1679 until his death in 1707, some of that time in the Bastille. The Invisible Girl probably refers to the poem "To the Invisible Girl," by English poet Thomas Hood (1799–1845), which is included in *English Minstrelsy* (vol. 2, 1810), edited by Sir Walter Scott. The Pig-faced Lady is a folk story, popular in Europe during the Middle Ages, in which a wealthy woman insults the child of a beggar by saying, "Take away your nasty pig; I shall not give you anything," and is cursed to bear a daughter with the face of a pig.

4. (p. 203) *The Stout Gentleman*: The title character of this story is said to be Sir Walter Scott, who had become a literary celebrity despite the fact that he published his novels anonymously until 1827. The story is significant, however, because it offers a glimpse of the development of a modern readership for commercial fiction. Stuck in the "travellers'-room" of an inn and surrounded by salesmen whom he ironically describes as "commercial knights-errant" (p. 204), the narrator strives to catch a glimpse of the patron he assumes is a celebrity only after he has exhausted all of the light reading at his disposal—"Old newspapers, . . . Good-for-nothing books, . . . [and] an old volume of the Lady's Magazine" (p. 205)—in other words, reading material exactly like the story of "The Stout Gentleman."

5. (p. 213) *The Historian*: "The Historian" is a frame-narrative designed to introduce "a manuscript tale from the pen of my fellow-countryman, the late Mr. Diedrich Knickerbocker" (p. 214), which includes the sequence of stories that follows: "The Haunted House," "Dolph Heyliger," and "The Storm-Ship."

6. (p. 213) *the "Arabian Nights"*: Available to Irving in a number of translations, *The Arabian Nights* or *The Thousand and One Nights* is a collection of Oriental stories that influenced Irving's use of embedded narratives. In the following story sequence the narration of Geoffrey Crayon is turned over to Diedrich Knickerbocker, who in turn relates Antony Vander Heyden's telling of "The Storm-Ship," which Vander Heyden claims to give "in the very words in which it had been written out by Mynheer Selyne, an early poet of New Netherlandts" (pp. 253–254).

7. (p. 216) *The Haunted House*: "The Haunted House" introduces the succeeding story, "Dolph Heyliger," the only story in *Bracebridge Hall* that is set in America. "Dolph Heyliger" is notable for its descriptions of the Hudson River valley. Along with "Rip Van Winkle" and "The Legend of Sleepy Hollow," it contributed to the formation of a regional cultural heritage for New York comparable to that provided for New England in the short stories of Nathaniel Hawthorne.

8. (p. 279) *The Author's Farewell*: "The Author's Farewell" to *Bracebridge Hall* is significant because of the way Irving returns to the cultural conflict between England and America he described in "English Writers on America." Despite Irving's effort to "[awaken] a chord of sympathy between the land of my fathers and the dear land which gave me birth," some American critics condemned him as an Anglophile and an imitator of British and European literary models (p. 283).

Tales of a Traveller

1. (p. 287) *To The Reader*: *Tales of a Traveller* was published in 1824, two years after *Bracebridge Hall*. Irving thought it contained "some of the best things I have ever written," but it was not well received by critics in England and America, partly because it was made up wholly of stories and lacked the familiar essays and sketches readers had come to expect from Irving. The selections in this edition are meant to illustrate the Gothic influence on Irving's writing; also included are two of the tales attributed to Diedrich Knickerbocker, "Kidd the Pirate" and "The Devil and Tom Walker."

2. (p. 293) *The Hunting-Dinner*: "The Hunting-Dinner" is the frame-narrative Irving designed to introduce the sequence of stories that comprise the first part of *Tales of a Traveller*. The last four tales of that sequence are included in this edition: "Adventure of the German Student," "Adventure of the Mysterious Picture," "Adventure of the Mysterious Stranger," and "The Story of the Young Italian."

3. (p. 297) *the old gentleman with the haunted head proceeded*: The subsequent tale is not "The Adventure of My Uncle" referred to here, but a later tale in the sequence that is also narrated by "the old gentleman with the haunted head."

4. (p. 298) *Adventure of the German Student*: The conservatism of this story can be seen in its association of "the liberal doctrines of the day" (p. 302) with a gruesome conclusion that drives the protagonist insane. More importantly for students of American literature, the woman dressed in black

introduces a figure and a theme whose psychological depths Edgar Allan
Poe would explore in stories such as "Morella" and "Ligeia."

5. (p. 304) *Adventure of the Mysterious Picture*: With this story Irving is attempting a Gothic tale of greater intensity than the stories that figure in
"Dolph Heyliger" or "The Legend of Sleepy Hollow." It is not the features of
the painting that terrorize the narrator but "some horror of the mind, some
inscrutable antipathy awakened by this picture" (p. 306). Whereas the
reader of "The Legend of Sleepy Hollow" realizes that Ichabod Crane is
being chased by Brom Bones disguised as the Headless Horseman, the
reader of "The Mysterious Picture" participates in the narrator's "state of
nervous agitation" (p. 307).

6. (p. 312) *Adventure of the Mysterious Stranger*: Presented as an explanation
of "Adventure of the Mysterious Picture," this story anticipates the theme
of alienation central to stories such as Nathaniel Hawthorne's "Wakefield"
or Edgar Allan Poe's "The Man of the Crowd." However, the subsequent
"The Story of the Young Italian" provides a solution to the mystery that
renders this sequence more conventional than Hawthorne's or Poe's narratives of isolation in the midst of society.

7. (p. 320) *The Story of the Young Italian*: "The Story of the Young Italian" concludes the sequence of stories that began with "Adventure of the Mysterious
Picture." Irving set "Adventure of the German Student" in Paris and "The
Story of the Young Italian" in Genoa, cities he stayed in on more than one
occasion; but his descriptions lack the verisimilitude of his evocative accounts of the Hudson River Valley. This may in part explain why a critic for
Blackwood's Edinburgh Magazine (September 1824) found *Tales of a Traveller* to be derivative, except for the concluding stories set in America, which
were "not only worth the bulk of it five hundred times over, but really, and
in every respect, worthy of the author and his fame."

8. (p. 346) *About six miles . . . within its clutches*: This description of the strait
at the mouth of the East River, which provides access to Long Island Sound
from New York Harbor, provides the frame-narrative for the fourth part of
Tales of a Traveller. Irving uses it to establish the narrative voice of Diedrich
Knickerbocker (fictional narrator of *A History of New York*), with his characteristic allusions to classical antiquity and New York's Dutch colonial
history.

9. (p. 349) *Kidd the Pirate*: "Kidd the Pirate" is a second frame-narrative for
the fourth part of *Tales*; it is designed to bridge the gap between history

and fiction. Irving begins with a popular history of William "Captain" Kidd (c.1645–1701), a Scottish privateer who was ultimately convicted of piracy and murder and hung for his crimes in London. This history provides the basis for the stories that follow.

10. (p. 355) *The Devil and Tom Walker*: This is one of the few stories Irving sets in New England. Walker's encounter with the Devil in the swamps of Back Bay perhaps anticipates Nathaniel Hawthorne's "Young Goodman Brown," but Irving's characteristic vein of light humor sets a very different tone than Hawthorne's puritan sensibility.

A History of New York

1. (p. 369) *The following work . . .* : Irving first published *A History of New York* in 1809, but he significantly revised it on five separate occasions throughout his career, culminating with the Author's Revised Edition of 1848. This last version is the one included in this edition, and as it reflects Irving's later style and political sensibilities, it has been placed at the end of the volume. The selections included here are designed to introduce readers to the major historical figures around whom Irving chose to organize his work: Oloff Van Cortlandt, founder of the Dutch colony at Manhattan, and the subsequent director-generals of the colony, Wouter Van Twiller, Willem Kieft, and Peter Stuyvesant. Irving's decision to limit his *History* to the Dutch colonial period preceding England's control of the colony is significant insofar as it provided his contemporary readers with an historical past free from the influence of English cultural traditions (see the Introduction, pp. xviii, xix and xxx).

2. (p. 373) *Notices*: In the weeks prior to the publication of *A History of New York*, Irving published these notices as a promotional hoax to increase sales (see the Introduction, p. xxiii). His ploy was successful, and a second edition of *A History* was printed in 1812.

Inspired by Washington Irving

Let us not, then, lament over the decay and oblivion into which ancient writers descend; they do but submit to the great law of nature, which declares that all sublunary shapes of matter shall be limited in their duration, but which decrees, also, that their elements shall never perish. Generation after generation, both in animal and vegetable life, passes away, but the vital principle is transmitted to posterity, and the species continue to flourish. Thus, also, do authors beget authors, and having produced a numerous progeny, in a good old age they sleep with their fathers, that is to say, with the authors who preceded them—and from whom they had stolen.

—Washington Irving, from "The Art of Book-Making"

Literature

America's first man of letters inspired a host of American authors who alternately revered, questioned, lambasted, and imitated him. The first generation of great American writers—Nathaniel Hawthorne, Herman Melville, and Edgar Allan Poe, among others—all explicitly acknowledged Irving's influence. Some of them even published their works in *Knickerbocker Magazine*, one of the many invocations of Diedrich Knickerbocker, Irving's narrator in *A History of New York* (1809). The term "Knickerbocker" eventually came to refer to the descendants of the Dutch of New York and finally to identify all New Yorkers; it is now found in dictionaries.

Poe's tales of horror—some of them blackly comic and dealing with the supernatural—are often cited as the first American works that distinctly show Irving's influence. Primarily a poet and writer of short stories, Poe struggled through most of his writing life for favorable attention. Looking to establish a reputation for himself in the American press, he courted Irving, and Irving, in his way, mentored the younger author. When he began to receive letters from Irving, the famously insecure Poe was jubilant. "I am sure you will be pleased to hear that Washington Irving has addressed me 2 letters, abounding in high passages of compliment in regard to my Tales—passages which he desires me to make public," Poe wrote in a November 11, 1839, letter to his old friend Joseph Evans Snodgrass. "Irving's name will afford me a complete triumph over those little critics who would endeavor to put me down by raising the hue & cry of *exaggeration* in style, of *Germanism* & such twaddle." Poe built on the foundation of American folklore and mystery found in Irving's works, adding to it his own lyricism and quiet beauty. Despite this, Poe never enjoyed literary success during his lifetime to rival Irving's.

Another writer to whom Irving played mentor is *Twice-Told Tales* author, Nathaniel Hawthorne. Hawthorne is said to have modeled "The Custom-House," a chapter that precedes the action in *The Scarlet Letter* (1850), after Irving's work. Following publication of that novel, Hawthorne's celebrity soared, and Irving became of one of the many admirers of Hawthorne's genius. Their mutual affection established, Hawthorne sent the following letter to Irving on July 16, 1852, along with a copy of his newest effort, *The Blithedale Romance* (1852):

I beg you to believe me, my dear Sir, that your friendly and approving word was one of the highest gratifications that I could possibly have received, from any literary source. Ever since I began to write, I have kept it among my cherished hopes to obtain such a word; nor did I ever publish a book without debating within myself whether to offer it to your notice. Nevertheless, the idea of introducing myself to you as an author, while unrecognized by the public, was not quite agreeable; and I saw too many faults in each of my books to be altogether willing to obtrude it beneath your eye. At last, I sent you 'The Wonder Book,' because, being meant for children, it seemed to reach a higher point, in its own way, than anything that I had written for grown people.

Pray, do not think it necessary to praise my "Blithedale Romance"—or even to acknowledge the receipt of it. From my own little experience, I can partly judge how dearly purchased are books that come to you on such terms. It affords me—and I ask no more—an opportunity of expressing the affectionate admiration which I have felt so long; a feeling, by the way, common to all our countrymen, in reference to Washington Irving, and which, I think, you can hardly appreciate, because there is no writer with the qualities to awaken in yourself precisely the same intellectual and heartfelt recognition.

Poetry

American poet Philip Freneau, in "To a New England Poet" (1823), derides Irving's seeming subservience to Britain's popular literary tastes: "Lo! he has kissed a Monarch's—hand! / Before a prince I see him stand, / And with the glittering nobles mix, / Forgetting times of seventy-six." But a host of American poets emerging in Irving's wake thought him to be the most important literary figure among them. Henry Wadsworth Longfellow was one such writer who in his works gave Irving his due. In addition to his prose volume *Outre-Mer: A Pilgrimage Beyond the Sea* (1833–1834), which is heavily influenced by Irving, Longfellow composed the poem "In the Churchyard at Tarrytown" in tribute to the author:

> Here lies the gentle humorist, who died
> In the bright Indian Summer of his fame!
> A simple stone, with but a date and name,
> Marks his secluded resting-place beside
> The river that he loved and glorified.
> Here in the autumn of his days he came,
> But the dry leaves of life were all aflame
> With tints that brightened and were multiplied.
> How sweet a life was his; how sweet a death!
> Living, to wing with mirth the weary hours,
> Or with romantic tales the heart to cheer;
> Dying, to leave a memory like the breath
> Of summers full of sunshine and of showers,
> A grief and gladness in the atmosphere.

Another poetic tribute to the writer of the *The Sketch-Book* came in the form of *A Fable for Critics* (1848), by James Russell Lowell. Lowell's ten-part poem reads like a who's who of American letters, including nods to Ralph Waldo Emerson, Poe, Longfellow, and Lowell himself. The stanza concerning Irving follows:

> To a true poet-heart add the fun of Dick Steele,
> Throw in all of Addison, minus the chill,
> With the whole of that partnership's stock and good will,
> Mix well, and while stirring, hum o'er, as a spell,
> The fine old English Gentleman, simmer it well,

Sweeten just to your own private liking, then strain
That only the finest and clearest remain,
Let it stand out of doors till a soul it receives
From the warm lazy sun loitering down through green leaves,
And you'll find a choice nature, not wholly deserving
A name either English or Yankee,—just Irving.

Film

Today, encomiums to an author's genius usually come in the form of film adaptations rather than verse. Washington Irving's "The Legend of Sleepy Hollow" has been the stuff of spine-tingling cinema for more than a century, with versions including a handful of shorts from the silent era; the beloved Disney cartoon of 1958, narrated and with songs sung by Bing Crosby; a humorous 1980 television adaptation starring Jeff Goldblum; and, perhaps the most faithful adaptation, a 1999 movie made for Canadian television. The most innovative of the lot is by auteur director Tim Burton. Known for his macabre humor, Burton lends his visionary genius to the Headless Horseman myth with 1999's *Sleepy Hollow*. The film's lush atmosphere is accented by poignant and memorable images: a horse carriage careening through a valley reminiscent of Hudson River School paintings; a moonlit New England village enclosed, even preserved, in curtains of fog and mist; and, of course, an epic and unforgettable Headless Horseman, with a cloud of flittering fallen leaves in his terrible wake.

Burton's film, featuring a screenplay by Andrew Kevin Walker, takes place in 1799. The coming century seems to promise order for the newly minted American nation, but for now, superstition reigns supreme. Ichabod Crane, played by a typically eccentric Johnny Depp, is a Manhattan-based, rational-to-a-fault solicitor, rather than the guileless schoolteacher of Irving's narrative. Crane is investigating a series of gruesome decapitations, attributed by village locals to the legendary Headless Horseman. Scoffing at what he considers superstitious imaginings, Crane conducts his inquiry with a Holmesian levelheadedness, only to discover that his modern methods and theories are no match for the supernatural phenomena local to Sleepy Hollow. Though the film sags beneath a belabored plot, its heavily atmospheric setting is pitch perfect.

Sleepy Hollow, as its truncated title seems to suggest, is less reverent to its source than are other Irving adaptations. In fact, Burton seems to have cast his eye elsewhere, including at the campy horror films of the 1950s and 1960s produced by the British company Hammer Film Productions Ltd. It is Hammer luminary Christopher Lee playing an imperious New York judge who banishes Crane to Sleepy Hollow in Burton's film. The Headless Horseman, played by a grotesque Christopher Walken and shown in various flashbacks, is revealed in all manner of gory detail to be a serial decapitator—the ghost of a Hessian soldier who fought in the Revolutionary War on the British side and who was buried sans head. The ensemble cast includes Christina Ricci and Miranda Richardson.

Comments & Questions

In this section, we aim to provide the reader with an array of perspectives on the text, as well as questions that challenge those perspectives. The commentary has been culled from sources as diverse as reviews contemporaneous with the work, letters written by the author, literary criticism of later generations, and appreciations written throughout the work's history. Following the commentary, a series of questions seeks to filter Washington Irving's The Legend of Sleepy Hollow *and* Other Writings *through a variety of points of view and bring about a richer understanding of this enduring work.*

Comments

WALTER SCOTT

I beg you to accept my best thanks for the uncommon degree of entertainment which I have received from the most excellently jocose history of New York. I am sensible that as a stranger to American parties and politics I must lose much of the conceald satire of the piece but I must own I have never read anything so closely resembling the stile of Dean Swift as the annals of Diedrich Knickerbocker. I have been employed these few evenings in reading them aloud to Mrs. S. and two ladies who are our guests and our sides have been absolutely tense with laughing. I think too, there are passages which indicate that the author possesses powers of a different kind & has some touches which remind me much of Sterne. I beg you will have the kindness to let me know when Mr. [Irving] take[s] pen in hand again for assuredly I shall expect a very great treat which I may chance never to hear of but through your kindness.

—from a letter to Henry Brevoort (April 23, 1813)

WILLIAM HAZLITT

Mr. Irving is by birth an American, and has, as it were, *skimmed the cream*, and taken off patterns with great skill and cleverness, from our best-known and happiest writers, so that their thoughts and almost their reputation are indirectly transferred to his page, and smile upon us from another hemisphere, like 'the pale reflex of Cynthia's brow.' He succeeds to our admiration and our sympathy by a sort of prescriptive title and traditional privilege . . .

Mr. Washington Irving's acquaintance with English literature begins almost where Mr. Lamb's ends,—with the *Spectator*, Tom Brown's works and the wits of Queen Anne. He is not bottomed in our elder writers, nor do we think he has tasked his own faculties much, at least on English ground. Of the merit of his *Knickerbocker* and New York stories we cannot pretend to judge. But in his *Sketchbook* and *Bracebridge-Hall* he gives us very good American copies of our British Essayists and Novelists, which may be very well on the other side of the water, or as proofs of the capabilities of the national genius, but which might be dispensed with here, where we have to boast of the originals. Not only Mr. Irving's language is with great taste and felicity modelled on that of Addison, Goldsmith, Sterne, or Mackenzie: but the thoughts and sentiments are taken at the rebound, and, as they are brought forward at the present period, want both freshness and probability . . .

Mr. Irving's writings are literary *anachronisms*.

—from *The Spirit of the Age* (1825)

CHARLES DICKENS
There is no living writer, and there are very few among the dead, whose approbation I should feel so proud to earn. And with everything you have written upon my shelves, and in my thoughts, and in my heart of hearts, I may honestly and truly say so. If you could know how earnestly I write this, you would be glad to read it—as I hope you will be, faintly guessing at the warmth of the hand I autobiographically hold out to you over the broad Atlantic.

—from a letter to Washington Irving (1842)

EDGAR ALLAN POE
The *Spectator*, Mr. Irving, and Mr. Hawthorne have in common that tranquil and subdued manner which we have chosen to denominate *repose*; but, in the case of the two former, this repose is attained rather by the absence of novel combination, or of originality, than otherwise,

and consists chiefly in the calm, quiet, unostentatious expression of commonplace thoughts, in an unambitious, unadulterated Saxon. In them, by strong effort, we are made to conceive the absence of all.

—from *Graham's Magazine* (May 1842)

WILLIAM CULLEN BRYANT

The "Sketch Book," and the two succeeding works of Irving, "Bracebridge Hall" and the "Tales of a Traveller," abound with agreeable pictures of English life, seen under favorable lights and sketched with a friendly pencil. Let me say here, that it was not to pay court to the English that he thus described them and their country; it was because he could not describe them otherwise. It was the instinct of his mind to attach itself to the contemplation of the good and the beautiful, wherever he found them, and to turn away from the sight of what was evil, misshapen and hateful. His was not a nature to pry for faults, or disabuse the world of good-natured mistakes; he looked for virtue, love and truth among men, and thanked God that he found them in such large measure. If there are touches of satire in his writings, he is the best natured and most amiable of satirists, amiable beyond Horace; and in his irony—for there is a vein of playful irony running through many of his works—there is no tinge of bitterness.

—from "A Discourse on the Life, Character and Genius of Washington Irving" (1860)

WILLIAM MAKEPEACE THACKERAY

Was Irving not good, and, of his works, was not his life the best part? In his family, gentle, generous, good-humoured, affectionate, self-denying: in society, a delightful example of complete gentlemanhood; quite unspoiled by prosperity; never obsequious to the great (or, worse still, to the base and mean, as some public men are forced to be in his and other countries); eager to acknowledge every contemporary's merit; always kind and affable to the young members of his calling: in his professional bargains and mercantile dealings delicately honest and grateful; one of the most charming masters of our lighter language; the constant friend to us and our nation; to men of letters doubly dear, not for his wit and genius merely, but as an exemplar of goodness, probity, and pure life.

—from *Cornhill Magazine* (January 1860)

EDMUND GOSSE

It is in the *Sketch-Book* that Irving first appeals to us as a torchbearer in the great procession of English prose-writers. In *Knickerbocker* he had been dancing or skipping in the lightness of his heart to a delicious measure of his own; in *Salmagundi* he had waked up to a sense of literary responsibility, without quite knowing in what direction his new-found sense of style would lead him. In the *Sketch-Book* he is a finished and classic writer, bowing to the great tradition of English prose, and knowing precisely what it is that he would do, and how to do it. He sustains this easy mastery of manner through his next book, *Bracebridge Hall,* and then, if he wrote no less well in future, the voice at least had become familiar, and the peculiar wonder and delight with which his age received him faded into a common pleasure. The *Sketch-Book* and *Bracebridge Hall,* then, remain the bright original stars in this gracious constellation.

—from *Critic* (March 31, 1883)

EDWIN P. WHIPPLE

The "revival" of American literature in New York differed much in character from its revival in New England. In New York it was purely human in tone; in New England it was a little superhuman in tone. In New England they feared the devil; in New York they dared the devil; and the greatest and most original literary dare-devil in New York was a young gentleman of a good family, whose "schooling" ended with his sixteenth year, who had rambled much about the island of Manhattan, who had in his saunterings gleaned and brooded over many Dutch legends of an elder time, who had read much but had studied little, who possessed fine observation, quick intelligence, a genial disposition, and an indolently original genius in detecting the ludicrous side of things, and whose name was Washington Irving. After some preliminary essays in humorous literature his genius arrived at the age of *in*discretion, and he produced at the age of twenty-six the most deliciously audacious work of humor in our literature, namely, The *History of New York,* by Diedrich Knickerbocker. It is said of some reformers that they have not only opinions, but the courage of their opinions. It may be said of Irving that he not only caricatured, but had the courage of his caricatures. The persons whom he covered with ridicule were the ancestors of the leading families of New York, and these families prided themselves on their descent. After the publication of such a book he could hardly enter the "best society" of New York, to which he naturally belonged, without running the risk of being insulted, especially by the elderly women of fashion; but he conquered their prejudices by the same grace and geniality of manner, by the same unmistakable tokens that he was an inborn gentleman, through which he afterward won his way into the first society of England, France, Germany, Italy, and Spain. Still, the promise of Knicker-bocker was not fulfilled. That book, if considered as an imitation at all, was an imitation of Rabelais, or Swift, or of any author in any language who had shown an independence of all convention, who did not hesitate to commit indecorums, and who laughed at all the regalities of the world. The author lived long enough to be called a timid imitator of Addison and Goldsmith. In fact, he imitated no-body. His genius, at first riotous and unrestrained, became tamed and regulated by a larger intercourse with the world, by the sadden-ing experience of life, and by the gradual development of some deep sentiments which held in check the audacities of his wit and humor. But even in the portions of *The Sketch-Book* relating to England it will be seen that his favorite authors belonged rather to the age of Elizabeth than to the age of Anne. In *Bracebridge Hall* there is one chapter called "The Rookery," which in exquisitely poetic humor is hardly equalled by the best productions of the authors he is said to have made his models. That he possessed essential humor and pathos, is proved by the warm admiration he excited in such masters of humor and pathos as Scott and Dickens; and style is but a sec-ondary consideration when it expresses vital qualities of genius. If he subordinated energy to elegance, he did it, not because he had the ignoble ambition to be ranked as "a fine writer," but because he was free from ambition, equally ignoble, of simulating a passion which he did not feel. The period which elapsed between the publication of Knickerbocker's history and *The Sketch-Book* was ten years. During this time his mind acquired the habit of tranquilly contemplating the objects which filled his imagination, and what it lost in spontaneous vigor it gained in sureness of insight and completeness of representation. "Rip Van Winkle" and "The Legend of Sleepy Hollow" have not the humorous inspiration of some passages in

Knickerbocker, but perhaps they give more permanent delight, for the scenes and characters are so harmonized that they have the effect of a picture, in which all the parts combine to produce one charming whole. Besides, Irving is one of those exceptional authors who are regarded by their readers as personal friends, and the felicity of nature by which he obtained this distinction was expressed in that amenity, that amiability of tone, which some of his austere critics have called elegant feebleness.

—from *American Literature, and Other Papers* (1887)

Questions

1. Is there anything *American* about Irving's writing other than the occasional settings and characters, anything in his spirit or sensibility or way of looking at things that strike you as typically American?

2. Analyze a typical passage of Irving's prose. What's good about it? What's not so good?

3. Hazlitt writes that Irving's writings are "literary *anachronisms.*" Poe pretty much agrees. Thackeray describes him as "one of the most charming masters of our lighter language." Edwin Whipple describes "that amenity, that amiability of tone, which some of his austere critics have called elegant feebleness." Is this condescension deserved? Or can Irving's absence of bite or partisanship be evidence of great tolerance, or even an aloof philosophic perspective in which everything is understood and therefore forgiven?

4. In some of Irving's tales there is what we might call a "spooky" or gothic dimension. Is this dimension the supernatural, or is the supernatural used as a metaphor for the psychological realm or for fear of the unknown?

For Further Reading

Bell, Michael Davitt. *The Development of American Romance: The Sacrifice of Relation*. Chicago: University of Chicago Press, 1980.

Irving, Pierre M. *The Life and Letters of Washington Irving*. 4 vols., 1862–1864. 3 vols. New York: Putnam, 1973.

McClary, Ben, ed. *Washington Irving and the House of Murray: Geoffrey Crayon Charms the British, 1817–1856*. Knoxville: University of Tennessee Press, 1969.

McLamore, Richard V. "The Dutchman in the Attic: Claiming an Inheritance in *The Sketch Book of Geoffrey Crayon*." *American Literature* 72 (March 2000), pp. 31–57.

Rubin-Dorsky, Jeffrey. *Adrift in the Old World: The Psychological Pilgrimage of Washington Irving*. Chicago: University of Chicago Press, 1988.

Tuttleton, James W., ed. *Washington Irving: The Critical Reaction*. New York: AMS Press, 1993.

Wagenknecht, Edward. *Washington Irving: Moderation Displayed*. New York: Oxford University Press, 1962.

Other Works Cited in the Introduction

Emerson, Ralph Waldo. *The Collected Works of Ralph Waldo Emerson*. General editors: Joseph Slater and Douglas Emory Wilson. 6 vols. Cambridge, MA, and London: Belknap Press of Harvard University, 1971–2003.

Hawthorne, Nathaniel. *The Centenary Edition of the Works of Nathaniel Hawthorne*. General editors: William Charvat, Roy Harvey Pearce, Claude M. Simpson, and Thomas Woodson. 23 vols. Columbus: Ohio State University Press, 1962–1997.

Horwitz, Howard. " 'Rip Van Winkle' and Legendary National Memory." *Western Humanities Review* 58:2 (Fall 2004), pp. 34–47.

Irving, Washington. *The Complete Works of Washington Irving*. General editors: Henry A. Pochmann, Herbert L. Kleinfield, and

Richard Dilworth Rust. 30 vols. Madison: University of Wisconsin Press, 1969–1970, and Boston: Twayne, 1976–1989.

Pattee, Fred Lewis. *The Development of the American Short Story: An Historical Survey.* New York: Harper and Brothers, 1923.

Spencer, Benjamin T. *The Quest for Nationality: An American Literary Campaign.* Syracuse, NY: Syracuse University Press, 1957.

Thoreau, Henry David. *The Writings of Henry David Thoreau.* 20 vols. Edited by Bradford Torrey and F. B. Sanborn. Boston: Houghton Mifflin, 1906.

Williams, Stanley T. *The Life of Washington Irving.* 2 vols. New York and London: Oxford University Press, 1935.

TIMELESS WORKS • NEW SCHOLARSHIP • EXTRAORDINARY VALUE

Look for the following titles, available now from
BARNES & NOBLE CLASSICS

Visit your local bookstore for these and more fine titles.
Or to order online go to: WWW.BN.COM/CLASSICS

Adventures of Huckleberry Finn	Mark Twain	1-59308-112-X	$6.95
The Adventures of Tom Sawyer	Mark Twain	1-59308-139-1	$6.95
The Aeneid	Vergil	1-59308-237-1	$7.95
Aesop's Fables		1-59308-062-X	$5.95
The Age of Innocence	Edith Wharton	1-59308-143-X	$5.95
Agnes Grey	Anne Brontë	1-59308-323-8	$5.95
Alice's Adventures in Wonderland and Through the Looking-Glass	Lewis Carroll	1-59308-015-8	$5.95
Anna Karenina	Leo Tolstoy	1-59308-027-1	$8.95
The Arabian Nights	Anonymous	1-59308-281-9	$9.95
The Art of War	Sun Tzu	1-59308-017-4	$7.95
The Autobiography of an Ex-Colored Man and Other Writings	James Weldon Johnson	1-59308-289-4	$5.95
The Awakening and Selected Short Fiction	Kate Chopin	1-59308-113-8	$6.95
Babbitt	Sinclair Lewis	1-59308-267-3	$7.95
The Beautiful and Damned	F. Scott Fitzgerald	1-59308-245-2	$7.95
Beowulf	Anonymous	1-59308-266-5	$4.95
Billy Budd and The Piazza Tales	Herman Melville	1-59308-253-3	$5.95
Bleak House	Charles Dickens	1-59308-311-4	$9.95
The Bostonians	Henry James	1-59308-297-5	$7.95
The Brothers Karamazov	Fyodor Dostoevsky	1-59308-045-X	$9.95
Bulfinch's Mythology	Thomas Bulfinch	1-59308-273-8	$12.95
The Call of the Wild and White Fang	Jack London	1-59308-200-2	$5.95
Candide	Voltaire	1-59308-028-X	$4.95
The Canterbury Tales	Geoffrey Chaucer	1-59308-080-8	$9.95
A Christmas Carol, The Chimes and The Cricket on the Hearth	Charles Dickens	1-59308-033-6	$5.95
The Collected Oscar Wilde		1-59308-310-6	$9.95
The Collected Poems of Emily Dickinson		1-59308-050-6	$5.95
Common Sense and Other Writings	Thomas Paine	1-59308-209-6	$6.95
The Communist Manifesto and Other Writings	Karl Marx and Friedrich Engels	1-59308-100-6	$5.95
The Complete Sherlock Holmes, Vol. I	Sir Arthur Conan Doyle	1-59308-034-4	$7.95
The Complete Sherlock Holmes, Vol. II	Sir Arthur Conan Doyle	1-59308-040-9	$7.95
Confessions	Saint Augustine	1-59308-259-2	$6.95
A Connecticut Yankee in King Arthur's Court	Mark Twain	1-59308-210-X	$7.95
The Count of Monte Cristo	Alexandre Dumas	1-59308-151-0	$7.95
The Country of the Pointed Firs and Selected Short Fiction	Sarah Orne Jewett	1-59308-262-2	$6.95
Crime and Punishment	Fyodor Dostoevsky	1-59308-081-6	$8.95
Daisy Miller and Washington Square	Henry James	1-59308-105-7	$4.95
Daniel Deronda	George Eliot	1-59308-290-8	$8.95
Dead Souls	Nikolai Gogol	1-59308-092-1	$7.95
The Deerslayer	James Fenimore Cooper	1-59308-211-8	$7.95

(continued)

(continued)

The Magnificent Ambersons	Booth Tarkington	1-59308-263-0	$7.95
Main Street	Sinclair Lewis	1-59308-386-6	$7.95
Man and Superman and Three Other Plays	George Bernard Shaw	1-59308-067-0	$7.95
The Man in the Iron Mask	Alexandre Dumas	1-59308-233-9	$8.95
Mansfield Park	Jane Austen	1-59308-154-5	$5.95
The Mayor of Casterbridge	Thomas Hardy	1-59308-309-2	$5.95
The Metamorphoses	Ovid	1-59308-276-2	$7.95
The Metamorphosis and Other Stories	Franz Kafka	1-59308-029-8	$6.95
Moby-Dick	Herman Melville	1-59308-018-2	$9.95
Moll Flanders	Daniel Defoe	1-59308-216-9	$5.95
My Ántonia	Willa Cather	1-59308-202-9	$5.95
My Bondage and My Freedom	Frederick Douglass	1-59308-301-7	$6.95
Narrative of Sojourner Truth		1-59308-293-2	$6.95
Narrative of the Life of Frederick Douglass, an American Slave		1-59308-041-7	$4.95
Nicholas Nickleby	Charles Dickens	1-59308-300-9	$8.95
Night and Day	Virginia Woolf	1-59308-212-6	$7.95
Nostromo	Joseph Conrad	1-59308-193-6	$7.95
O Pioneers!	Willa Cather	1-59308-205-3	$5.95
The Odyssey	Homer	1-59308-009-3	$5.95
Oliver Twist	Charles Dickens	1-59308-206-1	$6.95
The Origin of Species	Charles Darwin	1-59308-077-8	$7.95
Paradise Lost	John Milton	1-59308-095-6	$7.95
The Paradiso	Dante Alighieri	1-59308-317-3	$7.95
Pere Goriot	Honoré de Balzac	1-59308-285-1	$7.95
Persuasion	Jane Austen	1-59308-130-8	$5.95
Peter Pan	J. M. Barrie	1-59308-213-4	$4.95
The Phantom of the Opera	Gaston Leroux	1-59308-249-5	$6.95
The Picture of Dorian Gray	Oscar Wilde	1-59308-025-5	$4.95
The Pilgrim's Progress	John Bunyan	1-59308-254-1	$7.95
A Portrait of the Artist as a Young Man and Dubliners	James Joyce	1-59308-031-X	$6.95
The Possessed	Fyodor Dostoevsky	1-59308-250-9	$9.95
Pride and Prejudice	Jane Austen	1-59308-201-0	$5.95
The Prince and Other Writings	Niccolò Machiavelli	1-59308-060-3	$5.95
The Prince and the Pauper	Mark Twain	1-59308-218-5	$4.95
Pudd'nhead Wilson and Those Extraordinary Twins	Mark Twain	1-59308-255-X	$5.95
The Purgatorio	Dante Alighieri	1-59308-219-3	$7.95
Pygmalion and Three Other Plays	George Bernard Shaw	1-59308-078-6	$7.95
The Red Badge of Courage and Selected Short Fiction	Stephen Crane	1-59308-119-7	$4.95
Republic	Plato	1-59308-097-2	$6.95
The Return of the Native	Thomas Hardy	1-59308-220-7	$7.95
Robinson Crusoe	Daniel Defoe	1-59308-360-2	$5.95
A Room with a View	E. M. Forster	1-59308-288-6	$5.95
Scaramouche	Rafael Sabatini	1-59308-242-8	$6.95
The Scarlet Letter	Nathaniel Hawthorne	1-59308-207-X	$5.95
The Scarlet Pimpernel	Baroness Orczy	1-59308-234-7	$5.95
The Secret Agent	Joseph Conrad	1-59308-305-X	$6.95
The Secret Garden	Frances Hodgson Burnett	1-59308-277-0	$5.95
Selected Stories of O. Henry		1-59308-042-5	$5.95
Sense and Sensibility	Jane Austen	1-59308-125-1	$5.95
Siddhartha	Hermann Hesse	1-59308-379-3	$5.95

(continued)

Silas Marner and Two Short Stories	George Eliot	1-59308-251-7	$6.95
Sister Carrie	Theodore Dreiser	1-59308-226-6	$7.95
The Souls of Black Folk	W. E. B. Du Bois	1-59308-014-X	$5.95
The Strange Case of Dr. Jekyll and Mr. Hyde and Other Stories	Robert Louis Stevenson	1-59308-131-6	$4.95
Swann's Way	Marcel Proust	1-59308-295-9	$8.95
A Tale of Two Cities	Charles Dickens	1-59308-138-3	$5.95
Tarzan of the Apes	Edgar Rice Burroughs	1-59308-227-4	$5.95
Tess of d'Urbervilles	Thomas Hardy	1-59308-228-2	$7.95
This Side of Paradise	F. Scott Fitzgerald	1-59308-243-6	$6.95
Three Theban Plays	Sophocles	1-59308-235-5	$6.95
Thus Spoke Zarathustra	Friedrich Nietzsche	1-59308-278-9	$7.95
The Time Machine and The Invisible Man	H. G. Wells	1-59308-388-2	$6.95
Tom Jones	Henry Fielding	1-59308-070-0	$8.95
Treasure Island	Robert Louis Stevenson	1-59308-247-9	$4.95
The Turn of the Screw, The Aspern Papers and Two Stories	Henry James	1-59308-043-3	$5.95
Twenty Thousand Leagues Under the Sea	Jules Verne	1-59308-302-5	$5.95
Uncle Tom's Cabin	Harriet Beecher Stowe	1-59308-121-9	$7.95
Vanity Fair	William Makepeace Thackeray	1-59308-071-9	$7.95
The Varieties of Religious Experience	William James	1-59308-072-7	$7.95
Villette	Charlotte Brontë	1-59308-316-5	$7.95
The Virginian	Owen Wister	1-59308-236-3	$7.95
Walden and Civil Disobedience	Henry David Thoreau	1-59308-208-8	$5.95
War and Peace	Leo Tolstoy	1-59308-073-5	$12.95
The War of the Worlds	H. G. Wells	1-59308-362-9	$5.95
Ward No. 6 and Other Stories	Anton Chekhov	1-59308-003-4	$7.95
The Waste Land and Other Poems	T. S. Eliot	1-59308-279-7	$4.95
The Way We Live Now	Anthony Trollope	1-59308-304-1	$9.95
The Wind in the Willows	Kenneth Grahame	1-59308-265-7	$4.95
The Wings of the Dove	Henry James	1-59308-296-7	$7.95
Wives and Daughters	Elizabeth Gaskell	1-59308-257-6	$7.95
The Woman in White	Wilkie Collins	1-59308-280-0	$7.95
Women in Love	D. H. Lawrence	1-59308-258-4	$8.95
The Wonderful Wizard of Oz	L. Frank Baum	1-59308-221-5	$6.95
Wuthering Heights	Emily Brontë	1-59308-128-6	$5.95

BARNES & NOBLE CLASSICS

If you are an educator and would like to receive an
Examination or Desk Copy of a Barnes & Noble Classics edition,
please refer to Academic Resources on our website at
WWW.BN.COM/CLASSICS
or contact us at
BNCLASSICS@BN.COM

All prices are subject to change.